TO

PARADISE

ALSO BY HANYA YANAGIHARA

A Little Life

The People in the Trees

TO
PARADISE

———

Hanya Yanagihara

PICADOR

First published 2022 by Picador
an imprint of Pan Macmillan
The Smithson, 6 Briset Street, London ECIM 5NR
EU representative: Macmillan Publishers Ireland Ltd, 1st Floor,
The Liffey Trust Centre, 117–126 Sheriff Street Upper,
Dublin 1, DO1 YC43
Associated companies throughout the world
www.panmacmillan.com

ISBN 978-1-5290-7747-6

1 3 5 7 9 8 6 4 2

A CIP catalogue record for this book is available from the British Library.

Endpaper maps by John Burgoyne
Book design by Pei Loi Koay

Printed and bound by CPI Group (UK) Ltd, Croydon, CRO 4YY

Visit **www.picador.com** to read more about all our books
and to buy them. You will also find features, author interviews and
news of any author events, and you can sign up for e-newsletters
so that you're always first to hear about our new releases.

To Daniel Roseberry

who saw me through

and

To Jared Hohlt

always

CONTENTS

BOOK I

———

WASHINGTON SQUARE

He had come into the habit, before dinner, of taking a walk around the park: ten laps, as slow as he pleased on some evenings, briskly on others, and then back up the stairs of the house and to his room to wash his hands and straighten his tie before descending again to the table. Today, though, as he was leaving, the little maid handing him his gloves said, "Mister Bingham says to remind you that your brother and sister are coming tonight for supper," and he said, "Yes, thank you, Jane, for reminding me," as if he'd in fact forgotten, and she made a little curtsy and closed the door behind him.

He would have to go more quickly than he would were his time his own, but he found himself being deliberately contrary, walking instead at his slower pace, listening to the clicks of his boot heels on the pavestones ringing purposefully in the cold air. The day was over, almost, and the sky was the particular rich ink-purple that he couldn't see without remembering, achily, being away at school and watching everything shade itself black and the outline of the trees dissolve in front of him.

Winter would be upon them soon, and he had worn only his light coat, but nevertheless, he kept going, crossing his arms snug against his chest and turning up his lapels. Even after the bells rang five, he put his head down and continued moving forward, and it wasn't until he had finished his fifth circumnavigation that he turned, sighing, to walk north on one of the paths to the house, and up its neat stone steps, with the door opening for him before he reached the top, the butler reaching already for his hat.

"In the parlor, Mister David."

"Thank you, Adams."

Outside the parlor doors he stood, passing his hands repeatedly over his hair—a nervous habit of his, much as the repeated smoothing of his forelock as he read or drew, or the light drawing of his forefinger beneath his nose as he thought or waited for his turn at the chessboard, or any number of other displays to which he was given—before sighing again and opening both doors at once in a gesture of confidence and conviction that he of course did not possess. They looked over at him as a group, but passively, neither pleased nor dismayed to see him. He was a chair, a clock, a scarf draped over the back of the settee, something the eye had registered so many times that it now glided over it, its presence so familiar that it had already been drawn and pasted into the scene before the curtain rose.

"Late again," said John, before he'd had a chance to say anything, but his voice was mild and he seemed not to be in a scolding mood, though one never quite knew with John.

"John," he said, ignoring his brother's comment but shaking his hand and the hand of his husband, Peter; "Eden"—kissing first his sister and then her wife, Eliza, on their right cheeks—"where's Grandfather?"

"Cellar."

"Ah."

They all stood there for a moment in silence, and for a second David felt the old embarrassment he often sensed for the three of them, the Bingham siblings, that they should have nothing to say to one another—or, rather, that they should not know how to say anything—were it not for the presence of their grandfather, as if the only thing that made them real to one another were not the fact of their blood or history, but him.

"Busy day?" asked John, and he looked over at him, quickly, but John's head was bent over his pipe, and David couldn't tell how he had intended the question. When he was in doubt, he could usually interpret John's true meaning by looking at Peter's face—Peter spoke less but was more expressive, and David often thought that the two of them operated as a single communicative unit, Peter illuminating with his eyes and jaw what John said, or John articulating those frowns and grimaces and brief smiles that winked across Peter's face, but this time Peter was blank, as blank as John's voice, and therefore of no help, and so he was forced to answer as if the question had been meant plainly, which it perhaps had.

"Not so much," he said, and the truth of that answer—its obviousness, its undeniability—was so inarguable and stark that it again felt as if the room had gone still, and that even John was ashamed to have asked such a question. And then David began to try to do what he sometimes did, which was worse, which was to explain himself, to try to give word and form to what his days were. "I was reading—" But, oh, he was spared from further humiliation, because here was their grandfather entering the room, a dark bottle of wine furred in a mouse-gray felt of dust held aloft, exclaiming his triumph—he had found it!—even before he was fully among them, telling Adams they'd be spontaneous, to decant it now and they'd have it with dinner. "And, ah, look, in the time it took me to locate that blasted bottle, another lovely appearance," he said, and smiled at David, before turning toward the group so that his smile included them all, an invitation for them to follow him to the dining table, which they did, and where they were to have one of their usual monthly Sunday meals, the six of them in their usual positions around the gleaming oak table—Grandfather at the head, David to his right and Eliza to his, John to Grandfather's left and Peter to his, Eden at the foot—and their usual murmured, inconsequential conversation: news of the bank, news of Eden's studies, news of the children, news of Peter's and Eliza's families. Outside, the world stormed and burned—the Germans moving ever-deeper into Africa, the French still hacking their way through Indochina, and closer, the latest frights in the Colonies: shootings and hangings and beatings, immolations, events too terrible to contemplate and yet so near as well—but none of these things, especially the ones closest to them, were allowed to pierce the cloud of Grandfather's dinners, where everything was soft and the hard was made pliable; even the sole had been steamed so expertly that you needed only to scoop it with the spoon held out for you, the bones yielding to the silver's gentlest nudge. But still, it was difficult, ever more so, not to allow the outside to intrude, and over dessert, a ginger-wine syllabub whipped as light as milk froth, David wondered whether the others were thinking, as he was, of that precious gingerroot that had been found and dug in the Colonies and brought to them here in the Free States and bought by Cook at great expense: Who had been forced to dig and harvest the roots? From whose hands had it been taken?

After dinner, they reconvened in the parlor and Matthew poured the coffee and tea and Grandfather had shifted in his seat, just a bit, when Eliza suddenly sprung to her feet and said, "Peter, I keep meaning to show you the picture in that book of that extraordinary seabird I mentioned to you last week and promised I wouldn't let myself forget again tonight; Grandfather Bingham, might I?" and Grandfather nodded and said, "Of course, child," and Peter stood then, too, and they left the room, arm in arm, Eden looking proud to have a wife who was so well attuned to everything around her, who could anticipate when the Binghams would want to be alone and would know how to gracefully remove herself from their presence. Eliza was red-haired and thick-limbed, and when she moved through the parlor, the little glass ornaments trimming the table lamps shivered and jingled, but in this respect she was light and swift, and they had all had occasion to be grateful to her for this knowingness she possessed.

So they were to have the conversation Grandfather had told him they would back in January, when the year was new. And yet each month they had waited, and each month, after each family dinner—and after first Independence Day, and then Easter, and then May Day, and then Grandfather's birthday, and all the other special occasions for which the group of them gathered—they had not, and had not, and had not, and now here it was, the second Sunday in October, and they were to discuss it after all. The others, too, instantly understood the topic, and there was a general coming-to, a returning to plates and saucers of bitten-into biscuits and half-full teacups, and an uncrossing of legs and straightening of spines, except for

Grandfather, who instead leaned deeper into his chair, its seat creaking beneath him.

"It has been important for me to raise the three of you with honesty," he began after one of his silences. "I know other grandfathers would not be having this discussion with you, whether from a sense of discretion or because he would rather not suffer the arguments and disappointments that inevitably come from it—why should one, when those arguments can be had when one is gone, and no longer has to be involved? But I am not that kind of grandfather to you three, and never have been, and so I think it best to speak to you plainly. Mind you"—and here he stopped and looked at each of them, sharply, in turn—"this does not mean I plan on suffering any disappointments now: My telling you what I am about to does not mean it is unsettled in my mind; this is the end of the subject, not its beginning. I am telling you so there will be no misinterpretations, no speculations—you are hearing it from me, with your own ears, not from a piece of paper in Frances Holson's office with all of you clad in black.

"It should not surprise you to learn that I intend to divide my estate among the three of you equally. You all have personal items and assets from your parents, of course, but I have assigned you each some of my own treasures, things I think you or your children will enjoy, individually. The discovery of those will have to wait until I am no longer with you. There has been money set aside for any children you may have. For the children you already have, I have established trusts: Eden, there is one apiece for Wolf and Rosemary; John, there is one for Timothy as well. And, David, there is an equal amount for any of your potential heirs.

"Bingham Brothers will remain in control of its board of directors, and its shares will be divided among the three of you. You will each retain a seat on the board. Should you decide to sell your shares, the penalties will be steep, and you must offer your siblings the opportunity to buy them first, at a reduced rate, and then the sale must be approved by the rest of the board. I have discussed this all with you before, individually. None of this should be remarkable."

Now he shifted again, and so did the siblings, for they knew that what was to be announced next was the real riddle, and they knew, and knew that their grandfather knew, that whatever he had decided would make some combination of them unhappy—it was only to be a matter of which combination.

"Eden," he announced, "you shall have Frog's Pond Way and the Fifth Avenue apartment. John, you shall have the Larkspur estate and the Newport house."

And here the air seemed to tighten and shimmer, as they all realized what this meant: that David would have the house on Washington Square.

"And to David," Grandfather said, slowly, "Washington Square. And the Hudson cottage."

He looked tired then, and leaned back deeper still in his seat from what seemed like true exhaustion, not just performance, and still the silence continued. "And that is that, that is my decision," Grandfather declared. "I want you all to assent, aloud, now."

"Yes, Grandfather," they all murmured, and then David found himself and added, "Thank you, Grandfather," and John and Eden, waking from their own trances, echoed him.

"You're welcome," Grandfather said. "Although let us hope it might be many years still until Eden is tearing down my beloved root shack at Frog's Pond," and he smiled at her, and she managed to return it.

After this, and without any of them saying it, the evening came to an abrupt close. John rang for Matthew to summon Peter and Eliza and ready their hansoms, and then there were handshakes and kisses and the leave-taking, with all of them walking to the door and his siblings and their spouses draping themselves in cloaks and shawls and wrapping themselves in scarves, normally an oddly raucous and prolonged affair, with last-minute proclamations about the meal and announcements and stray, forgotten bits of information about their outside lives, was muted and brief, Peter and Eliza both already wearing the expectant, indulgent, sympathetic expressions that anyone who married into the Binghams' orbit learned to adopt early in their tenure. And then they were gone, in a last round of embraces and goodbyes that included David in gesture if not in warmth or spirit.

Following these Sunday-night dinners, it was his and his grandfather's habit to have either another glass of port or some more tea in his drawing room, and to discuss how the evening had unfolded—small observations, only verging on gossip, Grandfather's slightly more fanged as was both his right and his way: Had Peter not looked a touch wan to David? Did not Eden's anatomy professor sound insufferable? But tonight, once the door was closed and the two of them were again alone in the house, Grandfather said that he was tired, that it had been a long day, and he was going up to bed.

"Of course," he'd replied, though his permission wasn't being asked, but he too wanted to be alone to think about what had transpired, and so he kissed his grandfather on his cheek and then stood for a minute in the candlelit gold of the entry of what would someday be his house before he too turned to go upstairs to his room, asking Matthew to bring him another dish of the syllabub before he did.

II

He had not thought he'd be able to sleep, and indeed, for what felt like many hours he had lain awake, aware that he was dreaming and yet that he was still conscious, that beneath him he could feel the starched cotton of his bedsheets, and that the way he was resting, with his left leg bent into a triangle, would leave him sore and stiff the next day. And yet it seemed he had slept after all, for when he opened his eyes next, there were thin stripes of white light where the curtains hadn't quite met, and the sounds of horses clopping through the streets and, outside his door, the maids moving back and forth with their buckets and brooms.

Mondays were always dreary for him. He would wake with the previous night's dread undiluted, and usually he would try to rise early, even before Grandfather, so that he too might feel he was joining the slipstream of activities that animated most people's lives, that he too, like John or Peter or Eden, had duties to attend to, or, like Eliza, places he needed to be, instead of only a day as ill-defined as any other, one he would have to endeavor to fill on his own. It was not true that he had nothing: He was titularly the head of the firm's charitable foundation, and it was he who approved the disbursements to the various individuals and causes that, viewed collectively, offered a kind of family history—the resistance fighters leading the effort in the south and the charities working to house and reunite the escapees, the group advancing Negro education, the organizations addressing child abandonment and neglect, the ones educating the poor baying masses of immigrants arriving daily on their shores, the peoples one family member or another had encountered and been moved by in the course of their lives and now helped in some way—and yet his responsibility extended only to the approval of the checks, and of the monthly tally of figures and expenses that had already been submitted to the firm's accountants and its lawyers by his secretary, an efficient young woman named Alma who in practice ran the foundation herself; he was there only to offer his name as a Bingham. He also volunteered, in various capacities such as a well-brought-up, still-almost-young person might: He assembled packages of gauze and wrappings and herbal salves for the fighters in the Colonies; he knitted socks for the poor; he once-weekly taught a drawing class at the foundlings' school his family endowed. But all of those endeavors and activities, combined, occupied only perhaps a week's worth of hours every month, and so the rest of the time he was alone and purposeless. He felt at times as if his life were something he was only waiting to use up, so that, at the end of each day, he would settle into bed with a sigh, knowing he had worked through a small bit more of his existence and had moved another centimeter toward its natural conclusion.

This morning, though, he was glad to have woken late, because he was still uncertain how to understand the events of the night before, and was grateful that he might have a clearer mind with which to contemplate them. He rang for eggs and toast and tea and ate and drank in bed, reading the morning paper—another purge in the Colonies, its specifics withheld; a windy essay by an eccentric philanthropist well-known for his sometimes extreme views, raising again the argument that they must extend privileges of citizenship to the Negroes who had lived in the Free States before its founding; a long article, the ninth in as many months, celebrating the tenth anniversary of the completion of the Brooklyn Bridge, and how it had remade the city's commercial traffic, this time with large, detailed illustrations of its towering masts looming above the river—and then washed and dressed and left the house, calling out to Adams that he would have lunch at the club.

The day was chilly and sunny and had, it being well into the morning, that merry swinging energy to it: It was early enough so that everyone was still industrious and hopeful—today could be the day that life made a delightful and long-dreamed-of pivot, that there would be a windfall or the southern conflicts would cease or just that there might be two rashers of bacon at dinner tonight instead of one—and yet not so late that those hopes might be left unanswered once again. When he walked, he generally did so without a particular destination in mind, letting his feet decide his direction, and now he turned right up Fifth Avenue, nodding at the coachman as he passed, who was hitching up the brown horse in the mews in front of the carriage house.

The house: Now that he was no longer within its walls, he hoped he might be able to consider it a bit more objectively, although what would that even mean? He had not spent the first part of his childhood there, none of them had—that honor had belonged to a large, chilly manse far north, west of Park Avenue—but it had been there that he and his siblings and, before them, their parents had retired for every important family event, and when their parents had died, carried off by the sickness, it had been to that house that the three of them had moved. They had had to abandon every possession in their childhood home that was made of cloth or paper, anything that might have secreted a flea, anything that could be burned; he had remembered crying over a horsehair doll he had loved, and Grandfather promising him he could have another, and when the three of them had entered their respective rooms in Washington Square, there were their former lives re-created for them in faithful detail—their dolls and toys and blankets and books, their rugs and gowns and coats and cushions. On the bottom of the Bingham Brothers' crest were the words *Servatur Promissum*—A Promise Kept—and in that moment, the siblings were allowed to realize that those words were meant for them as well, that their grandfather would fulfill whatever he told them, and in all the more than two decades they had been in his charge since, first as children and then as adults, that promise had never been disproven.

So complete was their grandfather's command of the new situation in which both he and they had found themselves that there had been what he could only later remember as a near-immediate cessation of grief. Of course, that must not have been true, either for him and his siblings or for his grandfather, suddenly bereft of his only child, but so astonished was David by, he now thought, the confidence, the totality, of his grandfather and the realm he created for them that he could not now imagine those years any other way. It was as if his grandfather had been planning since their births for someday becoming their guardian and their moving into a house where he had once lived alone, its only rhythms his own, instead of having it dropped upon him. Later, David would have the sense that the house, already capacious, had cleaved new rooms, that new wings and spaces had magically revealed themselves to accommodate them, that the room he came to call his own (and still did) had been conjured out of need and not simply remade into what it was from what it had been, a little-used extra sitting room. Over the years, Grandfather would say that his grandchildren had given the house purpose, that without them it would have been just a jumble of rooms, and it was a testament to him that the three of them, even David, accepted this as true, had come to truly believe that they had provided the house—and, therefore, Grandfather's own life—with something crucial and rare.

He supposed that each of them thought of the house as his or her own, but he liked to fancy, always, that it was his especial lair, a place where he not just lived but was understood. Now, as an adult, he could occasionally see it for how it appeared to outsiders, its interiors a well-organized but still-eccentric collection of objects Grandfather had collected on his journeys through England and the Continent and even the Colonies, where he had spent time in a brief period of peace, but mostly, what persisted was the impression of it he'd formed as a child, when he could spend hours moving from floor to floor, opening drawers and cupboards, peering under beds and settees, the wood floors cool and smooth beneath his bare knees. He clearly remembered being a young boy and lying in bed late one morning, watching a band of sunlight that shone through the window, and understanding that this was where he belonged, and the sense of comfort that knowledge had brought him. Even later, when he had been unable to leave the house, his room, when his life had become only his bed, he had never considered the house as anything but a sanctuary, its walls not just holding out the terrors of the world but holding together his very self. And now it would be his, and he its, and for the first time, the house felt oppressive, a place that he might now not ever escape, a place that possessed him as much as he did it.

Such thoughts occupied him for the time it took him to reach Twenty-second Street, and although he no longer wanted to enter the club—a place he frequented less and less, out of reluctance to see his former classmates—hunger drove him inside, where he ordered tea and bread and sausages and ate, quickly, before leaving and heading once again north, strolling all the way up Broadway to the southern end of Central Park before turning and walking home. By the time he returned to Washington Square, it was past five, and the sky once again was shading itself its dark, lonely blue, and he had time only to change and tidy himself before he heard, beneath him, the sounds of his grandfather speaking to Adams.

He had not expected Grandfather to mention the previous night's events, not with the servants about, but even after they were in his drawing room and had been left alone with their drinks, Grandfather continued to speak only of the bank, and the day's goings-on, and a new client, an owner of a substantial fleet of ships, from Rhode Island. Matthew arrived with tea and a sponge cake frosted thickly with vanilla icing; Cook, knowing David's taste for it, had decorated the top with splinters of candied ginger. His grandfather ate his slice swiftly and neatly, but David was unable to enjoy it as much as he might, for he was too much anticipating what his grandfather might say about the previous night's conversation, and because he was afraid of what he himself might unintentionally say, that he might in some way reveal his own ambivalence, that he might sound ungrateful. Finally, though, his grandfather puffed twice on his pipe and, without looking at him, said, "Now, there is another matter I've to discuss with you, David, but of course couldn't do in the midst of last night's excitement."

This was his opportunity to once again offer his thanks, but his grandfather waved those away with the vapor of his smoke. "There is no need to offer gratitude. The house is yours. You love it, after all."

"Yes," he began, for he did, but he was thinking still of those queer feelings he'd had earlier that day, when he was examining, for those many blocks, why the prospect of inheriting the house filled him not with a sense of security, but, rather, a sort of panic. "But—"

"But what?" asked Grandfather, now looking at him with a queer expression of his own, and David, worried he had sounded doubtful, hurried on: "I'm just worried for Eden and John, is all," to which Grandfather flapped his hand again. "Eden and John will be fine," he said, briskly. "You needn't worry about them."

"Grandfather," he said, and smiled, "you needn't worry about me, either," to which his grandfather said nothing, and then they were both embarrassed, equally at the fact of the lie and at its enormity, so wrong that not even manners demanded a denial of it.

"I have had an offer of marriage for you," his grandfather said at last into this silence. "A good family—the Griffiths, of Nantucket. They began as shipbuilders, of course, but now they have their own fleet, as well as a small but lucrative fur trade. The gentleman's Christian name is Charles; he is a widower. His sister—herself a widow—lives with him, and they raise her three sons together. He spends the trading season on-island and lives on the Cape in the winters.

"I don't know the family myself, but they have a very respectable position—quite involved in local government, and Mister Griffith's brother, with whom he and his sister run their business, is the head of the merchant association. There is another sibling as well, a sister, who lives in the North. Mister Griffith is the eldest; the parents are still living—it was Mister Griffith's maternal grandparents who began the business. The offer came to Frances, through their lawyer."

He felt he should say something. "How old is the gentleman?"

Grandfather cleared his throat. "One-and-forty," he said, reluctantly.

"One-and-forty!" he exclaimed, more vehemently than he had

intended. "I apologize," he said. "But one-and-forty! Why, he is an old man!"

At this, Grandfather smiled. "Not quite," he said. "Not to me. And not to most of the rest of the world. But, yes, he is older. Older than you, at least." And then, when he said nothing, "Child, you know I don't mean for you to marry if you don't wish. But it *is* something we've discussed for you, it is something in which you've expressed interest, or I wouldn't have entertained the offer at all. Shall I tell Frances you decline? Or would you like to have a meeting?"

"I feel I'm becoming a burden to you," he murmured, finally.

"No," Grandfather said. "Not a burden. As I said, no grandchild of mine has need to marry unless he wishes. But I do think you might consider it. We needn't give Frances an answer immediately."

They sat in silence. It was true that it had been many months— a year, perhaps; more—since he had last had any offers, or even any interest, though he didn't know whether this was because he had declined the last two proposals so quickly and with such indifference, or whether it was because word of his confinements, which Grandfather and he had worked so diligently to conceal, had finally become known to society. It was true that the idea of marriage made him to some measure fearful, and yet was it not also worrisome that this latest offer was from a family unknown to them? Yes, they would be of adequate station and standing—Frances would not have dared to mention it to Grandfather were they not—but it also meant that the two of them, Grandfather and Frances, had decided they must now entertain prospects from beyond the people the Binghams knew and with whom they associated, the fifty-odd families who had built the Free States, and among whom not only he and his siblings but his parents, and Grandfather before them, had spent their entire lives. It was to this small community that Peter belonged, as well as Eliza, but it was now apparent that the eldest Bingham heir, were he to marry, would have to find his spouse from beyond this golden circle, would have to look to another group of people. They were not dismissive, the Binghams, they were not exclusive, they were not the sort of people who did not associate with merchants and traders, with people who had begun their lives in this country as one kind of person and had, through diligence and cleverness, become another. Peter's family was like that, but they were not. And yet he could not but feel that he had disappointed, that the legacy his ancestors had worked so hard to establish was, with his presence, being diminished.

But he also felt, despite what Grandfather said, that it would not do for him to immediately refuse this offer: He was the only person he might blame for his current situation, and as the presence of the Griffiths made clear, his choices would not be infinite, despite his name and his grandfather's money. So he told Grandfather that he would accept the meeting, and his grandfather—with what was, was it not, an expression of relief, barely concealed?—replied that he would tell Frances straightaway.

He was tired then, and made his excuses and went to his room. Though it was now unrecognizable from when he had first occupied it, he knew it so well that he could navigate it even in the dark. A second door led to what had been his and his siblings' playroom and was now his study, and it was to here he retreated with the envelope his grandfather had given him before he had taken his leave for the night. Inside it was a small etching of the man, Charles Griffith, and he looked at it, closely, in the lamplight. Mister Griffith was fair, with light eyebrows and a soft, round face, and a full, though not excessive mustache; David could see that he was heavyset even from the drawing, which showed only his face and neck and the top of his shoulders.

All at once he was gripped by a panic, and he went to the window and opened it, quickly, and inhaled the cold, clear air. It was late, he realized, later than he'd thought, and beneath him nothing stirred. Was he really to contemplate leaving Washington Square, so soon after reluctantly imagining he perhaps never would? He turned back around and studied the room, trying to imagine everything in it— his shelves of books; his easel; his desk with his papers and inks and the framed portrait of his parents; his chaise, its scarlet piping now flattened and splitting with age, which he had had since his college years; his paisley-embroidered scarf of the softest wool, which Grandfather had given him two Christmases ago, special-ordered from India; everything arranged for his comfort or for his delight, or both—relocated to a wooden house in Nantucket, and himself among them.

But he couldn't. These things belonged here, in this house: It was as if the house itself had grown them, as if they were something living that would shrivel and die were they moved elsewhere. And then he thought: Was the same not true for him? Was he not also something the house had, if not spawned, then nourished and fed? If he left Washington Square, how would he ever know where he truly was in the world? How could he leave these walls that had stared blankly, plainly back at him through all of his states? How could he leave these floors, upon which he heard his grandfather walking late at night, come himself with bone broth and medicine in the months he was unable to leave his room? It was not always a joyful place. It had at times been a terrible one. But how could anywhere else feel so exactly his?

III

Once a year, the week before Christmas, the wards of The Hiram Bingham Charitable School and Institution were treated to a luncheon in one of the Bingham Brothers boardrooms. There was ham, and sweetmeats, and stewed apples, and custards, and at its conclusion, Nathaniel Bingham, their patron and the owner of the bank, would himself come greet them, accompanied by two of his clerks, both of whom were alumni of their very school, and who offered a promise of an adult life that was still too (and would, for most of them, alas, remain) remote and abstract for them to conjure. Mister Bingham would offer a brief speech, encouraging them to be industrious and obedient, and then the children would assemble themselves into two lines and each receive, from one of the clerks, a flat, thick bar of peppermint candy.

All three siblings attended this luncheon, and David's favorite moment was not the expressions on the children's faces when they were greeted with the sight of their feast but, rather, the one they assumed when they stepped into the bank's lobby. He understood their awe, for he never failed to experience it as well: the vast floor of silvery marble, polished to a shining finish; the Ionic columns, hewn from the same stone; the grand rotunda ceiling, inlaid with a gleaming mosaic pattern; the three murals that occupied the length of three whole walls, painted so high that one was all but forced into a supplicative posture to properly see them—the first depicting his great-great-great-grandfather, Ezra, the war hero, distinguishing himself in the battle for independence from Britain; the second, his great-great-grandfather, Edmund, marching northward

with some of his fellow Utopians from Virginia to New York to
found what would become known as the Free States; the third, his
great-grandfather, Hiram, whom he had never known, founding
Bingham Brothers and being elected mayor of New York. In the
background of all the panels, rendered in browns and grays, were
moments from his family's and country's history alike: the Siege of
Yorktown, where Ezra had fought, his wife and young sons at home
in Charlottesville; Edmund marrying his husband, Mark, and the
first wars with the Colonies, which the Free States would win, but at
great human and financial cost; Hiram and his two brothers, David
and John, as young men, unaware that of the three of them, only
Hiram, the youngest, would live into his forties, and that only he
would produce an heir—his son, Nathaniel, David's grandfather. At
the bottom of each panel was a mounted marble plaque carved with
a single word—Civility; Humility; Humanity—which, along with
the phrase on the bank's crest, was the Bingham family's motto. The
fourth panel, the one over the grand front doors, which opened onto
Wall Street, was empty, a smooth blank expanse, and it was here that
David's grandfather's accomplishments would one day be recorded:
how he had grown Bingham Brothers into the wealthiest financial
institution in not only the Free States but also America; how, until
he had helped America fund its fight in the War of Rebellion and
secured his country's autonomy, he had successfully protected the
Free States' existence against every attempt to dismantle it and dissolve the rights of its citizenry; how he paid for the resettlement of
free Negroes who had entered the Free States, helping them establish new lives for themselves in the North or the West, as well as
escapees from the Colonies. True, Bingham Brothers was no longer
the only or, some might argue, the most powerful institution in the
Free States, especially with the recent flourishing of the arriviste
Jewish banks that had begun to establish themselves in the city, but
it was, all would agree, still the most influential, the most prestigious, the most renowned. Unlike the newcomers, David's grandfather liked to say, Bingham did not confuse ambition for greed, or
cleverness for wiliness—its responsibility was as much to the States
themselves as to the people it served. "The Great Mister Bingham,"

the journals called Nathaniel, occasionally mockingly, as when he attempted to initiate one of his more ambitious projects—such as his proposal, a decade ago, to advance universal suffrage throughout America as well—but mostly sincerely, for David's grandfather was, indisputably, a great man, someone whose deeds and visage deserved to be painted on plaster, the artist swinging perilously on a rope-and-wood seat high above the stone floor, trying not to look down as he stroked his brush, glossy with paint, over the surface.

But for all this, there was no fifth or sixth panel: No space had been allocated for his father, the family's second war hero, or for him and his siblings. Although—what would his third of the panel even depict? A man, in his grandfather's house, waiting for one season to shade into the next, for his life to announce itself to him at last?

Such pity, such indulgence, was unattractive and unbecoming, he knew, and he strode across the foyer to the towering oak doors at the back of the room, where his grandfather's secretary, a man whom he and his siblings had always known as Norris for as long as he could remember, was already waiting for him.

"Mister David," he said. "It's been quite a while."

"Hello, Norris," he said. "It has. I trust you've been well?"

"Yes, Mister David. And you?"

"Yes, very."

"The gentleman is here already; I'll take you to him. Your grandfather will want to see you afterward."

He followed Norris down the wood-paneled corridor. He was a trim, neat man, with delicate, fine-drawn features, whose hair, when David was young, had been a bright gold and had over the decades faded to the color of parchment. His grandfather was forthright about almost all the matters of his and his family's life, but about Norris he was evasive; it was accepted by everyone that Norris and his grandfather had an understanding, but despite Nathaniel Bingham's avowed tolerance for all social classes and his avowed impatience with propriety, he had never introduced Norris as his companion, nor had he ever suggested, to his grandchildren or to anyone, that he might become legally bound to him. Norris came and went from their house at his liberty, but he had no bed there, no room; he never addressed the Bingham children, from the time they were small, without preceding their names with "Master" or "Miss," and they had long ago ceased suggesting that he might; he was in attendance at certain family events, but he was never included in their after-dinner talks with Grandfather in the parlor, or at Christmas and Easter. Even now, David had no certainty of where Norris lived—he felt he had once heard, somewhere or other, that he resided in a flat near Gramercy Park that Grandfather had purchased for him, years ago—or any specific information about whence he had come, and who his people might have been; he had arrived, before David was born, from the Colonies, and had been working as a coal boy at Bingham Brothers when Grandfather met him. In the Binghams' company, he was unobtrusive and quiet but also at ease; he was so familiar that he was often forgotten—his presence was assumed, but his absence went unremarked.

Now Norris stopped outside one of the private conference rooms and opened the door, and both the man and the woman inside stood from their chairs and turned as he entered.

"I'll leave you be," Norris said, closing the door behind him quietly, as the woman advanced toward him.

"David!" she said. "I haven't seen you in such a while." This was Frances Holson, his grandfather's longtime attorney, who, along with Norris, was privy to almost every detail of the Binghams' lives. She, too, was a constant, but her place in the family firmament was both more important and better acknowledged—she had arranged both John's and Eden's marriages, and she was determined, it would seem, to arrange David's as well.

"David," she continued, "I am very pleased to present to you Mister Charles Griffith, of Nantucket and Falmouth. Mister Griffith, here is the young man about whom you have heard so much, Mister David Bingham."

He was not as old-looking as David had feared, and despite his fair complexion, he was not ruddy, either: Charles Griffith was tall, and large, but self-assuredly so, broad through the shoulders and wide in the torso and neck. His jacket was tailored precisely, the wool soft and fine, and beneath his mustache his lips were well-defined and still pink, and now turned upward in a smile. He was not handsome, not exactly, but he gave the impression of deftness, and vigor, and health, which combined to create an aspect of something almost pleasing.

His voice, when he spoke, was appealing too, deep and somehow furred at the edges: There was a softness, a gentleness to it that contrasted with his size and its suggestion of strength. "Mister Bingham," he said, as they shook hands. "It is a pleasure to meet you. I've heard so much about you."

"As I have about you," he said, though he'd not learned a significant amount more since first hearing Charles Griffith's name almost six weeks prior. "Thank you so much for coming down—I trust you had a good journey?"

"Yes, quite," Griffith replied. "And please—you must call me Charles."

"And you must call me David."

"Well!" said Frances. "I'll leave you two gentlemen to talk, then. When you're done, David, ring, and Norris will escort Mister Griffith out."

They waited until she had left, the door shutting behind her, and then they both sat. Between them was a small table with a plate of shortbread cookies and a pot of what David knew, simply by scent, was Lapsang souchong, wildly expensive and difficult to obtain and his grandfather's favorite tea, reserved for only the most special occasions. He knew this was his grandfather's way of wishing him good luck, and the gesture moved him and made him sad, both. Charles already had tea, but David poured himself some, and as he lifted his cup to his lips, Charles did as well, and they sipped in unison.

"It's rather strong," he said, because he knew the taste of the tea was overpowering to many; Peter, who detested it, had once described it as "an oversmoked wood fire in liquid form."

But "I'm very fond of it," Charles said. "It reminds me of my time in San Francisco—you used to be able to find it quite easily there. Expensive, of course. But not as rare as it is here in the Free States."

This surprised him. "You've spent time in the West?"

"Yes. This was, oh, twenty years ago. My father had recently renewed our partnership up North with our fur trappers, and San Francisco had, of course, become rich by that time. He had the idea that I should go out there and establish an office and make some sales. So I did. It was a wonderful experience, actually; I was young, and the city was growing, and it was a marvelous era to be there."

He was impressed by this—he had never known anyone who had actually lived in the West. "Are all the stories true?"

"Many of them. There's an air there of—of unhealthiness, I suppose. Certainly licentiousness. It felt dangerous, at times—so many people trying to make a new life for themselves; so many people yearning for wealth; so many people bound to be disappointed—but also liberating. Though it was unreliable, as well. Fortunes came and went so fast there, and so too did people: The man who owed you money might vanish the next day, and there'd be no way to find him again. We were able to maintain the office for three years, but then, of course, we had to leave in seventy-six, after the laws were passed."

"Still," he said, "I envy you. Do you know, I've never even been out West?"

"But you've traveled extensively through Europe, Miss Holson tells me."

"I took my Grand Tour, yes. But there was nothing licentious about that—unless you consider heaps of Canalettos, and Tintorettos, and Caravaggios licentious."

Charles laughed then, and after that, the conversation came naturally. They spoke further of their respective wanderings—Charles was remarkably well traveled, his business taking him not only to the West and Europe but to Brazil and Argentina, too—and of New York, where Charles had once lived and where he still maintained a residence, which he visited often. As they talked, David listened for the Massachusetts accent many of his school classmates had had, with its broad, flat vowels and particular galloping cadence, but in vain. Charles's was a pleasant voice but featureless, revealing little of his origins.

"I hope you won't think this too forward to mention," Charles said, "but we are all of us in Massachusetts intrigued by this tradition of arranged marriage, and long have been."

"Yes," he laughed, unoffended. "All of the other states are. And I understand why—it's a local practice, limited to New York and Connecticut." Arranged marriages had begun around a century ago as a way for the first families who settled the Free States to create strategic alliances and consolidate their wealth.

"I understand why it originated here—these were always the richest provinces—but why do you suppose it has so endured?"

"I can't say, quite. My grandfather's theory is that, because significant dynasties soon arose from those marriages, it became essential for the financial integrity of the States for them to continue. He speaks of them as one might the cultivation of trees"—here Charles laughed, a pleasing noise—"the maintaining of a web of roots upon which the nation thrives and flowers."

"Quite poetic for a banker. And patriotic."

"Yes—he's both, my grandfather."

"Well, I suppose the rest of us Free Staters have your proclivity for arranged marriages to thank for our ongoing well-being." He was teasing, David knew, but his voice was kind, and he returned Charles's smile.

"Yes, I suppose. I shall thank my grandfather on your and your fellow Massachusettans' behalf. Do you not practice them at all in New England? I had heard you do."

"Yes, but with far less regularity: When we do, the reasons are similar—to unite like-minded families—but the consequences are never as meaningful as they are here. My younger sister recently facilitated a marriage between her maid and one of our sailors, for instance, but that was because her maid's family has a small timber concern and the sailor's a rope workshop, and the two wanted to consolidate their resources—not to mention that the young people were rather fond of each other but were both too shy to begin the process of courtship themselves.

"But as I said: Nothing of consequence to the rest of the nation. So, yes, please do thank your grandfather on our behalf. Though it sounds as if you should thank your siblings as well—Miss Holson says both of them are in arranged marriages, too."

"Yes, from families long close to ours: Peter, my brother John's husband, is from the city, too; Eliza, Eden's wife, is from Connecticut."

"Do they have children?"

"John and Peter have one; Eden and Eliza have two. And you are helping to raise your nephews, I understand?"

"Yes, indeed, and they are very dear to me. But I should like to have children of my own, someday."

Here he knew he should agree, should say that he too yearned for children, but he found himself unable to do so. But Charles easily filled the space where his response should have been, and they spoke of his nephews, and sisters and brother, and his house on Nantucket, the conversation once again moving along, until Charles finally stood, and David did as well.

"I must leave," Charles said. "But I have had a lovely time, and am so glad you chose to meet me. I will be back in the city in another fortnight; I hope you might choose to see me again?"

"Yes, of course," he said, and rang the bell, and the two of them shook hands again before Norris escorted Charles back to the entrance, and David knocked on the door on the opposite side of the room, and when he heard a voice beckoning him, entered directly into his grandfather's office.

"Ah!" said his grandfather, standing from his desk and handing his accountant a stack of papers. "Here you are! Sarah—"

"Yes, sir, right away," Sarah said, and left, silently closing the door behind her.

His grandfather came out from behind his desk and sat in one of the two chairs facing it, indicating that David should sit in the other. "Well," said his grandfather, "I will not be coy, and neither must you; I have been eager to see you and hear your impressions of the gentleman."

"He was—" he began, and faltered. "He was agreeable," he said at last, "more agreeable than I'd imagined."

"That is a fine thing to hear," his grandfather said. "Of what did you speak?"

He told his grandfather about their conversation, saving the part about Charles's time in the West for last, and as he relayed it, he watched his grandfather's silvery eyebrows raise. "Is that so?" his grandfather asked, mildly, and David knew what he was thinking: that such information had not arisen in their investigation of Charles Griffith, and because Bingham Brothers had access to the most prominent figures in all professions—doctors, lawyers, investigators—he was wondering what other things they might not know, what other mysteries might remain to be uncovered.

"Will you meet him again?" Grandfather asked when he was finished.

"He will be back in a fortnight, and asked if he might see me again; I said he might."

He had thought his grandfather would be satisfied with this answer, but instead he stood, with a pensive expression, and walked to one of the large windows, lightly stroking the edge of its long, weighty silk curtain as he looked down at the street. For a moment he remained there, in silence, but when he turned again, he was smiling once more, his familiar, dear smile that always made David feel, no matter how dire his life seemed, that he was someplace comfortable.

"Well," his grandfather said, "then he is a very lucky man."

———

IV

The weeks passed swiftly, as they always seemed to in late autumn, and although of course the arrival of Christmas was never a surprise, they were doomed, it appeared, to be ill-prepared, no matter how strenuously they had vowed the previous year to plan further in advance, so that by *this* Thanksgiving, the menus might be determined, the gifts for the children bought and tied with ribbon, the envelopes of money for the servants sealed, the decorations hung.

It was in the midst of this activity that he met for a second time with Charles Griffith, in early December; they had attended a concert of early Liszt works performed by the New York Philharmonic-Orchestra, and afterward had walked north, to a café on the southern end of the Park where David sometimes paused in his perambulations of the city for cake and coffee. This time as well the conversation came easily, and they spoke of books they had read, and plays and exhibits they had seen, and of David's family—his grandfather and, briefly, his sister and brother.

Arranged marriages inevitably demanded an acceleration of intimacies, and, subsequently, a falling away of standard proprieties, and so, after they had spoken for a while, he was emboldened to ask Charles about his former husband.

"Ah," Charles said. "Well—I suppose you already know his name was William, William Hobbes, and he died nine years ago." David nodded. "It was a cancer that began in his throat and took him very quickly.

"He was a teacher at a little school in Falmouth, from a family of lobstermen in the North—we met shortly after I had returned from California. It was a very happy time for both of us, I believe; I was learning how to run my family's business alongside my sister and brother, and we were both young and adventurous. In the summer, when school let out, he would come with me to Nantucket, where all of us—my younger sister and her husband and their sons, my brother and his wife and their daughters, my parents, my other sister and her family on their visits from up North—lived together in the family house. One year, my father sent me to the border to meet some of our trappers, and we spent almost the entire season in Maine and Canada with our business partners, going from place to place: It is such a beautiful land there.

"I thought I would be with him my entire life. We decided we would become parents later: We would have a girl and a boy. We would go to London, to Paris, to Florence—he was so much smarter than I—I wanted to be the one who would show him the frescoes and statues he had read about all his life. I thought I would be the one to accompany him to those museums. I dreamed of it—we would tour the cathedrals, we would eat mussels by the river, I would get to see those places I thought beautiful but never appreciated as much as he would, and this time I would see them with him and therefore I would see them anew.

"When you are a sailor, or when you have spent significant time with them, you understand that to make plans is folly—God will do what he wishes, and our plans are nothing against His. I knew this, and yet I was unable to stop myself. I knew it was silly, and yet I was unable to stop myself—I dreamed and dreamed. I planned the house I would build for us, on a cliff overlooking the rocks and the sea, with lupines all around it.

"But then he died, and a year later my younger sister's husband died in the sickness of eighty-five, and since then, as you know, I have lived with her. The first three years after William was taken from me, I was consumed with work, and in work I found solace. But, curiously, it is as I have moved further from his death that I think of him more—and not only of him but of the companionship we had, and that I imagined we always would. And now my nephews are almost grown, and my sister betrothed, and I have come, these past few years, to realize that I—" And here Charles stopped, suddenly, his cheeks coloring. "I have spoken too long, and too plainly," he said, finally. "I hope you will accept my apologies."

"There is no need to apologize," David said, quietly, though in truth he was surprised, albeit not embarrassed, by the man's forthrightness, his near-confession of loneliness. But after this, they neither one knew how to re-begin their conversation, and their encounter ended soon after, with Charles thanking him, formally, but without offering a third meeting, and the two of them retrieving their coats and hats. Outside, Charles went north in his hansom, and David south in his, back to Washington Square. On his return, he considered this strange encounter, and how, despite its strangeness, it had not been unpleasant, and had indeed made him feel *consequential*— there could be no other word—to be brought into another's confidence as he had, to be allowed to be the witness of such vulnerability.

So he was more unprepared than he ought to have been when, sitting in the parlor after Christmas lunch (duck, its skin crisp and pimpled from the oven, and surrounded by pearl-like crimson currant berries), John announced, a trace of triumph in his voice, "So, David, I hear you are being courted by a gentleman from Massachusetts."

"Not courted," replied Grandfather, quickly.

"An offer, then? Well, who is he?"

He let Grandfather provide only the barest of sketches: shipper and trader, the Cape and Nantucket, widowed and childless. Eliza was the first to speak: "He sounds lovely," she said, staunchly—dear, cheerful Eliza, in her gray wool trousers and length of paisley silk knotted around her plump neck!—while the rest of his family sat in silence.

"Would you move to Nantucket, then?" asked Eden.

"I don't know," he said. "I haven't considered it."

"Then you haven't accepted," Peter said: a statement, rather than a question.

"No."

"But you plan to?" (Peter, again.)

"I don't know," he admitted again, feeling himself grow flustered. "But if—"

"Enough," said his grandfather. "It is Christmas, and besides, it is for David to choose, not the rest of us."

The party dissolved shortly after this, and his siblings went to gather their children and nannies from John's room, which had been made into a playroom for his and Eden's sons and daughter, and there were goodbyes and well-wishes, and then he and his grandfather were alone once more.

"Come back up with me," his grandfather said, and David did, resuming the same seat he always took in his grandfather's drawing room: across from his grandfather, slightly to his left. "I have not wanted to pry, but I admit I am curious: You have had two meetings now. Do you have any sense of whether you might want to accept the gentleman?"

"I know I ought, but I don't—Eden and John made their decisions so quickly. I wish I knew, as they had."

"You must not think of what Eden and John did. You are not they, and these decisions are not to be made rashly. The only thing you are required to do is consider the man's offer seriously, and, if the answer is no, inform him immediately, or have Frances do so—though really, after two meetings, it ought to be you. But you must take your time, and not feel bad for doing so. When your father was matched with your mother, it took her six months to accept." He smiled, slightly. "Not that that ought to be your example."

He smiled, too. But then he asked the question he knew he must: "Grandfather," he said, "what does he know of me?" And then, when his grandfather did not answer, only stared into his glass of whiskey, he ventured further. "Does he know of my confinements?"

"No," his grandfather said, fiercely, his head snapping back up. "He does not. And he does not need to know—it is not his business."

"But," he began, "is it not a kind of duplicity not to tell him?"

"Of course not. Duplicity suggests we would be intentionally withholding something meaningful from him, and this is not meaningful—it is not information that should affect his decision."

"Maybe it shouldn't—but wouldn't it?"

"If it did, then he would not be a man worth marrying to begin with."

His grandfather's logic, usually sterling, was here so faulty that, even were David in the habit of contradicting him, he would not, for fear that the entire edifice of his grandfather's story would come tumbling down. If his confinements were not meaningful, then why should they not be divulged? And was not the way to judge Charles Griffith's true character by telling him, fully and honestly, the truth of himself? Furthermore, if his illnesses were not in fact a source of shame, why had they both taken pains to conceal them? It was true that they had not beforehand learned everything about Charles that they might have—Grandfather had grumbled, after that first meeting, about being ignorant of his time in San Francisco—but what they *had* learned was simple and irrefutable. There was no evidence that Charles Griffith was not an honorable man.

He worried that, though he might not know it himself, and would be insulted to hear it, his grandfather had somehow decided that David's weaknesses were a reasonable burden for Charles to assume in exchange for marrying a Bingham. True, Charles was wealthy— not as wealthy as the Binghams, though no one would be—but his money was new. True, he was intelligent, but he was not educated; he had not attended college, he had no Latin or Greek, he had traveled the world not in the pursuit of knowledge but in the pursuit of business. True, he was worldly, but he was not sophisticated. David had not thought himself someone who believed such things, but he wondered if he was defective enough so that his grandfather was thinking of him and Charles as belonging on two sides of a ledger: His illnesses for Charles's lack of refinement. His lack of industry for Charles's advanced age. At the bottom, would the two of them come out the same, a zero underlined once in ink in his grandfather's hand?

"It will soon be a new year," his grandfather said into this silence, "and new years are always more revealing than old ones. You will make your decision, and it will be yes or no, and the years will keep ending and beginning and ending and beginning, whatever you choose." And with this, David understood he was being dismissed, and he stood and then bent to kiss his grandfather good night before climbing to his own room.

Then, too soon, the new year was almost upon them, and the Binghams gathered once again to toast its arrival. It was their tradition that on the last day of the year, all the servants should be invited to have a glass of champagne with the family in the dining room, and the group of them—the grandchildren and great-grandchildren, the maids and footmen, the cook and butler and housekeeper and coachman and their various underlings—stood gathered around the table where the maids had earlier placed bottles of champagne wedged into crystal bowls of ice and arrangements of oranges pierced with cloves and dishes of roasted walnuts and platters of mincemeat pies, to listen to Grandfather salute the new year. "Six more years until the twentieth century!" Grandfather crowed, and the servants tittered nervously, because they disliked change and uncertainty, and the thought of one epoch ending and another beginning made them fearful, even as they knew that in the house at Washington Square, nothing would change: David would occupy the room he had always, and his siblings would come and go, and Nathaniel Bingham would be their master forever and ever.

Several days after that celebration, David took one of the hansoms to the orphanage. This was one of the first institutions of its kind in the city, and the Binghams had been its primary patron since its founding, which was only a few years after the Free States' own founding. Over the decades, its population shrank and grew as the Colonies passed through periods of either relative wealth or worsening poverty; the journey north was a difficult and arduous one, and many of the children had been orphaned when their parents died en route, attempting to escape to the Free States. The worst period was three decades ago, during and directly after the War of Rebellion, just before David was born, when the refugee population in New York reached its peak and the governors of New York and Pennsylvania had sent mounted soldiers down to the latter's southern border on a humanitarian mission, to find and relocate escapees from the Colonies. Any unattended children they encountered—as well as some with parents, but parents clearly unfit to tend to them—

were, depending on their age, sent either to one of the Free States' trade schools or to one of their charitable institutions, where they would become available for adoption.

Like most charities of its kind, Hiram Bingham's housed very few infants and toddlers—there was such a demand for them that they were adopted quickly; unless they were sick or deformed or an imbecile, it was rare for a baby to remain more than a month in the orphanage. Both of David's siblings had procured their children from here, and if David himself were ever to desire an heir, he would find him within the institution as well. John and Peter's son was a Colony orphan; Eden and Eliza's children were saved from the squalid hovel of some wretched Irish immigrant couple who could scarcely afford to feed them. There were frequent lively debates, in the newspapers and in drawing rooms, about what to do with the ever-increasing number of immigrants finding their way to the Manhattan shores—these days from Italy, Germany, Russia, and Prussia, not to mention the Orient—but one thing everyone had to agree upon, even if grudgingly, was that the European immigrants provided children for couples who wanted them, not only in their own city but throughout the Free States.

So fierce was the competition for a child that recently the government had introduced a campaign encouraging people to adopt older children. But this had been largely unsuccessful, and it was well understood, even by the children themselves, that those over the age of six were unlikely to ever find a home. This meant that the Binghams' institution, like others, concentrated on teaching its wards how to read and do sums, so that they might be prepared to learn a trade; when they were fourteen, they would be apprenticed to a tailor or a carpenter or a seamstress or a cook or any number of people whose skills were essential to the continued prosperity and functioning of the Free States. Or they would join the militia or the navy, and serve their country in that way.

In the meantime, however, they were children, and as children, they attended school, as was required by law in the Free States. The new philosophy in education was that children would grow into healthier, better citizens and adults if they were exposed not just to the necessities of life (math, reading, writing) but to art and music and sport as well. And so, the previous summer, when his grandfather asked him if he might want to assist in the search for an art teacher for the institution, David had surprised even himself by volunteering for the responsibility—for had he not studied art for many years? Had he not been looking for something, some useful task, with which to define his days?

He taught his class every Wednesday, toward the end of the afternoon, just before the children had their supper, and initially, he had often wondered whether their fidgeting and tittering was at him or in anticipation of their meal—he had even considered asking the matron if he might teach his class earlier in the day, but she was fearsome to adults (though, curiously, beloved by her charges), and although she would have had to accede to his request, he was too intimidated to do so. He had always been wary of children, their unflinching, unbroken gazes that suggested they could see him in a way that adults no longer bothered to or could, but over time, he had grown first accustomed to and then fond of them, and as the months passed, they too grew steadier and calmer in his quiet presence, toiling away with their sticks of charcoal over their pads of paper, trying as best they could to reproduce the blue-and-white chinoiserie bowl filled with quince he had placed atop a stool at the front of the room.

He heard the music that day before he even opened the door— something familiar, a popular song, a song that he did not think was right for children to listen to—and he reached for the doorknob and turned it sharply, but before he could express either consternation or anger, he was struck at once by a number of sights and sounds that left him mute and motionless.

There, at the front of the room, was the decrepit, long-neglected piano that had been relegated to a corner of the classroom, its wood so buckled that, he had assumed, the instrument had been rendered hopelessly out of tune. But now it had been repaired, and cleaned, and positioned in the center of the room as if it were a grand, fine thing, and sitting at it was a young man, perhaps a few years younger than he, with dark hair slicked back as if it were evening and he were at a party, and a handsome, lively, beautiful face, one that complemented his handsome voice, with which he was singing: *Why are you single, why live alone? / Have you no babies, have you no home?*

The man's head was tipped back on his neck, which was long but supple and strong, like a snake, and as he sang, David watched a muscle move in his throat, a pearl traveling upward and then sliding down:

> *"Bright lights were flashing in the grand ballroom,*
> *Softly the music playing sweet tunes.*
> *There came my sweetheart, my love, my own,*
> *I wish some water, leave me alone!*
> *When I returned, dear, there stood a man,*
> *Kissing my sweetheart as lovers can . . ."*

It was the kind of song you heard at low places, at music halls and minstrel shows, and thus highly inappropriate to sing to children, especially children like these, who given their circumstances would be naturally inclined toward such sentimental entertainments. And yet David found himself unable to speak, as mesmerized by the man, by his sweet, low voice, as the children were. He had heard this song performed only as a waltz, syrupy and plaintive, but the man had changed it into something jolly and brisk, so that the mawkishness of its story—a young girl asking her ancient bachelor uncle to explain why he had never fallen in love, never coupled and had a family— was reborn into something winking and bright. It was a song David hated in part because he felt that it might be a tune he would someday be able to sing from experience, that in it was his inevitable fate, but in this version, the man in the song sounded jaunty and careless, as if by never marrying he had been not deprived but delivered from a dismal future.

> *"After the ball is over, after the break of morn,*
> *After the dancers' leaving, after the stars are gone,*
> *Many a heart is aching, if you could read them all—*
> *Many the hopes that have vanished after the ball."*

The young man finished with a flourish, and stood and bowed to the assembled twenty or so children, who had been listening raptly and now broke into cheers and applause, and David stood straighter and cleared his throat.

At this, the man looked at him and smiled, such a broad, brilliant smile that David was once again flustered. "Children," he said, "I believe I've made you late for your next lesson. Now, don't groan, it's very rude"—David flushed—"just go and get your drawing pads and I shall see you next week." He began, still smiling, to make his way over to David, still standing at the door.

"I say, that's a very strange song to play for children," he began, trying his best to sound severe, but the man laughed, unoffended, as if David had been only teasing him. "I suppose it is," he answered, good-naturedly, and then, before David could ask, "I am being very rude; not only have I made you late for your class, or, rather, your class late for you—*you* were on time!—but I haven't introduced myself. My name is Edward Bishop—I am the new music teacher here at this fine establishment."

"I see," he said, uncertain how the conversation had slipped from his control so quickly. "Well, I must say that I was quite surprised to hear—"

"And I know who *you* are," the young man interrupted him, but so charmingly, so warmly, that David once again found himself disarmed. "You're Mister David Bingham, of the New York Binghams. I suppose I don't need to say 'New York,' do I? Though surely there's another set of Binghams somewhere in the Free States, don't you think? The Chatham Binghams, for example; or the Portsmouth Binghams. I wonder how they must feel, these lesser Binghams, knowing that their name will always only mean one family, and they not a part of it, and therefore condemned to perpetually disappoint when people ask, 'Oh, of *the* Binghams?' and they having to apologetically say, 'Oh, I'm afraid not; we're of the Utica Binghams,' and watching their inquisitor's face fall."

He was made quite speechless at this delivery, which had unfurled with great gaiety and speed, so that all he could muster, stiffly, was "I had never thought of it like that," which made the young man laugh again, but quietly, as if he were laughing not at David but at something clever he had said, and the two had shared a confidence.

And then he placed his hand on David's arm, and said, still merrily, "Well, Mister David Bingham, it was very nice indeed to meet you, and I apologize once again for disrupting the schedule."

After the door closed behind him, something essential seemed to leach from the room; the children, who had been alert and attentive, suddenly became wan and defeated, and even David could feel himself slumping, as if his own body were no longer able to participate in the farce of enthusiasm, of uprightness, that a well-modeled life demanded.

Nevertheless, he plowed onward. "Good afternoon, children," he said, receiving a tepid "Good afternoon, Mister Bingham," in reply as he assembled on the stool the day's still life: a creamily glazed vase in which he arranged a few branches of holly. As usual, he took his position at the back of the room, both so he could supervise the children and so he too could sketch if he so chose. Today, though, it was as if the only object in the room he could see was the piano, which stood behind the stool with his poor arrangement and, for all its batteredness, seemed the most beautiful, most compelling object there: a beacon, something shining and pure.

He glanced over to the student on his right, a frowzy, tiny eight-year-old, and saw that she was sketching (poorly) not only the vase and the flowers but the piano as well.

"Alice, you are just to draw the still life," he reminded her.

She looked up, all eyes in her pinched little face, her two protruding teeth resembling chips of bone. "I apologize, Mister Bingham," she whispered, and he sighed. Why would she *not* want to include the piano, when he too was unable to stop himself from gazing at it, as if he too might be able to conjure its player simply by hoping, as if his ghostly form lingered still in the room? "It's all right, Alice," he said. "Just start again on a clean sheet." Around him, the rest of the children were silent and sullen; he could hear them shifting in their seats. It was foolish to feel so pained, but he did—he had always thought they had enjoyed his class, enjoyed it at least almost as much as he had come to enjoy teaching them, but after witnessing their earlier delight, he knew that even if that had once been true, it no longer was. He was a bite of an apple, but Edward Bishop was that apple baked into a pie with a shattery, lardy crust pattered with sugar, and after a taste of that, there was no going back to the other.

At dinner that night, he was morose, but Grandfather was in a cheery mood—was everyone in the world so happy?—and there was David's favorite roasted squab for dinner, and stewed cardoons, but he ate little, and when Grandfather asked, as he did every Wednesday, how his class had been, he murmured only "Fine, Grandfather," whereas normally he tried to make him laugh with stories of what the children had drawn, and what they had asked him, and how he had distributed the fruit or flowers from the still life among the students who had done the best work.

But Grandfather seemed not to notice his inwardness, or at least chose not to comment on it, and after dinner, as he was trudging upstairs to the drawing room, David had, preposterously, a vision of Edward Bishop, and what he might be doing as he himself prepared to spend another night indoors near the fire, across from his grandfather: In it, the young man was at a club, the kind David had been to only once, and his long throat was exposed, and his mouth was open in song, and around him were other handsome young men and women, all dressed in bright silks, and life was festive, and the air smelled of lilies and champagne as, above them, a cut-glass chandelier tossed wobbling spangles of light around the room.

V

───────

The six days until his next class passed even more slowly than usual, and the following Wednesday he arrived so early in anticipation that he determined to take a walk in order to calm himself and use up some time.

The institute was in a large, square building, simple but well-maintained, on the corner of West Twelfth and Greenwich Streets—a location that had become less salubrious over the decades with the arrival, three blocks north and one block west, of the city's brothel quarters. Every few years, the school's trustees would debate whether or not they might relocate, but they always chose in the end to remain, for it was the nature of the city that apparent opposites—the rich and the poor, the well-established and the newly arrived, the innocent and the criminal—should have to live in close proximity, as there was simply not enough territory available to make natural divisions otherwise possible. He walked south to Perry Street and then west and north on Washington Street, but after he completed the circuit twice, it was too cold even for him, and he was forced to stop, breathing on his hands and returning to the hansom to retrieve the package he'd brought.

For months now, he had been promising the children that he would let them draw something unusual, but he had been aware, as he handed the object over to Jane earlier that day to wrap in paper and twine, that he was also hoping that Edward Bishop might see him carrying such an unwieldy, odd thing in his arms and might be intrigued, might even stay to watch him unveil it, might be filled with awe. He was not proud of this, of course, or of the excitement he felt as he walked down the hall to his classroom: He was aware of his breath quickening, of his heart in his chest.

But when he opened the door to his classroom, there was nothing—no music, no young man, no enchantment—only his students, playing and scuffling and shouting at one another, then noticing him and shoving one another into silence.

"Good afternoon, children," he said, recovering himself. "Where is your music teacher?"

"He's coming on Thursdays now, sir," he heard one of the boys say.

"Ah," he said, and was aware of both his disappointment, an iron chain around his neck, and of his shame for it.

"What's in the package, sir?" asked another student, and he realized he was still leaning against the door, his numb hands gripping the object nestled in his arms. Suddenly it seemed foolish, a farce, but it was the only thing he had brought for them to sketch, and there was nothing else in the room with which to compose a tableau, and so he took it to the desk at the front of the class and unwrapped it, carefully, to reveal the statue, a plaster copy of a Roman marble torso. His grandfather possessed the original, bought when he was on *his* Grand Tour, and had had it copied when David was first learning to draw. It was of no real monetary value, but he had revisited it many times over the twenty-odd years he had owned it, and well before he saw another man's chest, the sculpture had taught him all he knew about anatomy, about the way muscle lay over bone, and skin over muscle, the single, womanly crease that appeared in the side of the abdomen when you bent in one direction, the two downward strokes, like arrows, that pointed toward the groin.

At least the children were interested, impressed even, and as he positioned it on the stool, he told them about Roman statuary, and how the greatest expression of an artist's skill was in the rendering of the human form. As he watched them draw, looking down at their paper and then up at the statue in brief, darting glances, he thought of how John considered his teaching foolish: "Why would you educate them in something that will be no part of their adult lives?" he had wondered. John was not the only one to think this—

even Grandfather, for all his indulgence of him, thought this pastime peculiar, if not cruel, exposing children to hobbies and interests that they would likely never have time, much less money, to pursue. But David maintained otherwise: He was teaching them something that you needed only a scrap of paper and a bit of ink or a stub of lead to enjoy; and besides, he told Grandfather, if you had servants who understood art better, who knew its value and worth, perhaps they would be more careful, more appreciative, of the artwork in the houses that they cleaned and tended, to which his grandfather—who had seen several of his objects inadvertently destroyed over the years by clumsy maids and footmen—had had to laugh, and admit that he could be correct.

That night, after sitting with Grandfather, he returned to his room and thought of how earlier, as he sat at the back of the classroom and drew along with his students, he had imagined Edward Bishop, not the plaster bust, perched on the stool, and he had dropped his pencil and then had made himself walk among the children, examining their attempts, in order to distract himself.

The next day was Thursday, and he was trying to invent a reason to once again visit the school when he received word that Frances needed to see him to review a discrepancy in the ledgers relating to the Binghams' foundation, which funded all of their various projects. He of course had no excuse for not being available, and he knew Frances knew this as well, and so he was made to go downtown, where the two of them examined the books until they realized that a one had been smudged into a seven, thus throwing the accounts into disarray. A one to a seven: such a simple mistake, and yet, had they not found it, Alma would have been brought in for questioning, and perhaps even terminated from the Binghams' employ. By the time they had finished, it was still early enough for him to reach the school before Edward's class concluded, but then his grandfather asked him to stay for tea, and, again, he had no reason to refuse—his leisure was so well-known that it had become its own kind of prison, a schedule in the absence of one.

"You seem very anxious about something," observed his grandfather, as he poured tea into David's cup. "Is there somewhere you need to be?"

"No, nowhere," he replied.

He left as soon as he politely could, pulling himself into the hansom and telling the driver to hurry, please, but it was already well past four when they reached West Twelfth Street, and it was unlikely that Edward would have loitered, especially in such cold. Nevertheless, he bade the driver to wait and walked purposefully toward his classroom, closing his eyes and drawing his breath before turning the doorknob, and exhaling when he heard nothing but silence within.

And then: "Mister Bingham," he heard a voice say, "what a surprise to see you here!"

He had of course been hoping for this moment, and yet, upon opening his eyes and seeing Edward Bishop before him, wearing his same bright smile, holding his gloves in one hand, his head tipped to one side as if he'd just asked David a question, he found himself unable to answer, and his expression must have given away something of his confusion, because Edward moved toward him, his face changing into a look of concern. "Mister Bingham, are you quite all right?" he asked. "You look very pale. Here, come sit in one of these chairs and let me get you some water."

"No, no," he managed at last. "I'm perfectly fine. I'm just—I had thought I left my sketchbook here yesterday—I was looking for it today and was unable to find it—but I can see I haven't left it here, either—I'm sorry to interrupt you."

"But you are not interrupting me at all! To lose your sketchbook—how awful: I don't know what I would do with myself if I lost my own notebook. Let me look around a bit."

"There is no need to," he began, faintly—it was a shoddy lie: The room had so little furniture that there were few places his imaginary sketchbook could even be—but Edward had already begun looking, opening the empty drawers of the desk at the front of the room, peering into the empty cupboard that stood behind the desk, next to the chalkboard, even lowering to his knees, despite David's protestations, to look beneath the piano (as if David would not have seen it immediately had the sketchbook—safe at home in his study—been somehow here). All the while, Edward was making exclamations of alarm and dismay on David's behalf. He had a theatrical, deliberately old-fashioned, deeply affected manner of speech—all *Oh!*s and *Ah!*s—but it irritated less than it ought: It was both unnatural and genuine, and felt less a pretension than a reflection of an artistic sensibility, a suggestion of liveliness and good humor, as if Edward Bishop were determined to not be too serious, as if *seriousness*, the kind with which most people greeted the world, was the affectation, and not enthusiasm.

"It seems not to be here, Mister Bingham," Edward declared at last, standing and looking at David directly with an expression, an almost-smile, that David wasn't able to interpret: Was it one of flirtation, or even seduction, an acknowledgment of both their roles in this particular pantomime? Or was it (more likely) teasing in its nature, even mocking? How many men with foolish plans and affections had Edward Bishop endured in his short life? How long was the list to which David must now add his own name?

He would have liked to end this piece of theater but was uncertain how to do so: He had authored it, but he realized too late that he'd not conceived of a conclusion before he began. "You were very kind to search," he said, miserably, looking toward the floor. "But I'm sure I simply misplaced it at home. I oughtn't've come—I won't trouble you any longer." *Never*, he promised himself. *I will never trouble you again.* And yet he made no move to leave.

There was a silence, and when Edward spoke next, his voice was different, less fulsome, less everything. "It was no trouble, not at all," he said, and, after another pause, "It's very cold in this room, isn't it?" (It was. Matron kept the facility chilly during school hours, which she claimed sharpened her charges' sense of concentration and taught them resolve. The children had grown accustomed to it, but adults never could: Every teacher or staff member was always seen swaddled in layers of coats and shawls. David had visited the institute once in the evening and had been surprised to find it warm, even cozy.)

"It always is," he replied, still unhappily.

"I thought I might warm myself with a cup of coffee," Edward said, and when David made no response, uncertain once again how to interpret this statement, "There is a café around the corner if you'd care to join me?"

He agreed before he even knew he was doing so, before he could demur, before he was able to examine what this offer might really mean, and then, to his surprise, Edward was fastening his coat and they were leaving the school and walking east and then south on Hudson Street. They did not speak, though Edward hummed something as they went, another popular song, and for a moment, David doubted himself: Was Edward all surface and gloss? He had been assuming there was a serious person beneath his smiles and gestures, his white, neat teeth, but what if there was not? What if he was a mere flibbertigibbet, a man who sought only pleasure?

But then he thought: And so what if he is? It was coffee, not an offer of marriage, and, assuring himself of this, he thought then of Charles Griffith, and how he had not heard from him since their last meeting, before Christmas, and felt his neck grow hot, even in the cold.

The café, when they reached it, was less a café than a kind of teahouse, a cramped, rough-floored place with rickety wooden tables and backless stools. The front part was a shop, and they had to inch past a crowd of patrons examining barrels containing, variously, coffee beans and dried chamomile flowers and mint leaves, which the establishment's two Chinamen employees would scoop into paper sacks and weigh on a brass scale, totting up the numbers on a wooden-bead abacus, whose constant, rhythmic clacking provided the place with its own percussive music. Despite this, or perhaps because of it, the mood was lively and convivial, and the two men found a place to sit near the fireplace, which sent a stream of snapping embers spiraling through the air like fireworks.

"Two coffees," Edward told the waitress, a plump Oriental girl, who nodded and trotted off.

For a moment, they sat staring at each other across the small table, and then Edward smiled, and David smiled back at him, and they smiled at each other smiling at each other, and then both began, at once, to laugh. And then Edward leaned close to him, as if to deliver an intimacy, but before he could speak, a large group of young men and women—university students, by the look and sound of them—came in, settling down at a table near theirs, not even pausing in their debate, one that had been fashionable for college-age young men and women to have for decades, since even before the War of Rebellion: "I am only saying that our country can hardly consider itself free if we cannot welcome Negroes as whole citizens," a pretty, sharp-featured girl was saying.

"But they *are* welcome here," countered a boy across from her.

"Yes, but only to pass through on their way to Canada or to the West—we do not wish them to stay, and when we say we open our borders to anyone from the Colonies, we do not mean them, and yet they are even more persecuted than the ones to whom we offer shelter! We think ourselves so much better than America and the Colonies, and yet we are not!"

"But Negroes are not people like us."

"But they are! I have known—well, not I, but my uncle, when he was traveling through the Colonies—Negroes who are *just* like us!"

There was jeering from some of the group at this, and then one boy said, in a lazy, arrogant drawl, "Anna would have us believe that there were even *redskins* like us, and we ought never to have eradicated them but left them to their savagery."

"There *were* Indians like us, Ethan! *That* has been documented!"

This was greeted with the entire table shouting their response, and between the ruckus they made, and the click-click of the abacus, now louder than before, and the heat of the fire on his back, David began to feel woozy. It must have shown on his face, for Edward leaned again across the table and asked him, in a near-shout, if he might want to go elsewhere, and David said he would.

Edward went to find the waitress to tell her they didn't need the coffees, and the two of them shouldered past the table of students and the customers waiting for their bags of tea, and out into the street once more, which felt, for all its activity and life, a relief, spacious and quiet.

"It can get quite loud in there," said Edward, "especially toward late afternoon—I should have remembered. But it's nice, usually, really."

"I've no doubt," he murmured, politely. "Is there somewhere else we can go?" For, although he had been teaching at the school for six months, it was not a neighborhood in which he dallied—his visits there were short and purposeful, and he felt himself too elderly to frequent the pubs and inexpensive coffeehouses that made the area so attractive to students.

"Well," said Edward after a moment's silence, "we could go to my flat, if you could bear it—it's very nearby."

He was surprised by this offer, but also gratified—for was this not exactly the kind of behavior that drew him to Edward initially? A promise of free-spiritedness, a blithe disregard for conventions, a dispensing of old modes of behavior and formality? He was modern, and in his presence, David felt modern as well, so much so that he accepted straightaway, emboldened by his new friend's irreverence, and Edward, nodding as if he'd expected this answer (even as David was momentarily stunned by his own boldness), led him first north and then west on Bethune Street. There were handsome houses on this street, newly built brownstones in whose windows tapers of candles flickered—it was only five in the afternoon, but already the night was drawing around them—but Edward strode past them all to a large, shabby, once-grand structure quite close to the river, a mansion of the kind David's grandfather had been raised in, although in ill condition, with a swollen wooden door that Edward had to tug at repeatedly to open.

"Watch the second step; there's a stone missing," he warned, before turning to David. "It's not Washington Square, I'll grant you, but it's home." The words were an apology, but his smile—that beam!—made them into something else: not quite a boast, perhaps, but a statement of defiance.

"How did you know I live on Washington Square?" he asked.

"Everyone knows," Edward replied, but in a way that made it sound as if living on Washington Square had been David's own accomplishment, something worthy of congratulation.

Once inside (having taken care to avoid the troublesome second step), David could see that the mansion had been converted into a boardinghouse; to the left, where the parlor would be, was a breakfast room of sorts, with a half-dozen tables of different styles and a dozen chairs, also of different designs. He could tell, by just a glance, that the furniture was poorly made, but then he noticed, in a corner, a handsome, turn-of-the-century secretary of the kind his grandfather had in his own parlor, and moved to examine it. The wood had not been polished in apparently months, and its finish had been destroyed by some inferior oil; its surface, when he touched it, was sticky, and when he brought his hand away, his fingers were padded with dust. But it had once been a fine piece, and before he could ask, Edward, behind him, said, "The proprietress of this place was once wealthy, or so I've heard. Not Bingham wealthy, of course"— there it was again, a mention of his family and their fortune—"but moneyed."

"And what happened?"

"A husband given to excess gambling, who then ran away with her sister. Or so I've been told. She lives on the top floor, and I rarely see her—she's quite elderly—her distant cousin manages the place now."

"What's her name?" David asked—if the owner had truly once been rich, his grandfather would know of her.

"Larsson. Florence Larsson. Come, my room is this way."

The carpet on the staircase was frayed in some places, worn clean through in others, and as they climbed the flights, Edward explained how many boarders lodged there (twelve, including him) and how long he'd lived there (a year). He seemed not a bit embarrassed by his surroundings, its poverty and disrepair (water had discolored the posy-print wallpaper, rendering it a haphazard pattern of large, irregular splotches of yellow), nor to be living in a boardinghouse at all. Of course, many people lived in boardinghouses, but David had never met one, much less been inside this kind of building, and he looked about him with curiosity and some small measure of trepidation. How people lived in this city! According to Eliza, whose own charity work involved the resettlement and housing of refugees from the Colonies and of immigrants from Europe, the conditions of most new residents were deplorable; she had told them of families crammed ten to a single room, of windows that went uncaulked even in the coldest weather, of children who were scalded while edging too close to a grateless fire in a wretched attempt to warm themselves, of roofs that wept rain directly into the living quarters. They would listen to these stories and shake their heads and Grandfather would cluck his tongue, and then the talk would turn to something else—Eden's studies, perhaps, or a show of paintings Peter had recently seen—and Eliza's deplorable residences would fade from their memories. And yet here he was, David Bingham, in a home of the kind none of his siblings ever would have dared enter. He found himself aware that he was having an adventure, and then ashamed at his pride, for, in truth, being a visitor demanded no kind of bravery at all.

On the third-floor landing, Edward turned right and David followed him to a room at the end of the hall. Around them, all was silent, though as he unlocked his door Edward held a finger to his lips and pointed to the door next to him: "He'll be asleep."

"So early?" he whispered in return. (Or was it in fact so late?)

"He works nights. A longshoreman—he doesn't leave the house until past seven or so."

"Ah," he said, and once more, he was struck by how little he knew of the world.

They entered the room, and Edward shut the door quietly behind them. It was so dark David was unable to see anything, but he could smell smoke and, faintly, tallow. Edward announced that he'd light some candles, and with each hiss of the match, he watched as the room clarified itself into shapes and colors. "I keep the curtains closed—it's warmer that way," Edward said, but now he drew them open, and the space was revealed at last.

It was smaller than David's study at Washington Square, and in one corner was a narrow bed, over which a rough wool blanket had been pulled tight and neat. At the foot of the bed was a trunk, its leather peeling in strips, and to its right was a wooden wardrobe that had been built into the wall. On the other side of the room was a meager slice of table, atop which sat an old-fashioned oil lamp and a sheaf of papers and a blotter, and around it were stacks of books, all of them worn. There was a stool as well, obviously inexpensive, like the rest of the furniture. In the corner opposite the bed was a substantial brick fireplace, and hanging from an iron arm was a heavy, black, old-fashioned pot, the kind he remembered from his childhood, when he would stand in the back courtyard of their house uptown and watch the maids stir their laundry in great cauldrons of boiling water. On either side of the fireplace was a large window, against which the bare branches of the alder trees traced cobwebbed shadows.

To David, it was a remarkable place, like something out of the newspapers, and he once again marveled at his presence, the fact of his being in the room even more notable than the fact of being in the company of the person whose room it was.

Then he remembered his manners and returned his gaze to Edward, who was standing in the center of the space, his fingers laced together before him in what David knew, already, to consider an uncharacteristic expression of vulnerability. And for the first time in their brief acquaintance, David recognized a sort of tentativeness on the other man's face, something he'd not seen before, and understanding this made him feel both more tender and braver as well, so that when Edward at last said, "Shall I make us some tea?" he was able to step forward—just a single step, but the space was so minute that it delivered him within a few inches of Edward Bishop, so close that he could see his each individual eyelash, each as black and wet as a stroke of ink.

"Please," he said, and he kept his voice especially soft, as if anything louder would bring Edward to his senses and startle him away. "I would like that very much."

And so Edward went to fetch the water, and after he left, David was able to inspect the room and its contents more closely and carefully, and to realize that the equanimity with which he had accepted the reality of Edward's home was actually not equanimity at all, but shock. He was, David could now recognize, poor.

But what had he expected? That Edward was someone like himself, of course, a well-brought-up, educated man who was teaching at the school as an act of charity, and not—as he was now made to consider was probable, even certain—for money. He had registered the beauty of his face, the cut of his clothes, and had assumed a kinship, a likeness, where none existed. But now he sat on the trunk at the end of the bed and looked at Edward's coat, which he had laid there before leaving the room; yes, the wool and construction were fine, but the lapels (when he turned them over to examine them more closely) were just a touch too wide to be fashionable, and the shoulders had been worn to a satiny sheen, and a piece of the placket had been darned with rows of tiny stitches, and there was a pleat in the sleeve where a hem had been let out. He shivered a little, both at his miscalculation and also at what he knew to be a flaw in himself: Edward had not tried to deceive him; David had simply decided that Edward was one thing and had ignored the evidence to the contrary. He looked for signs of himself, and for others of his world, and when he found them, or something close enough, he had simply stopped looking, had simply ceased to see. "A man of the world," Grandfather had greeted him the day after he'd returned from his yearlong tour through Europe, and David had believed him, agreed with him, even. But was he indeed a man of the world? Or was he only a man of the Bingham-created world, one that was rich and varied but, he knew, vastly incomplete? Here he was, in a room in a house that was less than a fifteen-minute hansom ride from Washington Square, and yet it was more foreign to him than London, than Paris, than Rome; he might have been in Peking, or on the moon, for all he recognized in it. And there was something worse in him as well—a sense of incredulity that spoke to a naïveté that was not just distasteful but perilous: Even as he had entered the house, he had persisted in thinking Edward lived here as a lark, as an affectation of poverty.

This knowledge, coupled with the room's chill, a cold that felt almost wet, it was so pervasive and insistent, made him realize the absurdity of his being here, and he stood, re-buttoning his coat, which he'd not even removed, and was about to leave, to prepare to encounter Edward Bishop on the stairs and make his excuses and apologies, when his host returned, lugging a sloshing copper pot.

"Stand aside, please, Mister Bingham," he said with mock formality, his earlier confidence already recovered, and poured the water into the kettle before kneeling to build a fire, the flames snapping to life as immediately as if he'd summoned them. All the while, David stood, helpless, and when Edward turned to face him again, he sat down on the bed, resigned.

"Oh, I shouldn't be so presumptuous as to sit on your bed!" he said, bolting to his feet.

Edward smiled, then. "There is nowhere else to sit," he said, simply. "Please." And so David sat again.

The fire made the room seem friendlier, less bleak, the windows turning opaque with steam, and by the time Edward had poured his tea—"Not really tea, I'm afraid; only dried chamomile buds"—David felt less uncomfortable, and for a moment, there was a companionable silence, as the two of them drank.

"I've biscuits, if you want them?"

"No, no thank you."

They both sipped. "We shall have to go back to the café again—earlier in the day, perhaps."

"Yes, I should like that."

For a moment, it seemed they both struggled to speak. "Do *you* think we should allow the Negroes in?" asked Edward, teasingly, and David, smiling back, shook his head. "I feel for the Negroes, of course," he said, staunchly, echoing his grandfather's opinion, "but it is best that they find their own places to live—in the West, perhaps." It was not, his grandfather said, that the Negroes were uneducable—in fact, the opposite was true, and that was the trouble, for once the Negro became learned, would he not want to enjoy the opportunities of the Free States himself? He thought of how his grandfather would only refer to the Negro question as "the Negro issue," never the Negro dilemma or the Negro problem, for "once we call it that, it becomes ours to solve." "The Negro issue is the sin at America's heart," he often said. "But we are not America, and it is not our sin." On this matter, as on many others, David knew his grandfather to be wise, and it had never occurred to him to believe differently.

Another silence, broken by only the sound of the china cups tapping against their teeth, and Edward smiled at him. "You are shocked by how I live."

"No," he said, "not shocked," though he was. He was so stunned, indeed, that his conversational abilities, his manners, had deserted him altogether. When he had been a shy schoolboy, slow to make friends and often ignored by his classmates, Grandfather had once told him that all one had to do to seem interesting was to ask questions of others. "People adore nothing more than to speak of themselves," Grandfather had said. "And if you ever find yourself in a circumstance in which you fear your place or standing—though you should not: You are a Bingham, remember, and the best child I know—then all you must do is ask the other person something about him- or herself, and they will forever after be convinced that you are the most fascinating individual they have ever encountered." This was an exaggeration, naturally, but his grandfather had not been incorrect, and this advice, once followed, had, if not transformed his place among his peers, then certainly prevented what would have promised to be a lifetime of ignominy, and he had relied upon it on countless occasions since.

Even now, he was aware that, of the two of them, Edward was by far the more mysterious, the more compelling figure. He was David Bingham, and everything about him was known. What would it be like to be someone anonymous, someone whose name meant nothing, who was able to move through life as a shadow, who was able to sing a music-hall ditty in a classroom without word of it traveling among everyone one knew, to live in a frigid room in a boardinghouse with a neighbor who woke when others were settling in their parlors for drinks and conversation, to be someone who was beholden to no one? He was not so romantic as to desire this, necessarily; he would not much like to live in this cold little cell so near the river, to have to fetch water every time one wanted to have a drink instead of merely giving a single sharp yank to a bell pull—he was not even convinced he would be capable of it. Yet to be so known was to trade adventure for certainty, and therefore to be exiled to an unsurprising life. Even in Europe, he had been passed from acquaintance to acquaintance of his grandfather's: His path was never his own to forge, for someone had already done it for him, clearing obstacles he would never know had once existed. He was free, but he was also not.

So it was with genuine longing that he began asking Edward about himself, about who he was and how he had come to live the life he had, and as Edward talked, as naturally and fluently as if he'd been waiting for years for David to come into his life and question him, David found himself aware, even as he listened with interest to Edward's story, of a kind of new and unpleasant pride in himself—that he was here in this unlikely space, and that he was talking to a strange and beautiful and unlikely man, and that, although he could see that beyond the mist-shrouded window the sky was becoming black and that therefore his grandfather would be sitting down to dinner and wondering where he was, he made no move to make his apologies, no move to leave. It was as if he had been bewitched and, knowing it, had sought not to fight against it but to surrender, to leave behind the world he thought he knew for another, and all because he wanted to attempt to be not the person he was—but the one he dreamed of being.

VI

O ver the following weeks, he saw Edward first once, then twice, then three, then four more times. They would meet after Edward's class or his own. For their second meeting, they maintained the pretense of going to the café first, but thereafter they went directly to Edward's room, and there they stayed as late as David dared before he had to return to his hansom, waiting for him in front of the school, and hurry home before Grandfather announced himself for dinner—he had been not angry, but curious when David had come in so late after that first encounter, and although David had evaded his questions then, he knew they would soon become more insistent if there were to be a second incident of tardiness, and he was unequipped to answer them.

Indeed, he was unsure how, if forced, he might characterize his friendship with Edward. At night, after he and Grandfather had had their drinks and talk in the drawing room—"Are you quite all right?" his grandfather asked, after David's third secret meeting. "You seem unusually . . . distracted"—he would retire to his study and record in his diary what he had learned of Edward that day, and then sit and reread it as if it were one of those mystery novels Peter liked, and not things that he had actually heard firsthand.

He was twenty-three, five years younger than David, and had attended, for two years, a conservatory in Worcester, Massachusetts. But although he had had a scholarship, he hadn't the money to earn his degree, and so had moved to New York four years ago to find work.

"What did you do?" David had asked him.

"Oh, a bit of everything," had been the reply, and this had turned out not to be untrue, or at least not completely: Edward had been, for brief periods, a cook's assistant ("Ghastly. I can scarcely boil water, as you've seen for yourself"), a nanny ("Terrible. I neglected my charges' education entirely and just let them eat sweets"), a coalman's apprentice ("I'm simply not sure why I even thought it might be work for which I'd be the least suited"), and an artist's model ("Much duller than you'd imagine. One perches in an impossible position until one's aching and cold while a class of simpering dowagers and leering codgers make attempts to sketch you"). Finally, though (through means which remained unexplained), he found work as a pianist in a small nightclub.

("A nightclub!" David was unable to stop himself from exclaiming.

"Yes, yes, a nightclub! Where else would I have learned all those inappropriate songs that so offend the Bingham ears?" But this last was said teasingly, and they smiled at each other.)

From the nightclub, he had received an offer to teach at the institute (this too was left unexplained, and David entertained a brief and satisfying fantasy of Matron marching down into a dark room, grabbing Edward by the back of his collar, and yanking him up a flight of stairs, down the street, and into the school); lately, he had been trying to supplement his income by giving private lessons, though he knew that finding such work would be difficult, if not near-impossible.

("But you *are* qualified," David had protested.

"But there are many others more qualified and better credentialed than I. Come—you have nieces and nephews, do you not? Would your brother or sister ever hire someone like me? Or would they hire—be truthful, now—tutors trained at the National Conservatory, or professional musicians, to teach their darlings? Oh, no, don't feel bad, you needn't apologize; I know it to be true, and it is simply how things are. A poor and unestablished young man without a degree even from a third-rate seminary is not much in demand, and never shall be.")

He enjoyed teaching. His friends (he offered no details of them) teased him for his job, modest as it was in all ways, but he was fond of it, fond of the children themselves. "They remind me of what I was," he said, though, again, he did not explain how. He, like David, knew that his charges would never be able to become musicians, might never even have the luxury of attending a musical performance, but he thought that he would at least be able to give them a spot of delight, of joy, in their lives, something they might carry with them, a source of pleasure they might always be able to call their own.

"That is how I feel, too," he'd cried, excited that someone should see the children's education as he did. "They may never play music themselves—none of them will, most likely—but it will give them a certain refinement of the spirit, won't it? And isn't that worthwhile?"

At this, something, some cloud, had moved quickly and briefly across Edward's face, and for a moment, David wondered if he had said something to offend. But "You are very right" was all his new friend said, and then the conversation had turned to a different subject.

All this he had recorded, along with the details Edward told him of his neighbors, which made him laugh and marvel, too: an elderly bachelor who never left his room, and yet whom Edward had seen lower his shoes in a bucket to a waiting bootblack on the sidewalk below; the longshoreman, whose snores they could occasionally hear purring through the thin wall; the boy in the room above his, who Edward swore spent his days giving dancing lessons to elderly ladies, the evidence the noise of their heels clopping across the wood. He was aware that Edward thought him naïve, and also of his delight in astonishing him, of trying, often, to shock him. And he was happy to comply: He *was* naïve. He *enjoyed* being astonished. In Edward's presence he felt both older and younger, and weightless, too—he was being given the opportunity to relive his youth, to finally experience that sense of abandon that young people felt, except he was now old enough to know to treasure it. "My innocent," Edward had begun calling him, and although he might have felt patronized by the affection—for it *was* patronizing, was it not?—he did not. To Edward, he was not ignorant after all but innocent, something small and precious, something to be protected and cherished from everything that existed outside the boardinghouse walls.

But it was what Edward had told him on their third meeting that had since come to occupy much of his time and many of his thoughts. They had been intimate for the first time that day, Edward standing, mid-sentence (he had been speaking of a friend of his who was a math tutor for a purportedly rich family of whom David had never heard), and drawing the curtains, and then matter-of-factly joining him on the bed, and although this was of course not his first encounter—he, like every man in the city, rich or poor, would from time to time take a hansom to the eastern mouth of Gansevoort Street, a few blocks north of the boardinghouse, where men like him would head to the southern row of houses, and men who wanted women to the northern row, and the ones who wanted something else altogether would go to the western end of the street, where there were a few parlors that fulfilled more specific desires, including a single, tidy house that was meant only for female customers—it felt extraordinary, as if he were relearning how to walk, or eat, or breathe: a physical sensation that he had for so long accepted as feeling one way but that had been revealed to be something entirely different.

Afterward, they had lain together, and so narrow was Edward's bed that they had both had to turn on their sides, else David would have tumbled out altogether. They laughed about this, too.

"Do you know," he had begun, moving his arm from beneath the wool blanket, which he found almost unbearably scratchy, like being covered with a skein woven from nettles—I shall have to get him another one, he thought—and placing it atop Edward's soft skin, beneath which he could feel the ridges of his rib cage, "you have told me so much of yourself, but you have still not told me where you are from, or who your people are." This reticence had initially intrigued him, but now he found it slightly troubling—he feared that Edward was ashamed of his origins, that he might think David would be disapproving. And yet he was not that sort of person: Edward had nothing to fear from him. "Where are you from?" he asked, into Edward's silence. "Not from New York," he continued. "Connecticut? Massachusetts?"

Finally, Edward spoke. "The Colonies," he said, quietly, and at this, David was speechless.

He had never known someone from the Colonies. Oh, he had seen them: Every year, Eliza and Eden hosted a salon in their home to raise money for the refugees, and there was always an escapee, usually recent, to speak tremblingly about his or her experience in the lovely, honeyed voice that the Colonists had. Increasingly, they came not for religious reasons, or to escape persecution, but because, in the decades since it had been defeated (though its citizens would never use this term) in the War of Rebellion, the Colonies had become steadily more impoverished—not entirely, of course, and not ruinously so, but it would never again have the sort of wealth it once did, much less the sort that the Free States had accumulated in the century-odd period since its founding. But it was not these kinds of migrants that his sister and her wife hosted but the rebels, the ones who came north because to remain where they had been born and raised would have been to court danger, because they wanted to live freely. The war was over but the fighting continued; there were many for whom the Colonies remained a miserable place, full of skirmishes and late-night raids.

So, yes, he was not unacquainted with the chaos of the Colonies. But *this* was a different matter entirely: *This* was someone he was coming to know, with whom he had spoken and laughed, and in whose arms he now lay, the both of them unclothed.

"But you don't sound like you're from the Colonies," he said at last, and at this, to his relief, Edward laughed.

"No, I don't—but I have lived here for many years," he said.

Slowly at first, and then in a rush, his story emerged. He had arrived in the Free States, to Philadelphia, as a child. The family had lived for four generations in Georgia, near Savannah, where his father had been a schoolteacher at a boys' school. When he was almost seven, though, he had announced that they were to leave on a trip. There were six of them: he, his mother, his father, and his three sisters—two older, the third younger.

David calculated. "So this would have been in seventy-seven?"

"Yes. That autumn."

What followed was a typical escapee's tale; before the war, the southern states had disapproved of the Free States, but did not adjudicate their citizens' movements through the nation. After the war, however, and the south's subsequent secession from the Union, it became illegal for those in the Free States to travel to the south, now renamed the United Colonies, or for the Colonists to travel north. Yet many of the Colonists did so anyway. The trip north was arduous, and long, and was generally made on foot. Common wisdom suggested that it was safest to move in a group, but that group ought not number more than, say, ten and ought not contain more than five children, as they tired quickly and were less likely to remain calm in the case of a patrol's appearance. One heard dreadful stories of aborted attempts: of children being torn, wailing, from their parents and, it was rumored, sold to local families to work as farmhands; wives being separated from their husbands and forced to remarry; imprisonment; death. The worst stories were of the people like them, people who came to the Free States in hopes of living legally. Not long ago, Eliza's guests had been two men, recently arrived, who were traveling with their friends, another couple, from Virginia. They were less than half a mile from Maryland, whence they would carry on to Pennsylvania, and had stopped to rest against an oak tree. There they lay, in each other's arms, but just as they had begun to relax, they heard the first hoofbeats, and immediately leapt to their feet and began running. But the second couple was slower, and when they heard the cries of their friends as they fell, the first couple did not turn back but instead ran harder and faster than they had ever dreamed themselves capable. Behind them, closer and closer, drew another set of hoofbeats, and it was only by meters that they made it across the border, and only then that they turned, and saw the patrol, his face obscured by his hood, pulling tight on his horse's reins, skidding to a halt, before raising his rifle at them. It was illegal for a patrol to cross the border in order to claim an escapee, much less kill one, but everyone knew that it took only a single bullet to render that law useless. The couple turned and ran again, with the horse's whinny echoing in the air behind them for what seemed like miles, and it was not until the next day, once they were safely in the state's interior, that they allowed themselves to weep for their friends, not only because they had imagined beginning their lives in the Free States together but because everyone knew what happened to people like them who were caught: beatings, burnings, torture— death. Telling the story in Eliza and Eden's parlor, the men had wept again, and David, like everyone else in attendance, had listened in spellbound horror. That night, back at Washington Square, he had thought of how dearly blessed he was to have been born in the Free States; how he had never known and would never know such barbarism as those gentlemen had endured.

Edward's family had been alone on their journey. His father had not hired a smuggler, who, if he was trustworthy (and some were), greatly improved your chances of a successful escape; they had not traveled with another family, which was preferable because it meant one couple could sleep while the other looked after the children. From Georgia, the trip required around a fortnight, but by the end of the first week, the weather had grown chilly, and then bitter, and the family's food reserves were nearly depleted.

"My parents would wake us very early, at daybreak, and my sisters and I would forage for acorns," Edward said. "We couldn't risk building a fire, but my mother would pound them into a paste, and we would eat it mashed atop hardtack."

"How awful," he murmured. He felt foolish—but there was nothing else he might say.

"Yes—it was. Most awful for my younger sister, Belle. She was only four and didn't understand that she had to be quiet; she only knew she was hungry and didn't know why. She cried and cried, and my mother had to hold her hand over her mouth so she wouldn't give us away."

Neither of his parents ate breakfast or lunch. They saved their remaining food for dinner, and at night, the family would huddle together for warmth. Edward and his father would try to find a copse of trees for them to sleep in, or at least a gully, and they would cover themselves with leaves and branches, both to protect themselves from the wind and to try to conceal their scent from the patrol's dogs. What was worse, Edward remembered thinking, even then—the terror or the hunger? Both defined his every day.

When they finally made it to Maryland, they went straight to one of the centers a friend had told Edward's father about, where they remained for several months. Edward's father taught classes in reading and mathematics to some of his fellow escapees' children; Edward's mother, a skilled seamstress, repaired damaged clothes, which the center took in to earn its residents a pittance. By spring, they had left the center and had embarked upon their travels once again—a difficult but less arduous journey, since now they were at least in the Union—this time to the Free States, where they continued northward to New York. Here, in the city, Mister Bishop had eventually found work at a printing press (there being a certain prejudice in the Free States and the Union against the educational standards of people from the Colonies, meaning that many learned escapees found themselves in reduced circumstances), and the six of them had settled into a small apartment on Orchard Street.

Still, Edward said (and David detected a note of sincerity, of pride, in his voice), they had most of them done well for themselves. His parents had died, carried away by the flu of '90, but his two older sisters were both schoolteachers in Vermont, and Belle, a nurse, lived with her husband, a doctor, in New Hampshire, in Manchester.

"Indeed, I am the only failure," he said, and sighed, dramatically, although David sensed that Edward in some way believed this to be true, and that it troubled him.

"You are not a failure," he told Edward, and pulled him closer to his body.

For a while, they were silent, and David, his chin resting atop Edward's dark head, traced patterns on Edward's back. "Your father," he said, at last, "had he been like us?"

"No, not like us, though if he had objections to our kind, he never said. I do not think he did."

"Had he been a believer of Reverend Foxley's, then?" Many of the escapees were secret believers in the preachings of the famous Utopian, an advocate of open love and one of the Free States' founders.

He was considered a heretic in the Colonies, where possession of his texts was illegal.

"No, no—he'd not been very religious."

"Then—if you do not mind my asking—why did he want to come north?"

Here David felt Edward sigh, his warm breath against his chest. "I must be honest and say that, even after all this time, I don't know myself. We had a good life in Georgia, after all. We were known; we had friends.

"When I was older and therefore impertinent enough, I asked him why we had made the journey. And all he would say is that he wanted us to have a better life. A better life! He had gone from being a respected teacher to being a printer—a perfectly fine occupation, of course, but a man who works with his mind does not usually consider a life working with his hands a better one. So I have never understood, not to my satisfaction—and, I suppose, I never shall."

"But maybe," David said, quietly, "maybe he did it for you."

Edward was quiet, too. Then, "I don't imagine he would have known when I was six."

"Perhaps he did. My father did; I believe he knew it of all of us. Well, not Eden, perhaps—she was still little more than a baby when he and my mother died. But John and I, even though we were so young . . . Yes, I believe he knew."

"And he was not bothered by this?"

"No, and why should he have been? His own father was like us. We were not foreign to him, nor distasteful."

At this, Edward gave a laugh like a puff of air and rolled away from him, onto his back. By now, it was evening, and the room had grown dark—David would have to leave soon, lest he miss another dinner. But all he wanted to do was lie in Edward Bishop's hard, narrow bed, feeling the terrible itch of the poor wool blanket atop him, the lingering warmth from the fire burning low in the hearth, and Edward's skin beside him. "You know what they call the Free States in the Colonies, don't you?" Edward asked, and David, though he did not put much stock in what the Colonies thought of them or not, was not of course ignorant of the cruel and vulgar nicknames by which they referred to his country, and instead of answering Edward's question, he put his palm over his mouth.

"I do," he said. "Kiss me." And Edward did.

He had returned to Washington Square after that, reluctantly dressing and venturing into the cold, but later, up in his study, he was able to recognize that that discussion, that encounter, had left him changed. He had a secret, and his secret was Edward, and not just him, his smooth white skin and his soft dark hair, but Edward's experiences, what he had seen and what he had endured: He was from another place, another existence, and in sharing his life with David, he had made David's own suddenly richer, more profound and ecstatic and mysterious all at once.

Now, in his study, he reviewed his journal again, poring over details he well knew as if he were learning them for the first time: Edward's middle name (Martins—his mother's maiden name); Edward's favorite piece of music (Bach's Cello Suite no. 1 in G Major); Edward's favorite food ("Don't laugh—it's hominy, with bacon. No, you *mustn't* laugh! I am from Georgia, after all!"). He read through the pages he'd written with a greed he'd not felt for many years, and when he finally retired, unable to stop yawning, it was with pleasure, for he knew that it would soon be the next day, and that would mean he would see Edward once more. The affinity he felt for Edward was thrilling, but equally as thrilling was the *intensity* of that affinity, and the speed with which it had developed. He felt, for the first time in perhaps his whole life, reckless, wild—as if he were atop a runaway horse, scarcely holding on as it galloped down a long stretch of plain, gasping with laughter and fear.

For many years—so many years—he had wondered if there was something not just amiss with him but deficient within him. It was not that he was not invited to the same parties as John and Eden; it was what happened at them. This was back when they were younger and simply known as the Bingham siblings, and he was only identified as the eldest, not "the bachelor" or "the unmarried one" or "the one who still lives at Washington Square": They would enter the party, ascending the low, wide stone steps of a recently built Park Avenue manse, Eden and John first, her arm looped through his, he bringing up the rear, and upon entering the glittering, twinklingly lit space, he would hear what sounded to him like a cheer, as John's and Eden's faces were kissed by well-wishers sighing in delight at their arrival.

And he? He would be greeted as well, of course; they were well-brought-up, their acquaintances and peers, and he was a Bingham, and no one would dare be anything less than cordial, not to his face. But for the rest of the party, he would feel strangely elsewhere, as if floating above the room, and at dinner, where he would be seated not with the bright young things of the gathering but, rather, among their parents' friends and relations—the father's sister, for example, or the mother's elderly uncle—he would feel the full force of his undeniable otherness, how what he had striven to conceal had been recognized and accounted for by everyone in their circle. From the other end of the table would occasionally come gusts of laughter, and his seatmate would shake his or her head indulgently, before turning to him and commenting on the irrepressible frivolity of the young, and how one must allow them such latitudes. Sometimes after saying this they would realize their mistake, and hastily add that he, too, must have his moments of mirth, but other times they would not; he would be aged before his time, cast from the island of youth not by his years but by his temperament.

Or perhaps it was not temperament at all but something else. He never had been jolly or lighthearted, not even as a child. He had once overheard his grandfather remarking on his somberness to Frances, adding that it was because he was the eldest, and therefore his grief had been the most intense when he and his siblings lost their parents. But the qualities that often attended his sort of inwardness—a studiousness, a seriousness of purpose, a scholarliness—were absent in him. He was attuned to the dangers of the world but not to its delights and joys; even love, to him, was not a state of elation but a source of anxiety and fear: Did his beloved actually love him? When might he be abandoned? He had watched first Eden and then John in their courtships, had witnessed their returning home late in the evening, their cheeks pink with wine and dancing, had seen how quickly they snatched letters from the tray proffered by Adams, tearing open the envelopes even as they hurried from the room, their lips already lifting into smiles. The fact that he had not experienced the same kind of happiness was a source of both sorrow and concern; of late, he had been beginning to fear that it was not just that no one might love him but that he might be incapable of *receiving* such love, which seemed altogether worse. His infatuation with Edward, then, the awakening he felt within him, was not just transporting for the sensation itself but intensified by his sense of relief: There was nothing wrong with him after all. It was not he who was damaged; it was only that he had yet to find the person who would rouse in him his full capacity for pleasure. But now he had, and he was at last experiencing the sort of transformation that love had visited on everyone he knew but that had always eluded him.

That night, he had a dream: It was years in the future. He and Edward were living together in Washington Square. The two of them were sitting, side by side, in chairs in the parlor, where a piano now stood beneath the window that overlooked the park's northern boundary. At their feet lay three dark-haired children, a girl and two boys, reading picture books, the girl wearing a scarlet velvet bow atop her glossy head. There was a fire burning and boughs of pine arranged atop the mantelpiece. Outside, he knew, it was snowing, and from the dining room came the fragrance of roasted partridge, and the sounds of wine glugging into glasses and of china being arranged on the table.

In this vision, Washington Square was not a prison, or something to dread—it was his home, their home, and this was their family. The house, he realized, had become his after all—and it had become his because it had become Edward's, too.

VII

The following Wednesday, he was leaving for his class when Adams hurried to the door. "Mister David, Mister Bingham sent word from the bank this morning—he requests you be home precisely at five o'clock today," he said.

"Thank you, Matthew, I'll take it from here," he said to the valet, assuming the box of fruit he was bringing for the students to draw and turning his attention to the butler. "Did he say why, Adams?"

"No, sir. Only that he asks for your presence."

"Very well. You can tell him to expect me."

"Very good, sir."

It was politely stated, but David knew it was no request but a command. A mere few weeks ago—a few weeks! Had it only been a scant month since he had met Edward, since his world had been redrawn?—he would have been frightened, anxious about what his grandfather might have to say to him (for no good reason, as his grandfather had never been unkind to him, had rarely rebuked him, even in childhood), but now he felt only irritation, for it meant that he would have less time with Edward than he otherwise might. After class, then, he went directly to Edward's, and it seemed as if in no time at all he was having once more to dress and leave, with a promise he would soon return.

At the door to Edward's room, they lingered, David in his coat and hat, Edward wrapped in his horrid scratchy blanket.

"Tomorrow, then?" Edward asked, with such unabashed yearning that David—unused to being the party who would provide the affirmative answer upon which another's happiness would be determined—smiled and nodded. "Tomorrow," he agreed, and finally Edward released him and David tripped down the stairs.

As he climbed the steps to his house, he found himself nervous to see his grandfather in a way he never was, as if this were to be their first encounter after months of distance, rather than less than twenty-four hours. But his grandfather, already in his drawing room, merely received David's kiss as he always did, and the two of them sat with their sherry and chatted about topics of little consequence until Adams came to announce dinner. It was only as they were going down that he whispered to his grandfather. But "After dinner," his grandfather replied.

Dinner, too, was uneventful, and near its conclusion, David found himself experiencing a rare resentment toward his grandfather. Was there no news, nothing for his grandfather to relay? Was this only a gambit to remind him of his own dependency, of the fact—which he knew very well—that he was indeed not the master of this house, that he was not even an adult but someone who was allowed only in theory to come and go as he pleased? He heard his answers to his grandfather's inquiries become curt, and had to correct himself before he crossed from being taciturn into being rude. For what could he do, what could he argue? It was not his house. He was not his own man. He was no different from the servants, from the bank's employees, from the students at the institute: He was dependent on Nathaniel Bingham, and always would be.

And so he was seething with emotions—irritation, self-pity, anger—by the time he was settled in his usual chair by the fire upstairs, when his grandfather handed him a thick letter, much battered, its edges crisped with dried water.

"This arrived at the office today," his grandfather said, expressionless, and David, wonderingly, turned it over and saw his name, addressed care of Bingham Brothers, with a Massachusetts postmark. "An express delivery," his grandfather said. "Take it, read it, and return," and David stood, wordlessly, and went to his own study, sitting for a moment with the envelope in his hands before at last slicing it open.

My dear David,   January 20, 1894

There is nowhere for me to begin this letter but with my deep-
est and most sincere apologies for not having written earlier. I am
wretched at the thought of any pain or upset I might have caused
you, though perhaps I am only flattering myself—perhaps you have
not thought of me as often as I have thought of you these past almost
seven weeks.

I do not wish to make excuses for my poor manners, but I do want
to explain why I have not communicated, because I do not wish that
my silence should be mistaken for lack of devotion.

Shortly after I left you in early December, I was obligated to make
a trip up North to visit our fur trappers. As I think I mentioned, my
family has had a long-standing agreement with a family of trappers
in northern Maine, and over the years, it has become an important
aspect of our business. On this trip, I was accompanied by my eldest
nephew, James, who had left college the previous spring to work in
our business. My sister, understandably, was not enthusiastic about
this idea, and nor was I—he would have been the first among us
to graduate from college—but he is grown and we finally had no
choice but to acquiesce. He is a wonderful young man, high-spirited
and enthusiastic, but as he has no sea legs and is indeed given to
sickness, my siblings and parents and I decided that he might be
trained to eventually oversee our fur trade.

The North has been unusually cold this year, and as I had mentioned, our trappers live very close to the Canadian border. Our
visit was largely a ceremonial one; I would introduce James to them,
and they would take him out to demonstrate how they caught the
animals and skinned and cured them, and then we would return to
the Cape in time for Christmas. But that was not what happened.

Initially, everything proceeded as planned. James immediately
formed a friendship with one of the members of the family, a very
likable and intelligent youth named Percival, and it was Percival who
spent several days introducing James to their trade while I stayed
behind in the house to discuss how we might expand our offerings.

You may well be wondering why we are concerning ourselves with fur when the industry has been in decline for the past sixty years; certainly our partners did. But it is precisely because the British have now all but abandoned the area that I think we have the opportunity to make our business there more robust, by selling not just beaver but, crucially, mink and stoat, which are much softer and finer and for which I believe there will be a small but meaningful group of dedicated customers. This family, the Delacroix, are also one of the very few European families left in the trade, which means they are much more reliable and much more suited to the realities and complexities of business.

The afternoon of the fifth day of our visit was reserved for leisure, to be followed by a dinner to celebrate our partnership. Earlier, while touring the Delacroix property, we had passed a pretty little pond, now frozen over, and James had been excited to skate on it. It was a frigid day, but clear and calm, and as the pond was just a few hundred meters from the main house, and he had comported himself well, I said he might.

He had not been gone an hour when, abruptly, the weather changed. In minutes, the skies had turned first white, then a deep pewter, and then nearly black. And then, at once, it was snowing, the flakes falling in clumps.

My first thought was of James, and it was the first thought as well of Olivier, the family's patriarch, who came running to find me as I was running to find him. "We will send Percival with the dogs," he said. "He can walk this route in the dark, he knows it so well." To ensure his safety, he tied one end of a long length of rope to the bottom of the staircase banister and the other to his nephew's belt, and told the boy, armed with an ax and a knife as a precaution, to return as quickly as he was able.

Off the boy set, unafraid and calm, while Olivier and I stood at the staircase, watching as the rope unspooled itself and, eventually, grew taut. By this time the snow was so thick that I, standing at the door, was unable to see anything but white. And then the wind began, gently at first, and then so fierce, so howling, that I was forced inside altogether.

Yet still the rope remained taut. Olivier gave it two sharp tugs, and a few seconds later, received two sharp tugs in response. By this time, the boy's father, Marcel, Olivier's younger brother, had joined us, silent and anxious, as well as their other brother, Julien, and their respective wives and their aged parents. Outside, the wind blew so loudly that even the sturdy cabin shook.

And then, suddenly, the rope went slack. It had been some twenty minutes since Percival had left, and when Olivier yanked on the cord once more, no one returned his signal. They are stoic people, the Delacroix: One cannot live in the part of the world they do, with the weather they have (not to mention the other dangers—the wolves and the bears and the cougars, and of course the Indians), and not remain calm under dire circumstances. And yet they all treasured Percival, and a hum of nervousness immediately circulated through the entryway.

There was some swift, murmured discussion about what to do. Percival had two of the family's best hunting dogs with him, which would offer him some protection—the dogs were trained to work as a unit, and one could be trusted to stay with him while the other returned to the house for help. This was assuming the dogs had not, for example, been urged by Percival to find and remain with James. By now the snow and wind were so intense that it seemed the entire house was listing to and fro, the windows rattling in their casements like chattering teeth.

We had all been timing how long he had been gone: Ten minutes. Twenty minutes. Half an hour. At our feet, like a dead snake, lay the length of rope.

Then, nearly forty minutes after Percival had left, there was a thudding at the door, one we at first mistook for the wind and then realized was the noise of a creature tossing itself against it. Marcel, with a cry, quickly threw off the heavy wooden bolt and he and Julien pulled it open to discover one of the dogs, his coat crusted so thickly with snow it appeared as if he'd been baked in salt, and, clutching at his back, James. We pulled him in—he was still wearing his skates, which had, we later realized, probably saved him, allowing him purchase as he made the walk uphill—and

Julien's and Olivier's wives fell upon him with blankets and hustled him away to a bedroom; they had been heating water for the boys' return, and we could hear them running back and forth with pails full, and the sound of water splashing into the metal tub. Olivier and I tried to interrogate him, but the poor boy was so chilled, so exhausted, so hysterical, that he was making very little sense. "Percival," he kept saying, "Percival." His eyes flicked back and forth in a way that made him seem crazed, and I was, I will admit, frightened. Something had happened, something that had terrified my nephew.

"James, where is he?" Olivier demanded.

"Pond," James babbled, "pond." But we could get no more information from him.

At the entryway, Julien told us later, the returned dog was pawing and scratching, whining to be let out. Marcel grabbed him by his collar and yanked him back, but the dog was desperate, yelping and straining, and finally, on their father's command, they again unbolted the door and the dog ran out into the white.

Once again, the waiting commenced, and after I had dressed James in clean flannels and held him while Julien's wife had him drink some hot toddy and then put him to bed, I rejoined the party in the entryway in time to once again hear that sickening thump against the door, which Marcel this time opened at once, with a cry of relief that soon became a wail. There, at the door, were both of the dogs, frozen and exhausted and panting, and, between them, Percival, his hair in icicles, his young handsome face the particular unearthly shade of blue that means only one thing. The dogs had dragged him all the way from the lake.

The next hour was awful. The rest of the children, Percival's brothers and sisters and cousins, who had been instructed by their parents to stay upstairs, came running down and saw their beloved brother frozen to death, and their father and mother keening, and began to sob as well. I cannot remember how we managed to calm them, nor how we managed to make everyone go to bed, except that the night felt interminable, and outside the wind continued to scream—spitefully, it now seemed—and the snow to fall. It was not until well into the following afternoon, when James had finally awoken and become sensate once more, that he was able to relay, tremblingly, what had happened: When the storm had come, he had panicked, and had tried to make his way back on his own. But the snow was so blinding, and the wind so ferocious, that he was driven back again and again to the pond. Then, just when he had convinced himself he would die there, he had heard the faint sound of barking, and had seen the top of Percival's bright-crimson cap, and knew he was to be saved.

Percival had reached out his arm, and James had grabbed it, but at that moment there had been a particularly strong gust of wind, and Percival had skidded onto the ice with him, and the two had tumbled into a heap. Again they stood, inching together to the edge of the pond, and again they fell. But this second time, after being once again pushed by the wind, Percival fell at a strange angle. He had had his ax drawn—James said he meant to stick it into the shore and use it as a lever to pull themselves out—but it instead pierced the ice, which cracked beneath them.

"Christ," James said Percival had shouted. "James, get off the ice."

He did—the dogs moving close to the water so he could grab them by their ruffs to steady himself—and then turned to reach for Percival, who was once again sliding on his boots across the frozen surface toward ground, but before he could reach it, he was buffeted by another gale, and fell back a third time, this time landing on his back near the spiderwebbed crack. And now, James said, the ice gave a groaning, sickening noise, and split, and Percival was swallowed by the water.

James yelled, from fright and desperation, but then Percival's head emerged. My nephew grabbed the end of the rope, now no longer attached to Percival's belt, and threw it to him. But when Percival tried to pull himself out, the hole in the ice split further, and his head once again slipped beneath the surface. By now, of course, James was frantic, but Percival, he recounted, was very calm. "James," he said, "go back to the house and tell them to send help. Rosie"—one of the dogs—"will stay with me. Take Rufus and tell them what happened." And, when James hesitated, "Go! Hurry!"

So James left, turning to watch Rosie pick her way across the ice toward Percival, and Percival reaching toward her.

They'd not gotten more than a few meters when they heard a dull sound behind them; the wind was so loud that it muffled all noise, but James turned, and he and Rufus returned to the pond, scarcely able to see through the snow. There, they saw Rosie running in circles on the ice, barking and barking, and then Rufus ran to her, and the two stood there together, whimpering. Through the snow, James could see Percival's red glove clutching at the surface, though not Percival's head. But he could see a thrashing from the water, a kind of violence. And then the red glove slipped, and Percival was gone. James hurried to the pond, but when he stepped atop the surface, it broke into plates, soaking his feet, and he only managed to scrabble up to the shore again before it split once more. He shouted for the dogs, but Rosie, no matter how much he called for her, wouldn't move from her floe of ice. It was Rufus who guided him back to the house, but for many minutes, he could hear Rosie's whining, her cries carried by the wind.

He had been crying as he told this story, but now he began to sob, gulping for breath. "I'm sorry, Uncle Charles!" he said. "I'm so sorry, Mister Delacroix!"

"He didn't even have time to sink," Marcel said in a strange, faint, strangled voice. "Not if the dogs were able to rescue him."

"He couldn't swim," Olivier added, in a low voice. "We tried to teach him, but he never learned."

As you can imagine, it was another dreadful night, and I spent it with James, holding him against me and murmuring to him until he at last fell asleep again. The snow and wind stopped the next day, and the skies turned brilliant and blue, and the weather even colder. I and some of Percival's cousins shoveled a path to the ice house, where Marcel and Julien would keep Percival's body until the ground had thawed enough for them to bury him properly. The day after, James and I left, detouring to Bangor to send word of what had happened to my sister.

Since then, as you can imagine, things have been much changed. I do not even mean from a business perspective, about which I dare not ask—I have sent the Delacroix our deep condolences, and my father ordered they be given the monies for a smokehouse they'd intended to build. But we have heard nothing from them in response.

James is very different now. He has spent the holiday season in his room, hardly eating, rarely speaking. He sits and stares, and sometimes he cries, but mostly he is silent, and nothing his brothers or mother or I can do seems able to bring him back to us. It is apparent he blames himself for the tragedy of Percival's passing, no matter how many times I tell him he is not at fault. My brother has temporarily assumed control of the business while my sister and I spend every moment we can with him, hoping we might be able to puncture his fog of grief, hoping we might once again hear his dear laugh. I fear for him, and for my beloved sister.

I know it will sound terrible, and selfish, to say this, but as I sit with him these days and weeks, I find myself returning repeatedly to our conversation, which I left feeling embarrassed—of how much I had said, of how emotional I let myself become, of how much I burdened you—and wondering what you must think of me. I say this not as a rebuke, but I wonder if this is why you've not chosen to write me, though of course you might have mistaken my silence for lack of interest and been offended, which I would understand.

Percival's death has made me think more often as well of William, of how wild with misery I was when he died, and of how, in my brief time spent with you, I began to imagine that I might be able to live again with a companion, someone with whom I might share the joys of life, but also its sorrows.

I hope you can forgive me for my poor communication, and that this very long letter might go some way in assuring you of my continued interest and affection. I will be back in your city in a fortnight and do hope I may be allowed to call on you again, if only to ask your forgiveness in person.

I wish you and your family all good health and belated holiday greetings. I await your reply.

Yours very sincerely,
Charles Griffith

VIII

F or a few moments, David merely sat, stunned by the story that Charles had related, a story that had the effect of abruptly deflating his own giddy happiness, but also any annoyance he may have felt for his grandfather. He thought with pity of poor young James, whose life was now, as Charles had said, transformed, and who would be haunted by this event forever—he was not to blame, but he would never quite believe that fact. He would spend his adulthood either trying to apologize for what he thought he had done or denying it. One path would make him feeble; the other, bitter. And poor Charles, to have once again brushed against death, to once again be associated with the loss of someone so young!

But he was also aware of a shame of his own, for until his grandfather had handed him the letter, he had quite forgotten about Charles Griffith.

Or—not forgotten, perhaps, but ceased to be curious about him. The idea of marriage itself had similarly lost any of the sense of intrigue it had once had, even if that intrigue had been tempered by wariness. It seemed, suddenly, a declaration of timidity to allow oneself to be shuttled into a marriage, to surrender the idea of love for stability, or respectability, or dependability. And why would he resign himself to a dun-colored life when he could have another? He pictured himself—unfairly, he knew, for he had never seen Charles Griffith's house—in a spacious but plain white clapboard structure, prettily bordered with hydrangea bushes, sitting in a rocking chair, a book in his lap, staring at the sea like an old lady, waiting for his husband's heavy tread on the front porch. In that instant, he was again furious at his grandfather and his grandfather's desire to condemn him to a colorless existence. Did his grandfather think that was the best he might imagine for himself? Did he, despite his protestations to the contrary, believe that the best place for him was an institution, if not a literal one, then a domestic one?

It was with these confused thoughts that he entered his grand-father's drawing room, shutting the door behind him a touch too forcefully, which caused his grandfather to look up at him, sur-prised. "I apologize," he mumbled, to which his grandfather said only, "What had he to say?"

He handed his grandfather the pages, silently, and his grandfa-ther took them, and unfolded his glasses, and began to read. David watched him, able to discern by his deepening frown how far into Charles's narrative he had ventured. "My goodness," said his grand-father, at last, removing his glasses and refolding them. "Those poor boys. That poor family. And poor Mister Griffith—he sounds wretched."

"Yes, it's a terrible thing."

"What does he mean when he says he was embarrassed by your last conversation?"

He told his grandfather, briefly, about Charles's loneliness, about how forthcoming he had been, and his grandfather shook his head, not with disapproval but with sympathy.

"So," he said, after a silence, "are you planning on seeing him again?"

"I don't know," David replied, after his own silence, looking into his lap.

A third silence ensued. "David," said Grandfather, gently. "Is something the matter?"

"What do you mean?"

"You've been so—distant. Are you feeling all right?"

He realized then that his grandfather thought he was entering one of his illnesses, and as bothered as he was by this, he also wanted to laugh at how incorrectly his grandfather had interpreted his life, at how little he truly knew of him, though understanding this made him sad as well.

"I am perfectly fine."

"I thought you enjoyed talking to Mister Griffith."

"I do."

"He certainly seems to enjoy talking to you. David. Don't you think?"

He stood then, seizing the poker and jabbing at the fire, watching the neatly stacked logs spit and tumble. "I suppose." And then, when Grandfather said nothing: "Why do you want me to get married?"

He could hear the surprise in his grandfather's voice. "What do you mean?"

"You say it is my decision, but it certainly seems as though it is yours. Yours and Mister Griffith's. Why do you want me to get married? Is it because you think I cannot do better for myself? Is it because you think I cannot take care of myself?"

He could not turn to look at his grandfather's face, but he felt his own grow hot, both from the fire and from his display of impertinence.

"I do not know, nor understand, what prompted this," his grandfather began, slowly. "As I have told not just you but all of you, I have worked to ensure that the only reason my grandchildren need marry is for companionship. You, David, *you* had indicated you were interested in the possibility; it is only because of that that Frances began indicating that we were open to offers. As you know, it was *you* who had declined a number of offers before even meeting the gentlemen—perfectly good candidates, I might as well tell you—and so, when Mister Griffith's offer arrived, Frances suggested, and I agreed, that I ought to urge you to at least *try* to entertain the idea of indulging the man before wasting yet more of everyone's time.

"This is for *your* future happiness, David—all of it. It is not for my pleasure, nor for Frances's, I assure you. This is being done for *you*, and only for you, and if I sound resentful, or peeved, I do not mean to be—only bewildered. *You* are the one responsible for making the decisions, and it is at *your* prompting that this process is even underway."

"And so, because I had rejected so many previous candidates, I was left with—who? People no one else would consider? A widower? An old man with no education?"

At this, his grandfather rose to his feet so swiftly that David was afraid he meant to strike him, and grabbed David's shoulders and made him face him.

"You astound me, David. I did not raise you nor your siblings to speak of other people like this. You are young, yes, younger than he is. But you are—I had thought—wise, and he is clearly tenderhearted, and many marriages are made on much, much less. I don't know what has inspired this—this tantrum, this suspicion of yours.

"He is obviously fond of you. He may even love you. I imagine he would be amenable to discussing whatever concerns you may have, about where you might live, for example. He has a house in the city; he had never indicated to Frances that you must live in Massachusetts, if that's what's troubling you. But if you are truly not interested in him, you are obligated to tell him. You owe the gentleman that. And you must do so in person, and do so with kindness and gratitude.

"I don't know what is happening to you, David. Over the past month, you have changed. I have meant to speak to you of it, but you have been so unavailable."

His grandfather stopped, and David turned away again to look at the fire, hot with shame.

"Oh, David," his grandfather said, softly. "You are so dear to me. And you are indeed correct—I *do* want you to be with someone who will care for you: not because I think you incapable of caring for yourself but because I believe you would be happiest with another. In the years since you returned from Europe, you have become less and less a part of the world. I know your sicknesses have been trying—I know how depleted they leave you and, moreover, how ashamed you are of them. But, child, this is a man who has endured great sorrow and illness in his past and has not run from them; he is therefore a man worth considering, because he is a man for whom your happiness will always be his concern. *That* is who I want for you."

Together, they stood in silence; his grandfather looked at him, and David looked at the floor. "Tell me, David," said his grandfather, slowly, "is there somebody else in your life? You can tell me, child."

"No, Grandfather," he said to the ground.

"Then," his grandfather said, "you must write to Mister Griffith at once and tell him you accept his offer to see him again. And at that meeting, you must either break off relations entirely or you must tell him of your intentions to continue communications. And if you *do* decide to keep speaking with him, David—and though you have not asked me, I think you ought—then you must do so with sincerity and with a generosity of spirit of which I know you to be capable. You owe the man that. Will you promise me this?"

And David said he would.

IX

The next few days were unusually busy—the family gathered for Wolf's birthday one evening, and Eliza's the evening after—and so it was not until the following Thursday that he was able to meet Edward outside the school after his class, and then walk with him to his boardinghouse. Along the way, Edward slipped his left arm through David's right, and David, who had never before walked arm in arm with someone, squeezed Edward's closer, though he had first looked behind him to see if the coachman had witnessed it, for he did not want it reported to Adams and, therefore, to his grandfather.

That afternoon, as they lay together—David had brought with him a fine wool blanket in a soft pigeon-gray that Edward had exclaimed over, and in which they now swaddled themselves—Edward talked of his friends. "A misfit bunch," he laughed, almost boastfully, and so they seemed to be: There was Theodora, the prodigal daughter of a rich family in Connecticut, who aspired to be a singer in "one of your dreaded nightclubs"; Harry, a penniless but exceedingly handsome young man who was the companion of "a very wealthy banker—your grandfather would likely know him"; Fritz, a painter, who sounded like little more than a wastrel (though of course David did not say this); and Marianne, who was attending art school and gave drawing lessons for money. They were of a kind: young, poor (though only some by circumstance of birth), carefree. David pictured them—Theodora, pretty, slim, nervous, with lustrous dark hair; Harry, blond and black-eyed and full-lipped; Fritz, sallow and twitchy with a long, thin smirk; Marianne, with a guileless smile and heaps of peach-colored curls. "I'd very much like to meet them someday," he said, though he wasn't sure he did—he wanted to pretend they did not exist, that Edward was his alone—and Edward, as though he knew this, merely smiled and said he someday might.

Too soon, it was time for him to leave, and as he was buttoning his coat, he said, "I'll see you tomorrow, then."

"Oh, no—I forgot to mention it, I'm leaving tomorrow!"

"Leaving?"

"Yes, one of my sisters—one of the two in Vermont—she's soon to have a baby, and I'm going to see her and the others."

"Oh," he said. (Would Edward not have told him if he hadn't asked to see him? Would David have announced himself as usual at the boardinghouse and sat in the parlor, waiting for him to make an appearance? How long would he have waited—hours, yes, but how many?—before admitting failure and retreating to Washington Square?) "When will you be back?"

"At the end of February."

"But that's so long!"

"Not so long! February is brief. Besides, it shan't be the very end—February twentieth. Not long at all! And I'll write you." A slow, insinuating smile crept over Edward's face, and he flung the blanket aside and stood and wrapped his arms around David. "Why? Shall you miss me?"

He colored. "You know I shall."

"But that is so dear! I am so honored." Over the weeks, Edward's speech had lost some of its theatricality, its dramatic expressiveness, but now it had returned, and, hearing its inflections once more, David was suddenly uncomfortable—what had not perturbed him before seemed now false and insincere and oddly troubling, and it was with genuine sadness, but also some other feeling, something unnamable but unpleasant, that he bade Edward goodbye.

But by the following week, any discomfort he had felt had dissipated, replaced by pure longing. How swiftly had Edward transformed him! How dreary life was without him! Now his afternoons were once again empty, and he spent them as he once had: reading and drawing and embroidery, though most of his time was spent daydreaming, or on listless strolls through the park. He even found himself walking to the café where they had almost had their first coffee, and this time sitting and ordering a cup, which he drank, slowly, darting glances at the door whenever it opened as if the person who stepped through it might be Edward.

He was returning from a visit to the café when Adams told him a letter had arrived for him, which turned out to be from Charles Griffith, inviting David to dinner at his house when he was in the city the following week. He accepted, politely but with no sense of anticipation, meaning only to honor his grandfather's request, and Charles's own to apologize in person, and the evening of their meeting he arrived home from the café so late that he barely had time to change and pat some water on his face before he'd had to climb into the waiting hansom.

Charles Griffith's house was near David's childhood home, although directly off Fifth Avenue. That house had been large, but Charles's was even larger, and notably grander, with a wide, curved marble staircase that led to the parlor floor, where his host awaited him, standing as soon as David entered. They shook hands, formally.

"David—it is so good to see you."

"And you," he said.

And to his surprise, this was to be true. They sat in the splendid parlor—David thinking of how sniffy Peter, who cared about such things, would be if he saw this space, with its overly rich textiles and colors, its overly plush sofas, its profusion of glittering lamps, its brocade-hung walls almost bare of paintings—and once more, conversation came naturally. David inquired about James, and saw an expression of sorrow move across Charles's face ("I thank you for asking, but he is very much the same, I'm afraid"), and they spoke of the continuing silence from the Delacroix family, and how they had each spent the holidays.

As they were seated for dinner, Charles said, "I remember you said oyster stew was one of your favorites."

"It is," he said, as a tureen wafting a delectably scented steam was brought to the table, and a ladleful of soup placed in his bowl. He tasted it—the broth was rich and well-seasoned, the oysters fat and buttery. "It's delicious."

"I'm glad you like it."

He was touched by the gesture, and something about the stew— such a humble, honest dish, made more humble and honest in this overwrought dining room, with its long, shining table that could have accommodated twenty but instead sat only two, its bowls of fresh-cut flowers wherever he looked—and the kindness that had inspired it made him feel warmly toward Charles, made him want to offer him something in return. "Do you know," he began, accepting a second serving of the stew, "that I was born quite near here?"

"I wondered," Charles said. "You had earlier mentioned your parents died when you were still young."

"Yes, in seventy-one. I was five, John was four, and Eden was two."

"Was it the flu?"

"Yes—they died so fast. My grandfather took us in immediately afterward."

Charles gave a shake of his head. "The poor man—to lose his son and daughter-in-law—"

"Yes, and to be saddled with three little devils, all in less than a month!"

Charles laughed. "I'm sure you weren't."

"Oh, but we were. Though, as difficult as I was, John was worse."

They both laughed at this, and he found himself, as he'd not done in some time, recounting the few memories he had of his parents: They had both worked for Bingham Brothers, his father as a banker, his mother as a lawyer. In his memories, they were always leaving—in the morning, to work; in the evening, to dinners and parties or to the opera or theater. He had a vague, gauzy image of his mother as a neat, slender woman with a long, straight nose and masses of dark hair, but he could never be certain whether this was truly his memory of her, or whether it was one he had constructed based on a small drawing of her that he had been given when she died. Of his father, he could remember even less. He knew he was fair-haired and green-eyed—his grandfather had adopted him as an infant from a German family in his employ with too many children and too little money, and had raised him alone—and that it was from him that David and his siblings had inherited their coloring. He remembered that he had been gentle, but also more playful than their mother, and that on Sundays, after they'd returned from church, he would have David and John stand in front of him as he stretched out two closed fists. They would get to choose—David one week, John the next—which fist secreted candy, and if they guessed incorrectly, he would always turn to walk away, and they would protest, and he would return, smiling, and distribute it to them anyway. Grandfather would always say that David was like their father in temperament, and John and Eden resembled their mother.

Mentioning his siblings led to a discussion of them, and he described how John and Peter had grown increasingly alike in sensibility and habit in the years since they married, and how they both worked for Bingham Brothers—in an echo of their parents, John was a banker and Peter a lawyer. Then there was Eden, and her studies at medical school, and Eliza's charitable work. Charles knew of their names—everyone did, for they were always appearing in the society columns, spotted attending this gala or hosting that costume party, Eden written of admiringly for her sense of style and wit, John for his conversational skills—and asked if he was fond of them, and although David was not overly concerned with Charles's opinion, he found himself fibbing and saying he was.

"And so you and Eden are the rebels, then, for not entering the family business. Or perhaps John is the rebel, for he is outnumbered, after all!"

"Yes," he said, but he was growing anxious, for he knew the direction the conversation would now take, and before Charles could ask, he offered, "I *did* want to work with my grandfather—I did. But I—" And, to his embarrassment and horror, he was unable to speak further.

"Well," said Charles, quietly, into the silence David had left, "but you are a wonderful artist, I am told, and artists should not spend their lives toiling in banks. I'm sure your grandfather would agree. Why, if any member of *my* family were to ever demonstrate any artistic skill in the slightest, you can be certain we wouldn't expect them to spend their time tallying numbers and charting sea routes and appeasing traders and brokering arrangements! But, sadly, it seems that there is very little chance of that, as the Griffiths are, I'm sorry to say, workaday people in the extreme!" He laughed, and the mood grew lighter, and David, having recovered himself, finally laughed with him, feeling a swell of gratitude for Charles.

"Practicality is a virtue," he said.

"Perhaps. But too much practicality, like too much of any virtue, is very dull, I think."

After their dinner and drinks, Charles walked him down to the entryway. David could tell, from the way he tarried, the way Charles held his hand in both of his, that he wished to kiss him, and although he had had a pleasant evening, although he could even admit to himself that he liked the man, indeed, liked him very much, he was unable to stop himself from looking up at Charles's face, flushed red from wine, and the stomach that not even his cleverly cut waistcoat could conceal, and comparing him unfavorably with Edward, his spare, slim frame, his smooth, pale skin.

Charles would not demand affection from him, he knew, and so David merely put his other hand atop Charles's own in what he hoped was a conclusive gesture, and thanked him for a lovely evening.

If Charles was disappointed, he did not betray it. "You are most welcome," he said. "Seeing you has been a bit of happiness for me in a very trying year."

"But the year is young."

"True. Though, if you might see me again, it would guarantee that it will only improve."

He knew that he ought to say yes, or if not yes, that he must tell Charles he would have to decline his offer of marriage, and was so deeply grateful for it and honored by it—and he was—and wished him every happiness and good fortune.

But for the second time that evening, speech failed him, and

Charles, as if understanding that David's silence was a kind of acquiescence, merely bent and kissed his hand and opened the door to the chilled night, where the Binghams' second coachman stood on the sidewalk, snow speckling his black coat, patiently holding open the hansom door.

X

Over the next week (as he had the week before), he wrote every day to Edward. Edward had promised that he would send him his sister's address in his first letter, but he had been gone almost two weeks and there had been not a single piece of correspondence. David had inquired at the boardinghouse if they had an address for him, and had even suffered an encounter with the terrifying Matron, but neither had yielded further information. And yet he continued to write, a letter a day, which he had one of the servants leave at Edward's boardinghouse in case he should inform them of his location.

He could feel his aimlessness transforming itself into desperation, and every evening he set himself a plan for the following day, one that would keep him away from Washington Square until just past the first post delivery, by which point he would be either alighting from the hansom or rounding the corner on foot, returning from his trip to the museum, or the club, or a chat with Eliza, who was the sibling he liked best and to whom he sometimes paid a visit when he knew Eden was attending class. Grandfather had, pointedly, asked him nothing about his dinner with Charles Griffith, and nor had David volunteered anything. Life resumed its pre-Edward rhythms, but this time, the days were grayer than before. Now he made himself wait until half past the hour when the mail arrived before finally ascending the stairs, and he made himself not ask Adams or Matthew whether anything had come for him, as if, by not doing so, he might cause a letter to materialize to reward him for his discipline and patience. But day after day passed, and the post brought only two letters from Charles, both asking if he might want to attend the theater: The first one he declined, courteously and quickly, begging family obligations; the second he ignored, angry at it for not being from Edward, until he was on the verge of being rude, whereupon he jotted a brief note apologizing and saying he had caught a chill and was staying indoors.

At the beginning of the third week of Edward's absence, he took the hansom west and, the day's letter in hand, determined to uncover answers himself about Edward's whereabouts. But the only person he found at the boardinghouse was the wan little maid who seemed to spend most of her time lugging a pail of brackish-looking water from one floor to the next. "I dunno, sir," she mumbled, looking doubtfully at David's shoes, recoiling from the letter he held out for her as if it might burn her, "he dinna say when he'll be back." He left the house, then, but stood on the sidewalk, looking up at Edward's windows, over which the dark curtains were fully drawn, the same as they had been for the past sixteen days.

That evening, though, he remembered something that might help him, and as he and his grandfather assumed their after-dinner positions, he asked, "Grandfather, have you heard of a woman named Florence Larsson?"

His grandfather appraised him, coolly, before tamping down the tobacco in his pipe and puffing. "Florence Larsson," he repeated. "That's a name I've not heard in a very long time. Why do you ask?"

"Oh, Charles was mentioning that his clerk lived in a boardinghouse she owns," he said, dismayed not just by the speed of his duplicity but by his involving Charles in it.

"So it's true," his grandfather murmured, almost to himself, before sighing. "I never knew her myself, mind you—she is even older than I am; frankly, I'm surprised she's still alive—but when she was around your age, she was involved in an awful scandal."

"What happened?"

"Well. She was the only daughter of a quite well-to-do man—a doctor, I believe—and was herself studying to be a doctor. Then, one night, she met a man—I cannot remember his name—at a party thrown by her cousin. He was, apparently, spectacularly handsome and deeply charming, and utterly penniless—one of those men who seem to come from nowhere, and are connected to no one, and yet, through their appearance and witty conversation, are able to find themselves in society, among all the best people."

"And so what happened?"

"What often happens in these circumstances, I'm sorry to say. He wooed her; she fell in love; her father threatened to disown her if she married the man . . . and she did so anyway. She had a fortune bestowed upon her by her late mother, and soon after they married, the man absconded with it all, every last cent. She was left destitute, and while she was able to return to her father's house, he was so spiteful—a very coldhearted man, everyone said—that he did as he'd threatened and disinherited her entirely. If she's still alive, she'd be living in her late aunt's house, which I suppose she's been in ever since her father's death. She was, by all accounts, bereft. She never continued her studies. And she never married again—never even flirted with the possibility, from what I understand."

He felt a coldness move over him. "And what happened to the man?"

"Who can say? For many years, there were rumors about him. He was sighted here or there, he emigrated to England or the Continent, he remarried this or that heiress—but no one ever knew for sure, and at any rate, he was never heard from again. But David—what's wrong? You've gone pale!"

"It is nothing," he managed to say. "I think the fish tonight disagreed with me, somewhat."

"Oh dear—I know you love sole."

Upstairs, back in the safety of his study, he tried to calm himself. The comparisons, which had risen unbidden, were ludicrous. Yes, Edward knew of his money, but he had never asked for any—he had even been bashful about accepting the blanket—and they were certainly not discussing marriage. But still, something about the story upset him, as if it were an echo of another story, a worse story, a story he had heard once but could not, however he tried, recall.

He was unable to sleep that night, and for the first time in a long while, he spent the following morning in bed, waving away the maids' offers of breakfast, staring at a water stain along the baseboard, where the two walls met in a V. It was his secret, this patch of yellow, and when he had been confined, he had gazed at it for hours, certain that were he to turn from it, or to blink, when he opened his eyes next the room would be transformed into an unfamiliar place, someplace terrifyingly dark and small: a monk's cell, the hold of a ship, the bottom of a well. The stain was what was keeping him in the world, and it demanded all of his concentration.

In his confinements, he was sometimes unable to even stand, but now he was not ill, only fearful of something he could not name, and so, finally, he made himself wash and dress, and by the time he'd ventured downstairs, it was already late in the afternoon.

"A letter for you, Mister David."

He felt his heart quicken. "Thank you, Matthew." But once he had plucked the letter from the silver tray, he set it on a table and sat, folding his hands in his lap, trying to still his heart, to lengthen and slow his breaths. Finally, cautiously, he stretched out his arm and picked up the letter. *It is not from him,* he told himself.

And it was not. It was another note from Charles, inquiring about his health and asking if he might like to accompany him to a recitation that Friday evening: *It is of Shakespeare's sonnets, of which I know you are fond.*

He sat, holding the letter, his disappointment mingling with something he was once again unable to identify. Then, before he could hesitate, he rang for Matthew and asked for paper and ink, and quickly scrawled a response to Charles, accepting his invitation, and handed the envelope back to Matthew, telling him to deliver it immediately.

Once this was done, his final reserves of strength left him, and he stood and made his slow way upstairs, back to his chambers, where he rang for the maid and told her to tell Adams to tell his grandfather that he was still feeling poorly and would have to miss dinner tonight. And then he stood in the center of his study and looked about him, trying to find something—a book, a painting, a portfolio of drawings—to distract him, to quell the feeling of unease that now arose within him.

XI

The sonnets were recited by an all-female troupe, more enthusiastic than talented, but young enough so that, despite their lack of skill, they were still fresh and appealing to watch—it was easy to applaud them at the show's conclusion.

He wasn't hungry afterward, but Charles was, and suggested—hopefully, David thought—that they might have something to eat at his house. "Something simple," he said, and David, from lack of anything to do and in need of distraction, agreed.

Back at the house, Charles suggested they sit in his upstairs parlor, which, though as inappropriately extravagant as the downstairs one—carpets so thick they felt like pelt beneath the foot; curtains of gloria that crackled, like burning paper, when one brushed against them—was at least smaller, friendlier in its scale. "Shall we just eat in here?" David asked him.

"Shall we?" Charles asked, raising his eyebrows. "I had told Walden to set the dining room. But I would far prefer to stay here, if you would."

"Anything you decide," he replied, suddenly losing interest, not only in the meal but in the conversation about it.

"I shall tell him," said Charles, and pulled the bell. "Bread and cheese and butter and maybe a little cold meat," he instructed the butler when he returned, turning to David for his approval, which he gave with a small nod.

He was determined to be silent and childish and sullen, but once again, Charles's pleasant way soon coaxed him into conversation. He told David about his other nephews: Teddy, in his final year at

Amherst ("So he will now take James's title as first in our family to graduate college, and I mean to reward him for it"), and Henry, soon to matriculate at the University of Pennsylvania ("So, you see, I shall be having to come south—well, yes, *I* consider this south!—much more often"). He spoke of them with such love, such affection, that David found himself irrationally jealous. He of course had no reason to be—his grandfather had never said an unkind word to him, and he had known only ease. But perhaps his envy was misdirected; perhaps it was understanding how proud Charles was of them, and knowing that he had done nothing to bring his grandfather the same kind of pride.

Into the evening they talked of various aspects of their lives: their families; Charles's friends; the wars down south; their country's détente with Maine, where, given that state's semi-autonomy from the Union, Free State citizens were better tolerated, while not quite accepted; and their relations with the West, where the potential for danger had become much greater. Despite the occasionally grim subjects, their company was easy, and David found himself in several moments on the verge of confiding to Charles as if to a friend, and not someone who had offered marriage, about Edward: his dark, quick eyes; the pink that rose in the hollow of his throat when he was speaking of music or art; the various struggles he had overcome to make his way in the world alone. But then he remembered where he was, and who Charles was, and bit back his words. If he could not have Edward in his arms, he wanted Edward's name on his tongue; by speaking of him, he would bring Edward alive. He wanted to show him off, wanted to tell anyone who would listen that *this* was who had chosen him, that *this* was who he spent his days with, that *this* was who had brought him alive once again. But in the absence of that, he would have to be satisfied with the secret of Edward, which he carried inside him like a lick of bright-white flame; something that burned high and pure and which warmed only him, and which he feared would vanish if he examined it too closely. By thinking of him, he felt almost as if he'd conjured him, a phantom only he could see, leaning against the secretary at the back of the room behind Charles, smiling at David and David alone.

And yet—he knew—Edward was not there, not just in body but in essence as well. Over the weeks, as he waited and waited to hear from Edward, dutifully writing his letters (whose ratios of what he hoped were amusing news about his life and the city versus expressions of affection and yearning had tipped almost wholly in the direction of the latter), his concern had been replaced by confusion, and confusion by bewilderment, and bewilderment by hurt, and hurt by frustration, and frustration by anger, and anger by desperation, until he was back at the beginning of the cycle once more. Now, at any moment, he felt all of these sensations all at once, so that he was unable to distinguish one from the other, and these were heightened by a pure and profound craving. Curiously, it was being in the presence of Charles, someone kind and in whose company he could relax, that made these feelings the more potent, and therefore oppressive—he knew that, if he told Charles of his agony, he would have advice, or at least sympathy, but of course the cruelty of his situation was that Charles was the one person whom he could never tell.

He was thinking all this, reviewing his predicament again and again, as if in the next revisitation of the problem a solution would magically announce itself, when he realized that Charles had stopped speaking, and that he had been so deeply consumed with his own dilemma that he had altogether ceased to listen.

He apologized hurriedly and profusely, but Charles only shook his head, and then stood from his chair and crossed to the divan where David sat, and joined him.

"Is something the matter?" Charles asked.

"No, no—I'm very sorry. I think I'm only tired, and this fire is so lovely and warm, I'm afraid I've grown somewhat sleepy—you must excuse me."

Charles nodded, and took his hand. "You seem very distracted, though," he continued. "Troubled, even. Is it not something you can tell me?"

He smiled, so Charles wouldn't worry. "You're so kind to me," he said, and then, more fervently, "so kind. I wonder what it would be like, to have a friend like you."

"But you do have me as a friend," said Charles, smiling back at him, and David understood that he had said the wrong thing, that he was doing exactly what Grandfather had said he oughtn't: The fact that he was doing so unintentionally made no difference.

"I hope you should see me as your friend," Charles continued, his voice low, "but also as something else," and he put his hands on David's shoulders and kissed him, and continued kissing him until he finally pulled David to his feet and began to unbutton his trousers, and David let Charles undress him and waited as Charles then undressed himself.

In his hansom home, he bemoaned his own stupidity, at how he had, in his confused state, let Charles believe that he might be interested in being his husband after all. He knew that with each occasion he saw Charles, with each conversation they had, with each communication he answered, he was going farther and farther down a path that would lead, inexorably, to one destination. It was not too late for him to stop, to announce his intention to turn and retreat—he had not given his word, they had signed no papers, and even if he had behaved poorly, misleadingly, he would not be breaking a promise—but if he did, he knew that both Charles and his grandfather would be justifiably wounded, if not livid, and that the blame would be entirely his. He had acquiesced to Charles in part from gratitude for his compassion (and, David had to admit, to reward Charles for being fond of him when he was uncertain of fondness from Edward), but his other reasons were altogether less honorable and generous: a sense of misplaced and unfulfilled lust, a desire to punish Edward for his silence and unreachability, a need to distract himself from his own difficulties. By doing so, he had made another difficulty, one entirely of his own creation, in which he was undeniably the pursued, the object of another's longing. It chilled him to realize that these were his thoughts, that he was so proud and selfish that he had encouraged not just another person, but a good person, to form false hopes and expectations simply because his pride was injured and he wanted to be flattered.

Yet so powerful was this feeling, this hunger to subdue the disagreeable sentiments that Edward's absence and persisting silence awakened in him, that over the next three weeks—three weeks in which February twentieth came and passed, three weeks in which he heard nothing from Edward—he returned to Charles's house again and again. Seeing Charles, the enthusiasm and excitement that he made no efforts to conceal, made David both powerful and scornful; watching Charles fumble with his buttons, clumsy in his impatience, the upstairs parlor's door hastily closed and locked as soon as Walden had delivered him inside, he felt a seducer, an enchanter, but later, hearing Charles whisper endearments into his ear, he felt only embarrassment for the man. He knew what he was doing was wrong, even wicked—intimacy was encouraged before an arranged marriage between men, but it was usually to be explored only once or twice, and only to determine one's compatibility with one's possible intended—and yet he found himself unable to stop, even as, privately, his motivations became less and less defensible, even as his new, wholly unjustifiable disdain for Charles began to curdle into a kind of disgust. But here too he was confused. He did not enjoy relations with Charles, not exactly—although he came to welcome the attention, and Charles's consistent and sustained excitement and physical strength, he thought the man too earnest, both dull and inelegant—but continuing them made his memories of Edward inexplicably sharper, for he was always measuring one against the other, and finding the former wanting. Feeling Charles's girth moving against him, he yearned for Edward's sylphlike lean-ness, and imagined how he might tell Edward about Charles, and how Edward would laugh, his low, mesmerizing chuckle. But of course—there was no Edward to tell, to share in his unkind, unspo-ken mocking of the person who *was* before him, steadfast and true and responsive in every way: Charles Griffith. Charles had become disagreeable to him *because* he was available, and yet that same gen-erous availability also made David feel less vulnerable, less helpless in the face of Edward's continuing silence. He had come to nurse a small hatred for Charles, for loving him so much, and, mostly, for not being Edward. His budding disgust for Charles made being with him feel sacrificial, a delicious self-punishment, an almost religious act of degradation that—if only to him—proved what he was willing to withstand in order to someday be reunited with Edward.

"I believe I am in love with you," Charles said to him one night in early March as he was preparing to leave, buttoning up his shirt and looking about for his tie. But although he had spoken clearly enough, David pretended he'd not heard him, and said only a cursory goodbye over his shoulder as he left. He could tell that by now Charles was bewildered, even hurt, by his coolness, by David's now unignorable unwillingness to reciprocate his declarations of affection, and he was aware as well that in his behavior toward Charles he was perpetuating a small but very real sort of evil, one in which he was repaying honor with cruelty.

"I must go," he announced into the quiet that greeted Charles's proclamation, "but I shall write you tomorrow."

"Shall you?" asked Charles, softly, and David felt again that mingling of impatience and tenderness.

"Yes," he said. "I promise."

He saw Charles next on a Sunday afternoon, and as he was leaving, Charles asked him—as he always did after their encounters—whether he might like to stay for supper, whether he might like to attend this concert or that theater performance. He always demurred, aware that with each successive encounter the question David knew Charles dared not ask loomed larger and larger, until it began to feel as if it had somehow materialized as a fog, so that every movement the two of them made brought them deeper into its obfuscating, impermeable murk. David had once again spent most of his time with Charles thinking of Edward, trying to imagine Charles to *be* Edward, and although he was, as always, polite to Charles, he was increasingly formal, despite the increasing intimacy of their behavior.

"Wait," Charles said, "don't get dressed so quickly—let me look at you a while longer." But David said his grandfather was expecting him, and left before Charles could ask again.

After each visit, he was increasingly miserable: at how he was treating poor, decent Charles; at how he was conducting himself as a

Bingham, and his grandfather's charge; at how his desperate hunger for Edward was driving him to behave. Though he could not blame his choices on Edward, no matter his reasons for not writing—it was his decision, and only his, and instead of bearing his anguish alone, and bravely, he had now let it infect Charles as well.

And although he returned to Charles to distract himself, being with him also inspired unwanted questions, new doubts: Whenever Charles spoke of his friends, of his nephews, of his business associates, he was reminded that Edward had made it impossible for David to ever locate him. Edward's friends had been identified only by their Christian names, never their family ones—David realized that he didn't even know the sisters' married names. Whenever Charles asked him questions about himself, his childhood and school years, his grandfather and siblings, he was reminded that Edward had rarely asked him such questions: He had not noticed it at the time, but he remembered it now. Was he not interested? He thought bitterly of how he had once felt that Edward had been seeking his approval and was grateful when David gave it to him, and recognized now how wrong he'd been, how, all along, it had always been Edward who had been in control.

The following Wednesday, he was tidying the classroom after his lesson when he heard the sound of his name echoing through the hallway. The previous week, the piano, which until then had remained standing at the front of the room, a monument to Edward and then to his disappearance, had been relegated to its corner, where neglect would return it to its natural state of disrepair.

He turned, and into the classroom marched Matron, looking at him disapprovingly, as always. "Go back to your rooms now, children," she told the few stragglers, patting them on the heads or shoulders as they greeted her. And then, to him, "Mister Bingham. How are the classes coming along?"

"Very well, thank you."

"It is very good of you to come teach my children. You know they are very fond of you."

"And I of them."

"I came to bring you this," Matron said, and drew from her pocket a thin white envelope, which he took and nearly dropped when he saw the handwriting.

"Yes, it is from *Mister Bishop*," she said, witheringly, spitting out Edward's name. "He has at last deigned to return to us, it seems." In the weeks since Edward's disappearance, Matron had been David's only, unlikely, and unwitting ally, the sole person in David's life who was as interested in Edward's whereabouts as he was. Her motivations for recovering him, however, were rather different—Edward, she had confided in David when he had finally forced himself to ask her, had begged her for leave because of an emergency in his family; he was to return to class on February twenty-second, but that date had passed and there had been no word from him, and Matron was finally forced to terminate the class altogether.

("I believe his mother, who lives in New England, is very ill," Matron had said, sounding put out by the fact of the ill mother.

"I believe he is an orphan," David had ventured, after a pause. "I believe it was his sister who had had a baby?"

Matron stopped and considered this. "I'm fairly certain he had said his mother," she said. "I would not have given leave for a baby. But, well," she said, softening—at some point in every interaction with David, she would visibly recall that he was her school's patron and would adjust her voice and manners accordingly—"perhaps I am mistaken. Goodness knows there are people telling me things about their lives and difficulties all day long and I am simply unable to keep track of every last detail. He said she was in Vermont, is she not? There are three sisters?"

"Yes," he'd said, relief filling him. "Exactly.")

"When did you receive this?" he asked, faintly, wanting both to sit down and for Matron to leave, immediately, so he could tear into the letter.

"Yesterday," Matron huffed. "He came by—the nerve!—to ask for his final payment, and I gave him a piece of my mind as well; told him how he had disappointed the children, how selfish he'd been, taking off and not returning when he promised he would. And he said—"

David interrupted her. "Matron, I'm very sorry," he said, "but I really must leave; I've an appointment I mustn't be late for."

Matron drew herself very straight, her dignity clearly injured. "Of course, Mister Bingham," she said. "I certainly wouldn't want to inconvenience *you*. I shall see *you* at least next week."

It was only a few meters from the front of the school to his hansom, but he was unable to wait even that long, and he opened the letter directly on the front steps, nearly dropping it again, his fingers trembling from the cold and the anticipation.

My dearest David—   March 5, 1894

What must you think of me. I am so ashamed, so embarrassed, so deeply, profoundly apologetic. I can only say that my silence was not by choice, and that I thought of you every minute of every hour of every day. It was all I could do, upon my return yesterday, to not throw myself onto the steps of your house at Washington Square and wait for you to beg your forgiveness, but I was unsure of how I might be received.

I am unsure now, as well. But if you will give me the privilege of attempting to make my amends to you, I beg you to come by the boardinghouse, anytime.

Until then, I remain—
Your loving Edward

———

XII

There was no choice for him. He sent the hansom driver home with a message for his grandfather saying he was meeting Charles Griffith that night, and then, turning and wincing from the lie, he watched the driver round the corner before he began running, not caring about the spectacle he made. His potential embarrassment now meant nothing against the promise of seeing Edward once more.

At the boardinghouse, he was let in by the same whey-faced maid, and hurried up the flights of stairs. It was only at the final landing that he hesitated, aware that beneath his excitement lurked another set of sensations as well: doubt, confusion, anger. But it was not enough to deter him, and even before he'd finished knocking, the door was opening, and Edward was in his arms, kissing him wherever he could, as eager as a pup, and David in turn felt his earlier misgivings disappear, swept away by happiness and relief.

But when he managed to hold Edward at arm's length, he noticed his face: his right eye blackened, his bottom lip split and seamed with dried blood. "Edward," he said, "my dear Edward! Whatever is this?"

"This," said Edward, almost pertly, "is one of the reasons I was unable to write you," and after they were able to calm themselves, he began to explain what had happened on his ill-fated visit to his sisters.

In the beginning, Edward said, all went well. His trip was uneventful, if bitterly cold, and he detoured to Boston to spend three nights visiting some old family friends before continuing onward to Burlington. There, he was greeted by his three sisters: Laura, who was soon to deliver her baby; Margaret; and of course Belle, visiting from New Hampshire. Laura and Margaret, who were close in age and in everything else, shared a large wooden house, with each sister and her respective husband occupying a different floor, and Belle was settled in Laura's section and Edward in Margaret's.

Margaret left in the mornings to her schoolhouse, but Laura and Belle and Edward spent the days talking and laughing, admiring the tiny sweaters and blankets and socks Laura and Margaret and their husbands had knitted, and when Margaret returned in the afternoon, they sat before the fire and talked of their parents, and their memories of growing up together, while Laura's and Margaret's husbands—Laura's husband, a teacher as well; Margaret's, an accountant—completed the chores the sisters would normally have done themselves so that they might have more time with one another.

("I of course told them about you," Edward said.

"Oh?" he asked, flattered. "What did you say?"

"I said I had met a beautiful, brilliant man, and that I missed him already."

David found himself blushing with pleasure, but said only, "Go on.")

Six days into this blissful visit, Laura gave birth to a healthy baby, a boy, whom she named Francis, after their father. This was the first child born to the Bishop siblings, and they all rejoiced as if he were their own. It had been planned that Edward and Belle would stay for an additional two or so weeks, and despite Laura's exhaustion, they were content: There were six adults to dote on one baby. But being together, the four of them, after such a long time, made them think as well of their parents, and on more than one occasion there were tears as they discussed how much their mother and father had sacrificed on their behalf to give them better lives in the Free States, and how, whatever their disappointments, they would be so pleased to see their children together.

("We were all so busy that I scarcely had time to do anything else," said Edward, before David could ask him why he'd not written. "I thought of you always; I began a hundred letters to you in my head. And then the baby would cry, or there would be milk to heat, or I would need to help my brothers-in-law with the chores—I'd no idea how much labor one small baby could generate!—and any time in which I might have set pen to paper would vanish."

"But why did you not write me with your sisters' address, at least?" he asked, hating himself for the tremor in his voice.

"Well! *That* I can only attribute to my idiocy—I was certain, *certain* that I had given it to you before I left. In fact, I thought it very peculiar that *you* hadn't written *me* at all; every day, when one of my sisters came in with the post, I would ask if there was something from you, but there never was. I cannot tell you how sorrowful it made me: I feared you had forgotten me."

"As you can see, I had not," he murmured, trying to keep the petulance from his voice as he indicated the embarrassingly fat bundle of letters that the maid had tied with twine and which now sat, unread, on the trunk at the foot of Edward's bed. But Edward, once again anticipating David's injury, put his arms around him. "I saved them in hopes I might see you and be able to explain my absence in person," he said. "And then, after you had forgiven me—as I so desperately hoped, and hope, you will—that we might read them together, and you could tell me everything you were feeling and thinking when you wrote them, and it would be as if our time apart had never happened, and we had been together always.")

After almost a fortnight, Edward and Belle prepared to leave; they would go to Manchester, where Edward would stay with his sister for several days before finally making his way back to New York. But when they reached Belle's home, Belle calling out for her husband as they entered the front door, they were greeted only with silence.

At first, they were unconcerned. "He must still be at the clinic," Belle said, cheerfully, and sent Edward up to the spare room while she went to the kitchen to make them something to eat. But when Edward came back downstairs, he found her standing immobile in the middle of the room, looking at the table, and when she turned to look at him, her face was very white.

"He is gone," she said.

"What do you mean, he is gone?" Edward asked her, but as he looked about him, he noticed that the kitchen had not been occupied for at least a week: The hearth was blackened and cold, the dishes and kettles and pots dry and traced with a light layer of dust. He seized the note Belle held and saw it was in his brother-in-law's hand, apologizing to her and telling her he was unworthy, but he had left to make a life with another.

"Sylvie," Belle whispered. "Our maid. She's not here, either." She swooned, and Edward caught her before she could fall, and helped her into bed.

How upsetting the next few days were! Poor Belle vacillated between silence and weeping, and Edward sent word to their sisters to inform them of the unhappy news. He stormed down to his brother-in-law Mason's clinic, but both of his nurses claimed ignorance; he even went to report Mason's absence to the police, but they said they were unable to involve themselves in domestic affairs. "But this is no mere domestic affair," Edward cried. "This man has abandoned his wife, my sister, a good and faithful woman and spouse, stealing away while she was attending to her pregnant sister in Vermont. He must be found and brought to justice!" The police were sympathetic but claimed powerlessness, and with each day, Edward felt his anger rise, along with his sense of despair—seeing his sister staring mutely into the empty hearth, her hair twisted sloppily into a bun, kneading her hands and wearing the same wool dress she'd worn for the past four days, made him ever-more aware of his impotence, and ever-more determined to, if not recover his beloved little sister's husband, then to at least avenge her.

And then, one night, he was out at the local tavern, drinking a cider and thinking of his sister's predicament, when who should he see walk in but Mason.

("He looked the same as ever," Edward replied to David's question. "I realized then that I had thought that if I saw him again he would look somehow transformed, as if his poor character and caddish ways would somehow have announced themselves on his countenance. But they had not. Thank goodness he was not with that girl, Sylvie, or I'd not have been able to do what I did.")

He'd no plan when he stalked over to Mason, but just as he could see his brother-in-law recognizing him, Edward drew back his fist and walloped Mason in the cheek. Mason, once he'd recovered from his initial shock, responded, but their tussle was quickly ended by a number of the other patrons, who separated them—though, Edward noted with some satisfaction, not before he was able to tell them of his erstwhile brother-in-law's despicable behavior.

"Manchester is a small place," he said. "Everyone knows everyone else, and Mason is not the only doctor in town. His reputation will never recover, and why should it, for he has damaged his own prospects by his poor behavior."

Belle, Edward said, expressed horror at his actions—and, indeed, Edward was remorseful as well: not for assaulting Mason but because his confrontation brought her further pain and embarrassment—but, he ventured to think, she was also secretly pleased. The two engaged in a long conversation the following day, after Belle had cleaned his face and sutured his lip ("I do not mean to boast, but I'm certain Mason got the worst of it, though I also must admit that throwing punches wasn't the wisest recourse, given my profession"), and agreed that Belle could not stay in either Manchester—where Mason's entire extended family lived—or the marriage. Laura and Margaret had already sent first a telegram and then a letter urging Belle to come live with them in Vermont—there was plenty of room in their house, and Belle, who, David would recall, was trained as a nurse, would be able to find good work there. But Belle was reluctant to interfere in such a joyous and busy time for Laura, and besides, she confided in Edward, she yearned for some quiet, some time and room to think. And so the siblings decided that Belle would accompany Edward to Boston, where he would once again stay for several nights in the home of their family friends before at last returning to New York. Belle was very fond of these friends, and they of her, and there she would be able to consider her options more calmly: She would divorce Mason, that was certain, but whether she would stay in Manchester or perhaps join her sisters in Vermont was undetermined.

"So you see," Edward concluded, "the trip was by no means what

I'd anticipated, and every good intention I had vanished in the face of Belle's difficulties. It was wrong of me—so *very* wrong of me—not to communicate with you, but I was so consumed with my sister's struggles that I neglected everything else. It was terrible of me, I know—but I hope you can understand. Please tell me you forgive me, dear David. Please tell me you do."

Did he? He both did and didn't—he felt for Belle, of course, and yet, in his selfishness, he could not but persist in thinking that Edward might have found time to jot him even the briefest of notes; even that Edward *ought* to have, because if he had confided in him, he might have been able to help somehow. *How* was unclear—but he would have liked the opportunity to try.

Though to say any of this would have been too childish, too small. So "Of course," he told Edward. "My poor Edward. Of course I forgive you," and was rewarded with a kiss.

But Edward's story was not yet finished. By the time they arrived at their friends', the Cookes, Belle was already much calmer, more resolved, and Edward knew that a few days with them would steady her further. The Cookes, Susannah and Aubrey, were a married couple a little older than Margaret; Susannah, herself a Colony escapee, had lived with her parents in the building next to the Bishops', and she and her siblings and Edward and his had grown up as great friends. Now she and her husband owned a small textile factory in Boston and lived in a handsome new house near the river.

Edward was pleased to see the Cookes again, not least because Susannah and Belle were so fond of each other, with Susannah assuming the role of a third elder sister—the two would repair to Belle's room and talk late into the night, while Edward and Aubrey remained in the parlor playing chess. On the fourth evening of their visit, though, Aubrey and Susannah told the Bishop siblings that they wished to speak to them about an important matter, and so, after dinner, they all retired to the parlor together, and the Cookes announced that they had important news.

A little more than a year ago, the couple had been contacted by a Frenchman with whom they had traded over the years, and who presented them with an irresistible proposal: to establish California as the New World's preeminent silk-growing region. The French-man, Étienne Louis, had already secured a lot of nearly five thou-sand acres north of Los Angeles, planted almost a thousand trees, and established nurseries that could house tens of thousands of worms and eggs. Eventually, the farm would become its own self-sustaining colony: Already, Louis was employing the first of what was anticipated to be one hundred people expert in various aspects of the silk-making process, from tending the trees to feeding the worms to harvesting the cocoons to, of course, spinning and then weaving the silk itself. The workers would be, for the most part, Chinamen—many left indolent after the completion of the trans-continental railroad, unable either to return home or, due to the laws of '92, to bring over their families from the Orient. An alarm-ing number had fallen into destitution, depravity, and opium addic-tion, among other unsavory activities—the Cookes and Louis would need to pay them only a pittance; the city of San Francisco, where most of them lived, was even helping Louis find likely candidates that he might convince to come south. The plan was that the colony would begin its operations in the early fall.

The Bishop siblings took nearly as much excitement from the Cookes' announcement as the Cookes did in the telling. It was, they all four agreed, a brilliant plan—the population in California was growing so rapidly, and there was so little organized textile industry, that they were certain of a handsome return. Everyone knew the sort of money a clever and industrious person could make in the West, and the Cookes were not just one clever and industrious person but two. They were bound for success. It was a cheering development, made more so after a difficult week.

But this was not the only surprise the Cookes had. For they intended to ask Belle and Edward to oversee their enterprise. "We were going to ask you anyway," Susannah said. "You both and Mason. But now—and dear Belle, you will know I mean this with no malice—it seems providential. It is a new opportunity for you, a new life, a chance to begin again."

"That is so generous of you," said Belle, once she'd recovered herself. "But—neither Edward nor I know anything about textiles, nor running a factory!"

"It's true," Edward said. "Dear Susannah and Aubrey—we are very flattered—but surely you need someone with experience in such matters."

But Susannah and Aubrey persisted. There would be a foreman, and Aubrey himself would travel west in the autumn to meet with Louis and oversee the business during its early days. Once Belle and Edward arrived, they would learn as they worked. The important thing was that the Cookes might have people they trusted. So much about the West was mysterious to them that they needed business partners they could rely upon, whose histories and characters they knew completely. "And whom do we know better or trust more wholly than you?" Susannah cried. "You and Belle are almost siblings to us as well!"

"But what about Louis?"

"We trust him, of course. But he is not known to us as you are."

Belle laughed. "Dear Aubrey," she said, "I am a nurse; Edward is a pianist. We know nothing of silkworm cultivation, or mulberry trees, or textiles, or business! Why, we would ruin you!"

Back and forth the four of them argued, spiritedly but good-naturedly, until, finally, Aubrey and Susannah extracted a promise from the Bishops that they would consider their offer, and then, it being very late, they went to bed, but with smiles and congratulations on their lips, for although the Bishops still thought the idea improbable, they were flattered to be asked, and full of new gratitude for their friends' generosity and faith.

The next day, Edward was to depart, but after bidding the Cookes goodbye and before catching his coach, he and Belle took a short stroll. For a while, the siblings walked in silence, arm in arm, pausing to look at the few ducks who flew down to the river and, upon dipping their webbed feet into the water, flew off once more, cawing loudly and angrily, offended by the water's chill.

"You would think they would know better," Edward said, watching them. And then, to his sister, "What shall you do?"

"I'm not quite certain," she said. But then, as they neared the Cookes' house once again, where Edward's luggage waited, she said, "But I do think we might consider their offer."

"My dear Belle!"

"It could be a new life for us, Edward, an adventure. We are both still young—I am only one-and-twenty! And—don't speak—we wouldn't be completely alone: We would have each other."

Now it was the two of them who argued back and forth, until Edward was in danger of missing his coach, and they finally parted, tenderly, Edward promising Belle that he would consider the Cookes' proposal, even though he had no intention of doing so. But once he was in the coach, and then over the many hours of the first part of his journey, he found himself thinking more and more about the idea. Why *would* he not go west? Why *would* he not try to make his fortune? Why *would* he not want to have an adventure? Belle was correct—they were young; the venture's success was assured. And even were it not, had he not always yearned for excitement? Had New York ever really felt like his home? Already his sisters were far from him, and he was alone in a city whose casual brutalities—of money, of status, of climate—chipped and chafed at him, so that even though he was only twenty-three, he felt much older, weary of living in a place where he was never warm, where he was always scrabbling for money, where he still felt, more often than he would have imagined, that he was only a visitor, a Colony child waiting to alight on his final destination. And, too, he thought once more of his parents, who themselves had made a long, transformative journey from one place to another—was it not time for him to make his own, mirrored journey? Laura and Margaret had found their home, and it was in the Free States, and he was happy for them. But if he were to be honest with himself, he would have to admit that his entire life, for as long as he could remember, he too had been hoping for that sense of contentment, of security they possessed, only to have it elude him year after year.

After several days of thinking like this, he was back again in New York, and it was as if the city, sensing his wavering conviction, had amassed its most unpleasant qualities to visit upon him in an endeavor to help him reach the correct, the inevitable conclusion. His first step back on city soil was not upon earth but into a large puddle that had formed in a rut in the road, a lake of icy, scummy water that soaked him to mid-calf. Then there were the smells, the sounds, the sights: the peddlers pulling their wooden carts with their misshapen wheels that jostled off the sidewalk into the mud-lapped streets with a thunk, the men bent like mules; the gray-faced, starved-eyed children filing dully from the factory where they'd spent hours sewing buttons to poorly made garments; the hawkers desperately trying to sell their few wares, things that no one wanted except the most destitute, the devils without even a penny coin to pay for an onion as stunted and dry and hard as an oyster shell, a tin cup's worth of beans that writhed with gray-white grubs; the beggars and touts and pickpockets; all the poor, cold, struggling hordes of people trudging through their small lives in this impossible, proud, heartless city, the only witness to so much human misery the stone gargoyles that leered, meanly, with their sneering smiles, from their perches on grand buildings high above the teeming streets. And then there was the boardinghouse, where he was handed by the maid a letter threatening eviction by the unseen Florence Larsson, whom he appeased by paying an extra month's rent in advance along with the rent his long trip had made delinquent, and where he climbed the stairs once more, those stairs that smelled of cabbage and damp even in the summer, and then into his freezing room with its meager possessions and bleak view of the bare black trees. And it was then, breathing on his fingers so he would have enough feeling in them to go fetch some water so he might begin the wearying labor of warming himself, that he made his decision: He would go to California. He would help the Cookes begin their silk concern. He would become a rich man, his own man. And if he ever returned to New York—though he did not imagine why he ever would—he would do so without feeling a pauper, without feeling apology. New York could never make him free, but California might.

There was a long silence.

"You're leaving, then," David said, though he could barely speak the words.

Edward had been looking above and beyond him as he spoke, but now he turned his gaze to David's. "Yes," he said. And then: "And you are coming with me."

"I?" he finally managed. And then: "I! No, Edward. No."

"But why ever not?"

"Edward! No—I—no. This is my home. I could never leave it."

"But why not?" Edward slipped from the bed and knelt at his feet, taking both of David's hands in his own. "Think of it, David—think of it. We would be together. It would be a new life for us, a new life together, a new life together in the sunshine, in the warmth. David. Do you not want to be with me? Do you not love me?"

"You know I love you," he admitted, wretchedly.

"And I love you," Edward said, fervently, but those words, which David had waited and wanted, so keenly, to hear, were eclipsed by the extraordinariness of the context in which they were spoken. "David. We could be together. We could be together at last."

"We can be together here!"

"David—my darling—you know that's not true. You know your grandfather would never let you be with someone like me."

To this he could say nothing, for he knew it was true, and he knew Edward knew it, too. "But we could never be together in the West, Edward. Be sensible! It is *dangerous* to be like us out there—we would be imprisoned for it; we could be killed."

"Nothing will happen to us! We know how to be careful. David, the people who are in peril are people who are, who are—*excessive* in who they are, who *flaunt* who they are, who *ask* to be noticed. We are not those kinds of people, and we never will be."

"But we *are* those kinds of people, Edward! There is no difference between us! If we were ever suspected, if we were ever caught, the consequences would be dire. If we couldn't live as who we are, then how would we be free?"

And here Edward stood, and pivoted from him, and when he turned back, his face was gentle, and he sat next to David on the bed and reclaimed his hands. "Forgive me, David, for asking this," he said, quietly, "but are you free now?" And, when David was unable to answer him: "David. My innocent. Have you ever thought of what your life might be if your name meant nothing to no one? If you were able to escape from who you are meant to be and become instead who you want to be? If the name Bingham were just another, like Bishop or Smith or Jones, instead of a word chiseled into marble atop a great monolith?

"What if you were merely Mister Bingham, as I am merely Mister Bishop? Mister Bingham of Los Angeles: A talented artist, a dear and good and clever man, the husband—secretly, perhaps, yes, but no less true for that secrecy—of Edward Bishop? Who lived with him in a little house on a vast orchard of silvery-leafed trees in a land where there was no ice, no winter, no snow? Who came to understand who he might want to be? Who, after a period—maybe a few years, maybe many—might move back east with his husband, or might come alone to visit his beloved grandfather? Who would have me in his arms every night and every morning, and who would be loved by his husband always, and more loved because his husband would be only his, and his alone? Who could choose, whenever he wished, to be Mister David Bingham of Washington Square, New York, the Free States, eldest and most cherished grandchild of Nathaniel Bingham, but would also be something less, and therefore something more; who would belong to someone he chose, and yet would belong, too, only to himself. David. Could this not be you? Could this not be who you really are?"

He stood, yanking himself from Edward's grip, and walked the single step over to the fireplace, which was cold and black and empty, and yet into which he stared as if gazing at the flames.

Behind him, Edward still spoke. "You are frightened," he said. "And I understand. But you will always have me. Me, my love, my affection for and admiration of you—David, you will always have that. But would living in California really be so different in certain ways from being here? Here, we are free as a people but not as a couple. There, we would not be free as a people, but we *would* be a couple, real to each other and living with each other, and with no one to tut at us, no one to stop us, no one to tell us that within the walls of our home we might not be together. David, I ask you: What use is the Free States if we cannot be truly free?"

"Do you really love me?" he finally managed to ask.

"Oh, David," said Edward, standing and coming behind him and wrapping his arms about him, and David remembered, involuntarily, the feeling of Charles's bulk against him, and shuddered. "I want to spend my life with you."

He turned to face Edward, and in that instant, they were tearing at each other, and when, later, they lay spent, David found the bewilderment come over him again, and he sat, and began to dress, as Edward watched him.

"I must go," he announced, retrieving his gloves, which had fallen beneath the bed.

"David," Edward said, wrapping the blanket about himself and climbing to his feet, standing in front of David and making him look up. "Please consider my offer. I have yet to even tell Belle. But now that I have spoken to you, I shall tell her of my decision—though I would like to inform her, in either this letter or in one soon after, that I will join her as a married man, with my husband.

"The Cookes had suggested that, were we to accept, one of us should leave in May, the other no later than June. Belle has no one else to consider but herself—I shall have her be the pioneer, and she will not only be worthy of it, she will enjoy it as well. But, David—I *will* go in June. I will, no matter what. And I hope, David, I do hope—I cannot convey to you how much so—that I will not be making the journey alone. Please tell me you'll consider it. Please—David? Please."

XIII

It was a Bingham family tradition to throw a party on March twelfth, on the anniversary of the Free States' independence, though the gathering was meant to be less festive than reflective, an opportunity for the Binghams' friends and acquaintances to review the family's collection of artifacts and ephemera that documented the establishment of their country and the significant role that the Binghams had played in its founding.

This year, though, the date would coincide with the opening of a small museum that Nathaniel Bingham had founded. The family's papers and memorabilia would constitute the primary holdings, but the hope was that other of the founding families would donate pieces, letters and diaries and maps, from their own archives as well. Several, including Eliza's family, had already done so, and it was expected that many more would follow after the museum's unveiling.

The night of the inauguration, David stood in his bedroom before his mirror, brushing his jacket. It had already been brushed, and rebrushed, by Matthew, and was not in need of further grooming. He was hardly paying attention to his ministrations, at any rate; the movement was meaningless, but soothing.

It would be his first evening outside the house since he last had seen Edward, now almost a week ago. After that extraordinary night, he had returned home and had taken to bed, and for the next six days, he had not left. His grandfather had been alarmed, certain his illness had returned, and although David had felt deeply guilty for this deception, it also seemed an easier explanation than trying to convey the profound disquiet he felt—for even had he the words to communicate it, he would have also to find a way to introduce the idea of Edward, who he was and who he was to David, and that was a conversation for which he felt completely unprepared. And so he had lain there, mute and unmoving, allowing their family doctor, Mister Armstrong, to come and examine him, to prize open his eyes and mouth, to measure his pulse and grunt at the results; the maids to deliver trays of his favorite foods, only to retrieve them, untouched, hours later; Adams to bring (at his grandfather's order, he knew) fresh flowers—anemones and posies and peonies—daily, acquired from places unknown at prices unbelievable during the bleakest weeks of late winter. All the while, for those many hours, he had stared at the water stain. But unlike a true spell of sickness, in which he would have thought of nothing, here he could do nothing *but* think: of Edward's inevitable departure, of his shocking offer, of their conversation, which David had not fully comprehended in the moment but to which he now returned, again and again—he argued with Edward's definition of freedom, and his suggestion that David was chained, bound to his grandfather and his name and therefore to a life not fully his own; he argued with Edward's assuredness that they would be somehow spared from the punishments visited upon anyone found to have violated the region's anti-sodomy laws. Those laws had always existed, but since their reinforcement in '76, the West, once a promising place—so promising that a number of the Free States' legislators had even considered trying to bring the territory under their control—had become in certain ways even more perilous than the Colonies; it was not legal, as it was in the Colonies, to pursue discovery of their kind of illegal activity, but if it *was* discovered, the consequences were both severe and unpardonable. Not even money could secure the freedom of an accused. The one thing he could not do was argue with Edward himself, for Edward had not called upon him or sent any sort of message, a fact that would have bothered David had he not been so preoccupied by the quandary with which he had been presented.

But though Edward had not communicated with him, Charles had, or had at least tried to. More than a week had now passed since

David had last seen him, and Charles's notes to him had, over the days, become beseeching, unable to quite disguise their author's desperation, a desperation David remembered from his own latter letters to Edward. But the day before, an enormous arrangement of blue hyacinths had been delivered, the card—"My dearest David, Miss Holson told me you were feeling poorly, which I am deeply sorry to hear. I know you are in excellent care, but if you should need or desire anything at all, you need only say so and I shall be at your service immediately. In the meantime, I send you my good wishes, along with my devotion"—expressing what David interpreted as a palpable relief that his silence was not due to lack of interest after all, only illness. He looked at the flowers, and at Charles's card, and realized that he had once again forgotten his very existence, that all it had taken was the reappearance of Edward in his life for everything else in it to dim or become inconsequential.

Mostly, though, he contemplated leaving—or not even that, but contemplated whether he could even contemplate leaving. His fear of the West and what might happen there to him, to them, was inarguable and, he felt, justified. But what of his fear of leaving his grandfather, of leaving Washington Square? Was that not also what stopped him? He knew Edward was correct: For as long as he remained in New York, he would always be his grandfather's, his family's, his city's, his country's. That too was inarguable.

What was not was whether he even desired another life, a different life. He had always thought he had. When he was on his Grand Tour, he had in fact tried to experiment with being someone else. One day in the Uffizi, he had stopped in the hallway to gaze down the Vasari Corridor, its symmetry that discomfited in its inhuman perfection, when a young man, dark and slender, had stepped beside him.

"It is unreal, is it not?" he had asked David, after the two of them had stood in silence for a moment, and David turned to look at him.

His name was Morgan, and he was from London, on his own Grand Tour, the son of a barrister, a few months from returning home to, he said, "Nothing. Or nothing interesting, at any rate. A position at my father's firm—he insists—and, eventually, I suppose, marriage to some girl my mother will find for me. *She* insists."

They had spent the afternoon together, walking through the streets, stopping for coffee and pastry. Up to this point in David's trip, he had spoken to almost no one but the various friends of his grandfather's who greeted him and hosted him at each stop, and talking with another man his age was like slipping back into water and recognizing its silk on his skin, remembering how comfortable it could be.

"Have you a girl at home for you?" Morgan asked him as they walked through the Piazza Santa Croce, and David, smiling, said he hadn't.

"Just a moment," said Morgan, peering at him. "Where in America did you say you were from, exactly?"

"I didn't," he said, smiling again, knowing what would follow. "And I'm not. I'm from New York."

At this, Morgan's eyes widened. "Then you are a Free Stater!" he exclaimed. "I've heard so much about your country! You must tell me everything," and the conversation turned to the Free States: their now mostly cordial relations with America, in which they maintained their own laws of marriage and religion but adopted for themselves the Union's laws of taxation and democracy; their support, financial and military, of the Union in the War of Rebellion; Maine, which was mostly sympathetic to them, and where Free Staters' safety was more or less assured; the Colonies and the West, where they would be in varying degrees of peril; how the Colonies had lost their war but seceded anyway, sinking further into poverty and degradation by the year, even as their debt to and therefore resentment toward the Free States burned hotter and brighter; the Free States' ongoing struggle to be recognized as its own, distinct nation by other countries, a recognition denied them by everyone besides the kingdoms of Tonga and of Hawaii. Morgan had studied modern history at university and asked scores of questions, and in answering them, David was made aware both of his love for his nation and of how dearly he missed it, a sensation made more acute after he and Morgan had repaired to Morgan's dingy room in his ill-maintained pensione. As David walked back to his host's house late that evening, he was reminded, as he often had been on this trip, how fortunate he was to live in a country where he would never have to hide behind a door, waiting for someone to tell him that it was safe for him to leave without being seen, where he might stroll arm in arm across a city square with his beloved (should there ever be one), the way he saw male-and-female couples (but no other variants) do in squares across the Continent, where he might one day marry a man he loved. He lived in a country in which every man and woman could be free and could live with dignity.

But the other aspect of that day that had been memorable was that in it, David had not been David Bingham; he had been Nathaniel Frear, a name hastily patched together from his grandfather's and mother's, a son of a doctor, taking his year in Europe before he would return to New York to attend law school. He had invented a half-dozen brothers and sisters, a modest and cheerful house in an unfashionable but homey part of town, a life lived comfortably but not excessively. When Morgan had told him about a great residence of his former classmate's that was to have hot running water in all its water closets, David did not reveal that the house on Washington Square already had hot-water plumbing, and that he had only to nudge a faucet handle to one side for a clear stream to at once gurgle forth. Instead, he marveled with Morgan at the classmate's good fortune, the innovations of modern life. He would not deny his country—to do so seemed a form of treason—but he did deny his own biography, and there was something about doing so that made him giddy, even light-headed, so much so that when he finally entered his host's home—a grand palazzo owned by his grandfather's old college chum, a Free States expatriate, and his wife, a frowning, clomping contessa whom the man had obviously married for her title—his grandfather's friend had looked him over and smirked.

"A good day, then?" he'd drawled, seeing David's dreamy, unfocused expression, and David, who had spent his week in Florence leaving the house early in the morning and returning late at night, so as not to suffer his grandfather's friend's hands, which seemed always to be finding ways to float over his body, birds of prey that would one day dive and grab onto something, only smiled and said it had been.

He did not think often of this incident, but now he did, trying and failing to remember how he had felt in the moment of invention, and realizing that whatever ecstasy he had experienced was partly attributable to his being aware of the flimsiness of his deception. At any moment, he could have declared his actual self, and even Morgan would have known his name. It was a performance known only to him, but beneath the performance was something true, something meaningful: his grandfather, his wealth, his name. Were he to move to the West, his name would stand only for vice, if it stood for anything. In the Free States and in the North, to be a Bingham was to be respected and even revered. But in the West, to be a Bingham was to be an abomination, a perversion, a threat. It was not that he *could* change his name in California but, rather, that he would have to, because to be who he was would be too perilous.

Even entertaining these thoughts made him remorseful, especially because he was often jolted from his reverie by the appearance of his grandfather, who visited him before he left for the bank in the morning, and then twice in the evening, once before he dined, once after. This third visit was always the longest, and Grandfather would sit in the chair near David's bed and, without preamble, begin reading to him from the day's paper, or from a volume of poetry. Sometimes he would merely speak of his day, delivering a calm, unbroken monologue that David experienced as if floating in a placid, flowing river. This, to sit by him and talk or read, was Grandfather's method for treating all of his previous illnesses, and although his gentle constancy was not in any way proven to help—or so David had once overheard his doctor informing his grandfather—it was stabilizing, and predictable, and therefore reassuring, something that, like the wallpaper stain, kept him in the world. And yet, because this was not one of his illnesses, just a self-imposed simulacrum of it, David felt only shame listening to his grandfather now—shame that he was causing him concern; further shame that he would even consider leaving him, and not just him but the rights and safety that his grandfather, and forebears, had fought to secure for him.

His grandfather had not reminded him of the museum's unveiling, but it was to alleviate this shame that, on the day of the opening, he rang for a bath to be prepared and his suit to be pressed. He looked at himself in his brushed clothes and saw he was pale and drawn, but there was nothing to be done about that, and after he'd shakily descended the stairs and tapped on the door to his grandfather's study—"Come in, Adams!"—he was rewarded with his grandfather's astonishment: "David! My dear boy—are you better?"

"Yes," he lied. "And I wouldn't miss tonight."

"David, you needn't attend if you're still ill," his grandfather said, but David could hear how much he wanted him to come, and it seemed the least and only thing he could do after so many days spent contemplating betrayal.

It would have been only the briefest of walks to the townhouse on Thirteenth Street, just west of Fifth Avenue, that his grandfather had purchased for his museum, but Grandfather declared that, given the cold and David's weakened state, it was best to take a hansom. Inside, they were met by John and Peter and Eden and Eliza, and by Norris and Frances Holson, and by others of his family's friends and acquaintances and business associates, along with a number of people unknown to David but whom his grandfather greeted warmly. As the museum's director, a trim little historian long employed by the family, was explaining to some guests an exhibit featuring drawings of the Binghams' onetime property near Charlottesville, the farm and acreage that Edmund, a wealthy landowner's son, forsook in order to venture north and found the Free States, the Binghams followed their patriarch as he moved about the room, exclaiming over things both remembered and not: Here, under a sheet of glass, was the piece of the parchment, now almost in tatters, on which David's great-great-grandfather Edmund had drafted the Free States' ur-constitution in November 1790, signed by all fourteen of the founders, the original Utopians, including Eliza's maternal great-great-grandmother, promising freedom of marriage and abolishing slavery and indentured servitude and, though not allowing

Negroes full citizenry, also outlawing their abuse and torture; here was Edmund's Bible that he had consulted in his studies with Reverend Samuel Foxley when the two were law-school students in Virginia, and with whom he had conceived of their future country, a place where there might be freedom for both men and women to love whom they wished, an idea that Foxley had formulated after an encounter in London with an idiosyncratic Prussian theologian who would later count Friedrich Daniel Ernst Schleiermacher among his students and disciples, and who encouraged him toward an emotionally and civically minded interpretation of Christianity; here were the first designs for the Free States' flag by Edmund's sister, Cassandra: a rectangle of scarlet wool at whose center a pine tree, a woman, and a man were arranged in a pyramid, with eight stars, one for each of the member states—Pennsylvania, Connecticut, New Jersey, New York, New Hampshire, Massachusetts, Vermont, and Rhode Island—arcing above them, and the motto, "For freedom is dignity, and dignity freedom," stitched beneath them; here were proposals for laws allowing women to be educated and, in 1799, to vote. Here were letters dated throughout 1790 and 1791 from Edmund to a college friend testifying to the future Free States' squalid conditions, the forests full of vengeful Indians, the bandits and thieves, the battle to win over the existing residents, one swiftly accomplished, not with guns and bloodshed but with resources and infrastructure, the religiously fervent, those who found the Free States' beliefs repellent, paid off and sent south, the Indians driven west in hordes or slaughtered, quietly, in mass roundups in the very forests they had once terrorized, the native-born Negroes who had not assisted in their fight to gain control over the land (as well refugee Negroes from the Colonies) ferried to Canada or west in caravans. Here was a copy of the papers hand-delivered to the President's House in Philadelphia on March 12, 1791, announcing the states' intention to secede from America, but vowing to stand with the country against any attacks, domestic or foreign, in perpetuity; here was President Washington's biting response, accusing Foxley and Bingham, the letter's authors, of treason, of starving their country of its wealth and resources; here were the pages and pages of negotiations, Washington finally, grudgingly, granting the Free States' right to existence, but only at the pleasure of the president, and only if the Free States swore that they would never recruit any future American states or territories to their cause, and continued to pay taxes to the American capital as if they were its vassal.

Here was an engraving, from 1793, of Edmund's wedding to the man he had lived with since the death of his wife in childbirth three years prior, and the first legal union between two men in their new country, officiated by Reverend Foxley, and another, from fifty years later, documenting the marriage of two of the Binghams' longest-serving and most loyal footmen. Here was a drawing of Hiram being sworn in as mayor of New York in 1822 (a tiny Nathaniel, then just a boy, was shown standing by his side, his eyes lifted adoringly); here was a copy of Nathaniel's letter to President Lincoln, pledging the Free States' loyalty to the Union at the beginning of the War of Rebellion and, beside it, the original of Lincoln's reply thanking him, a letter so famous that every Free State child could recite by heart its contents, the American president's implicit promise to respect their rights of autonomy, the vow that had been invoked, time and time again, to justify the States' existence to Washington, D.C.: ". . . and you shall have not only my eternal Gratitude but our sworn recognition of your Nation as one within our Own." Here was the agreement drafted shortly after this letter between America's Congress and the Free States' own in which the latter promised to pay enormous taxes to America in exchange for their uncontested freedoms of religion, education, and marriage. Here was the legal declaration allowing Delaware to join the Free States shortly after the war's end, a voluntary decision that had nonetheless once again imperiled the country's existence. Here was the charter from the Free States Society of Abolitionists, cofounded by Nathaniel, which provided Negroes passage through the country and financial assistance to resettle in America or the North—the Free States had had to protect itself from an influx of escaping Negroes, as its citizens of course did not want to find their land overrun with them, and yet were also sympathetic to their miserable plight.

America was not for everyone—it was not for them—and yet

everywhere were reminders of the careful, constant work that had been and was still being done to appease America, to keep the Free States autonomous and independent: Here were the early plans for the arch that would crown the Square, commemorating, as did the Square itself, General George Washington, that the Binghams' next-door neighbor had had built five years ago, from plaster and wood; here were the subsequent drawings of the arch, now to be rebuilt in glittering marble quarried from Bingham family land in Westchester, for which David's grandfather—who had bristled at the idea of being upstaged by a minor businessman who lived across Fifth Avenue from them, in a house not quite as stately—had largely paid.

All these David had seen many times before, but even so, he, like the others, found himself perusing everything as carefully as if it were altogether new to him. Indeed, the room was hushed, the only sound the women's swishing silk skirts, the men's occasional coughs and cleared throats. He was examining Lincoln's spiky hand, the ink faded to a dark mustard, when he felt rather than heard the presence of someone behind him, and when he straightened and turned, he saw it was Charles, his expression shifting between surprise and happiness and sorrow and pain.

"It is you," Charles said, in a small, strangled voice.

"Charles," he replied, not knowing how to proceed, and there was a silence before Charles bumbled onward.

"I heard you were sick," he began, and, after David nodded, "I'm very sorry to sneak up on you like this—Frances invited me—I had thought—that is to say—I do not wish to embarrass you, nor for you to think I was trying to catch you unawares."

"No, no—I didn't think that. I have been sick—but it was important to my grandfather I come, and so"—David made a helpless gesture with his hands—"I did. Thank you for the flowers. They were quite beautiful. And the card."

"You're welcome," said Charles, but he looked so unhappy, so distraught, that David was about to step toward him, thinking he might collapse, when Charles instead moved to him. "David," he said, in a low, urgent voice, "I know this is neither the place nor the time for me to speak to you like this, but—I am—that is to say—do you—why have you not—I have been waiting—" He was quiet, his movements contained, but David froze, thinking that everyone in the room must sense the fervor, the anguish, that surrounded the man, and that everyone too must know that he was the cause of such anguish, that he was the source of such distress. Even in his horror, for Charles and for himself, he could see how Charles had been affected—his jowls gone slack, his round, good-natured face blotchy and damp.

Charles was opening his mouth to speak again when Frances appeared at his elbow, patting him on the arm. "Charles!" she said. "My goodness—you look as if you're to faint! David, do get someone to fetch Mister Griffith some water!," and there was a general parting of the crowd as she led Charles to a bench and Norris slipped away to find some water.

But before Frances escorted Charles away, David had seen the look she darted at him—disapproving; disgusted even—and he abruptly turned to leave, understanding that he must get away before Charles recovered and Frances sought him out. As he did, though, he nearly collided with his grandfather, who was peering over his shoulder at Frances's back. "What on earth is happening?" Grandfather asked, and, before David could form an answer, "Why, is that Mister Griffith? Is he feeling ill?" He began moving toward Charles and Frances, but as he did, turned around to look at the room. "David?" he asked the space where his grandson had once stood. "David? Where are you?"

But David had already left.

XIV

When he opened his eyes, he was for a moment bewildered—where was he? And then he remembered: Ah, yes. He was at Eden and Eliza's, in one of their bedrooms.

Since fleeing the party two nights ago, he had been staying at his sister's house on Gramercy Park. He'd not heard a word from his grandfather—although Eden, before disappearing for her class the following morning, had assured David that he was livid—or from Edward, to whom he had sent a brief note, or from Charles. He was, at least for the present, spared from explaining himself.

Now he washed and dressed and visited the children in their nursery before going downstairs, where Eliza was in the parlor, kneeling on the floor in her trousers, the carpet covered with fuzzing balls of yarn and gray woolen socks and stacks of cotton nightshirts. "Oh, David!" she said, looking up and giving him one of her beaming smiles. "Do come in and help me!"

"What are you doing, dear Liza?" he asked, crouching next to her.

"I'm assembling these supplies for the refugees. See, each bundle gets a pair of socks, two nightshirts, two of these balls of yarn, and two of these knitting needles—they're in the box next to you. You tie them like so—here's twine and a knife—and then put the finished packages into this box, here, near me."

He smiled—it was difficult to feel too despairing around Eliza—and the two of them fell to their tasks. After they had worked in silence for several minutes, Eliza said, "So, you must tell me about your Mister Griffith."

He winced. "He is not mine."

"But he seemed rather nice, or what I saw of him anyway, before he took ill."

"He *is* nice, very nice indeed." And he began to tell Eliza of Charles Griffith—of his kindness and generosity; of his sense of industry; of his practical nature, with its unexpected flights into the romantic; of his authority, which never shaded into pedantry; of the heartbreaks he had suffered and the elegant sense of forbearance with which he bore them.

"Well," said Eliza, after a pause. "He does sound lovely, David. And it does sound as if he loves you. But—you do not love him back."

"I don't know," he admitted. "I do not think I do."

"And why not?"

"Because," he began, and then realized what his answer would be: Because he is not Edward. Because he did not feel like Edward did in his arms, because he did not have Edward's sprightly manner, Edward's unpredictability, Edward's charm. Compared with Edward, Charles's consistency felt like stodginess, his solidity like timidity, his industriousness like dullness. They both, Edward and Charles, wanted companions, but Charles's companion would be a fellow in complacency, in regularity, whereas Edward's would be a fellow in adventure, someone bold and brave. One offered a vision of who he was, the other of who he hoped to become. He knew what life with Charles would be. Charles would leave for work in the morning and David would stay home, and when Charles returned in the evening, there would be a quiet dinner together and then he would be obliged to submit to Charles's meaty hands, his prickly mustache, his overly enthusiastic kisses and compliments. Occasionally, he would accompany Charles to a dinner with his business associates—Mister Griffith's handsome, rich, young husband—and after David had excused himself, Charles's friends and colleagues would congratulate him on his catch—young and lovely *and* a Bingham! Griffith, you sly thing, what a lucky man you are!—and

Charles would chuckle, embarrassed and proud and besotted, and that night he would want to be with David again and again, padding into his bedroom and lifting up a corner of his bedcover, his paw reaching for him. And then, one day, David would look at himself in the mirror and realize that he had become Charles—the same thickened waist, the same thinning hair—and realize too that he had given his last years of youth to a man who had made him old before he needed to be.

But ever since Edward had made his proposal, David had had a different daydream, of a different kind of day. He would return from whatever he would do on the silk farm—perhaps he could become a documenter of the trees, making botanical sketches of them and overseeing their health—to the bungalow in which he and Edward lived together. There would be two bedrooms, each with a bed, in case they were someday reported and their house raided, but once the night had drawn its curtain over the land, it was to one room they would repair, and it was in that room, in that bed, where they would do whatever they wished, a never-ending continuation of their encounters in the boardinghouse. To live a life in color, a life in love: Was that not every person's dream? In less than two years, when he was thirty, he would come into some of his fortune, the part bequeathed him by his parents, but Edward had not even mentioned his money—he had mentioned only him, and their life together— and so how, and for what reason, could he say no? True, his forefathers had fought and toiled to establish a land in which he was free, but had they not also ensured and therefore encouraged a different kind of freedom, one greater because it was smaller? The freedom to be with the person he desired; the freedom to place above all other concerns his own happiness. He was David Bingham, a man who always behaved correctly, who always chose deliberately: Now he would begin again, just as his great-great-grandfather Edmund had, but his would be the bravery of love.

The recognition of this made him feel light-headed, and he stood and asked Eliza if he might use her hansom, and she said he might, though as he was leaving she plucked at his sleeve and brought him close to her. "Be careful, David," she said, gently, but he only brushed her cheek with his lips and hurried down the stairs to the street, understanding that he must speak the words aloud in order to make them real, and he must do so before he set to deliberating once more.

He'd realized on the way over that he'd no way of knowing whether Edward would be at the boardinghouse, but up he went, and when Edward opened the door, David was at once in his arms. "I will go," he heard himself saying. "I will go with you."

What a scene it was! Both of them crying, crying and grabbing at each other, at each other's clothes, each other's hair, so that if you were watching them you would not be able to tell whether they were in a state of violent mourning or of ecstasy.

"I thought for certain you had decided against it after I'd not heard a reply from you," Edward confessed after they'd calmed themselves somewhat.

"A reply?"

"Yes, to the letter I sent you four days ago—telling you I'd told Belle I had hopes of convincing you and asking you to do me the favor of letting me try again."

"I received no such letter!"

"No? But I sent it—I wonder where it could be!"

"Well—I—I've not been home, as such. But—I shall explain later," for again, the urge, the passion, had overtaken them.

It was only much later, as they lay in their usual positions in Edward's hard little bed, that Edward asked, "And what has your grandfather said to all of this?"

"Well, you see—I haven't told him. Not yet."

"David! My dearest. What shall he say?"

Just then, there it was: the slightest of tears in their happiness. But "He shall come around," David said, staunchly, more to hear himself say it than because he believed it. "He will. It may take some time, but he will. And anyway—he cannot stop me. I am an adult, after all, no longer under his legal protection. In two years, I shall come into part of my money."

Beside him, Edward moved closer. "Can he not withhold it from you?"

"Certainly not—it's not his to withhold, after all: It's from my parents."

They were quiet, and then Edward said, "Well—until then—you needn't worry. I will be drawing a salary, and I shall take care of both of us," and David, who had never before had anyone offer him financial sustenance, was moved, and kissed Edward's upturned face.

"I have saved almost every penny of my allowance since I was a child," he reassured Edward. "We shall have thousands, easily. I do not mean for you to worry about me." Indeed, *he* would take care of Edward, he knew. Edward would want to work, because he was industrious and ambitious, but David would make their lives not just bold but comfortable. There would be a piano for Edward, and books for him, and everything—rose-hued Oriental carpets and thin white china and silk-upholstered chairs—that he had at Washington Square. California would be their new home, their new Washington Square, and David would make it as familiar and pleasant as he could.

They lay there through the afternoon, and then into the evening, and for once, there was nowhere for David to be: He did not snap awake from his doze only to panic at the sight of the darkening sky, frantically dress, and leave Edward's beseeching arms so he could bolt back to the hansom and implore the coachman—why: Was he *smirking*? At *him*? How *dare* he!—to go as fast as he could, as if he were back in school, a child about to miss the final bell, after which the doors to the dining hall would be locked and he would have to go to bed without his supper. That day, and then that night, they slept and woke, slept and woke, and when they finally rose to boil some eggs over the fire, Edward stopped him from checking his pocket watch. "Why does it matter?" he asked. "We have all the time we want, do we not?" And instead he was set to slicing a loaf of brown bread, which they toasted over the flames.

The next day they woke late, and talked and talked about their new life together—of the flowers David would plant in their garden, of the piano Edward would buy ("But only after we have become secure," he said earnestly, and David had laughed. "I shall buy you one," he promised, spoiling his own surprise, but Edward shook his

head: "I do not want you spending your money on me—it is yours"),
of how much David would like Belle, and she him. Then it was time
for David's class—he had been absent the previous two weeks, and
had told Matron he would hold a special class on Thursday instead
of Wednesday—and he made himself dress and go see his students,
whom he instructed to draw whatever they pleased, and then drifted
among them as they did, glancing occasionally at their sketches of
lopsided faces, of dogs and wild-eyed cats, of crudely executed dai-
sies and pointy-petaled roses, smiling all the while. And after, when
he returned home, there was a freshly made fire, and a table of food
he had given Edward money to buy, and Edward himself, to whom
David now told stories of his afternoon—stories of the sort he had
once told Grandfather, which he blushed to remember: a grown
man with only his grandfather for company! He thought of the two
of them, their quiet nights in his grandfather's drawing room, his
retreats afterward to his study, where he would draw in his notepad. It had been an invalid's life, but now he had been restored to
health—now he was cured.

He had sent back Eden and Eliza's hansom with a note the evening of his arrival at Edward's, but on the third night, there was a
thumping on the door, and David opened it to find a slattern of a
maid, holding out a letter, which he took and replaced with a coin.

"Who is it from?" Edward asked.

"Frances Holson," he frowned. "Our family lawyer."

"Well, read it—I shall turn to face this wall and pretend I have
gone to another room, thus giving you some privacy."

Dear David,   March 16

I write with unfortunate news. Mister Griffith has taken ill. He
became feverish the night of the museum opening—your grandfather saw that he reached home safely.

I cannot be certain what has transpired between you, but I can
tell you that he is devoted to you, and that if you are the man I know

you to be and have known since he was a small boy, then you will do him the kindness of calling on him, especially as he believes there is an understanding between you and him. He was to have left for the Cape directly after the party, but has been forced to stay longer. And not only forced, I suspect—he has wanted to, in hopes of seeing you. I hope your conscience and good heart will oblige him.

I see no reason to mention any of this to your grandfather.

Sincerely, F. Holson

Frances must have learned of his whereabouts from Eden, who had no doubt learned it from her driver, that traitor, though he could not but be grateful to their longtime lawyer and family intimate for her discretion—as scolding as her note was, he knew she would not betray him to his grandfather, for she had always indulged him, even when he was a small boy. He crumpled the paper in his hand, hurled it into the fire, and then, in defiance of Frances, slipped back into bed, waving away Edward's concerns. But later, as they once more lay in each other's arms, he thought of Charles and was overcome with sorrow and rage: sorrow for Charles, rage at himself.

"You are so serious," Edward said to him, softly, stroking his cheek. "Will you not tell me?"

And so, finally, he did: of his grandfather's proposal, of Charles's offer, of Charles himself, of their encounters together, of how Charles had fallen in love with him. His earlier imaginings, that he and Edward would laugh together about Charles's bumbling gestures in bed, now made him prickle with shame, and were at any rate not to be. Edward listened quietly and sympathetically, and as he did, David felt himself become more regretful: He had treated Charles abominably.

"The poor man," said Edward at last, feelingly. "You must tell him, David. Unless—unless you are in fact in love with him?"

"Of course not!" he said, hotly. "I am in love with you!"

"Well, then," said Edward, pressing close to him, "you truly must tell him. David, you must."

"I know," he said. "I know you're right. My good Edward. Let me just stay with you here one more night, and tomorrow I'll go to him."

And then they agreed that they would sleep, for as much as they still wanted to talk, they were both very tired. So they blew out the candles, and though David thought he might be kept awake from worrying about the task he had to endure the next day, he was not—it seemed that he had only to lay his head against Edward's sole, thin pillow and close his eyes when sleep blanketed him, and his concerns vanished into the murk of his dreams.

XV

M ister Bingham," said Walden, dryly. "I'm very sorry to keep you waiting."

David stiffened—he had never much liked Walden, for he knew his type: A Londoner, hired away by Charles at no doubt enormous expense, he struggled between feeling diminished for being the butler to a man of new money and no name . . . and feeling proud of himself for having a sense of authority so unimpeachable that a rich man had sought and wooed him from across the sea. Like all seductions, of course, the romance of his had ebbed, and now Walden was trapped in this vulgar territory in the New World, working for someone with means but with gaudy taste. David was a reminder to Walden that he might have done better for himself, might have found himself in the employ of new money that was at least not quite *so* new.

"That's quite all right, Walden," said David, coolly. "My visit is unannounced, after all."

"Indeed. We have missed seeing you here for some time, Mister Bingham."

The comment was impertinent, and made to fluster him, and did, but he said nothing, until finally Walden continued, "I'm afraid Mister Griffith is still quite weak. He wonders—but will understand if you'd rather not—if you might come see him in his chambers?"

"Of course—that would be fine, if he's certain?"

"Oh, yes. He is quite certain. Please: I believe you know the way."

Walden had spoken mildly, but David bolted to his feet, furious, following Walden up the staircase, blushing as he remembered how

Walden had several times witnessed him being steered by an eager Charles into his bedroom, his palm on his lower back, and how David had detected on the butler's face as he passed him a shadow of a smirk, one both lascivious and mocking.

At the door, he brushed past Walden, his formal, ironic bow—"Mister Bingham"—and then into the room, which was dark, its shades drawn against the late-morning skies, and lit only by a single lamp near Charles's bedside. Charles himself sat in bed, propped up against tiers of pillows and still clad in his dressing gown. Around him were scatters of papers, and a little table with an inkwell and a quill, which Charles moved from atop his knees.

"David," he said, quietly. "Come here, so I can see you." He reached over and lit the lamp on the other side of the bed, and David advanced, drawing close a chair as he did.

He was surprised by how poorly Charles looked, his face and lips gray, the pouches beneath his eyes pleated and sagging, his sparse hair uncombed and floaty, and some of this surprise must have shown in his face, for Charles gave a twitching sort of smile and said, "I ought to have warned you before you entered."

"Not at all," he said. "It is always lovely to see you," a statement both true and not, and Charles, as if understanding this, winced.

He had been fearing—and, he would have to admit to himself later, half hoping—that Charles was lovesick, lovesick for him, and so, when Charles explained that he had been felled with a cough, he experienced a slight, unbidden prick of disappointment, coupled with a larger measure of relief. "It is like nothing I've experienced in many years," Charles said. "But I believe I am beyond the worst of it, though it still tires me to walk up and down the stairs. I'm afraid I've been trapped in this room and my study for the most part, examining these"—he indicated the wash of paper—"accounts and ledgers, and writing my correspondence." David began to murmur his sympathies, but Charles stopped him with a gesture that was not unkind but declarative. "There is no need," he said. "I thank you, but I shall be fine; I am on the mend already."

For a long moment, there was a silence, during which Charles looked at him and David looked at the floor, and when he finally spoke, Charles did, too.

"I'm sorry," they said to each other, and then, at the same time, "Please—you first."

"Charles," he began. "You are a wonderful man. I so enjoy speaking to you. You are not only a good person but a wise one as well. I have been, and am, honored by your interest and by your affections. But—I cannot marry you.

"If you had been a callous man, or a selfish one, my behavior toward you would be unacceptable. But considering the sort of man you are, it is reprehensible. I have no explanations for myself, no justifications, no defense. I was and am completely in the wrong, and my sorrow for any pain I might have caused you will haunt me for the rest of my life. You deserve much better than me, that is for certain. I hope someday you might forgive me, though I do not expect it. But I will always wish well for you—that I know."

He had not quite known what he was to say, even as he mounted the stairs to Charles's room. It had been a season of apologies, he now saw: Charles to him, for not writing; Edward to him, again for not writing; he to Charles. There was only one other apology to make, and that was to his grandfather, but he could not contemplate that, not now.

Charles was quiet, and for a time they sat in the echo of David's words, and when Charles finally did speak, his eyes were closed, and his voice was broken and hoarse. "I knew this," he said. "I knew this was to be your answer. I knew it, and I had days—weeks, if I am to be honest—to prepare myself. But hearing it from you—" He fell silent.

"Charles," he said, gently.

"Tell me—no, don't. But—David, I know I am older than you, and not even a quarter as handsome. But—I have given this a great deal of thought as I anticipated this conversation—and wondered if there might be a way for us to be together in which—in which you might also find satisfaction with others."

He did not immediately comprehend what Charles meant, but

once he did, he sighed, deeply moved. "Oh, Charles, you are very handsome," he lied, to which Charles made a sad little smile but said nothing. "And you are very kind. But you would not want to be in a marriage like that."

"No," Charles admitted, "I would not. But if it might be a way of being with you—"

"Charles—I cannot."

Charles sighed, and turned his head on the pillow. For a while he did not speak. Then: "Are you in love with another?"

"Yes," he said, and his answer startled them both. It was as if he had shouted a horrible word, a terrible slur, and neither of them knew how to respond.

"How long?" asked Charles at last, in a low, dull voice. And then, when David did not respond, "Before we were intimate?" And then, again, "Who is he?"

"Not long," he mumbled. "No. No one. A man I met." It was a betrayal to reduce Edward to a nobody, a nameless figure, but he knew as well that he had to spare Charles's feelings, that it was enough to simply recognize Edward's existence aloud without specifying his particulars.

A third silence, and then Charles, who had been slumping against his pillows, his face turned from David, sat up with a rustling of his sheets. "David, I have something I must say to you, or I shall always regret it," he began, speaking slowly. "I must take your declaration of love for another seriously, as much as it pains me—and it does. But for some time now I have wondered if you might be—frightened. If not of matrimony, then about having to keep your secrets from me, and if this is what has made you reluctant, what has made you stay distant from me.

"I know about your illnesses, David. Do not ask me from whom, but I have known for some time, and I wish to tell you now—perhaps, almost certainly, I should have said this earlier—that this knowledge has never deterred me from wanting to make you my husband, from wanting to spend my life with you."

He was glad to be sitting, for he felt he might faint, and worse, as if his clothes had been ripped from him and he was standing in the middle of Union Square, surrounded by crowds, all jeering and pointing at his nakedness, throwing slimy leaves of rotting cabbage at his head, dray horses prancing about him. Charles was correct: There was no point in trying to discover who had revealed his secret. He knew it was not his family, however cool his relationship with his siblings might be; such information was almost invariably spread by servants, and although the Binghams' were loyal, and some had been in their employ for decades, there were always a few who left, seeking other, better work, and even those who did not talked among their own kind. All it would take was one chambermaid telling her sister, a scullery maid at another house, who would then tell her beau, a coachman at another house, who would then tell the second valet, who would then tell *his* beau, the cook's assistant, who, in order to curry favor with his master, would tell the cook himself, who would then tell his sometimes-friend and always-nemesis, the butler, the figure who, even more than the master of the house, dictated the rhythms and therefore petty comforts of his life, who then, after his master's young friend had left for the night, back to his manse on Washington Square, would tap on his master's bedroom door and be bidden to enter and, clearing his throat, would begin, "Forgive me, sir—I have deliberated whether I might say something, but I feel that it is my moral obligation to do so," and his master, irritated and accustomed to these kinds of dramas that servants so indulged in, who understood the way they both resented and relished being so privy to the most intimate aspects of their employers' lives, would say, "Well, what is it? Out with it, Walden!," and Walden, dipping his head in a pantomime of humility, as well as to hide the smile he could not keep from forming on his long, thin lips, would begin, "It is about young Mister Bingham, sir."

"Do you mean to threaten me?" he whispered, when he had recovered himself.

"Threaten you! No, David, of course not! You mistake me. I mean only to reassure you, to tell you that if your past has made you understandably wary, that you have nothing to fear from me, that—"

"Because you shall not. You forget—I am still a Bingham. While you? You are nobody. You are nothing. You may have money. You may even have some standing back in Massachusetts. But here? No one will ever listen to you. No one will ever believe you."

The ugly words hung in the air between them, and for a long while, neither of them spoke. And then, in a quick, sudden movement, so sudden that David rose to his feet, thinking that Charles might strike him, Charles threw back his covers and stood, resting one hand against the bed to balance himself, and when he spoke, his voice was like metal, like nothing David had heard before.

"It seems I have been mistaken. About what I thought might be your fear. About you, in general. But now I have said all I mean to, and now we need never speak again.

"I wish you well, David—I do. I hope this man you love loves you back, and always will, and that you have a long life together, and that you will not find yourself as I do at my age, a fool standing in your bedclothes before a beautiful young man you trusted with your heart and whom you thought decent, and good, and who has revealed himself to be neither, but instead a spoiled child."

He turned his back to David. "Walden will see you out," he said, but David, recognizing the moment he had spoken the horror of what he had done, simply stood frozen in place. Seconds passed, and when it was clear Charles would not face him again, he too turned, and walked to the door, where he was certain that on the other side Walden waited, his ear pressed to the wood, a smile playing on his mouth, already planning how he would relay this remarkable story to his colleagues at that night's staff meal.

XVI

H e found himself leaving the house in a trance, and once outside, he stood dazed on the pavement. Around him, the world was impossibly vivid: the sky assaultively blue, the birds oppressively loud, the smell of horse manure, even in the cold, unpleasantly strong, the stitches in his fine kid gloves so precise and tiny and numerous that he could easily become lost in counting them.

There was a storm roiling within him, and to counter it, he began one of his own, directing his hansom to shop after shop, spending money in a way he never had, on boxes of fragile meringues, as snowy as lard; on a cashmere scarf the same black as Edward's eyes; on a bushel of oranges, plump and as fragrant as blossoms; on a tin of caviar, each bead as shimmery as a pearl. He spent extravagantly, and only on extravagant things—nothing he purchased was necessary, and indeed most of them would decay or sour before there would be time to reasonably consume them. On and on he bought, taking some of the packages with him but sending most directly to Edward's house, and so, by the time he finally reached Bethune Street, he had to wait at the bottom of the steps as two deliverymen hoisted between them a flowering kumquat tree through the entryway and another two exited, carrying an empty crate that had once held a complete Limoges tea service painted with animals of the African jungle. Upstairs, Edward was standing in the center of his room, his palms on either side of his head, directing—or, rather, not—the placement of the tree. "My goodness," he kept repeating. "I suppose put it here—or, no: here, maybe. But—no, not there either—" And when he saw David, he gave a cry of surprise and relief and perhaps exasperation as well. "David!" he said. "My darling! What is the meaning of all this? No, please, over there, I should think"—this to the deliverymen—"David! My dear, you're back so late! What have you been doing?"

In response, he began pulling things from his pockets, tossing them onto the bed: the caviar, a triangle of White Stilton cheese, a little wooden box containing shards of his favorite crystallized ginger, liqueur-filled bonbons, each wrapped in a scrap of gaily colored tissue—everything sweet, everything delicious, things meant only to delight, to enchant away the regret that surrounded him like a cloud. He had been in such a frenzy that he had purchased things in multiples: not one bar of chocolate stippled with gooseberries but two; not one cone of candied chestnuts but three; not one more fine wool blanket to match the one he'd already bought Edward but two more.

But this they only discovered, laughingly, after they had gorged themselves, and by the time they were able to come to their senses— unclothed yet perspiring even in the damp chill of the room, lying on the floor because the bed was covered with packages—they were both holding their stomachs and moaning, theatrically, from all of the sugar, the rich creamy fat, the smoked duck and pâté that they had just consumed.

"Oh, David," said Edward, "will you not regret this?"

"Of course not," he said, and he didn't—he had never behaved like this in his life. His actions had been necessary, he felt—his fortune would never feel his own until he behaved as if it were.

"We shall not live like this in California," Edward murmured, dreamily, and instead of answering, David stood and found his trousers—thrown to a far corner (such as it was) of the room—and reached inside its pocket.

"What is this?" Edward asked, taking the little leather case from him, and opening its hinged lid. "Oh," he said.

It was a small porcelain dove, perfectly captured, its tiny beak open in song, its black eyes bright. "It is for you, because you are my little bird," David explained, "and because I hope you will be forever after."

Edward took the bird from its case and cupped it in his palm. "Are you asking me to marry you?" he asked, quietly.

"Yes," David told him, "I am," and Edward flung his arms around him. "I of course accept," he said. "Of course I do!"

They would never be as happy again as they were that night. All around them, all within them, was pleasure. David especially felt himself born anew: In one day, he had lost an offer of marriage, and yet he had made his own. He felt, that night, invincible; every piece of happiness the room contained was because of him. Every sweet taste on their tongues, every soft cushion they lay their heads upon, every scent that perfumed the air: All of it was because of *him*. All of it *he* had provided. Running beneath these triumphs, though, like a dark and poisoned river, was his disgrace—the unconscionable things he'd said to Charles and, below that, the fact of his behavior, of how disrespectfully he had treated Charles, how he had used him out of restlessness and fearfulness and in desire of praise and attention. And beneath *that* was the specter of his grandfather, whom he had betrayed and to whom no apology would ever suffice. Whenever knowledge of these things bubbled up within him, he pushed them down again by slipping another bonbon into his or Edward's mouth, or by making Edward turn him on his stomach.

Yet he knew that it would never be enough, that he had stained himself, and that the stain was irreversible. And so, the next morning, when the little maid tapped on the door, her eyes agoggle at the scene within the room, and presented him with a terse and inarguable note from his grandfather, he knew both that he had been found out at last and that there was nothing to do but return to Washington Square, where he would answer his shame—and declare his freedom.

XVII

H ome! He had been away for only a little less than a week, and yet how strange it already seemed—how strange and yet how familiar, its fragrance of furniture wax and lilies, of Earl Grey tea and fire. And, of course, of his grandfather: his tobacco and orange-blossom cologne.

He had told himself he would not be nervous entering Washington Square—it *was* his house; it would *be* his house—and yet, when he reached the top of the flight of stairs, he hesitated: Normally, he would stride in, but for a moment he felt as if he should knock, and had the door not suddenly opened (Adams, showing Norris out), he might have remained there forever. Norris's eyes perceptibly widened upon seeing him, but he quickly recovered himself and wished David a pleasant evening, adding that he hoped to see him again soon, and even Adams, who was much better trained than the loathsome Walden, involuntarily raised his eyebrows before quickly and severely lowering them into a scowl, as if punishing them for their disobedience.

"Mister David, you look very well. Welcome home. Your grandfather is in his drawing room."

He thanked Adams, handing him his hat and allowing him to take his coat, and then up he went. Dinner was served early on Sundays, and so he too had arrived early, just past his grandfather's lunchtime. Being away from Washington Square had made him realize how he had come to measure time by its metronome: Noon was not just noon, it was when he and his grandfather finished their weekend midday meal; five-thirty p.m. was not just five-thirty p.m., it was when they would sit again for dinner. Seven a.m. was when his grandfather would leave for the bank; five p.m. was when he would return. His clock, his days, were determined by his grandfather, and he had for all his years yielded unthinkingly to him. Even in exile, he could feel the old ache of those Sunday-night dinners, could see, as clearly as if it were a painting, his siblings and grandfather gathered around the mirrored shine of the dining-room table, could smell the rich fattiness of the roasted quail.

Outside his grandfather's drawing room, he stopped again and paused, inhaling deeply, before finally tapping his knuckle against the door and, hearing his grandfather's voice, entering. When he did, his grandfather rose, unusually for him, and the two stood in silence, each staring at the other as if he were someone he had seen once and then forgotten.

"David," said his grandfather, blandly.

"Grandfather," he said.

His grandfather came to him. "Let me look at you," he said, and took David's cheeks in his palms, turning his head slightly this way and that, as if the riddles of David's current life might be writ on his face, before dropping his hands to his side again, his expression betraying nothing. "Sit," he told David, and David did, in his usual chair.

For a period, they were silent, and then his grandfather began to speak. "I shall not begin where I might: by rebuking you, or questioning you, though I cannot promise I will be able to resist either for the entirety of our conversation. For now, though, I have two things I mean to show you." He watched as his grandfather reached into a box on the table next to him and drew out a bundle of letters, dozens of them, tied with string, and upon receiving them, David saw that they were all from Edward, and looked up, outraged. "*Do not*," his grandfather said, before he could speak. "You *dare* not." And David, though furious, hurriedly untied the knot and tore at the first one in silence. Inside was the first of the letters he had written to Edward when Edward had left to see his sisters and, on a separate sheet, Edward's reply. The second enve-lope, cut open and resealed, contained another of his letters, and another of Edward's replies. So did the third, and the fourth, and the fifth—all the letters Edward had never replied to, finally answered. As he read, he could not stop himself from beaming, or his hands from trembling: at the romance of the gesture, from realizing how much he had needed these responses, from the cru-elty of their being withheld from him, from relief that they had been left unopened for him to read, for him alone to see. Here too was the letter that Edward had referred to, the one he had had delivered two days before the museum show, when David had been lying in his bed, insensate and tormented, here it was, and many more besides. *Here* was proof of Edward's love for him, his devotion in every word, in every sheet of onionskin—*here* was why he had not heard from Edward during his confinement: because Edward had been writing him these letters. He suddenly had a vision of himself, in bed and staring at the stain, and, west from here, Edward scrib-bling by candlelight, his hand stiff and sore, each of them unaware of the other's discomfort, but both thinking only of each other.

And then he was incensed, and yet once again, his grandfa-ther began speaking before he could. "You must not judge me too harshly, child—though I do apologize for keeping these from you. But you were so ill, so upset, that I could not know if these would harm you further. It was such an extraordinary quantity of letters, that I thought they might be from—from—" He stopped.

"Well, they were not," he snapped.

"I know that now," his grandfather continued, and his face became grim. "And this leads me to the second thing I need you to read," and once again he reached into the box and this time handed David a large brown envelope, which contained a sheaf of stitched pages, the top sheet marked, in large letters, "Confidential—for Mister Nathaniel Bingham, upon request," and suddenly David felt a fear ripple through him, and he held the pages in his lap, careful not to look at them.

But "Read it," his grandfather said, in that same tight, bland voice. And, when David refused to move, "*Read it.*"

Dear Mister Bingham,   March 17, 1894

We have completed the report on the gentleman in question, Edward Bishop, and have recorded the details of the subject's life within these pages.

The subject was born Edward Martins Knowlton on August 2, 1870, in Savannah, Georgia, to Francis Knowlton, a schoolteacher, and Sarabeth Knowlton (née Martins). The Knowltons had one other child, a daughter, Isabelle (known as Belle) Harriet Knowlton, born January 27, 1873. Mister Knowlton was a beloved teacher, but he was also a known and inveterate gambler, and the family was often in debt. Knowlton borrowed heavily from his and his wife's extended family, but it was when he was discovered to be stealing money from the school's coffers that he was fired and threatened with probable imprisonment. At the same time, Knowlton was found to be much more indebted than even his family knew—he had accrued hundreds of dollars' worth, with no way to repay it.

The night before he was to be arraigned, Knowlton fled with his wife and two children. His neighbors found the house almost exactly as they'd left it, though with signs that they had departed in great haste; the larder had been ransacked for dry goods, and drawers had been left ajar. A child's forgotten sock lay on the staircase. The authorities immediately began pursuit, but it is thought that Knowlton sought refuge in one of the underground houses, likely claiming religious persecution.

From here, the trail on Knowlton and his wife ends. The two children, Edward and Belle, are recorded as registered in a safe house in Frederick, Maryland, on October 4, 1877, but they are identified as orphans. According to notes from the shelter, neither child could or would talk about what had happened to their parents, but the boy did at one point say that "the man with the horse found them and we hid," which led the facility director to believe that the Knowlton parents were captured by a Colony patrol just before crossing into Maryland and the children were later found and taken to the shelter by a good Samaritan.

The siblings remained at the house for another two months before being moved with a number of other parentless children found in the area to an institution for Colony orphans in Philadelphia on December 12, 1877. Here they were almost immediately adopted by a couple from Burlington, Vermont, Luke and Victoria Bishop, who already had two daughters, Laura (eight) and Margaret (nine), also Colony orphans, though both were adopted in infancy. The Bishops were wealthy, upstanding citizens: Mister Bishop owned a successful lumber concern, which he managed with his wife.

But the early, pleasant relations between the Bishops and their new son were soon to sour. While Belle adjusted quickly to her new life, Edward resisted it. The boy was highly attractive, as well as intelligent and charming, but, as Victoria Bishop put it, "lacked any true sense of industry or self-control." Indeed, while his sisters dutifully completed their chores and homework, Edward was forever finding ways to shirk responsibility; he even engaged in petty blackmail to coerce Belle into doing his chores for him. Though obviously quick-witted, he was an indifferent student and indeed was suspended from school after he was found to have cheated on a mathematics exam. He loved sweets, and several times filched candy from the general store. And yet, as his adoptive mother emphasized, he was also beloved by his sisters, especially Belle, despite the small ways in which she was often manipulated by him. He was, she says, exceptionally patient with animals, including the family's lame dog, as well as a gifted singer, an excellent writer and reader, and deeply affectionate. Though he had very few true friends, preferring to be with Belle, he was well-liked and had many acquaintances and never seemed to be lonely.

When the boy was ten years old, the family acquired a piano— Mister Bishop had learned to play in his youth—and although all the children were given lessons, it was Edward who demonstrated the most talent and natural skill. "It seemed to quiet something within him," Missus Bishop said, adding that she and her husband were "relieved" that their son might have found an affinity for something. They engaged additional tutors for him, and were gratified to see Edward at last applying himself so diligently to something.

As Edward grew older, the Bishops' difficulties with him increased. He was, his mother notes, something of a conundrum for them; though capable, he was bored by school and began to skip classes, and was again caught committing a series of petty thefts—pencils and small change and the like—from his classmates, which bewildered his parents, as they had never denied him anything he wished. After he was expelled from his third preparatory school in as many years, his parents hired a private tutor so that he might finish his education; he managed to earn his degree, barely, and thence attended a conservatory of little prestige in western Massachusetts, where he completed only one year before taking a small inheritance he had from one of his uncles and decamping for New York City, where he moved into the Harlem house of his maternal great-aunt Bethesda. Both of his parents approved of the situation: Since she became widowed nine years prior, Bethesda's mind had slipped considerably, and though she had plenty of attendants—she was quite wealthy—they felt that Edward's presence would be soothing for her; she had always been deeply fond of him, and, being childless, had considered him as her own son.

The first autumn after leaving school, Edward returned to visit his family for Thanksgiving, where they all spent a pleasant weekend. After Edward had left for New York, and his sisters to their homes—Laura and Margaret, who was newly married, were living in Burlington, near their parents, and Belle was preparing to attend nursing school in New Hampshire—Missus Bishop decided she would do some tidying. It was then, in her bedroom, that she discovered that her favorite necklace, a pearl on a gold strand that her husband had given her for their anniversary, was missing. She immediately set to searching, but after many hours, after checking every place it could possibly be, she was still not able to locate it. It was then that she realized where it might have disappeared to, or, rather, who might have disappeared it, and as if to banish the thought from her mind, she embarked upon a resorting and refolding of all of her husband's handkerchiefs, which she did not of course need to do but felt she must.

She was too frightened to ask Edward if he had taken her necklace, and she dared not mention it to her husband, who was far less tolerant of their son than she was and, she knew, would say something he would later regret. She promised herself she would not suspect her son, but after Christmas came and went, and with it, her children, and with them, or one of them, rather—as she later discovered—a silver filigree bracelet, she was forced to confront her suspicions again. She did not know why Edward would not just tell her that he needed money, for she would have given it to him, even if her husband would not. But the next time he came to visit, she hid everything he might be able to easily locate in a box deep within the locked trunk she kept in her closet, secreting her valuables from her own child.

Of Edward's present life, she knew very little. She had heard from acquaintances that he was singing in a nightclub, which worried her—not for her family's reputation but because her son, though intelligent, was so young and could, she felt, be easily influenced. She wrote him letters, but he rarely responded, and in his silence, she tried not to wonder whether she knew him at all. But at least she knew he was with her aunt, and although Bethesda's mind continued to deteriorate, she would receive an occasional lucid letter in which Bethesda would write warmly and appreciatively of her grand-nephew and his presence.

Then, a little more than two years ago, her associations with Edward came to an end. She received one day a frantic telegram from her aunt's attorney informing her that he had been alerted by Aunt Bethesda's bank that large amounts of money had been withdrawn from her account. Missus Bishop left immediately for New York, where a dismaying round of meetings revealed that, over the past twelvemonth, Edward himself had signed for increasingly substantial sums from his aunt's trust; an investigation by the bank (one of your competitors, you will be relieved to hear) revealed that Edward had seduced Bethesda Carroll's trustee's assistant, a plain and gullible young man, who gulpingly confessed that he had knowingly violated company bylaws in order to help Edward secure the funds—thousands of dollars, though Missus Bishop declined to specify an exact number—that he desired. Back at the house, Missus Bishop discovered her aunt cared for but completely unaware of her surroundings or even who Edward was; she discovered as well that small things—pieces of silver and china, her aunt's diamond necklace—were also missing. I asked her how she could be certain it was her son, and not one of her aunt's many attendants or staff, who had taken it, and here she began to cry and said that they had been in her aunt's employ for years, and nothing had ever vanished—the only new addition to her aunt's life was, she admitted through tears, her son.

But where *was* her son? He seemed to have disappeared. Missus Bishop searched for him and even hired an investigator, but he had not been recovered by the time she was forced to return to Burlington.

All along, she had successfully concealed from her husband Edward's lapses. Now, though, that Edward's activities had crossed into the criminal, she was forced to confess. As she feared, her husband reacted violently, disowning Edward entirely, and, after summoning his daughters to tell them of their brother's wickedness, forbidding them from speaking to him again. All three wept, for they loved their brother, with Belle especially distraught.

But Mister Bishop remained unmoved: They were never to speak to him again, and if he should try to contact them, they must ignore him. "We made a mistake," his wife remembers him saying, and although he hastened to add, "Not you, Belle," Missus Bishop says, "I saw her face and knew it was too late."

Even if they *had* been allowed to contact Edward, however, they would have been unable, for he seemed to have vanished completely. The investigator his mother had hired continued to search but concluded he must have left the city, and likely the state, and, perhaps, the Free States altogether. For almost a year, there was silence. And then, about six months ago, the investigator wrote once more to Missus Bishop: Edward had been located. He was in New York and playing piano in a nightclub near Wall Street, one popular with moneyed young society people, and living in a single room in a boardinghouse on Bethune Street. Missus Bishop was perplexed by this revelation: A boardinghouse! But where had the money gone, the monies he had taken from her aunt? Was Edward a gambler, as his late father had been? There had been no signs of such behavior, but, given how much she apparently did not know about her son, it did not seem implausible. She ordered the investigator to monitor Edward's comings and goings for a week to see if she might glean more information from his daily movements, but these too proved frustrating: Edward never went into a bank, nor did he visit any gambling dens. Instead, his movements were restricted to his room and to a grand house near Gramercy Park. Upon further investigation, this was determined to be the residence of a Mister Christopher D. (I have struck his name from this record to protect his and his family's privacy), a well-born man of nine-and-twenty who lived with his aging parents, Mister and Missus D., who own a trading concern and are of considerable wealth. The young Mister D. was described by the investigator as "lonely" and "homely," and it appears that Edward Bishop was able to quickly seduce him, to such an extent that Mister D. proposed marriage—and was accepted—three months into their acquaintance. It appears, though, that his parents, learning of their son's proposal and strongly disapproving, called upon Edward for a meeting, during which they offered to secure him a job as a teacher at a charitable foundation of which they knew, as well as a quantity of cash, in return for his promise that he would conclusively end all relations with their son and heir. Edward agreed, the monies were delivered, and he ceased contact with young Mister D., who is said to this day to be "bereft," and, the Bishops' investigator told me, has made regular and increasingly desperate attempts to contact his former fiancé. (The charitable foundation, I am sorry to report, is The Hiram Bingham Charitable School and Institution, where until February Edward Bishop was employed as a music teacher.)

And here we come to Mister Bishop's current state of affairs. According to the matron of the institution, Mister Bishop—whom she described, dismissively, as "fey" and "a flibbertigibbet" while admitting he was enormously popular with his students: "The most popular teacher we have ever had, I am sorry to say"—requested a period of leave toward the end of January in order to tend to his sick mother in Burlington. (Obviously, a lie, as Missus Bishop is and has always been in excellent health.) Edward did indeed venture north, but here again, his account diverges from the truth. His first stop was to friends of his in Boston, the Cookes, a brother-and-sister duo who pose as a young married couple for reasons I will return to later in this narrative. His second stop was to Manchester, where Belle was living in a respectable boardinghouse and finishing her training as a nurse. It appears that Belle, despite her father's admonishments, had remained in communication with Edward since his banishment from the family, even sending him a portion of her monthly allowance. It is unclear what exactly transpired between the siblings, but late in February, at least a week past the date Edward told the matron he would return, the two traveled to Burlington, where, it seemed, Belle hoped to reconcile her brother with his father. Laura, the younger of their elder sisters, had recently given birth, and Belle must have assumed that her parents would be in a forgiving mood.

Needless to say, the visit did not unfold as the siblings had hoped. Mister Bishop, upon seeing his wayward son, exploded in anger, and there was a heated exchange; he had by this point learned of his son's theft of his wife's jewelry and personal items, and confronted Edward with this information. Edward, hearing this, made a sudden lunge for his mother, who, even now, remains confident that Edward was simply reacting to the fever of the moment and had no intention of actually harming her, but his action alarmed Mister Bishop, who threw a punch at his son, which knocked the latter to the floor. A scuffle ensued, with all the women attempting to separate the two, and in the melee, Missus Bishop was struck in the face.

It was not certain that Edward had been the one to land the blow, but it no longer mattered: Mister Bishop ordered Edward out of the house, and then told Belle she had a choice—she could remain in the family, or she could leave with her brother, but she could not do both. To the Bishops' great astonishment, she left, turning her back without a word on the family that had raised her. (Such, Missus Bishop weepingly told me, is the power of Edward's charm and the spell he is able to cast over those he has seduced.)

Together, Edward and Belle—she now entirely dependent upon her brother—fled. They returned to Manchester to gather Belle's valuables (and, certainly, her money), and then continued onward to Boston, to the Cookes'. Like the Bishops, the Cookes too were Colony orphans, and, like them, they too were adopted into a wealthy family. It is thought that Aubrey, the brother, met Edward in New York when Edward was living with Aunt Bethesda, and began a relationship—by all accounts deeply passionate and true—that endures to this day. Aubrey was, and is, a spectacularly handsome man of some seven-and-twenty years, educated and familiar with the ways of good society, and he and his sister were all but assured an easy life. However, when Aubrey was twenty and his sister, Susannah, nineteen, their parents died suddenly in a road accident, and when their affairs were settled, it was revealed that the money their children had always assumed would be theirs was nonexistent, diminished by years of bad investments and overwhelming debts.

A different man or woman would have turned to honest work, but that was not Aubrey and Susannah's way. Instead, under the guise of being young newlyweds, they separately began to prey upon lonely, married men and women—they were indiscriminate about which—of great wealth, often in loveless unions, offering their friendship and company. Then, once they had made them fall in love, they would demand money on threat of exposing them to their spouses. To a one, their victims paid, too fearful of the consequences and too humiliated by their own gullibility, and together, the Cookes amassed a good sum, which, along with, presumably, the money Edward stole from his aunt and was paid by poor Mister D.'s parents, they intend to use to open a silk-weaving concern in the West. My sources indicate that Edward, along with the Cookes, have been arranging this for at least a year; their scheme is that, being mindful of the laws of '76, Edward will pretend to be married to Susannah Cooke, and Belle to Aubrey.

As of November of last year, the plan was almost ready to execute when a blight killed the majority of the mulberry trees. Panicked, Aubrey and Edward agreed that they would try to find one last source of money. They know that it is only a matter of time before one of the Cookes' victims speaks and they find themselves in grave legal trouble. All they needed was one final sum, enough to see them through the farm's opening and first few years of operation.

And then, in January of this year, Edward Bishop met your grandson.

XVIII

There was more, but he could not bear to read it. Already, he was trembling so much—and the room was so silent—that he could hear the dry, rattling noise the paper made in his hands, his short, broken gasps. He felt as if he had been walloped about the head with something dense but yielding, a cushion perhaps, and it had left him breathless and confused. He was aware of his fingers releasing the page, and of rising, unsteadily, to his feet, and then tipping forward, and then of someone—his grandfather, whose presence he had almost forgotten—catching him and lowering him onto the settee, repeating his name. As if from far away, he heard his grandfather call out for Adams, and when he returned to himself, he was once again sitting upright, and his grandfather was holding a teacup to his lips.

"There's some ginger in this, and honey," Grandfather said. "Sip it slowly. There's a good boy. Yes, very good. And there's a molasses cookie—can you hold it? Very good."

He closed his eyes and leaned back his head. Once again, he was David Bingham, and he was weak, and his grandfather was soothing him, and it was as if he had never read the investigator's report, as if he had never learned what was within its pages, as if he had never met Edward. He was in too much of a muddle. It was dangerous. And yet, no matter how much he tried, no matter how he tried to separate one strand of the story from the next, he could not. It was as if he had *experienced* the story rather than read it, and at the same time, he did not feel that it had anything to do with him, or with the Edward he knew, who was, after all, the only version of Edward that mattered. There was the story he had just consumed, and it was an anchor falling rapidly through the water many thousands of leagues, falling and falling until it was swallowed by the sand at the bottom of the sea. And above this was Edward's face and Edward's eyes, Edward turning to him and smiling, asking, "Do you love me?," his body skimming above the water like a bird, his voice made whispery by the wind. "Do you trust me, David?" asked the voice, Edward's voice, "Do you believe me?" He thought of Edward's skin on his, the delight in his face when he saw David in his doorway, how he had stroked the tip of David's nose and had told him that in a year's time it would be freckled, each speck the color of caramel, a gift from the California sun.

He opened his eyes and looked into his grandfather's stern, handsome face, his flint-gray eyes, and knew he had to speak, though when he did, his words surprised them both: David because he knew it was what he really felt, Grandfather because—although he would like to pretend otherwise—he knew as well.

"I do not believe it," he said.

He watched his grandfather's worried expression become incredulous. "Do not believe it? Do not *believe it*? David—I hardly know what to say. You know this comes from Gunnar Wesley, the best private investigator in the city, perhaps in the Free States?"

"But he has made mistakes in the past. Did he not miss the fact of Mister Griffith's time in the West?" Though even as he spoke, he knew he should not have mentioned Charles's name.

"Oh, come, David. That is a minor matter. And that was not a period Mister Griffith sought to conceal—Wesley's oversight was simply that, and of no harm to anyone. But the information he *did* gather was all correct.

"David. David. I am not angry. I assure you, I am not. I *was*, when I received this. But not at you, but at this—this *confidence* man, who has taken advantage of you. Or has tried to, at least. David. My child. I know this is difficult for you to read. But is it not better to know now, before serious harm is done, before it jeopardizes your relationship with Mister Griffith? If he were to discover that this was the sort of person with whom you were associating—"

"This is of no concern to Mister Griffith," he heard his voice say, a voice he did not recognize, it was so cold and clipped.

"Of no concern! David, he is making great allowances for you—unusually large ones, I should say. But not even a man as devoted as Mister Griffith could overlook this. Of *course* this would matter to him!"

"But it does not, and it will not, for I have declined his offer," David said, and he felt, deep within him, a hard kernel of triumph at his grandfather's mute astonishment, and at the way he drew back as if he had been singed.

"You have declined! David, when did you do this? And why?"

"Recently. And before you ask, no, there is no reconsidering, on my part or his, for it was ended badly. As for why, it is simple: I do not love him."

"You do not—!" At this, his grandfather suddenly stood, and walked to the opposite corner of the room, before turning to face David once again. "With all respect, David—you are not one to judge that."

He heard himself laugh, a loud, ugly bark. "And so who is? You? Frances? Mister Griffith? I am an *adult*. In June I will be twenty-nine. I am the *only* one to judge. I am in love with Edward Bishop, and I will be with him, no matter what you or Wesley or anyone says."

He thought his grandfather would erupt, but instead he grew very still, and before he spoke next, he gripped the back of his chair with both hands. "David, I promised myself I would never speak of this again. I vowed. But now I must, and for the second time tonight, because it is relevant to your current situation. Forgive me, my child, but: You had thought yourself in love before. And you were proven incorrect, in the most horrible way.

"You think I am lying. You think I am mistaken. I assure you, I am not. And I assure you as well that I would give all my fortune to be wrong about Mister Bishop. And all yours to stop you from getting hurt by him.

"He doesn't love you, my child. He is already in love, with another. What he loves is your money, the idea of its being his. It pains me, as someone who *does* love you, to tell you this, to have to speak it aloud. But I must, for I will not see your heart broken again, not when I could have kept it whole.

"You asked me earlier why I wanted Mister Griffith for you, and I answered you honestly: because I sensed from Frances's report of him that he was someone who would not harm you, who would want nothing from you but your company, who would never abandon you. You are intelligent, David; you are perceptive. But in this matter, you are unwise, and long have been, have been since you were a boy. I cannot take credit for your gifts—but I *can* protect you from your deficiencies. I can no longer send you away, though if you would, if you cared to, I would gladly do it. But I *can* warn you, with everything I have, to not make the same mistake again."

He had not thought, despite his grandfather's earlier allusion, that he would mention the events of seven years ago, the events that, he sometimes thought, had changed him forever. (And yet he knew that was wrong: It was almost as if what had happened was preordained.) He had been twenty-one, just out of college, taking a year of art school before joining Bingham Brothers. And then, one day early in the term, he had been walking out of class and had dropped his supplies, and when he knelt to retrieve them, there was someone by his side, a classmate of his named Andrew who was so sunlit, so effortless in his charm, that David, upon registering his existence the first day of class, had not spent any further time observing him—he was so far beyond the kind of person who might ever want to know him. Instead, he had talked to and made efforts to befriend the men like him: the quiet, sober, mouselike ones, the ones who, in recent weeks, he had succeeded in meeting for a cup of tea or a lunch, where they would together talk about books they'd read, or works of art they were hoping to copy as they became more skilled. *These* were the people to whom he belonged—usually the younger siblings of more dynamic elder sisters or brothers; competent students but not distinguished; pleasing in looks but not exceptional; able but not memorable conversationalists. They were, all of them, heirs to fortunes that ranged from good to extraordinary; they had, all of them, moved from their parents' houses to their boarding schools to their colleges and then back to their parents', where they would remain until a marriage could be arranged for them with a suitable man or woman—some would even marry one another. There was a group of them, artistic-minded and sensitive boys, granted a year of indulgence by their parents before they would be sent back to school or join their parents' companies, as bankers, as shippers, as traders, as lawyers. He knew this, and he accepted it: He was one of them. Even then, John was first in his class at college, studying law and banking—though he was only twenty, his marriage to Peter, also his classmate, had already been arranged—and Eden the head girl at her school. His grandfather's annual midsummer party was crammed with their friends, rafts of them, all shouting and laughing beneath the net of candles that the servants had hung earlier across the garden.

But that had never been David, and he knew it never would be. He was, for most of his life, left alone: His name had protected him from abuse and harassment, but he was largely ignored, never sought, and never missed. And so, when Andrew had, that afternoon, first spoken to him and then, over the successive days and weeks, talked to him more and more, David had felt himself becoming unrecognizable. Here he was, laughing out loud, in the street, like Eden; here he was, arguing petulantly and being thought adorable for it, as John did when he was with Peter. He had always enjoyed being intimate with others, though he long had been too shy to pursue it—preferring to visit the brothel he had been patronizing since he was sixteen, where he knew he would never be rejected—but with Andrew, he asked for what he wanted and received it; he was emboldened, elated with his new understanding of what it meant to be a man, a person in the world, young, rich. Ah, he remembered thinking, so *this* is it! This is what John felt, what Peter felt, what Eden felt, what all his class-mates with their merry voices, their echoing laughter, felt!

It was as if he had been seized by a madness. He introduced Andrew—the son of doctors from Connecticut—to Grandfather, and when, afterward, Grandfather, who had remained mostly silent during their dinner, a dinner through which Andrew had been at his sparkling best and David had smiled at everything he said, wondering at his grandfather's silence, had told him he thought Andrew "too studied and pert," he had dismissed him, coldly. And when, six months later, Andrew became vague in his presence, and then stopped calling on him, and then began avoiding him altogether, and David began sending him bouquets of flowers and boxes of chocolates—excessive, embarrassing declarations of love—only to receive no messages at all, and then, later yet, the chocolate boxes returned with their ribbons uncut, his letters still sealed, his packages of rare books unopened, he ignored his grandfather still, his kind inquiries, his efforts to distract him with offers of the theater, the symphony, a trip abroad. And then, one day, he had been desultorily pacing around the perimeter of Washington Square when he saw, their arms linked, Andrew with another man he knew from their class, the class David had stopped attending. He knew the man by face but not by name, but he knew that he was from the kind of people to whom Andrew belonged, and from which people he had strayed to spend time—from curiosity, perhaps—with David. They were alike, two spirited young people, walking together and chatting, their faces bright with happiness, and David found himself first walking and then sprinting toward them, falling upon Andrew and crying out his love and yearning and hurt, while Andrew, at first agog and then alarmed, tried initially to appease him and then to push him away, his friend swatting about David's head with his gloves in a scene made more ghastly by the passersby who had gathered to watch and point and laugh. And then Andrew gave him a mighty shove, and David fell backward, and the two ran away, and David, still desperate, found himself in Adams's arms, Adams, who shouted at the gawkers to get away as he half carried, half dragged David back to the house.

For days, he did not leave: not his bed, not his room. He was tormented by thoughts of Andrew, and of his degradation, and if he was not thinking of one, he was thinking of the other. It seemed that if he stopped engaging with the world, then it too might stop engaging with him, and as days turned into weeks, he lay in his bed and tried to think of nothing, certainly not of himself within the world's dizzying vastness, and finally, after many weeks, the world did indeed shrink to something manageable—his bed, his room, his grandfather's undemanding daily and nightly visits. Finally, after nearly three months, something broke, as if he had been encased in a shell and someone—not him—had tapped it open, and he emerged feeble and pale and hardened, he thought, against Andrew and his own mortification. He swore, then, that he would never again let himself feel so passionately, never let himself be so full of adoration, so replete with happiness, a vow that he would extend not just to people but to art as well, so that when Grandfather sent him to Europe for a year under the guise of a Grand Tour (but really, they both knew, as a way to avoid Andrew, who was still living in the city, still with his beau, who was now his fiancé), he moved lightly among the frescoes and paintings that loomed down from every ceiling, from every wall: He looked up and at them and felt nothing.

When he returned home to Washington Square fourteen months later, he was cooler, more distant, but also more alone. His friends, those quiet boys he had neglected and then discarded once he had begun seeing Andrew, had found their own lives—he rarely saw them. John and Eden too seemed to have become more capable than ever before: John was soon to be married; Eden was in college. Something had been gained, a sense of remoteness, a greater strength, but something had also been lost: He tired quickly, he craved solitude, and his first month at Bingham Brothers—where he began as a clerk, as his father and grandfather had both done upon their entry into the company—was so taxing as to be almost debilitating, especially when compared with John, who was training alongside him and yet whose numerical dexterity and general ambition distinguished him from the beginning. It was Grandfather who suggested that David might have contracted an illness, something unknown and depleting, on the Continent, and might do with a few weeks' rest, but they both knew that this was a fiction, and that he was giving David a way to excuse himself without having to actually admit failure. Weary, David accepted, and then those weeks became months, and then years, and he never returned to the bank.

He did his best to forget the wildness of emotion, the passion, that he had felt around Andrew, but sometimes he was gripped with the memory of that time, and its humiliation, and he would retreat once more to his room and take to his bed. These episodes, what he and his grandfather would come to call his confinements—and what his grandfather characterized, delicately, to Adams and his siblings as his "nervous trouble"—would usually be preceded or succeeded by a period of mania, frenzied days he would spend feverishly shopping, or painting, or walking, or at the bordello: all things he did in his normal life, but intensified and excessively writ. They were, he knew, ways for him to escape himself, and yet he had not invented these methods; they had been invented for him, and he was at their mercy, they made his body move either too quickly or not at all. Two years after his return from Europe, he had received a card from Andrew announcing the adoption of his and his husband's first child, a girl, and he had written a congratulatory note back. But then, that night, he had begun to wonder: What was the purpose of Andrew's note? Had it truly been sent intentionally, or was it an oversight? Was it a gesture of friendship, or was it meant to ridicule? He sent a longer letter to Andrew, inquiring about him and confessing how he missed him.

And then it was as if something had been undammed in him, and he began to write letter after letter, by turns accusing Andrew and pleading with him, condemning him and imploring him. After dinner, he would sit with Grandfather in his drawing room, trying to stop his fingers from twitching with impatience, looking at the chessboard but seeing in his mind his desk with its paper and blotter, and as soon as he was able, he would leave, running up the final steps, and write Andrew again, ringing for Matthew late into the night to post his most recent missive. His disgrace, when it came—as even he knew it would—was great: An attorney who represented Andrew's husband's family asked for a meeting with Frances Holson and gravely drew from his case a stack of David's letters to Andrew, dozens of them, the last twenty or so not even opened, and told Frances that David must stop bothering his client. Frances spoke to his grandfather, and his grandfather spoke to him, and though he had been gentle, David's anguish had been so intense that this time it had been his grandfather who had confined him to his room, with one of the maids to watch over him day or night, so worried was he that David might harm himself. This, David could see, was when his siblings had lost their final residue of respect for him, was when he became, truly, an invalid; someone whose normal state went from being one of health to one of illness, so that wellness was something to be measured in interludes, a respite before he was returned to his native lunacy. He knew he had become a problem for his grandfather, and although his grandfather never mentioned it, he feared he would soon graduate from being a difficulty into being a burden. He did not go out, he knew no one; a marriage would clearly have to be found for him, for he was incapable of finding his own. And yet he rejected all of Frances's candidates, unable to contemplate the energy and deception it would take to trick someone into marrying him. Gradually, the offers had thinned, and then stopped, until, at some point, Frances and Grandfather must have talked about finding a different caliber of man—that is how Frances would have stated it: *A different caliber, perhaps someone slightly more mature*, what did Nathaniel think?—and Charles Griffith had been contacted by the marriage broker, and David's dossier presented to him as a possible candidate.

This was the end for him. This year, he would be twenty-nine. If Charles knew of his confinements, others did as well—he must not delude himself about that. With each year, his money meant less, for the world was growing wealthier: Not now, but within the next few decades, there would emerge a family richer than the Binghams, and he would have rejected all his opportunities, and still be living in Washington Square, his hair gone white, his skin lined, spending his money on amusements—books and drawing paper and paints and men—as a child does on candy and toys. He did not only *want* to believe Edward, he *had* to believe him; if he went to California, he would be leaving behind his home and his grandfather, but might he not also be leaving behind his sickness, his past, his mortifications? His history, so entangled with New York itself that every block he walked was the scene of some past embarrassment?: Could it not be draped in a sheet and hung in the back of his closet like his winter coat? What was life worth if he might not have his chance, slim as it might be, of feeling that it was truly his, his to make or destroy, his to mold like clay or shatter like china?

Grandfather was waiting for his reply, he realized. "He loves *me*," he whispered to his grandfather. "And I know this."

"My child—"

"I have asked him to marry me," he continued, helplessly. "And he has accepted. And we are going to California together."

At this, his grandfather sank into his chair, and rotated his body to look into the fire, and when he turned around once more, David was amazed to see that his eyes were shining. "David," he began, quietly, "if you marry this man, I will have to cut you off—you know that, don't you? I will do it because I must, because it is my only way to protect you."

He knew this, and yet, hearing it, he felt as if the floor had sunk from beneath him. "I will still have my parents' trust," he said, at last.

"Yes, you will. I cannot stop that—as much as I wish I could. But *my* allowance to you, David, *my* bestowment: That will end. Washington Square will no longer be yours, not unless you promise me you will not go with this person."

"I cannot promise you," he said, and now he too was beginning to feel himself on the verge of tears. "Grandfather—please. Don't you want me to be happy?"

His grandfather inhaled, and then exhaled. "I want you to be safe, David." He sighed again. "David, child—what is the hurry? Why can you not wait? If he truly loves you, he will wait for you. And what about this Aubrey fellow? What if Wesley is indeed correct, and you go with your Edward all the way to California—a dangerous place for us, may I remind you, a potentially fatal one, indeed—only to discover that you have been hoodwinked, that they are a couple and you their stooge?"

"It is not true. It cannot be true. Grandfather, if you could see the way he is with me, how much he loves me, how good he is to me—"

"Of *course* he is being good to you, David! He *needs* you! *They* need you—Edward and his beloved. Don't you see?"

He was angry then, an anger that had been building inside him but that he dared not voice because he did not want to make it true by saying it aloud. "I was unaware you thought so little of me, Grandfather—is it so difficult, so impossible, to believe that someone might actually love me for the fact of me? Someone young and beautiful and self-made?

"I see now that you have never thought me worth someone like Edward—you have been ashamed of me, and I understand that, I understand why. But is it not possible that I am someone else, someone you do not see, someone who has been loved twice, by two different men, in the space of a year? Is it not possible that, for as well as you know me, you have known only one aspect of me, that you have been blinded to who I might be, because of your familiarity with me? Is it not possible that, in your protectiveness, you have discounted me, that you have lost any ability to see me in any other way?

"I must go, Grandfather—I must. You say I will be throwing my life to the winds if I leave, but I think I will be burying it if I stay. Can you not grant me this right to my own life? Can you not forgive me for what I will do?"

He was begging, but his grandfather again stood: not angrily, not declaratively, but with a great weariness, as if he were experiencing a terrible pain. And suddenly, and with great violence, he turned his head sharply to the right and brought his right hand up to shield his face, and David realized that his grandfather was crying. It was an amazing sight, but for a moment, he was unable to comprehend the feeling of devastation that swiftly descended upon him.

But then he knew. It was not just the fact of his grandfather's tears; it was because he knew that, with them, his grandfather was acknowledging that he understood that David would, finally, disobey him. And with that, David knew as well that his grandfather would not yield, and that when he left Washington Square, he would be leaving it behind forever. He sat, immobile, understanding that this would be the last time he would sit in this drawing room, before this fire, the last time this would be his home. He understood that now his life was not here. Now his life was with Edward.

—————

XIX

Late April was the one time the city could be described as
soft, and for a few precious weeks, the trees would be clouds
of pink-and-white blossoms, the air cleansed of its grit, the
breezes gentle.

Edward had already left for the day, and David had to leave as
well. But he was glad of the silence—though it was never quite completely silent in the boardinghouse—for he felt the need to compose
himself before he stepped outside.

He had been living with Edward in the boardinghouse room
for little more than four weeks. After leaving his grandfather and
Washington Square that night, he had gone directly to the boardinghouse, but Edward was out. The little maid let David into his
cold and dark room, though, and David had sat still for a few minutes before he had stood and begun, at first methodically and then
feverishly, an examination of the room, pulling and replacing clothes
from Edward's trunk, paging through every one of his books, rifling
through his papers, stamping upon the floorboards to see if any
might be loose, with secrets hidden beneath. He found answers, he
supposed, but there was no way of telling if they were answers he
sought: A small etching of a pretty, dark-haired girl, tucked into a
copy of the *Aeneid*—was this Belle? A daguerreotype of a handsome
man with a knowing smile and a hat tipped rakishly on his head—was
this Aubrey? A roll of money, secured with a length of string—was
this stolen from Aunt Bethesda, or his earnings from the institute?
A sheet of crackling onionskin, pressed between the pages of his
Bible, inscribed "I will always love you" in a fluttery hand—was this

from one of his mothers, his first or his second? Belle? Bethesda? Aubrey? Somebody else entirely? The second trunk, which he had bought Edward, with its brass clasps and leather straps, held the little porcelain bird and a few blank music-composition books, but the tea set he had placed in it before leaving to see his grandfather—a ceremonial gesture toward packing, toward the creation of the new house they would have together—was missing, as was the silver set he'd bought.

He was contemplating what this might mean when Edward walked in, and David turned and saw the mess he had made, all of Edward's possessions strewn about him, and Edward himself before him with an unreadable expression, and after his first, absurd question burst from his mouth, the only question he could think to ask because he did not know where to begin with the rest—"Where is the tea set I bought you?"—he began to weep, sinking to the floor. Edward picked his way across the piles of clothes and books and crouched next to him, holding him in his arms, and David turned and sobbed into his coat. Even after he was able to speak, his questions came as staccato explosions, one following the next with no apparent logic or order, but all seeming equally urgent: Was Edward in love with another? Who was Aubrey to him, really? Had he lied about who he was, who his family was? Why had he really gone to Vermont? Did he love him? Did he love him? Did he *truly* love him?

Edward had attempted to answer his questions as he asked them, but David interrupted before he was able to finish any of his explanations; he was unable to comprehend anything Edward said. The only things he had brought with him from Washington Square were the bundle of Edward's letters answering his own, and the report from Wesley, which he finally retrieved, still sobbing, from his own coat pocket and handed to Edward, who took the pages and began to read, first with curiosity and then with anger, and it was witnessing this anger, Edward's explosions of "Blast!" and "The devil!" that, curiously, quieted David's own upset. When he was finished, Edward threw the pages across the room, into the blackened hearth, and then turned to David. "My poor David," he said. "My poor innocent. What must you think of me?" And then his face hardened. "I never thought she would do this to me," he muttered. "But she has, and has placed in peril the relationship I value most."

He said he would explain, and so he did: His parents were indeed dead, his elder sisters in Vermont, his younger in New Hampshire. But, he admitted, there *had* been a schism between himself and his mother's sister, Lucy, who was his great-aunt Bethesda's caretaker. He *had* lived with Bethesda for a period after leaving the conservatory—"I did not want to tell you, because I wanted you to think me independent; I wanted you to admire me. It would be too cruel if this omission, one motivated by my own fears, becomes the thing that now makes you doubt my truthfulness"—but had left to find his own lodgings after a matter of months: "I am enormously fond of my great-aunt; I always have been. She and my aunt arrived soon after we settled in the Free States, and she has been the closest I have to a grandmother. But the idea that she is wealthy, much less that I have stolen money from her, is laughable."

"So why would Lucy have said you did?"

"Who can know? She is a spiteful, petty woman, never married, never made a mother, friendless, but possessed of a vivid imagination—as you can see. My mother used to tell us all that we were to be kind to her, as her sourness was a reaction to her enduring loneliness, and we were, all to the best of our abilities. But this is too much, too far. And at any rate, my aunt Bethesda died two years ago; I have not seen my aunt Lucy—my aunt in name only—since; but this is proof, though of the worst kind, that she is still alive and still vengeful, still irreparably destructive."

"Dead? But earlier when you spoke of Bethesda, you said you were enormously fond of her, as if she were still alive."

"She is not. But can I not be enormously fond of her still? My affection for her hardly ended with her death."

"And so you were not adopted by a Free State couple?"

"No, of course not! Lucy's lies about my supposed thievery—conjured out of what I can only imagine is sport and resentment for my youth—appalls, but her denial of my family (and hers, might I add) absolutely sickens. For her to deny my parents that—! She is an unwell woman. I wish Belle were here so she could tell you herself what absolute rubbish this all is, and about my aunt's character."

"Well—can she not?"

"Of course, and it is an excellent notion—I shall write her tonight and have her answer any questions you might have."

"Well, I have more—many more."

"And how could you not, after that report? (I have only the greatest respect for your grandfather, but must admit I'm somewhat shocked that he would place so much trust in someone who would believe everything told him by one lonely, clearly deranged woman.) Oh, my poor David! I cannot tell you how disgusted I am that this woman's—*mischief-making* should have caused you such distress. You must allow me to explain."

So he did. Edward had an answer for all of David's concerns. No, he was assuredly *not* in love with Aubrey, who, anyway, was married to Susannah (His sister! My God, of *course* not! The depravity in this report!) and not one of their kind besides. The two were dear friends, but nothing more—David would see for himself in California, and "I would not be surprised if you and he should become even better friends than he and I are; you are both highly practical people, you see. And then I shall be the suspicious one!" Yes, he had been in a relationship with Christopher D., and yes, it had ended poorly ("He had become—and I say this not to boast, but as fact—besotted with me, and after he proposed marriage and I declined, he became fixated on me, and I, I am ashamed to say, began to avoid him, for I knew not how to convince him I was not in love with him. Although he was overbearing, my cowardice was my fault, and mine only, and I am deeply remorseful about it"), but, no, Edward had certainly never been with him for his money, nor had his parents ever tried to intervene on their son's behalf: He would introduce David to Mr. D. so he could ask for himself. No, he would! He absolutely would! He had nothing to hide. No, he had never stolen anything from anyone, least of all his parents, who, after all, had nothing for him to steal, even if he had been that sort of person: "Of all the cruelties of this report, the cruelest is the denial of my parentage, of my childhood, of the sacrifices my mother and father made for me and my sisters, of the slander levied against my father: A gambler? A runaway? A cheat? He was the most honest man I ever knew. For him to be manipulated into this . . . this *criminal* is a level of evil to which I had not known even Lucy capable of sinking."

On and on they talked, and after an hour and more had passed, Edward seized David's hands. "David—my innocent. I can and will refute everything in these pages. But the primary thing I must disabuse you of is this: I do not love you, I do not want to make a life with you, for your money. Your money is yours, and I have no need of it. I have not ever lived with it—I would not know what to do with it. Besides, I shall soon have my own, and—though I intend no ingratitude—I prefer it that way.

"You asked what I had done with the tea set. I sold it, David, and it was not until afterward that I realized what a mistake I had made, that it was something you had given me out of love, and I, in my desire to prove to you that I could take care of you, take care of *us*, exchanged it for money. But do you not see that it was done out of my own sense of love? I never want to ask you for anything—I never want you to be in discomfort. I will take care of us both. Dear David. Do you not want to be with someone who will not expect you to be David Bingham but merely beloved companion, trusted husband, dearest spouse? Here"—and here Edward reached into his trouser pocket and drew out a purse, which he pressed into David's hand— "here is the money from it. I will go buy it back tomorrow, if you wish. It, and the silver set, too. But either way, the money is yours to keep. We shall spend it on our first meal in California, on your first set of new paints. But the important thing is that we shall spend it together, making our life together."

His head ached. He was overwhelmed. The tears had dried on his cheeks and left his skin stiff and itchy. His limbs felt boneless, and he was taken by a tiredness so intense that when Edward began to undress him and then laid him in the bed, he felt none of the anticipation or excitement he usually did in those moments, just a kind of dullness, and although he responded to Edward's commands, he did so as if in a daze, as if his arms and legs were moving of their own accord and he was no longer their master. He kept thinking of what his grandfather had said—"*They* need you: Edward and his beloved"—and when he woke early in the morning, he slipped out from beneath Edward's arm and silently dressed and left the boardinghouse.

It was so early that the candles still flickered in the lamppost lanterns, and the light was drawn in shades of gray. He walked along the cobblestones, his boot heels echoing, to the river, where he watched the waters slap against the wooden pier. It would be a damp day, damp and chill, and he wrapped his arms around himself and gazed out toward the opposite shore. He and Andrew had sometimes strolled along the river and talked, though those events now seemed very long ago, incidents from decades past.

What would he do? Here, on one side of the river, was the Edward he knew, and there, on the other, the Edward his grandfather thought he knew, and between them was an impassable body of water, not wide but deep and apparently unbreachable. If he left with Edward, he would forever lose his grandfather. If he stayed, he would lose Edward. Did he believe Edward? He did; he did not. He kept remembering how upset Edward had been the night before—upset but, he reminded himself, not flustered; there were no inconsistencies, or very few, in his reassurances, and those that existed did not seem worrisomely consequential—and how that alone proved his truthfulness. He thought of the tenderness with which Edward spoke to him, touched him, held him. Surely he was not imagining it? Surely that could not be a pantomime? The passion they felt for each other, the fever of their encounters—that could not be a charade, could it? Here was New York, and everything he knew. There, with Edward, was someplace else, someplace he had never before been but, he could recognize, he had been searching for his entire life. He had thought he might have found it with Andrew, but it had been a mirage. He would never have found it with Charles. Was this not the point of life, the reason his ancestors had established this country at all? So he might be allowed to feel the way he did, so that he might entitle himself to happiness?

He had no answers for himself, and he turned and walked back toward the boardinghouse, where Edward was waiting for him. The next several days passed in the same manner: David would wake first and walk to the river, and then he would return and continue his interrogation, which Edward bore patiently, even indulgently. Yes, the girl in the illustration was Belle; no, the man in the daguerreotype was not Aubrey, but an old beau, from the conservatory, and if it bothered David, he would—See? He was doing it now!—burn the image, for the man meant nothing to him, not any longer; yes, the note was from his mother. Always he was full of explanations, which David drank and drank until, by evening, he was disoriented and exhausted again, whereupon Edward would undress him and lead him to the bed, and then the cycle would begin again.

He could not settle. "My dearest David, if you have any further doubts, then we should perhaps not marry," Edward said one afternoon. "I shall still want to be with you, but your fortune will be safe."

"So you *don't* want to marry me?"

"I do! Of course I do! But if this is the way I might convince you that I have no intentions, no desire, to possess your money—"

"But our marriage would not be recognized in California at any rate, so it would not be much of a sacrifice for you, would it?"

"It would be *more* of a sacrifice, had I any intentions to steal your money, for if I did, I should marry you now and take everything you own and *then* leave you. But that is *not* my intention, which is why I am suggesting it!"

In the coming months and years, he would reflect upon this period and wonder if he was misremembering: Had there not been a moment, an hour, a day, in which he decided, declaratively and definitively, that he loved Edward, and that his love for him would overcome all of the uncertainties that still lingered in his mind, despite all of Edward's reassurances? But no—there was no single episode, no revelation that he might date and commemorate on paper. It was simply that, with every day he failed to return to Washington Square, with every letter—at first just from his grandfather, but then from Eliza and John and Eden and Frances and even Norris—that he ignored, either throwing them into the fire or securing them, unopened, into the bundle of Edward's letters he'd brought with him, with every item of clothing and book and notepad he asked to be sent him from his grandfather's house, with every day he decided not to send a note to Christopher D., asking him to meet and talk, with every week he did not inquire whether Edward had in fact sent a letter to Belle asking her to corroborate his account, and with every week that passed without a reply from her, he was declaring his intention to begin another life, a new life, a life anew.

In this way, close to a month had elapsed, and although Edward had never demanded a conclusive commitment from David that he would accompany him to California after all, David did not protest when Edward bought two tickets on the Transcontinental Express, did not object when his own belongings disappeared into one of the trunks, secreted between Edward's own. Edward was abustle with activity—packing, planning, full of chatter—and as he grew more industrious, David grew less. Every morning, he reminded himself that he could still stop what seemed now fated to happen, that it was still within his power, however humiliating it would be, for now and for ever; but by evening, he would have been carried along a little more on the slipstream of Edward's excitement, so that with each day he had drifted farther from land. And yet he was also not desirous of resisting, and why should he? How lovely, how seductive, it was to be wanted as much as Edward wanted him, to be cherished and kissed and whispered to and thought so dear, to never once be asked for or about his fortune, to be undressed with such avidity and regarded with such unembarrassed lust. Had he ever experienced these things? For he had not, and yet he knew: *This* was happiness, *this* was life.

Still, in colder moments—those just before dawn—David could see too that the month had not been without its difficulties. He knew so little, he had never before completed a chore, and there had been times when his ignorance had made things tense between them; he did not know how to boil an egg or darn a sock or hammer a nail. The boardinghouse had no indoor lavatories but only an outdoor washroom, and the first, freezing time David had visited it, he had, unaware, used all the water that was to have been shared among the house's residents, and Edward had been terse with him. "What *do* you know?" he had snapped after David had confessed he'd never before built a fire, and "We shan't be able to survive on your knitting and drawings and embroidery, you know," at which David had stormed out and walked the streets, tears stinging his eyes, and when he finally returned to the room—it being cold and he having nowhere else to go—Edward had been there (a fire crackling) to greet him with tenderness and apologies, to guide him to the bed, where he promised to make him warm again. After, he had asked Edward if they might move elsewhere, somewhere more commodious and modern, for which he would gladly pay, but Edward had only kissed him between the eyes and told him that they must be frugal and, at any rate, that David had to learn these skills, for he would need them in California, where, after all, they would be living on a farm. And so he tried to improve. But his success was limited.

And then, suddenly, it was five days, four days, three days, two days before they were to depart—their leave-taking accelerated so that they would now reach California only days after Belle's own arrival—and the tiny room had gone from being full of things to abruptly empty of them, everything they owned packed into three large steamer trunks, the last of which David had sent for from Washington Square. The night before their penultimate day in the city, Edward had suggested that it might be useful to have any monies David might have available secured before they left: The next day, he would leave early to purchase some final supplies he thought they might need, and, it was left unspoken, David would go visit his grandfather.

It was not an unreasonable request; it was, indeed, an inevitable one. And yet that morning, when David left the boardinghouse for what was to be one of the last times of his life, descending the cracked stairs onto the street, he felt as if he had been struck in the face by the raw, dirty beauty of the city; by the trees above him feathered with tiny, bright-green leaves; by the pleasing, hollow clops of the passing horses; by the sights of industry all around him: the charwomen mopping their front steps; the coal boy pulling his cart behind him, inch by slow inch; the chimney sweep with his bucket, whistling a merry tune. They were not his people, of course, but they also were: They were citizens of the Free States, and it was together that they had made their country, their city, what it was—they through their labor, and David through his money.

He had thought to take a hansom, but he instead walked slowly, first south, then east, moving dreamily through the streets, his feet somehow knowing where to sidestep a pile of dung, a scrap of turnip, a scampering feral kitten, before even his eyes did; he felt himself a slim cone of fire, licking his way down the dear filthy streets he had walked his entire life, his shoes leaving no imprint, making no sound, the people parting for him before he even had to announce himself with a clear of his throat. And so it was that, when he finally reached Bingham Brothers, he was quite far from himself, afloat even, and it was as if he were hovering meters above the city, swooping slowly around the stone building, before being landed gently on its steps, and walking through its doors, the same as he'd done for nearly twenty-nine years, and yet of course not the same at all.

Down the hall he walked, through the doors to the bank's offices, and then to the left, where he met with the banker who was responsible for the family's accounts, and where he withdrew all of his savings; the Free States' currency was accepted in the West, but only grudgingly, and David had sent word beforehand that he needed his money in gold. He watched as the ingots were weighed and wrapped in cloth and then stacked inside a small black leather case and its straps buckled.

As he handed him the case, the banker—someone new, unknown to him—bowed. "May I wish you the best of luck, Mister Bingham," he said, somberly, and David, suddenly breathless, his arm tugged downward by the weight of the metal, could only nod his thanks.

Once again, his story was apparently known, and as he left the banker and made his final walk down the long, carpeted hallway toward his grandfather's office, he sensed a collective murmuring, almost a hum, though he encountered no one. It was not until he had almost reached the office's closed doorway that he did see someone, Norris, stepping quickly into the hallway from an antechamber.

"Mister David," he said. "Your grandfather is awaiting you."

"Thank you, Norris," he managed. He could hardly speak; the words were choking him.

He turned to knock on the door, but as he did, Norris touched him, suddenly, on the shoulder. David was startled; Norris never touched him or his siblings, and when he looked at the man again, he was shocked to see his eyes were wet. "I wish you all the happiness, Mister David," Norris said. And then he had vanished, and David was pressing the brass handle on his grandfather's door and entering the room, and—ah!—there was his grandfather, rising from behind his desk, not beckoning him as he usually did but waiting for him to walk across the soft carpet, one so plush that you could, as David once did when he was a boy, drop a crystal goblet upon it and it would not shatter but bounce, gently, off the surface. He saw, at once, his grandfather's eyes flicker to his case, and knew he knew what was secured within; indeed, knew to the cent how much gold it contained, and as he sat, his grandfather yet to say a single word, he smelled smoke, earth, and opened his eyes to watch Lapsang souchong being poured into a cup, and his eyes once more stung with tears. But then he realized: There was only one cup, and it was his grandfather's.

"I have come to say goodbye," he said after a silence so dense he could not bear it, though he could hear the tremble in his voice as he spoke. And then, when his grandfather did not respond, "Are you not going to say anything?" He had intended to re-present his case—Edward's denials, how much Edward cared for him, how Edward had assuaged his concerns—and then he realized: He did not have to. At his feet was a trunk of gold, like something from a fairy tale, and it was his, and a little more than a mile from here was a man who loved him, and together they would travel many more miles, and David would hope that their love would come with them—because he believed it; because he must.

"Grandfather," he said, hesitantly, and then, when his grandfather responded only with a sip of his tea, David repeated it, and then again, and then in a shout—"*Grandfather!*"—and still the man remained impassive, lifting his cup to his mouth.

"It is not too late, David," his grandfather said at last, and the sound of his grandfather's voice—its patience, its authority that David had never before seen need or reason or desire to doubt—filled him with an ache, and he had to stop himself from bending over and clutching his stomach in pain. "You can choose. I can keep you safe—I can still keep you safe."

He knew then, as he had always known, that he would never be able to explain himself—he would never have the argument, he would never have the words, he would never be more than Nathaniel Bingham's grandson. What was Edward Bishop against Nathaniel Bingham? What was love against all his grandfather symbolized and was? What was he against any of it? He was no one; he was nothing; he was a man who was in love with Edward Bishop and he was, for perhaps the first time in his life, doing something he wanted, something that frightened him, but something that was his own. He was choosing foolishly, perhaps, but he was choosing. He reached his arm down to his feet; he slid his fingers through the case's handle; he tightened his hand around it; he stood.

"Goodbye," he whispered. "I love you, Grandfather."

He was halfway to the door when his grandfather cried out, in a voice David had never before heard from him, "You are a fool, David!" And still he kept walking, and as he was closing the door behind him, he heard his grandfather not so much call as groan his name, two anguished syllables: "David!"

No one stopped him as he left. Down the carpeted hallway he walked once more, and then through the spectacular doors, and then across the marble lobby. And then he was outside, with Bingham Brothers to his back and the city before him.

Once, when he and his siblings were still quite young, probably soon after they came to live in Washington Square, they had had a conversation with their grandfather about Heaven, and after Grandfather had explained it, John had promptly said, "I'd like mine to be made all of ice cream," but David, who did not care, then, for cold things, had disagreed: His Heaven would be made of cakes. He could see it—oceans made turgid with buttercream; mountains made of sponge; trees dangling candied cherries. He did not want to be in John's Heaven; he wanted to be in his own. That night, when his grandfather came to wish him good night, he had asked him, anxious: How could God know what each person wanted? How could He be certain they were in the place they had dreamed of? His grandfather had laughed. "He knows, David," he had said. "He knows, and He will make as many Heavens as He needs."

And so what if this was Heaven? Would he know it if it were? Perhaps not. But he knew it was not whence he had come: That was someone else's Heaven, but it was not his. His was somewhere else, but it would not appear in front of him; rather, it would be his to find. Indeed, was that not what he had been taught, been made to hope for, his entire life? Now it was time to seek. Now it was time to be brave. Now he must go alone. So he would stand here for another moment, the bag leaden in his hand, and then he would take a breath, and then he would make his first step: his first step to a new life; his first step—to paradise.

BOOK II

LIPO-WAO-NAHELE

The letter arrived at the office on the day of the party. He rarely got mail, and when he did, it wasn't actually for him—just subscription offers for magazines and law journals that were addressed to "Paralegal" and dropped in a bundle on one of their desks by the mailroom clerk—so it wasn't until he was drinking his afternoon cup of coffee that he bothered to scrape the rubber band off the stack of envelopes and flick through them, only to suddenly see his name. When he saw the return address, he experienced a loss of breath, one so profound that for a moment all sound disappeared except for that of a hot, dry wind.

He took the envelope and stuffed it into his pants pocket and hurried to the archive room, which was the most private place on the floor, where he held it against his chest for a moment before opening it, tearing the letter itself in his haste. But then, midway through removing the sheet of paper inside, he instead replaced it in its envelope, folded it in half, and jammed it into his shirt pocket. And then he had to sit on a stack of old law books, puffing air onto his clasped hands, which was something he did when he was anxious, until he was ready to leave.

By the time he returned to his desk, it was a quarter of four. He had already requested permission to leave at four today, but he went to ask his manager if he might go a few minutes earlier. Of course, she said—it was a slow day; she'd see him on Monday. He thanked her, and shoved the letter into his bag.

"Have a good weekend," she said as he left.

You too, he said.

He had to pass Charles's office on the way to the elevator, but he didn't look in to say goodbye to him, because they had agreed that it was safest if they pretended not to be any more familiar with each other than a senior partner would be with a junior paralegal. When they had first begun seeing each other, he would find himself walking by Charles's office a dozen times a day, hoping to catch a glimpse of him doing something mundane, the more mundane the better: smoothing back his hair as he read a brief; dictating a memo into his recorder; flipping through the pages of a law book; talking on the phone while looking out the window to the Hudson River, his back to the door. Charles never acknowledged him, but David was certain he was aware of his passings.

That had been the source of one of their early disagreements: Charles's lack of acknowledgment. "Well, what can I do, David?" Charles had asked him, not defensively, as they lay in bed one night. "It's not like I can stop by the paralegals' area whenever I want. Or even call you: Laura can see on her phone who I'm calling, and she'd eventually put two and two together."

He didn't say anything, just pressed his face into the pillow, and Charles sighed. "It's not that I don't *want* to see you," he said, gently. "It's just complicated. You know how it is."

Finally, they had worked out a code: Whenever he passed Charles's office, and Charles wasn't busy, he would clear his throat and twirl a pencil between his fingers; that would be his signal that he'd seen David. It was silly—David wouldn't dare tell his friends that this was how he and Charles interacted in the office; they already didn't trust Charles—but it was also satisfying. "Larsson, Wesley owns me by day, but you own me by night," Charles always said, and that was satisfying, too.

But they still get more billable hours from you than I do, he'd said to Charles, once.

"Not true," said Charles. "You get weekends, and holidays, and nights as well." He reached over then and grabbed his calculator— Charles was the only person he had ever slept with, or dated, who kept a calculator on his bedside table, much less consulted it regularly during their arguments and discussions—and began punching the buttons. "Twenty-four hours in a day, seven days a week," he said. "Larsson, Wesley gets—what? Twelve hours over five days, plus, okay, another seven combined on the weekend. That's sixty-seven total. One hundred sixty-eight hours in a week, take away sixty-seven—that means that for a hundred and one hours every week, minimum, I am at your complete and utter disposal. And that doesn't count the hours at Larsson that I spend thinking about you, or thinking about you and trying not to think about you."

How many are those? he asked. They were both smiling by then.

"Loads," said Charles. "Countless. Tens of thousands of dollars in billable hours. More than any other client I have."

Now he walked by Charles's office, and Charles cleared his throat and spun a pencil between his fingers, and David smiled: He'd been seen. Now he could go.

———

At home, everything was under control. That's what Adams told him when he came in: "Everything is under control, Mister David." As always, he seemed faintly puzzled—by the fact of David, by his presence in the house, by having to serve David, and now by David's belief that he could contribute anything to a dinner party, the kind Adams had been arranging for years, more years than David had been alive.

When he moved into the house a year ago, he had asked Adams again and again to call him David, not Mister David, but Adams never would, or at least never did. Adams would never be used to him, and he would never be used to Adams. After one of the first nights he had spent with Charles, they had been in bed making out, near sex, when he heard someone speak Charles's name gravely, and he had yelped and jolted and looked up to see Adams standing in the doorway of Charles's room.

"I can bring breakfast now, Mister Charles, unless you'd rather wait."

"I'll wait, Adams, thank you."

After Adams left, Charles had pulled him close again, but David pushed away, and Charles laughed. "What *was* that sound you made?" he teased, and gave a few short, high barks. "Like a porpoise," he said. "Adorable."

Does he *always* do that? he asked.

"Adams? Yes. He knows I like my routine."

It's a little creepy, Charles.

"Oh, Adams is harmless," Charles said. "He's just a little old-fashioned. And he's an excellent butler."

Over the months, he had tried to talk to Charles about Adams, but he was never successful, in part because he could never quite articulate his objections. Adams never treated him with anything but a somber, distant respect, and yet David knew somehow that Adams disapproved of him. When he told his best friend and former roommate, Eden, about Adams, she had rolled her eyes. "A *butler*?" she had said. "Give me a break, David. Anyway, he probably hates all of Chuck's tricks." (That was what Eden called Charles: Chuck. Now all their friends called him Chuck as well.)

I'm not a trick, he'd corrected Eden.

"Oh, right, I'm sorry," Eden had said. "You're his *boyfriend*." And she had pursed her lips and fluttered her eyelashes—she didn't approve of monogamy, and neither did she approve of men: "Except for you, David," she'd say. "And you barely count."

Gee, thanks, he'd say, and she'd laugh.

But he knew it wasn't true that Adams disapproved of all of Charles's boyfriends, because he'd once overheard a conversation that Adams and Charles had had about Charles's former boyfriend Olivier, whom Charles had dated before he met David. "And Mister Olivier called," Adams had said, giving Charles his messages, and David, standing just outside the doorway to the study, could hear something different in Adams's voice.

"How did he sound?" Charles asked. He and Olivier were still friendly but only saw each other once or twice a year at most.

"Very well," said Adams. "Please give him my regards."

"I absolutely will," Charles said.

Anyway, trying to complain about Adams was useless, because Charles would never abandon him: He had been Charles's parents' butler when he was a teenager, and when they both died, Charles, who was their only child, inherited not only their house but Adams as well. He could never tell his friends that; they would see Charles's employment of a seventy-five-year-old man in a physically demand-ing position as a form of geriatric exploitation, despite the fact that David knew that Adams enjoyed having his job as much as Charles enjoyed providing it to him. His friends never understood that— how, for some people, work was the only thing that made them feel real to the world.

"I know it seems anachronistic to have a butler," Charles had said—few of his own friends did, even the ones who were richer or from older money than he was—"but when you're raised with one, it's a hard habit to give up." He sighed. "I don't expect you, or anyone, to understand." David said nothing. "This is as much Adams's house as it is mine," Charles often said, and David knew he meant it in a way, even if it wasn't true. Habitation is not equiv-alent to ownership, he'd reminded Charles, quoting his first-year law-school professor, and Charles had grabbed him (they'd been in bed then, too). "Are you *actually* explaining legal principles to me?" he'd asked, teasing. "To *me*? You really are adorable." *You wouldn't understand,* Charles said to him, about this and so many other matters, and when he did, David's grandmother's face would suddenly flash through his mind. Would his grandmother have ever said that their house was as much Matthew's and Jane's as it was theirs? He didn't think so. Their house belonged only to the Binghams, and the only way to become a Bingham was to be born one or to marry one.

It certainly would never have occurred to Matthew or Jane to consider the Bingham house theirs either, and David suspected that Adams felt the same way: This was Charles's house, and always would be, and although he might be a part of it, it was only as a chair or a sidewall cabinet was part of it—a fixture, but nothing with its own desires or motivations or sense of autonomy. Adams could *behave* as if it were his—look at him now, ignoring the pres-ence of the party planner to order the caterers into the kitchen and the furniture movers into the dining room—but though his author-

ity was in part innate, much of it was due to his association with
Charles, whose name he invoked only when necessary, though still
not infrequently. "You *know* Mr. Griffith doesn't like them," he was
now chiding the florist, who stood before him, protesting, trying to
persuade, clutching a green plastic bucket of partially opened Easter
lilies against her chest. "We discussed this. He thinks their scent is
funereal."

"But I ordered all of these!" (The florist, in a near-wail.)

"Then I suggest you contact Mr. Griffith and try to convince
him," Adams said, knowing she never would, and, indeed, the florist
turned and walked away, calling to her crew as she did, "We have to
eighty-six the lilies!" and, lower, "Asshole."

David watched her go, feeling triumphant as she did. *He* was
to have coordinated the flowers. After the last big party—this was
shortly after David had moved in—he had suggested to Charles that
the flowers were a little listless, and far too fragrant: overly perfumed flowers distracted from the food. "You're right," Charles had
said. "Next time, you'll be in charge of them."

Will I really?

"Of course. What do I know about flowers? You're the expert,"
Charles had said, and had kissed him.

At the time, this had felt like a privilege, a gift, but since then
he had come to learn that when Charles declared his ignorance
it was only because he thought the subject inconsequential. He
could make his lack of knowledge—about flowers, baseball, football, modernist architecture, contemporary literature and art, South
American food—sound like a boast; he didn't know because there
was no reason to know. *You* might know, but then *you* had wasted
your time—*he* had other, more important things to learn about and
remember. And anyway, it hadn't happened: Charles had remembered to tell the party planner not to hire the same florist, but had
forgotten to tell her that David would be in charge. David had spent
the past month planning his arrangements, calling different shops in
the Flower District to ask if they could special-order stephanotis and
protea, and it had only been two weeks ago, when he and Charles
were having a drink in the living room and Charles had asked Adams

for an update about the party planner—"Yes, she's hired a different florist"—that David had realized that he wasn't to be responsible for the flowers after all.

He had waited until Adams left to ask Charles about it, both because they tried not to argue in front of Adams and because he wanted to rehearse the words to himself, to make sure he didn't sound like he was whining. But he had anyway. I thought *I* was overseeing the flowers, he'd said, once Adams exited the room.

"What?"

Remember? You said I could?

"Oh, god. Did I?"

Yes.

"I don't remember. But if you say I did, then I did. Oh, David, I'm sorry." And then, when he didn't answer, "You're not mad, are you? It's just a bunch of silly flowers. David. Are you upset?"

No, he lied.

"But you are. I'm sorry, David. You can do the next one, I promise."

He had nodded, and then Adams had reappeared to announce that dinner was served, and the two of them had gone to the dining room. As they ate, he tried to be cheerful, because that was what Charles liked, but later, in bed, Charles had turned to him in the dark and asked, "You're still annoyed, aren't you?"

It was difficult to explain why he was—he knew he would sound petty. I just want to help you, he'd begun. I just want to feel like I'm *doing* something here.

"But you *are* helping me," Charles had said. "Every night you're here with me, you're helping me."

Well—thank you. But—I want to feel like we're doing something together, like I'm *contributing* something to your life. I feel like—like I'm just taking up room in this house, but I'm not actually doing anything, do you know what I mean?

Charles had been quiet. "I understand," he said, finally. "Next time, David, I promise. And—I've been thinking—why don't we have some of your friends over for a dinner? Just your friends. You know all of mine, but I feel I've hardly met yours."

Really?

"Yes. This is your house, too; I want them to feel welcome here."

He had been relieved that night, but since then, Charles hadn't repeated his offer, and David hadn't reminded him, partly because he wasn't sure whether Charles had meant it, but also because he wasn't certain he wanted his friends meeting Charles at all. The fact that they hadn't been introduced by now, so long into their relationship, had gone from being unusual to being suspicious: What was David hiding? What didn't he want them to see? They already knew how old Charles was, and how rich, and how they had met, so what else was he embarrassed about? So, yes, they would come, but they would come to gather evidence, and after dinner they would all go out together and talk about why David was with Charles to begin with, and what he could possibly see in a man thirty years older than he was.

"I know one thing," he could hear Eden saying.

Yet David often wondered whether it was only the difference in their ages that made him feel like such a child around Charles, in a way that he had never felt around his own father, who was five years younger than his boyfriend. Look at him now: He was hiding in the stairway that connected the parlor and second floors, crouching on a step that he knew afforded him an excellent view of downstairs while concealing him completely, and from which he could watch the florist, still grumbling, snipping the twine off cords of juniper branches and, just behind her, the two movers, white cotton gloves on their hands, hoisting the eighteenth-century wooden sidewall cupboard from its spot in the dining room and carrying it slowly toward the kitchen, like a coffin, where it would remain for the evening. As a child, he had also hidden on the stairs, listening first to his father and grandmother arguing and later Edward and his grandmother arguing, ready to get up and run back toward his room, back under the sheet, if he needed to.

His role tonight had been demoted to that of a supervisor. "You're quality control," Charles had said to him. "I need you there to make sure everything looks as it ought to." But he knew this was a kindness on Charles's part—his presence here, as in many things, was amorphous and ultimately impotent. What he thought, his opinions, would make little difference. Here, in Charles's house, his suggestions were as meaningless as they were at work.

"Self-pity is an unattractive quality in a man," he heard his grandmother say.

What about in a woman?

"Also unattractive, but understandable," his grandmother would say. "A woman has much more to pity herself for."

His real job tonight (as on every night), he knew, was to be attractive and presentable, and this, at least, he could do, so he stood and climbed the next flight of stairs, to his and Charles's room. Until five years ago, when Charles had bought a small condominium in a building one block north, Adams had slept directly above, on the fourth story, in what was now another guest suite. David imagined him kneeling on the floor, still in his black suit, his ear pressed to the rug, listening to Charles and Olivier beneath him. He didn't like this vision, in which Adams's face was always turned away from him because he could never determine what his expression would be, and yet he kept seeing it.

The party tonight was for another of Charles's ex-boyfriends, but this one from so long ago—boarding school—that David saw no threat and no need for jealousy. Peter was the first person Charles had ever slept with, when Peter was sixteen and Charles was fourteen, and they had been friends ever since, their relationship sometimes sliding into a sexual one for months or years, though not in the past decade.

But now Peter was dying. This was why the party was on a Friday, not Charles's preferred Saturday—because the next day Peter had a ticket to Zurich, where he was going to meet an old Swiss classmate of his from college who was now a doctor, and who had agreed to give him an injection of barbiturates that would stop his heart.

It was difficult for David to comprehend how Charles truly felt about this. He was upset, of course—"I'm upset," Charles said—but what did "upset" mean, really? Charles had never cried, or gotten angry, or gone blank, not as David had when his first friend had died, seven years ago, and as he had with all the rest since; when he told David about Peter's decision, he had done so matter-of-factly, almost as an afterthought, and when David gasped and nearly started crying himself (despite the fact that he didn't know Peter very well and didn't much like him besides), it had been Charles who had had to comfort him. Charles had wanted to accompany Peter, but Peter had refused—it would be too difficult for him, he said. He would spend his final evening with Charles, but then, the next morning, he would board the plane with only the nurse he had hired for company.

"At least it's not the disease," Charles had said. He said that often. Sometimes he said it directly to David, and sometimes he said it in random moments, almost as an announcement, though the only person to hear it was David. "At least it's not the disease—at least that's not how he's going to die." Peter was dying of multiple myeloma, with which he'd lived for nine years.

"And now my time is up," he'd said, with a deliberate, ironic cheerfulness, to a long-unseen acquaintance of his and Charles's at Charles's last dinner. "No more extensions for little old me."

"Is it—"

"Oh, god, no. Boring old cancer, I'm afraid."

"You always were behind the curve, Peter."

"I prefer to think of it as traditional. Traditions matter, you know. Someone has to maintain them."

Now David changed into a suit—all of his good suits had been bought by Charles, but he had stopped wearing them to work when another of the paralegals had commented on them—and chose a tie, before deciding against it: The suit would be enough. He was the only twenty-five-year-old he knew who wore suits outside of work except for Eden, who wore them to be subversive. But as he went to his side of the closet to replace the tie, he passed his bag, and, stuffed down its side, the letter.

He sat on the bed, contemplating it. There would be nothing good in that letter, he knew; it would be about his father, and the news would be bad, and he would have to go home, to his real home, and see him, a person who in certain respects had ceased to become real to him: He was an apparition, someone who appeared only in

David's dreams, someone who had long ago wandered away from the realm of consciousness into wherever he was, someone lost to him. Over the decade since David had seen him last, he had worked hard to never think about him, because thinking about him was like succumbing to a riptide so powerful that he was afraid he would never emerge from it, that it would carry him so far away from land that he would never be able to return. Every day he woke and practiced not thinking about his father, as an athlete practices his sprints or a musician his scales. And now that diligence was about to be upset. Whatever was inside that envelope would begin a series of conversations with Charles, or at least one very long one, one that he would have to start by telling Charles he needed to go away. *Why?* Charles would ask. And then: *Where? Who? I thought you said he was dead. Wait, slow down*—who?

He wouldn't have that conversation tonight, he decided. It was Peter's party. He had already mourned his father, mourned him for years, and now whatever was in that envelope could wait. And so he buried it deep in his bag, as if by not reading it he was also making not real whatever the letter said—it was suspended, somewhere between New York and Hawai'i: something that had almost happened, but that he, through not recognizing it, had kept at bay.

———

The party was starting at seven, and Charles had sworn he would be home by six, but at six-fifteen there was still no sign of him, and David stood at the window, looking out onto the street and the shadowy stage of Washington Square beyond, waiting for Charles to arrive.

When he was in college, the school's drama club had staged a play about a nineteenth-century heiress who hoped to be married to a man her father was convinced was courting her only for her money. The heiress was plain, and the man was handsome, and no one— not her father, not her simpering spinster aunt, not her friends, not the playwright or the audience—believed that she could be of any genuine attraction to her beloved; the heiress was the only one who believed otherwise. The stubbornness of her belief was meant to be proof of her foolishness, but David saw it as steeliness, the kind born of a great self-possession, the kind he admired in Charles. The opening scene of the second act was of the woman standing in the window of her house, her hair parted in the center and drawn back into a bun at the nape of her neck, with two ringlets, like curtains, hanging on each side of her round, sweet face, and her dress, of crisp peach silk, rustling about her. She looked calm and unworried; her hands lay one atop the other at her waist. She was watching for her beloved; she was certain he would come for her.

Now here he was in a similar pose, waiting for *his* beloved. He, unlike the heiress, had fewer reasons to be anxious, and yet he was. But why? Charles loved him, he would always care for him, he had given him a life he could never have afforded on his own, even if it sometimes felt as if he didn't truly possess it but was an understudy, hurried onstage in the middle of a scene he couldn't remember, trying to read his fellow actors' cues, hopeful his lines would return to him.

When he had met Charles, a year and a half ago, he had been living in a one-bedroom apartment with Eden on Eighth Street and Avenue B, and although Eden had found their street exciting—the moaning drunks who shouted at you, inexplicably, just to make you jump; the long-haired boys they occasionally found passed out on their stoop in the morning—he had not. He had learned to leave for the law firm at seven a.m. exactly: any earlier and he would find himself encountering partiers and unsuccessful drug dealers stumbling home from the night before; any later and he would have to pass the first panhandlers of the day, mumbling for change as they shuffled west from Tompkins Square Park to St. Marks Place.

"Got a quarter? Got a quarter? Got a quarter?" they would ask.

Sorry, no, I don't, he had murmured one morning, his head down as if ashamed, trying to sidestep the man.

Normally, this was enough, but this time, the man—white, with a ragged blond beard knotted with filth, a twist tie wrapped around a clump of it—began to follow him, so closely that David could feel the tips of the man's shoes ticking at the heels of his, could smell his peppery, porky breath. "You're lying," he had hissed. "Why do you lie? I can hear it in your pocket: all that jingle-jangle of coins. Why are you lying? Because you're one of them, a fucking spic, a fucking spic, aren't you?"

He had been scared—it was only seven-thirty, and the street was mostly deserted, but there were a few other people out, who stood and gawped at them, as if the two of them were putting on a performance for them to enjoy. (This was something he had quickly grown to hate about this place: how New Yorkers congratulated themselves for ignoring the famous, while watching with unabashed avidity the minor dramas of the plain and average as they played themselves out on the street.) He was almost at Third Avenue by then, and in one of the rare salvations the city sometimes offered, the bus was pulling up to his stop—ten steps, and he would be safe. Ten, nine, eight, seven. And then he was boarding, and he turned and yelled at the man, his voice shrill with fear: I'm not a spic!

"Oh!" said the man, who made no move toward the bus himself. A kind of glee had entered his voice, a delight in getting a response. "Fucking gook! Fucking Chink! Fucking fag! Fucking wop! Fuck you!" As the door had closed, the man had bent, and as the bus pulled away, there had been a thunk on its side, and David had turned and looked out the window and had seen the man, now wearing only one shoe, limping into the street to retrieve its companion.

By the time he reached the office, walking crosstown on Fifty-sixth Street to Broadway, he had managed to compose himself, but then he had seen his reflection in the plate-glass window of the building and realized his pen had leaked, and the entire right-hand side of his shirt was saturated with dark-blue ink. Upstairs, he had gone to the lavatory, only to find it inexplicably locked, and, nearly breathless with panic, had gone instead to the executive washroom, which was empty. There he had begun to dab, fecklessly, at his shirt, the ink dissipating, but not enough. Now his fingers and cheek were stained blue as well. What would he do? It had been a warm day; he hadn't worn a jacket. He would have to go to a store and buy himself a shirt, and he didn't have money for that—not money for the shirt itself, not money to lose the pay for the hour it would take to buy it.

It was as he was blotting, cursing, that the door opened, and he looked up and saw Charles. He knew of Charles; he was one of the senior partners, and he was, he supposed, handsome. He had never thought much about it beyond recognizing that he was—Charles was powerful, and old. Spending further time considering his handsomeness was both counterproductive and potentially dangerous. He did know that the secretaries thought Charles was handsome, too. He knew as well that Charles wasn't married—this was a topic of speculation among them.

"You think he's a homosexual?" he had overheard one of the secretaries whisper to another.

"Mr. Griffith?" she said. "No! He's not like one of them."

Now he began to apologize—for being in the executive washroom, for being covered in ink, for being alive.

Charles ignored his apologies, however. "You do know that shirt's a goner, right?" he asked, and David looked up from his dabbing to see him smiling. "I'm assuming you don't have another."

No, he admitted. Sir.

"Charles," said Charles, still smiling. "Charles Griffith. I'll shake your hand later."

Yes, he said. Right. I'm David Bingham.

He resisted the impulse to apologize again for being in the executive washroom. *No land is owned land*, Edward used to tell him, back when he was still called Edward. *You have the right to be wherever you want.* He wondered if Edward would think that same principle would apply to a senior-management bathroom in a midtown Manhattan law firm. He probably would, though the very concept of a law firm, of a law firm in New York, of David working in a law firm in New York, would disgust him even before he got to the absurdity of there being separate bathrooms in the law firm based upon its employees' rank. *Shame on you, Kawika. Shame on you. I taught you better than that.*

"Wait here," said Charles, and left, and David, looking up into the mirror and realizing the extent of his dishevelment—there was a clot of ink above his right eye that was sinking into his skin like a bruise—took his wad of paper towels and went into one of the stalls in case another of the partners came in. But when the bathroom door opened next, it was only Charles, with a flat cardboard box tucked beneath his arm. "Where are you?" he asked.

He peered around the stall door. Here, he said.

Charles looked amused. "What are you doing, hiding in there?" he asked.

I'm not supposed to be here, he said. I'm a paralegal, he added, as clarification.

Charles's smile became a bit wider. "Well, Paralegal," he said, lifting the lid of the box to reveal a white shirt, clean and folded, "this is all I have. I think it might be a little big on you, but it's better than walking around looking like the dark side of the moon, right?"

Or topless, he heard himself say, and he saw Charles's look turn sharp and appraising. "Yes," he said, after a short silence. "Or topless. We can't have that."

Thank you, he said, taking the box from Charles. He could feel from the cotton that the shirt was expensive, and he pulled out its stays and the cardboard beneath its collar and unbuttoned it with his inky fingers. He was about to hang it on the back of the stall door and begin unbuttoning his own shirt when Charles reached out his hand: "Let me take it," he said, and he draped his own, clean shirt over his arm, like a caricature of an old-fashioned waiter, while David began undressing. It seemed churlish to close the door at that point and ask for privacy, and, indeed, Charles didn't move, but stood there, silently, watching him unbutton his shirt, remove it, exchange it for the one he held, and then button up the new one. He was very aware of the sound of their breaths, and of how he hadn't worn an undershirt, and of how his skin was pimpling even though the bathroom wasn't especially cold. When he had finished buttoning it and then stuffing it into his pants—turning from Charles as he did to unfasten his belt: How clumsy and graceless it was, this process of dressing and undressing—he thanked Charles again. Thank you for holding my shirt, he said. For everything. I'll take it back. But Charles grinned. "I think you'd better just throw it away," he said. "I don't think it's salvageable." Yes, he agreed, but he didn't add that he had to try—he only had six shirts, and he couldn't afford to lose one.

Charles's shirt sat around him, a balloon of crisp, dry cotton, and as he stepped out of the stall, Charles made a little sound of amusement, saying, "I'd forgotten about that," and David had looked down at his left side, where, just above his kidney, were Charles's initials stitched in black: CGG. "Well," Charles said, "I'd cover that up, if I were you. We can't have people thinking you stole a shirt from me." And then he winked at him and left, while David stood there, stupidly. A moment later, the door opened again and Charles's face appeared. "Incoming," he said. "Delacroix." Delacroix was the managing director of the firm. Then he winked again and was gone.

"Hello," said Delacroix, entering and studying him, clearly not recognizing him, but wondering if he ought to—he didn't look like someone who'd be using the executive washroom, but these days, anyone under fifty looked like a child to him, so who knew? Maybe this fellow was a partner, too.

Hello, David responded as confidently as he could, and then he scuttled out.

For the rest of the day, he held his arm bent at a right angle over his stomach, concealing the monogram. (That night, it occurred to him that he could have just taped a patch of paper over the spot.) And though no one noticed, he felt marked, branded, and when, leaving the archives room, he saw Charles walking toward him with another partner, he flushed and nearly dropped his books, catching a glimpse of Charles's back before he rounded the corner. By the end of the day, he was exhausted, and that night his arm floated toward his torso, already disciplined into submission.

The next day was Saturday, and despite his vigorous scrubbing, Charles was proven right—the shirt was hopeless. He had debated whether he could get away with washing and ironing Charles's shirt himself, but that would have meant adding it to his own bag of laundry and taking it all to the laundromat, and something about putting the shirt in the mesh bag containing his underwear and T-shirts made him embarrassed. So he'd had to take the shirt to the dry cleaners, spending money he didn't have.

On Monday, he made sure to arrive at the firm particularly early, and was heading toward Charles's door when he realized he couldn't just leave the box outside of his office. He stopped, and was thinking about what to do when, suddenly, there was Charles, in his suit and tie, holding his briefcase, regarding him with the same amused expression he'd given him the previous week.

"Hello, Paralegal David," he said.

Hi, he said. Um—I brought back your shirt. (Belatedly, he realized he should have brought something for Charles, to thank him, though he couldn't think of what that might possibly be.) Thank you—thank you so much. You saved me. It's clean, he added, stupidly.

"I should hope so," Charles said, still smiling, and he unlocked his office, and took the box, which he set on his desk while David waited in the doorway. "You know," Charles said, after a pause, turning back to him, "I think you owe me a favor after this."

Do I?, he finally managed to say.

"I think so," Charles said, stepping close to him. "I saved you, didn't I?" He smiled, again. "Why don't you come have dinner with me sometime?"

Oh, he said. And then again: Oh. Okay. Yes.

"Good," said Charles. "I'll call you."

Oh, he repeated. Right. Yes. Okay.

They were the only ones in the office, and yet they both spoke quietly, almost in whispers, and when David walked away, back to the paralegals' area, his face was hot.

The dinner was arranged for the following Thursday, and on Charles's instructions, he had left the office first, at seven-thirty, and had gone alone to the restaurant, which was dark and hushed, where he was seated in a booth and handed a large menu in a leather case. A few minutes past eight, Charles arrived, and David watched as he was greeted by the maître d', who whispered something in his ear that made Charles smile and roll his eyes. After he sat, a martini was brought to him, unbidden. "He'll have one, too," Charles said to the waiter, nodding at David, and when he had been given his, Charles had raised his glass, ironically, and touched it to his. "To non-exploding pens," he said.

To non-exploding pens, he'd echoed.

Later, he would look back on that night and realize it had been the first real date he had ever been on. Charles had ordered for both of them (a porterhouse, rare, with sides of spinach and rosemary-roasted potatoes) and had led the conversation. It soon became clear that he had certain ideas about David, which David hadn't corrected. Besides, most of them weren't wrong: He *was* poor. He *hadn't* had a fancy education. He *was* naïve. He *hadn't* been anywhere. And yet beneath those truths were a set of what Charles, in the courtroom, would have characterized as mitigating factors: He hadn't always been poor. He had once had a fancy education. He wasn't completely naïve. He had once lived somewhere neither Charles nor anyone he knew could ever go.

They were halfway through their steak when David realized that he hadn't asked Charles anything about himself. "Oh, no, what is there to say? I'm afraid I'm very boring," Charles said, in the careless way that only people who knew they weren't boring at all could. "We'll get to me. Tell me about your apartment," and David, drunk on both gin and the unusual sensation of being treated as if he were a source of great fascination and wisdom, did: He told Charles about the mice and the window casements seamed with grime, and the sad drag queen whose favorite resting place was their stoop and whose favorite two a.m. ballad to bellow was "Waltzing Matilda," and about his roommate, Eden, who was an artist, a painter, mostly, but whose day job was as a proofreader at a book publishing company. (He didn't mention that Eden called him every day at the firm at three p.m. and that the two of them talked for an hour, David whispering into the phone and feigning coughing fits to disguise his laughter.)

"Where are you from?" Charles asked, after he had smiled or laughed at all of David's stories.

Hawai'i, he said, and then, before Charles could ask, O'ahu. Honolulu.

Charles had been there, of course, everyone had, and for a while David spoke around the edges of his life: Yes, he still had family there. No, they weren't close. No, his father was dead. No, he never knew his mother. No, no siblings, and his father had also been an only child. Yes, one grandparent—his paternal grandmother.

Charles tilted his head and studied him for a moment. "I hope this doesn't sound rude," he said, "but what are you? Are you—" He stopped, stymied.

Hawaiian, he said, staunchly, though it wasn't the whole truth.

"But your last name—"

It's a missionary name. American missionaries started arriving in the islands in significant numbers in the early nineteenth century; a lot of them intermarried with the Hawaiians.

"Bingham . . . Bingham," Charles said ruminatively, and David knew what he would say next. "You know, there's a dormitory at Yale called Bingham Hall. I lived in it freshman year. Is there any relation?" He grinned, his eyebrow lifted; he already assumed there wasn't.

Yes—he's an ancestor.

"Really," Charles said, and leaned back in his seat, his smile fading. He was quiet, and David understood that, for the first time, he had surprised Charles, surprised and disconcerted him, and that Charles was wondering if his assessments of David had been correct after all. He had spent less than an hour with Charles, but he knew already that Charles did not like to be surprised, did not like having to recalibrate his opinions, the way he had decided to see things. Later, after he had moved in with Charles, he had looked back at that moment and had recognized that he could have redirected the course of their relationship; what if, instead of responding as he had, he had instead said something like: *Oh, yes, I'm from one of the oldest families in Hawai'i. I'm descended from royalty. Everyone there knows who we are. If things had gone differently, I would have been king.* It would have been true.

But what point was the truth? When he had been at his third-rate college, he had once told his boyfriend at the time—a lacrosse player who, outside of his bedroom, either ignored David or pretended he didn't exist—the abbreviated story of his family, and the boy had scoffed. "Very funny, man," he'd said. "And I'm descended from the queen of England. Right." He had insisted, and finally his boyfriend had rolled over onto his side, away from him, bored by David's stories. After that, he had learned not to say anything, because it seemed easier and better to lie than it was to be disbelieved. His family was a remote fact, but even so, he didn't want to hear them mocked; he didn't want to be reminded how the source of his grandmother's pride was for most people a subject of ridicule. He didn't want to think about his poor lost father.

So: We're from the penniless side of the family, he said instead, and Charles had laughed, relieved.

"It happens to the best of us," he said.

In the taxi downtown, they had been quiet, and Charles, staring straight ahead, had placed his hand on David's knee, and David had taken it and moved it atop his groin, and had seen, in shadows, Charles's profile change as he smiled. They had parted chastely that night—Charles dropping him off on Second Avenue, because he had been too embarrassed for Charles to see the building where he actually lived: Charles's house was only a mile west from him, but it might as well have been another country altogether—but over the following weeks they met again and again, and six months after their first date, he had moved into Charles's house on Washington Square.

He felt he had grown simultaneously older and younger over the months he and Charles had been together. Isolated from his own friends, he spent more time with Charles's, sitting at dinners at which Charles's polite friends tried to include him in the conversation, and his not-so-polite ones made him the subject of conversation. Eventually, however, both groups would forget about him, their talk turning to more arcane points of the law or the stock market, and he would excuse himself and creep off to bed to wait for Charles. Sometimes they would go to Charles's friends' houses for dinner, and there he would listen in silence as they discussed things—people he had never heard of, books he had never read,

movie stars he didn't care about, events he hadn't been alive for—
until it was time to go home (early, thankfully).

But he was also aware of feeling like a child. Charles chose his
clothes and where they would vacation and what they would eat: all
the things he had had to do for his father; all the things he wished
his father would have done for him. He knew he should feel infan-
tilized by how obviously unequal their life together was, and yet he
didn't—he liked it, he found it relaxing. It was a relief to be with
someone so declarative; it was a relief not to think. Charles's self-
assuredness, which extended to every aspect of their lives, was reassuring. He gave orders to Adams or to the cook with the same brisk,
warm authority that he used with David when they were in bed. He
sometimes felt as if he were reliving his childhood, this time with
Charles as his father, and that made him queasy, because Charles
wasn't his father; he was his lover. Yet the sensation persisted—here
was someone who allowed him to be the object of worry, never the
worrier. Here was someone whose rhythms and patterns were explicable and dependable and, once learned, could be relied upon to be
maintained. All along he had known that something had been absent
from his life, but it wasn't until he met Charles that he understood
that that quality was logic—fantasy, in Charles's life, was confined to
bed, and even there it made sense in its own way.

He had never thought too much about what kind of man he
might someday live with, but he had slipped so easily into his role
as Charles's boyfriend, as Charles's, that it was only in rare moments
that he realized with a flop of his stomach that he had in fact come
to resemble his father in ways he had never foreseen or imagined—
someone who yearned only to be loved and taken care of, to be
instructed. And it was in those moments—moments in which he
stood in the gloom at the front window, his hand on the shutter,
looking out into the darkened square for Charles, waiting like a cat
for its owner to come home—that he was able to recognize who he
reminded himself of: not just the heiress, in her much too lovely
pink dress, but his father. His father, standing at the window of their
house, near sundown, exhausted from the anxiety and hopefulness

of waiting all day, still scanning the street for Edward to arrive in his puttery old car, waiting to run down the porch steps and join his friend, waiting to be taken away from his mother and his son, and all the disappointments of his small and inescapable life.

————

The first doorbell chime sounded as Charles was still getting dressed. "Damnit," he said. "Who comes exactly when they're supposed to?"

Americans, he said, which was something he had read in a book, and Charles laughed.

"That's true," he said, and kissed him. "Will you go down and talk to whoever it is? I'll be down in ten minutes."

Ten? he asked, in mock outrage. You still need ten more minutes to get ready?

Charles swatted him with his towel. "We can't all look like you do just out of the shower," he said. "Some of us need to work at it."

So he went down, grinning. They had exchanges like that often—complimenting each other's appearance while diminishing their own—but only in private, because they both knew they were handsome and also both knew that recognizing it aloud was not just unappealing but, these days, potentially cruel as well. They were both vain, and yet vanity was an indulgence, a sign of life, a reminder of good health, a thanksgiving. Sometimes when they were out together, or even in someone's apartment with a group of other men, they would look at each other quickly and then turn away, because they understood there was something obscene about their cheeks, still plumped with fat, and their arms, still layered with muscle. They were, in certain company, a provocation.

Downstairs, there were no lilies to be seen or smelled, only Adams returning to the kitchen with a now empty silver drinks tray. In the dining room, which David had checked earlier, the catering staff was arranging plates of food around the vases of holly and freesia: Charles had suggested sushi to Peter, but Peter had rejected that suggestion. "Now, on my deathbed, is not when I need to start eating *fish*," he said. "Not after a lifetime of studiously avoiding it. Just

get me something normal, Charles. Something normal and good."
So Charles had had the party planner hire a caterer who specialized
in Mediterranean-inspired food, and now the table was being set
with terra-cotta dishes of sliced steak and grilled zucchini and bowls
of angel-hair pasta tossed with olives and sundried tomatoes. The
waitstaff in their black pants and shirts were women—although he
hadn't been able to oversee the flowers, David *had* found a way to
request only female caterers from the company Charles preferred.
David knew he'd be irritated when he saw that the usual crew—
uniformly young, blond, and male, and who at the last party David
had seen eyeing Charles, and Charles enjoying their attention—had
been replaced, but knew too that he would be forgiven by the time
they went to bed, because Charles liked it when David was jealous,
liked being reminded that he still had options.

The dining room, where he and Charles ate dinner every night
if they didn't go out, was old-fashioned and fusty, left mostly intact
from when Charles's parents had lived there. The rest of the house
had been renovated a decade ago, when Charles moved in, but this
room still had its original long, polished mahogany table, and its
matching Federal-period cupboard, and its dark-green wallpaper
with its pattern of morning-glory vines, and its dark-green dupioni
silk drapes, and its side-by-side portraits of Charles's ancestors, the
first Griffiths to arrive in America from Scotland, their clock with
its creamy, whale-ivory face—an heirloom of which Charles was
very proud—sitting atop the mantel between them. Charles had no
good explanation for why he hadn't changed the room, and when
David was in it, he would always think of his grandmother's dining
room, a place very different in appearance and detail, but similarly
unchanged—and more than the room itself, he would think of their
family dinners: how his father would get nervous and drop the ladle
into the tureen, splashing the tablecloth with soup; how his grandmother would get angry. "For heaven's sake, son," she would say.
"Can't you be more careful? Do you see what you've done?"

"I'm sorry, Mama," his father would murmur.

"You see the kind of example you're setting," his grandmother
would continue, as if his father hadn't spoken at all. And then, to

David, "You're going to be more careful than your father, aren't you, Kawika?"

Yes, he would promise, though he would feel guilty doing so, as if he had betrayed his father, and when his father came into his room that night to tuck him in, he would tell him that he wanted to be just like him. Tears would come to his father's eyes then, both because he knew David was lying and because he was grateful to him for it. "Don't be like me, Kawika," his father would say, kissing him on his cheek. "And you won't be. You're going to be better than I am, I know it." He never knew what to say to this, and so usually he would say nothing, and his father would kiss his fingertips and place them on his forehead. "Go to sleep, now," he would say. "My Kawika. My son."

He was suddenly dizzy. What would his father think of him now? What would he say? How would he feel if he knew his son had received a letter that probably contained news, bad news, about him, and had chosen not to read it? *My Kawika. My son.* He was seized by an impulse to run upstairs, tear the letter out of its envelope, and devour it, whatever it might say.

But, no, he couldn't; if he did, the evening would be lost. Instead, he made himself go into the living room, where three of Peter and Charles's old friends were sitting: John and Timothy and Percival. These were the nicest friends, the kind who would only look him up and down once, quickly, when he walked in, and for the rest of the evening would keep their eyes on his face. "The Three Sisters," Peter called them, because they were all single and unglamorous, and because Peter found them insufficiently exciting: "The Spinsters." Timothy and Percival were both sick; Timothy visibly so, Percival secretly. He had confided in Charles seven months ago, and Charles had told David. "I look fine, don't I?" Percival asked Charles whenever they saw each other. "I look the same, don't I?" He was the editor in chief of a small, prestigious publishing house—he was afraid he'd get fired if the company's owners found out.

"You won't get fired," Charles always said. "And if they try, I know exactly the person you should call, and you'll sue the hell out of them, and I'll help."

Percival ignored this. "But I look the same, don't I?"

"Yes, Percy—you look the same. You look great."

He looked over at Percival now. The others had glasses of wine, but Percival was holding a teacup in which David knew he was soaking a teabag of medicinal herbs that he got from an acupuncturist in Chinatown who he swore was strengthening his immune system. He studied Percival as he was distracted by his tea: *Did* he look the same? It had been five months since he'd seen him last—was he thinner? Did his complexion seem dustier? It was difficult to say; all of Charles's friends looked slightly unhealthy to him, whether they were or not. Something, some quality, had disappeared from all of them, no matter how well maintained or robust—light seemed to vanish into their skin, so that even when they were sitting here, in the forgiving candlelight that Charles had grown to favor for these gatherings, they seemed made not from flesh but from something silty and cold. Not marble, but chalk. He had once attempted to explain this to Eden, who spent her weekends drawing nudes, and she had rolled her eyes. "It's because they're old," she had said.

He looked next at Timothy, who was now clearly ill, his eyelids as violet as if he'd smudged them with paint, his teeth too long, his hair a fuzz. Timothy had been in boarding school with Peter and Charles, and back then, Charles said, "You wouldn't believe how beautiful he was. The most beautiful boy in the school." This was after the first time he'd met Timothy, and the next time, David had examined him, looking for the boy Charles had fallen in love with. He was an actor, an unsuccessful one, and had been married to a beautiful woman, and then for decades had been the lover of a very rich man, but when the man died, his adult children had made Timothy leave their father's house, and Timothy had moved in with John. No one knew how John, who was jolly and large, made his money—he was from a modest family in the Midwest and had never had a job that lasted longer than a few months and wasn't handsome enough to be kept—and yet he occupied an entire townhouse in the West Village and ate extravagantly (though, as Charles pointed out, usually only when someone else was paying). "When people like John stop being able to survive through mysterious means in this city is the day this city is no longer worth living in," Charles would say, fondly. (For someone who was adamant about people earning their way, he had an unusual number of friends who seemed to do nothing at all: It was something David liked about him.)

As always, the three said hello to him, asked him about what he was doing and how he was, but he had little to say, and eventually, their conversation turned back to themselves, to recounting things they'd done together when they were younger.

". . . Well, that's not as bad as when John dated that homeless guy!"

"First of all, we were hardly *dating*, and second . . ."

"Tell that story again!"

"Well. This was, oh, about fifteen years ago, when I was working at that framing shop on Twentieth between Fifth and Sixth—"

"Where you got fired for stealing—"

"*Excuse* me. I did *not* get fired for stealing. I got fired for being chronically tardy and incompetent, and for providing poor customer service. I got fired from the *bookstore* for stealing."

"Oh, well, *excuse me*."

"Anyway, can I continue? So I'd get off the F at Twenty-third Street, and I'd always see this guy, *very* cute, kind of a scruffy artist type, plaid shirt and a little beard, carrying a grocery bag, standing on Sixth near the empty lot on the southeast corner. So I cruise her, and she cruises back, and this goes on for a few days. And then, on the fourth day, I go up to her and we talk. She says, 'Do you live around here?' And I say, 'No, I work down the block.' And she says, 'Well, we can go into this alley'—it wasn't really an alley, but there was this little channel between the back wall of the parking lot and this other building they were tearing down—and, you know, we did."

"Spare us the details."

"Jealous?"

"Uh, no."

"Anyway, the next day, I'm walking down the street and there she is again, and back we go into the alley. And then, the day after that, I see her *again*, and I think: Huh. Something's off here. And then I realize she's wearing the *exact same thing* as the previous two times! Right down to the underwear. And also that she's kind of smelly. Actually, let me correct that: She's *very* smelly. Poor old girl. She didn't have anywhere to go."

"So did you leave?"

"Of course not! We were there, weren't we?"

They all laughed, and then Timothy began singing: "La da dee la dee da, La da dee la dee da," and Percival joined in: "She's just like you and me, but she's homeless; she's homeless." David left them, smiling—he liked watching the three of them together; he liked how no one else seemed to interest them as much as they did themselves. How would his father's life have been different if Edward had been more like Timothy or Percival or John, if his father had had a friend who would make the stuff of their past into a story to entertain instead of to control? He tried to picture his father in Charles's house, at this party. What would he think? What would he do? He imagined his father, his shy, slight smile, standing behind the staircase banister, looking at the other men but afraid to join them, assuming they would ignore him as he had been ignored almost all of his life. What would his father's life have been like had he left the island, had he learned to ignore his mother, had he found someone to cherish him? It might have resulted in a future in which David might not exist. He stood there, conjuring this other life for him: His father, strolling alongside the arch at the north of the Square, a novel tucked under his arm, walking beneath the late-fall trees, their leaves as red as apples, his face lifted to the sky. It would be a Sunday, and he would be on his way to meet a friend for a movie and then dinner. But then the vision faltered: Who was this friend? Was it a man or a woman? Was theirs a romantic relationship? Where was his father living? How was he supporting himself? Where would he go the next day, and the day after? Was he healthy, and if he wasn't, who was taking care of him? He felt a kind of despair steal over him: for how his father eluded him even in fiction, for how he was unable to construct a happy life for him. He had been unable to save him; he was unable even to summon the courage to learn of his fate. He had abandoned his father in life, and now he was abandoning him again, in fantasy. Should he not at least be able to dream him into a better existence, a kinder one? What did it say about him, as his son, that he was incapable of even that?

But maybe, he thought, maybe it wasn't a lack of empathy that was to blame for his inability to project his father into a different life—maybe it was how childlike his father was, how his father had behaved like no other parent, like no other adult, he had known, then or since. There were, for example, their walks, which had begun when David was six or seven. He would be woken late at night by his father, holding out his hand, and David would take it, and together they would walk the streets of their neighborhood in silence, showing each other how familiar things became different in the nighttime: the bush dangling flowers that resembled upside-down cornets, the acacia tree on their neighbor's property that in the dark appeared enchanted and malevolent and like something from a country far from their own, where they would be two travelers moving through snow that squeaked beneath their boots, and in the distance would be a farmhouse with a single window lit a smoky yellow by a single candle, and inside would be a witch disguised as a kindly widow, and two bowls of soup as thick as porridge, salty with cubes of fatback and sweet with chunks of roasted yam.

On those walks, there would always be a moment in which he realized that he could see, that the night, which had at first seemed a featureless screen of black, toneless and silent, was brighter than it appeared, and although he always promised himself that he would determine the exact moment when it happened, when his eyes adjusted themselves to this different, filtered light, he never could: It happened so gradually, so without his participation, that it was as if his mind existed not to control his body but to marvel at its abilities, its capacity for adaptation.

As they walked, his father would tell him stories from his childhood, would show him places where he had played or had hidden as a boy, and in the night, these stories wouldn't seem sad the way they did when David's grandmother had told them, but simply stories: about the other boys in the neighborhood, who threw avocados from one of their trees at his father as he walked home from school;

about the time they had made him climb the mango tree in his own front yard and then had told him he couldn't come down or they'd beat him, and for hours, until it turned dark, until the last of them finally had to leave his post to go home for dinner, his father had stayed in the tree, crouched in the flat, shallow space made by the limbs meeting the trunk, and when he had finally climbed down—his legs shaking from hunger and exhaustion—he had had to go inside his own house and explain where he'd been to his mother, who had been waiting for him at the dining-room table, silent and livid.

Why didn't you just tell her then what had happened to you? he had asked his father.

"Oh," his father had said, and then stopped. "She didn't want to hear it. She didn't want to hear that those boys weren't really my friends after all. It was embarrassing for her." He was silent, listening to him. "But that won't happen to you, Kawika," his father had continued. "You have friends. I'm proud of you."

He had been quiet then, his father's story and its sadness sinking into him, past his heart and down to his intestines, a leaden anvil, and, remembering this, he felt the same sorrow, this time spreading through his body as if it were something that had been injected into his bloodstream. He turned then, and was intending to go to the kitchen on some made-up pretense—to check on the plating of the food; to tell Adams that Percival would need more hot water soon—when he saw Charles descending the stairs.

"What's wrong?" Charles asked, upon seeing him, his smile vanishing. "Did something happen?" No, no, nothing happened, he said, but Charles held out his arms anyway, and David walked into them, into Charles's warm solidity, his reassuring bulk. "It's all right, David, whatever it is," Charles said, after a pause, and he nodded into Charles's shoulder. It would be all right, he knew—Charles said so, and David loved him, and he was far from where he'd been, and nothing would happen to him that Charles wouldn't be able to solve.

———

By eight, all twelve of the guests had arrived, Peter last of all—it was snowing by then, and Charles and David and John had carried Peter, in his heavy wheelchair, up the front steps: David and John on either side of him, Charles propping up the rear.

He had just seen Peter at Thanksgiving, and he was stunned by how much he had deteriorated in three weeks. The most noticeable evidence of this was the wheelchair—a high-backed one with a headrest—but also his weight loss, the way the skin on his face in particular seemed to have shrunk, so that his lips couldn't quite close over his teeth. Or maybe it wasn't that it had shrunk so much as it had been yanked, as if someone had gathered a fistful of scalp at the back of Peter's skull and pulled, stretching the skin taut and painful and bulging his eyes out of their sockets. Once he was inside, Peter's friends gathered around him, but David could tell they too were shocked by his appearance; no one seemed to know what to say.

"What, you've never seen a dying man before?" Peter asked, coolly, and everyone looked away.

It was a rhetorical question, and a cruel one, but "Of course we have, Peter," Charles said in his businesslike way. He had retrieved a wool blanket from the study and was now wrapping it about Peter's shoulders, tucking it around his rib cage. "Now, let's get you something to eat. Everyone! Dinner's set out in the dining room; please help yourselves."

It had been Charles's original plan to host a sit-down dinner, but Peter had discouraged that. He didn't know if he would have the strength to sit through a long meal, he said, and besides, the point of this gathering was for him to say goodbye to everyone. He needed to be able to circulate, to talk to people, and then to get away from them when he wanted. Now, as everyone filed slowly, almost reluctantly, toward the dining room, Charles turned to him: "David, would you get Peter a plate? I'm going to settle him on the couch."

Of course, he said.

In the dining room, there was an atmosphere of excessive merriment, as people served themselves more food than they would ever eat, and made loud pronouncements about how they were putting their diets on hold. They had come for Peter, but no one mentioned him. It would be the last time they would see him, the last time they would say goodbye, and suddenly the party seemed ghoulish, grotesque, and David hurriedly went from platter to platter, cutting into the line, loading Peter's plate with meats and pastas and braised vegetables before getting a second plate and arranging it with all of Charles's favorites, eager to get away.

Back in the living room, Peter was sitting at one end of the sofa, his legs on the ottoman, and Charles was leaning against him, his right arm around Peter's shoulders, Peter's face pressed into Charles's neck, and when David approached them, Charles turned and smiled and David could see he had been crying, and Charles never cried. "Thank you," he said to David, and, holding the plate out for Peter: "See? No fish. Just like you commanded."

"Excellent," said Peter, turning his skull-like face to David. "Thank you, young man." That was what Peter called him: "young man." He didn't like it, but what could he do? After this weekend, he would never have to bear Peter calling him "young man" again. Then he realized he had thought that and felt ashamed, almost as if he'd spoken aloud.

But for all of Peter's strong opinions about the food, he had no appetite for any of it—even the smell made him gag, he said. And yet, for the rest of the evening, the plate David had brought for him sat on the side table to his right, a cloth napkin bundled around a set of utensils tucked beneath its lip, as if he might at any moment change his mind, pick it up, and consume everything it held. It wasn't the illness that had eliminated his appetite: It was the new course of chemotherapy he had begun taking a little over a month ago. But the drugs had once again proven useless; the cancer remained, but Peter's physical strength had not.

He had been bewildered by this when Charles had told him. Why had Peter started a course of chemotherapy when he already knew he was going to kill himself? Beside him, Charles had sighed, and was silent. "It's hard to give up hope," he said at last. "Even until the very end."

It was only after more people had drifted back into the living room with their own plates of food, tentatively arranging themselves onto chairs and footrests and the second sofa like courtiers assembling around the king's throne, that David felt he could go get himself something to eat. The dining room was empty, the platters diminished, and as he was filling his plate with what he could, a waiter entered from the kitchen. "Oh," he said, "I'm sorry. We're bringing out more right now." He saw that David had been reaching for the steak. "I'll bring out a fresh batch."

He left, and David looked after him. He was young and handsome and male (everything that he'd strictly forbidden), and when he returned, David stood aside silently and let him remove the empty platter and put the new one down.

That went quick, he said.

"Well, it should. It's really good. We had a tasting beforehand." The waiter looked up and smiled, and David smiled back. There was a pause.

I'm David, he said.

"James."

"Nice to meet you," they both said at the same time, and then laughed.

"So, is this a birthday party?" James asked.

No—no. It's for Peter—the guy in the wheelchair. He's—he's sick.

James nodded, and there was another silence. "This is a nice house," he said, and David nodded back. Yeah, it is, he said.

"Who owns it?"

Charles—the big blond guy? The one in the green sweater? *My boyfriend*, he should have said, but he didn't.

"Oh—oh yeah." James was still holding the platter, and now he rotated it in his hands and then looked up again and smiled. "And what about you?"

What about me? he asked, flirting back.

"What's your deal?"

I don't have a deal.

James gestured with his chin toward the living room. "One of them your boyfriend?"

He didn't say anything. Eighteen months after their first date, he still found himself occasionally surprised that he and Charles were a couple. It wasn't just that Charles was so much older than he was; it was that Charles wasn't the sort of man he had ever been attracted to—he was too blond, too rich, too white. He knew what they looked like together; he knew what people said. "Well, so what if they think you're trade?" Eden had asked when he confessed to her. "Trade are people, too." I know, I know, he said. But it's different. "Your problem," Eden said, "is that you can't accept that people just think of you as some brown-skinned nothing." And, indeed, it bothered him that people assumed that he was poor and uneducated and using Charles for his money. (Eden: "You *are* poor and uneducated. Besides, what do you care what these old fucks think about you?")

But what if, instead, he and this James were a couple, both of them young and poor and not-white together? What if he were with someone whom he could look at and see, if only superficially, himself? Was it Charles's wealth, or his age, or his race that made David feel so often helpless and inferior? Would he be more purposeful, less passive, if things between him and his boyfriend were more equitable? Would he feel like less of a traitor?

And yet he was being a traitor now, by not claiming Charles, by his guilt. Yes, he told James. Charles is. He's my boyfriend.

"Oh," said James, and David watched something—pity? disdain?— flicker across his face. "Too bad," he added, and he grinned and pushed open the double doors to the kitchen, disappearing with his platter, leaving David alone once more.

He grabbed his plate and left, feeling both an intense embarrassment and, less explicably, a kind of rage at Charles, for not being the sort of person he ought to be with, for making him feel ashamed. He knew this was unfair: He wanted Charles's protection, and he wanted to be free. Sometimes, when he and Charles were sitting in the study on a Saturday night they had chosen to stay in the city, watching a video of one of the black-and-white movies Charles loved from his youth, they would hear the sounds of a group of people on the sidewalk below them, passing beneath the house on their way to a club or bar or party. He would recognize them by their laughter, by the pitch of their voices—not who they were specifically but the kind of people they were, the tribe of the young and broke and futureless to which he himself had belonged until eighteen months ago. He sometimes felt like one of his ancestors, coaxed onto a ship and sent bobbing around the world, made to stand on plinths at medical colleges in Boston and London and Paris so that doctors and students could examine his elaborately tattooed skin, his necklace of twisted ropes of plaited human hair—Charles was his guide, his chaperone, but he was also his warden, and now that he had been taken from his people, he would never be allowed to return to them. The sensation was most profound on summer nights, when they kept the windows open, and at three a.m. he would be awoken by groups of passersby, singing drunkenly as they rounded the Square, their voices gradually disappearing among the trees. Then he would look at Charles in bed by his side, and feel a mix of pity and love and revulsion and irritation—dismay that he was with someone so different; gratitude that that someone was Charles. "Age is just a number," one of his more vapid friends had said, trying to be nice, but he was wrong— age was a different continent, and as long as he was with Charles, he would be moored there.

Not that he had anywhere else to be. His future was a vague, vaporous thing. He wasn't alone in this; so many of his friends and classmates were like him, drifting from home to their jobs and then home again before going out at night to bars or clubs or other people's apartments. They didn't have money, and who knew how long they would have life? Preparing to be thirty, much less forty or fifty, was like buying furniture for a house made of sand—who knew when it would be washed away, or when it would start disintegrating, falling apart in clots? It was far better to use what money you could make proving to yourself that you were still alive. He had one friend who, after his lover had died, had started gorging himself. Anything he had, he spent on food; David had gone out to dinner with Ezra once and had watched in horrified awe as he had eaten a bowl of wonton soup followed by a plate of wok-fried snow peas and water chestnuts followed by a dish of braised beef tongue followed by a whole Peking duck. He had eaten with a kind of steady, joyless determination, tracing his finger through the last streaks of sauce, stacking the empty plates atop one another as if they were completed paperwork. It had been repellent, but David had understood it as well: Food was real, food was proof of life, of how your body was still yours, of how it still could and still would respond to whatever you put inside it, of how it could be made to work. To be hungry was to be alive, and to be alive was to need food. Over the months, Ezra gained weight, at first slowly and then quickly, and now he was fat. But as long as he was fat, he wasn't sick, and no one would ever think he was: His cheeks were hot and pink; his lips and fingertips were often slicked with grease—wherever he went, he left evidence of his existence. Even his new grossness was a kind of shout, a defiance; he was a body that took up more space than was allowed, than was polite. He had made himself into a presence that couldn't be ignored. He had made himself undeniable.

But David's distance from his own life made less sense to him. He wasn't sick. He wasn't poor, and as long as he was with Charles, he never would be. And yet he was unable to imagine what he might be alive for. He had completed one year of law school before his finances had forced him to drop out and take the job as a paralegal at Larsson, Wesley three years ago, and Charles was always telling him he should reenroll. "Anywhere you want, the best place you can get in," he'd say. (David had been attending a state school beforehand; he knew Charles would expect better from him.) "I'll pay for all of it." When David demurred, Charles would be puzzled. "Why?" he'd ask. "You did a year—you clearly wanted to do it before. And you have a good mind for it. So why not continue?" He couldn't tell Charles that he hadn't actually had a particular passion for the law, that he didn't understand why he had applied for law school in the first place—except that it had seemed like something his father might have wanted for him, something that might have made his father proud. Going to law school fell into the vast category of being able to take care of himself, a virtue his father had always impressed upon him—a skill his father was never able to possess.

Do we have to talk about it? he'd ask Charles.

"No, we don't," Charles would say. "But I just don't like seeing someone as bright as you waste his time being a paralegal."

I like being a paralegal, he'd say. I'm not as ambitious as you want me to be, Charles.

Charles would sigh. "I don't want you to be anything but happy, David," Charles would say. "I just want to know what you want in life. When I was your age, I wanted everything. I wanted influence, and I wanted to argue in front of the Supreme Court, and I wanted to be respected. What do *you* want?"

I want to be here, he'd always say, with you, and Charles would sigh again but also smile, frustrated but also pleased. "David," he'd groan, and the argument, if that's what it was, would end.

And yet sometimes, on those summer nights, he thought he knew exactly what he wanted. He wanted to be somewhere between where he was, in a bed dressed in expensive cotton sheets next to the man he had grown to love, and on the street, skirting the edge of the park, squealing and clinging to his friends when a rat darted from the shadows inches from his feet, drunk and wild and hopeless, his life burning away, with no one to have dreams for him, not even himself.

———

In the living room, two of the waitstaff were circulating, refilling water glasses, removing empty plates; Adams was delivering drinks. There was a bartender among the catering crew, but David knew that she was being held hostage in the kitchen, her attempts to help rebuffed by Adams, who liked to make the drinks himself and would allow no one to disrupt his methods. And so, for every party, Charles would remind the party planner to instruct the caterer not to bring a bartender, and every time, the caterer would bring someone along "just in case," and every time, he would be consigned to the kitchen and not allowed to do his job.

From his position beside the staircase, he watched as James entered the room, watched the other guests watch him, watched them register his ass, his eyes, his smile. Now that David wasn't in the room, he was the only nonwhite person there. James bent over the Three Sisters and said something that David couldn't hear but that made them all laugh, before straightening and leaving with a stack of plates. A few minutes later, he returned with clean plates and the platter of pasta, which he offered around the room, balancing the dish atop the palm of his right hand while holding his left hand in a fist behind his back.

What if he were to say James's name as James exited the room? James would look about, surprised, and then see him and smile and come to him, and David would take his hand and lead him to the slant-ceilinged closet beneath the staircase, where Adams stored the house's supply of mothballs and candles and the burlap bags of cedar chips that he tucked between Charles's sweaters when he was packing them up for the summer, and which Charles liked to toss into the fireplace to make the smoke more fragrant. The space was just high enough to stand in, and just deep enough for one person to kneel in; he could already feel James's skin beneath his fingers, already hear the sounds they'd both make. And then James would leave, returning to his duties, and David would wait, counting to two hundred, before he too left, running upstairs to his and Charles's bathroom to rinse out his mouth before returning to the living room, where James would already be offering people another helping of steak or chicken, and sitting down next to Charles. For the rest of the evening, they would try not to look at each other too much, but with every rotation through the room, James would glance at him, and he would glance back, and when the catering crew was cleaning up, he would tell Charles that he thought he'd forgotten his book and would slip downstairs before Charles could respond, where he would find James just as he was putting on his coat, press into his palm a piece of paper with his telephone number at work, tell him to call. For weeks, maybe months, thereafter they would meet, always at James's, and then, one day, James would start dating someone or move away or simply grow bored, and David would never hear from him again. He could see and feel and taste it so vividly that it was as if it had already happened and he was reliving a memory, but when James finally did come into view, walking back to the kitchen, he made himself hide, turning his face to the wall to keep from the temptation of speaking.

This constant desire! Was it the fact that it was dangerous to have sex the way he used to, or that he and Charles were monogamous, or was he just restless? "You're young," Charles had said, laughing, unoffended, when he had told him. "It's normal. You'll grow out of it in the next sixty years or so." But he wasn't sure it was that, or perhaps not only that. He just wanted more life. He didn't know what he would do with it, but he wanted it—and not just his own but everyone's. More and more and more, until he had stuffed himself with it.

He thought, inevitably, of his father, of what his father had craved. Love, he supposed, affection. But nothing else. Food did not interest him, or sex, or travel, or cars or clothes or houses. One Christmas—the year before they left for Lipo-wao-nahele, which means he would have been nine—they had been assigned at school to find out what their parents wanted for the holiday, and then they would make that thing in art class. Of course, what their parents really wanted they couldn't make, but other children's mothers and fathers seemed to understand that, and had answered with something plausible. "I've always wanted a nice drawing of you," someone's mother said, or "I'd love a new picture frame." But David's father had only taken his hand. "I have you," his father said. "I don't need anything else." But you must want *something*, he had insisted, frustrated, and his father had shaken his head. "No," he repeated. "You're my greatest treasure. If I have you, I don't need anything else." Finally, David had had to explain his dilemma to his grandmother, who had stood and marched over to where his father lay on the porch, reading the paper and waiting for Edward, and snapped at him, "Wika! Your son is going to fail his school assignment unless you tell him something he can make for you!"

In the end, he had made his father a clay ornament, which was fired in the school's kiln. It was a lumpy thing, only half glazed, in the shape of what was meant to be a star, with his father's name— their name—scratched into its surface, but his father had loved it and had hung it above his bed (they hadn't bought a tree that year), hammering the nail in himself. He remembered how his father had almost cried, and how he had been embarrassed for him, for his happiness over something so stupid and ugly and inexpert, something he had made hastily, in just a few minutes, eager to go outside to play with his friends.

Or, perhaps, this constant yearning for sex was Charles's fault. He had not been attracted to Charles when they met—his flirting had been automatic, rather than from any genuine feeling—and when he had accepted his invitation for dinner, it was out of curiosity, not desire. But midway through the meal, something had shifted, and the second time they met, at Charles's house the following day, their encounter had been feverish and almost wordless.

Yet, despite their mutual attraction, they delayed actually having sex for weeks, because they both wanted to avoid the conversation they would first need to have, the conversation that was written on the faces of so many people they knew.

Finally, he had brought it up himself. Listen, he'd said, I don't have it, and he had watched Charles's face sag.

"Thank god," he had said. He had waited for Charles to say that he didn't have it, either, but he didn't. "Nobody knows," he said. "But you should. But aside from Olivier—my ex—no one else does: Just my doctor, him, me, and now you. Oh, and Adams, of course. But no one at work. They can't."

He had been momentarily speechless, but Charles had spoken into his silence. "I'm very healthy," he said. "I have the drugs, I tolerate them well." He paused. "No one has to know."

He had been surprised, and then surprised at his surprise. He had made out with and even dated men with the illness, but Charles seemed the antithesis of the disease, a person in whom it would dare not reside. He knew that was silly, but it was also how he felt. After they became a couple, Charles's friends would ask him—half teasing, half serious—what on earth he had seen in their old, *old* friend ("Fuck you," Charles would say, grinning), and David would say that it was Charles's confidence ("Note that he didn't say your looks, Charlie," Peter would say). And while that was true, it wasn't only what attracted him, or rather not just; it was Charles's ability to project a certain indestructibility, his radical conviction that anything was solvable, that anything could be fixed as long as you had the right money and connections and mind. No less than death would have to yield to Charles, or so it seemed. It was a quality he would have for the rest of his life, and the thing David would miss the most about him when he was gone.

And it was that same quality that allowed David to forget—not always, but for periods of time—that Charles was infected at all. He saw him take his medication, he knew that he saw his doctor at lunchtime on the first Monday of every month, but for hours, days, weeks, he was able to pretend that Charles's life, and his life with him, would go on and on, a roll of parchment unscrolling down a long grassy path. He was able to tease Charles about how much time he spent in front of the mirror, the way he patted creams on his face before they went to bed, flexing his mouth into different grimaces, the way he would examine his reflection after getting out of the shower, holding his towel in place around his waist with one hand as he twisted his neck to examine his back, the way he would bare his teeth, tapping at his gums with his fingernail. Charles's self-scrutiny was the result of middle-aged vanity and insecurity, yes, the kind that was exacerbated by David's presence, by his youth, but it was also, David knew—knew, but tried to ignore—an expression of Charles's fear: Was he losing weight? Were his fingernails discoloring? Were his cheeks hollowing? Had he sprouted a lesion? When would the illness write itself on his body? When would the drugs that had so far kept the illness away do the same? When would he become a citizen in the land of the sick? Pretending was foolish, and yet they both did it, except when it was perilous to do so; Charles pretended and David let him. Or was it that David pretended and Charles let him? Either way, the outcome was the same: They rarely discussed the disease; they never even said its name.

But though Charles refused to claim the disease for himself, he never denied it in his friends. Percival, Timothy, Teddy, Norris: Charles gave them money, he arranged appointments with his doctor, he hired cooks and housekeepers and nurses who would dare, would deign, to help them. He had even moved Teddy, who had died shortly before David had begun seeing Charles, into the study next to his bedroom, and it was there, surrounded by Charles's collection of botanical prints, that Teddy had spent his final months. When Teddy had died, it had been Charles, along with Teddy's other friends, who had found a sympathetic priest, who had arranged the wake, who had divided Teddy's ashes among them. The next day, he had gone to work. Work was one realm, and outside of work was another, and he seemed to accept that the two would never overlap, that his friend's death would never be an adequate excuse for coming in late or for not coming in at all. His grief, like his love, was something he would never expect anyone at Larsson, Wesley to understand or share. He was exhausted, David would later understand, but he never complained about it, because exhaustion was a privilege of the living.

And here, too, David felt ashamed, ashamed because he was frightened, because he was repulsed. He didn't want to look at Timothy's shrunken face; he didn't want to confront Peter's wrists, grown so bony that he had exchanged his metal watch for a child's plastic one, which even so slid down his arm like a bangle. He had had friends who had gotten sick, but he had shrunk from them, blowing them kisses goodbye instead of kissing them on the cheek, crossing the street to avoid talking to them, dawdling outside buildings he used to dash into, standing in corners when Eden went to hug them, skirting out of rooms that were desperate for visitors. Wasn't it enough that he was twenty-five and had to live like this? Wasn't that courage enough? How could he be expected to do more, to be more?

His behavior, his cowardice—they had been the source of his and Eden's first big fight. "You're such an asshole," Eden had hissed at him when she found him downstairs, sitting on one of their friends' stoops, waiting for her in the cold for thirty minutes. He hadn't been able to take it—the smells of the room, its closeness, the fear and resignation. "How would you feel, David?" she'd yelled at him, and, when he admitted he was scared, she'd snorted. "You're *scared*," she said. "*You're* scared? God, David, I hope you grow a fucking pair by the time I die." And he had: By the time Eden herself was dying, twenty-two years later, it was he who sat by her side, night after night, for months; it was he who picked her up from her chemotherapy appointments; it was he who held her that final day, he who stroked her back as the skin turned cold and smooth. In the way that people decided they would become healthier, he had decided to become better, braver, and when Eden finally died, he had sobbed, both because she had left him but also because no one had been prouder of him, no one had seen how hard he had worked at not running away. She had been the final witness of the person he had been, and now she was gone, and her memory of his transformation was gone with her.

Decades later, when Charles was long dead and David was an old man himself, his husband, who was much younger than he was—history repeating itself, but inverted—would have a curious nostalgia for these years, and a curious wonder for the disease, which he insisted on calling "the plague." "Didn't you just feel that everything was falling to pieces around you?" he'd ask, ready to be outraged on David's and his friends' behalf, ready to offer him sympathy and solace, and David, who had by then lived with the disease for almost as long as his husband had been alive, would say he hadn't. Maybe Charles did, he said, but I didn't. The year I started having sex was the year the disease was given a name—I never knew sex, or adulthood, without it. "But how could you even function when it killed so many? Didn't it feel impossible?" his husband would ask, and David would struggle to articulate what he wanted Aubrey to understand. Yes, he'd say slowly, it sometimes did. But we all functioned; we all had to. We went to funerals and to hospitals, but we also went to work and to parties and to gallery shows and ran errands and had sex and dated and were young and stupid. We helped each other, it's true, we loved each other, but we also gossiped about people and made fun of them and got into fights and were shitty friends and boyfriends, sometimes. We did both—we did it all. He didn't say that it was only years later that he came to an understanding of how extraordinary that period had been, of how numerous its terrors, of how strange that some of what he remembered most clearly were the mundanities, stray details, little things significant to no one but himself: not the hospital rooms or faces but the evening he and Eden decided they were going to stay up until dawn, drinking cup after cup of coffee until they were so punchy they lost the ability to speak, or the gray-and-white cat that lived in the little flower shop he used to visit on Horatio and Eighth Avenue, or the kind of bagels that Nathaniel, the man he had lived with and loved after Charles, liked to eat: poppy seed, with a smoked-salmon-and-chive spread. (He had named his and Aubrey's son after Nathaniel—the first firstborn male Bingham in generations not to be called David.) It was also not until years later that he came to realize how much he had simply accepted as fact, when, really, he should never have accepted it at all—that he should have spent his twenties going to memorial services instead of plotting his own future; that his fantasies never extended beyond the year. He had, he was able to see, drifted through that decade, moving through it with the cool detachment of a sleepwalker—to have awakened would have been to be overwhelmed with all he had seen and withstood. Others had been able to do this, but he had not; he had sought to cosset himself, to invent a place of safety, one in which the outside world was unable to fully intrude. Theirs had been a generational suspension—some had found solace in anger, and others in silence. His friends marched and protested and shouted against the government and the pharmaceutical companies; they volunteered, they submerged themselves into the horror that surrounded them. But he did nothing, as if doing nothing meant that nothing would be done to him; it was a noisy time, but he had chosen quiet instead, and although he had been ashamed of his passivity, of his fear, not even shame had been enough to motivate him to seek a greater engagement with the world around him. He wanted protection. He wanted to be removed. He sought, he knew, what his father might also have sought in Lipo-wao-nahele. And like his father, he had chosen incorrectly—he had attempted not to reckon with his own anger but to hide from it. But hiding hadn't stopped things from happening. The only thing it prevented was eventually being found.

———

Now it was nine p.m., and the dishes on the dining-room table had been removed and replaced with desserts, and once again, everyone roused themselves to cut slices of pine-nut tart and polenta cake, its surface glazed with candied rounds of orange, and a double-chocolate cake made from a recipe invented by Charles's grand-mother's cook, and which he served at every dinner he hosted. Once again, David followed the guests into the dining room to fix plates for Peter and Charles.

When he returned, James was setting a platter of dried apricots and figs and salted almonds and shards of dark chocolate on the cof-fee table near the sofa where Charles and Peter still sat, and David watched the two men watch James, their faces alert but unreadable. "*Thank* you, young man," Peter said, as James straightened.

He avoided looking at James as they passed each other in the entryway, James's left arm brushing against his right one, and set Peter's plate at his side, and handed Charles his, Charles grabbing his hand as he did. Next to them, Peter watched, his expression still unreadable.

He had met all of Charles's other close friends before Peter, and the combination of Charles's apparent reluctance to introduce them and his frequent invocation of Peter's name and opinions—"Peter saw that new production at the Signature already and says it's gar-bage"; "I want to stop by Three Lives and buy this biography that Peter recommended"; "Peter said we must go to the Adrian Piper show at Paula Cooper as soon as it opens"—made him nervous. By the time they met, three months into his and Charles's relationship, his nervousness had hardened into anxiety, which was compounded by Charles's own. "I hope the food's okay," Charles fretted, as David hunted for one of his socks, only to realize it was on the bed, where he'd left it five minutes earlier. "Peter's a very picky eater. And he has excellent taste, so if it's not good enough, he'll say something." ("Peter sounds like an asshole," Eden had said when David had told her about him, or at least the secondhand Peter he knew, and David had to now stop himself from echoing her aloud.)

He was both fascinated and alarmed by this version of Charles, so flustered and discombobulated. It was something of a relief to see that even Charles could feel inadequate; on the other hand, they couldn't *both* begin the evening feeling this insecure—he was counting on Charles to be his defender. Why are you so nervous? he asked Charles. This is your oldest friend.

"It's *because* he's my oldest friend that I'm nervous," said Charles, stroking his razor beneath his chin. "Don't you have a friend whose opinion matters more to you than anyone's?"

No, he said, though he thought of Eden as he did.

"Well, you will someday," said Charles. "Damnit." He had nicked himself, and he grabbed a square of toilet paper and held it against his skin. "If you're lucky, that is. You should always have a close friend you're slightly afraid of."

Why?

"Because it means that you'll have someone in your life who really challenges you, who forces you to become better in some way, in whatever way you're most scared of: Their approval is what'll hold you accountable."

But was that really true? He thought of his father, who definitely had been afraid of Edward. He had wanted Edward's approval, that was true; and Edward had challenged him, that was also true. But Edward hadn't wanted his father to become *better*—not smarter or more educated or more independent-minded. He had simply wanted his father to—what? Agree with him; obey him; keep him company. He had pretended that such obedience was in the service of a greater mission, but it hadn't been—it had been about finding someone who might finally look up to him, which is all anyone seemed to want. The kind of friend Charles was describing was someone who wanted you to become more yourself. But Edward had wanted the opposite for David's father. He had wanted to reduce him into something that didn't think at all.

Well, he said, but isn't your friend supposed to be nice to you?

"That's what I have you for," Charles said, smiling at him in the mirror.

When he finally did meet Peter, he was surprised by how mesmerizingly ugly he was. It wasn't that any one feature was so disagreeable—he had large, light-colored eyes, like a dog's, and a bony, confident nose, and long dark eyebrows that seemed to have grown as a single unit rather than as a collection of individual hairs—but the combination was unharmonious, if compellingly so. It was as if every aspect of his face was determined to be a soloist, rather than a member of an ensemble.

"Peter," Charles said, hugging him.

"Charlie," Peter replied.

For the first part of dinner, Peter talked. He was someone, it seemed, who had a strong and informed opinion on virtually any topic, and his soliloquy, fueled by small comments and questions from Charles, went from the repointing work on Peter's building to the revival of certain nearly extinct squash varietals to the flaws of a highly acclaimed recent novel to the charms of an obscure, newly republished collection of brief essays by a fourteenth-century Japanese monk to the connections between anti-modernists and anti-Semites to why he would no longer holiday in Hydra but, rather, in Rhodes. David was ignorant about all of these subjects, yet through his mounting unease, he found himself intrigued by Peter. Not so much by what he said—he was unable to follow most of it—but by how he said it: He had a lovely, deep voice, and he spoke as if he enjoyed the feel of the words coming off his tongue, as if he were saying them only because he liked the sensation of doing so.

"So, David," said Peter, turning to him as David knew he must. "Charles has already told me how you met. But tell me about yourself."

There's really not much to tell, he began, looking briefly at Charles, who gave him an encouraging smile. He recited the facts that Charles already knew, as Peter stared at him with his pale, wolfish eyes. He had expected Peter to be interrogatory, to start asking him the questions everyone always did—So your father never worked, ever? *Never?* You didn't know your mother? Not even a little?—but he had only nodded, and then said nothing.

I'm boring, he'd concluded, apologetically, and Peter had nodded, slowly and gravely, as if David had said something profound. "Yes," he said. "You are. But you're young. You're supposed to be boring." He had been uncertain how to interpret this, but Charles had only smiled. "Does that mean *you* were boring when you were twenty-five, Peter?" he asked, teasingly, and Peter had nodded again. "Of course I was, and you too, Charles."

"So when did we start becoming interesting?"

"That's a big assumption to make, isn't it? But I'd say in the last ten years."

"That recently?"

"I'm just talking about myself now," Peter said, and Charles laughed. "Bitch," he said, fondly.

"I think that went well," Charles had said that night in bed, and David had agreed, though he actually didn't. Since that night, he had had to see Peter on only a few more occasions, and each time, there would be a pause in the conversation in which Peter would turn his large head in David's direction and ask, "So what's happened to you since I saw you last, young man?," as if life was something that David wasn't experiencing but was, rather, having bestowed upon him. And then Peter had gotten sicker, and David had seen him even less, and after tonight, he would never see him again. Charles had said that Peter was dying a disappointed man: He was a renowned poet, but for the past three decades he had been writing a novel, yet it had never found a publisher. "He had assumed it would be his legacy," Charles said.

He couldn't completely understand Charles's and his friends' interest in their legacy. Sometimes at these parties, talk would turn to how they might be remembered when they died, to the things they would leave behind. Sometimes their tone would be content, or defiant, or, more often, plaintive; it wasn't only that some of them didn't feel they were leaving enough but that what they were leaving was too complicated, too compromised. Who would remember them, and what would they remember? Would their children think of how they had had tea parties with them, or read to them, or taught them how to catch a ball? Or would they instead recall how they had left their mothers, how they had moved out of their houses in Connecticut and into apartments in the city that were never comfortable enough for children, no matter how hard they tried? Would their lovers think of them when they were so bright with health that they could walk down the street and men would literally turn around to look at them, or would they think of them as they were today, as old men who weren't even old, from whose faces and bodies people shied? The knowledge and recognition of who they were in life had been hard-won, but they wouldn't be able to control who they became in death.

And yet who cared? The dead knew nothing, felt nothing, were nothing. When he told Eden of Charles's and his friends' concerns, she had said that it was a very white male fixation to be concerned with legacy. How do you mean? he'd asked. "Only people who have a plausible hope of being immortalized in history are so obsessed about how they might get immortalized," she said. "The rest of us are too busy trying to get through the day." At the time, he'd laughed and called her melodramatic, and a reactionary man-hater, but that night, as he lay in bed, he had thought about what she said and wondered if she was correct. "If I had had a child," Charles occasionally said, "I'd feel like I was leaving something behind—like I had left my mark on the world." He knew what Charles meant by this, but he was also puzzled by his inability to see the assumptions inherent in that statement: How did having a child guarantee anything? What if your child didn't like you? What if your child didn't care about you? What if your child became a terrible adult, an association you were ashamed of? Then what? A person was the worst legacy, because a person was by definition unpredictable.

His grandmother had known this. When he was very young, he had asked his grandmother why he was called Kawika if his real name was David. All of the firstborn males in their family were named David, and yet all of them were known as Kawika, the Hawaiianization of David. If we're all called Kawika, why is our name David? he had wondered aloud to her, and his father—they had been at the dinner table—had made that little chirping noise he did when he was fearful or worried.

But there had been nothing to be frightened of, for his grandmother had not only not been angry, she had even smiled a bit. "Because," she said, "the king was named David." The king, their ancestor: He knew that much.

That night, his father had come to see him before he went to sleep. "Don't ask your grandmother questions like that," he'd said. Why? he had asked: She hadn't been mad. "Not with you," his father said. "But later, with me—she asked me why I wasn't teaching you these things better." His father had looked so upset that he had promised, and apologized, and his father had exhaled in relief and leaned over and kissed him on his forehead. "Thank you," he said. "Good night, Kawika."

He hadn't the words for it, he was too young, but he knew even then that his grandmother was ashamed of his father. In May, when they went to her society's annual party, it would be David who would walk into the palace with his grandmother, David whom his grandmother would introduce to her friends, beaming as they kissed him on the cheek and told him how handsome he looked. Somewhere behind them, he knew, would be his father, smiling at the ground, not expecting recognition and not receiving any, either. After the guests had moved outdoors for dinner on the palace grounds, David would sneak back into the building and find his father still in the throne room, sitting half shrouded by silk curtains in one of the window bays, looking out at the torchlit lawn.

Da, he'd say. Come join the party.

"No, Kawika," his father would say. "You go, have fun. I'm not wanted there."

But he would insist, and finally his father would say, "I'll only go if you come with me." Of course, he'd say, and hold out his hand, which his father would take, and they'd walk outside together toward the party, which had continued without them.

His father had been his grandmother's first disappointed legacy; David knew he was her second. When he had left Hawai'i for what he knew would be forever, he had gone to tell her—not because he wanted her approval (he had told himself at the time that he didn't care either way), and not because he expected her to argue with him, but because he wanted to ask her to take care of his father, to protect him. He knew that, by leaving, he would be forsaking his birthright as well—the land, the money, his trust. But it seemed a small sacrifice, small and theoretical, because none of it had ever been his to begin with. It had belonged not to him specifically but to the person who happened to possess his name, and he would renounce that as well.

By then he had been living for two years on the Big Island. Back he had gone to the house on Oʻahu Avenue, where he had found his grandmother in the sunroom, sitting in her cane-backed chair, gripping the ends of its arms with her long, strong fingers. He had spoken, and she was silent, and at the end, she had finally looked at him, once, before turning away again. "You're a disappointment," she said. "You and your father, both. After all I did for you, Kawika. After all that I did."

My name's not Kawika anymore, he said. It's David. And then he had turned and fled before his grandmother could say anything else: *You don't deserve to be called Kawika. You don't deserve that name.*

Months later, he would think of this conversation and cry, because there had been a time—years—when he was his grandmother's pride, when she would have him sit next to her on the love seat, pressed against her side. "I'm not afraid of death," she'd say, "and do you know why, Kawika?"

No, he'd say.

"Because I know I'll live on in you. My purpose—my life—will live on in you, my pride and joy. My story, and our history, lives in you."

But it hadn't, or at least not in the way she'd intended. He had failed her in so many ways. He had left her, he had rejected his home, his faith, his name. He was living in New York with a man, with a white man. He never spoke of his family, or his ancestors. He never chanted the songs he had been taught to chant, he never danced the stories he had been taught to dance, he never recited the history he had been taught to revere. She had assumed that she would be preserved in him—and not just her but his grandfather and his grandfather's grandfather. He had always told himself that he had chosen to betray her because she hadn't loved his father well enough, but lately, he had been wondering whether his betrayal was deliberate or whether it was attributable to something deficient within him, some fundamental coldness. He knew how happy Charles would be if, after one of their conversations, David would promise Charles that *he* would be Charles's legacy, that Charles would always live on in him. He knew how moved Charles would be if he did. And yet he never could. Not because it wasn't true—he *would* love Charles, he would tell all his future lovers, his future husband, his future son, his future colleagues and friends, about Charles for decades after his death: the lessons he had learned from him, the places they had visited together, the way he smelled, how brave and generous he had been, the way he had taught him to eat marrow, escargot, and artichokes, how sexy he had been, how they had met, how they had parted—but because he had had enough of being someone's legacy; he knew the fear of feeling inadequate, the burden of disappointing. He would never do it again; he would be free. What he wouldn't know until he was much older was that no one was ever free, that to know someone and to love them was to assume the task of remembering them, even if that person was still living. No one could escape that duty, and as you aged, you grew to crave that responsibility even as you sometimes resented it, that knowledge that your life was inextricable from another's, that a person marked their existence in part by their association with you.

Now, standing beside Charles, he took a breath. He would have to speak to Peter at some point; he would have to tell him goodbye. He had thought for weeks about what he might say, but anything he deemed meaningful he knew Peter would find trite, and anything pleasant and uncontroversial seemed like a waste of time. He had something that Peter did not—life, the promise and expectation of years—and yet he remained intimidated by him. Do it now, he told himself. Talk to him now, while the room's still empty and no one will be listening to you.

But when he finally sat down on Charles's left, Charles and Peter didn't pause in their low, murmured conversation, and so he instead leaned against Charles, who took his hand again and squeezed it, before turning to him and smiling. "I feel like I haven't seen you all night," he said.

The night is young; and so am I, he said, an old joke of theirs, and Charles put his hand on the back of David's head and brought his face close. "Will you help me?" he asked.

He had been warned beforehand that Charles would need his assistance with Peter, and so he stood and helped Peter into his chair before pushing him out of the room and down the hallway to the left, past the slant-ceilinged closet, to the little bathroom wedged beneath the stairs. This bathroom, Charles had told him, was legendary: At earlier parties, in earlier years, when Charles was younger and wilder, it was to here that people would sneak away, in twos and threes in the midst of dinners and late-night gatherings, with everyone else sitting in the dining room or living room and making jokes about the disappeared, greeting them upon their return with hoots and laughter. Did you ever go in there with anyone? he had asked, and Charles had grinned. "Of course I did," he said. "What do you think? I'm a red-blooded American male." Adams called this bathroom the powder room, which he intended to be decorous, but which Charles's friends had found hilarious.

Now, though, the powder room was only what it was—a bathroom—and these days, there were two people inside of it only because one was helping the other use the toilet. David helped Charles help Peter stand (for, as thin as he was, he was, curiously, heavier than he appeared, his legs almost useless beneath him), and once Charles had his arms wrapped around Peter's chest, he nodded at them and closed the door and stood outside, trying not to listen to the sounds Peter was making. He was always perplexed and impressed by how much waste the body was able to create until the very end, even when it was given little to digest. On and on it went, the enjoyable things—eating, fucking, drinking, dancing, walking—falling away one by one, until all you were left with were the undignified motions and movements, the essence of what the body was: shitting and peeing and crying and bleeding, the body draining itself of liquids, like a river determined to run itself dry.

There was the noise of the tap turning on, and hands being washed, and then Charles calling his name. He opened the door and maneuvered the chair into position and then helped lower Peter into it, replacing the pillow behind his back. David had been avoiding Peter's eyes, certain that Peter resented his presence, but as he straightened, Peter looked up, and the two of them looked at each other. It was a brief exchange, so brief that Charles, arranging Peter's sweater around him, didn't even notice, but after they returned Peter to the living room—now filled once more with their guests, the air scented with sugar and chocolate and the coffee Adams was pouring into cups—David again pressed himself against Charles's side, feeling childish but also in need of protection from the anger, the fury, the terrible *want* he had seen in Peter's face. It was not, David knew, directed at him specifically but, rather, at what he represented: He was alive, and when this night was over, he would climb two flights upstairs and maybe he and Charles would have sex and maybe they wouldn't, and the next day he would wake and choose what he wanted for breakfast, and what he wanted to do that day—he would go to the bookstore, or to the movies, or to lunch, or to a museum, or simply take a walk. And in that day he would make hundreds of choices, so many he would lose count, so many he would forget to notice he was doing it, and with every choice he would be asserting his presence, his place in the world. And with every choice he made, Peter would be receding further from life, further from his memory, would be becoming a matter of history with each minute, each hour, one day to be forgotten altogether: a legacy of nothing; a memory of no one.

———

For most of the night, Peter's guests had been circling about him rather than engaging him directly. Sometimes someone near him would turn to him in the course of conversation with someone else— "Do you remember that night, Peter?"; "That guy, Peter, what was his name? You know, the one we met in Palm Springs"; "Peter, we're talking about that trip we went on in seventy-eight"—but mostly, they talked only with one another, leaving Peter to sit there on the far end of the sofa, Charles at his side. They were all scared of Peter, David had long since realized, and now they were especially scared of him, because this was the last time they would see him and the pressure to say goodbye to him was so great that they were ignoring him instead. Peter, however, seemed content with his position. There was something majestic about his calm, the way he moved his gaze over his friends, all gathered there for him, occasionally nodding at something Charles said to him, like a massive old dog that sits by his master's side and surveys the room, knowing that there would be no threats to his owner's safety that night.

But now, suddenly, as if commanded by a call only they could hear, people began approaching Peter, one by one, bending and talking into his ear. John was among the first, and David nudged Charles, who made to stand, to leave and give Peter some privacy, but Peter placed his hand on Charles's leg and Charles sat back down. And so, instead, he and David stayed, watching as John returned to his place in the chair on the other side of the room, and was replaced by Percival, and then Timothy, and then Norris and Julien and Christopher, who all in turn took Peter's hands in their own and bent or knelt or sat beside him and spoke softly to him, having their final conversations. David was unable to hear most, or even all, of what they said, but he and Charles remained still, as if Peter were the emperor and these his ministers, come to deliver bits of news from across the realm, and they were servants, never meant to hear any of it and yet unable to flee back to the kitchen where they belonged.

Of course, what Peter's friends had to say wasn't confidential at all but banalities delivered with the intimacy of a secret. They spoke as if Peter were ancient, and his memory long gone. "I *do* remember, you know," Peter would normally say, as he always did when someone prefaced a story with "Do you remember?" "I'm not *that* far gone." But in this moment he seemed to have acquired a new kind of grace, one that manifested itself as patience, and he allowed each person to hold him against them, talking at him without seeming to need a response. He had not thought Peter would be interested in, much less capable of, being good at dying, but there he sat, generous and stately, listening to his friends, smiling at various moments, nodding his head and letting his hand be held:

"Do you remember that summer ten years ago when we took that tumbledown house in the Pines, Peter, and how one morning you went downstairs and there was that deer standing in the middle of the living room, eating the nectarines that Christopher had left on the counter?"

"I've always felt bad about that time we fought—you know what I'm talking about. I've always regretted it; I always wanted to take it back. I'm so sorry, Peter. Please tell me you forgive me."

"Peter, I don't know how I'm going to do this—all this—without you. I know it wasn't always easy between us, but I'm going to miss you. You taught me so much—I just want to thank you."

He had come to realize that it was when you were dying that people most wanted things from you—they wanted you to remember, they wanted reassurance, they wanted forgiveness. They wanted acknowledgment and redemption; they wanted you to make them feel better—about the fact that you were leaving while they remained; about the fact that they hated you for leaving them and dreaded it, too; about the fact that your death was reminding them of their own inevitable one; about the fact that they were so uncomfortable that they didn't know what to say. Dying meant repeating the same things again and again, much as Peter was doing now: *Yes, I remember. No, I'll be fine. No, you'll be fine. Yes, of course I forgive you. No, you shouldn't feel guilty. No, I'm not in any pain. No, I know what you're trying to say. Yes, I love you, too, I love you, too, I love you, too.*

He listened to all of this, still pressed against Charles's side, Charles's left arm around him, his right arm around Peter's shoulders. He had burrowed his face into Charles's rib cage, like a child, so he could listen to Charles's slow, steady breaths, so he could feel the heat of his body against his cheek. Charles's left hand was tucked beneath his left arm, and now David reached up his hand and laced his fingers through Charles's. The two of them were unnecessary to this part of the evening, but if you were observing them from above, the three of them would have appeared to be a single organism, a twelve-limbed, three-headed creature, one head nodding and listening, the other two silent and immobile, the three of them kept alive by a single, enormous heart, one that steadily, uncomplainingly beat in Charles's chest, sending bright, clean blood through the yards of arteries that connected all three of their forms, filling them with life.

––––––––

It was still early, but people were already preparing to leave. "He's tired," they said of Peter to one another, and, to him, "Are you tired?," to which Peter replied, time after time, "Yes, a little," until a certain weariness entered his voice, one that could have been from his patience finally depleting or from genuine fatigue. He spent most of his days sleeping, he had told Charles, and in the evenings he would doze until midnight and then wake and "take care of things."

Like what? he had asked at a lunch about six months ago, shortly after Peter had decided on his Switzerland plan.

"Gathering my papers. Burning letters I don't want getting into the wrong hands. Finalizing the gift list appended to my will—deciding who gets what. Making a list of people I want to say good-bye to. Making a list of people I don't want invited to my funeral. I had no idea how much of dying involves list-making: You make lists of people you like and people you hate. You make lists of people you want to say thanks to, and people you want to ask forgiveness from. You make lists of people you want to see and people you don't. You make lists of songs you want played at your memorial service, and poems you might want read, and who you might want to invite.

"Of course, this is if you've been lucky enough to keep your mind. Though lately I've been wondering if it's so lucky at all, being so conscious, being so aware that, from now on, you'll never progress. You'll never become *more* educated or learned or interesting than you are right now—everything you do, and experience, from the moment you begin actively dying is useless, a futile attempt to change the end of the story. And yet you keep trying to do it anyway—read what you haven't read and see what you haven't seen. But it isn't *for* anything, you see. You just do it out of practice—because that's what a human does."

But does it have to be *for* anything? he had asked, tentatively. He

was always nervous about addressing Peter directly, but he hadn't
been able to stop himself—he had been thinking about his father.

"No, of course not. But we've been taught that it must, that experience, that learning, is a pathway to salvation; that it's the point of
life. But it isn't. The ignorant person dies the same way as the educated one. It makes no difference in the end."

"Well, but what about pleasure?" Charles had asked. "That's a
reason to do it."

"Certainly, pleasure. But pleasure doesn't change anything, really.
Not that one should do or not do things because they make no difference in the end."

Are you scared? he had asked.

Peter had been quiet, and David had worried he had been rude.
But then Peter spoke. "I'm not scared because I'm worried it's going
to hurt," he said, slowly, and when he looked up, his large, light
eyes looked even larger and lighter than usual. "I'm scared because
I know my last thoughts are going to be about how much time I
wasted—how much life I wasted. I'm scared because I'm going to
die not being proud of how I lived."

There had been a silence after that, and then the conversation
had somehow changed. He wondered if Peter still felt that way; he
wondered if he was thinking even now that he had wasted his life.
He wondered if that was why Peter had tried chemotherapy after all,
if he had decided he was going to try once more, if he was hoping
he could change his mind, hoping he could feel differently. David
hoped he *did* feel differently; he hoped Peter didn't still feel as he
had. It was an impossible thing to ask—*Do you still feel you've wasted
your life?*—and so he didn't, though later he would wish he had been
able to find a way to do so. He thought, as he always did, of his
father, of how he had willed his life away—or was it that he had
willed himself away from it? It was his sole act of disobedience, and
David hated him for it.

In the living room, the Three Sisters were putting on their coats,
winding scarves around their throats, kissing Peter and then Charles
goodbye. "You'll be okay?" he heard Charles ask Percival. "I'll see

you next week, all right?" And Percival's response: "Yes, I'm fine. Thanks, Charlie—for everything." David was always moved by this side of Charles: his motherliness, his care. He had a sudden vision of one of the mothers in the picture books he and his father used to read together, babushkaed and aproned and pleasantly fat and living in a stone house in some unnamed village in some unnamed European country, slipping into her children's pockets pebbles that she had heated in the oven so their fingers would stay warm on their walk to school.

He knew Charles had asked Adams to instruct the caterers to pack up all the leftover food so any of their guests could take some, though he knew Charles meant for the majority of it to go to John and Timothy. In the kitchen, he found some of the waitstaff placing the last of the cookies and cakes into cardboard containers, and the containers into paper bags, and others hefting large crates of dirty dishes out to their van, which was parked behind the house, in the courtyard that had once separated the main building from the carriage house, which was now a garage. James, he was disappointed and relieved to discover, was nowhere in sight, and for a moment he watched, mesmerized, at the tenderness with which one young woman lowered the remaining quarter of the cheesecake into a plastic tub, settling it as if it were a baby she was tucking into its cradle.

The only thing not put away was the misshapen brick of dark chocolate, scarred and dusty in parts like an oversize car battery. This, like the double-chocolate cake, was a signature of Charles's parties, and the first time David had seen it, seen how one of the waiters had taken an awl and stuck it in its side, tapping it with a small hammer as another waiter held aloft a plate to catch the splinters that fell from it, he was enraptured. It seemed both improbable and ridiculous that people should order a cube of chocolate so big that they had to actually carve it with a hammer and chisel until its sides appeared to have been gnawed on by mice, and even more unlikely that he should be dating someone who thought this was unexceptional. He had described it later to Eden, who had scoffed and said unhelpful things like "This is why the revolution is coming" and "You better than anyone should know that eating sugar is an act of hostile colonialism," but he could tell she was entranced as well by something that seemed like a child's fantasy brought to life—after this, why shouldn't one expect to find the house made of gingerbread, the clouds made of cotton candy, the trees in the Square made of peppermint bark? It became a running joke of theirs: The omelet she made was good, he said, but not chocolate-mountain good. The girl she'd had sex with the night before had been fine, she said, but she was no chocolate mountain. "The next party, you have to take a picture and prove to me the depth of Charles's capitalist depravity," she told him. She was always asking him when the next gathering would be, when she would finally get to see the evidence.

And so he had been excited to invite Eden to Charles's next party, his annual pre-Christmas gathering. This had been last year, shortly after he'd moved in, and he had been nervous to ask, but Charles had been enthusiastic. "Of course you should bring her," he said. "I'm looking forward to meeting this spitfire of yours." Come, he had told Eden. Come hungry.

She had rolled her eyes. "I'm only coming for the chocolate mountain," she said, and although she had tried to sound blasé, David had known she was excited as well.

But the night of the party, he had waited and waited, and she had never appeared. This had been a sit-down dinner, and her place had sat empty, her napkin still pleated on her plate. He had been embarrassed and concerned, but Charles had been kind. "Something must have come up," he had whispered to David as he slid back into his chair after calling her for the third time. "Don't worry, David. I'm sure she's okay. I'm sure there's a good reason."

They were drinking coffee in the living room when Adams approached him, looking disapproving. "Mister David," he said to him in a low voice, "there's a person—a *Miss* Eden—asking for you."

He was relieved, and then angry: at Adams, for his condescension, and at Eden, for being late, for making him wait and worry. Please bring her in, Adams, he said.

"She won't come in. She asked for you to come out. She's waiting in the courtyard."

He had gotten up, grabbed his coat from the closet, and pushed past the scrum of waiters and out the back door, where Eden stood on the cobblestones. But just before he exited the building, he had stopped and seen her, looking up at the warm-lit windows that were fogging over with steam, at the handsome waiters in their shirt-sleeves and black ties, her breath coming out in puffs. And suddenly he'd understood, as clearly as if she'd said it aloud, that she had been intimidated. He could see her marching west down Washington Square North, stopping in front of the house and checking and rechecking the number, and then, slowly, climbing the stairs. He could see her looking inside, seeing a roomful of middle-aged men, most of them somehow discernibly rich even in their sweaters and jeans; he could see her faltering. He could see that she would have hesitated before lifting her finger to press the buzzer, that she would have reminded herself that she was just as good as they, that she didn't care about their opinions anyway, that they were just a bunch of old, rich white men, and that she had nothing to apologize for and nothing to be ashamed about.

And then he could see her watching Adams enter the living room to tell them dinner was served, and although she knew already that Charles had a butler, she hadn't actually expected to *see* him, and as the room cleared, she would have squinted and realized that the painting on the far wall, the one that hung over the sofa, was a Jasper Johns, a real Jasper Johns—not the reproduction she had tacked up in her bedroom—and one which Charles had bought himself as a thirtieth-birthday present, and which David had never told her about. She would have turned then, and stumbled down the stairs, and walked a lap around the Square, telling herself that she could go inside, that she belonged there, that her best friend lived in that house, and that she had every right to be there, too.

But she couldn't. And so she would have stood outside, just across the street from the house, leaning against the cold iron fence surrounding the Square, watching the waiters present the soup, and then the meat, and then the salad, and wine being poured, and, although she wouldn't have been able to hear, jokes being told and everyone laughing. And it was only when all the guests had stood that she, by now so chilled she could barely move, her feet numb in her old combat boots that she'd mended with electrical tape, would see one of the waiters duck onto Fifth Avenue for a smoke and then disappear into the back of the house and realize that there was a service entrance, and she would go there, leaning on the buzzer, announcing David's name, refusing to enter that golden house.

He knew, looking at her, that part of her would never forgive him, would never forgive the fact that he had—even unintentionally—made her feel so uncomfortable, like such a nothing. He stood on the other side of the door, in the sweater and pants Charles had bought him, the softest clothes he had ever worn, and looked at her in what she called her fancy outfit—a frayed wool herringbone man's coat, so long it brushed the ground; a brown thrift-store suit worn shiny from use; an old rep tie in stripes of orange and black; a fedora pushed back from her round, plain face; the thin mustache she drew with eyeliner above her upper lip for special occasions—and understood that inviting her here, having her witness his life here, had taken from her the joy of wearing those clothes, of being who she was. She was dear to him, she was his closest friend, she was the only one he had told the real story of what happened to his father. "I'll cut anyone who messes with you," she would say to him as they walked through a dangerous part of Alphabet City or the Lower East Side, and he would try not to smile, because she was more than a foot shorter than he was, and so plump and ticklish that just the thought of her barreling toward an assailant, knife in hand, made him grin, but he also knew she meant it: She would protect him, always, against anyone. But by inviting her here, he had failed to protect her. In their world, among their friends, she was Eden, brilliant and witty and singular. In Charles's world, though, she would be whom everyone else saw: a mannish, overweight, short Chinese American woman, unfeminine and unattractive, charmless and loud, in cheap secondhand clothes and a mustache made of makeup, someone whom people ignored or laughed at, as Charles's friends surely would have, despite their efforts not to. And now Charles's world had become his world as well, and for the first time in their friendship there was a trench, and there was no way for her to come to him, and no way that he could return to her.

He opened the door and went to her. She looked up, and saw him, and they stared at each other in silence. Eden, he said. Come in. You're freezing.

But she shook her head. "No way," she said.

Please. There's tea, or wine, or coffee, or cider, or—

"I can't stay," she said. *Then why have you come?* he wanted to say, but didn't. "I have places to be," she continued. "I just came to give you this," and handed him a lumpy little package wrapped in newsprint. "Open it later," she instructed, and he slipped it into his coat pocket. "I'd better go," she said.

Wait, he said, and hurried back inside, where the staff was wrapping up the last of the leftovers, shrouding the chocolate mountain in tinfoil. He grabbed it—Adams raising his eyebrows but saying nothing—and staggered back downstairs, both of his arms wrapped around it.

Here, he said to Eden, handing it over to her. It's the chocolate mountain.

She was surprised, he could tell, and adjusted it in her arms, listing a little beneath its weight. "What the fuck, David?" she said. "What'm I going to do with this?"

He had shrugged. I don't know, he said. But it's yours.

"How'm I going to get it home?"

A cab?

"I don't have money for a cab. And I *don't*," she said, as David reached *into* his pocket, "I don't want your *money*, David."

I don't know what you want me to say, Eden, he said, and then, when she said nothing, I love him. I'm sorry, but I do. I love him.

For a while they had stood there, quiet, in the cold night. From inside, he could hear the thump-thump-thump of house music begin to play. "Then fuck you, David," said Eden, quietly, and she had turned and left, still lugging the chocolate mountain, the hem of her coat dusting the ground behind her in a way that made her appear, for a moment, grand. He had watched her round the corner. Then he went back into the house and returned to Charles's side.

"Everything okay?" Charles asked, and David nodded.

They did the best they could, afterward. The next day he called

Eden at home, and spoke into the answering machine—the message still in his voice—but she didn't pick up, and she didn't call him back. For a whole month, they didn't speak, and every afternoon David would stare at his phone at Larsson, Wesley, willing that it would ring and he would hear Eden's dry, throaty croak on the other end. And then, finally, she did call, one afternoon in late January.

"I'm not apologizing," Eden said.

I'm not expecting you to, he said.

"You won't believe what happened to me on New Year's Eve," she said. "Remember that girl I was fucking? Theodora?"

You wouldn't believe what happened to me, either, he could have said, because by that point he had been taken by Charles on a surprise trip to Gstaad, his first time out of the country, where he had learned how to ski and had eaten pizza that had been covered with a drift of shaved truffles and a velvety soup made of pureed white asparagus and cream, and where he and Charles had had a threeway—David's first—with one of the ski instructors, and for a few days, he had forgotten who he was entirely. But he never said that to her; he wanted her to think that nothing at all had changed, and she, for her part, let him pretend that she believed that, too.

What he also never said was thank you. That night, after she left and then the guests did as well, he and Charles had gone up to their room. "Is your friend all right?" Charles asked, as they climbed into bed.

Yes, he lied. She got the date wrong. She's really sorry and sends her apologies. Eden and Charles would never meet, he now knew, but manners mattered to Charles and he wanted him to like her, or at least the idea of her.

Charles fell asleep, but David lay awake, thinking of Eden. And then he remembered that she had given him something, and he got out of bed and went downstairs to grope in the closet for his coat, and then for the hard little package. It had been bundled in the page from *The Village Voice* advertising escorts, their standard wrapping paper, and then tied with twine, and he had had to knife through its bindings.

Inside had been a small clay sculpture of two forms, two men, standing pressed against each other, holding hands. Eden had begun working with clay only a few months before David moved out, and although the forms were imperfect, he could see that she'd improved—the lines were more fluid, the forms more confident, the proportions more refined. But the piece still looked primitive, somehow, lively rather than lifelike, and that too was intentional: Eden was trying to repopulate the world with statuary of the sort that had been destroyed over the centuries by Western marauders. He examined the work more closely and realized that the two men were meant to be him and Charles—Eden had rendered Charles's mustache as a series of short vertical strokes, had captured the sharp side part of his hair. On the bottom she had etched their initials and the date, and beneath those, her own initials.

She didn't like Charles—on principle, and because he'd taken her closest friend from her. But in this sculpture, she had united the three of them: She had carved herself into David's and Charles's lives.

He climbed the stairs, back up to his and Charles's room; he had gone to his and Charles's closet, had worked the sculpture into a gym sock, and had shoved it into the back of his and Charles's underwear drawer. He never showed it to Charles, and Eden never asked him about it. But years later, when he was moving out of Charles's house, he found it, and in his new apartment, he set it on the mantel, and every now and again, he would pick it up and hold it in his palm. He had spent so much of his childhood feeling alone that when he began seeing Charles, he felt like he would never be alone, or lonely, ever again.

He was wrong, of course. He was still lonely with Charles; he was lonelier after Charles. That was a feeling that never went away. But the sculpture was a reminder of something else. He hadn't been alone before he met Charles after all—he had been Eden's. He just hadn't known it.

But she had.

———

The guests had left, the caterers had left, and the house had taken on that particular desolate mood that it always did in the aftermath of a party: It had been called on to perform, brilliantly, for a few hours, and now it was being returned to its normal, dull existence. The Three Sisters, who had lingered the longest, had finally departed with half a dozen paper bags stacked with containers of food, John purring with delight as he received them. Even Adams had been dismissed, though before he had left, he had bowed, formally, before Peter, and Peter had bent his head in return. "Godspeed, Mister Peter," Adams had said, solemnly. "I hope your journey is safe."

"Thank you, Adams," said Peter, who had used to call Adams "Miss Adams" behind his back. "For everything. You've been so good to me over the years—to all of us." They shook hands.

"Good night, Adams," said Charles, who was standing behind Peter. "Thank you for tonight—everything was perfect, as usual," and Adams nodded again and walked out of the living room, toward the kitchen. When Charles's parents were alive, and there had been a full-time cook and a full-time housekeeper and a maid and a chauffeur as well as Adams, all of the staff were expected to use the back door for their comings and goings. And although Charles had long since revised that rule, Adams still only arrived or departed through the kitchen entrance—initially because, Charles thought, he was uncomfortable disrupting such a long-standing tradition, but recently because he was old, and the back staircase was shallower, its steps wider.

As David watched him go, he wondered, as he sometimes did, what Adams's life was outside of the house. What did Adams wear, to whom and how did he speak, when he wasn't in Charles's house, when he wasn't in his suit, when he wasn't serving? What did he do in his apartment? What were his hobbies? He had every Sunday off, as well as the third Monday of every month, and five weeks of vacation, two of which he took in early January, when Charles was skiing. When David asked, Charles had said that he thought that Adams had a rental cabin down in Key West, and that he went fishing there, but he hadn't been sure. He knew so little about Adams's life. Had Adams been married? Did he have a boyfriend, a girlfriend? Had he ever? Did he have siblings, nieces or nephews? Did he have friends? In the early days of their relationship, when he was still getting accustomed to Adams's presence, he had asked Charles all of these questions, and Charles had laughed, embarrassed. "This is terrible," he said, "but I don't know how to answer any of these." How could you not? he'd asked, before he was aware of what he was saying, but Charles hadn't been offended. "It's difficult to explain," he said, "but there are some people in your life where it's just—it's just easier not to know too much about them."

He wondered now if he was another one of those people in Charles's life, someone whose appeal would not only be ruined by the complications of his history but who had indeed been chosen because he seemed to have no history at all. He knew Charles was unafraid of difficult lives, but perhaps David had been attractive because he had appeared so simple, someone not yet marked by age or experience. A dead mother, a dead father, a year in law school, a childhood spent far away in a middle-class family, handsome but not intimidatingly so, smart but not memorably so, someone who had preferences and desires, but not so strongly held that he would be unwilling to accommodate Charles's. He could see how, to Charles, he was defined by his absences—no secrets, no troublesome ex-boyfriends, no illnesses, no past.

Then there was Peter: someone whom Charles knew intimately, and who in turn, David was belatedly realizing, knew more about Charles than he ever would. No matter how long he stayed with Charles, no matter how much he might learn about him, Peter would always possess more of him—not just years but epochs. He had known Charles as a child, and as a young man, and as a middle-aged one. He had given Charles his first kiss, his first blow job, his first cigarette, his first beer, his first breakup. Together, they had learned what they liked in the world: what food, what books, what plays, what art, what ideas, what people. He had known Charles before he became Charles, when he was just a sturdy, athletic boy to whom Peter had found himself attracted. David could see, too late, after months of struggling to find a way to talk to Peter, how he could have and should have simply asked Peter about the person they shared: about who he'd been, about the life he'd had before David had entered it. Charles may have been incurious about David, but David was guilty of the same incuriousness; each of them wanted the other to exist only as he was currently experiencing him—as if they were both too unimaginative to contemplate each other in a different context.

But suppose they were forced to? Suppose the earth were to shift in space, only an inch or two but enough to redraw their world, their country, their city, themselves, entirely? What if Manhattan was a flooded island of rivers and canals, and people traveled in wooden longboats, and you yanked nets of oysters from the cloudy waters beneath your house, which was held aloft on stilts? Or what if they lived in a glittering, treeless metropolis rendered entirely in frost, in buildings made from stacked blocks of ice, and rode polar bears and kept seals as pets, against whose jiggling sides you'd press at night for warmth? Would they still recognize each other, passing each other in different boats, or crunching through the snow, hurrying home to their fires?

Or what if New York looked just as it did, but no one he knew was dying, no one was dead, and tonight's party had been just another gathering of friends, and there was no pressure to say anything wise, anything conclusive, because they would have hundreds more dinners, thousands more nights, dozens more years, to figure out what they wanted to tell one another? Would they still be together in that world, where there was no need to cling together from fear, where their knowledge of pneumonia, of cancers, of fungal infections, of blindness, would be obscure, useless, ridiculous?

Or what if, in this planetary shift, they were knocked sideways, west and south, and returned to consciousness somewhere else entirely, in Hawai'i, and in that Hawai'i, that other Hawai'i, there was no reason for Lipo-wao-nahele, that place to which his father had removed him so long ago, because what it had tried to conjure was in fact real? What if, in this Hawai'i, the islands were still a kingdom, not part of America at all, and his father was the king, and he, David, was the crown prince? Would they still know each other? Would they still have fallen in love? Would David still have need for Charles? There, he would be the more powerful of the two—he would no longer be in need of another's largesse, another's protection, another's education. Who would Charles be to him there? Would David still find something to love in him? And what of his father—who would he be? Would he be more confident, more self-assured, less scared, less lost? Would he still have had use for Edward? Or would Edward be a speck, a servant, a nameless functionary his father passed, unseeing, on his way to his study to sign documents and treaties, his handsome face aglow as he walked barefoot across the gleaming floors, the wood polished every morning with macadamia oil?

He would never know. For in the world in which they lived, he and his father, they were only who they were: two men, both of whom had sought succor from another man, one each hoped might save him from the smallness of his life. His father had chosen poorly. David had not. But in the end, they were both dependents, disappointed by their past and frightened by their present.

He turned to watch Charles wrap a scarf around Peter's throat. They were silent, and David had the feeling, as he often had when watching them, but which he had most acutely that evening, that he was a trespasser, that their intimacy was never his to witness. He didn't move, but he didn't need to—they had forgotten he was even there. Peter had originally thought he might spend the night in the house with Charles, but the day before had decided against it. His nurse had been called, and was coming with an assistant to pick him up and escort him home.

It was time to say goodbye. "Just give me a second," Charles announced to them both in a strangled voice, and left the room, and they could both hear him running up the stairs.

And then David was alone with Peter. Peter was in his wheelchair, swaddled in his coat and hat; the top and bottom of his face were obscured by layers of wool, as if he wasn't dying but mutating, as if the wool were creeping over him like a skin, turning him into something cozy and soft—a couch, a cushion, a bundle of yarn. Charles had been sitting on the sofa to talk to him, and Peter's chair was still angled toward what was now an empty seat in an empty room.

He went to the sofa and sat where Charles had sat, the cushions still warm beneath him. Charles had been holding Peter's hands, but he did not. And still—*still:* Even as Peter gazed at him, he could think of nothing to say, nothing that was not impossible. It would have to be Peter who spoke first, and, finally, he did, David leaning toward him to hear what he would say.

"David."

Yes.

"Take care of my Charles. Will you do that for me?"

Yes, he promised, relieved that more hadn't been asked from him, and that Peter hadn't taken the opportunity to deliver some devastating observation he'd made, some truth about himself that David would never be able to forget. Of course I will.

Peter made a soft dismissive noise. "'Of course,'" he murmured.

I will, he told Peter, fiercely. *I will.* It was important that Peter believed him. But as David was promising him, Peter was already looking away, toward the sound of Charles's reentry, reaching his arms toward his friend in a gesture so childlike, so loving, that forever after, David was unable to imagine him in any other way: Peter, his arms open and empty, bundled like a toddler about to go out and play in the snow, and walking toward them, to fill them with his presence, Charles, his face crumpling, looking only at Peter, as if nobody else existed in the world.

———

They lay in bed that night, he and Charles, not touching, not speaking, their preoccupation so complete that, had anyone seen them, he would have mistaken them for strangers.

Peter was gone, lifted downstairs by his nurse and the assistant and accompanied by David and Charles, fed into a car that Charles had called for him. And then the car had driven away, back to Peter's warm, cluttered second-floor apartment in an old house on Bethune Street near the river, with its crumbling staircase and painted brick facade, and David and Charles had remained on the sidewalk in the cold. He had always known that the end of the evening would be the end of Peter in their lives—in Charles's life—and now that it had

actually happened, it seemed too abrupt, too abbreviated, like something out of a fairy tale: a clock striking midnight and the world
being misted with gray, potential lives together dissolving into nothingness.

They had stood there, together, long after the car had vanished
from sight. It wasn't so late, but the cold had kept almost everyone indoors, and only a few stray people, wrapped in black, passed
before them. Across the street, the park glittered with snow. Finally,
he had taken Charles's arm. It's chilly, he said. Let's go back inside.
"Yes," Charles agreed, his voice faint.

Back inside, they shut off the living-room lights, Charles did a
check of the back-door locks as he always did, and then they climbed
the stairs to their room, undressed and dressed, and brushed their
teeth in silence.

Around them, the night thickened and settled. Eventually, after
what felt like an hour, he heard Charles's breathing change, grow
slow and deep, and when he did, he got out of bed and went quietly
to the closet, retrieved the letter from his bag, and crept downstairs.

For a while he sat on the sofa in the darkened living room, holding the envelope in both hands. This was his last moment of ignorance, of pretending, and he didn't want it to end. But finally, he
turned on the lamp, and removed the sheet of paper, and read what
it said.

He woke to the sound of his name and Charles's palm on his
cheek, and when he opened his eyes, he knew from the clarity of
light that filled the room that it was snowing again. Before him,
on the ottoman, sat Charles, wearing his robe and what they called
his old-man pajamas, striped blue cotton with his initials stitched
in black on the breast pocket. Charles never came downstairs until
he had combed his hair, but now it stood about his head in clumps,
so that David could see the white of his scalp where the hair had
become thin at the crown.

"He's gone," Charles said.

Oh, Charles, he said. When?

"About an hour ago. His nurse called me. I woke up, and looked
over, and you weren't next to me"—he began to apologize, but

Charles put his hand on his arm, stopping him—"and I was disoriented. For a moment, I didn't know where I was. But then I remembered: I was in my house, and it was the day after the party, and I had been waiting for this call—I knew what it would be. I had just thought it would be tomorrow, not today. But it wasn't—he never even made it to the airport.

"So I didn't answer it. You didn't hear it ring? I just lay there and listened to the phone ringing and ringing and ringing: six, ten, twenty times—I'd turned the answering machine off last night. It was so loud. Such an insistent, *rude* noise: I never realized. Finally, it stopped, and I sat up, on the edge of the bed, and listened.

"I found myself in that moment thinking of my brother. Oh, right—you don't know. Well, when I was five, my mother gave birth to another son. My brother, Morgan. She and my father had been trying to have a child for years, I later learned. Ten weeks before her due date, she went into labor.

"Back then—this would have been 1943—there was nothing you could do for such a premature baby: There was no such thing as neonatal care; the incubators were primitive compared to what we have now. It was extraordinary he was alive at all. The doctor told my parents he would die within forty-eight hours.

"No one told me this, of course. These days, I'm always shocked by how much information parents give their children, information those children aren't yet equipped to understand. When I was a child, I knew *nothing*, and the people who looked after me were charged with keeping me ignorant. What I learned I gathered from whispers and eavesdropping. And yet I don't remember feeling frustrated; I would never have considered my parents' lives part of mine. My world was the fourth floor, with my toys and books. My parents were visitors; the only adults who belonged were my nanny and my tutor.

"But even I knew that something was wrong—I knew from the way the adults whispered in the hallway, falling silent when they spotted me; the way even my nanny, who loved me, seemed distracted, looking toward the door when the maid came in with my lunch, raising her eyebrows inquiringly at her, tightening her mouth when she shook her head in response. Downstairs, everything was silent. The servants—this was long before Adams's time—spoke in low voices, and for three days, I went to bed without being taken downstairs to be presented to my parents first.

"On the fourth day of this, I decided I was going to sneak downstairs and figure out what was happening. And so I pretended to be asleep when Nanny came to check on me that night, and then I waited and waited, until I heard the last maid walking upstairs toward her bedroom. And then I got out of bed and tiptoed down to my parents'. As I did, I noticed a faint light, candlelight, coming from the parlor next door to their room, and as I noticed that light, I also heard a small, strange sound that I couldn't identify. I crept closer to the parlor. I was so careful, so quiet. Finally, I was at the door, which was ajar, and I looked inside.

"I saw my mother, sitting on a chair. There was a candle on the table by her side, and in her arms, she held my brother. The thing I remember thinking later was how beautiful she looked. She had long, reddish hair that she always wore pinned up, but now it hung about her like a veil, and she was wearing a lilac-colored silk robe and a white nightgown beneath it; her feet were bare. I had never seen my mother look like this—I had never seen my parents in any way other than how they wanted me to see them: fully dressed, capable, competent.

"In her left arm, she was cradling the baby. But in her right hand she was holding an odd instrument, a clear glass dome, and she would fit the dome over the baby's mouth and nose and then squeeze the rubber bulb attached to it. That was the sound I'd heard, the rubber bulb wheezing as it filled and emptied with air, air she was giving to Morgan. She kept up a steady rhythm, and she didn't rush: not too fast, not too much. Every ten squeezes or so she would stop for a second, and I could hear, barely, the baby's breath, so quiet.

"I don't know how long I stood there, watching her. She never looked up. The expression on her face—I can't describe it. It wasn't despairing, or sorrowful, or desperate. It was just—nothing. But not blank. Attentive, I suppose. As if there were nothing else in her life—no past, no present, no husband or son or house—as if she existed only to try to pump air into her baby's lungs.

"It didn't work, of course. Morgan died the next day. Nanny told me about it at last: that I'd had a brother, and that his lungs had been faulty, and that he had died, and that I wasn't to be sad because he was now with God. Later, when my mother was dying, I learned that my parents had fought; that my father had disagreed with her trying, that he had forbade her from using that instrument. I don't know where she got it from. I don't know that she ever forgave him: for not believing, for dissuading her from trying. My father, I learned, hadn't even wanted to bring him home from the hospital, and when my mother fought to do so—they donated so much to the place that they wouldn't deny her—he had disapproved of that as well.

"My mother wasn't a sentimental woman. She never spoke of Morgan, and after he died, she eventually recovered herself. Over the decades, she ran charities, she hosted dinners, she rode horses and painted, she read and collected rare books, she volunteered at a home for unwed young mothers; she made a life in this house for me and my father.

"I never considered myself much like her, and neither did she. 'You're just like your father,' she'd sometimes say to me, and she always sounded a little rueful. And she was right—I was never one of those gay men who found an affinity with their mothers. Except for the fact that we never discussed who I loved, I *did* have a kinship with my father. For a long time, I was able to pretend that we never talked about who I was, or part of who I was, because we had so many other things to talk about. The law, for example. Or business. Or biographies, which we both liked to read. By the time I stopped pretending, he was already dead.

"But lately, I've been thinking about that night more and more. I wonder if I'm actually more like her than I knew. I wonder who will hold that little air pump for me when it's my turn. Not because they think it'll revive me, or save me. But because they want to try.

"I was sitting there, thinking all of this, when the phone rang again. This time I got up and answered it. It was Peter's new day-shift nurse—a nice guy. I'd met him a few times. He told me Peter had died, and that it had been peaceful, and that he was very sorry for my loss. And then I hung up and I went looking for you."

He was quiet, and David realized that it was the end of his story. As Charles had talked, he had looked out the window, which had become a screen of white, and now he turned to David again, and David pressed his back into the sofa's cushions and beckoned to Charles, who lay down next to him.

They were silent for a long time, and although David was thinking many things, he mostly thought about how good this moment was, lying next to Charles in a warm room, with snow outside. He thought that he should tell Charles that he would hold the air pump for him, but he couldn't. He wanted so much to give Charles something, some measure of the consolation that Charles had given him, but he couldn't. Much later, he would wish, again and again, that he had said something, anything, no matter how clumsy. In those years, fear—of sounding dumb, of being inadequate—kept him from the generosity he should have shown, and it was not until he had accumulated many regrets that he had learned that his comfort could have taken any form, that what had been important was that it was offered at all.

"I came down here," Charles finally said, "I came down here and found you. And"—he took a breath—"and you were asleep, with a letter on your chest, beneath your hand. And—I took it from you, and I read it. I don't know why. I'm sorry, David." He was quiet. "And I'm sorry for what's in it. How come you never told me?"

I don't know, he said, at last. But he wasn't angry that Charles had read his letter. He was relieved—that Charles knew, that, once again, Charles's decisiveness had made a difficult task easier.

"So—your father. He's still alive."

Barely, he said. For now.

"Yes. And your grandmother wants you to come see him."

Yes.

"And that place he lived in—"

It wasn't what you were thinking, he interrupted Charles. I mean, it was. But it wasn't. How could he tell Charles? How could he make him understand? How could he make Lipo-wao-nahele sound like something different, something better, something saner than what it was? Not a folly, not make-believe, not an impossibility, but something his father—and even he—had once believed in with all the hopefulness they had, a place where history was meaningless, a place that would finally feel like home, a place where his father had gone in anticipation as much as in fear. He couldn't. His grandmother had never understood it; Charles certainly wouldn't, either.

I can't explain it, he said at last. You wouldn't understand.

"Try me," said Charles.

Well, maybe, he said, but he knew he would. Charles knew how to help everyone—what if he knew how to help David, too? What was the point of loving him, of being loved back, if he wasn't going to try?

But first, he had to eat something; he was hungry. He wriggled himself off the sofa, and held out his hand for Charles, and as they went to the kitchen, he thought of his father again. Not as he was in the care home he lived in now; not as he had been in the last days of his stay at Lipo-wao-nahele, his eyes vacant, his face streaked with dirt; but as he had been when they lived together in their house, when he was four, five, six, seven, eight, nine, when they were a father and a son, and he had never had to consider anything other than the fact that his father would always take care of him, or at least would always try, because he had promised he always would, and because he knew his father loved him, and because that was the way of things. Loss, loss—he had lost so much. How would he ever feel complete again? How could he make up for all those years? How could he forgive? How could he be forgiven?

"Let's see," said Charles, as they stood in the kitchen together, surveying their options. On the counter, there was a loaf of sourdough bread wrapped in brown paper that Adams had set aside for them, and Charles sawed off slices for both of them before holding his aloft. "To your father," he said.

To Peter, he responded.

"An early New Year's toast," Charles announced: "Six more years until the twenty-first century."

They touched their pieces of bread against each other, solemnly, and ate. Behind them, the windows rattled from the wind, but they couldn't feel it themselves—the house was too well made. "Let's see what Adams saved for us," Charles said after they had finished, and opened the refrigerator, removing a jar of mayonnaise, a container of cold steak, a jar of mustard, a wedge of cheese. "Jarlsberg," he said, and then, almost to himself, "Peter's favorite."

He put his arms around Charles, and Charles leaned against him, and for a moment they were quiet. It was then that he had a sudden vision of the two of them many years later, in some undated time far into the future. Outside, the world had changed: The streets had been overgrown with weeds, and the cobblestones in the courtyard were shaggy with pampas grass, and the sky was a viscous green, and a creature with rubbery, webbed wings glided past them. A car puffed south down Fifth Avenue, hovering a few inches above the ground, hissing air as it went. The garage was a ruin, half decayed, its bricks soft and cakey, and in the middle of it, thrusting its way through the crumbling roof, grew a mango tree, just like the one that had grown in the front yard of the house where he had once lived with his father, its branches bulbous with fruit. If it wasn't quite the end of things, then it was close—the fruit was too poisoned to eat; the car was windowless; the air shimmered with oily smoke; the creature had settled atop the building across the street, its talons gripping the parapet, its black eyes searching for something to swoop down upon and devour.

But inside, he and Charles were somehow the same as they were: still healthy, still there, still magically themselves. They were two people in love, and they were making themselves something to eat, and there was plenty of food, and as long as they stayed indoors, together, no harm would come to them. And to their right, at the far end of the kitchen, was a door, and if they opened that door and walked through it, they would find themselves in a replica of this house, except in that house would be Peter, alive and sarcastic and intimidating, and in the house to the right of his would be John and Timothy and Percy, and in the house to the right of theirs, Eden and Teddy, and on and on and on, an unbroken chain of houses, the people they loved resurrected and restored, an eternity of meals and conversations and arguments and forgivenesses. Together they'd walk through these houses, opening doors, greeting friends, closing doors behind them, until, at last, they'd come to what they somehow knew was the final door. And here they'd pause a moment, squeezing each other's hands, before turning the knob and entering a kitchen just like their own, the same jade-green walls, the same gilt-edged china in the cupboards, the same framed etchings on the walls, the same soft linen dish towels hung on the same ash-carved pegs, but in which a mango tree was growing, its leaves brushing the ceiling.

And here, sitting on a chair and patiently waiting, would be his father, and when he saw David, he would spring to his feet, his face alight, crying with joy. "My Kawika," he'd say, "you've come for me! You've finally come for me!" He wouldn't hesitate, but would run toward him, while behind him, Charles stood and beamed, watching this final reunion, a father and son finding each other at last.

M y son, my Kawika—what are you doing today? I know where you are, because Mama told me: New York. But where in New York, I wonder? And what are you doing there? She said you were working in a law firm, though not a lawyer, but you mustn't think I'm any less proud of you for that. I visited New York once, did you know that? Yes, it's true—your papa has some secrets of his own.

I think about you often. When I'm awake, but also when I'm asleep. All of my dreams are about you in one way or another. Sometimes I dream about the time before we went to Lipo-wao-nahele, when we were together in your grandmother's house, and we used to take our midnight walks. Do you remember those? I would wake you up, and we'd sneak outside. Up Oʻahu Avenue to East Manoa Road we'd go, and then up Mohala Way, because one of the houses there had a trumpet bush in its front yard that fascinated you, do you remember this? It had pale-yellow flowers, the color of ivory, that grew upside down and looked like the bell of a cornet. At least that's what people said. You didn't agree, however. "The upside-down tulip tree," you used to call it, and I could never see it any other way after that. Then down Lipioma Way we'd go, and over to Beckwith, and then down Manoa Road, and then home. It's funny—of all the things I was scared of, I was never scared of the dark. In the dark, everyone was helpless, and, knowing that, that I was just like everyone else, no less, made me feel braver.

I loved those walks of ours. I think you did, too. We had to stop them after you told your teacher about them—you were falling asleep in class, and your teacher asked why, and you told her it was because of our nighttime walks, and your teacher called me in to see her and I got in trouble. "He's growing, Mr. Bingham," she said, "he needs his sleep. You can't be waking him up in the middle of the night to go on walks." I felt foolish, but she was kind to me. She could have told your grandmother, but she didn't. "I just want to spend more time with him," I told the teacher, and she looked at me in the way that people often did, that made me realize I'd said something wrong, something queer, but finally she had nodded. "You love your son, Mr. Bingham," she said, "and that's a wonderful thing. But if you really love him, you'll let him sleep." I was embarrassed then, because of course she was right: You were just a child. I had no right to wake you and take you from your bed. The first time I did so, you were confused, but then you grew to expect it, and you would rub your eyes and yawn, but you never complained— you would put on your slippers and take my hand and follow me down the path. I never had to tell you not to tell your grandmother; you already knew not to. Later, I told Edward that I had gotten in trouble with the teacher, and why. "You dumbass," he said, but in a way so that I knew he wasn't mad, just frustrated. "They could've called Child Services and taken Kawika away for that." "Could they have?" I asked. It was the worst thing I could imagine. "'Course they could've," he said. "But don't worry. When we go to Lipo-wao-nahele, you can raise Kawika however you want, and no one can say anything about it."

What else do you remember? All I can do is remember. I can see, a little, but just light and darkness. Do you remember how we used to go to the Chinese cemetery and sit near the monkeypod tree at the top of the hill? We'd lie right on the grass, with our faces turned up to the sun. "Keep your eyes shut," I'd tell you, but even though we did, we could still see a field of orange, little blobs of black flickering across it like flies. After I told you how vision worked, you asked me if you were seeing the back of your eye, and I told you that maybe you were. Anyway, it's like that—I can see color and those blobs, but not much else. When they take me outdoors, though, they put sunglasses on me first. This is because, according to one of the doctors here, I should still be able to see—there's nothing wrong with my eyes, as such, and so they need to be protected. Until recently, your grandmother used to bring pictures of you, which she'd hold in front of me, so close that the paper tickled against my nose. "Look at him, Wika," she'd say. "*Look* at him. Stop this nonsense. Don't you want to see pictures of your son?" Of course I did, and I tried, I tried hard. But I could never see more than the outline of the square of paper, maybe the dark of your hair. Or maybe it wasn't a picture of you at all that she was showing me. Maybe it was a picture of a cat, or a mushroom. I couldn't tell the difference. The point is that I never see everything new; everything I see I've seen before.

But although I can't see, I *can* hear. Most of it doesn't make much sense to me, not because I can't understand it, exactly, but because I'm so often asleep that it's difficult for me to keep track of what I'm actually hearing and what I'm imagining. And sometimes when I'm trying to figure it out, I fall asleep again, and then, when I wake next, I'm more confused—assuming I can recall what I was trying to sort out before I fell asleep, I by then don't know whether I really heard what I thought I heard, or whether I had been hallucinating. Your being in New York, for example: I woke with the strong feeling you were there. But were you, really? Had someone told me that, or had I invented it? I thought and thought, so hard that I could hear myself begin to whimper with frustration and confusion, and then someone came into my room, and then there was blankness. When I woke again, I remembered only that I had been upset, and it wasn't until later that I remembered why. I had no way to ask whether you were in New York or not, of course, and so I just had to wait until someone—your grandmother—came to visit me again, and hope that she would mention you. And eventually, she did come, and said that she'd gotten a letter from you, and that the weather in New York was hot, hot and rainy, and that you wanted me to get better. Now I suppose you're wondering how I knew that this was actually happening, that I wasn't dreaming it, and the answer is because that day I could smell the flowers your grandmother was wearing. Do you remember how, when the pakalana vine was in bloom, she'd send you to the side of the house to pick a few clusters, and then she'd put them in that little silver brooch she had, the one shaped like a vase that could actually hold a few blossoms? That was how I knew it was real, and also that it was summer, because pakalana only blooms in summer. It's also why, whenever I think of you, and New York, I smell pakalana.

I don't know how long you've been away. I think it must be a very long time. Years. Maybe even a decade. But then I realize that, if that's so, it means that I've been here, in this place, for years, maybe even a decade. And then I can hear myself beginning to moan, louder and louder, and thrash my arms and legs, and piss myself, and then I can hear the sound of people running toward me, and sometimes I hear them say my name: "Wika. Wika, you need to calm down. You need to calm down, Wika." Wika: They only call me Wika. No one here calls me Mr. Bingham unless your grandmother is visiting. But that's fine. It never felt right, being called Mr. Bingham.

But I can't calm down, because now I'm thinking about how I'll never get out of here, about how my life—my entire life—has been spent in places I can't escape: Your grandmother's house. Lipo-wao-nahele. And now here. This island. I could never really leave. But you did. You got away.

And so I keep making the sounds I can, slapping away their hands, wailing over their attempts to soothe me, and I keep doing it until I feel the medication entering my veins, warming my body, calming my heart, delivering me back to a state of forgetting.

I want to talk to you, my son, my Kawika, though I know you will never hear me, as I will never be able to say any of this aloud to you, not anymore. But I want to talk to you about everything that happened, and try to explain to you why I did what I did.

You have never visited me. I know this, and yet I also don't. Sometimes I'm able to pretend that you *have* visited me, that I'm just confused. But I know you haven't. I don't know what your voice sounds like anymore; I don't know what you smell like. The image I have of you is from when you were fifteen, and leaving me after one of our weekends together, and I didn't know—maybe you didn't,

either, maybe you still loved me a little then, despite everything—
that I would never see you again. Of course this makes me sad. Not
just for my sake—but for yours as well. Because you have a father
who is both alive and yet not, and yet you are still a young man, and
a young man needs his father.

I can't tell you exactly where I am, because I don't know. Sometimes I imagine I must be on Tantalus, high up in the forest, because
it's cool and rainy and very quiet, but I could also be in Nu'uanu, or
even in Manoa. I do know I'm not at our house, because this place
doesn't smell like our house. For a long time I thought I was in a
hospital, but it doesn't smell like a hospital, either. But there are
doctors and nurses and orderlies, and they all take care of me.

For a long time I didn't leave my bed at all, and then they started
making me. "C'mon, Wika," a man's voice would say. "C'mon, brud-
dah." And I could feel a hand on my back, helping me sit, and then
four hands on me, two wrapped around my waist, lifting me up and
setting me down again. Then I was being pushed, and I could feel
that we had left the building, I could feel the sun on my neck. One
of the hands tipped my chin up; I closed my eyes. "That feels good,
doesn't it, Wika?" said the voice. But then he let go of my chin and
my head flopped forward again. Now when they take me around the
building or out to the garden, they strap something around my forehead so that my head stays in place. Sometimes a woman comes and
moves my arms and legs and talks to me. She bends and straightens
each limb, and then she rubs me before turning me onto my stomach and kneading my back. There would have been a time when that
would have made me embarrassed, to be lying there without any
clothes on and with a strange woman touching me, but now I don't
mind. Her name is Rosemary, and as she massages me, she talks
about her day and her family: her husband, who's an accountant;
her son and daughter, who're still in elementary school. Occasionally, she'll say something that makes me realize how much time has
passed, but then, later, I get confused because—once again—I don't
know if she actually said it or if I just made it up. Did the Berlin Wall
fall, or did it not? Are there now colonies on Mars, or are there not?
Did Edward triumph after all, and has the monarchy been restored,

and I named king of the Hawaiian islands, and my mother the queen regent, or has it not? One time she said something about you, about my son, and I became agitated and she had to buzz for help, and since then she's never mentioned you again.

Today I thought of you as they were feeding me my dinner. Everything I eat is soft, because sometimes I think too much about swallowing and then I start panicking and gagging, but if I don't have to chew I think about it less. Dinner was congee with preserved egg and scallions, which is one of the dishes I used to have Jane make you when you were sick—one of the dishes she made me when I was a child. It was one of my father's favorites as well, although he liked his with boiled chicken.

I think Jane is dead. Matthew, too. No one has told me this, but I know, because they used to come visit me and now they don't. Don't ask me how long ago, or how; I wouldn't be able to tell you. But they were old—older than your grandmother. I once overheard her telling you that her father had given her Jane and Matthew as a wedding present: two servants from her father's household that would help her run her own. But that isn't true. Jane and Matthew were in the house well before your grandmother joined it. And besides, by that point her father didn't have the money for a single servant, much less two, much less two he could give away. And if he had, it's unlikely he would have given them to her, when legally she wasn't even related to him by blood.

I never knew what to do when I heard your grandmother tell you things that weren't true. I didn't want to contradict her. I knew better. And I wanted you to trust her, and to love her—I wanted things to be easier for you than they were for me, and that meant having a good relationship with her. I worked hard to make that happen, and I think I succeeded, which means I didn't completely fail you; I made sure your grandmother loved you. But now you are grown, grown and safe and living in New York, and I feel I can tell you the truth.

I will say this for your grandmother: She took nothing she had for granted. What she had she had fought for and earned, and her life was dedicated to ensuring it never slipped away from her. She raised me to feel the opposite, and yet there were times I think she felt resentful that I did, even though it had been her intention. She never resented my father for it, and yet she resented me, because I was partially hers, and I should therefore be aware of how precarious my position was, because then her own anxiety would feel less lonely. We often end up resenting our children when they achieve what we've wished for them—although this isn't my way of saying that I resent you, even though my only wish was that you grow up and leave me behind.

About my father I have little to say that you don't already know. I was already eight, almost nine, when he died, and yet I have few memories of him—he is a blurred, jovial presence, sporty and hearty, swinging me up in the air when he came home from work, dangling me upside down as I squealed, trying and failing to teach me how to hit a ball. I wasn't like him, but he didn't seem dissatisfied with me, the way I knew my mother to be from almost the time I had a sense of her opinions at all; I liked reading, and he would call me "Professor," never sarcastically, even though what I liked to read were just comic books. "This is Wika, the reader in the family," he'd introduce me to acquaintances, and I would feel embarrassed, because I knew that I was reading nothing important, that I didn't really have the right to call myself a reader. But it hadn't mattered to him; if I had ridden horses, I would have been the Rider, and if I had played tennis I would have been the Athlete, and it wouldn't have made a difference if I had distinguished myself or not.

Most of the money had been spent by the time my father joined the family firm, and he didn't seem interested in replenishing its coffers. We'd spend weekends at the club, where we'd have lunch together—people stopping by our table to shake my father's hand and smile at my mother; the slice of coconut layer cake, soapy-sweet and shagged like a carpet, that my father always ordered for me at the end, despite my mother's protestations, placed in front of me— before my father joined his golf game and my mother sat with her stack of magazines beneath an umbrella near the pool, where she could watch me. Later, when Edward and I were becoming friends, I would stay quiet as he talked about going to the beach on the weekends with his mother; they would pack containers of food and spend all day there, his mother sitting on a blanket with her friends, Edward running into the water and then back out, in and then out, until the sky began to darken and they packed their things to leave. The club was near the ocean—when you were on the course, you could see stripes of it through the trees, a band of glinting blue—but we would never have thought of going there: It was too sandy, too wild, too poor. But I never said this to Edward; I said I loved going to the beach as well, even though, when we started going together, part of me was always thinking about when we could leave, when I could take a shower and become clean again.

It wasn't until my father died that I realized we were rich, and by then, we were far less rich than we had been. But the kind of wealth my father had possessed wasn't of an obvious kind—our house was large, but it was like everyone else's, with a wide porch and a large, crowded sunroom, and a small kitchen. I had all the toys I wanted, but my first bike was secondhand, a hand-me-down from a boy on the next street. We had Jane and Matthew, but our meals were simple—rice and meat of some kind for dinner; rice and fish and eggs for breakfast; a metal bento box I took to school for lunch—and it was only when my parents entertained, and the candles were lit and the chandelier was cleaned, that the house looked grand, and that I was able to recognize that there was something stately in its simplicity: the dark, shining dining-room table; the smooth white wood of the walls and ceiling; the vases of flowers that were replaced every other day. This was in the late '40s, when our neighbors were laying linoleum over their floors and replacing their dishware with plastic, but ours was not, as my mother said, a house of convenience. In our house, the floors were wood and the cutlery was silver and the plates and bowls were china. Not expensive china, but not plastic, either. The postwar years had brought new wealth to the islands, new things from the mainland, but here again our household did not indulge in what my mother considered trends. Why would you buy expensive oranges from Florida when the ones from our yard were even better? Why should you buy raisins from California when the lychee from our trees were even sweeter? "They've gone mainland mad," she would say about our neighbors; she was dismissive of what she saw as their gullibility, in which she saw a kind of self-loathing for where we lived and who we were. Edward was never able to see that aspect of her, her fierce nationalism, her love for her home—he saw only the inconsistency with which that pride was expressed, the way she scorned other people for wanting the latest music and food from the mainland while also wearing the pearls she had bought in New York, the long cotton skirts that she ordered from her dress-maker in San Francisco, where she and my father had made annual trips, a habit she continued after his death.

Twice a year, the three of us would drive out to Lāʻie, on the North Shore. Here there was a small coral-rock church for which my great-grandfather had been the benefactor since he was a young man, and it was from here that my father would distribute enve-lopes of money, twenty dollars for each adult, to celebrate my great-grandfather's birthday and then the day of his death, by giving a gift to the people of the town his grandfather had loved. As we approached the church, turning off the road onto a dirt path, we would see the townspeople clumped around the door, and as my father climbed out and advanced toward the building, they would bow. "Your Highness," they would murmur, these big dark people, their voices unnaturally soft, "welcome back, King." My father would nod at them, offer his hands to be taken and squeezed, and inside, he would distribute the money and then would sit to listen to the best singer among them, who would sing a song, and then someone else, who would chant, and then we would get into the car and drive back to town.

These visits always made me uncomfortable. I felt, even as a young boy, as if I were a fraud—what had I done to be called "Prince," to have an old woman, so old that she spoke only Hawaiian, bow before me, her hand clenching the head of her cane so she wouldn't fall? On the ride home, my father was cheery, whistling the song that had just been performed for him, while my mother sat by his side, straight and silent and regal. After my father died, I had gone with her alone, and although the townspeople had been respect-ful, they had acknowledged only me, not her, and although she was always polite to them, she didn't have my father's good humor, or his ability to make people far poorer than he feel like his equal, and the occasion took on a strained quality. By the time I was eighteen, and expected to discharge this duty myself, the entire enterprise had begun to feel anachronistic and condescending, and from then on, my mother just sent an annual donation to the local community center, for it to distribute in whatever way benefited its members. Not that I was capable of being my father, anyway. That was what I had told her—that I wasn't a substitute for him. "You don't understand, Wika," she had said, wearily, "you're not his substitute. You're his heir." But she hadn't contradicted me, either: We both knew I couldn't equal my father.

Things changed after he died, of course. For my mother, the changes were more profound and threatening. Once his debts had been paid—he had liked to gamble and had liked cars—there was less money left than she had assumed. She had also lost with him a sense of security in who she was—he had legitimized who she always claimed to be, and without him, she would forever be defending her right to call herself nobility.

But the other change was that my mother and I were left with only each other, and it wasn't until my father had left us that we both realized that it was he who had provided us our identities: She was Kawika Bingham's wife; I was Kawika Bingham's son. Even now that he was gone, we still defined ourselves in relation to him. But without him, our relation to each other seemed more capricious. She was now Kawika Bingham's widow; I was Kawika Bingham's heir. But Kawika Bingham himself no longer existed, and without him, we no longer knew how to relate to each other.

After my father's death, my mother became increasingly involved with her society, Kaikamahine kū Hawai'i. The group, whose members referred to themselves as the Daughters, was open to anyone who could prove noble lineage.

My mother's own claim to noble blood was a complicated subject. Her adopted father, who was a distant cousin of my father's, had been noble: He, like my father, could trace his family all the way back to before the Great King. But my mother's origins were more opaque. As I grew older, I would hear various stories about who she was. The most common was that she was in fact her adopted father's illegitimate child, and that her mother had been a fling, a haole cocktail waitress who'd returned home to America soon after giving birth. But there were other theories as well, including that she was not only not noble but not even of Hawaiian blood, that her mother had been her adoptive father's secretary, and that her father had been her adoptive father's manservant—her father had been known to prefer hiring haoles, because he liked to show off that he had the stature and money to have white people work for him. When she occasionally spoke about her adoptive father, she would say only that he was always kind to her, though from someone—who, I don't know—I must have gotten the sense that, while he might have been kind to her, it was in a vague sort of way; he was strict with his own children, his daughter and his son, because he expected more from and for them. They had the power to disappoint him, but they also had the power to please him. They were embodiments of him in a way my mother was not.

Marrying my father had quieted most of the rumors—*his* origins were inarguable, unimpeachable—but with his death, I believe she felt she was once again on the defensive, alert and attuned to any challengers. It was why she did so much work with the Daughters— why she hosted their annual fund-raisers, why she led committees, why she chaired charity initiatives, why she tried, in all the ways appropriate for her imagination and her era, to be the ideal Hawaiian woman.

The problem, though, with trying to be the ideal anything is that eventually the definition changes, and you realize that what you'd been pursuing all along was not a single truth but a set of expectations determined by context. You leave that context, and you leave behind those expectations, too, and then you're nothing once again.

When Edward first met my mother, he was careful and polite. It wasn't until later, when we became close again as adults, that he became suspicious of her. She couldn't speak Hawaiian, he pointed out (neither could I; aside from the few phrases and words we all knew, and a dozen songs and chants, I spoke only English and some French). She didn't support the struggle. She didn't support the return of the Hawaiian kingdom. But he never mentioned, as others had, how light-skinned she was; he was lighter still, and if you hadn't grown up on the islands, you wouldn't know to look past his hair and eyes to see his Hawaiianness, a secret hiding just beneath. By that point, he had grown envious of my own appearance, my own skin and hair and eyes. Sometimes I'd look up to catch him staring at me. "You should grow your hair out," he said to me, once. "More authentic that way." It bothered him that even then, when everyone was wearing their hair long, I still wore mine as my father had worn his—tidy and very short—because it was woolly and dense, and if it got too long, it puffed out around my head.

"I don't want it to look like an Afro," I said, and he sat up from his usual slouch, leaning forward.

"What's wrong with an Afro?" he asked, giving me that unblinking stare he sometimes did, when his eyes darkened, turned a deeper blue, and I began to stammer, as I did when I was nervous.

"Nothing," I said. "Nothing's wrong with an Afro."

He leaned back and gazed at me for a long moment, and I had to look away. "A real Hawaiian wears his hair big," he said. His own hair was curly but fine, like a child's, and he wore it tied back with an elastic band. "Big and proud." He began calling me Accountant after that, because he said I looked like I should be working in a bank somewhere, counting other people's money. "Howzit, Accountant," he'd say in greeting when he came to pick me up. "Business good?" It was a taunt, I knew, but at times it felt almost loving, a term of affection, something only we shared.

I never knew what to say when he criticized my mother. By this time, it had long ago been made clear that I could never make her happy, and yet I couldn't help but feel protective of her, even though she'd never asked for my protection, and, indeed, I had none to give her. I would like to think, in retrospect, that part of what made me uncomfortable was his implication that there was only one way to be

Hawaiian. But I hadn't been sophisticated enough to think in those terms back then—the idea that my race compelled me to *be* one way or another at all was so foreign that it would have been like telling me that there was another, more correct way to breathe or swallow. I now know that all around me there were people my age who were having those very conversations: how to be black, or Oriental, or American, or a woman. But I had never heard those conversations, and when I finally did, it was in Edward's company.

So instead I would just say, "She's Hawaiian," though even as I said it I could hear it sounded like a question: "She's Hawaiian?"

Which is maybe why Edward answered as he did.

"No, she's not," he said.

———

But let me go back to when we first met. I was ten at the time, recently made fatherless. Edward was new that year. The school admitted new waves of students in kindergarten, fifth grade, seventh grade, and ninth grade. Later, Edward would curse the fact that we'd attended this school when we could have attended the school that only admitted students with Hawaiian blood. Our school had been granted by the king's charter but was founded by missionaries. "Of course we didn't learn about who we are and where we came from," he'd said. "Of course we didn't. That damn school's entire mission was to colonize us into submission." And yet he'd gone there as well. It was one of the many examples of things in my and Edward's shared life that he would come to hate or be ashamed of, and my refusal or inability to be equally ashamed—though I was ashamed of plenty of other things—came to infuriate him, too.

I attended the school because members of my family had always attended the school. On the high-school part of the campus there was even a building called Bingham Hall, one of the first structures the missionaries had built, named for one of the reverends who would later marry the crown princess. Every Kawika Bingham who had attended the school—my father, and grandfather, and great-grandfather, and great-great-grandfather—posed for a photograph or drawing in front of the building, standing beneath the name, which had been tapped into stone.

No one from Edward's family had ever attended the school, and it was only—he told me—because of a scholarship that he was able to go at all. He told me these things matter-of-factly, without self-pity or embarrassment, which I found remarkable.

We became friends slowly. Neither of us had any others. When I had been younger, there were some boys whose mothers wanted them to befriend me because of who my father was, who my mother was. It makes me cringe even now, the memory of one of them trudging across the playground toward me, introducing himself, asking if I wanted to play. I always said yes, and there'd be a lackluster game of catch. After a few days of this, I'd be invited to his house; Matthew would drive me if they didn't live in the valley. There, I'd meet the boy's mother, who would smile at me and serve us a snack: Vienna sausages and rice, or bread and passion fruit jam, or baked breadfruit with butter. There'd be another, silent game of catch, and then Matthew would drive me home. Depending on how ambitious the boy's mother was, there might be another two or three invitations, but eventually they would stop, and at school, the boy would bolt toward his real friends at recess, never looking at me. They were never cruel to me, they never bullied me, but that was only because I wasn't worth bullying. In the neighborhood, as I told you, there *were* boys who bullied me, but I grew used to that as well—it was a kind of attention.

I was friendless because I was boring, but Edward was friendless because he was strange. He didn't *look* strange—his clothes weren't as new as ours, but they were the same clothes, the same Hawaiian shirts and cotton pants—but he had, even then, a kind of inwardness; he was somehow able to suggest, without ever saying it, that he needed no one else, that he knew something that none of the rest of us did, and until we did, it wasn't worth his trying to have a conversation with us.

It was early in the school year when he approached me one recess period. I was sitting, as I always did, at the base of the giant monkeypod tree, reading a comic book. The tree was at the top of the field, which sloped gently toward the southern end of campus, and as I read, I could watch my classmates—the boys playing soccer, the girls jumping rope. Then I looked up and saw Edward loping toward me, but something in his air made me think he was just walking in my direction, not that I was his destination.

Yet it was in front of me that he stopped. "You're Kawika Bingham," he said.

"Wika," I said.

"What?" he asked.

"Wika," I said. "People call me Wika."

"Okay," he said. "Wika." And then he walked off. For a moment, I felt uncertain—*was* I Kawika Bingham?—and then I realized I was, because he had confirmed it.

The next day, he returned. "My mother wants you to come over after school tomorrow," he said. He had a way of speaking in which he looked not at you but at a point beyond you, which meant that when he finally did turn his gaze directly to you—as he did now, waiting for my answer—it felt particularly intense, almost interrogatory.

"Okay," I said. I didn't know what else to say.

The following morning, I told Matthew and Jane that I was going to a classmate's house after school. I told them quickly, quietly, as I ate my breakfast, for I knew, somehow, that my mother would not approve of Edward. This may have been unfair—my mother was not dismissive of people with less money than she had, at least not in a way I would have recognized at the time—but I knew I couldn't tell her.

Matthew and Jane looked at each other. All of my other play dates had been arranged by the boys' mothers with my mother; I had never arranged one on my own. I could tell they were happy for me, and trying not to make me self-conscious.

"You need me to come get you afterward, Wika?" asked Matthew, but I shook my head—I already knew that Edward lived near the school, which meant I'd be able to walk home, as usual.

Jane got up. "You'll want to bring something to give his mother," she said, and went to the pantry for one of her jars of mango jam. "Tell her she can send back the jar with you when she's done and I'll refill it next season, all right, Wika?" That seemed very optimistic—mango season had just ended, so, in order to get a refilled jar, Mrs. Bishop would have to count on her son and me remaining friends for another year. But I only said thank you, and put the jar in my backpack.

Edward and I were in adjoining classrooms, and he waited for me at the building's exit. We walked in silence through the middle-school campus, and then hopped over the low wall that encircled the school. He lived just a block south of this wall, in the middle of a poky street I'd often driven down with Matthew.

My first thought was that the house was charmed. The street was lined with small, single-story shops and businesses—a dry-goods shop, a hardware store, a grocer—and then, suddenly, as if conjured, was a tiny wooden house. The rest of the block was denuded of greenery, but looming over the structure was a large mango tree, so domineering and leafy that it seemed to be protecting the little building from sight. Nothing else grew in the lawn, not even grass, and the concrete path leading to the front porch had buckled from the tree's roots, one of which had split a paving stone in two. The house itself was a miniature version of the kind you saw in my neighborhood—a plantation house, as I learned to call them, with a wide lanai and large windows shaded by metal awnings.

The next surprise was the door itself, which was actually closed. Everyone I knew kept their doors open until they went to bed; there was only the screen door, which you banged through as you entered and exited. I watched as Edward reached down the front of his shirt and drew out a key, which dangled from a cotton string that hung around his neck, and unlocked the door. He slipped off his zoris and walked in, and I waited, stupidly, for an invitation before I realized I was to follow him.

Inside, it was close, and dark, and after relocking the door, Edward went around the living room, cranking open the jalousies to let in the breeze, though the mango tree blocked all the light.

But its shade also kept the house cool and heightened its sense of bewitchment.

"Do you want a snack?" Edward asked, already walking to the kitchen.

"Yes, please," I said.

He returned to the living room a few moments later with two plates, one of which he gave to me. On it were arranged four soda crackers, each with a daub of mayonnaise. He sat down on one of the rattan couches, and I sat on the other, and we ate our snack in silence. I had never had mayonnaise on crackers before and wasn't sure I liked it, or even if I was supposed to like it.

Edward ate his crackers quickly, as if it were a chore to be dispensed with, and then stood again. "Do you want to see my room?" he asked, and again, he asked almost sideways, as if he were addressing someone else in the room, although there was only me.

"Yes," I said.

There were three closed doors to the left of the living room. He opened the one on the right, and we entered a bedroom. This room too was small, but it was also cozy, like the lair of a harmless animal. There was a narrow bed with a striped blanket on it, and strung across the ceiling from one corner to the opposite were chains of bright-colored construction paper. "My mother and I made those," Edward explained, and although later I would remember how remarkable his tone was—so matter-of-fact, almost proud, when we were coming to an age in which announcing you made crafts, much less with your mother, was inadvisable—what I thought then was how foreign the idea was of making *anything* with your mother, especially something that you would hang from your ceiling, deliberately transforming your room into someplace messier and stranger than it had to be.

Now Edward turned and retrieved an object from the drawer beneath the table next to his bed. "Look at this," he said, solemnly, and held out a black velvet box about the size of a deck of playing cards. He opened the hinged lid, and inside was a medal made of coppery metal: It was the seal of our school and, on a scroll beneath, the words "Scholarship: 1953–1954." He flipped it over to show me his name engraved on the back: Edward Paiea Bishop.

"What's it for?" I asked, and he made a small, impatient sound.

"It's not *for* anything," he said. "They gave it to me when I got my scholarship."

"Oh," I said. I realized I was supposed to say something, but couldn't decide what it might be. I didn't know anyone else who was on a scholarship. In fact, until I had met Edward, I didn't even know what a scholarship was, and had had to ask Jane for an explanation. "It's nice," I said, and he made the sound again.

"It's stupid," he said, but when he replaced the box in its drawer, he did so tenderly, smoothing his hand across its furred surface.

Then he reached into another drawer, this one tucked beneath his bed—over time, I would realize that, although the room was minute, it was as well-organized and efficient as a sailor's berth, and that whoever had arranged it had accounted for all of Edward's interests, all of his needs—and retrieved a cardboard box. "Checkers," he said. "Want to play?"

As we played game after game of checkers, mostly in silence, I had time to consider what was most unusual about Edward's house. It was not its size, or its darkness (though, curiously, the dim made it not gloomy but snug, and even as the afternoon stretched on, there was no need to turn on a lamp), but the fact that we were there all alone. In my house, I was never alone. If my mother was at one of her meetings, there was Jane, and, sometimes, Matthew. But Jane was always there. She was cooking in the kitchen, or she was dusting in the living room, or she was sweeping the upstairs hallway. The farthest she strayed was to the side of the house, to hang the laundry on the line, or, occasionally, to the driveway, to bring Matthew, who was washing the car, his lunch. Even at night, she and Matthew were only a few hundred feet away, in their apartment above the garage. But I had never before been to a classmate's house where there was no mother. You didn't expect to see a father—they were creatures who materialized only at dinnertime, never in the afternoon—but the mothers were always there, a presence as reliable as a couch or a table. Sitting there, on Edward's bed, playing checkers, I had the sudden notion that he lived by himself. I had a vision of Edward making himself dinner on the stove (I was not allowed to touch the stove in my house), eating it at the kitchen table, washing the dishes, taking a bath, and putting himself to bed. There had been plenty of times when I had resented the lack of any true, meaningful privacy in my house, but suddenly the alternative—an absence of people, nothing but time and silence—seemed horrible, and it seemed to me that I should stay with Edward as long as I could, for when I left, he would have no one.

But as I was thinking this, there was a sound of the door opening, and then a woman's voice, bright and cheerful, calling Edward's name. "My mother," Edward said, and for the first time, he smiled, a quick, bright grin, and climbed off the bed and hurried into the living room.

I followed, to see Edward's mother kissing him, and then, before he could say anything, approaching me with her arms held out. "You must be Wika," she said, smiling. "Edward's told me so much about you," and she pulled me close.

"It's nice to meet you, Mrs. Bishop," I remembered to say, and she beamed and squeezed me again. "Victoria," she corrected me, and then, seeing my face, "or Auntie! Just not Mrs. Bishop." She turned to Edward, her arms still wrapped around me. "Are you boys hungry?"

"No, we had a snack," he said, and she smiled at him, too. "Good boy," she said, and yet her praise seemed to include me as well.

I watched her as she went to the kitchen. She was the most beautiful mother I had ever seen, so beautiful that if I had encountered her in another context, I would never have associated her with motherhood at all. She had dark-blond hair twisted into a bun at the base of her head, and her skin was a dark gold as well—more light-filled than mine, but darker than her son's—and she wore what was in those days considered a low-cut dress of pink cotton, with white bands at the sleeves and throat, and a full skirt that spun around her legs as she moved. She smelled delicious, like a combination of fried meat and, beneath that, the gardenia blossom she wore pinned behind her ear, and she didn't walk but twirled through the little house as if it were a palace, someplace expansive and dazzling.

It was only when she said that she hoped I was staying for dinner that I looked at the round-faced clock above the sink and realized that it was almost five-thirty, and I had told Matthew and Jane I'd be home an hour ago—never would I have assumed I would have wanted to stay at another boy's house for so long. I could feel myself entering that stage of distress I often did when I knew I had done something wrong, but Mrs. Bishop told me not to worry, just to call home, and when Jane picked up, she sounded relieved. "Matthew will come get you now," she said, before I even had a chance to ask if I could stay for dinner (which I wasn't sure I wanted to do, anyway). "He'll be there in ten minutes."

"I have to go home," I told Mrs. Bishop, when I had hung up, "I'm sorry," and she smiled at me again.

"You'll stay next time," she said. She spoke in a slight singsong. "We'd like that, right, Edward?" And Edward nodded, though he was already moving about the kitchen with his mother, removing things from the refrigerator, and seemed to have forgotten I was still there.

Before I left, I gave her the jar of mango jam in my bag. "This is for you," I said. "She"—I knew not to clarify that "she" was the housekeeper, and not my mother—"said you could give it back to me when it's empty and then she'll refill it next season." But then I remembered the tree outside, and felt foolish, and was about to apologize when Mrs. Bishop pulled me close again.

"My favorite," she said. "Tell your mother thank you." She laughed. "I may need to ask her for the recipe—every year I swear I'm going to make jam, and every year I never do. I'm such a klutz in the kitchen, you see," and she actually winked at me, as if she were letting me know a secret that no one else was privy to, not even her son.

I heard Matthew's car pull up outside, and said goodbye to them both. But on the lanai, I turned and looked through the screen door and saw the two of them, mother and son, in the kitchen making dinner. Edward said something to his mother and she tipped her head back and laughed, and then reached over and rubbed the top of his head, playfully. They had turned the kitchen light on, and I had the strange sense that I was looking inside a diorama, at a scene of happiness I could witness but never enter.

"Bishop," said my mother, later that night. "Bishop."

I knew, even then, what she was thinking: Bishop was a famous name, an old name, almost as famous and old as our own. She was thinking that Edward was someone like us, and yet I knew he wasn't, not in the way she meant.

"What does his father do?" she asked, and as I admitted I didn't know, I realized that I hadn't thought about his father at all. Part of this was, as I have said, because fathers were shadowy presences in all of our lives. You saw them on weekends and in the evenings, and if you were lucky, they were benevolent, distant beings, with an odd piece of candy for you, and if you were unlucky, they were chilly and remote, dispensers of whippings and spankings. My understanding of the world was very limited, but even I somehow comprehended that Edward didn't have a father—or, more accurately, that Mrs. Bishop didn't have a husband. The two of them, mother and son, were so complete together, cooking in that miniature kitchen, she playfully butting her hip against his side, he dramatically skidding to the right, his mother laughing at him, that there was no room for a father or a husband: They were a matched set, one female, one male, and another man would simply disrupt their symmetry.

"Well," my mother said, "we should have them over for tea."

And so, the following Sunday, they came. They couldn't come on Saturday, I heard Jane tell my mother, because Mrs. Bishop had to work her shift. ("Her *shift*," my mother echoed, in a tone that conveyed some meaning I couldn't quite interpret. "All right, Jane, tell her Sunday.") They arrived on foot, yet weren't hot or flushed, which meant they had taken the bus and had walked to our house from the closest stop. Edward was wearing his school clothes. His mother was wearing another full-skirted cotton dress, this one hibiscus-yellow, her dark-blond hair in its knot, her lips painted a cheery red, even more beautiful than I'd remembered.

She was smiling as my mother approached her. "Mrs. Bishop, such a pleasure to meet you," she said, to which Mrs. Bishop responded, as she had to me, "Please, call me Victoria."

"Victoria," my mother repeated, as if it were a foreign name and she wanted to make sure she was pronouncing it correctly, but she did not reciprocate the offer, though Mrs. Bishop seemed not to expect it.

"Thank you so much for having us over," she said. "Edward"— she turned her beam to her son, who was looking at my mother with a steady, serious expression, not quite suspicious, but alert—"is new this year, and Wika has been so kind to him." And now she turned to look at me, with that little wink, as if I had done her son a favor by talking to him, as if I had departed from my busy schedule in order to do so.

Even my mother seemed slightly taken aback by this. "Well, I'm very glad to hear Wika has a new friend," she said. "Won't you come in?"

We filed into the sunroom, where Jane served us shortbread, pouring the women coffee—"Oh! Thank you—Jane? Thank you, Jane, this looks delicious!"—and Edward and me guava juice. I had seen other acquaintances of my mother grow silent and awestruck in this room, which to me was simply a room, sunlit and dull, but to them was a museum of my father's ancestors: the scarred wooden surfboard my great-grandfather, known as the Portly Prince, had ridden in Waikīkī; the daguerreotypes of my great-great-grandfather's sister, the queen, in her black taffeta gown, and a great-great-cousin, an explorer who had a building at a famous university named for him. But Mrs. Bishop seemed unintimidated, and looked about herself openly, with genuine delight. "What a lovely room this is, Mrs. Bingham," she said, smiling at my mother. "My entire family has always been great admirers of your husband's family, and how much he did for the islands."

It was exactly the right thing to say, done simply and well, and

I could tell my mother was surprised. "Thank you," she said, a bit stiffly. "He loved his home."

For a while, my mother talked to Edward, asking him if he liked his new school (yes), and if he missed his old friends (not really), and what his hobbies were (swimming, hiking, camping, going to the beach). When I became the parent of a young boy myself, I was able to appreciate Edward's composure, his apparent unflappability; as a child, I was eager, too eager, to please, smiling desperately through conversations with my parents' friends, hoping I wouldn't shame them. But Edward was neither ingratiating nor awkward—he answered my mother's questions straightforwardly, without any pandering or apology. Even then, he possessed an unusual dignity, one that made him seem invincible. It was almost as if he didn't care about anyone else, and yet that would suggest that he was aloof, or proud, and he wasn't either of those things.

Finally, my mother was able to ask about Mr. Bishop: Certain members of the Bishop family had been distant cousins of my father, the way that all the old missionary families who had married into Hawaiian royalty were distant cousins—was it possible that there might be a connection?

Mrs. Bishop laughed. There was no bitterness in that laugh, no falsity: It was a sound of pure merriment. "Oh, I'm afraid not," she said. "I'm the only Hawaiian, not my husband." My mother looked blank, and Mrs. Bishop smiled again. "It was quite a shock for Luke, a haole boy from a small town in Texas whose father was a construction worker, to understand that, here, his last name made him something special."

"I see," said my mother, quietly. "So is your husband in construction as well?"

"He could be." Again, the smile. "But we just don't know, do we, Edward?" Then, to my mother, "He left long ago, when Edward was a baby—I haven't seen him since."

I can't say, of course, that men didn't leave their families all the time in the early fifties. But I *can* say—and this was true even decades later—that to have your husband or father leave was something shameful, as if the responsible party was the abandoned, the wife and children. If people spoke about it, they did so in whispers. But not the Bishops. Mr. Bishop had left, but *they* weren't the losers—*he* was.

It was one of those rare moments in which my mother and I were united in our discomfiture. Before the Bishops left, we learned that Sunday was Mrs. Bishop's day off; the other six days, she worked as a waitress at a busy diner a few blocks from their house called Mizumoto's, which my mother hadn't heard of but Jane and Matthew had, and that she was from Honoka'a, a tiny town, a village, really, on the Big Island.

"What an extraordinary woman," my mother said, watching as mother and son turned right at the end of our driveway and walked out of sight toward the bus stop. I could tell she didn't quite mean it as a compliment.

I agreed with her—she *was* extraordinary. They both were. I had never encountered two people who seemed less abashed by the circumstances of their lives. But whereas that lack of apology manifested itself in Mrs. Bishop as an irrepressible buoyancy, the kind of cheer that exists only in the rare people who have never felt embarrassed for who they are, they were realized in Edward as a defiance, one that in later years curdled into anger.

I see this now, of course. But it took me a long time. And by that point, I had already given up my life, and therefore your life, for his. Not because I shared his anger—but because I craved his certainty, this strange and wondrous notion that there really was a single answer, and that, by believing in it, I would cease to believe everything that had bothered me about myself for so long.

———

And now, Kawika, I will skip forward a number of years. First, though, I want to tell you about something that happened to me yesterday.

I was lying in bed as usual. It was the afternoon, and hot. Earlier in the day they had opened the windows and turned on the fan, but now the breeze had died, and no one had returned to switch on the air-conditioning. This occasionally happened, and then someone would enter the room, exclaiming at how hot it was, scolding me a bit, as if I had the ability to call out for them and had simply refused to do so out of stubbornness. Once, they had forgotten to turn on the air-conditioning at all and my mother had made a surprise visit. I had heard her voice, and her feet marching in, and then I heard her march back out again, and return a few seconds later with an orderly, who was apologizing again and again as my mother rebuked him: "Do you know how much I pay for my son to be looked after? Get me the manager on duty. This is unacceptable." I was humiliated hearing this, being so old and still in my mother's care, but also comforted, and I fell asleep to the sound of her anger.

Normally, the heat didn't bother me so much, but yesterday, it was oppressive, and I could feel my face and hair becoming damp; I could feel sweat trickling into my diaper. Why won't someone come help me? I thought. I tried to make a sound, but I of course couldn't.

And then something very strange happened. I stood. I cannot explain how this happened—I have not stood for years, not since I was rescued from Lipo-wao-nahele. But now I was not only standing, I was trying to walk, trying to move toward where I knew the air-conditioning unit was. As I realized this, however, I fell, and after a few minutes, someone came into the room and started making a fuss, asking me why I was on the floor, and if I'd rolled out of bed. For a minute I worried she might strap me down, as has happened before, but she didn't, just buzzed for help, and then another person came in and they returned me to bed and then, thank goodness, switched on the air conditioner.

The point, though, is that I had stood; I had been standing. It felt both foreign and also familiar to be upright again, even if I trembled for a long time afterward because my limbs were so wasted. Last night, after I had been fed and washed and the space was dark and silent, I began to think. It had been luck that no one had seen me standing, because if they had, there would have been questions, and my mother would have been called, and there would have been tests, the sorts I had had when I first came here: Why would I not walk?

Why would I not speak? Why would I not see? "You're asking the wrong questions," my mother had snapped to someone, a doctor. "You should be asking why he *can't* do those things." "No, Mrs. Bingham," the doctor replied, and I could hear an edge in his voice. "I am asking exactly the right questions. It's not that your son *can't* do these things—it's that he *won't*," and my mother had been silent.

Now, however, I realized: What if I *could* learn how to walk again? What if every day I practiced standing? What would happen? The thought scared me, but it was exciting as well. What if I was getting better after all?

But I meant to continue my story. Throughout the remainder of fifth grade, Edward and I saw a lot of each other. Occasionally, he came to my house, but more often, I went to his, where we would play checkers or cards. When he came to my house, he'd want to play outside, as his yard was too small to toss a ball in, but he soon realized I wasn't much of an athlete. The strange thing, though, was that we never seemed to grow closer in any meaningful way. Boys that age may not exchange intimacies or secrets, but they do become more physical with each other: I remember you at that age, how you would tussle on the grass with your friends like little animals, how much of the fun you had with them was getting dirty together. But Edward and I weren't like that—I was too fastidious, and he was too composed. I sensed, early on, that he would never be someone I could relax around, and I didn't mind that.

Then came summer. Edward went to the Big Island to stay with his grandparents; my mother and I went to Hāna, where we at the time had a house that had been in my father's family since before annexation. And by the time school had resumed, something had shifted. Friendships at that age are so fragile, because who you are—not just the physical dimensions of you but the emotional ones, too—change so dramatically from month to month. Edward joined the baseball team and swim team and made new friends; I reverted to my solitude. I now suppose I must have been sad about this, but, curiously, I remember no feelings of sorrow, no feelings of anger—it was like the previous year had been a mistake, and I had known that things would at some point return to normal. Also, it wasn't as if there was any animosity—we had only drifted, not split, and when we saw each other across campus or in the hallways, we would both nod or wave, gestures you'd make across a wide sea, where you knew your voice couldn't carry. When we reunited more than a decade later, it felt somehow inevitable, as if we had both drifted for so long that we were bound to find each other again.

There are, however, two encounters from those years apart that stood out for me. The first took place when I was around thirteen. I had overheard an exchange between two girls in my grade. One of the girls, it was well-known, had a crush on Edward. But her friend disapproved. "You *can't*, Belle," she hissed. "Why not?" Belle asked. "Because," said the first girl, her voice dropping, "his mother. She's a *dancer*."

Since he had matriculated, Edward was occasionally the subject of—not rumors, because they were all true, but stories. Eventually, we came to learn who the scholarship students were, and their parents' occupations were sometimes whispered from child to child, all mimicking the voices their own parents used to discuss the newcomers. Edward had no father, and his mother was a waitress, but he was spared from outright ridicule: He was good at sports, and moreover, he didn't seem to care what people said, which was partly what motivated the stories—I think the other students hoped that they might provoke him to react, but he never did.

At least he wasn't Oriental. This was in the years of the quota, when only ten percent of the school's population was Oriental, even though the territory's actual population was around thirty percent. Most of the Orientals who did attend arrived, in some cases, having never worn shoes, just rubber slippers. They were all on scholarships, identified by their public-school teachers as promising and bright, and subjected to multiple tests before they gained admission. Their parents worked on the island's final sugarcane plantation or in the canning factories, and on weekends and in the summer, they worked there, too, cutting cane or picking pine, as they called it, in the fields, loading it onto the trucks. There was a boy, Harry, who had begun at the school in seventh grade whose father was a night-soil collector, someone who cleaned out the plantation outhouses and transferred the human feces there to—where, we didn't know. It was said he smelled like shit, and although he too always sat alone at lunch, eating his rice sandwiches, I never thought of introducing myself to him: I looked down on him as well.

Hearing about Mrs. Bishop made me miss her. Indeed, she was what I missed most about my friendship with Edward: the way she held me by the shoulders and then pulled me in for a hug, laughing; the way she kissed me on the forehead when I left their house for the evening; the way she told me she hoped she'd see me again soon.

I had never listened to the talk about Edward, but now I did, and after a few weeks, I learned that, while Mrs. Bishop was still a waitress at Mizumoto's, she was now also dancing three nights a week at a restaurant called Forsythia. This was a popular place near Mizumoto's, a hangout for union men of all ethnicities. Matthew's brother, of whom he was very proud, was a union representative for the Filipino cannery employees, and I knew he sometimes went to Forsythia, because occasionally Jane would beckon me into the kitchen after school and, with a flourish, present the restaurant's yellow bakery box, in which would sit a guava chiffon cake, its surface a glossy rose-pink.

"From Matthew's brother," she'd say—she was proud of him, too, and pride made her even more generous. "Have a big slice, Wika. Have more."

I didn't understand why I wanted to see her so badly. But one Friday afternoon, I told Matthew and Jane I had to stay late to help paint sets for the annual school play, and then I cycled over. Forsythia (much later, I would wonder who had chosen this name, as it wasn't a plant that grew in Hawai'i, and no one knew what it was) was at the end of a row of small, mostly Japanese-owned stores of the sort that surrounded the Bishops' house, and though its stucco exterior had been painted a bright yellow, it was designed to resemble a Japanese teahouse, with a peaked roof and small windows cut high into the walls. In the rear of the building, though, near one of the corners, there was a long, skinny window, and it was to here that I quietly wheeled my bike.

I sat down to wait. The kitchen entrance was a few feet away, but there was a dumpster, and I hid behind that. A Hawaiian music group performed here on Fridays and the weekends, playing all the big-band standards, music my father had liked to listen to—"Nani Waimea," "Moonlight in Hawai'i," "Ē Lili'u ē"—and it was after the fourth song that I heard the guitarist announce, "And now, gentlemen—and some ladies, yeah?—please join me in welcoming the lovely Miss Victoria Nāmāhānaikaleleokalani Bishop!"

The crowd cheered, and I looked through the window to see Mrs. Bishop, in a close-fitting yellow holokū printed with white hibiscus, a lei of orange puakenikeni around her head, her hair coiled into a bun, her lips scarlet, ascend to the small stage. She waved to the audience, which was clapping, and I watched as she danced to "My Yellow Ginger Lei" and "Pālolo." She was a beautiful dancer, and although I didn't speak more than a few words of Hawaiian, I understood the lyrics from watching her movements.

It occurred to me as I watched her, her face lit with happiness, that, although I had always liked her, part of me had wanted to see her degraded in some way. "Dancing," in my classmates' voices, had sounded so sordid, something a desperate woman would have to do, and something in me had craved witnessing it. Watching her now, queenly and elegant, was both a relief and, as much as I hated to admit it, a disappointment—I realized that I resented her son after all, that I wanted him to have something to be ashamed of, and that I had wanted that something to be his mother, who had always been kind to me, kind in a way her son could never be. She was not dancing because she had been forced to out of circumstance—she was dancing because she loved to dance, and although she dipped her head graciously at the crowd's applause, it was also clear that her joy was separate from their approval.

I left before her set was over. But in bed that night, I lay awake thinking of the night I had departed the Bishops' house for the first time and had turned back to see them in the kitchen together, laughing and talking in the house's warm yellow light. Now I revised that memory: They had put a record on the player, and Mrs. Bishop, still in her Mizumoto's uniform, was dancing, and Edward was strumming his ukulele, playing along. Outside, in the tiny yard, were crowded all of Edward's and my classmates, and all of the patrons from Forsythia as well, all of us watching and clapping, though mother and son never turned to acknowledge us—to them, there was only each other, and it was as if we didn't exist.

That was the first incident I wanted to tell you about. The second occurred three years later, in 1959.

It was August 21, and the school year had just begun. I was in tenth grade, almost sixteen. Now that we were in high school, I saw more of Edward than I had in the previous years, when we had been assigned to single, different classrooms. Now we moved from teacher to teacher, and sometimes we were in the same class. His earlier spell of popularity, when it had been discovered he could play sports, had tempered, and now I mostly saw him around the same three or four boys. As always, we nodded at each other in passing, and sometimes we even spoke a few words if we were in proximity—*I think I messed up on that chem test. Oh, me too*—but no one would have identified us as friends.

I was in English class when the intercom crackled and the principal's voice, rapid and emotional, started speaking: President Eisenhower had signed a bill granting Hawai'i statehood. We were now officially the fiftieth American state. Many of the students, and my teacher, began clapping.

We were given the rest of the day off in celebration. For most of us, this was a formality, but I knew that Matthew and Jane would be excited; they had lived in the territory for thirty years—they wanted to be able to vote, which was not something I'd considered.

I was walking up toward the campus's western gate when I saw Edward heading south. The first thing I noticed was how slowly he was moving; other students were passing him by, talking about what they were going to do with their unexpected free day, but he appeared to be sleepwalking.

I was nearing him when he suddenly looked up and saw me. "Hi," I said, and then, when he didn't respond, "What're you going to do with your day off?"

For a moment, he didn't answer, and I thought that he perhaps hadn't heard me. But then he said, "This is horrible news."

He spoke so quietly that I at first thought I'd misheard him. "Oh," I said, stupidly.

But it was like I'd tried to argue with him. "It's horrible news," he repeated tonelessly, "horrible." And then he turned from me and kept walking. I remember thinking he looked lonely, even though I'd seen him alone many times and had never associated his aloneness with loneliness, the way I did with mine. This time, though, something felt different. He looked—though I wouldn't have had the word for it then—bereft, and although I couldn't see his face, there was something about his back, the slump of his shoulders, that, had I not known better, would have made me think he had just suffered a terrible loss.

I understand that that incident, knowing what you do of Edward, might not seem particularly notable. But it was uncharacteristic of the Edward I knew—admittedly not very well—back then. However, I would have known—through him or through gossip—if he had expressed any strong sentiments about native Hawaiian rights, even given the fact that the very *idea* of native Hawaiian rights had not yet been invented. (Now I can hear Edward saying, "Of *course* it had been invented." So, all right: It had not yet been named. Named, or popularized, not even on a small scale.) There were a few boys in our grade who were interested in politics—one, whose father was the territorial governor, even got it into his head that he would one day be president of the United States. But Edward was not one of them, which made what happened later all the more surprising.

I should add, though, that Edward was not the only person who was upset that day. Back home, I found my mother sitting in the sunroom, quilting. This was unusual, as she was typically with the Daughters on Friday afternoons, volunteering at a food kitchen that served Hawaiian families. When I entered the room, she looked up, and we stared at each other in silence.

"They let us out early," I said. "Because of the announcement."

She nodded. "I stayed home today," she said. "I just couldn't bear it." She looked down at her quilt—it was a breadfruit pattern, dark green on white—and then back up at me. "This doesn't change anything, you know, Kawika," she said. "Your father should still be king. And someday, you should still be king, too. Remember that."

It was a strange mix of tenses, a sentence of promises and grievances, reassurances and consolations.

"All right," I said, and she nodded.

"This changes nothing," she said. "This land is ours." And then she looked back at her quilting ring, my signal that I was dismissed, and I went upstairs to my room.

I had no strong feelings about statehood. I thought of it as falling under the broad roof of "government," and I had no interest in government. Who was in charge, which decisions were made—none of it affected me. A signature on a piece of paper was irrelevant to the facts of my own life. Our house, the people within it, my school: These things wouldn't change. My burden was one not of citizenry but of legacy; I was David Bingham, my father's son, and all that went with it. I suppose, looking back on it, I might even have been relieved—now that the islands' fate was settled, it would perhaps mean that I would no longer bear the responsibility and obligation of trying to correct a history I had no hopes of changing.

It would be another decade, almost, before I returned to Edward's orbit, but in those years, many things happened.

The first thing is that I graduated—we all did. Most of my classmates went to college on the mainland; it was what we had been groomed to do, after all—it was the entire point of the school. We were to go away and get our degrees, maybe do a bit of traveling, and then we would return after college or law school or medical school and get jobs in the most prestigious local banks and law firms and hospitals, which were owned or founded by our relatives and ancestors. Quite a few of us would go into government, leading the Departments of Transportation or Education or Agriculture.

At first, I was among their number. The dean had directed me toward an obscure liberal-arts school in the Hudson Valley of New York, and in September 1962, I left home.

It quickly became clear that I was not meant for the college. It may have been small, and expensive, and unknown, but the other students, most of whom were from rich but vaguely bohemian New York City families, were somehow much more sophisticated and much better educated than I was. It wasn't that I had never traveled, but my travels had been oriented toward the East, and none of my new classmates seemed to care about the places I'd been. They'd all traveled to Europe, some of them every summer, and I was soon made aware of my own provinciality. Few of them knew that Hawai'i had been a kingdom; more than one asked if I lived in a "real" house, by which they meant one made of stone, with a shingled roof. The first time, I hadn't known how to reply, the question was so ludicrous, and stood there blinking until the other person moved away. The references they made, the books they quoted, the vacations they took, the food and wine they preferred, the people they all seemed to know—all of it whirred past me.

The strange thing, though, is that I didn't resent them: I resented where I had come from. I cursed my school, where generations of Binghams had gone, for not better preparing me. What had I learned there that was useful? I had taken all the same subjects my new classmates had, but so much of my education, it seemed, had been taken up with learning Hawaiian history and bits of Hawaiian language, which I couldn't even speak. How was that knowledge meant to be useful to me, when the rest of the world simply didn't care? I didn't dare bring up who my family was—I sensed that half of them wouldn't believe me, and the other half would mock me.

I knew this for certain after the variety show. Every December, the college presented a series of brief sketches by different students satirizing various professors and administrators. One of the sketches was about the school's president, who was always talking about recruiting students from new countries and unlikely places, trying to convince a Stone Age tribe boy—Prince Woogawooga of the Ooga-ooga, was his name—to attend the school. The student playing the tribe member had darkened his skin with brown shoe polish and wore an oversize diaper; on either side of his nose was taped one half of a cardboard bone, so that it looked as if the length of it had pierced though the bridge. On his head he wore a mop, its ropes dyed black and tied back from his face.

"Hello there, young man," the student playing the president said. "You look like an intelligent young person."

"Ooga booga, ooga booga," hooted the student playing the tribesman prince, scratching beneath his arms like an ape and bouncing from foot to foot.

"We teach everything that a young man needs to learn in order to be considered educated," the president continued, stoically ignoring the tribesman's antics. "Geometry, history, literature, Latin; and, of course, sports: lacrosse, tennis, football, badminton." And here he held out a badminton ball to the tribesman, who immediately stuffed it into his mouth.

"No, no!" cried the president, finally flustered. "This is not for eating, good man! Spit it out at once!"

The tribesman did, scratching and jumping, and then, after a pause during which he looked at the audience, his eyes opened wide, his mouth, which had been circled with red lipstick, stretched taut, he made a lunging leap at the president, trying to take a bite out of his cheek.

"Help!" shouted the president. "Help!" The two began to run around the stage, the tribesman's teeth coming together in a sharp wooden click as he bit down on air, cackling and whooping as he chased the president into the wings.

The two actors returned to the stage to loud applause. The audience had been laughing the entire time, in an exaggerated, obscene way, almost as if they'd never laughed before and were just learning how. Only two of us were silent: me, and an upperclassman from Ghana whom I didn't know. I watched him watching the stage, his face still and clenched, and realized he thought it was about him and his home, but I knew it was about me and mine—the cardboard palm trees, the ferns tied in clumsy bunches around the savage's ankles and wrists, the lei made of cut-up plastic straws and newsprint flowers. It was a cheap, coarse costume, cheaply and coarsely made, dismissive even in its ridicule. This is what they thought of me, I realized, and later, when Edward first mentioned Lipo-wao-nahele, it was this night that I remembered, the sensation of watching, frozen, as everything I was, and everything my family was, was brutally dismembered, stripped naked, and pushed onto the stage to be howled at.

How could I have remained there, after that? I packed a bag and took a bus south, to Manhattan, where I checked in to the Plaza, the only hotel whose name I knew. I sent a telegram to my uncle William, who managed my father's estate, asking him to wire me money and not tell my mother; he sent one back saying he would, but he wouldn't be able to keep this from her forever, and he hoped I was being smart.

I spent the days walking. Every morning, I went to a diner near Carnegie Hall for breakfast, where I could have fried eggs and potatoes and bacon and coffee for far less than I'd have to pay at the hotel, and then I walked north or south or east or west. I had a tweed coat, expensive and handsome but not quite warm enough, and as I walked, I breathed on my hands, and when I could bear the cold no longer, I would find a diner or coffee shop and go inside to have a hot chocolate and get warm.

My identity changed with the neighborhood I found myself in. In midtown, they thought I might be black, but in Harlem, they knew I wasn't. I was spoken to in Spanish and Portuguese and Italian and even Hindi, and when I answered, "I'm Hawaiian," I would invariably be told that they or their brother or cousin had been there after the war, and asked what I was doing up here, so far from home, when I could be on the beach with a pretty little hula girl. I never had an answer to these questions, but they didn't expect one—it was all they knew to ask, but no one wanted to hear what I had to say.

On my eighth day, though—Uncle William had sent me a telegram that morning saying that my mother had been alerted by the bursar's office that I had left school, and was instructing him to send me a ticket home, which would be waiting for me that evening—I was walking back to the hotel from Washington Square Park, where

I'd gone to see the arch. It was very cold that afternoon, whipping wind, and the city seemed to mirror my mood, which was gray and bleak.

I had walked north on Broadway, and as I turned east on Central Park South, I almost stumbled into a beggar. I had seen him before; he was a squat, dark, beaten man, always on this corner, in a much too long black coat—he held before him with both hands an old-fashioned felt bowler, the kind that had been fashionable thirty years ago, and which he shook as people passed. "Spare a dime, sir?" he would call. "Spare a nickel?"

I was passing him, about to murmur my regrets, when he saw me, and as he did, he suddenly snapped, soldierlike, to his full height, before bowing at the waist. I heard him gasp. "Your Highness," he said, to the pavement.

My first reaction was shame. I looked around me, but no one was staring at us; no one had seen.

He gazed up at me, his eyes wet. I could see now that he was one of mine, one of us: His face was one I knew in shape and color and form, if not in its specifics. "Prince Kawika," he said, his voice slurry with emotion and alcohol; I could smell it on him. "I knew your father," he said, "I knew your father." And then he shook his hat at me. "Please, Your Highness," he said, "please give something to one of your subjects, so far from home."

There was nothing sly in his voice, only beseechment. Only later, back in my room, would I wonder *why* he was so far from home, how he had ended up begging on a street corner in New York, and if he had really known my father—it was possible, after all. For true royalists, which this man seemed to be, statehood was an insult, a loss of hope. "Please, Your Highness, I'm very hungry." His hat was dark, and I could see only a few coins inside, sliding around in the bowl of shiny felt.

I took out my wallet and hurriedly gave him everything I had—about forty dollars, I thought—and then I hurried on, moving away from his cries of thanks. I was Prince Woogawooga of the Ooga-ooga, except, instead of running after someone, I was running from him, as if he would pursue me, this man who called himself my subject. He was hungry, and he would open his mouth, and when he closed his jaws, I would be within them, my head being chewed to bits, waiting for the play to be over.

I went home; I enrolled in the University of Hawai'i, which the graduates of my school only attended if they were poor or had poor grades. Upon graduating, I was given a job at what had been my father's company, except it wasn't actually a company, insofar as it produced nothing, sold nothing, and bought nothing—it was a collection of my family's remaining real-estate holdings and investments, and aside from Uncle William, who was a lawyer, and an accountant, there was a clerk and a secretary.

Initially, I showed up every day at eight. But within a few months, it became clear that my presence was superfluous. My title was "estate manager," but there was nothing to manage. The trust was conservative, and a few times a year, some stocks would be bought or sold and the dividends reinvested. A rabbity Chinese man was contracted to gather rents from the various residential properties and, if the renters refused to or were unable to pay, a Samoan, enormous and terrifying, was sent on a follow-up visit. The trust's goals were deliberately unambitious, because ambition entailed risk, and after the resolution of my father's debts, the focus was on maintenance, on providing enough for my mother and me to live on, and, if they planned correctly, my great-grandchildren and great-great-grandchildren as well.

Once it became clear that the firm would totter on whether I was there or not, I began taking long breaks. The offices were downtown in a beautiful old Spanish-style building, and I would leave at eleven, before the lunch crowds, and walk the few blocks to Chinatown. I drew a salary, but I lived modestly—I would go to a restaurant that served a bowl of pork-and-shrimp wonton min for a quarter, and after paying I would wander the streets, past the hawkers arranging their pyramids of starfruit and rambutan, past the apothecaries with their bins of shriveled roots and dried seeds, their rows of glass jars filled with a cloudy liquid and curls of herbs and different unidentifiable animal paws, shorn of their fur. Nothing ever changed in Hawai'i; it was as if every day I walked onto a stage set, and every morning, long before I woke, it was unfurled, swept clean, and readied for me to pass through it again.

Of course I was lonely. Some of the boys who I had been able to pretend were my friends in high school came back to town as well, but they were busy with graduate school or their new jobs, and much of my time was spent as it had been when I was a child: in my bedroom at my mother's house, or in the sunroom watching television on the little black-and-white set I had bought with some of my salary. On weekends, I went to watch the fishermen at Waimānalo or Kaimana; I went to the movies. I turned twenty-two, and then twenty-three.

One day when I was twenty-four, I was driving back to town. It was late in the evening. By this time, I had stopped going to work entirely, phasing myself out of the life of the office until I simply never returned. No one seemed upset or even surprised by this; it was my money, after all, and it continued to come to me in the form of a paycheck, every two weeks.

I was driving through Kailua, which was at the time a very small town, with none of the stores and restaurants it would have a decade later, when I passed a bus stop. Two times a month, I drove around the entire island, one week going east, the next, west. It was a way to pass the time, and I would sit on the beach near the stone church in Lā'ie, where my father had once handed out money, and look at the sea. The bus stop was beneath a streetlamp, one of the few on the road, and seated at its bench was a young woman. I was driving slow enough so that I could see she had dark hair pulled back from her face, and wore a printed-orange cotton skirt—in the light, she appeared to be glowing. She sat very straight, her legs together, her hands folded in her lap, her purse strap looped over one wrist.

I don't know why I didn't just drive on, but I didn't. I turned around in the road, which was deserted, and returned to her.

"Hello," I said, when I was close to her, and she looked back at me.

"Hello," she said.

"Where are you going?" I asked.

"I'm waiting for the bus to town," she said.

"The bus doesn't run this late," I said, and for the first time, she looked worried.

"Oh, no," she said. "I have to get back to the dorm or they'll lock the doors."

"I can drop you off," I offered, and she hesitated, looking up and down the dark, empty road. "You can sit in the back seat," I added.

At this she nodded, and smiled. "Thank you," she said, "I'd be very grateful."

She sat the same way as she had at the bus stop: erect and poised, her eyes straight ahead. I studied her in the rearview mirror. "I'm a student at the university," she finally said, as if by way of an offering.

"What year are you?" I asked.

"A junior," she said, "but I'm only here for the year."

She was on an exchange program, she said; the next year she would return to Minneapolis, and graduate from her college there. Her name was Alice.

I began seeing her. She lived in one of the girls' dormitories, Frear Hall, and I would wait in the lobby until she came down. Every Wednesday, she took weaving lessons in Kailua with an old Hawaiian lady, for which she always wore a modest, knee-length skirt and her hair pulled back. Otherwise, she wore jeans and let her hair loose. I could tell from its texture and the shape of her nose that she wasn't entirely haole, but I didn't understand what she actually was. "I'm Spanish," she said, but I knew from my time on the mainland that "Spanish" could sometimes mean Mexican, or Puerto Rican, or something else altogether. She talked about her studies, and how she had come here because she wanted to be somewhere warm for once in her life, but had grown to love it, about how she wanted to go back home and become a teacher, and about how she missed her mother (her father was dead) and little brother. She talked about how she wanted a life full of adventure, about how living in Hawai'i was a little like living abroad, and someday, she would live in China, and India, and, when the war was over, Thailand, too. We talked about what was happening in Vietnam, and about the election, and about music; in each case, she had more to say than I did. Sometimes she asked about my life, but there wasn't much to tell. And yet she seemed to like me well enough; she was very gentle with me, and when I made mistakes, fumbling for too long with her clothes, she placed my hands on her shoulders and unbuttoned her dress herself.

We had sex in her room one night when her roommate was out. She had to tell me what to do, and how, and at first I was embarrassed, and then I felt nothing at all. Afterward, I thought about the experience: It had been neither pleasant nor unpleasant, but I was glad I had done it and glad it was over. I felt I had crossed some important threshold, one that marked me as an adult even as my daily life belied it. If it had been less enjoyable than I had assumed it would be, it had also been easier, and we met for a few times more, and it made me feel like my life was moving forward.

Now comes the part you know, Kawika, which is also the hard part.

Of course Alice knew who my family was, but it seemed she hadn't realized its full implications until she had returned home. By the time the letter arrived at the firm, I had had the first of my seizures. Initially, I assumed they were headaches: The world would quiet and flatten, and shifting fields of color—of the kind we used to see together after we stared at the sun and then shut our eyes— would float across my field of vision. When I came to, it might be a minute later or an hour, and then I would be woozy and disoriented. After I was diagnosed, I lost my driver's license; from there on, Matthew would have to drive me, and if Matthew was unavailable, my mother.

So I cannot quite remember the exact sequence of events that brought you home to me. I know your grandmother told you that your mother had effectively abandoned you, writing to Uncle William and telling him that someone had to come retrieve you because she was leaving Minneapolis again, this time to study in Japan, and her own mother was in no position to take care of a baby. Later, Uncle William told me that, while Alice had contacted the firm, it was your grandmother who, upon receiving evidence that you were in fact a Bingham, offered your mother money. Alice, your mother, countered with a different sum, one that Uncle William warned your grandmother would necessitate selling the house in Hāna. "Do it," she told him, and she didn't need to explain why: You would be the heir of the family, and there was no guarantee that I would ever produce another. She had to take the opportunity she was presented. A month later, Uncle William flew to Minnesota and had the papers countersigned; when he returned, it was with you. It was an echo of my mother's own alleged origins, though neither of us ever acknowledged that.

I cannot say which version was true. I *can* say she had never told me—not that she was pregnant, not that she had given birth. She disappeared from my life after the end of the 1967 school year. I do know that she is indeed dead—she married at some point in the early seventies, to a man she met while a student in Kobe; they were killed in a boating accident in '74. But as for why neither she nor her family ever made contact with you—I can only imagine it was because the terms of arrangement she made with your grandmother prohibited it.

You cannot be bitter about this, Kawika—not bitter toward your grandmother, or toward Alice. One wanted you very badly, and the other hadn't planned on becoming a mother.

I can also say that you are and always were the joy of my life, that having you made me feel I might have something to contribute after all. You were still a baby when I got you, and in those years when you were learning to roll over, and sit, and walk, and talk, my mother and I were in harmony—because of you. Sometimes we would sit on the floor in the sunroom, watching you kick your legs and babble, and as we laughed or clapped at your efforts, we would sometimes catch each other's eye, and it was as if we were not mother and son but husband and wife, and you were our child.

She was always proud of you, Kawika, as I was and as I am. She still is, I know it—she's just disappointed, because she misses you, as I miss you too.

And here I must restate that I never blamed you for leaving me. I was not your responsibility; you were mine. You had to find your way out of a situation you should never have been in at all.

Over the years, I kept waiting for the day you would ask about your mother, but you never did. I'll admit that I was relieved, although, later, I came to realize that you might not have asked because you wanted to protect me, because you were always trying to protect me, when I was the one who should have been protecting you. Your apparent lack of interest in your mother was the subject of a fight I had with your grandmother, one of the few times I stood up to her. "It's strange," she had said, after a parent-teacher conference we had attended, in which your teacher had mentioned that she didn't know anything about your mother, "strange how incurious he is." She was implying that this meant you were slow, somehow, slow or tepid, and I barked at her. "So you want him to start asking?" I demanded, and she shrugged, slightly, not lifting her eyes from her quilting ring. "Of course not," she said. "I just think it's odd that he doesn't." I was furious with her. "He's just a little boy," I said, "and he believes what you told him. I can't believe you're complaining about the fact that he trusts you, that you're trying to make it sound like a flaw." I got up and left the room, and that night, she had Jane prepare rice pudding, your favorite, which I knew was her way of apologizing to you, even though you would never know that it was an apology.

Eventually, it became easy for us to pretend that you'd never had a mother at all. There was a Japanese folktale that you had liked me to tell you, about a boy who was born from a peach and found by an old childless couple. "Read me 'Momotaro' again," you'd say, and then, when I had, "Again." After a while, I began telling you a version about a boy, Mangotaro, who was discovered inside a mango hanging from the tree in our yard, and how that boy grew up to have many adventures and make many friends. The story always ended with the boy leaving his father and grandmother and aunt and uncle and going far away, where he would have new adventures and make new friends. I knew, even then, that my job was to remain, and yours was to leave, to go somewhere I would never see, to have a life of your own.

"What happens next?" you'd ask when the story was over, and I'd kissed you good night.

"You'll have to come back and tell me someday," I'd say.

————

Kawika: It happened again. I had a dream that I was standing, and not just standing but walking. My hands were extended before me, like a zombie, and I was shuffling one foot and then the other. And then I realized that, again, I wasn't dreaming but really walking, and I began to concentrate, using my hands to touch the walls, edging my way around the room.

My bed is in the center of the room, which I knew because I'd heard my mother complain about it—Why, she wondered, was it in the *center*, instead of pressed up against one wall or another?—and yet I was glad of it, because it made the space easier to navigate. Here was the wall of windows that looked over the garden; here was the doorway to the bathroom where I was taken for my baths and showers; here was the door—locked—to, I imagined, the hallway. Here was a chest of drawers, on top of which were a few bottles, some heavy, some light, some glass, some plastic. I opened the top drawers and felt my shorts, my T-shirts. The floor was cold, tile or stone, but as I neared my bed, I encountered a different surface, which I recognized as a woven lauhala mat, satiny beneath my feet, the same kind as I'd had in my room back home. They kept the whole room cool, Jane used to say, and even though they splintered and shagged, they were easy to replace every few months.

After I found my way back to bed, I lay awake for a long time, for I had realized: What if I *were* to leave? If I could walk, was it not possible that other things would return to me as well? My eyesight, for example? My speech? What if I were to walk out of here one night? What if I were to come find you? Wouldn't that be a surprise? To see you again, to hold you again? I knew that, in the meantime, I wouldn't tell anyone, not until I'd practiced more, and, indeed, the walk, as short as it was, had left me panting. But now you know, too. I'm going to come find you—I'm going to walk there myself.

I had been walking as well the day I reencountered Edward. It was 1969, and I had had you for just four months—you weren't yet a year old. A few times a week, I had Matthew drive us down to Kapi'olani Park, where I'd push you among the monkeypod and shower trees; sometimes we'd stop to watch the cricket club play their matches. Or sometimes I'd walk you over to Kaimana Beach, where I used to linger to watch the fishermen.

Back then—and maybe even now—it was unusual to see a young man pushing a carriage, and sometimes people would laugh. I never said anything, though, never spoke back, just kept moving. So that morning, when I felt, rather than saw, someone stop to stare, I didn't think anything of it, and it wasn't until the person spoke my name that I too stopped, and then only because I recognized the voice.

"How've you been?" he asked, as if it had been just a week, rather than nearly a decade, since we had seen each other last.

"Pretty good," I said, shaking his hand. I had heard he had moved to Los Angeles, where he had gone to college, and told him so, but he shrugged. "I just came back," he said. Then he looked into the carriage. "Whose baby is that?" he asked.

"Mine," I said, and he blinked. Another person might have brayed in astonishment, or thought I was joking, but he only nodded. I remembered that he had never joked, and never thought anyone else was joking, either.

"Your son," he said, as if tasting the word. "Little Kawika," he said, testing out the name. "Or does he go by 'David'?"

"No, Kawika," I said, and he smiled, slightly.

"Good," he said.

Somehow it was arranged that we should go get something to eat, and we loaded everything into his beat-up car and drove to Chinatown, where we went to my twenty-five-cent wonton min restaurant. On the way, I asked about his mother, and I knew by his silence, the way his face twisted before he answered, that she was dead—breast cancer, he said. It was why he was home.

"I wish I had known," I said; I felt as if I had been punched. But he shrugged. "It was slow, and then quick," he said. "She didn't suffer too much. I buried her in Honoka'a."

After that lunch, we began seeing each other again. It wasn't as if we discussed it: He just told me he'd pick me up on Sunday at noon and we could go to the beach, and I agreed. Over the weeks and then months, we saw more and more of each other, until I was seeing him at least every other day. Curiously, we rarely discussed where he'd been, or where I'd been, or what we'd done in the years since we saw each other last, or why we had drifted apart in the first place. But although the past was not so much forgotten as it was excised, we were both careful—again, without ever discussing it—about not letting my mother discover our renewed communication. When he came, I would wait (sometimes with you, sometimes alone) on the porch if she was out, or at the bottom of the hill if she was home, which is where Edward dropped me off as well.

It's difficult to remember what we discussed in those days. This may surprise you to hear, but it took me many months to realize that Edward had changed in some fundamental way—I don't mean the kind of change we all experience when we move from childhood to adulthood, but that, in his beliefs and convictions, he had become someone I no longer recognized. Part of this, I'm embarrassed to say, is that, because he *looked* very much the same, I assumed he *was* very much the same. I knew, from television news reports, that the mainland was full of long-haired hippies, and while there were hippies in Honolulu as well, there was no sense of rage, of revolution. Everything came late to Hawai'i—even our papers carried day-old news—and so, if you had seen Edward then, you wouldn't have been able to immediately identify him as a political radical by sight alone. Yes, his hair was longer, fluffier, than mine, but it was always clean; the effect was less intimidating than it was merely pretty.

Neither of us worked. Unlike me, Edward had not finished his degree; he had, he eventually explained, dropped out at the beginning of his senior year and had spent the rest of the fall hitchhiking through the West. When he needed money, he returned to California and picked grapes or garlic or strawberries or walnuts, whatever was being harvested—he would never eat another strawberry in his life, he said. Now, back in Honolulu, he found short-term jobs. He helped a friend paint houses, or joined a moving crew for a few days.

The little house he'd shared with his mother was a rental, the land-lord an old Chinese man who'd fancied Mrs. Bishop, and he'd have to move out of it eventually, but he didn't seem concerned about this, or his future. He seemed concerned about very little, and it reminded me of his childhood self-assurance, his complete lack of insecurity.

But it was toward the end of that year that I realized how truly different a person he had become. "We're going to an event," he said as he picked me up at the foot of the hill one evening, "to meet some friends of mine." He didn't offer any further information, and I, as usual, didn't ask. But I could tell he was excited, even nervous—as he drove, he beat out a twitchy rhythm on the steering wheel with one finger.

We drove deep into Nuʻuanu, down a narrow, private road so shrouded by trees and so ill-lit that even with the headlights I had to hold up a flashlight to guide our way. We passed a series of gates, and at the fourth, Edward stopped and got out of the car; there was a key attached to a long piece of wire on the gatepost, and he unlocked the gate and we drove through, stopping again to close the gate behind us. Ahead of us was a long dirt driveway, and as we bumped along, I could see and smell that it was lined with clumps of white ginger, their flowers ghostly in the dusk.

At the end of the driveway was a large white wooden house, once grand, once well-maintained, that resembled my own, except parked in front of it were at least twenty cars, and even from outside, we could hear people talking, their voices echoey in the valley's quiet.

"Come on," Edward said.

There were perhaps fifty people inside, and after I had recovered from my initial shock, I was able to observe them more closely. Most of them were our age, and all of them were local, and some of them were clearly hippies, and many of them were standing around a very tall black man, whose back was toward me, so that all I could see was his Afro, which was large and thick and glistening. As he shifted, the top of his hair brushed against the bottom of the ceiling pendant light, making it sway, the light rocking about the room.

"Come on," Edward said, again, and this time, I could hear the excitement in his voice.

The crowd began to stir as a single organism, and we found ourselves being moved from the entryway and into a large open space. Here, as in the first room, there was no furniture, and some of the floorboards had cracked and split from the moisture. In this room, above the chatter, I heard a roaring, like an airplane passing overhead, but then I looked out the window and realized the sound was coming from a waterfall at the bottom of the property.

After we had all settled ourselves on the floor, there was a nervous silence, one that seemed to lengthen and deepen. "The fuck's happening?" someone, a guy, asked, and was shushed; someone else giggled. On and on the silence went, and finally, the shuffling and whispering quieted, and for at least a minute, we sat there, together, mute and immobile.

It was then that the tall black man picked himself up from where he'd been sitting in the middle of the crowd and loped to the front of the room. The combination of his height and our position on the ground, staring up at him, made him seem towering, an edifice rather than a man. He was not so black—I was darker than he was—nor was he exactly handsome: His skin was shiny, and he had a patchy beard and a smattering of pimples across his left cheek that made him look more childlike than I think he'd have preferred. But there was something indisputable about him; he had a wide, gap-toothed smile that he could make look either goofy or fierce, and long, liquid arms and legs that he bent and twisted into shapes as he moved, so that you were forced to not only listen to him but to watch him as well. But it was his voice that really captivated: what he said, but also how he said it, gentle and low and furred; his was a voice you'd like to hear telling you how much he loved you, and why, and how.

He began with a smile. "Brothers and sisters," he said. "Aloha." The crowd clapped then, and his smile widened, sleepy and seductive. "Aloha and mahalo for bringing me to this beautiful land of yours.

"It seems particularly right to me that we should be at this house tonight, for do you know what I was told the name of this house is? Yes, that's right, it has a name, that's something all fancy houses do, I guess, all over the world—it's Hale Kealoha, the House of Aloha: the House of Love, the House of the Beloved.

"And that's particularly interesting to me, because I too am named after a house: Bethesda. Who of you here remember your Bible, your New Testament? Ah, I see a hand in the back; there's another. You, sister in the back, tell me what it means. That's right, the Pools of Bethesda, Bethesda meaning the house of mercy, the pools being the place where Christ healed a crippled man. So here I am: the House of Mercy in the House of Love.

"I was asked to come, not just here, tonight, but to your islands, your home, by my good friend, the brother sitting all the way to the right, Brother Louis. Thank you, Brother Louis.

"I'm ashamed to say this now, but when I was invited to come here, I thought I knew everything about what this place was. I thought: pineapples. I thought: rainbows. I thought: hula girls, swaying their hips back and forth, all nice and sweet. I know, I know! But that's what I thought. But within a few days, even before I left California, I realized I was wrong.

"I'm also ashamed to say that I didn't even want to come here, not at first. You know, what you have here, I thought, is not reality. It's not part of the world. I live near Oakland—*that* is part of the world. You see what's happening there, what we're *struggling* against there, what we're fighting against there: the oppression of the black man and woman, the oppression that's gone on since America was founded and will go on and on until it burns down to the ground and we begin something new. Because there is no fixing what America is—there is no way to do work around the margins and say justice has been restored. No, brothers and sisters, that's not how justice works. My mother worked as a nurse's aide in what they used to call the Houston Negro Hospital, and she would tell me stories of the men and women who came in with heart attacks, about how they'd be gasping for breath, about how their nails would turn blue because they weren't getting enough oxygen. My mother would be told by the senior nurses to massage her patients' hands, to get the blood flowing through the extremities, and as she did, she'd watch their nails turn pink again, and feel their hands warm up with her touch. But one day she realized that this wasn't solving anything—she was making their hands prettier, maybe even work better, but their hearts were still sick. Nothing had really changed after all.

"And in the same way, nothing has really changed here. America is a country with sin at its heart. You know what I'm talking about. One group of people sent away from their land; another group of people stolen from their land. *We* replaced *you*, and yet we never wanted to replace you—we wanted to be left where we were. None of our ancestors, our great-great-great-grandparents, ever woke up one day and thought: *Let's sail halfway around the world, be part of a land grab, pit ourselves against some other native peoples.* No way, no how. That is not how normal people, decent people, think—that is how the devil thinks. But that sin, that mark, never goes away, and although we didn't cause it, we are all infected by it.

"Let me tell you why. Imagine that heart again, but this time swiped with a smear of oil. Not cooking oil but motor oil, the thick, gluey black kind, the kind that sticks to your hands and clothes like tar. It's just a small bit of oil, you think, and eventually it'll get washed away. And so you try to forget about it. But that isn't what happens. What happens instead is that with each beat, with each thump of your heart, that oil, that little mark, spreads and spreads. The arteries carry it away; the veins carry it back. And with each journey through your body, it leaves a deposit, so that eventually—not right away, but over time—every organ, every blood vessel, every cell, has been tainted by that oil. Sometimes you can't even see it—but you know it's there. Because by this time, brothers and sisters, that oil is everywhere: It's coating the inside of your veins; it's lining your large intestine and liver; it's slicking your spleen and kidneys. Your brain. That little bit of oil, that little splotch that you thought you could ignore, it's now everywhere. And now there is no way to clean it out; the only way to clean it out is to stop the heart altogether—the only way to clean it out is to burn the body pure of it. The only way to clean it is to end it. You want to eliminate the stain, you've got to eliminate the host.

"Now. Now. What does this have to do with us here in Hawai'i, you might be saying. The country, you might be saying, is not a body. The metaphor doesn't hold. But doesn't it? Here we sit, brothers and sisters, in this beautiful place far from Oakland. And yet it's not far at all. Because here's the thing, brothers and sisters: You *do* have pineapples here. You *do* have rainbows. You *do* have hula girls. But none of those things are *yours*. Those pineapple fields Brother Louis took me to see? Who're they owned by? Not by you. Those rainbows? You have them, but can you see them for those high-rises going up, those hotels and condominiums in Waikīkī? And who owns those buildings? Do you? How about you? Those hula girls—those are your sisters, your brown-skinned sisters, and yet you're letting them dance . . . for whom?

"This is the dissonance of living here. This is the lie you've been fed. I look at all of you here, your brown faces, your kinky hair, and then I look at who's running this place. I look at who your elected officials are. I look at who runs your banks, your businesses, your schools. They don't look like you. So: You're poor? You got no money? You want to go to school? You want to buy a house? And yet you can't? And why? Why do you think that is? Is it because you're all stupid? Is it because you don't deserve to go to school, to have someplace to live? Is it because you're bad?

"Or is it because you've let yourselves sleep, because you've let yourselves forget? You live in a land not of milk and honey but of sugar and sun, and yet you've become *drunk* on it. You've become *lazy* on it. You've become *complacent* on it. And what's happened, while you surfed and sang and swayed your hips? Your land, your very soul, has been taken from you, bit by bit by bit, right beneath your brown noses, while you watched it happen and did nothing— *nothing*—to stop it. Anyone watching you would think you *wanted* to give it all up. 'Take my land!' you said. 'Take it all! Because I don't care. I won't stand in your way.'"

He took a breath then, rocked back on his heels, swiped a red bandanna across his forehead. The crowd had been utterly still, but now a hiss sizzled in the air, like a flock of insects, and when he spoke next, his voice was kinder, softer, almost placating.

"Brothers and sisters. We have something else in common. We are both from lands of kings. We both were kings and queens and princes and princesses. We both had wealth, handed down from father to son to grandson to great-grandson. You all are lucky, though. Because you remember your kings and queens. You *know* their names. You *know* where they're buried. It's 1969, my friends. Nineteen sixty-nine. That means it's only been seventy-one years since your land was stolen by the Americans, seventy-six since your queen was betrayed by the American devils. And here you are—not all of you, mind, but enough of you, brothers and sisters, enough of you—calling yourselves American. *American?* You believe that 'America is for everyone' bullshit? America is *not* for everyone—it is not for us. You know that, don't you? In your hearts and in your souls? You know that America despises you, don't you? They want your land, your fields, and your mountains, but America don't want *you*.

"This land was never their land. Legally, it's barely their land. This land was taken. That is not your fault. But letting it *stay* taken? Well, that *is* your fault.

"You've let them buy you off, brothers and sisters. You've let them promise that they would give you some of your land back. But look around you: You know that there are more of you in prison than anyone else here? You know that there are more of you in poverty than anyone else? You know that there are more of you that go hungry than anyone else? You know that you die younger, that your babies die sooner, that you die in childbirth more than anyone else? You are *Hawaiians*. This land is yours. It's time to take it back. Why are you living on your land like tenants? Why are you scared to ask for what's yours? When I walk through Waikīkī—as I did yesterday—why are you smiling, thanking these white devils, these thieves, for coming to your land? 'Oh, thank you for visiting! Aloha for visiting! Thank you for coming to our islands—we hope you have a good time!' *Thank you?* Thank you for *what*? For making you beggars in your own land? For turning you, you kings and queens, into jesters and clowns?"

Again, that hiss, and the audience seemed to recoil as one, leaning away from him. Throughout this part of the speech, he had grown quieter and quieter, but when he spoke again, after letting the silence hang in the air a few unbearable seconds, his voice was strong once more.

"This is *your* land, brothers and sisters. It is up to *you* to reclaim it. You *can* do it. You *must* do it. If you don't do it for yourself, no one will. Who should respect you if you don't ask for respect?

"Before I came here, before I came to visit your land—*your* land—I did some research. I went to the public library, and I started reading. And although there were a lot of lies in the books, as there are in almost *all* books, my brothers and sisters, it doesn't matter, because you learn how to read between the lies; you learn how to read the truth that lurks behind those falsehoods. And it was there, in my reading, that I found this song. I know many of you will know this song, but I'm going to recite to you without music, in English, so you can really hear the words:

> *"Famous are the children of Hawai'i*
> *Ever loyal to the land*
> *When the evil-hearted messenger comes*
> *With his greedy document of extortion—"*

He had only said the first line when the singing began, and although he'd said he wanted us to listen to the lyrics, he clapped his hands together when the melody started, and then again when the first person, his friend Brother Louis, stood to dance. This was a song we all knew, written shortly after the queen was overthrown. I had always considered it an old song, even though, as Bethesda had said, it wasn't so old at all—there were people alive today who would have heard it played by the Royal Hawaiian Band shortly after it had been written; there were people in the room whose grandparents would have remembered seeing the queen in her black bombazine, waving to them from the palace steps.

Now he stood and watched us, his smile wide again, as if he had willed all of this to happen, as if he had brought us back to life after a long hibernation and was witnessing us remember who we were. I hadn't liked the pride on his face, as if we were his clever children and he our tireless teacher. Each stanza was sung once in Hawaiian and then again in English, and I hadn't liked how he recited along with the translation, referring to the sheet of paper he'd taken from his pants pocket.

But mostly, I hadn't liked the look I'd seen on Edward's face when I had glanced his way: rapt as I'd never before seen him, his fist raised in the air like Bethesda's, practically bellowing the song's most famous lyrics, as if there were before him an audience of thousands, and all of them had gathered to hear him say something they had never heard before.

'A'ole a'e kau i ka pūlima *Do not fix a signature*
Maluna o ka pepa o ka 'enemi *To the paper of the enemy*
Ho'ohui 'āina kū'ai hewa *With its sin of annexation*
I ka pono sivila a'o ke kanaka *And sale of the civil rights of the people*

'A'ole mākou a'e minamina *We do not value*
I ka pu'u kālā a ke aupuni *The government's hills of money*
Ua lawa mākou i ka pōhaku *We are satisfied with the stones*
I ka 'ai kamaha'o o ka 'āina *The wondrous food of the land.*

If you were to ask my mother what happened next—not that I can, and not that anyone else would—she would say it was sudden, a complete surprise. But that isn't true. Though I can also understand why she might feel that way. There were years of apparent inactivity followed by—without warning, she would probably say—a rupture. One night, you and I were there in the house on O'ahu Avenue, lying in our beds; the next night, we were not. Later, I know, she would discuss our departure as a disappearance, something abrupt and unexpected. Sometimes, she would characterize it as a loss, as if the two of us were buttons or safety pins. But I knew it was more of a vanishing, a bar of soap smoothing and rounding itself into nothingness, diminishing beneath her fingertips.

There was another person, however, who would have agreed with my mother's characterization of the events that followed, and ironically, that person was Edward. Later, he would say that he had been "transformed" by that night at Hale Kealoha, that it had been a kind of resurrection. I believe he felt that. On the ride back to town that night, we had been mostly silent, me because I was uncertain what I thought about Bethesda and what he had said, Edward because he had been so thunderstruck by it. As he drove, he would occasionally strike the steering wheel with the heel of his hand, bursting out with a "Damn!" or "Man!" or "Christ!," and had I not been so unsettled, I might even have thought it was funny. Funny, or alarming—Edward, who showed so little excitement about anything, capable only of expulsions of sound, rather than speech.

Bethesda's lecture had been recorded, and Edward procured a copy. In the weeks that followed, we would lie on the mattress in the bedroom he was renting from a family in the valley, listening to it again and again on his reel-to-reel, until we both had it memorized—not just the speech itself but the audience's angry gasp, the creak of the floor as Bethesda shifted his weight from one foot to the other, the crowd's singing, faint and tinny, atop of which Bethesda's occasional claps were like explosions.

And yet, even after that night, it took some months for me to realize that something irrevocable had changed for Edward. I had never known him (insofar as I knew him at all) to be a dabbler or a bounder, someone who vaulted from one enthusiasm to another, so it wasn't as if I witnessed his increasing interest in Hawaiian sovereignty and thought it was just a phase—rather, I'm convinced that he hid something of his transformation from me. I don't believe it was because he was being duplicitous; I think it was because it was precious to him, precious and personal and also to some degree unfathomable, and he wanted to nurture it in private, where no one could see it and comment on it.

But if I could date the beginning of his different self, it was probably in December 1970, about a year after we listened to Bethesda in that house in Nuʻuanu. Even then, my mother was largely unaware that Edward had reentered my life—he still dropped me off at the bottom of the hill; he had still never come to the house. Before I got out of the car, I'd ask him if he wanted to come in, and every time, he'd say no, and I'd be relieved. But one night, I asked and he said, "Sure, why not?," as if accepting were a regular occurrence, based on nothing more than his mood.

"Oh," I replied. I couldn't pretend he was kidding—as I've said, he didn't kid. And so I got out of the car and he, after a second, followed.

As we walked up the hill, I grew more and more anxious, and when we reached the house, I mumbled something about needing to check on you—on the days I brought you with me, I'd sit in the back seat and hold you in my arms—and sprinted upstairs to look at you, asleep in your bed. We'd recently moved you into a little bed of your own, low to the ground and surrounded by cushions, because you were an active, squirmy sleeper and sometimes rolled off the futon and onto the floor. "Kawika," I remember whispering to you, "what should I do?" But you didn't answer, of course—you were asleep, and you were only two.

By the time I returned downstairs, my mother and Edward had already encountered each other and were waiting for me at the dinner table. "Edward tells me that you've reacquainted yourselves," she said, after we'd served ourselves, and I nodded. "Don't nod, speak," she said, and I cleared my throat and made myself speak.

"Yes," I said.

She turned to Edward. "What are you doing this Christmas?" she asked, as if she saw Edward every month, as if she knew enough about how he normally spent Christmas to understand whether this year's celebrations would be typical or unusual.

"Nothing," he said, and then, after a pause, "I see you have a tree."

He spoke neutrally enough, but my mother, already suspicious of him, and therefore alert, straightened. "Yes," she replied, also neutrally.

"That's not very Hawaiian, is it?" he asked.

We all looked at the tree in the corner of the sunroom. We had a tree because we always had a tree. Every year, a limited number were imported from the mainland and made available to buy at great expense. There was nothing special about it except its sweet, uriney scent, which for many years I associated with the entire mainland. The mainland was asphalt and snow and highways and the fragrance of pine trees, the country trapped in perpetual winter. We took no particular pains in decorating it—indeed, it was Jane who did most of the ornamentation—but this year it seemed more interesting than before, because now you were here, and old enough to pull on its branches and laugh when you were scolded for doing so.

"It's not a matter of being Hawaiian or not Hawaiian," my mother said, "it's tradition."

"Yes, but whose tradition?" Edward asked.

"Why, everyone's," she said.

"Not mine," Edward said.

"I should think it is," my mother said, and then, to me, "Please pass me the rice, Wika."

"Well, it's not mine," Edward repeated.

She didn't respond. It wasn't until many years later that I was able to appreciate my mother's equanimity that night. There was nothing obviously argumentative in Edward's tone, but she had known anyway, known long before I had—I hadn't grown up with anyone challenging who I was or what I deserved, but she had. Her right to her name and her birth had always been questioned. She knew when someone was trying to provoke her.

"It's a Christian tradition," he finally said into her silence. "Not ours."

She allowed herself a small smile, looking up from her plate to do so. "So there aren't such things as Christian Hawaiians, then?" she asked.

He shrugged. "Not if you're a real Hawaiian."

Her smile grew wider, tenser. "I see," she said. "My grandfather would be surprised to hear that—he was a Christian, you know; he served in the king's court."

He shrugged again. "I'm not saying there *aren't* such things as Christian Hawaiians," he said, "just that the two are in opposition to each other." (Later, he would repeat the same thing to me, extending the point past what he knew firsthand: "It's like how people always talk about the black Christian experience. But don't the blacks know that they're celebrating the tools of their oppressor? They were encouraged to be Christian so they would think something better awaited them in the afterlife, after years of being abused. Christianity was a form of mind control, and it still is. All that moralizing, all that talk of sin—they swallowed it, and now they're kept imprisoned by it.") When she still said nothing, he kept talking. "It was Christians who took away our dance, our language, our religion, our land—even our queen. Which you should know." She looked up then, startled, as did I—no one had ever before confronted my mother like that—and he stared back at her. "So it just seems bizarre that any true Hawaiian could believe in an ideology whose practitioners robbed them of everything."

(Real Hawaiian, true Hawaiian—it was the first time I would hear him use those phrases, and soon I would be sick of the terms, as much because I felt accused by them as because I didn't understand them. All I knew was that a real Hawaiian was something I was not: A real Hawaiian was angrier, poorer, more strident. He spoke the language, fluently; he danced, powerfully; he sang, soulfully. He was not only not American, he would be angry if you ever called him that. The only thing I had in common with a real Hawaiian was my skin and my blood, though later, even my family would become a deficit, proof of my accommodationist tendencies. Even my name would be deemed not Hawaiian enough, even though it had been the name of a Hawaiian king—it was the Hawaiianization of a Christian name, and therefore not Hawaiian at all.)

We might have sat there, frozen, forever had my mother not looked over to me—no doubt in anger—and gasped. "Wika!" I heard her say, and when I opened my eyes next, I was in my bed in a darkened room.

She was sitting next to me. "Careful," she said, when I tried to sit, "you had a seizure and hit your head. The doctor said you should stay in bed for another day. Kawika's fine," she continued, when I began to speak.

For a while, we were silent. Then she spoke again. "I don't want you to see Edward anymore, do you understand me, Wika?" she asked.

I could have laughed, I could have scoffed, I could have told her that I was an adult, that she could no longer tell me who I could talk to or not. I could have told her that I found Edward alarming as well, but exciting, too, and that I was going to keep seeing him.

But I did none of those things. I simply nodded, and closed my eyes, and before I fell asleep again, I heard her say, "Good boy," and then felt her lay her palm on my forehead, and as I lost consciousness, I had the feeling that I was a child again, and that I was being given the chance to live my life all over, and this time, I would do everything correctly.

———

I kept my promise. I did not see Edward. He called, but I didn't come to the phone; he stopped by the house, but I made Jane say I wasn't there. I stayed inside and I watched you grow. When I went out, I was anxious: Honolulu was (and is) a small town on a small island, and I was always afraid I would encounter him, but I somehow never did.

Nothing changed for me in those three years I was in hiding. But you changed: You learned to speak, first in sentences and then paragraphs; you learned to run, and to read, and to swim. Matthew taught you to climb up to the lowest branch of the mango tree; Jane taught you how to tell a juicy mango from a fibrous one. You learned a few words in Hawaiian, which my mother taught you, and a few in Tagalog, which Jane taught you, but only in secret: Your grandmother didn't like the sound of the language, and you knew not to speak it in front of her. You learned which foods you liked—like me, you preferred salt over sugar—and you made friends, effortlessly, in a way I had never been capable of doing. You learned to call for help when I had one of my seizures, and then, when I emerged from it, to come pat the side of my face, and I would grab your hand in mine. These were the years when you loved me the most. You could never love me more than, or even as much as, I loved and love you, but in that period, we were closest in mutual affection.

You changed, and so did the rest of the world. Every night on television there was at least one report about the day's protests: First there were people protesting against the war in Vietnam, and then there were people protesting for blacks, and then for women, and then for homosexuals. I watched them on our little black-and-white set, those swaying, shifting masses of people in San Francisco, and Washington, D.C., and New York, and Oakland, and Chicago—I always wondered if Bethesda, who had left the island directly after his speech, was in one of those crowds. The protestors were almost always young, and although I too was young, not yet thirty in 1973, I felt much older—I didn't recognize myself in any of them; I felt no affinity for them or their struggles or their passions. It wasn't just that I didn't look like them; it was that I couldn't understand their fervor. They had been born with access to and an understanding of extremes, but I had not. I wanted time to slip past me, one year indistinguishable from the next, you the only calendar I had. But they wanted to stop time—stop it, and then speed it up, making it go faster and faster until the entire world burst into flames and would have to start over.

There were changes here, too. Sometimes there would be stories on TV about the Keiki kū Ali'i. This was a group of native Hawaiians who, depending on which member you asked and on which day, were demanding either Hawai'i's secession from the United States, or the restoration of the monarchy, or nation-within-a-nation status for native Hawaiians, or the creation of a Hawaiian state. They wanted Hawaiian language classes to be mandatory in schools, and they wanted a king or queen, and they wanted all haoles to get out. They didn't even want to call themselves Hawaiian anymore: Now they were kanaka maoli.

Watching these reports always felt like an illicit activity, and fear that one of them might air while I was in the room with my mother made me stop watching the early-evening news altogether. I only did so when I knew she'd be out of the house, and even then, I kept the volume low, so if she came back early I'd be able to hear her and turn off the television. I'd sit close to the set, ready to switch it off in a flash, my palms tacky with sweat.

I felt oddly protective—not of my mother but of the protestors, those wild-haired young men and women, my peers, chanting and raising their fists in an imitation of the Black Power members. I already knew what my mother thought of them—"What fools," she'd murmured, almost sympathetically, after the end of the first segment that had aired and which we had watched together, in mesmerized silence, a year ago, "they don't even know what they want. And how do they think they'll get it? You can't ask for the restoration of the monarchy *and* a new state at the same time"—and I for some reason didn't want to hear her insult them further. I knew this was irrational, in part because I didn't disagree with her: They *did* look ridiculous, in their T-shirts and big hair, breaking into ragged chants and song when the camera turned to them; their spokespeople could barely speak proper English, yet they stumbled in Hawaiian, too. I was embarrassed for them. They were so loud.

And yet I also envied them. Except for you, I had never felt such ardor for anything. I looked at those men and women and I knew what they wanted—their want was greater than logic or organization. I had always been told that I should try to live my life with happiness, but could happiness give you the zeal, the energy, that anger clearly could? Theirs was the kind of avidity that seemed to override any other desire—if you had it, you might never want again. At night, I'd experiment with pretending I was one of them: Could I ever be that incensed? Could I ever desire something so much? Could I ever feel that wronged?

I could not. But I began trying. As I have said, I had never before much considered what it meant to be Hawaiian. It was like considering being male, or human—they were things I was, and the fact that I was them seemed always to be enough to me. I began wondering if there was in fact another way to be, if I had been wrong this entire time, if I was somehow incapable of seeing what these other people seemed to see so clearly.

I went to the library, where I read books I had already read about the overthrow; I went to the museum, where my great-grandfather's feather cape was displayed in a glass case, donated—the cape and the case—by my father. I tried to feel something—but all I could feel was a faint sense of amused disbelief that it was not the haoles who were doing things in my name but these activists themselves. Keiki kū Ali'i: the children of royalty. But I really *was* a child of royalty. When they talked of a king who would be someday restored, they meant me, by rights, and yet they didn't know who I was; they spoke of the king returning, yet they never thought to ask the king himself if he would want to return. But I also knew that *what* I was would always be more significant than *who* I was—indeed, what I was was the only thing that made who I was significant at all. Why *would* they ever think to ask me?

They wouldn't, but Edward would. I'll admit that, while I was too cowardly to speak to him, I was always looking for him. I squinted at the television, scanning the gang of protestors trying to infiltrate the governor's office, the mayor's office, the university president's office. But although I saw Louis—Brother Louis—once or twice, I never saw Edward. Yet I always believed that he was there anyway, just out of camera range, leaning against a wall and surveying the crowd. In my imaginings, he even became something of a leader, elusive and evasive, bestowing his rare smile like a blessing on his followers when they did something to please him. At night, I dreamed of him standing in a shadow-filled house much like Hale Kealoha, giving a speech, and when I woke, I was astonished and full of admiration for him, his eloquence and elegance, until I realized that the words I had been so captivated by were not his but Bethesda's, now recited back to myself so many times that they had become a hymn of my subconscious, like the state anthem or the song that Jane had sung to me as a boy, and which I now sang to you: *Yellow bird, up high in banana tree / Yellow bird, you sit all alone like me* . . .

So, when I finally did encounter him, I was only surprised it had taken as long as it had. It was a Wednesday, which I know because every Wednesday, after dropping you off at school, I took a long walk, all the way to Waikīkī, where I sat beneath one of the trees in Kapiʻolani Park we had sat beneath together when you were a baby, and ate a package of crackers. Each package had eight crackers, but I'd only eat seven; the last I'd crumble into ash and feed to the mynah birds, and then I'd get up again and keep walking.

"Wika," I heard someone say, and when I looked up, there he was, walking toward me.

"Well, well," he said, smiling. "Long time, no see, brother."

The smiling was new. So was the "brother." His hair was even longer now, almost blond in parts from the sun, and twisted into a bun, though strands of it floated around his head. He was tanner, which made his eyes look lighter and brighter, but the skin around them had wrinkled, and he had lost weight. He wore a faded aloha shirt, bleached a pale blue, and cutoff jeans—he looked both younger and older than I'd remembered him.

What remained the same was his lack of surprise at encountering me. "You hungry?" he asked, and when I said I was, he said we should walk to Chinatown and get some noodles. "Don't have the car anymore," he said, and when I made a sound of concern, or sympathy, he shrugged. "Doesn't matter," he said. "I'll get it back. I just don't have it now." His left incisor was stained the color of tea.

The biggest change was his new volubility. (In those first six months of our most recent reacquaintance, I was always measuring what was different in him and what was familiar, which invariably led to the same unnerving realization: I didn't know who he was. I knew a few facts, I had a few impressions, but the rest I had conjured, making him into whoever I needed him to be.) Over lunch, and then the following months, he talked more and more, until there were days when we would drive for hours (the car, which had vanished mysteriously, had reappeared just as mysteriously) and he would talk and talk and talk, and at times I would stop listening altogether, just lean my head back against the seat and let his words wash over me, as if it were a boring news report on the radio.

What did he talk about? Well, first, there was how he talked; he had adapted a kind of pidgin inflection, except because he hadn't grown up speaking pidgin—he was a scholarship boy, after all; he wouldn't have gotten into the school if his mother hadn't been vigilant about his speaking standard English—it sounded artificial and weirdly formal. Even I could appreciate how rich and robustly casual pidgin sounded when spoken by natives: It wasn't a language for exchanging ideas but one for trading jokes and insults and gossip. But Edward made it, or tried to make it, a language of instruction.

He didn't need to ask if I understood the way things were—he knew I didn't. I didn't understand why our fate as Hawaiians was linked to black people's fate on the mainland ("There are no black people in Hawai'i," I reminded him, echoing my mother's statement as we watched a news report about some protest among blacks on the mainland one day. "There are no Negroes in Hawai'i," she had announced, the ghost of what she didn't bother to say next—*Thank goodness*—hovering in the air between us). I didn't understand how we'd been used as pawns, or his argument that the Orientals were taking advantage of us—many of the Orientals I knew and saw were clearly poor or, at the very least, far from rich, and yet, to Edward, they were as much to blame as the haole missionaries for the disappearance of our land. "You see them now, buying houses, opening businesses," he said. "If they're poor, they won't stay poor forever." Yet it seemed impossible to separate the Orientals and the haoles from who we were—every Hawaiian I knew was also part Oriental, or part haole, or both, or in some cases, like Edward's (though I did not say this), mostly haole.

One of the most difficult concepts for me to understand was this idea that I, and my mother, belonged to an *us* at all. Those thick brown men, slow-moving and massive, whom I saw drunk and dozing in the park: They may have been Hawaiian, but I felt no kinship toward them. "They're kings too, brother," Edward reprimanded me, and although I didn't say it, I thought of what my mother would tell me when I was young: "Only a few people are kings, Wika." Perhaps I was like my mother in the end, though I meant no harm; she would have seen those people as unlike her because she thought them beneath her, while I saw them as unlike me because I was scared of them. I wouldn't deny that we were of the same race, but we were different sorts of people, and that was what divided us.

I had assumed all along that Edward was a member of Keiki kū

Ali'i—in my dreams, as I have said, he was not only a member but their leader. But that turned out not to be true. He *had* been a member, he told me, but he had soon afterward left. "Bunch of ignoramuses," he scoffed. "Didn't know how to organize themselves." He had tried to teach them what he knew about organizing from his time on the mainland; he had pushed them toward being more expansive, more radical in their approach. But they had wanted only small things, he said: more land set aside for poor Hawaiians, more social welfare programs. "That's the problem with this place—it's too provincial," he often said. For, as appalled as he would be if this were pointed out to him, he too could be a snob; he too thought himself better.

I had played an unwitting role in his disenchantment with the group, he said. It was he who had pushed for the restoration of the monarchy, he who had introduced the language of secession and overthrow. "I told them, I already know the king," he said, and although it was less a compliment than a statement of fact—I *would* be king, after all; would have been king—it was as if he'd praised me anyway, and I felt my cheeks grow warm. Yet talk of secession and overthrow had proven, he said, too intimidating for most of the members, who feared it would jeopardize their chances to earn other concessions from the state; they quarreled, and Edward lost. "A shame," he told me now, letting his fingers flutter out the car window. "They're so small-minded." We were on our way toward Waimānalo, on the eastern coast, and as he zagged down the road, I stared out at the ocean, a wrinkled sheet of blue.

We had meant to stop at a plate-lunch place Edward liked just before Sherwood Forest, but we instead drove on. At some point I had a seizure, and I could feel my head slumping against the seat and hear the sound of Edward's voice, even though I couldn't distinguish his words, and the sun throbbed behind my eyelids. When I woke, we were parked beneath a large acacia tree. The car smelled like fried meat, and I looked over to see Edward staring back at me and eating a hamburger. "Wake up, lolo," he said, but good-naturedly, "I got you a burger," but I shook my head, which made me dizzier—I was too nauseated to eat after one of my attacks. He shrugged. "Suit yourself," he said, and ate the other burger, and by the time he was done, I was feeling a little better.

He had something to show me, he said, and we got out of the car and began walking. We were somewhere in the very northern part of the island—I could tell by how empty it was. We were standing in a large plain of sun-dried, unshorn grass, and around us was nothing: no houses, no buildings, no cars. Behind us were the mountains, and in front of us was the ocean.

"Let's go to the water," Edward said, and I followed him. On our way, we walked across a bumpy, silty dirt path; there was no paved road in sight. As we went, the tall grasses grew sparser and thinner and eventually gave way to sand, and then we were on a beach, where waves lapped against the shore and withdrew, again and again.

I cannot describe to you what made it seem so foreign. Perhaps it was the lack of people, though back then there were still places on the island where you could go and be alone. Yet there was something that felt especially isolated about this area, isolated and abandoned. Though I was unable—and am still now not able—to say why: Here was sand, grass, mountain, the same three elements you would find all over the island. The trees, palms and monkeypods and halas and acacias, were the same as we had in the valley; the stalks of heliconia were the same. And yet it was different in some unexplainable way. Later, I would try to tell myself that I had known from the moment I saw this land that I would return to it, but that was fiction. What is more likely is the opposite: That, given what happened there, I've begun to remember it differently, as a place that felt meaningful, when at the time it hadn't struck me as special at all, just a piece of unoccupied land.

"What do you think of it?" Edward asked, finally, and I looked up at the sky.

"It's pretty," I said.

He nodded, slowly, as if I'd said something profound. "It's yours," he said.

This was the kind of thing he'd taken to saying, gesturing out the window at beaches, where kids ran up and down the sand, lofting kites in the air, or at parking lots, or on our walks through Chinatown: *This land is yours*, he'd say, and sometimes he meant it was mine because of who my ancestors were, and sometimes he meant it was mine because it was also his, and the land belonged to us because we were Hawaiians.

But when I turned, I found he was staring at me. "It's yours," he repeated. "Yours and Kawika's. Here," he continued, before I could speak, and pulled from his pocket a piece of paper, which he quickly unfolded and presented to me. "I went down to the property records office in the state building," he said, excited. "I looked up your family's records. You own this land, Wika—it was your father's, and now it's yours."

I looked at the paper. "Lot 45090, Hau'ula, 30.3 acres," I read, but I was suddenly unable to read anything else, and I handed it back to him.

I was at once very tired and thirsty; the sun above us was too hot. "I need to lie down again," I said to him, and felt the ground beneath me crater and then sink, and my head fall, as if in slow motion, into Edward's palms. For a while, there was silence. "You big lolo," I heard him say at last, but as if from far away, and his voice was fond. "You dummy," he said, "you dummy, you dummy, you dummy," repeating the word like a caress, while above me the sun stopped in its path, turning everything around me a bright, unyielding white.

———

Kawika: I can now walk all the way around my room without getting tired. I keep the wall on my right and use my hand to guide me: The walls are stucco and cool and bumpy, and I can sometimes convince myself I'm feeling something living, like the skin of a reptile. Tomorrow night I'll attempt walking down the hallway. Last night I tried the handle for the first time, assuming it was locked, but it depressed easily in my hand, so easily I was almost disappointed. But then I remembered that I had something new to try, and that with each night I was able to prove myself able to walk farther and farther, I was getting closer to you.

Your grandmother came to visit me today. She talked about the price of pork, and her new neighbors, of whom she clearly disapproves—he's Japanese, raised in Kaka'ako; she's haole, from Vermont; they're both research scientists who got rich manufacturing some sort of antiviral—and a blight that's infected the 'ōhai ali'i tree; I had hoped she might have news of you, but she didn't. It's been so long since she's mentioned you, and sometimes I worry that something's happened. But this is only during daylight—somehow, at night, I know you're safe. You may be far from me, maybe too far, but I know for certain that you're alive, alive and healthy. Recently, I've been having a dream of you with a woman; you two are walking down Fifty-seventh Street, just as I once did, your arms linked. You turn to her and she smiles. I can't see her face, only that she's dark-haired, like your mother was, but I know she's beautiful, and that you're happy. Maybe this is what you're doing right now? I like to think it is.

But this is not what you want to hear. You want to hear about what happened next.

The day after my trip to Hau'ula, I went to visit Uncle William, who was surprised to see me—it had now been more than five years since I had stopped by the office—and asked him if he could explain to me, in detail, the family's real-estate holdings. It now seems absurd, even shameful, that I had never asked him before, but there was no reason for me to be concerned. There was always money when I needed it; I never had to consider its origins.

Poor Uncle William was delighted that I was expressing an interest in the trust, and he began detailing what land we had and where. It was far more than I had expected, though all of it was modest. There were seven acres outside Dallas, two parking garages in North Carolina, ten acres of farmland outside Ojai. "Your grandfather bought cheap land on the mainland all his life," said William, as proud as if he had bought it himself.

Finally, I had to interrupt him. "But what about Hawai'i?" I asked, and then, when he drew out a map of Maui, I stopped him again: "O'ahu, specifically."

Once again, I was surprised. Along with our house in Manoa, there were two run-down apartment buildings in Waikīkī, and three consecutive storefronts in Chinatown, and a small house in Kailua, and even the church in Lāʻie. I waited as Uncle William worked his way around the state counterclockwise from southern Honolulu, pitying him as I never had before for the caress in his voice, for the pride he took in this land that wasn't even his.

But if I felt pity for William, I felt disgust for myself. What had I done to earn any of this? Nothing. Money, my money, *did* grow on trees: on trees, and in fields, and between blocks of concrete. It was harvested and cleaned and counted and stored, and whenever I wanted it, even before I knew I wanted it, there it was, stacks of it, more than I could ever know to desire.

I sat in silence as Uncle William talked, until, finally, I heard him say, "And then there's the property in Hauʻula," at which I sat up and leaned toward him, looking at the map of the island he was lovingly gliding his fingers across. "Just over thirty acres, but a useless piece of land," he said. "Too arid and too small for significant farming; too remote to be a good homestead. The beach is no good, either—too rough and too much coral. The road's just dirt, and the state has no plans to extend asphalt out that far. No neighbors, no restaurants, no grocery stores, no schools."

On and on he went, detailing the property's flaws, until I finally asked, "Then why do we have it at all?"

"Ah," he smiled. "It was a whim of your grandfather's, and your father was too sentimental to sell it. Yes," he said, mistaking my look for surprise, "he could be sentimental, your father." He smiled again and shook his head. "Lipo-wao-nahele," he added.

"What's that?" I asked.

"That's what your grandfather called this land," he said. "The Dark Forest, technically, but he translated it as the Forest of Paradise." He looked at me. "You'd think it'd be Nahelekūlani, wouldn't you?" he asked, and I shrugged. Uncle William's Hawaiian was much better than my own; my grandfather had paid for him to study it when he was a college student and had just begun working for the family practice. "Technically, you'd be right, but your grandfather

Kawika said it was lazy Hawaiian, tacked on, that it'd be akin to calling it, oh, Kawikakūlani." *Kawikakūlani:* David of Heaven. He began to sing:

"*He ho'oheno kē 'ike aku*
Ke kai moana nui lā
Nui ke aloha e hi'ipoi nei
Me ke 'ala o ka līpoa

"You know that song, of course." (I did; it was popular.) "'Ka Uluwehi O Ke Kai': 'The Bounty of the Sea.' *Lipoa:* It sounds the same, doesn't it? But it isn't—here, the word is *līpoa,* and it refers to the seaweed. But your grandfather used *lipoa,* as in *ua lipoa wale i ka ua ka nahele,* 'the forest dark with rain'—very beautiful, don't you think? So, '*Lipo wao nahele*': the Dark Forest. But your grandfather preserved the *mana* of the name: 'the Forest of Heaven.'"

He sat back in his seat and smiled, such a gentle smile, filled with the joy of understanding a language I didn't speak and couldn't properly comprehend. Suddenly I hated him—he possessed something I could not, and it wasn't money but those words, rolling like smooth, shiny pebbles in his mouth, white and clean as the moon.

"Is there a forest out there?" I asked, finally, though I had been about to pose it as a statement: *There's no forest there.*

"Not anymore," he said. "But there once was, or so your grandfather said. He planned to plant it again someday, and it would be his paradise.

"Your father didn't share his father's appreciation for this land—he thought it wasn't worth the bother. But he didn't sell it, either. He always said it was because no one would buy it, it being so far out and so far from prime. Though I long suspected it was another form of sentimentalism. You know that the two weren't terribly close, or at least that was what they'd both say, and yet I think that wasn't really true. They were just too much alike, and both of them grew accustomed to this narrative, which seemed easier and more dignified than actually trying to close the distance between them. But I wasn't fooled. Why, I remember . . ."

And then he was off, telling stories I had already been told: about how my father had wrecked my grandfather's car and never apologized; about how my father had been a poor high-school student and my grandfather had had to make an additional donation to the school to ensure his graduation; about how my grandfather had wanted my father to be more of a scholar, whereas my father wanted to be an athlete. They were typical father-and-son problems, yet they felt as remote and uninteresting as something I might read in a book.

And behind this all were the words *Lipo wao nahele*, a phrase meant to be chanted, to be carried beneath the tongue, and although I was looking at Uncle William, smiling and nodding as he talked and talked, I was thinking of that land that was mine after all, where I had lain beneath an acacia tree and watched as, just a few yards away, Edward shucked off his shorts and shirt and ran, whooping, into the glittering water, and dived beneath a wave so large that, for a few seconds, it was as if he had been a victim of some kind of alchemy, and his bones had been turned to foam.

Finally, I had information to tell Edward: He may have discovered that the land belonged to me, but I was able to tell him what it had meant to my grandfather, the last person in our family to be addressed as Prince Kawika. Today I am embarrassed about how gratified I was by his excitement, to finally have something to give him and to have it be so enthusiastically received, with all the self-ishness of the gift-giver.

It became a shorthand between us. Not quite a joke. But not something I thought I took seriously. I had little imagination, and he had less, but we began to speak of it as someplace real, as if, every time we mentioned its name, a new tree would begin to sprout, as if we were speaking the forest into being. Sometimes we would take you with us on our weekend road trips, and in the afternoons, after you and Edward swam, you would come lie by my side and I would tell you stories I remembered from when I was little, replacing every magic forest, every haunted glen, with Lipo-wao-nahele. The witch's house in "Hansel and Gretel," which had so confounded me when I was a child, with its gingerbread walls and gumdrop-trimmed eaves (What was gingerbread? What were gumdrops? What were eaves?), became a palm hut in Lipo-wao-nahele, its roof made of scallops of dried mango, its doorway a curtain of strings of crack seed, their salt-and-sugar perfume filling the witch's kitchen. Sometimes I would tell you about it as if it were a place that actually existed—or, rather, I would let you believe it was anything you wanted it to be: "Are there bunnies there?" you'd ask (you were fixated on bunnies, in those years). "Yes," I'd say. "Is there ice cream there?" you'd ask. "Yes," I'd say. Was there a model train set in Lipo-wao-nahele? Was there a jungle gym you could have all to yourself? Was there a tire swing? Yes, yes, yes. Anything you wanted could be found in Lipo-wao-nahele, which was equally defined by what it lacked: bedtime, bath time, homework, onions. There was no room for things you hated at Lipo-wao-nahele. It was heaven as much for what it excluded.

What was I doing? These were the years when you were five, six, seven, eight, still young enough to believe that, because I told you wonderful things, I was wonderful as well. Back then, it seemed not just harmless but helpful. It made me feel, for the first time in my life, like I might be a king after all. Here was this land that my grandfather thought was paradise, and so why should I not agree? Who was I to say that he might not be right?

You may be wondering what your grandmother thought of all this. When she discovered I was with Edward again—and of course she was going to discover it, that was an inevitability—she didn't speak to me for a week. Though such was the power of Lipo-wao-nahele that, as I remember it, I didn't even care. I had a different, bigger secret, and that secret was a place where I would feel invincible, where I for once would feel like I belonged, where I would never feel shame or apology for who I was. I had never rebelled as a child, not ever, and yet I had still disappointed her, because I had never been able to be the son she had wanted. But I hadn't done that on purpose, and if I'm to be honest, there was a thrill in defying her, in being the agent of her dismay, of inviting Edward back to our house, my house, to have him at our table, my mother a hostage.

We began driving out there every weekend, Edward and I, and although the first time we went I was deflated, thinking only of Uncle William's dismissals (*a useless piece of land*), Edward was so excited that I let myself become excited as well. "Here's where my offices will be," he said, pacing out a square around the acacia. "We'll keep the tree and build the courtyard around it. And there is where we'll build the school, where we'll teach the kids only in Hawaiian. And there's where your palace will be, near that monkeypod tree. See? We'll situate it facing the water, so when you wake you'll be able to see the sun rise over the ocean." The following weekend, we spent the night there, camped out on the beach, and after the sun had gone down, Edward scooped up a dozen of the tiny firefly squid that had washed onto shore, and skewered them on 'ōhi'a branches and roasted them for us. The next morning, I woke early, before Edward, and looked toward the mountains. In the dawn, the land, which normally looked so scorched, appeared lush and soft and vulnerable.

Now, however, I can see that Lipo-wao-nahele meant different things to us—different, but the same as well. It was, for both of us, a fantasy of usefulness, our own usefulness. Edward had inherited a small amount of money from his mother, enough to rent a single-room cottage on a Lower Valley property owned by a Korean family about a five-minute walk from me; he had an occasional job painting rooms for a construction crew. I didn't even have that—after you left for school for the day, I had nothing to do but wait for you to come home. Sometimes I helped my mother with simple things, like stuffing envelopes with solicitations for the Daughters' annual fund-raiser, but mostly I just waited. I read magazines or books, I took long walks, I slept. I hoped for my attacks in those days, for they would prove that my inactivity wasn't laziness or driftiness but a necessity. "Are you taking it easy?" my doctor—my doctor since childhood—would ask me at my appointments, and I would always say I was. "Good," he would say, solemnly, "you mustn't overtax yourself, Wika," and I would promise him I wasn't.

We were inessential in every way. I to you and my mother; the both of us to Hawai'i. That was the irony—we needed the idea of Hawai'i more than it needed us. No one was clamoring for us to take over; no one wanted our help. We were playacting, and because our pretending affected no one—until, of course, it did—we could be as indulgent as we wanted. The things we convinced ourselves! That I would be king, that he would be my first adviser, that in Lipo-wao-nahele we would rebuild the paradise my grandfather had supposedly dreamed of, though he certainly couldn't have dreamed that someone like me would be his representative. In reality, we did nothing—we didn't even try to plant the forest he wanted.

The difference between us, however, is that Edward believed. He was rich in belief; it was all he had. Lipo-wao-nahele was a retreat and a pastime for him just as it was for me, but it was something more, too. Looking back, I can understand how Edward *needed* to be Hawaiian, or at least this idea of Hawaiian he had created. He needed to feel that he was a part of some larger, greater tradition. His mother was dead, and he had never known his father; he had few friends and no family. To be Hawaiian was not a political imperative for him but, rather, a personal one. Yet here, too, he was unconvincing to others, kicked out of Keiki kū Ali'i, unwelcome (or so he said) in the Hawaiian-language classes he tried to take, expelled from the hālau because a painting job had meant he would miss too many practices. This was his birthright, and even here he was unwanted.

But at Lipo-wao-nahele, there was no one to tell him no, and no one to tell him that his way of being Hawaiian was incorrect. There was only me, and sometimes you, and we believed whatever he said. I was the king, but he was the leader, and over the years, those thirty acres were being reclassified in his mind from metaphor to something else. It would be his kingdom after all, and we his subjects, and no one would be able to deny him ever again.

The first step was changing our names.

This was 1978, a year before we left. He had already changed his, the previous year. First he had become Ekewaka, the Hawaiianization of Edward, and a strange and awkward name to say aloud. I had been relieved when he told me he was changing it again, to Paiea, his middle name. "A real Hawaiian name," he said, proudly, as if he had thought of it himself, instead of merely remembering that it had been there all along. Paiea: the crab, and Kamehameha the Great's given name. And now Edward's, as well.

I should have anticipated his wanting to change our names too, but somehow, like so much else, it never occurred to me that he might ask for something so large. "A Hawaiianization of a Christian name is still a Christian name, just in brownface," he said. It was clear that he had learned this term, "brownface," recently, because uncertainty softened his voice a bit as he said it.

"But it was the king's name," I said, in a rare show of resistance, though I wasn't arguing so much as I was bewildered. Was the king not Hawaiian enough, either?

"That's true," he admitted, and looked momentarily confused. Then his face cleared. "But we're going to begin again out in Lipo-wao-nahele. Your blood gives you a right to the throne, but we're going to begin a new dynasty for it."

He had begun keeping a list of what he considered "true" Hawaiian names, those that predated Western contact. But he bemoaned how few there were, how they had gone almost extinct from lack of interest. It had stupidly never occurred to me that a name, as much as a plant or a creature, could vanish from lack of popularity, nor did I quite see the point of Edward's quest: You couldn't force a name back into existence. A name was not a plant or an animal—it flourished from desire, not need, and therefore was subject to all the fickle attentions of humans. Had the old names disappeared because, as he claimed, they had been banned by the missionaries, or had they disappeared simply because they couldn't withstand the novelty of the Western ones? Edward would have said that both arguments began in the same place: They had been shoved aside by the interlopers. But shouldn't a name that was meaningful be meaningful enough to hold its place, even in the face of insurrection?

I didn't ask this. And I didn't even protest too much when he gave first me and then you our new names. But you know—or I hope you know—that I didn't let our name be taken from us. I hope you noticed that I only called you by the name he gave you when he was present, that at all other times, you were still my Kawika, and always will be. And I resisted in another small way as well—although I learned, eventually, to call him Paiea, in my head I continued to think of him, to refer to him, as Edward.

I am struck, now, telling you all of this, by how make-believe it was. We knew almost nothing of anything: nothing of history, nothing of work, nothing of Hawai'i, nothing of responsibility. And the things we *did* know we tried to unknow: My great-grandfather's sister, the one who had succeeded him as monarch after he had died prematurely, the one who was overthrown, the one with whom the kingdom died—had she not been a Christian herself? Had she not given power and wealth to some of the very men, Christian, white, missionary men, who had later taken her throne? Had she not watched as her people were taught English and encouraged to go to church? Had she not worn silk gowns and diamonds in her hair and at her throat like an English queen, had her black hair oiled and tamed? But these were facts that complicated our imaginings, and so we chose to ignore them. We were grown men, long past the age at which we should have been pretending, and yet we were pretending as if our lives depended upon it. What did we—what did I—think would happen? What did I think our pretending would amount to? The most pathetic answer is that I didn't. I pretended because, when I was pretending, I had given myself something to do.

It's not that we wanted something to happen—we wanted the opposite. The world was becoming less explicable to me the older you got. At night, I watched the news, the reports of strikes and protests, marches and the occasional celebration. I watched the war end, and fireworks exploding over the Statue of Liberty, the water beneath shimmering as if flooded with oil. I watched a new president be sworn in and images of a man in San Francisco who was assassinated. How was I going to explain the world to you when I couldn't understand it myself? How could I let you go into it when all around us were terrors and horrors, nightmares from which I'd never be able to wake you?

But inside Lipo-wao-nahele, nothing ever changed. It was not so much a fantasy as a suspension—if I was there, then time would stop. If you never got older, there would never come the day when your knowledge surpassed mine, when you learned to look at me with scorn. If you never got older, I would never disappoint you. Sometimes I prayed time would start traveling backward—not, as Edward would have it, two centuries back, so I could see the islands as they once were, but eight years back, when you were still my baby and learning to walk, and everything I did was marvelous to you, when all I had to do was say your name and your face would open in a smile. "Never leave me," I'd whisper to you then, even as I knew that my job was to raise you to leave me, that your purpose as my child was to leave me, a purpose I myself had failed to fulfill. I was selfish. I wanted you to always love me. I didn't do what was best for you—I did what I thought was best for me.

But as it happened, I was wrong about that, too.

———

Kawika, something very important happened to me last night: I went outdoors.

For months, I was only able to walk around my room before losing my breath, not to mention my courage. And then, last night, for no particular reason, I pressed the handle of my room door and stepped into the hallway. One second, I was in my room, and the next, I was outside of it, and nothing had changed in that moment except that I had tried. It's like that, sometimes, you know; you wait and wait and wait—because you're frightened, because you've always waited—and then, one day, the wait is over. In that moment, you forget what it was to wait. This state that you'd lived in for sometimes years is gone, and so is your memory of it. All you have at the end is loss.

At the doorway, I turned right, and down the hall I went, running my right hand against the side of the wall to guide my way. Initially, I was so nervous I thought I might vomit, and every small noise I heard made my heart seize.

But then—I can't say how far I'd walked, in length or minutes—something very strange happened. I felt a kind of elation overcome me, an ecstasy, and suddenly, as suddenly as I'd pressed on the door handle, I dropped my hand from the wall and stepped into the center of the hallway and began to walk with a swiftness and certainty I couldn't remember ever experiencing. Faster and surer I walked, and it was as if with each step I was creating new stone beneath my feet, as if the building was growing up around me, and the hallway, if I never turned off it, would stretch on infinitely.

At some point, I turned right, reaching in front of me with my hand, and there, once again as if I'd willed it, was a handle. For some reason, I don't know why, I understood that this door led to the garden. I pressed down on the handle, and even before I felt the door yield, I smelled pīkake, which I knew—because Mama had told me—had been planted all along the walls.

I began to walk through the garden. I had never thought I had paid much attention to its dimensions and paths while I was being pushed through it, but after almost nine years—I stopped when I realized this, my elation abruptly vanishing—I must have memorized its contours after all. So confident was I that for a disorienting moment I wondered if I could see again, if vision itself had changed and this was what it now felt like. Because although all I could discern was the same dark-gray screen I saw every day, it seemed not to matter. Up and down the paths I marched, and I never had to stop to grope before me, I never had to rest—though, if I had, I knew, intuitively, where the benches were.

At the far end of the garden there was a door, and I knew that if I turned its handle I would be outside—not just outside in the still, warm air but outside of this place, out in the world. For a while, I stood with my palm against the door, thinking of what I'd do, of how I'd leave.

Although then I realized: Where would I go? I could not return to my mother's house. And I could not return to Lipo-wao-nahele. The first because I knew exactly what I'd find there, and the second because it had disappeared. Not physically, but the idea of it—it had vanished with Edward.

But, Kawika, you would have been proud of me. Once, I would have been dispirited by this. I would have lost my bearings, I would have lain on the ground and moaned for help, I would have put my arms over my head and begged, aloud, for the mountains to stack themselves atop me, for everything to stop *moving* so much and so fast. You saw me do this, many times. The first time it happened was the winter after we left for Lipo-wao-nahele, and I had been overcome by what I had done—how I had taken you from your home, how I had enraged my mother, how nothing had changed after all: How I was still a disappointment, and frightened, and how I hadn't grown out of those traits but had instead grown into them, so that these qualities had not kept me from becoming someone else but in fact had become who I was. You had been visiting that weekend, and you had been scared, you had held my hand as you knew to do when I was having a seizure, and when it became clear that this was no seizure but, rather, some other kind of state, you had dropped my hand and run across the plain, yelling for Edward, and he had returned with you and shaken me, hard, yelling at me to stop acting like such a dummy, like such a baby. "Don't call my father a dummy," you'd said, so brave even then, and Edward had hissed back at you, "I'll call him a dummy if he acts like a dummy," and you had spit at him then, not to actually hit him but just to do it, and he had raised his hand. From my position on the ground, it looked almost as if he were trying to blot out the sun. And you, so brave, stood there, your arms crossed in front of you, even though you were only eleven, and you must have been terrified. "I'll spare you this one time," Edward had said, "because I respect my prince," and if I had been able to laugh, I would have at his pomposity, at his pretension. But it would be a long time before I would think that, and in the moment, I was as scared as you were, except the difference was that I was supposed to take care of you, not just lie on the ground and watch.

Anyway—I did not fall to the garden floor; I did not weep and wail. I instead sat with my back against one of the trees (I could feel it was a skinny little banyan) and thought about you. I understood then that my job was to keep practicing. Tonight I had navigated my way through the garden; tomorrow, or perhaps next week, I would try to leave this property. Every night I would go farther. Every night I would get stronger. And one day, someday soon, I would see you again, and say all this to you in person.

————

You remember the day we left. It was the day after you graduated from fourth grade. You were ten. In June, you would turn eleven.

I had packed a bag for you, which I had stored in the trunk of Edward's car. Over the previous two months, little things had been disappearing from your room—underwear and T-shirts and shorts and your favorite deck of cards, one of your skateboards, your favorite stuffed animal: the plush shark you were too embarrassed to admit you still occasionally slept with, which you kept hidden beneath your bed. You didn't notice the clothes, but you did notice the skateboard: "Da, have you seen my skateboard? No, the purple one. No, I looked—it's not there. I'll go ask Jane again."

I had packed food as well, tins of Spam and cans of corn and kidney beans. A saucepan and a kettle. Matches and lighter fluid. Packages of crackers and instant noodles. Glass jugs of water. Every weekend, we took a little more. In April, we'd set up the tarp and hidden the tents beneath a pile of coral rocks we lugged from the sea. "Later, we'll build a real palace," Edward said, and as always when he said such things, such improbable things, I remained silent. If he meant them, I was embarrassed for him. If he did not, I was embarrassed for me.

Here my story joins your own, and yet there's so much I don't know about how you felt and what you saw. What did you think that afternoon we arrived at Lipo-wao-nahele and saw the tents—one for me and you; one for Edward—arranged under the acacia, the tarp stretched taut between four metal poles we'd scavenged from the abandoned cement plant on the western side of the island, the cardboard boxes of our food and clothes and supplies beneath it? I remembered you smiling, a little uncertainly, looking from me to the tarp to Edward, who was unloading the hibachi grill from his car. "Da?" you had asked me, looking up into my face. But you hadn't known what to say next. "What is this?" you finally asked, and I pretended I hadn't heard you, though of course I had—it was only that I didn't know what to say.

That weekend, you played along. When Edward woke us early Friday morning to recite a chant, you did so, and when he said that, beginning that day, the three of us were going to take Hawaiian lessons together, that this would be a place where only Hawaiian was spoken, you looked at me, and when I nodded, you shrugged, acquiescent. "Okay," you said.

"'*Ae*," he corrected you, sternly, and you shrugged again.

"'*Ae*," you repeated.

Most of the time, you were inscrutable, but I watched bemusement scud across your face, and amusement, too. Did Edward *really* expect you to fish for your food? Were you *really* to learn to cook it over the fire? Would we *really* go to bed at eight, so we could wake with the dawn? Yes, it seemed; yes, and yes. You were smart even then, you didn't challenge him—you knew as well that he didn't play, that he didn't have a sense of humor. "Edward," you once said, and he didn't look up, he pretended he hadn't heard you, and I watched as a kind of understanding came over you. "Paiea," you said, and he turned: "'*Ae?*"

I think it was because you were never able to trust my abilities as a father that you learned early that people would not behave as they should, and things were not what they appeared. Here we were, your father and his friend, whom you had known since you were a baby, and we were having a fun beachside camping trip. And yet was this really what it seemed? No one had said anything about fun, and, indeed, there was something toilsome about your time at Lipo-wao-nahele, even though here you were getting to do everything you liked to do—fish and swim and climb up the edge of the nearby mountain, foraging for greens. But something was amiss—something was wrong. You couldn't articulate how, but you sensed it.

"Da," you whispered to me the second night, as I blew out the candle in the hurricane lamp between us. "What're we doing here?"

I took so long to answer that you poked me, gently, in my arm. "Da?" you asked. "Did you hear me?"

"We're camping, Kawika," I said, and then, when you were silent, "Aren't you having a good time?"

"I guess," you said, reluctantly, finally. You weren't, but you couldn't explain why you weren't. You were a child, and the problem isn't that children don't possess the full range of emotions that adults do—it is only that they don't possess the vocabulary to express them. I *was* an adult, I *did* have the vocabulary, and yet I too couldn't explain what was wrong about the situation, I too couldn't express what I was feeling.

That Monday was the same: the Hawaiian lessons, the long hours of boredom, the fishing, the fire. I saw you staring at the car at odd moments, as if you might be able to call it like a dog, have it come revving to your side.

On Thursday, you were to begin attending a camp where you'd learn to build robots. You were so excited about this camp: You had been speaking of it for months, rereading the brochure, telling me about the kind of robot you were going to build—it'd be called the Spider, and it'd be able to climb up to the tops of shelves and retrieve things that Jane couldn't reach. Three of your friends would be attending as well.

The day before, you said to me, "What time are we leaving?" And, when I didn't answer you, "Da. Camp starts at eight tomorrow morning."

"Talk to Paiea," I finally said, in a voice I didn't recognize.

You stared at me, disbelief on your face, and then got up and hurried over to Paiea. "Paiea," I heard you say, "when are we leaving? I have camp tomorrow!"

"You're not going to camp," Edward said, calmly.

"What do you mean?" you asked, and, before he could answer, "Edward—I mean, Paiea—what do you mean?"

Oh, how we both wished Edward were teasing, were capable of teasing. But although I knew he was not, I never believed, truly believed, until it was too late, that he would always do exactly what he said he was going to do—yet he was the least secretive person I knew, the least conniving. What he said he was going to do was what he did.

"You're not going," he repeated. "You're staying here."

"*Here?*" you asked. "Where?"

"Here," he said. "At Lipo-wao-nahele."

"But that's make-believe!" you cried, and then, turning to me, "Da! Da!" But I didn't say anything, I couldn't, and you didn't try harder with me—you knew I would be of no use, of no help—before swiveling back to Edward. "I want to go home," you said, and then, when he too didn't respond, your voice took on a hysterical edge. "I want to go home. I want to go home!"

You ran to the car, you got in the driver's seat, you began to pound on the horn, which made sharp little bleats. "Take me home!" you yelled, and by that time you were crying. "Da! Da! Edward! Take me home!" *Honk, honk, honk.* "Tutu!" you shouted, as if your grandmother might emerge from one of the tents, "Jane! Matthew! Help me! Help me! Take me home!"

Another man would have laughed at you, but he didn't—the one good thing about his lack of humor was that he wasn't a humiliator; he took you seriously in his own way. He simply let you yell and shout for a few minutes, until you slumped out of the car, exhausted and crying, and then he picked himself up from beneath the acacia and came and sat down next to you, and you sagged against him, despite yourself.

"It's okay," I heard him say to you, and he put his arm around you and began stroking your hair. "It's okay. You're home, little prince. You're home."

What did you think of Edward? I never asked you, because I never wanted to know the answer, and anyway, it would have been a strange and impossible question for a parent to ask his child: What do you think of my friend? But now we're both adults, and I can ask: What did you think?

I'm still afraid of the answer. You knew, knew long before I did, that there was something to fear in him, something to not trust. Even as a very little child, you would look from your grandmother to me to your uncle Edward on the occasions he stayed for supper, and although you were unable to articulate the tension between us all, of course you could sense it. You saw how silent I grew around him, you saw how I waited for permission to speak before I said anything in his presence. Once, when you were around ten, we were spending the day by the beach at Lipo-wao-nahele. It was late afternoon, almost time for us to leave, and I asked Edward if I could go relieve myself first. "Yes," he said, and I did. It was unremarkable to me—I asked him whether I could do things all the time: Could I eat? Could I have seconds? Could I go home? The only things I didn't ask him were things that involved you—and it wasn't until I was tucking you into bed that night that you asked me why I hadn't just gone, why I had needed permission. It wasn't like that, I tried to tell you, but then I couldn't explain why it wasn't, why you were wrong, why I hadn't just gotten up and gone when I had wanted to—when I had needed to. It is a terrible thing for a child to have to realize that their parent is weak, too weak to protect them. Some children react with scorn, and some—as you did then—with sympathy. I believe it was then that you realized that you were no longer a child, that you had to protect me, that I needed your help. It was when you realized that you would have to figure things out on your own.

Sometimes Edward would give you lectures, clumsy versions of the ones Bethesda had given us. He would try for Bethesda's poetry, his sense of rhythm, but aside from a few borrowed lines, which he repeated as punctuation—"America is a country with sin at its heart"—he was incapable, and his attempts were disjointed and repetitive, dull and circular. I would hear myself thinking this and feel guilty for my betrayal, though I never said it aloud, never said it to you. "No land is owned land," Edward would say to you, forgetting, or perhaps ignoring, the fact of Lipo-wao-nahele, whose ownership was central to his fantasy of it. "You have the right to be whatever you want," he'd say, although this too he didn't mean— you would be a Hawaiian man, a young prince, as he called you, though he had little conception of what that meant, and neither did I. If you had said then, as you had every right to, that you wanted to grow up, marry the blondest woman you could, live in Ohio, and manage a bank, he would have been horrified, but would he have been horrified by your choices or by your ambition? How brave you'd be, to go all the way to Ohio, to leave behind all the privileges your name guaranteed you, to go where you might as well be Prince Woogawooga, foreign and laughable, your status vanished as soon as you climbed into your little coconut-tree canoe and pushed off the sandy shore of Ooga-ooga!

His idea of what Hawai'i was, what we were as Hawaiians, was so shallow that, of all the things I am ashamed of today, it is that which affects me the most. Not the fact of it but that I blinded myself to it, that I allowed him to play, and that I sacrificed our lives for that play. All those years he tried to teach you Hawaiian, using an old primer stolen from the university library—you never learned, because he never learned. His lessons about Hawaiian history too were mostly invented, projections of what he hoped had happened rather than what actually had. "We are a land of kings and queens and princes and princesses," he would say to you, but the truth was that there were only two princes on our land, and they were you and I, and that you cannot have a land full of royalty, because royalty needs people to revere them, or they cease to be royalty.

I would hear him give you these lectures and I would be unable to stop them. With each day, I felt myself less capable of undoing what I had allowed to happen. It was as if I had been delivered to Lipo-wao-nahele—I had not chosen to come there; I had been deposited there, as though some wind had blown me across the island and dropped me beneath the acacia tree. My life, where I lived, had become foreign to me.

It was the Sunday after I had failed to take you to robotics camp that we heard the car. We heard it, and then we saw it, jogging along the stony road. You had spent the last three days stunned by what had happened to you: On Thursday, the day you were to be at robotics camp, you had woken to find yourself still at Lipo-wao-nahele—I think you had hoped that it might be a dream, that you might wake up in your bed at your grandmother's house—and had flung yourself down upon the ground and sobbed, actually striking your arms and legs against the earth like a parody of a temper tantrum. "Kawika,"

I had said, creeping toward you (Edward was walking along the beach), "Kawika, it'll be okay."

Then you had sat abruptly upright, your face wet. "How will it be okay?" you had shouted. "Huh? How?"

I had sat back on my heels. "I don't know," I'd had to admit.

"Of *course* you don't know," you'd snarled. "You don't know *anything*. You never do." And then you had returned to crying, and I had crept away. I didn't blame you. How could I? You were right.

On Friday and Saturday, you lapsed into a silence. You wouldn't leave the tent, not even to eat. I was worried about you, but Edward was not. "Leave him alone," he said. "He'll come out eventually."

But you didn't. And so, when the car arrived, you were slow to emerge from the tent, blinking in the sun and staring at it like it was a hallucination. It was only when Uncle William got out from behind the wheel that you gave a weak, animal cry, a kind I'd never heard from you before, and began running toward him, wobbly from dehydration and hunger.

He hadn't come alone. Your grandmother was in the passenger seat, and Jane and Matthew, looking scared, were in the back. It was your grandmother who took you, pushing you behind her and standing between you and Edward as if he might reach out and hit you. "I don't know what you're playing at, I don't know what you're doing," she said. "But I am taking my grandson, and I'm leaving with him."

Edward had shrugged. "I don't think that's really up to you, lady," he said, and I had stepped backward, despite myself. *Lady.* I had never heard my mother addressed so disrespectfully. "It's up to your son."

"That's where you're wrong, Mr. Bishop," she said, and to you, more gently: "Get in the car, Kawika."

But you wouldn't. Instead you looked around her, at me. "Da?" you asked.

"Kawika," she said, "get in the car. Now."

"No," you said. "Not without him." *Him:* You meant me.

"For heaven's sakes, Kawika," she said, impatient. "He doesn't want to come."

"Yes, he does," you'd insisted. "He doesn't want to be here, do you, Da? Come home with us."

"This is his land," Edward said. "Pure land. Hawaiian land. He'll stay."

They began to argue, Edward and your grandmother, and I turned my face to the sky, which was white and hot, too hot for May. They seemed to have forgotten that I existed, that I was standing there, a distance from both of them, the third point in the triangle. But I was no longer listening to them, to Edward's pablum or your grandmother's commands; instead, I was looking at Uncle William and Jane and Matthew, the three of them staring not just at the three of us but at the land itself. I saw them noticing the tents, the blue plastic tarp, the cardboard boxes. It had rained two nights before, and the wind had made one side of the tent you and I shared collapse, so that when I slept beneath it, the nylon covered me like a shroud. Our boxes were still damp, and the contents of them—our clothes and your books—were scattered across the field to dry; it appeared as if a bomb had exploded and everything had been tossed about. The tarp was muddy; from the acacia tree hung a dozen plastic bags containing our food supplies, protecting them from the ants and the mongoose. I saw what they were seeing: an unremarkable piece of scrubby land littered with ugly debris—plastic bottles and broken plastic forks, the tarp rustling in the breeze. Lipo-wao-nahele, but we had planted no trees, and the ones that were already there we were using as furniture. The place was now worse than unloved; it was degraded, and it was Edward and I who had degraded it.

They took you away that day. They tried to have me declared incompetent. They tried to declare me an unfit parent. They tried to take away my trust. I say "they," because Uncle William was the one who was dispatched to (discreetly) talk to someone at Child Protective Services and then to consult an old law-school classmate of his, now a Family Court judge, but I really mean not "they" but "she": your grandmother.

I cannot blame her now, and I couldn't then, either. I knew that what I was doing was wrong. I knew that you should stay where you were, that there was no life for you at Lipo-wao-nahele. So why did I let it happen? How could I let it happen? I could tell you that it was because I wanted to share something with you, something that—rightly or wrongly—I had created for us, a realm in which I made decisions for you that I thought might help you in some way, that might enrich you in some way. But that would be untrue. Or I could tell you that it was because I had initially had hopes for Lipo-wao-nahele, for the life we might have there, and that I had been surprised when those hopes were unfulfilled. But that would be untrue as well.

The truth is neither of those things. The truth is far more pathetic. The truth is that I had simply followed someone, and I had surrendered my own life to somebody else, and that, in surrendering mine, I had surrendered yours, too. And that, once I had done so, I didn't know how to fix what I had done, I didn't know how to make it right. The truth is that I was weak. The truth is that I was incapable. The truth is that I gave up. The truth is that I gave you up, too.

By fall, we had come to an agreement. I would get to see you two weekends a month at Lipo-wao-nahele, but only if proper accommodations were built for you. You would otherwise reside full-time with your grandmother. If I challenged this in any way, I would be committed. Edward had raged about this, but there was nothing I could do; my mother was still able to circumvent certain processes, and we both understood that if there were a fight between us I would lose—I would lose you, and I would lose my freedom. Though I suppose, by that point, I had already lost both.

My mother came to talk to me just once more, shortly after we had both signed the agreement. It was November, a week or so before Thanksgiving—I was still trying to keep track of the days then. I hadn't known she was coming. For the past week, a crew of carpenters had been building what would be a small house on the northern edge of the property, in the shadow of the mountain. There would be a room for me, a room for Edward, and a room for you, but furnishings would be provided only for your room. This was not an act of meanness—it had been Edward who had refused

Uncle William's offer, telling him we would sleep outside on lauhala mats.

"I don't care where you sleep, as long as you sleep inside when the boy's here," Uncle William had said.

Our experiment was being tested, Edward said; we must not surrender. We would continue to live as our ancestors once had when you weren't with us. When you *were* here, food would be delivered and we would eat it, but when you weren't, we would catch or forage only, and we would cook it over a fire. We would grow our own taro and sweet potatoes; it was my responsibility to muck out the trench I had dug for our feces and to use it to fertilize our plants. The phone, which had been installed at great expense—there were no telephone lines in the area—would be unplugged once you left; the electricity, which Uncle William had somehow arranged with the state, would go unused. "Don't you see they're trying to break us?" he had asked. "Don't you see this is a test, a way for them to find out how passionate we are?"

It had been raining on the morning your grandmother came to visit me, and I watched as she picked her way across the muddy expanse of grass to where I was lying on the tarp beneath the acacia. The tarp, once a ceiling, was now a floor, and I spent most of my day there, sleeping, waiting for one day to end and the next to begin. Sometimes Edward would try to rouse me, but that happened less and less frequently, and often he would vanish for what might have been hours or might have been days—even as I tried, I was less and less able to distinguish time—and I would be left alone to doze, waking only when I was too hungry to sleep. Sometimes I dreamed of that night in the house when we had heard Bethesda, and would wonder if he had been real or if we had summoned him from some other realm.

She stood over me for a few seconds before she spoke. "Wake up, Wika," she said, and, when I didn't move, she knelt and shook my shoulder. "Wika, get up," she repeated, and I finally did.

She stared at me for a bit, and then she stood. "Get up," she instructed. "We're walking."

I got up and followed her. She was carrying a cloth bag and a

tatami mat, which she passed to me. Although it was no longer raining, the sky was still gray, and there was no sun. We walked toward
the mountain, and at the monkeypod tree, she gestured for me to
unfurl the mat. "I brought us a picnic," she said, and before I could
look around, she added, "He's not here."

I wanted to tell her I wasn't hungry, but she was already unloading
the food: bento boxes of rice and mochi fried chicken and nishime,
cucumber namasu, and cut muskmelon for dessert—all the things I
had once loved to eat. "It's all for you," she said, as I began to serve
her. "I already ate."

I ate so fast and so much I gagged, but she never scolded me,
and even after I had finished, she was still silent. She had taken off
her shoes, which she'd placed neatly by the edge of the mat, and
had stretched her legs out before her; I remembered she had always
worn her nylons a shade darker than her skin. She was wearing a
lime-green skirt printed with white roses, now very faded, that I
remembered from my childhood, and as she looked up at the sky
through the branches, leaning back her head and then closing her
eyes, I wondered if she too—as I was occasionally able to myself,
though with far less frequency—was able to appreciate the land's
difficult beauty, the way it seemed to yield to no one. Some yards
away from us, the builders had finished their lunch break and were
once again pounding and sawing; I had overheard one saying that
the land was far too wet for a wooden house, and another disagree-
ing, saying the problem wasn't the humidity but the heat. They had
had to delay the foundation work, and then re-site it, when it had
been discovered that the original location had abutted a swamp,
which had been drained and then filled. For a while, we listened to
the construction, and I waited to hear what she was going to say.

"When you were almost three, I took you to the mainland to see
a specialist," she began. "Because you didn't speak. It was clear you
weren't deaf, which was what we first thought. But when your father
or I said your name, you turned to us, and when we were outside
and you heard a dog bark, you would get excited and smile and clap.

"You liked music as well, and when we played your favorite songs,
you would even sometimes—not hum along, quite, but you would

make little noises. Still, you wouldn't speak. Your doctor said we perhaps weren't speaking enough to you, so we spoke to you constantly. At night, your father would seat you next to him and read the sports section to you. But since I was the one who was with you the most, I talked to you most of all. Ceaselessly, in fact. I took you with me wherever I went. I read books to you, and recipes, and when we were in the car, I'd tell you everything we were passing. 'See,' I'd say, 'there's the school you're going to attend someday, when you're a little older; over there, that's the house your father and I lived in right after we got married, before we moved to the valley; up that hill is where your father's high-school friend lives—they have a little boy just your age.'

"Mostly, though, I talked to you about my life. I told you about my father and my siblings, and how, when I was a girl, I wanted to move to Los Angeles and be a dancer, except of course that wasn't the sort of thing that I would be allowed to do, and anyway, I wasn't a very good dancer. I even told you about how your father and I had tried so many times to give you a sister, and each time, she slipped away from us, until the doctor told us that you would be our only.

"How much I talked to you! I was lonely in those days; I hadn't yet joined the Daughters, and most of my friends from school had large families or were busy running their own households, and I was already estranged from my siblings. So I just had you. At times I would lie in bed in the evening and think of all that I'd told you and feel frightened that I had perhaps damaged you by telling you things I shouldn't tell a child. Once, I became so worried that I even confessed to your father, and he laughed and took me in his arms and said, 'Don't be silly, pet'—he called me 'pet'—'he doesn't even understand what you're saying. Why, you could curse at him all day long and it wouldn't make a difference!' I swatted him on the arm and scolded him, but he just laughed again, and he made me feel a little better.

"On the flight to San Francisco, though, I thought again of how much I'd told you, and do you know what I wished? I wished you would never speak at all. I was afraid that if you did, you would tell someone the things I had told you, all of my secrets. 'Don't tell anyone,' I whispered into your ear as you lay asleep on my lap. 'Don't ever tell what I told you.' And then I felt horribly guilty—that I should hope my only child never spoke, that I should be so selfish. What kind of mother was I?

"But at any rate, I didn't have to worry. Three weeks after we came home—the San Francisco doctor had no greater insight than our own doctor—you began to talk, not just in single words but in whole sentences. I was so relieved: I wept with joy. Your father, who hadn't been as concerned as I, teased me, but nicely, in that way he had. 'You see, pet?' he asked me. 'I knew he was going to be all right! Just like his old man, didn't I tell you? Now you're going to pray for the day he *stops* talking!'

"That was what everyone told me—that I would someday pray for you to stop talking. But I never had to pray for that, because you were so quiet. And sometimes, as you got older, I wondered: Was I being punished? I had asked you not to say anything, and so you hadn't. And then you said less and less and less, and now—" She stopped, cleared her throat. "And now we're here," she concluded.

We were both quiet for a long time. "For god's sakes, Wika," she said, at last. "*Say* something."

"There's nothing to say," I said.

"This isn't a life here, you understand," she said in a rush. "You're thirty-six; you have an eleven-year-old son. This place—what do you call it? Lipo-wao-nahele? You can't stay here, Wika. You don't have any skills, you or your friend. You don't know how to cook for yourself, or take care of yourself, or, or—*anything*. You know nothing, Wika. You—"

Once again, she stopped speaking mid-sentence. She shook her head, quickly; she seemed to refocus herself. And then she stacked the now empty containers inside one another and placed them in her bag, and rocked back on the balls of her feet into a standing position. She stepped into her shoes, and picked up her bag.

I looked up at her, and she looked down at me. She would say something terrible, I thought, something so insulting that I would never be able to forgive her, and she might never be able to forgive herself.

But she didn't. "Why am I worrying," she said, coolly, as she studied not just my face but the whole of me, my unwashed T-shirt and torn board shorts and the patchy beard that made my cheeks itch. "You won't be able to survive out here. You'll be home before I know it."

And then she turned and walked away from me, and I watched her go. She slid into her car; she put the bag of empty containers onto the seat next to her; she checked her reflection in the rearview mirror, running a hand along the side of her face, as if reminding herself that it was still there. Then she started the engine and drove away.

"Goodbye," I said to her, as the car disappeared. "Goodbye." Overhead, the clouds were turning gray—I could hear the foreman urge his crew to hurry, to finish their work before the rain came.

I lay back down. I closed my eyes. Eventually, I fell asleep, one of those sleeps that feel more real than waking life, so that when I woke—early the next day, Edward still nowhere in sight—I was almost able to convince myself that I could still begin anew.

In the end, my mother was wrong: I didn't go home again. Not before she knew it, and not ever. Over time, Lipo-wao-nahele became where I was and who I was, although it never stopped feeling temporary, someplace intended only for waiting, though the only thing I was waiting for was the next day to begin.

All around us were signs that the land, never inhabited, would frustrate any attempts to be inhabited, and that any human accommodations it made would be temporary. The house, which was concrete and wood, was ugly and boxy and cheap; only your room was painted, with a bed and a mat on the floor and a light fixture in the ceiling—the other rooms had unfinished Sheetrock walls and, also at Edward's insistence, plain cement floors.

Even you spent most of your time outdoors on your visits. Not because you liked being outdoors—or at least, not outdoors at Lipo-wao-nahele—but because the house was so bleak, so obviously hostile to human comfort. I looked forward to your visits, too. I wanted to see you. But I also knew that when you were there, and for the days that followed, the food would be better and more diverse and plentiful. On the Thursdays before your visits, Uncle William would drive out with sackloads of groceries; I would keep the empty bags for our supplies. He would plug in the refrigerator—Edward didn't like to use it—and unload the bottle of milk, the cartons of juice, the oranges and heads of lettuce and patties of beef: all the lovely super-market goods I had once had whenever I wanted. If Edward wasn't around, he'd sneak me a few bars of chocolate. The first time he had tried to give them to me, I had refused, but eventually I accepted, and when I did, tears came to his eyes, and he turned away from me. I hid them in a hole I'd dug behind the house, where they would keep cool and where Edward wouldn't find them.

It was always Uncle William who came, never the clerk or some other functionary from the office, and I wondered why until I real-ized that it was because my mother didn't want anyone else to see me, her son, living like this. Uncle William she could trust, but no one else. It was Uncle William, I presumed, who paid for the elec-tricity and the phone line, Uncle William who paid for our fresh water. He brought us toilet paper, and when he left, he took our bundle of trash with him, as there was no garbage service in our area. When our blue tarp finally became so tattered that it resem-bled a spiderweb, it was Uncle William who brought us a new one, which Edward—for a time—refused to use, until even he had to admit its necessity.

Every time, before he departed for home, he asked me if I wanted to come with him, and every time, I would shake my head. One time, he didn't ask, and I had been bereft when he left, as if that door too had finally shut, and I was truly all alone, stranded here by only my weakness and my stubbornness: two contradictory qualities, one canceling out the other, so that what remained was stasis.

By the third year, Edward was more and more often away. Uncle William had bought you a kayak for your twelfth birthday and had delivered it to Lipo-wao-nahele; it was a two-seater, so that you and I could go together. But you weren't interested, and I was too tired, and so Edward commandeered it, and most days he would leave early in the morning and paddle out, past the bay, rounding one of the outcroppings and disappearing. Sometimes he didn't return until it was dark, and if there wasn't food left over, I would have to eat what I could find. There was an apple banana tree on the eastern edge of the property, and there were nights in which all I had were those stubby green bananas, starchy and underripe, which gave me stomach cramps but which I was forced to eat. I had become like a dog to him; most days, he remembered to feed me, but when he didn't, there was little I could do but wait.

We had few possessions, yet somehow the land always appeared to be littered with trash. There were always empty plastic bags, torn and useless, floating about; you had left one of the Hawaiian-language primers outside on one of your visits—intentionally or not, I couldn't say—and its pages had become fat with water and then had crisped in the sun, and now crackled when a breeze passed over it; debris from projects we'd never begun (a pyramid of coral rocks, another of kindling) were stacked near the acacia. On your visits, you would pace, bored and disgusted, between the house and the tree, back and forth, as if you might walk something else—your friends, a new father—into existence. Once, Uncle William had brought a kite for me to give you on your visit, and although you tried, you could never get it airborne; even the wind had abandoned us.

When you left on Sunday, it was so painful that I couldn't even get up from beneath the tree to see you to your grandmother's car. The first time this happened, you called my name three times, coming over and shaking my shoulder. "Tutu!" you shouted. "There's something wrong with him!"

"No, there's not, Kawika." Her voice was weary. "He just can't get up. Say goodbye and come on now. We have to get home; Jane made you spaghetti and meatballs for dinner."

I felt you crouch by my side. "Bye, Da," you said, quietly, "I love you," and then you leaned over and kissed me, your touch as light as wings, and left. Earlier that day, you'd come upon me holding the side of my face and rocking, which was something I'd begun doing because my tooth hurt so much. "Da, let me see," you had said, your face worried, and then, when I finally, reluctantly, opened my mouth for you, you had gasped. "Da," you said, "your tooth looks—looks really gross. Don't you want to come back into town and get it fixed?" And when I shook my head, groaning again at the pain such a simple movement caused, you sat next to me and patted my back. "Da," you said, "come home with me." But I couldn't. You were thirteen. Every time you visited, it was a reminder of how time had spun forward; every time you left, it was as if time was slowing down again, where I had no future and no past, and had made no mistakes because I had made no decisions, and all there was was possibility.

Eventually, as I knew you must, you stopped coming. You were getting older; you were becoming a man. You were so angry when you came out to Lipo-wao-nahele—angry at your grandmother, angry at Edward, but mostly angry at me. One weekend, one of the last before you stopped coming altogether, shortly after you turned fifteen, you were helping me harvest bamboo shoots, which you had discovered growing on the far side of the mountain two years earlier. They saved me, those bamboo shoots, though they had become too difficult for me to unearth. I was now so weak that Uncle William had stopped asking me to come back to town to see a doctor and had started sending one to me every month. He gave me some drops to keep my eyes from burning, and some drinks that helped make me stronger, and some salves for the insect bites on my face, and some pills to help with my seizures. A dentist came to pull my tooth; he packed the crater with gauze, and left me a tube of ointment to rub into the gum as it healed.

That day, I was very tired. My only job was to hold open an old rice sack so you could drop the shoots into it. After you'd finished, you took the sack from me and slung it over your shoulder, holding out your other hand for me to take so you could lead me back down the hill. You were as tall as I by this point, but much stronger; you held the tips of my fingers gently, like you were afraid of breaking them.

Edward was there that day but not speaking to either of us, and that was fine. I was nervous he might be angry with me, but you had long ago ceased caring what Edward thought of you, and long ago learned that you had nothing to fear from him—he too had disintegrated, although in a different way than I had. He was irritating, not dangerous, if he had ever been, and when you came to see us, you doled out our meals and handed them to us as we sat on the floor, reaching up to you like children, even though we were already—or only—forty, before finally sitting down yourself. Only Edward spoke during those meals, telling you old stories, worn stories, about how we were going to restore this island to what it had been, about how we were doing it for you, our son of Hawai'i, our prince. "That's nice, Paiea," you'd sometimes say, indulgently, as if he were a repetitive child. Once, he looked at you, confused. "Edward," he said. "My name is Edward." But mostly he didn't say anything, just kept talking and talking, until, finally, his voice faded and he stood and walked outside, to the beach, to stare at the sea. We had both become diminished—we had come to give the land life, but it had ended up taking life from us.

We went to the kitchen and you began making us dinner. I sat and watched you move about, putting the shoots aside so I could eat them when you had left, taking the ground pork out of the refrigerator. Even then my eyesight was vanishing, but I could still sit and watch you and admire how handsome you were, how perfectly you had been made.

Jane had been teaching you to cook—just simple things, like noodles and fried rice—and when you came to stay with us, you were the chef. Recently, you had learned to bake, and on this trip, you had brought fresh eggs and flour with you, as well as milk and cream. The next morning you would make me banana bread, you said. The previous two times you had come, you had been surly and snappish, but when you arrived this morning, you were merry and light, whistling as you unloaded the groceries. I was watching you, so full of affection and yearning that I could barely speak, when I suddenly recognized your state of happiness—you were in love.

"Da, will you put the cream and milk in the refrigerator?" you asked. "I have some more supplies to bring in." When you were young, Uncle William had never sent you with supplies, but now he sometimes did, and I would watch as you unloaded rolls of toilet paper and bags of food and even, sometimes, cords of wood, while your grandmother sat behind the wheel of the car, looking out the window toward the sea.

You left, and I remained on my chair (our only chair), staring at the kitchen wall, wondering who you were in love with and if she loved you back. I sat there, dreaming, until you called me again—you had to beckon us both like dogs by then, the two of us obediently answering to our names, trudging toward you—and I followed you to dig up the bamboo shoots.

I was thinking of this, that morning, your dreamy, inward smile, as you muttered to yourself, reaching into the refrigerator for the peppers and zucchini you'd need for your stir-fry, when I heard you curse. "Jesus Christ, Da!" you said, and I focused my gaze to see you holding up the bottle of cream, which I'd forgotten to put away when you told me to. "You left out the cream, Da! And the milk! Now they're ruined!"

You slammed the cream down in the sink and turned back to me. I could see your teeth, your bright black eyes. "Can't you do anything? The only thing I asked you to do was put away the cream and milk, and you can't even do that?" You came over to me, grabbed me by the shoulders, and started to shake me. "What's wrong with you?" you cried. "What's the matter with you? Can't you do anything?"

I had learned, over the years, that the best thing to do when you were being shaken was not to try to fight back but to go slack, and so I did, letting my head loll on its stem, letting my arms go limp, and finally you stopped and pushed me so hard that I fell from the chair to the ground, and then I saw your feet running away from me, and heard the front screen door bang shut.

When you returned, it was night. I was still lying where I had fallen. The pork, left on the counter, had spoiled as well, and in the glow of the lamp, I could see little gnats swarming above it.

You sat down beside me, and I leaned against your warm, bare skin. "Da," you said, and I struggled to sit up. "Here, let me help you," you said, and put your arm behind me and helped me sit. You gave me a glass of water. "I'm going to make something to eat," you said, and I heard you throw the pork into the garbage can, and then begin chopping vegetables.

You made us two plates of stir-fried vegetables with rice, and we both ate them right there, sitting on the kitchen floor.

"I'm sorry, Da," you said, eventually, and I nodded, my mouth too full to answer. "I get so frustrated with you sometimes," you continued, and I nodded again. "Da, can't you look at me?" you asked, and I lifted my head and tried to find your eyes, and you took my head between your palms and brought it close to your face. "Here I am," you whispered. "Do you see me now?" And I nodded once more.

"Don't nod, speak," you instructed, but your voice was gentle.

"Yes," I said. "Yes, I see you."

I slept indoors that night, in your room, in your bed: Edward wasn't around to tell me I couldn't, and you were going to go night fishing. "What about when you come back?" I asked, and you said you'd just climb in next to me, and we'd sleep side by side, like we used to in our tent. "Come on," you said, "take the bed," and although I should have argued with you, I did. But you never came to join me, to keep me company, and the next day, you were quiet and distant, the joy of the previous morning disappeared.

That weekend was the last time I ever saw you. Two weeks later, I was sitting on the tarp and waiting for you when Uncle William drove up, and when he got out of the car, his arms and hands were empty. He explained that you couldn't come this weekend, that you had a school function, something you couldn't miss. "Oh," I said, "will he come next weekend?" And Uncle William nodded, slowly. "I should think so," he said. But you didn't, and this time Uncle William didn't come to tell me, and it wasn't until another month that he arrived again, this time with food and supplies, and a message: You weren't returning to Lipo-wao-nahele, not ever. "Try to see it his way, Wika," he'd said, almost pleadingly. "Kawika's growing up, son—he wants to be with his friends and classmates. This is too hard a place for a young man to be." It was as if he was expecting me to argue, but I couldn't, because everything he said was true. And I knew what he meant, too: It wasn't that Lipo-wao-nahele itself was too difficult a place to be; the difficult part was being with me, the person I had become—or perhaps always had been.

A lot of people think they've wasted their lives. When I was in college on the mainland, it had snowed one night, and the following day, classes were canceled. My dorm room overlooked a steep hill that led to a pond, and I stood at my window and watched as my classmates spent the afternoon sledding and tobogganing, sliding down the hill before slogging back up, laughing and holding on to one another in exaggerated exhaustion. It was evening before they returned to the dorm, and through my door, I could hear them talking about the day they'd had. "What have I done?" I heard one boy groan, in mock despair. "I had a Greek paper to write for tomorrow! I'm wasting my life!"

They all laughed, because it was absurd—he wasn't wasting his life. He would go on to write the Greek paper, and then pass the class, and then graduate, and years later, when he was seeing his own son off to college, he'd say, "Have fun, but not too much," and he would tell him the story of when *he* was in college, and the day he'd wasted sledding in the snow. But there'd be no real suspense to the story, because they would both know the ending already.

I, however, *had* wasted my life. Aside from you, the only thing I had ever accomplished was not leaving Lipo-wao-nahele. But *not* doing something is not the same as doing something. I had wasted my life, but you weren't going to let me waste yours as well. So I was proud of you for leaving me behind, for doing what I was unable to do—you wouldn't let yourself be seduced or fooled or spellbound; you would leave, and not just leave me, and Lipo-wao-nahele, but you would leave everything else as well: the island, the state, history, who you were meant to be, who you might have been. You would discard it all, and when you had, you would find yourself so light that when you stepped into the ocean, your footfall wouldn't even sink but would instead skim atop the surface of the water: There you'd begin walking, east, toward a different life, one where no one knew who you were, not even yourself.

You know what happened next, Kawika, perhaps better than I do. It was some months after you left—Uncle William told me it was seven months—that Edward drowned, and while his death was declared an accident, I sometimes wonder whether it was intentional. He had come there to find something, but he hadn't had the strength to find it, and neither had I. I was meant to be his audience, and yet I hadn't been able to, and without me, he had given up as well.

It was Uncle William who found his body on the beach on one of his visits, and it was that same day—after the police questioned me—that he had taken me back to Honolulu and to the hospital. When I awoke, I was in a room, and I had looked up and had seen the doctor, who was repeating my name and shining a bright white light into my eyes.

The doctor sat next to me and asked me questions: Did I know my name? Did I know where I was? Did I know who the president was? Could I count backward in increments of six from one hundred? I answered, and he wrote my answers down. And then, before he left, he said, "Wika, you won't remember me, but I know you." When I didn't reply, he said, "My name's Harry Yoshimoto—we went to school together. Do you remember?" But it wasn't until that night, when I was alone in my bed, that I did remember him: Harry, the boy who had eaten rice sandwiches, and to whom no one had spoken; Harry, the boy I was grateful not to be.

And this was the end. I never returned to our house in the valley. After a while, they brought me here. Eventually, I lost the eyesight that remained; I lost the interest, and then the ability, to do anything. I lay in bed and dreamed, and time blurred and softened, and it was as if I had never made any mistakes. Even you—now, I was told, at another school, on the Big Island—even you, who never visited, even you I could conjure nearby, and sometimes, if I was very lucky, I could even fool myself into pretending I had never known you to begin with. You would be the first Kawika Bingham not to graduate from the school—who knew what else you would be the first Kawika Bingham to do? The first to live abroad, maybe? The first to be someone else? The first to go somewhere very far away, somewhere so far that it made even Hawai'i look close to someplace else?

I was thinking about this when I woke today, to the sounds of someone crying—crying, but trying not to, her breath coming out in hiccups. "I'm sorry, Mrs. Bingham," I heard someone say. "But it's as if he's willing himself to go—we can only keep him alive if he wants to be." And then the sound again, that desperate, sad sound, and the voice once more: "I'm sorry, Mrs. Bingham. I'm sorry."

"I shall have to write my grandson—my son's son," I heard her say. "I can't tell him this over the phone. Will I have time?"

"Yes," the man's voice said, "but tell him to hurry."

I wished I could have told them not to worry, that I was getting better, that I was almost well. It was all I could do to keep from smiling, from shouting with joy, from calling your name. But I want it to be a surprise—I want to see your face when you walk through the door at last, when you see me jump out of bed to greet you. How surprised you'll be! How surprised they'll all be. Will they applaud for me, I wonder? Will they be proud? Or will they be embarrassed, or even angry—embarrassed that they'd underestimated me; angry that I had made them into fools?

But I hope they don't feel that way, for there's no time to be angry. You are coming, and I can feel my heart pounding faster and faster, the blood thrumming in my ears. For now, though, I'm going to keep practicing. I'm so strong now, Kawika—I'm almost ready. This time, I'm ready to make you proud. This time, I won't let you down. All along, I had thought that Lipo-wao-nahele would be the only story I could tell about my life, but now I know: I'm being given another chance, a chance to make another story, a chance to tell you something new. And so tonight, when it's dark, and this place is quiet around me, I'll get up, I'll retrace my route to the garden, and this time, I'll let myself out through the back door and into the world. I can already see the treetops, black against the dark sky; I can already smell the ginger all around me. They were wrong: It's not too late, it's not too late, it's not too late after all. And then I'll start walking—not to my mother's house, not to Lipo-wao-nahele, but to somewhere else, the same place I hope you've gone, and I won't stop, I won't need to rest, not until I make it there, all the way to you, all the way to paradise.

ZONE EIGHT

———

Normally, I catch the 18:00 shuttle home, which drops me off at Eighth Street and Fifth Avenue somewhere between 18:30 and 18:40, depending on disruptions, but today I knew there was going to be a Ceremony, so I asked Dr. Morgan if I could leave early. I was worried the shuttle would get stalled near Forty-second Street, and then who knew how long I would be delayed, and then I might be too late to buy dinner for my husband. I was explaining all this to Dr. Morgan when he interrupted me. "I don't need to hear all the details," he said. "Of course you have permission. Take the 17:00 shuttle." So I thanked him and did.

The passengers on the 17:00 shuttle were different from the passengers on the 18:00 shuttle. The 18:00 passengers were other lab techs and scientists, even some of the principal investigators, but the only person I recognized on the 17:00 was one of the janitors. I even remembered to wave at her, just a second after she passed me, turning in my seat to do so, but I don't think she saw me, because she didn't wave back.

As I had predicted, the shuttle slowed and then stopped just south of Forty-second Street. The windows on the shuttle are covered with bars, but you can still see everything outside pretty well. I had chosen a seat on the right so I could see the Old Library, and sure enough, there were the chairs, six of them, arranged in a row facing the avenue, although no one was sitting in them and the ropes hadn't yet been uncoiled. The Ceremony wouldn't begin for another two hours, but there were already radio technicians strolling about in their long black coats, and two men were filling the wire trash cans with rocks from the back of a big truck. It was the truck that had stopped the flow of traffic, but there was nothing we could do except wait until the men had filled all the trash cans and then had climbed back into the truck and moved out of the way, and from there, the rest of the trip was very fast, even with the checkpoints.

By the time we reached my stop, it was 17:50, and while the drive itself had taken longer than normal, I was still home much earlier than usual. But I did what I always do after work, which was to go straight to the grocery store. Today was a meat day, and because it was the third Thursday, I was also entitled to our monthly ration of soap and toilet paper. I had saved one of my vegetable coupons from the previous week, so, along with the potatoes and carrots, I was also able to get a can of peas. That day, along with the usual assortment of flavored protein bricks and soy patties and artificial meats, there was also real horse meat, dog meat, deer meat, and nutria meat. The nutria meat was the cheapest, but my husband says it's too greasy, so I bought a half kilo of horse meat, and some cornmeal because we were almost out. We needed milk, but if I saved up another week of rations, I'd be able to buy a pint of pudding, so I instead bought the powdered version, which my husband and I both dislike but would have to do.

Then I walked the four blocks home to our building, and it was only when I was safe inside our apartment, browning the horse meat in vegetable oil, that I remembered that it was my husband's free night, and that he wouldn't be home for dinner. But by that time, it was too late to stop cooking, so I finished frying the meat and then ate it with some of the peas. Above me, I could hear the echoey sound of screams, and knew that the neighbors were listening to the Ceremony on their radios, but I didn't want to listen myself, and after cleaning the dishes, I sat on the couch and waited for my husband for a while, even though I knew he wouldn't be home anytime soon, before finally going to bed.

———

The next day, everything was as usual, and I caught the 18:00 shuttle home. As we passed the Old Library, I looked for remaining signs of the Ceremony, but there weren't any: The rocks were gone and the chairs were gone and the banners were gone and the steps were clean and gray and empty, just like normal.

At home, I was warming a little oil to fry some more of the meat when I heard my husband's knock on the door—tap-tap-thunk-thunk-thunk—and then his call—"Cobra"—to which I called back "Mongoose," and then the clunk of the bolts unlocking: one, two, three, four. And then the door opened and there he was, my husband, my Mongoose.

"Dinner's almost done," I said.

"I'll be right out," he said, and went back to our room to change.

I put a piece of meat on his plate and a piece on mine, as well as peas and half of a potato for each of us, which I'd baked that morning, after my husband left for work, and had reheated. And then I sat and waited for him to come sit down at the table across from me.

For a while, we ate in silence. "Horse?" my husband asked.

"Yes," I said.

"Hmm," my husband said.

Even though I've been married to my husband for more than five years, I still find it difficult to know what to say to him. It was like this when we first met, too, and as we left the marriage broker's office, Grandfather had put his arm around me and brought me close to his body, but he didn't speak until we were back home. "What did you think?" he had asked.

"I don't know," I said. I wasn't supposed to say *I don't know*—I had been told I said it too much—but in this case, I really didn't know. "I didn't know what to say to him when I wasn't answering his questions," I said.

"That's normal," said Grandfather. "But it'll get easier, over time." He was quiet. "You just have to remember the lessons we've had," he said, "the things we discussed. Do you remember?"

"Yes, of course," I said. "'How was your day?' 'Did you hear the story on the radio?' 'Did anything interesting happen today?'" We had made a list together, Grandfather and I, of all the questions one person might ask another. Sometimes, even now, I reviewed that list before I went to bed, thinking that the next day I might ask one of them to my husband, or to one of my colleagues. The problem was that some of the questions—What do you want to eat tonight? What books are you reading? Where are you taking your next vacation? The weather's been great/terrible, hasn't it? How are you feeling?—had become either irrelevant or unsafe to ask. When I looked at the list, I remembered having those practice conversations with Grandfather, but I was unable to remember his replies.

Now I said to my husband, "How is the meat?"

"Fine."

"Not too tough?"

"No, no, it's fine." He took another bite. "It's good."

This made me feel better, more relaxed. Grandfather had told me that when I was anxious I could help calm myself by adding numbers in my head, and that's what I had been doing until my husband reassured me. After that, I felt relaxed enough to say something else to him. "How was your free night?" I asked him.

He didn't look up. "Fine," he said. "Nice."

I didn't know what else to say. Then I remembered: "There was a Ceremony last night. I passed it on the ride home."

Now he did look at me. "Did you listen to it?"

"No," I said. "Did you?"

"No," he said.

"Do you know who they were?" I asked, even though we all knew not to ask that question.

I had asked just to make conversation with my husband, but to my surprise, he looked again at me, directly at me, and for a few seconds he said nothing, and I said nothing, too. Then "No," he said. It seemed to me like he wanted to say something else, but he didn't, and we finished eating in silence.

———

Two nights later, we woke to a pounding, and the sound of men's voices. My husband sprung out of his bed, cursing, and I leaned over and switched on the lamp. "Stay here," he told me, but I was already following him to the front door.

"Who's there?" he demanded of the closed door, and I was impressed, as I always was in these instances, by my husband's bravery, by how unafraid he seemed.

"Municipality Three Investigative Unit 546, Officers 5528, 7879, and 4578," replied a voice on the other side of the door. I could hear a dog barking. "Pursuing suspect accused of violating Codes 122, 135, 229, 247, and 333." Codes beginning with a one were crimes against the state. Codes beginning with a two were trafficking crimes. Codes beginning with three were crimes of information, which usually meant the accused had somehow accessed the internet or was in possession of an illegal book. "Permission to search the unit."

They weren't asking for permission, but you had to give it anyway. "Permission granted," my husband said, and unlocked the locks, and three men and a tall, lean, wedge-faced dog entered our unit. The biggest of the men remained in the doorway, pointing his gun at us, and we stood against the far wall facing him, our hands raised and elbows bent at right angles, while the other two men opened our closets and searched our bathroom and bedroom. These events were meant to be quiet, but I could hear the men in the bedroom lifting first one mattress and then the next, and the mattresses falling back onto the bed frames with a thud, and although the man in the doorway was large, I could still see other police units behind him, one entering the apartment to the left and the other running up the stairs.

Then they were done, and the two men and the dog came out of the bedroom and one of the men said "Clear" to the man in the door and "Signature" to us and we both applied our right thumbprints to the screen he held out and spoke our names and identity numbers into the scanner's microphone and then they left and we locked the door behind them.

Searches always made a mess, and all of our clothes and shoes had been yanked out of the closet, and the mattresses were askew in their frames, and the window had been opened when the officers had checked to see if there was anyone dangling from the windowsill or hiding in the trees, as had apparently happened a year ago. My husband made sure the folding iron gate outside the window was secure and locked, and then he closed the window and drew the black curtain across it and helped me straighten first my mattress and then his. I was going to start organizing at least a little of the closet, but he stopped me. "Leave it," he said. "It'll still be there tomorrow." And then he got into his bed and I got into mine, and he turned off the lamp and it was dark again.

Then it was quiet and yet not quite quiet. We could hear the officers moving around in the apartment above us—something heavy fell, and we could hear the light fixture in our ceiling rattle. There were muffled shouts, and the sound of a dog barking. And then we heard the units' footsteps descending again, and then the all-clear, announced over the speakers mounted atop one of the police vans: "Zone Eight; Thirteen Washington Square North; eight units plus basement; all units checked." After that, we heard the whup-whup-whup of the police helicopter's blades, and then it really was quiet again, so quiet we could hear the sound of someone crying, a woman, from either above or next to us. But then that too stopped, and there was a period of real silence, and I lay and watched my husband's back as the strobe light moved across it and up the wall and disappeared again out the window. The curtains were supposed to block the strobe, but they didn't entirely, though after a while you forgot it was happening.

Suddenly I was scared, and I scooted down the bed until my head was below the pillows and pulled the blanket over myself, the way I had as a child. I had still been living with Grandfather when I experienced my first search, and that night I had been so frightened afterward that I had started moaning, moaning and rocking, and Grandfather had had to hold me so I didn't hurt myself. "It'll be fine, it'll be fine," he repeated, again and again, and the next morning, when I woke, I was still scared, but less so, and he had told me that it was normal to be scared, and that I would get used to the searches with time, and that I was a good person and a brave person and that I shouldn't forget that.

But—like talking to my husband—it hadn't ever gotten easier, though in the years since the first search, I had learned how to make myself feel better afterward, had learned how, if I covered myself so that the air I breathed in was the same air I breathed out, so that, soon, the entire space I made for myself was filled with my hot, familiar breath, I would eventually be able to convince myself that I was someplace else, in a plastic pod tumbling through space.

That night, though, I couldn't make the plastic pod feel real. I realized then I wanted something to hold, something warm and dense and full of its own breath, but I couldn't think of what that might be. I tried to think of what Grandfather might say if he were here, but I couldn't imagine what that might be, either. So instead I did my math sums in my head, whispering into the sheets, and eventually I was able to calm myself and fall asleep.

———

The morning after the search, I woke later than usual, but I still wasn't going to be late: I typically get up in time to see my husband off to work, but today I missed him.

My husband's shuttle leaves earlier than mine, because he works in a higher-security location than I do, and every employee has to be scanned and examined before entering the site. Every day before he goes, he makes us both breakfast, and today, he had left mine in the oven: a stone bowl of oatmeal, with what I knew were the last of the almonds, toasted in a pan and crushed on top. As I ate my breakfast, I looked out the window in our main room through the metal grate. To the right you could see the remains of what had been a wooden deck attached to a unit in the building next to ours. I had liked looking at that deck, watching its pots of herbs and tomatoes grow taller and thicker and greener, and after it became illegal to grow food privately, the people in the unit had decorated the patio with fake plants made of plastic and paper they'd somehow painted green, and it had reminded me of Grandfather, how, even after things got bad, he had found paper to cut into shapes for us—flowers, snowflakes, animals he had seen when he was a child—and had stuck them to our window with a blob of porridge. The people in the building next door had eventually covered their plants with a piece of blue tarp they'd gotten somewhere, and as I ate breakfast, I would stand at the window and look at the tarp and imagine the fake plants and feel calm.

But then there had been a raid, and the people next door were found guilty of harboring an enemy, and the deck had been destroyed the same night they had been taken away. That had been the last search, five months ago. I never did know who they were.

My husband had begun putting things back in the closet before he left, but I was only able to do a little more cleaning before it was time for me to catch the 08:30 shuttle for work. Our shuttle stop was on Sixth Avenue and Ninth Street, just three blocks away. There were eight shuttles leaving every morning from Zone Eight, one every half hour from 06:00. The shuttles made four stops in Zone Eight and three in Zone Nine before stopping in Zone Ten, where my husband works, Zone Fifteen, where I work, and Zone Sixteen. Then, every evening beginning at 16:00 and until 20:00, it went in reverse, from Zone Sixteen to Zone Fifteen to Zone Ten, and then back to Zones Nine and Eight before cutting east to Zone Seventeen.

When I began taking the shuttle, I had liked to look at the other passengers and guess what they did and where they would disembark: The tall man, thin and long-legged like my husband, I imagined was an ichthyologist and worked in the Pond in Zone Ten; the mean-looking woman with small, dark, seedlike eyes was an epidemiologist who worked in Zone Fifteen. I knew they were all scientists or techs, but beyond that, I would never know anything more.

There was never anything new to see on the ride to work, but I always took a window seat anyway, because I liked to look outside. When I was young, we had had a cat, and the cat had liked car rides—he would stand between my legs and put his front paws on the bottom of the window and look outside, and I would look outside with him, and Grandfather, who sometimes sat in the front seat with the driver when I wanted extra room, would look back at us and laugh. "My two little cats," he would say, "watching the world go by. What do you see, little cats?" And I would tell him—a car, a person, a tree—and Grandfather would ask me, "Where do you think the car is going? What do you think that person had for breakfast this morning? What do you think those flowers on the tree would taste like, if you could eat them?," because he was always helping me make up stories, which I knew from my teachers was something I didn't do very well. Sometimes, on my ride to work, I would tell Grandfather in my head the things I saw: a brown brick building with a fourth-floor window over which two strips of black tape had been stuck in an X, and in the cleft of which a small boy's small face had briefly appeared, like a wink; a black police wagon, one of its back doors partially opened, from which I could see a long white foot emerge; a group of twenty children in their dark-blue uniforms, each holding on to a knot tied into a long piece of gray rope, queuing at the checkpoint at Twenty-third Street so they could cross into Zone Nine, where the elite schools were. And then I would think of Grandfather, and I would wish I had more to tell him, but the truth was that very little changed in Zone Eight, which was one of the reasons we were so lucky to live there. In other zones there was more to see, but we never saw those things in Zone Eight, which was another reason why we were lucky.

One day about a year ago, I was riding the shuttle to work when I did see something I had never seen before in Zone Eight. We were moving up Sixth Avenue, as usual, and crossing Fourteenth Street, when a man suddenly ran into the intersection. I had been sitting in the middle of the shuttle, on the left, and so I hadn't seen where the man had come from, but I could see that he didn't have a shirt on, and that he was wearing the gauzy white pants that people in the containment centers wore before they were sent to the relocation centers. The man was clearly saying something, but the windows on the shuttle, along with being bulletproof, were also soundproof, so I couldn't hear him, but I could still see he was shouting: His arms were stretched out in front of him, and I could see the muscles in his neck, so stiff and hard that for a minute he looked like he was carved out of stone. On his chest were about a dozen places where he had tried to hide signs of the illness, which people often did, burning the lesions with a match and leaving behind dull black scars that resembled leeches. I never understood why they did this, because even though everyone knew what the lesions meant, everyone knew what the scars meant as well, so it was really just exchanging one mark for another. This man was young, in his twenties probably, and white, and even though he was gaunt and his hair had almost disappeared, as happened in the second stage of the disease, I could tell he had once been nice-looking, and now he was standing in the street in his bare feet and yelling and yelling. And then two attendants came running toward him in their silver biohazard suits with the reflective screens over their faces, so that, when you looked into one, all you could see was your own face staring back at you, and one of them leapt at the man to try to tackle him to the ground.

But the man was surprisingly quick, and he darted out of the attendant's way and ran instead toward our shuttle, and everyone on board, who had been silent and watching, gasped, as a single great intake of breath, and the driver, who had had to stop the shuttle so he didn't hit the attendants, honked his horn, as if that might scare the man away. And then the man jumped up toward my window, and for just a moment, I saw his eye, the iris so large and glittering blue that I was very frightened, and I could finally hear what he was yelling, even through the window: Help me. And then there was a bang, and the man's head kicked backward, and he fell out of my sight, and I could see the attendants running toward him; one of them had his weapon still held aloft.

After that, the shuttle started moving again, quite fast, as if driving faster could erase what had happened, and everyone became silent again, and I felt as if everyone were looking at me, as if they thought it was my fault, as if I had asked the man to try to communicate with me. People rarely spoke on the shuttle, but I heard a man announce, in a low voice, "He shouldn't still have been on the island," and although no one responded, you could feel that people agreed with him, and even I could sense that they were frightened, and that they were frightened because they were confused. But although people were often frightened about things they couldn't understand, this time I agreed with them—someone that sick should have been sent away by now.

That day at work had been slow, which was unfortunate, because my mind kept returning to what had happened. But what I thought about most was not the man himself, or his bright eye, but about how, when he fell, he had made almost no noise at all, he was so light and soft. A few months after that, it was announced that the containment centers in Zones Eight and Nine were being relocated, and although there were stories about what that meant, we of course never knew for sure.

Since that day, there had been no further strange incidents in Zone Eight, and on this morning, I looked out the window and everything was the same, so predictable that it felt, as it sometimes did, less as if we were moving through it and more as if the city were a series of sets and performers moving past us on a track. Here came the buildings where people lived, and then the chain of children holding one another's hands, and then Zone Nine, the two large hospitals now empty, and here the clinic, and here, just before the Farm, the row of ministries.

This was the sign that you were crossing into Zone Ten, the most important zone. No one lived in Zone Ten. Aside from some of the ministries, the district was dominated by the Farm, which had once been an enormous park that had bisected the island. It had been so big, this park, that it had accounted for a significant percent of the island's acreage. I didn't remember it as a park, but Grandfather had, and he used to tell me stories of how it had been crisscrossed with paths, both cement and dirt, and how people would run through it, and bicycle and walk, and have picnics there. There had been a zoo, where people would pay just to go look at strange, useless animals, who were expected to do nothing but sit and eat the food they were provided, and a lake, on which people would row small boats, and in the spring, people would gather to look at colored birds that had flown up from below the equator, and to find mushrooms and look at flowers. At various points there had been sculptures made of iron in whimsical forms that were meant to entertain children. A long time ago, it had even snowed, and people would come to the park and strap long, thin planks to their feet and shuffle across the low icy hills, which Grandfather said were slick and could make you fall, but not in a bad way—in a way that made people want to do it again and again. I know it's now difficult to understand what this park had been meant for, but Grandfather said it hadn't been *for* anything: It was simply for people to spend time in and enjoy. Even the lake was meant only for enjoyment—you went to float paper boats on it, or walk around it, or just sit and look at it.

The shuttle stopped at the main entrance of the Farm, and people got off and began queuing for the entrance. Only the two thousand or so people who were certified to work at the Farm could get in, and even before you joined the queue, you had to have a retinal scan to prove you had the right to enter, and there were always guards waiting with weapons in case someone tried to dash inside, which people occasionally did. You heard rumors about the Farm: that they were breeding new kinds of animals there—cows with two sets of udders, to produce double the amount of milk; brainless, legless chickens that could be packed, fat and square, into cages and would be fed by tubes; sheep that had been engineered to eat only waste, so that you wouldn't have to use land and resources to grow grass. But none of these rumors had ever been confirmed, and if there were in fact new animals being made, we never saw them.

There are many other projects being worked on in the Farm as well. There are the greenhouses, where all sorts of new plants are being grown, both to eat and as possible medicines, and the Forest, where new kinds of trees are being raised, and the Lab, where scientists are working on creating new kinds of biofuels, and the Pond, where my husband works. The Pond is split into two parts: the animal-cultivating half and the plant-cultivating half. Ichthyologists and geneticists work in the first part, botanists and chemists work in the second. My husband works in the second, though he isn't a scientist because he hadn't been able to finish his graduate degree. He's an aquatic gardener, which means that he plants the specimens that the botanists have approved or engineered—different algae, mostly—and then oversees the specimens' growth and harvesting.

Some of those plants will be developed as medicines, and some will be made into food, and the plants that can be used as neither will be turned into compost.

But though I say this, the truth is that I don't actually know what my husband does. I *think* this is what he does—the planting and tending and harvesting—but I don't know for certain, just as he doesn't know for certain what I do.

This morning, as always, I looked out the shuttle window very hard, but, as always, there was nothing to see. The entire Farm is surrounded by a twelve-foot-high stone wall, and atop the wall, spaced a foot apart, are sensors, so that even if you were able to scale it, your presence would be detected almost immediately, and then you would be captured. Most of the Farm is beneath an enormous biodome, but there are a few feet near the southern wall that aren't protected, and just beyond that wall are two rows of acacia trees that stretch along the entire border, from Farm Avenue West to Fifth Avenue. There were trees all over the city, of course, but you almost never saw them with leaves, which people picked—to boil for tea or broth—as soon as they appeared. Picking leaves was against the law, naturally, but everyone did it anyway. But no one dared to touch the leaves inside or around the Farm, and whenever the shuttle rounded the corner and turned east onto Farm Avenue South, you would see them, clouds of bright green, and although I saw them five days a week, I was always surprised when I did.

After stopping at the Farm, the shuttle continued toward Madison Avenue, and then turned north, and then turned right again at Sixty-eighth Street, and then south on York Avenue, where it stopped in front of Rockefeller University, which is on Sixty-fifth Street. This is where I got off, as well as the other people who work either at Rockefeller or at the Sloan Kettering Research Facility, which is a block west. Everyone going into RU split into two lines: the scientists stood in one, the lab techs and support staff in another. We had to have our fingerprints checked and our bags searched and our bodies scanned before we entered the campus, and then again before we entered our buildings. Last week, my supervisor announced that, because of an incident, they were going to be initiating retinal scans as well. Everyone had been upset about this, because there's no canopy to stand under when it rains, not like at the Farm, and although the campus itself is beneath a biodome, the security area is not, which means we could be waiting for thirty minutes in the heat. My supervisor told us that they were going to set up cooling units in case the wait was excessive, but so far they haven't arrived. But they did start staggering our arrival and departure times, so we wouldn't all be waiting at once.

"What was the incident?" asked one of the techs from another lab, a man I didn't know, but the supervisor didn't answer, and no one had expected him to.

I work in the Larsson Center, which was constructed in the 2030s and is a building but also has a bridge that connects the main campus with a much smaller campus extension on a man-made island in the East River. There are nine labs in Larsson, and they all specialize in various kinds of influenza. One lab studies the descendants of the 2046 flu, which has proven to be evolutionarily aggressive; another studies descendants of the 2056 flu, which, according to Dr. Morgan, wasn't actually a flu at all. My lab, which is run by Dr. Wesley, specializes in predictive influenza, which means we try to anticipate the next unknown flu, which might be altogether different from the other two. Ours is one of the biggest labs in the institution: Aside from Dr. Wesley, who's the principal investigator, or lab chief, there are also twenty-four postdoctoral students—like Dr. Morgan—which means they have their Ph.D.s and are trying to discover something important so they can someday get their own lab; nine graduate students, who are called the Ph.D.s; and ten technical and support staff, of which I am one.

I work with the mice. At any given time, we have at least four hundred, which is significantly more than either of the other two labs have. I sometimes overhear my counterparts in those other labs discussing how their chiefs complain about how much money Dr. Wesley has, money he spends on "fishing expeditions," which is a term Grandfather taught me and means they think that he doesn't have any real evidence or information, that he's just looking for something he can't even identify. I repeated this once to Dr. Morgan, who frowned and said that it was inappropriate for them to be talking that way, and anyway, they were just lab techs. Then he asked me their names, but I pretended they had been temporary help and I hadn't known, and he looked at me for a long time and made me promise I would tell him if I ever heard such discussions again, and I said I would, but I haven't.

I am responsible for the mouse embryos. What happens is that the mice—already one week pregnant—are delivered in crates from the supply company. I get a list from the scientists telling me how old they need the embryos to be: usually ten days but sometimes a little older. Then I exterminate the mice and harvest their fetuses, which I prepare either in tubes or in dishes, depending, and then I shelve them in the refrigerator by age. My job is to make sure there's always mice when the scientists need them.

This all takes a lot of time, especially if you're careful, but there are still moments when I find myself with nothing to do. Then I ask for permission to use one of my two twenty-minute breaks. Sometimes I spend it taking a walk. All of the buildings at RU are connected by underground tunnels, so you never have to go outside. During the '56 epidemic, they built a series of storage rooms and safe rooms, but I've never seen them. Everyone says that beneath these tunnels are two more stories of rooms: operating rooms and laboratories and cold-storage units. But Grandfather always told me not to trust what I couldn't prove. "Nothing is true to a scientist until he proves it so," he used to say. And even though I am not a scientist, I remind myself of this whenever I walk through the tunnels and suddenly get scared, when I become certain that the air has grown colder and that I can hear, as if from very far away, the scrabbly sounds of mice far beneath me, and of groans and whispers. The first time it happened, I couldn't move, and when I did, I woke up in a corner of the corridor, near one of the staircase doorways, and I was yelling for Grandfather. I don't remember this, but later, Dr. Morgan told me that they'd found me and I'd urinated on myself, and I had had to sit in the reception room with a tech from another lab whom I didn't know until my husband came to pick me up.

That was shortly after we had been married, shortly after Grandfather had died, and when I woke, it was night and I was confused until I realized that I was in my bed, in our apartment. And then I looked over and saw someone sitting on the other bed and staring at me: my husband.

"Are you all right?" he'd asked.

I was feeling strange, sleepy, and I couldn't quite form the words I needed. He hadn't turned any of the lights on, but then the spotlight swept past the windows, and I could see his face.

I tried to say something, but my mouth was too dry, and my husband handed me a cup, and I drank and drank, and when the water was gone, too soon, he took the cup from me and left the room, and I could hear him remove the lid from the stone water-container in the kitchen, and the wooden dipper knocking against the inside, and the slish of liquid as he refilled the cup.

"I don't remember what happened," I said, after I'd drunk some more.

"You fainted," he said. "At work. They called me and I came to get you and brought you home."

"Oh," I said. Then I remembered, but only somewhat, as if it were a story that Grandfather had told me long ago. "I'm sorry," I said.

"Don't worry," my husband said. "I'm glad you're better."

He stood, then, and came toward me, and for a second, I thought he was going to touch me, maybe even kiss me, and I didn't know how I felt about that, but he only looked down into my face, and put his palm briefly on my forehead: His hand was cool and dry, and I suddenly wanted to grab his fingers, but I didn't, because we don't touch each other like that.

And then he left the room, closing the door behind him. I lay awake for a long time, listening for his footfall, or the sound of the main-room lamp turning on. But I heard nothing. He spent the night in the main room, in the dark, not doing anything, not going anywhere, but not in the same room as I was.

That night I thought of Grandfather. I thought about him often, but that night I thought about him especially hard: I repeated to myself all the nice things he had said to me that I could remember, and I thought of how, when I had done something good, he would grab me and squeeze me, and although I hadn't liked it, I had liked it, too. I thought of how he called me his little cat, and how, when I was scared, I would go to him and he would take me back to my bed and sit there next to me, holding my hand, until I fell asleep again. I tried not to think of the last time I saw him, when he was being led away, and he turned back and I saw his eyes scanning the crowd, looking for me, and how I had tried to scream out to him but hadn't been able to, I was so frightened, and how I had just stood there, my husband, whom I had just married, beside me, watching Grandfather's eyes track back and forth, back and forth, until, finally, as he was being led up the stairs to the stage, he had called out, "I love you, little cat," and I still wasn't able to say anything.

"Do you hear me, little cat?" he shouted, and he was still looking for me, but he wasn't looking in the right direction, he was shouting to the mass of people, and they were jeering at him, and the man on the stage was stepping forward with the black cloth in his hands. "I love you, little cat, never forget that. No matter what."

I lay in bed and rocked myself and talked to Grandfather. "I won't forget," I said aloud. "I won't forget." But although I hadn't forgotten, I *had* forgotten what being loved felt like: Once, I had understood it, and now I no longer did.

———

A few weeks after the raid, I was listening to the morning broadcast and learned that the air-conditioning system at RU had malfunctioned and everyone was being told not to come to work that day.

There were four daily morning bulletins—one at 05:00, one at 06:00, one at 07:00, and one at 08:00—and you had to listen to one of them, because they might have information that you needed. Sometimes, for example, the shuttle would be rerouted because of an incident, and the man or woman would tell you which areas were affected and where you should wait instead. Sometimes there was an announcement about the air quality, and you knew you should wear your mask, or about the sun index, and then you would wear your shroud, or the heat index, so you knew to wear your cooling suit. Sometimes there was news about a Ceremony or a trial, and you'd know to adjust your schedule accordingly. If you worked for one of the big state projects or institutions, like my husband and I did, there would also be information about any closures or strange circumstances affecting them. Last year, for example, there had been another hurricane, and while RU had been closed completely, my husband and other technical staff had still had to go to the Farm to feed and clean up after the animals and double-check the measurements of the water salinity in the classified tanks and do all the things the computers couldn't. A special shuttle, one that wound through all the zones, instead of just certain ones, came and picked my husband up and then dropped him off again, right in front of our building, just as the skies turned black.

When I began working at RU, six years ago, there were never air-conditioning malfunctions. But in the past year, there had been four. The buildings were never completely without power, of course: There were five large generators that were programmed to compensate for any loss of electricity almost immediately. But after the last blackout, in May, we were told not to come in if there was another, because the generators were running at full capacity just to keep the refrigerators at the proper temperature, and our collective body heat would tax the system further.

Even though I didn't have to go to work that day, I did everything I normally did. I had my oatmeal, I brushed my teeth, I cleaned myself with some hygiene wipes, I made my bed. Then I was done with everything I could do: I could only go to the grocery store during my allotted hours, and even if I had wanted to do the laundry, I could only do that on our extra-water day, which wasn't until next week. Finally, I got the broom out of the closet and swept the apartment, which I usually do on Wednesdays and Sundays. This didn't take up very much time, as it was Thursday and I had just swept the day before and the floors were still clean. Then I reread the monthly Zone Eight bulletin, which was distributed to every household and listed any upcoming repairs to streets in our area, as well as updates about the new trees that were being planted on Fifth and

Sixth Avenues, and new items that the grocery store would likely be stocking, and when they'd arrive and how many coupons each would cost. The bulletin also always featured a recipe from a Zone Eight resident, which I usually tried to make. This time, the recipe was for broiled raccoon with lovage and grits, which was especially interesting because I disliked cooking with raccoon and was always trying to find ways to improve the flavor. I cut this one out and put it in a kitchen drawer. Every few months or so, I submitted a recipe that I had invented, but mine were never chosen for publication.

After that, I sat on the sofa and listened to the radio. They played music between 08:30 and 17:00, when there would be three evening bulletins, and more music between 18:30 and 23:59. Then the station stopped broadcasting until 04:00, both so it could air encrypted messages for military personnel, which we heard as a long, low buzzing noise, and to encourage everyone to sleep, because the state wanted us to live healthily, which is also why the electricity grids halved their capacity during those same hours. I didn't know the name of the music, but it was nice, and it made me feel calm, and as I listened, I thought of the mouse embryos drifting in their saline pools, with their paws that hadn't yet developed completely and still looked like very tiny human hands. They didn't have tails yet, either, just slight elongations of the spine, and if you hadn't known what they were, you wouldn't be able to tell they were mouse embryos at all. They could be cats, or dogs, or monkeys, or humans. The scientists called them pinkies.

I worried about the embryos, though that was silly; the generators would keep them cold, and anyway, they were dead. What they were was what they would remain—they would never transform into anything else, they would never get bigger, their eyes would never open, and they would never grow white fur. And yet the embryos were why the air-conditioning was broken. This was because there were different groups of people who didn't like RU. Some people thought that the scientists there weren't working hard enough—that if they worked faster, then the sicknesses would be cured and things would become better, and maybe even go back to how they had been, back when Grandfather was my age. Some people thought that the scientists were working on the wrong solutions. Then there were some people who thought the scientists were creating the sicknesses in our labs, because they wanted to eliminate certain kinds of people or because they wanted to help the state maintain control of the country, and those were the most dangerous people of all.

The primary thing the second two groups tried to do was starve the scientists of the pinkies: If they didn't have the pinkies, they couldn't inject them with viruses, and if they couldn't do that, they would have to stop their work, or they would have to change how they did their work. That was what these groups thought. Along with the blackouts, there had been rumors of armored transport trucks of lab animals being attacked by insurgent groups on their way from the buildings where they were bred, out on Long Island. After the '88 incident, every truck driver was armed, and every truck was accompanied by three soldiers. But two years ago, something had happened anyway: A truck was successfully stopped by an insurgent group, and everyone on it was killed, and for the first time in the university's history, the specimens hadn't arrived. It was around then that there was the first attack on the electrical system. Back then, RU had only two generators, and it hadn't been enough, and the Delacroix wing had lost power altogether, and hundreds of specimens had spoiled, and months of work had been destroyed, and after that, the president of the university had gone to the state and appealed for more security, and more generators, and harsher punishments against the insurgents, and all of this was granted.

Of course, no one told me any of these things. I had to figure them out from eavesdropping on the scientists, who gathered in corners of the lab and whispered, and as I delivered the embryos and took others away, I lingered, not long enough to be noticed, and tried to overhear what they said. None of the scientists paid any attention to me as I came and went, even though everyone knew who I was, because of Grandfather. I always knew when the new postdocs or Ph.D.s learned who I was, because I would enter the room and they would stare at me, and then they would thank me when I gave them their new batch of mice, and thank me for taking away the old batch. But eventually they would get used to me, and they would stop thanking me, and they would forget I was even there, and that was fine.

I listened to the music for what felt like a long time, even though when I looked at the clock, I could see it had only been twenty minutes, and it was still just 09:20, which meant I had nothing to do until my grocery hours began at 17:30, which was a long way away. And so it was then that I decided that I would take a walk around the Square.

———

My husband's and my apartment is on the north side of the Square, on the eastern corner of Fifth Avenue. When I was a child, the building had been a house, and only Grandfather and I had lived there, along with a cook and two servants. But during the '83 uprising, the state divided it into eight apartments, two per floor, and let us choose which one we wanted. Then, when I was married, my husband and I remained in our apartment and Grandfather moved out. One unit on each floor faces the Square, and the other unit faces north. Our apartment faces north, which is quieter and therefore better, and is on the third floor. These units overlook what used to be the area where the family who built this house more than two hundred years ago kept its horses, which they kept not to eat but to pull them around the city.

I didn't really want to walk around the Square, first, because it was very hot, even hotter than usual for late October, and second, because walking around the Square could be frightening. But I also couldn't sit much longer in the apartment, with nothing to do and no one to look at, and so, finally, I put on some sunscreen and my hat and a long-sleeved shirt and walked downstairs and outside and across the street, and then I was in the Square.

You could get whatever you needed in the Square. In the northwest corner were the metalworkers, who could make you anything from a lock to a pan, and who would also buy any old metal you had. They would weigh it, and tell you what it was, whether it was cobalt mixed with aluminum or iron mixed with nickel, and give you gold or food or water coupons, whichever you wanted, and then they would smelt it and make it into something else. South of them were the cloth merchants, who weren't just merchants but also tailors and seamstresses, and who would also buy any clothes or fabrics that you didn't need anymore, or could remake old clothes into new clothes. In the northeast corner were the moneylenders, and next to them were the herbalists, and south of them were the carpenters, who could make or repair anything out of wood. There were also rubber repairmen and rope-makers and plastic merchants, who would buy or trade you anything made of plastic, and could also make you something new.

Not all of them were licensed to be in the Square, and every few months or so there'd be a raid, and everyone, even the vendors who had permits, would disappear for a week, and then they'd return. People—not all people, not people like the scientists and ministers, but most other people—depended on the vendors. Up in Zone Fourteen, there were stores you could go to and buy things, I don't know what, but except for the grocery, there were no stores in Zone Eight, and so instead we had the Square. Anyway, the officials didn't really care about the cloth merchants and carpenters and metalworkers: The ones they cared about were the people who moved among the vendors. These people didn't have fixed positions in the Square, like the vendors did—a wooden table, with a tarp stretched above to protect them from the sun or the rain. At most, these other people usually would have only a stool and an umbrella, and they would sit in a different spot every day. Sometimes they didn't even have that, and would just wander through the Square, walking between the stalls. Yet everyone, all the other vendors and regular shoppers, knew who they were and where to find them, though no one ever used their actual names. There were people who could help reset a bone or give you stitches, and who could help you get out of the prefecture, and who could help procure anything you wanted, from illegal books to sugar to even a specific person. There were people who could find you a child, and people who could take one away. There were people who could get someone into a good containment center, and people who could get someone out of one. There were even people who claimed they could cure you of the illnesses, and they were the ones that the authorities looked for the hardest, but it was said that they could disappear at will, and they could never be caught. This was illogical, of course: People can't disappear. And yet there were rumors about them, about how they could elude the authorities again and again.

In the center of the Square was a large, shallow cement pit in the shape of a ring, and in the middle of the pit, on an elevated pedestal, was a fire that was never extinguished, not even in the hottest weather, except during the raids, and surrounding the fire were more vendors. There were twenty to thirty of them, depending on the day, and they sat in the ring, and on the raised lip of the ring they each unrolled a plastic tarp, and on the tarps they displayed different cuts of meat. Sometimes you could tell what kind of animal the meat was from, and sometimes you couldn't. Each vendor had his own sharp knife and a pair of long metal tongs and a set of long metal skewers and a fan made from woven plastic that they would wave over the meat to keep the flies away. The vendors accepted gold or coupons, and they would either cut the meat for you and wrap it in a piece of paper so you could take it home, or they would stab a skewer through it and cook it for you right there in the fire, whichever you wanted. Around the fire were metal trays that collected the fat that dripped from the meat, and if you couldn't afford the meat, you could buy just the fat, and take that home and use it to cook. The strange thing was that all the vendors who worked in the pit were very skinny, and you never saw them eat. People always said that was because they would never dare eat the meat they sold, and every few months there were rumors that the meat was actually human, and had been procured from one of the camps. But that didn't stop people from buying it, from tearing the meat off the skewers with their teeth, sucking the metal clean and bright before handing it back to the vendor.

Even though the Square was right outside our building, I rarely visited it. Maybe my husband did. But I did not. It was too loud, it was too confusing, and the crowds and the smells and the vendors' shouting—*Brii-iing me your metal! Brii-iing me your metal!*—and the sounds of hammers constantly tocking against wood made me nervous. And it was so hot, the fire turning the air watery, that I thought I might faint.

I wasn't the only person the Square made uneasy, which was silly, really, because there were at least twenty Flies that monitored the area, buzzing back and forth from one end to the other, and if anything really bad were to happen, the police would be there in an instant. Still, there was a group of us who regularly walked the sidewalk that encircled its perimeter, looking at the activity through the fence but not stepping into it. Many of these people were old and out of work, though I didn't recognize any of them—they might not even have lived in Zone Eight but came from other zones, which was technically illegal but only rarely enforced. The southern and eastern zones had their own versions of the Square, but Zone Eight's was considered the best, because Zone Eight was a stable and healthy and calm place to live.

After walking around the Square several times, I was desperately hot. On the southern edge of the Square was a row of cooling stations, but there was a long queue for them and it was foolish to pay for one when I could just walk back to the apartment. When Grandfather was my age, there were no cooling stations and no vendors. Back then, the Square had been planted with trees and covered with grass, and the pit in the center had been a fountain, where water erupted in bursts and then fell back into the pit again. Over and over the water exploded and fell, exploded and fell, for no other reason than because people liked it. I know this sounds queer, but it's true: Grandfather showed me a photograph of it once. Back then, people lived with dogs, which they kept as companions, like children, and the dogs had their own special food, and they were all named, like they were people, and their owners would bring them to the Square and they would run around on the grass and their owners would watch them from benches that had been placed there for exactly that reason. That was what Grandfather said. Back then, he would come to the Square and sit on a bench and read a book, or walk through here on the way to Zone Seven, which wasn't called Zone Seven but had an actual name, also like a person. A lot of things were named, back then.

I was thinking about all this as I was walking along the southern side of the Square, when a group of people who had been gathered around one vendor close to the entrance moved away, and I saw that the vendor was standing near an instrument shaped like a giant metal clamp, and in the clamp he was fitting a large block of ice. It had been a long time since I had seen a piece of ice that big, and although it wasn't quite pure—it was a very light brown, and you could see little specks of gnats that had been trapped in it—it looked clean enough, and I was standing there looking at it when the vendor turned and saw me.

"Something cold?" he asked. He was an old man, older than Dr. Wesley, almost as old as Grandfather had been, and he was wearing a long-sleeved sweater, even in the heat, and plastic gloves on his hands.

I wasn't used to having strangers talk to me, and I felt panicked, but then I closed my eyes and breathed in and out, like Grandfather had taught me, and when I opened them, he was still there and still looking at me, though not in a way that made me nervous.

"How much?" I finally managed to say.

"One dairy or two grain," he said.

This was a lot to ask, because we only got twenty-four dairy coupons and forty grain coupons a month, and it was more so because I didn't even know what the man was selling. I know I could have asked him, but I didn't. I don't know why. *You can always ask*, Grandfather used to remind me, and although that wasn't true, not anymore, it *is* true that I could have asked the vendor. No one would have been mad at me; I wouldn't have gotten into any trouble.

"You look like you're hot," the man said, and when I didn't reply, he said, "I promise you it's worth it." He was a nice old man, I decided, and he had a voice a little like Grandfather's.

"Okay," I said, and I reached into my pocket and tore off a dairy coupon and gave it to him, and he tucked it away in his apron pocket. Then he positioned a paper cup into a hole in the machine directly beneath the ice and began to turn the crank very fast, and as he did, shavings of ice fell into the cup. When the ice had reached the top, he tapped the cup rapidly against the clamp, tamping it down, and set it back in its place and began turning the crank again, rotating the cup as he did until there was a mound of ice. Finally, he patted the ice into place and picked up from next to his feet a glass bottle containing a cloudy, pale liquid, which he poured atop the ice for what seemed like a long time, and then he handed it to me.

"Thank you," I said, and he nodded. "Enjoy it," he said. He brought his arm up to rub at his forehead, but when he did, his sweater sleeve drooped, and I saw from the scars on the inside of his forearm that he had survived the illness of '70, which had mostly affected children.

Then I felt very strange, and I turned and walked away as fast as I could, and it wasn't until I reached the west corner, with the queue of people waiting for the cooling stations, and felt the ice dripping down my hand that I remembered the treat. I licked it and found that the ice had been doused with syrup, and the syrup was sweet. Not from sugar—sugar was too rare—but from something that tasted like sugar and was almost as good. The ice was so cold, but by now I was upset, and after a few more licks, I threw the cup into a trash can and started moving as fast as I could toward our house, my tongue numb and burning.

———

I was relieved when I was safely back in our apartment, and I went to the sofa and sat there, taking deep breaths until I felt better. After a few minutes, I did, and I turned on the radio and sat down again and breathed some more.

But after a while, I began to feel bad. I had gotten scared for no reason, and I had spent one of our dairy coupons, and it was still only the middle of the month, which meant we would have to go an extra two days without milk or curds, and not only that but I had spent it on ice that was probably unhygienic, and to make matters worse still, I hadn't even eaten it. *And* I had gone outside, so I was now very sweaty, and it was only 11:07, which meant I would have to wait another nine hours, almost, until I could take my shower.

Suddenly I wished my husband were here. Not because I would tell him what I had done but because he was proof that nothing bad was going to happen to me, that I was safe, that he would always take care of me, just as he had promised.

And then I remembered that it was Thursday, which meant it was my husband's free night, and he wouldn't be coming home until after dinner, maybe even after I was asleep.

Remembering this gave me the funny, jumpy feeling that sometimes came over me, which was different from the nervous feeling I sometimes had and which occasionally even felt exciting, like something was going to happen. But of course nothing was going to happen: I was in our apartment, and we were in Zone Eight, and I would always be protected because Grandfather had made sure of that.

But I was still unable to sit quietly, and I got up and began walking round and round the apartment. Then I started opening doors, which is something I did when I was young, too, and I was looking for something I couldn't describe. "What are you looking for, little cat?" Grandfather used to ask me, but I was never able to respond. When I was small, he had tried to stop me, pulling me onto his lap and holding my wrists, whispering into my ear. "It's okay, little cat," he would say, "it's okay," and I would scream and thrash because I didn't like being held, I liked my freedom, I liked to roam. Then, when I was a little older, he would simply get up from whatever he was doing and start looking with me. I'd open a cupboard beneath the sink, and close it, and he would do the same, very serious, until I had opened and shut all the doors in the house, on every floor, and he had, too. By then I would be very tired, and I still wouldn't have found what I needed, and Grandfather would pick me up and carry me to bed. "We'll find it next time, little cat," he would tell me. "Don't worry. We'll find it."

Now, though, everything was where it was supposed to be: In the kitchen, there were the tins of beans and fish and the jars of pickled cucumbers and radishes and the containers of oats and dried tofu skin and the glass ampoules with artificial honey. In the front closet were our umbrellas and raincoats and our cooling suits and shrouds and masks and our emergency bag stocked with four-liter bottles of water and antibiotics and flashlights and batteries and sunscreen and cooling gels and socks and sneakers and underwear and protein bricks and fruit and nuts; in the hallway closet were our shirts and pants and underwear and extra shoes, and our fourteen-day supply of drinking water, and on the ground there was a box with our birth certificates and our citizenship and residence papers and copies of our security clearances and our most recent health records and a few pictures of Grandfather I had managed to keep; in the bathroom cupboard were our vitamins and backup supply of antibiotics, our extra sun cream and sunburn gel and shampoo and soap and hygiene wipes and toilet paper. In the drawer beneath my bed, there were our gold coins and paper chits. Our grade of state employee got paid enough allowance so we could buy two extra treats a week, like ice milk, or some combination of between three and six extra food coupons. But because neither of us bought anything extra, we had a lot saved, which we could use for something bigger, like new clothes or a new radio. But we didn't need anything else: Along with our uniforms, the state gave us each two new outfits a year, and a new radio every five years, so it was silly to spend our coins and chits on those. We didn't spend them on anything, even on things we wanted, like extra dairy coupons—I don't know why.

I went back to the hallway and pulled out the box, because I wanted to look at the pictures of Grandfather. But as I was removing the envelope with our birth certificates, the papers inside slid out and fell to the floor, and so did another envelope, one I hadn't seen before. It wasn't an old envelope, but it had clearly been used before, and I opened it, and inside were six pieces of paper. Actually, they weren't so much pieces as scraps, and they had been torn from different sheets: some were lined and others were obviously ripped from books, and none of them were dated or addressed to anyone or signed, and all of them had very little written on them, just a few words each, in black ink, and in a hurried, jagged hand. "I miss you," one read. Another read, "22:00, the usual spot." "20:00," read the third. The fourth and fifth said the same thing: "Am thinking of you." And then there was the sixth, which contained only one word: "Someday."

For a while, I sat there, looking at the pieces of paper, and wondering where they came from. But I knew they must have been my husband's, because they weren't mine, and no one else ever entered the apartment. Someone had written these notes to my husband, and he had kept them. I knew I wasn't supposed to ever see them, because they had been stored with our papers, and it was my husband, not me, who took care of our paperwork, who renewed our citizenship certificates every year.

It would be many hours still until my husband came home, and yet, after I finished reading the notes, I hurriedly shoved them back into the envelope and then replaced the box without even looking at the pictures I'd wanted to see, as if at any moment I might hear my husband's knock at the door. And then I went to our bedroom and lay down on my bed fully clothed, and stared at the ceiling.

"Grandfather," I said.

But of course there was no one to answer me.

I lay there, trying to think of something other than those torn pieces of paper with their statements and instructions, so complicated because they were so simple: I thought of the pinkies, Grandfather, the things I'd seen at the Square. But the entire time, all I could hear was the word on that final note, which someone had written to my husband, and which he had kept. *Someday*, someone had written, and he had saved it, and the left-hand edge of the paper was softer than the other, as if it had been rubbed between someone's fingers, as if it had been held many times as it was read again and again and again. *Someday, someday, someday.*

PART II

———

Autumn, fifty years earlier

Dear Peter,   September 1, 2043

Thanks so much for the flowers, which arrived yesterday and which you really didn't need to send. But they're gorgeous, and we love them—thank you.

Speaking of flowers, the florist messed up. I told them we wanted white or purple Miltonias, and what did they order? Bunches and bunches of chartreuse Cattleyas. The shop looked like it'd been hosed down in bile. How do things like this happen? As you know, I don't care that much, but Nathaniel is apoplectic, which means I must project sympathetic apoplexy if I'm to keep the household calm: peace over chaos, and all that.

Less than forty-eight hours until the big day. I still can't believe I agreed to this. Nor can I believe you're not going to be here with us. I forgive you, of course, but it won't be the same without you.

Nathaniel and the baby send their love. And so do I.

Dear P,   September 5, 2043

Well, I'm still alive. Barely. But alive.

Where to start? It rained the night before, and it never rains on the north side of the island. All night I had to listen to Nathaniel fretting—What about the mud? What if the rain didn't stop? (We didn't have a contingency plan.) What about the pit we'd dug for the pig? What if it was too damp for the kiawe branches to dry out? Should we ask John and Matthew to move them indoors?—until I finally had to tell him to shut up. When that didn't work, I made him take a pill, and he eventually fell asleep.

Naturally, once he did, I couldn't sleep myself, and at around three in the morning, I went outside to find that the rain had stopped and the moon was huge and silver and that the few shreds of clouds that remained were sailing north out to sea, and that John and Matthew had moved the cords of wood under the porch and had covered the pit with monstera leaves, and that everything smelled sweet and green, and I felt—not for the first time, and not the last—a sense of what can only be called wonder: that I was getting to live in this beautiful place, at least for a little while longer, and that I was having a wedding.

And then, thirteen hours later, Nathaniel and I got married. I'll spare you (most of) the details, but will say that I was, again, unexpectedly moved, and that Nathaniel cried (obviously), and that I cried as well. We had it on John and Matthew's back lawn, and Matthew had for unknown reasons built a chuppah-like structure from bamboo. After we'd said our vows, Nathaniel had the idea of jumping over the fence and running into the ocean, and so that's what we did.

So that was it, and now we're back to business as usual—the house is still in a terrific state of disarray, and the movers are coming in less than two weeks, and I haven't even begun sorting through the lab *and* I have to finish our review of my final paper of my life as a postdoc: The honeymoon (such as it'll be, with the baby in tow) will have to wait. By the way, he was very happy with your presents, and thank you for sending them—they were ingenious, and the perfect way to reassure him that, although it might've been the only day in his short life that wasn't meant to be all about him, it actually really was. (Before the wedding, he had a tantrum, and when Nathaniel and I, fluttering about him like distressed mother crows, begged him to calm down, he shouted: "And stop calling me 'the baby'! I'm almost *four*!" Well, we started laughing, and that made him even angrier.)

Now off to oversee his thank-you email to his uncle P.

Love, Me

P.S. I almost forgot: the Mayfair incident. Horrific. They keep playing clips of it on the news, again and again. Wasn't that café just down the street from that bar we went to a few years ago? I imagine it's keeping you very busy. Not that that's the worst part of it, of course. But still.

Dear Petey,   September 17, 2043

We made it. Phew. Nathaniel in tears, the baby too, and I'm not far behind. More soon. Love, Me

My dear Peter,   October 1, 2043

Sorry I've been such a bad correspondent: Every day for the past three-odd weeks I've thought, I must write Petey a long message of all the things that have happened today, and every night, all I manage to do is our standard How are you, miss you, have you read such-and-such article. So, my apologies.

This email is in two parts: the professional and the personal. One will be slightly more interesting than the other. Guess which.

We are now settled into Florence House East, which is an old high-rise just west of the FDR. It's almost eighty years old, but, like a lot of buildings constructed in the mid-sixties, feels both newer and older, misplaced in time and also not quite of it. Many of the postdocs and almost all of the principal investigators (a.k.a. the lab chiefs) live on campus in one of these units. Apparently, our arrival has caused some controversy because our unit is (1) on a high floor (twentieth); (2) a corner apartment; (3) faces southeast (best light, etc.); and (4) has three real bedrooms (as opposed to most of the other three-bedroom units, which are conversions of large two-bedroom units, which means the third bedroom doesn't have a window). According to one of our neighbors, there was supposed to be a lottery based on family size, tenure, and—as with everything here—volume of publication, but instead the place was assigned to us, which gives everyone yet another reason to preemptively hate me. Oh well. Story of my life.

The apartment is large and well-situated (I'd be bitter, too), with views of the old smallpox hospital on Roosevelt Island that they're now preparing to use as one of the new refugee camps. If the skies are clear, you can see all the way up the spine of the island, and when it's sunny, the river, which is normally brown and creamy, instead glitters and appears almost pretty. Yesterday we saw a tiny police boat chugging north, which, I was later told by the same neighbor, is a frequent occurrence: Apparently, people kill themselves by jumping off the bridge and float downstream, and the police have to drag them out. I like it when it's overcast and the sky turns metallic— yesterday it stormed, and we watched the lightning flicker over the water, and the baby jumped up and down and cheered.

Speaking of the baby, he's already enrolled in the on-campus school (subsidized, though still not cheap), which he can attend through eighth grade, after which—barring disaster, expulsion, or failure—he'll go directly into Hunter for high school (free!). The school is open to children whose parents are either professors or postdocs at RU or are fellows or post-fellows at Memorial Sloan Kettering, which is one block west and one block south, which means the student body showcases a vast range of racial diversity, from Indian to Japanese, and all the ethnicities in between. There's a Soviet-aesthetic cement bridge that connects the apartment building to the campus's old hospital-wing building, and from there you can descend to a series of tunnels that connect the entire campus, which people seem to prefer to, you know, the outdoors, and emerge in the basement of the Child and Family Center. So far, there seems to be little evidence of actual education—as far as I can tell, they spend most of their days going to the zoo and being read to—but Nathaniel claims this is what school is these days, and I defer to him on these subjects. Anyway, the baby seems happy, and I don't know what else I can reasonably expect from a four-year-old.

I only wish I could say the same for Nathaniel, who's pretty clearly miserable but also pretty clearly determined not to say anything, which I love him for but which also makes me a little heartsick. There was never any doubt that I'd take this job, but we both knew that there was unlikely to be a curatorial post in New York for an expert in 19th-century Hawaiian textiles and textile art, and this unfortunately has proven to be true. I think I told you that he'd been in touch with a friend from grad school who's a researcher in the Oceania department at the Met and thought there might be a way to get him in there, even as a part-timer, but it seems it's not to be, and that was really his best lead. We'd been talking, on and off, for the past year about what else he might do and how he might retrain, but neither of us allowed ourselves to engage as deeply in those conversations as we ought to have: on his part, I think, out of fear, and on mine, because I knew that any discussion would inevitably end up spotlighting how selfish this decision was, how our moving here deprives him of a livelihood and a professional identity. So, every morning, I leave early for the lab, and he drops off the baby and spends the rest of his day trying to decorate the apartment, which I know depresses him: the low ceilings, the hollow doors, the mauve bathroom tiles.

The worst thing is how his unhappiness makes me self-conscious about how much I discuss the lab with him, because I don't want to remind him of what I have and he doesn't. For the first time, we're keeping secrets from each other, and they're more difficult because they're so quotidian, the stuff we'd discuss when we were doing the dishes after the baby had been put to bed, or in the morning as Nathaniel made the baby his lunch. And there are so many of them! For example: I made my first hire the day after we arrived, a lab tech who'd been at Harvard and moved here because her husband's a jazz musician and thought there'd be better opportunities in New York;

she's probably in her early forties and worked in mouse immunology for ten years. This week I hired my second postdoc, a very smart guy from Stanford named Wesley. So I have funding for three more postdocs and four to five grad students, who cycle in and out of labs on twelve-week rotations. Grad students normally wait until a lab's up and running until they decide whether they want to join or not—it's a little like rushing a fraternity, I'm sorry to say—but I'm told that, given my "reputation," I may be able to get some earlier. Promise I'm not trying to brag here. Just repeating what I've been told.

My lab (*my* lab!) is in one of the newer buildings, Larsson, part of which literally forms a bridge between Manhattan and a man-made landmass adjacent to Roosevelt Island. From my office, I can look over a slightly different view than the one I see from home: the water, the highway, the cement bridge, and Florence Houses East and West. All the labs here have official titles; mine is the Laboratory of Emerging and Incipient Infections. But when one of the service guys came early this morning to deliver my supply of Erlenmeyers, he asked, "You the Department of New Diseases?" I laughed, and he said, "What? Did I get it wrong?" and I told him he'd gotten it just right.

Sorry this has been so self-absorbed, but you *did* ask for it. Next week we have our final interviews with Immigration, after which we will be, officially, full-time, legal, permanent United States residents (eek!). Tell me what's going on with you, and work, and that weirdo you're seeing, and everything else. In the meantime, sending you love from the Department of New Diseases.

Your loving old pal, C.

Dear Peter,   April 11, 2045

Thanks for your most recent note; it cheered me up a bit, which is a near-impossible feat these days.

I wonder, given how much you already know about these things (not to mention what's happening in your part of the world), whether you've already heard about the cutbacks, which are going to be rolled out before the end of summer and will supposedly affect every federal scientific agency in the country. The official line is that the money is being redirected toward the war, and in a way it is, but everyone in the community knows that the money is actually going to Colorado, where rumor has it they're working on a new bioweapon of some kind. I'm lucky insofar as RU isn't completely dependent on government grants, but it is still *largely* dependent on them, and I'm worried my own work is going to be affected.

Then there's the fact of the war itself, which is really hampering me in other ways. The Chinese are, as you know, responsible for the most advanced and most diverse infectious-disease scholarship in the world, and the new sanctions mean we can't communicate with them anymore—not officially, at least. There's been months of back-channeling between us and NIH and the CDC and Congress ever since the sanctions were proposed last year, but it hasn't seemed to make a difference. Again, my work isn't as affected as some of my colleagues', but all that means is that it someday *will* be as affected, and so far, there's nothing to be done.

It seems particularly insane that they should be doing this given the South Carolina incident—I don't know if word made it to you, but in early February, there was an outbreak of an unknown virus just outside the town of Moncks Corner, in the southeast of the state, which is also home to a landscaped blackwater swamp called Cypress Gardens. A local woman—forties, otherwise healthy—became ill with what seemed to be a flu after being bitten by a mosquito while kayaking through the swamp. Forty-eight hours after diagnosis, she began seizing; seventy-two hours after, she was paralyzed; ninety-six hours after, she was dead. By this time, however, the woman's son and their next-door neighbor, an elderly man, were displaying similar symptoms. It sounds, I know, a little like Eastern equine encephalitis, but it isn't; rather, it's a novel alphavirus. It was only good, weird, rare fortune that the town mayor had been, of all things, a missionary in East Africa during their '37 chikungunya outbreak and suspected that something might be amiss; he contacted the CDC, and they came and locked down the town. The old man died, but the son lived. Of course, the CDC is treating this as a major triumph: Not only did the disease not spread but they also kept it out of the national news. They kept it out of the news altogether, actually—they in fact urged the president to order the mayor not to speak of it to any media, much less his citizens, which he did, and it's rumored that this will lead next to an executive order that prohibits media outlets from publishing non-preapproved information about future outbreaks in the interest of national safety. The thinking is that panic would lead to people trying to flee the area, and early and aggressive containment is the only thing that halts a fast-spreading illness. I see the wisdom of this, of course, but I also think it's a dangerous solution. Information has a way of finding its way around bans, and once the population discovers they've been lied to, or at the very least kept ignorant, it'll only lead to greater mistrust and suspicion, and, therefore, even greater panic. But the government will do anything to delay confronting and correcting the actual problem: Americans' scientific illiteracy.

Anyway, as I was saying—*this* is the context in which our funding is being cut? Can they really be so shortsighted as to think that this'll be the last outbreak? There seems to be this unvoiced but persistent belief that illness is something that happens *over there*, and that, just because we have money and resources and a sophisticated research infrastructure, we'll be able to halt any future disease in its tracks before it "gets too bad." But what is "too bad," and how do they propose we do this with *less* intelligence and *fewer* resources? I'm not one of those scientists—not like Wesley, bless his shriveled heart—who see apocalypse around every corner, who predict with something near glee the imminence of "the big one." But I *do* think it's terrifically foolish to react to an outbreak by scaling back, as if, by starving us of a solution, we might also be starving the problem from even beginning. We've all become so inured to these outbreaks that we forget that there's no such thing as a minor virus; there are just those whose progress is halted early, and those that aren't. We've been lucky so far. But we won't be lucky forever.

So that's work. Home has been less than great as well. Nathaniel has finally found a job, and just in time—things have been very strained between us. Being in an apartment he hates all day has not been conducive to making new friends, and though, as you know, he's been trying to keep himself busy, volunteering at the baby's school and also at a homeless shelter, where he goes every Thursday morning to prepare meals, he feels (as he told me) "useless and meaningless." I mean, he *knew* he wasn't going to find work in his field, but actually accepting that, instead of just *saying* he accepts that, has taken the better part of two years. So now he's teaching art to fourth- and fifth-graders at a small, expensive, low-rated school in Brooklyn, one that attracts parents with dim kids and lots of money. Nathaniel has never actually taught before, and the commute is a hassle, but he seems much happier. He's a last-minute replacement for a woman who was diagnosed with third-stage uterine cancer and quit midterm.

One of the unforeseen consequences of this move—me being at work and satisfied, Nathaniel being at home and resentful—is that he and the baby have constructed a life that feels separate from me and mine. Now, Nathaniel was always the baby's primary parent anyway, but something seems to have shifted in the past year or so, and I find myself being frequently reminded that they have developed a relationship that in certain ways excludes me, that I am in certain ways ignorant of their daily lives. These reminders are manifested in tiny moments: a shared joke between them at the dinner table which I can't understand and which they sometimes don't bother to illuminate (and I, resentful myself, don't inquire about and feel ashamed about later); a guilt-driven purchase of a gift for the baby, an electric-purple tin robot, only to learn upon giving it to him that purple is no longer his favorite color, that his favorite color is red, information delivered in an impatient, disappointed tone that wounds me more than it ought to.

Then there was last night, when I was putting the baby to bed, and he announced, suddenly, "Mama's in heaven."

Heaven? I thought. From where did he learn that? And "mama"? We had never referred to Nathaniel's cousin as the baby's mama—we had always been truthful with him: Nathaniel's distant cousin had carried him, but he was ours alone, by our choice. And when she died, we had been exacting in our language: *Daddy's cousin, the one who helped make you, died last night.* But I suppose he took my silence for confusion of another sort, because he added, in a clarifying way, "She died. So she's in heaven."

For a moment, I was stymied. "Well, yes, she is dead," I said, weakly, thinking that I would ask Nathaniel to investigate where this talk of heaven was coming from (surely not the school?), and then couldn't think of anything else to say that wouldn't necessitate a much, much longer conversation.

He was silent for a moment, and I wondered, as I have many times, what happens in a child's brain, how they are able to hold two or three ideas, completely contradictory or completely different, in their consciousness at once, and how to them these are all not only related but intertwined, and dependent on one another. When do we stop being able to think like that?

Then he said, "Daddy and Mama made me."

"Yes," I said, at last. "Daddy and your mama made you."

He was quiet again. "But now I'm alone," he said, softly, and I felt something in me weaken.

"You're not alone," I said. "You have Daddy, and you have me, and we love you very much."

He thought about this. "Are you going to die?"

"Yes," I told him, "but not for a very long time."

"How long?" he asked.

"Too long," I said. "So long that I can't even count that high."

He finally smiled. "Good night," he said.

"Good night," I told him. I kissed him. "I'll see you in the morning."

I got up to turn off the light (noticing, as I left, the purple robot kicked into a corner, facedown, which made my throat hurt with sorrow, as if the stupid thing had feelings and wasn't just something I'd picked up from the toy store ten minutes before it closed for the night), and was about to march over to our bedroom and interrogate Nathaniel, when I was suddenly overcome with exhaustion.

Here I was, a man with my own lab and my own family and my own covetable apartment, and everything was good, or good enough, and yet I had the sensation at that moment that I was atop a large piece of white plastic tubing, and the tube was rolling down a dirt path, and I was surfing it, almost, my feet constantly moving, trying to stay upright. That was what life felt like. So I went to our room, but I didn't say anything about the conversation with the baby, and instead Nathaniel and I had sex for the first time in a long time, and he went to sleep, and eventually I did as well.

So. That's what's going on with me. I'm sorry this has been so self-pitying, and so self-absorbed. I know how hard you've been working, and I can only imagine the kinds of problems you've been dealing with. I know this won't mean much, but whenever my colleagues are complaining about the bureaucrats, I think of you, and how, as much as I may disagree with some of your brethren's conclusions, I know too there are some of you who are endeavoring to make the best decisions, the right decisions, and I know you're one of those people. If only you could be the right kind of bureaucrat here in America—I'd feel a lot better for all of us if you were.

With love, C.

Dear dear Petey,   November 22, 2045

Well, it happened. I know you've been following the news, and I know you know we were at risk for a big federal cut, but as you also know, I didn't *actually* expect it to happen. Nathaniel says I was being naïve, but was I really? Let's see: Nation barely stable from the flu of '35. At least six mini-outbreaks within North America in the past five years. Given these circumstances, what seems like the dumbest thing to do? Oh, I know, cut funding to one of the premier biological sciences centers in the country! The problem, one of the other lab chiefs told me, is that although *we* all know how closely we came to disaster in '35, the rest of the country does not. And we can't tell them now, because no one would care. (And we couldn't have told them *then*, because they'd all have panicked. It occurs to me, and not for the first time, that an increasingly and dismayingly large part of our jobs is spent debating how and when and if we should reveal findings that took years and millions of dollars to discover.) The point is that if we complain, no one will believe us. In other words, we're getting penalized for our competence.

Not that I'm supposed to say that to anyone outside the university. This is according to both the institute's head of communications, who gathered us in an auditorium to lecture us shortly before the news broke, and this is especially according to Nathaniel, as we sat in traffic last night on our way to dinner. Which is what this message is really about.

I haven't mentioned this for reasons I'll try to articulate later—maybe next week, when we see each other—but Nathaniel has made new friends. Their names are Norris and Aubrey (Aubrey!), and they're a pair of ancient and very rich queens whom Nathaniel met a few months ago when he was asked by an auction house to authenticate a private collection of what were allegedly 18th-century, allegedly Hawaiian kapa bedcovers that had been no doubt stolen from who knows whom. Anyway, Nathaniel examined them, and authenticated both their origin and the date—he thinks they're early 1700s, which would make them precontact and therefore extremely rare.

The point is that the auction house already had an interested buyer, a guy named Aubrey Cooke, who collects precontact Polynesian and Micronesian artifacts. So the house set up a meeting with him and Nathaniel, and the two of them fell in instant love, and now Nathaniel has a freelance consulting gig cataloguing Aubrey Cooke's collection, which is, according to Nathaniel, "diverse and spectacular."

I feel several ways about this. The first is relief. Ever since we moved here, I've been carrying within me a hollowness, an ache, over what I've done to Nathaniel and, even, the baby. They were so happy in Honolulu and, except for the fact of my own ambition, I was, too. But despite my frustrations, we belonged there. We all had work—me being a scientist at a small but respected lab; Nathaniel being a curator at a small but respected museum; the baby being a baby at a small but respected kindergarten—and I made us leave because I wanted to be at Rockefeller. I can't pretend, as I sometimes do, that it was because I wanted to save lives or I thought I'd do more good here: it's because I wanted to be at a prestigious facility, and because I love the hunt. I spend my days dreading a new outbreak, but I yearn for one as well. I want to be here when the next big pandemic happens. I want to be the one to discover it, I want to be the one to solve it, I want to be the one who looks up from his desk and sees the sky outside a dense black and realizes that he doesn't know how long he's been at the lab, that he's been so involved, so immersed, that the fact of a day has ceased to hold any significance. I know all this, and I feel guilty about it, and yet it doesn't stop me from wanting it. And so when Nathaniel came to me after that first meeting at the auction house, so happy—*so* happy—I felt exonerated. I realized how long it had been since I had seen him so excited, and how, always, I had been hoping for this, had been hoping that he would, as I kept telling him he would, find his place, find some meaning in this city and country he quietly hates. And then, when he came back joyful from meeting Aubrey Cooke, I was happy, too. He's made a few friends here, but not many, and most of them are parents of other kids at the baby's school.

That joy, however, soon shaded into something else, and although I'm ashamed to admit it, that something else is of course jealousy. Every Saturday for the past two-odd months, Nathaniel has taken the subway down to Washington Square, where Aubrey has an actual house on the park, and I stay home with the baby (the implicit message is that it's my turn to stay home with him after two years of spending every weekend at the lab while Nathaniel watched him). And when Nathaniel returns in the late afternoon, he's aglow. He picks up the baby, swings him around, and starts making dinner, and as he cooks, he tells me about Aubrey and his husband, Norris. How incredibly deep and rich Aubrey's knowledge of 18th- and 19th-century Oceania is. How gorgeous Aubrey's house is. How Aubrey made his money as a manager of a fund of funds. How Aubrey and Norris met. How and where Aubrey and Norris like to vacation.

How Aubrey and Norris have invited us "out east" to Frog's Pond Way, their "estate" in Water Mill. What Norris said about X book or Y play. What Aubrey thinks about the government. The brilliant idea Aubrey and Norris had about the refugee camps. What we *must* see/do/visit/eat/try, according to Aubrey and Norris.

To all of this, I say, "Wow," or "Wow, babe, that's great." I really try to sound sincere, but frankly, it wouldn't matter if I couldn't, because Nathaniel is barely listening to me. My life outside the lab has always consisted of two fixed poles: him and the baby. But now *his* life is (not in order of importance) me, the baby, and Aubrey and Norris. Every Saturday he springs out of bed, gets dressed for the gym (he's been going more since meeting Aubrey and Norris), works out, comes home to shower and feed the baby, kisses us both, and leaves for his day downtown. I want to be clear that it's not that I think he's in love with them, or that he's fucking them—you know neither of us is weird about that. It's that in his fascination with them, I hear a repudiation of me. Not us, not me *and* the baby, but *me*.

I had always thought that Nathaniel was content with our life. He's never been someone who's been seduced by money or ease or glamour. But after an evening spent listening to detailed descriptions of Aubrey and Norris's beautiful house, and their beautiful things, I lie awake staring at our low ceilings, at our flapping slatted plastic blinds, at the track light with its blackened bulb that I've been promising Nathaniel I'll change for the past six months, and wondering whether my accomplishments, and my position, have really given him what he wants and deserves. He has always been happy for me, and proud of me, but have I helped make a good life for him? Would he not leave me for another?

And so, last night. When the dinner invitation came, as I knew it would, I at first had the baby for an excuse. He's been suffering from minor respiratory issues all fall: The days are hot and then cool and then hot again, and the crocuses, which last year bloomed in October, started shooting in September, followed by the plum trees a month later, so he's been coughing and sneezing for weeks. But then he began to get better, and less physically miserable, plus Nathaniel found a babysitter he likes, and I was out of arguments. So last night we got in a taxi and went downtown to Aubrey and Norris's.

I hadn't been entirely sure who I had imagined Aubrey and Norris to be, other than people I needed to be suspicious of and whom I was already disinclined to like. Oh, and white—I had expected them to be white. But they weren't. The door was opened by a very handsome blond man in his early fifties wearing a suit, and I blurted out, "You must be Aubrey," only to hear Nathaniel's hiss of embarrassed laughter beside me. The man smiled. "If only I could be so lucky!" he said. "No, I'm Adams, the butler. But come in: They're waiting for you upstairs in the drawing room."

Up a gleaming dark staircase we went, me seething at Nathaniel, who had been embarrassed by me, of me, and as Adams led us through a pair of half-open double doors made of that same satiny wood, the two men inside stood.

I knew from Nathaniel that Aubrey was sixty-five and Norris a few years younger, though they both had that kind of ageless, shiny face that the very rich have. Only their gums gave them away: Aubrey's were a dark purple, and Norris's were the gray-pink of a much-used eraser. But the other surprise was their skin: Aubrey was Black, and Norris was Asian . . . but also something else. He looked, in fact, a little like my grandfather, and before I could stop myself, I was once again blurting: "Are you from Hawai'i?" Again, there was Nathaniel's uncomfortable titter, joined this time by Norris's and Aubrey's laughter. "Nathaniel asked me that same question when we met," Norris said, unoffended. "But no, I'm afraid not. I hate to be such a disappointment, but I'm just a dark Asian."

"Not just," Aubrey said.

"Well, part Indian," Norris said. "But that's Asian, Aub." And then to me: "Indian and English on my father's side; my mother was Chinese."

"So was mine," I said, stupidly. "Chinese Hawaiian."

He smiled. "I know," he said. "Nathaniel said."

"Why don't you sit?" Aubrey said.

We did, obediently. Adams returned with drinks, and we talked about the baby for a while, until Adams reappeared and said dinner was ready to be served, at which point we all stood again and went to the dining room, where there was a small round table covered with what I at first, heart-stoppingly, mistook for a piece of kapa cloth. I looked up to see Aubrey smiling at me. "It's a contemporary weaving, inspired by the real thing," he said. "It's beautiful, isn't it?" I swallowed, mumbled something vague.

We sat. Dinner—a "seasonal celebration" of sausage-and-pumpkin soup served from a massive, hollowed-out white squash; veal chops with buttery green beans; a tomato galette—was served. We ate. At some point, Norris and Nathaniel started talking, and I was left with Aubrey, who was sitting next to me. I had to speak. "So," I began, and then I couldn't think of a single thing to say. Or, rather, I could think of too many, but none of them seemed appropriate. I had, for example, been planning to try to pick a fight with Aubrey by subtly suggesting he was a cultural appropriator, but given the fact that he hadn't, as I feared, made me take a tour of his collection, and by the fact of his Blackness (later, Nathaniel and I would have an argument about whether Black people could indeed be cultural appropriators), that idea no longer seemed quite as exciting or provocative as it might have been.

I was quiet for so long that Aubrey finally laughed. "Why don't I start," he said, and although he was kind, I could feel myself flushing regardless. "Nathaniel's told us a little about what you do."

"I tried to, anyway," Nathaniel suddenly interjected from across the table, before turning back to Norris.

"He tried, and I tried to understand," Aubrey said. "But I'd be honored to hear it from the source, as it were."

So I gave him my short speech about infectious diseases and how I spent my days trying to anticipate the newest ones, playing up the statistics that civilians love hearing, because civilians love to panic: How the 1918 flu killed fifty million people, which led to additional, but less disastrous, pandemics in 1957, 1968, 2009, and 2022. How, since the 1970s, we've been living in an era of multiple pandemics, with a new one announcing itself at the rate of every five years. How viruses are never truly eliminated, only controlled. How decades of excessive and reckless prescribing of antibiotics had given rise to a new Family of microbes, one more powerful and durable than any in human history. How habitat destruction and the growth of megacities has led to our living in closer proximity to animals than ever before, and therefore to a flourishing of zoonotic diseases. How we're absolutely due for another catastrophic pandemic, one that this time will have the potential to eliminate up to a quarter of the global population, putting it on par with the Black Death of more than seven hundred years ago, and how everything in the past century, from the outbreak of 2030 through last year's episode in Botswana, has been a series of tests that we've ultimately failed, because true victory would be treating not each outbreak individually but developing a comprehensive global plan, and because of that, we're inevitably doomed.

"But why?" Aubrey asked. "We have immeasurably better public health systems, not to mention medications and sanitation, than in 1918, not to mention than we did just twenty years ago."

"That's true," I said. "But the only thing that ended up making the 1918 flu less disastrous than it should've been was the rate at which the infection was able to spread: The microbe traveled among continents by boat, and back then, it took a week, if you hurried, to get from Europe to America. The mortality rate of the infected on that journey was so great that you had far fewer carriers who were able to spread the illness on the other shore. But that's not true any longer, and hasn't been for more than a century. The only thing that contains a potentially rampant infectious disease now—and they are all potentially rampant, as far as we're concerned—is less technology than the swift segregation and isolation of the affected area, and *that* depends upon the local authorities reporting it to their national or local epidemiological center, which should in turn trigger an immediate lockdown of the site.

"The problem, of course, is that municipalities are reluctant to report new diseases. Besides the immediate overreaction and loss of business, a stigma attaches itself to the place, one that in many cases far outlasts the successful containment of the disease. For example: Would you go to Seoul now?"

"Well—no."

"Exactly. And yet it's been four years since the threat of EARS was for all purposes eradicated. And we were lucky there: The mayor was informed by a local councilperson after the third death, and after the fifth death, he'd contacted the National Health Services, and within twelve hours, they had tented the entirety of Samcheong-dong, and managed to contain fatalities to that neighborhood alone."

"But there were so many."

"Yes. And it was unfortunate. But there would have been far more had they not done what they did."

"But they killed those people!"

"No. They didn't. They just didn't let them leave."

"But the result ended up being the same!"

"No—the result ended up being *far* fewer deaths than there would have been otherwise: nine thousand deaths instead of, potentially, fourteen million. That, and the containment of a particularly pathogenic microbe."

"But what about the argument that isolating the district doomed them rather than helped them? That if they'd opened the area to international assistance, they could've saved them?"

"You're talking about the globalist argument, and in many cases, that's correct," I said. "Nationalism means that there's less exchange of information between scientists, and that's extremely dangerous. But that wasn't the case here. Korea isn't a hostile government; they didn't try to conceal anything; they freely and honestly shared what they were learning with the international scientific community, not to mention other governments: They behaved perfectly, exactly how a country should. What looked like a unilateral choice, to isolate the neighborhood, was in reality a selfless one—they prevented a potential pandemic by sacrificing a relatively small number of their own people. That's exactly the kind of calculation that we need any community to make if we're to contain, *truly* contain, a virus."

Aubrey shook his head. "I suppose I'm too old-fashioned to view nine thousand deaths as a happy outcome. And I also suppose that's why I've never been back: I can't unsee those pictures—those black plastic tents covering the whole neighborhood, and beneath them, you knew people were just waiting to die. You never saw them. But you knew they were."

There wasn't anything I could say to this without sounding callous, so I just drank my wine and said nothing.

There was a silence, and Aubrey shook his head again, quickly, as if collecting himself. "How did you get interested in Hawaiian antiquities?" I asked him, for I felt I must.

He smiled then. "I'd been visiting for decades," he said. "I love it there. I have some family history there, actually: My great-great-grandfather was stationed on Kahoʻolawe, when it was a U.S. military base, just before secession." He caught himself. "I mean Restoration," he said.

"It's okay," I said. "Nathaniel says you have an impressive collection."

He beamed at this, and babbled on for some time about his various holdings, and their provenances, and how he'd built a special climate-controlled room for some of them in the basement, which, were he to do it over, he would have instead put on the fourth floor, as basements are always inclined to be damp, and although he and his air-conditioning guy had managed to maintain a steady temperature of seventy degrees, they couldn't stabilize the humidity, which should be forty percent but was always creeping upward to fifty no matter what they did. Listening to him, I realized two things: first, that I had learned more by osmosis about 18th- and 19th-century Hawaiian weaponry, textiles, and objects than I had known I had; and second, that I would never understand the pleasure of collecting— all that hunting, all that dust, all that trouble, all that maintenance. And for what?

It was his tone—confiding, shyly proud—that made me look up at him again. "But my biggest treasure," he continued, "my biggest treasure never leaves my hand." He held up his right hand, and I saw that on his pinkie he wore a thick band of dark, battered gold. Now he turned the band, and I could see that he had kept facing toward his palm the band's stone, a clouded, opaque, inexpertly cut pearl. I already knew what he would do next, but I watched anyway as he squeezed the small latches at either side of the ring and the pearl hinged open, a little door, to reveal a tiny compartment. He angled it toward me, and I looked: empty. This was exactly the kind of ring my great-great-grandmother had once worn, the kind that hundreds of women had sold off to treasure hunters in their attempts to raise funds for their campaign to restore the sovereign. They had kept a few grains of arsenic in the chamber, a symbolic declaration of their willingness to commit suicide unless their queen was returned to her throne. And now here it was on this man's hand. For a moment, I was unable to speak.

"Nathaniel says you yourselves don't collect," Aubrey was saying.

"We don't need to *collect* Hawaiiana," I said. "We *are* Hawaiiana." I had spoken more fiercely than I knew I would, and for a moment, there was another silence. (Note: This sounded less pretentious in the moment than it does here.)

But the uncomfortable aftermath of my gaffe (though *was* it a gaffe, really?) was interrupted by the arrival of the cook, who was offering me a platter of blackberry cake. "Fresh from the farmers' market," he said, like he had invented the very idea of the farmers' market, and I thanked him and took a slice. And from here the conversation turned to the subjects that every conversation between friendly, like-minded people inevitably did: the weather (bad), the sunken boat of Filipino refugees off the coast of Texas (also bad), the economy (bad as well, but not as bad as it was going to get; like most money people, Aubrey was slightly gleeful about this, as, to be fair, am I when talking about the next big pandemic), the coming war with China (very bad, but would be over "within a year," according to Norris who, it turned out, was a litigator and had a client who "sold military equipment," i.e., an arms dealer), the latest news about the environment and the predicted onslaught of climatic refugees (extremely bad). I wanted to say, "My best friend, Peter, is very high up in the British government, and he says that the war with China is going to last three years minimum and is going to cause a global migration crisis that will number in the millions," but I didn't. I just sat there and said nothing, and Nathaniel didn't look at me, and I didn't look at him.

"This is quite a house," I said at one point, and although it wasn't quite a compliment, or meant as one (I could feel Nathaniel staring at me, hard), Aubrey smiled. "Thank you," he said. Then there was a long story about how he'd bought it from the scion of a supposedly storied banking family I'd never heard of, and how the man had been nearly destitute, full of tales about his family's lost wealth, and how it had been such a thrill to be a Black man, buying a house like this from a white man who'd assumed he'd have it forever. "Look at you," I heard my grandfather saying, "bunch of dark-skinned men trying to be white," although he wouldn't have said "white" but "haole." Anything I did that was foreign to him was haole: reading books, going to grad school, moving to New York. He saw my life as an indictment of his simply because it was different.

By then it was late enough to make a polite escape, and after sitting for what I judged to be about twenty minutes with my coffee, I made a big show of stretching and saying we had to get home to the baby: I had the sense, as one does about the person one's lived with for fifteen years, that Nathaniel was about to suggest we go see Aubrey's collection, and I had zero interest in that. I could also feel Nathaniel about to protest, but then I suppose he figured that he'd put me through enough (or that it was only a matter of time before I said something truly inappropriate), and we all stood and said our goodbyes, and Aubrey said we should get together again so I could see the collection, and I said I'd be honored, even though I have no intention of doing so.

On the way back uptown, I didn't say anything to Nathaniel and he didn't say anything to me. We didn't say anything as we entered the apartment, and as we paid the babysitter, and as we went to check on the baby, and as we got ready for bed. It was only when we were lying next to each other in the dark that Nathaniel finally said, "You might as well say it."

"What?" I said.

"Whatever it is you're going to say," he said.

"I'm not going to say anything," I said. (A lie, obviously. I had spent the last thirty minutes composing a speech, and then thinking about how I could make it sound spontaneous.) He sighed. "I just think it's a little odd," I said. "Nate, you hate people like that!

Haven't you always said that collecting native objects is a form of material colonization? Haven't you always argued for their return to the Hawaiian state, or at the very least to a museum? And now you're, what, best friends with this rich fuck and his weapons-dealing husband, and not only tolerating their trophy-collecting but complicit in it? Not to mention that he thinks the kingdom is a joke."

He was still. "I never got that impression."

"He called it *secession*, Nate. He corrected himself, but come on— we know the type."

He was quiet for a long time. "I promised I wouldn't get defensive," he said at last. Then he was quiet again. "You make it sound like Norris is an arms dealer."

"Well, isn't he?"

"He defends them. It's not the same thing."

"Oh, come on, Natey."

He shrugged: We weren't looking at each other, but I could hear the blanket move up and down on his chest.

"Also," I barreled on, "you never told me they weren't white."

He looked at me. "Yes, I did."

"No, you didn't."

"Of *course* I did. You just weren't listening to me. As usual. Anyway, why does it make a difference?"

"Oh, stop, Natey. You know why it does."

He grunted. There wasn't much he could say to that. Then— another silence. Finally, he said, "I know it seems strange. But—I like them. And I'm lonely. I can talk about home with them."

You can talk about home with me, I should have said. But I didn't. Because I knew, and he knew, that *I* was the one who had taken us from home, and that it was because of me that he had left a job, a life, that he was proud of. And now he had become someone he didn't recognize and didn't like, and he was doing everything he could to not blame me, even up to and including denying what and who he was. I knew this, and he knew this.

So I didn't say anything at all, and by the time I knew what to say, he was already asleep, or pretending to be, and I had once again failed him.

This was going to be our life, I realized. He would grow closer and closer to Aubrey and Norris, and I would have to encourage him, or else his resentment toward me would grow so large and unwieldy that he wouldn't be able to pretend it didn't exist. And then he would leave me, he and the baby, and I would be on my own, without my family.

So, that's all. I know you have much bigger problems to deal with than your old friend's, but I'd appreciate any words of comfort you might have. I can't wait to see you. Tell me everything on your end, or as much as you can. I will be silent as the tomb, or the grave, or however the expression goes.

Love you. C.

My dear Peter,   March 29, 2046

Instead of apologizing at the end of this message for being so self-absorbed, I'm going to *start* with an apology for being so self-absorbed.

But on the other hand, I don't feel I should have to be *so* apologetic, when last week was all about you, and gloriously so. It was such a beautiful wedding, Petey. Thank you so much for having us. I forgot to tell you that when we were leaving the temple, the baby looked up at me and said, solemnly, "Uncle Peter looked very happy." He was right, of course. You were very happy—you are. And I am happy, so happy, for you.

Right now, you and Olivier are somewhere over India, I expect. As you know, Nathaniel and I never took our honeymoon. We were supposed to, and then I had the lab to set up, and we had the baby to settle, and, I don't know, it just never happened. And then it kept not happening. (We had, as you remember, wanted to go to the Maldives. I have a way of picking them, don't I.)

I'm writing you from Washington, D.C., where I'm attending a conference on zoonoses—N and the baby are back home. Actu-

ally, they're not home at all: They're out with Aubrey and Norris at
Frog's Pond Way. It's the first weekend it's warm enough to swim,
and Nathaniel's trying to teach the baby how to surf. He had planned
to teach him in January, when we were back in Honolulu, but there
were so many jellyfish that we ended up avoiding the beaches altogether. But things are a little better between us, thank you for asking.
I've been feeling a bit more connected to both of them—though,
well, that could've just been because you and Olivier needed recep-
tacles to catch the overflow of love you have, and the three of us
were there to do just that. So we'll see. I think part of our renewed
semi-closeness is because, as you observed, I'm trying to get used to
the fact of Aubrey and Norris. They're in our lives for good, or so
it seems. For months, I fought against it. Then I resigned myself.
Now? Well. I suppose they're fine. They've been very generous with
us, that's for sure. Nathaniel's formal consulting work with Aubrey is
long over, but he's down there at least a couple of times a month. And
the baby likes them a lot, Aubrey in particular.

The mood here is grim. First, the rations are much more strin-
gent than they are in New York—last night the hotel lost water completely. It was just for an hour, but still. Second, and more worrisome,
everyone's funding has been cut—again. Our third round is probably
going to be announced next week. My lab is less exposed than some
of the others—we only get thirty percent of our funding from the
government, and the Howard Hughes Institute is making up some of
the shortfall—but I'm anxious. All the Americans are talking about
it between sessions: How much have you lost? Who's stepping in to
make up the difference? What's been imperiled, or is about to be?

But the mood is grim for other, more alarming reasons, far
beyond the Americans' administrative struggles and our collective
discomfort. The keynote was by two scientists from Erasmus University in Rotterdam, who had done early work on the Venice outbreak of '39, which as you know was attributed to a mutation of the
Nipah virus. Their session was unusual for a number of reasons,
primarily because it was more speculative than these speeches usually are. On the other hand, this has been happening with increasing
frequency—when I was a doctoral student, these sorts of presenta-

tions would largely concern lab findings and would usually address a second- or third-generation mutation of one virus or another. But now there are so many new viruses that these conferences have become opportunities to elucidate reports we've read about on our institutions' private networks, to which any scientist at an accredited university can upload their findings or questions. The absence of China from this network (and from the conference at large) is one of the international community's most pressing problems, and one of the revelations from this conference—whispered from one scientist to the next—is that a group of researchers within mainland China have created a secret portal, one to which they're uploading their own findings. My feeling is that if *we* know about it, so must their government, and so the information on it cannot be totally trustworthy—and yet not to take these reports seriously might lead to catastrophe.

Anyway. The Erasmus team claims to have discovered a new virus, which they claim once again originated in bats. It too is being classified as a Henipavirus, which means it's an RNA virus that mutates at a high rate. Back in the 20th century, this Family of viruses was thought to be endemic only in Africa and Asia—though, as the '39 outbreak proves, Nipah in particular has proven to be capable of frequent reemergence, and has inspired a good deal of research in the last seven years about its ability not only to withstand climatic changes but to adapt zoonotically in hosts—dogs, in the Italian case—it had never before infected. Though it had decimated livestock and other domesticated animals, Nipah had never been too serious a threat to us previously because it was a notably non-transmissible disease among humans, one unable to exist for more than a few days without a receptive host. By the time it *did* infect humans, it quickly lost steam: Transmission rates were poor, and the virus proved unable to transmit itself onward. After Venice eradicated its dog population, for example, the disease vanished as well.

But now the Erasmus team is suggesting that this new strain, which they're calling Nipah-45, is capable not just of infecting humans but is both highly contagious and extremely fatal. Like its parent virus, it can be transmitted through contaminated food as well as by the airborne route, and unlike its evolutionary ancestor, it can exist in the host for perhaps months. Their study was of a group of small villages north of Luang Prabang, where the government has been relocating Muslim minorities who come over the border from China. According to them, six months ago the virus was responsible for the decimation of this community: almost seven thousand people dead within eight weeks. The virus switched from bat to water buffalo, and from there into the food supply. The disease manifests itself in humans as a cough, which rapidly leads to full-blown respiratory failure, followed by organ failure—patients were dead within eleven days, on average, after diagnosis. And as shocking as the death rate is, the Erasmus team said that the community's isolation and inability to travel within the country (the group is denied movement by law) prevented widespread dissemination.

Half a year later, these villages remain isolated. Still, the Laotian government, abetted by the American one, is desperately trying to keep the story out of the news, because, along with the spread of disease, the gravest concerns are (1) the all-but-inevitable stigmatization of these poor people, which might easily lead to their mass murder, as we saw in Malaysia in '40; and (2) another refugee crisis. Hong Kong's borders are protected; so are Singapore's, India's, China's, Japan's, Korea's, and Thailand's. So, if there's another large-scale population shift, it seems inevitable that the refugees will attempt to make their way across the Pacific. Those who aren't shot on sight off the Philippine, Australian, New Zealand, Hawaiian, or American coasts will (the thinking goes) try to make their way to Oregon or Washington or Texas, and from those countries, over the border to the U.S.

Not surprisingly, the report kicked off a furor. Not about the team's findings—those were incontrovertible—but about their suggestion, never actually stated but heavily implied, that this virus might be the one we had all been waiting and preparing for. Mingled with the fear was a certain amount of professional jealousy, along with resentment (if *we'd* had governments as dedicated to funding our research as the Netherlands' is, then *we'd* have been the ones to discover this), as well as a certain amount of excitement. Someone on one of the bulletin boards had compared speculative virology to being an understudy in a long-running Broadway show: You wait and wait for the chance to go on, and most of the time it never happens, but you have to stay alert regardless, because what if someday it's your turn?

Now, because I know you'll ask: The answer is that I don't know. *Will* this be the one? I can't say. My sense is it won't be, that if Nipah-45 had the potential to be truly devastating we would have known about it far earlier. *You* would have known about it far earlier. It would have spread far beyond this network of villages. The fact that it hasn't should be comforting. But, then again, a lot of things should be comforting these days.

I'll keep you updated. You keep me updated, too. It seems remarkable that a deputy minister of the interior should increasingly have more information about global outbreaks than I do, but here we are. In the meantime: My love to you, always, and to Olivier as well. Stay out of trouble and keep away from bats.

Love, Me

My dearest Peter,   January 6, 2048

We are all transfixed with horror by what's happening over there. The labs more or less ceased operations today because everyone was watching the news, and when the bridge exploded, there was an audible gasp, not just in our lab but throughout the floor. That astonishing scene, of London Bridge collapsing, of those people and cars falling through the air—in the report we were watching, the newscaster cried out: no words, just a sound, and then was quiet, and all you could hear were the helicopters flying overhead. After, we sat around talking about who might be responsible, and one of my Ph.D.s said we should be thinking instead of who we hoped it *wouldn't* be, because there were so many possible culprits. Do *you* think it was an attack on the refugee camp? Or something else?

But mostly, Peter, I was so, so sorry to hear that Alice is one of the dead. I know how close you two were, and how long you'd worked together, and I can only imagine what you and your colleagues must be feeling right now.

Nathaniel and the baby join me in sending you love. Olivier is taking good care of you, I know, but text or just call me if you want to talk.

I love you. C.

Dearest Peter,   March 14, 2049

I'm writing you from our new apartment. Yes, the rumors are true: We've moved. Not far, and not really up—the new place, a two-bedroom, is on 70th and Second, on the fourth floor of a 1980s-era building—but we had to, for Nathaniel's happiness and therefore my sanity. It was, however, fairly cheap, and this is only because there are reports that the East River will finally flood the dams sometime between next year and never. (Of course, this is also why we should've stayed in RU housing, which is even more likely to be flooded than this new place, and therefore even less expensive, but Nathaniel had had it and there was no arguing with him.)

There's nothing much to say about the new neighborhood, because it's the same as the old neighborhood, more or less. The difference is that, here, the living-room windows look down onto a sanitation center across the street. You don't have those yet, do you? You will. They're abandoned storefronts (this one had been—irony of ironies—an ice-cream parlor) that the government's taken over and fitted out with industrial-grade air-conditioning, as well as, typically, ten to twenty air showers, which is a new technology they're testing out: You take off your clothes and go into the stall, which resembles an upright tubular coffin, and press a button and get blasted by powerful bursts of air. The concept is that you don't need to use water, because the force of the air will blast away the grime. It sort of works, I guess. At any rate, it's better than nothing. Anyway, they're opening these centers all over the city, and the idea is that you pay a monthly fee and can use them whenever you want; the really expensive ones, which are still federally regulated but privately owned, allow you to stay all day in the air-conditioning, and offer unlimited air shower time, and there are also work spaces and beds for people who need to spend the night because their building's had a blackout. The one across the street from us, however, is an emergency center, which means that it's for people whose buildings have lost water or electricity for an extended period (meaning more than ninety-six hours), or whose neighborhoods don't have enough generators to go around. So, all day long, you have these miserable people, hundreds of them—lots of children, lots of old people, none of them white—standing in the sweltering heat for literally hours, waiting to get in. And because of last month's scare, you're not allowed to enter if you have a cough, and even if you don't, you still have to submit to a temperature check, which is ridiculous because by that point you've been standing in the heat for so long that your body temperature will be naturally elevated. The city officials claim that the guards can tell the difference between a fever from infection and simple overheating, but I seriously doubt that. And to *further* complicate matters, you now also have to show your identity papers at the door: only U.S. citizens and permanent residents accepted.

One day last month, Nathaniel and I took over some of baby's old clothes and toys to donate, standing for a few minutes in a separate, much shorter queue, and though I'm not shocked by much anymore in this shit-ass city, I was shocked by that center: There were probably a hundred adults and fifty kids in a space meant for maybe sixty people, and the stench—of vomit, of feces, of unwashed hair and skin—was so overpowering that you could almost see it, coloring the room a dull mustard. But the thing that *really* struck us was how quiet it was: Except for one baby, who cried and cried in a thin, helpless way, there was no sound. Everyone was standing mutely in lines for one of the seven air showers, and when one person exited, the next would silently enter the shower space and draw the curtain closed.

We navigated through the crowds, which parted, wordlessly, to let us pass, and headed toward the back, where there was a plastic table, behind which stood a middle-aged woman. On the table was an enormous metal cauldron, and in front of the table was another queue of people, all holding ceramic mugs. When they reached the front of the line, they held out their cups, and the woman dipped a ladle into the pot and poured them a drink of cold water. Next to her were two more pots, their sides perspiring, and behind those pots was a guard, his arms crossed, a holster with a gun at his hip. We told the woman we'd brought some clothes for donation, and she told us we could put them in one of the bins beneath the windows, which we did. As we were leaving, she thanked us, and asked if we might have any liquid antibiotics at home, or diaper cream, or nutritional drinks. We had to say we didn't, that our son had long outgrown all of these things, and she nodded again, wearily. "Thanks anyway," she said.

We walked back across the street—the heat so thick and stunning it felt as if the air had been knitted from wool—and up to our apartment in silence, and once we were inside, Nathaniel turned to me and we put our arms around each other. It had been a long, long time since we'd held each other like that, and even though I knew he was clinging to me out of sorrow and fear more than affection, I was glad for it.

"Those poor people," he said into my shoulder, and I sighed back. Then he pulled away from me, angry. "This is *New York*," he said. "It's 2049! *Jesus* Christ!" Yes, I wanted to say, it's New York. It's 2049. That's exactly the problem. But I didn't.

We took a long shower then, which was a grotesque thing to do, given what we'd just seen, but there was something delicious about it, and defiant, too—a way of telling ourselves that we could get clean whenever we wanted, that we weren't those people, that we never would be. Or at least that's what I said as we lay there in bed, after. "Tell me that won't happen to us," Nathaniel said. "That will never happen to us," I said. "Promise me," he said. "I promise you," I told him. Though I couldn't promise. But what else was I going to say? Then we lay there for a while, listening to the purr of the air conditioner, and then he left to pick the baby up from swimming lessons.

I know I mentioned this briefly in my last communiqué, but aside from finances, the baby is the other reason we had to stay in this neighborhood, because we're trying to keep things as normal as possible for him. I told you about that incident on the basketball court last year, and two days ago, there was another: They called me at the lab (Nathaniel was upstate with his students on a field trip) and I had to hurry over to the school, where I found the baby sitting in the principal's office. He had clearly been crying but was pretending he hadn't, and I was so overcome—angry and afraid and helpless—that I think I probably just stood there for a moment, stupidly staring at him, before I ordered him out, and he left, feigning a kick toward the doorframe as he left.

What I *should* have done, though, is hugged him and told him everything was going to be okay. Increasingly, all of my human interactions seem to follow this pattern—I see a problem, I get overwhelmed, I don't offer compassion when I should, and the other person storms off.

The principal is this tough middle-aged dyke named Eliza, and I like her—she's the kind of person who's unimpressed by all adults and interested in all kids—but when she set the syringe down on the desk between us, I had to grip the sides of my chair to keep from slapping her: I hated the dramatics of it, the staginess of the presentation.

"I've worked at this school a long time, Dr. Griffith," she began. "My father was a scientist, too. So I don't need to ask where your son got this from. But I have never seen a child try to use a needle as a weapon." To which I thought: Really? *Never?* What's wrong with kids' imagination these days? I didn't say this, though—I just apologized on the baby's behalf, said he had an overactive imagination, and that he'd had a difficult time adjusting to America. All of which was true. I didn't say how shocked I was, though that was true, too.

"But you've been living in America, what"—she glanced at her computer screen—"almost six years now, am I right?"

"It's still hard for him," I said. "A different language, a different environment, different customs—"

"I hate to interrupt you, Dr. Griffith," she interrupted me. "I don't need to tell you that David is very, very bright." She looked at me sternly, as if the baby's brightness were somehow my fault. "But he's had consistent problems with impulse control—this isn't the first time we've had this conversation. And he's had some . . . challenges with socialization. He has difficulty comprehending social cues."

"So did I, when I was his age," I said. "My husband would say that I still do." I smiled, but she didn't smile back.

Then she sighed, and leaned forward in her chair, and something in her face—some veneer of professionalism—dropped. "Dr. Griffith," she said, "I'm worried about David. He'll be ten in November: He understands the consequences of what he's doing. He only has four more years here, and then he's off to high school, and if he doesn't learn lessons now, this year, about how to interact with kids his own age . . ." She stopped. "Did his teacher tell you what happened?"

"No," I admitted.

And out came the story. In brief: There's a clique of boys—not athletic, not good-looking: these are kids of scientists, after all—who're considered "popular" because they make robots. The baby wanted to join them, and had been trying to hang out with them at lunch. But they rebuffed him, multiple times ("Respectfully, I can assure you. We don't tolerate bullying or unkindness here"), and then I guess the baby brought in the syringe and told the head of the pack that he was going to give him a virus if he didn't let him join. The entire class witnessed this exchange.

Hearing this, I felt two competing sensations: First, I was horrified that my child was threatening another child, and not just threatening him but threatening him with what he claimed was a disease. And second, I was heartbroken for him. I have blamed and do blame the baby's loneliness on his homesickness, but the truth is that, even in Hawai'i, he never had many companions. I don't think I've ever told you this, but once, when he was about three, I saw him go over to some other kids on the playground who were playing in the sandbox and ask if he could join them. They said yes, and he got in, but as he did, they all got up and ran over to the jungle gym and left him there alone. They didn't say anything, they didn't call him names, but how could he see their departure as anything other than what it was—a rejection?

But the worst thing is what happened after: He sat there in the sandbox, looking at them, and then he slowly began playing by himself. Every few seconds he'd look over at them, waiting for them to come back, but they never did. After five or so minutes, I couldn't take it any longer, and I went and gathered him up and told him we could have ice cream but he wasn't to tattle on me to Daddy.

That night, though, I didn't tell Nathaniel what had happened in the sandbox. I felt ashamed, somehow, implicated in the baby's sorrow. He had failed, and I had failed to help him. He had been rejected, and I was somehow responsible for that rejection, if only because I had seen it and been unable to repair it. The next day, when we were walking to the playground again, he pulled on my hand and asked if we had to go. I told him no, we didn't, and instead we went to get another illicit ice cream. We never went back to that playground. But now I think we should have. I should have told him that those other children had been unkind, and that it had nothing to do with him, and that he would find other friends, people who really loved and appreciated him, and that anyone who didn't wasn't someone who deserved his attention anyway.

But I didn't. Instead, we never spoke of it. And over the years, the baby has become more and more withdrawn. Not necessarily with Nathaniel, maybe, but—well, maybe even with him. I just don't know if Nathaniel sees it. It's not something I could even accurately describe. But I increasingly feel as if he's not quite present, even when he is, as if he's already detaching himself from us. He has a couple of friends here, quiet, earnest boys, but they rarely come over to our apartment, and he's rarely invited to theirs. Nathaniel always says he's mature for his age, which is one of those things worried parents say about their children when their children baffle them, but I think what he's mature in is his loneliness. A child can be alone. But he shouldn't be lonely. And our child is.

Eliza recommended handwritten letters of apology, a two-week suspension, weekly counseling, an organized sport or two—"to chal-

lenge him, let him burn off some resentment"—and "greater participation from both of his parents," which was meant for me, because
Nathaniel attends every school meeting, game, event, and play. "I
know it's hard for you, Dr. Griffith," she said, and before I could protest or make some defensive remark, she continued, more gently, "I
know it is. I don't mean that sarcastically. We're all proud of the work
you're doing, Charles." Suddenly I could feel my eyes fill, stupidly,
with tears, and mumbled, "I'll bet you say that to all the virologists,"
and left, grabbing the baby by his shoulder and steering him out.

The baby and I walked back to the apartment in silence, but once
we were inside, I turned on him. "What the hell were you thinking, David?" I yelled. "You realize the school could've expelled you,
could've had you arrested? We're guests in this country—don't you
know you could've been taken from us, been sent to a state institution? You know kids have been sent away for less?" I was about to
continue when I saw the baby was crying, and that made me stop,
because the baby rarely cries. "I'm sorry," he was saying, "I'm sorry."

"David," I groaned, and I sat down next to him and pulled him
into my lap like I used to when he was in fact a baby, and rocked him,
also as I had done when he was a baby. For a while we were silent.

"Nobody likes me," he said, quietly, and I said the only thing
I could, which was "Of course they do, David." But really, what I
should have said is "No one liked me when I was your age either,
David. But then I grew up, and people *did* like me, and I found your
daddy, and we had you, and now I'm the luckiest person I know."

We sat there a while longer. It had been a long, long time—
years—since I had held the baby like this. Finally, he spoke. "Don't
tell him," he said.

"Daddy?" I asked. "I have to tell him, David, you know that."

He seemed resigned to this, and stood up to leave. But one thing had
been troubling me. "David," I said, "where did you get the syringe?"

I thought I might get some evasive answer, like "some kids" or "I
dunno" or "I found it." But instead he said, "I ordered it."

"Show me," I said.

And so he walked me over to the study, where I watched him log
on to my computer—bypassing the retinal scan by tapping in my

password with a deftness that proved this wasn't the first time he'd done so—and then onto a site so illegal that I would be forced to file a report explaining what had happened and requesting a new laptop. He stood back from my chair and dropped his hand by his side, and for a while we both stared at the screen, on which a graphic of an atom whirred. Every few revolutions, the atom would halt, and a new category of offerings would appear above it: "Viral Agents." "Needles and Syringes." "Antibodies." "Toxins and Antitoxins."

You can imagine how I felt. But my first questions were practical ones: How had he known about such a site? How had he breached the security walls in order to access it? How had he known what to order? Who had given him the idea?

Was this normal for a child his age?

Was there something wrong with him?

Who *was* my child?

I looked at him. "David," I began, though I had no idea what I was going to say next.

He wouldn't look up, not even when I repeated his name. "David," I said, for a third time, "I'm not angry"—which wasn't exactly true, but what I was, I couldn't identify—"I just need you to look at me," and when he finally did, I saw from his face that he was scared.

And then—I don't know why, I don't—I hit him: with the flat of my palm, across his face. He yelped and fell backward, and I jerked him upright and hit him again, this time on his left cheek, and he burst into tears. It relieved me, somehow, that he was still capable of being frightened, of being frightened by me; it reminded me that he was still a child after all, that there was hope for him, that he wasn't wrong or bad or evil. But I would only be able to articulate this to myself later—in that moment, I was only scared: scared for him, and also scared of him. I was about to hit him again when, suddenly, there was Nathaniel, pulling me off of him and shouting. "What the *fuck* are you doing, Charles?" he yelled at me. "You *fucking* asshole, you *psycho*, what the fuck are you doing?" He pushed me, hard, and I fell and hit my face on the floor, and then he took the baby, now sobbing, into his arms, consoling him. "Shh," he murmured. "It's okay, David, it's okay, sweetheart, I'm here, I'm here, I'm here."

"He's hurting people," I said, quietly, but my nose was bleeding so badly that my speech was garbled. "He was trying to hurt people."

But Nathaniel didn't answer me. He took off his shirt and pressed it against the baby's own bleeding nose, and then they stood and left, Nathaniel's arm around our son's shoulders. He never looked back at me.

All of this is a long way of saying: I'm in our new apartment. I'm writing you from the study, where I have been banished for the foreseeable future. Nathaniel still hasn't said a word to me, and neither has the baby. Yesterday I delivered my laptop to the head of technological security and explained what had happened—he seemed less shocked than I had anticipated, which made me think that there was less of a reason to be worried than I had feared. But as he was issuing me a new computer, he asked, "How old is your son, again?"

"Almost ten," I said.

He shook his head. "And you're foreign nationals, am I correct?"

"Yes," I said.

"Dr. Griffith, I know you know this, but—you have to be careful," he said. "If your son had accessed that site and you hadn't had the security clearances that you do—"

"I know," I said.

"No," he said, looking at me, "you don't. Be careful, Dr. Griffith. There's only so much the institute could do to protect your son if this happens again."

Suddenly I wanted to be far away from him. And not just him but all of it: Rockefeller, my lab, New York, America, even Nathaniel and David. I wanted to be back home, on my grandparents' farm, as miserable as I had been there, long before any of this—all of this—had ever happened. But I can never go home again. My grandparents and I don't speak, the farm is flooded, and this is my life now. I have to make the best of it. And I will.

But sometimes, I worry that I won't.

I love you—Charles

One nice memory I have is of Grandfather brushing my hair. I liked to sit in the corner of his study and watch him work; I could stay there for hours, drawing or playing, and rarely make a sound. Once, one of Grandfather's research assistants had come in and had seen me there, and I could see he was surprised. "I can take her away if she's bothering you," said the research assistant, quietly. Then it was Grandfather who was surprised. "My little one?" he asked. "She's no bother to anyone, especially to me." Hearing that, I had felt proud, like I had done something correct.

I had a cushion I sat on while Grandfather read or typed or wrote, and when I wasn't watching him, I had a set of wooden blocks I would play with. The wooden blocks were all painted white, and I was careful not to stack them too high, so they wouldn't topple over and make a noise.

But sometimes, Grandfather would stop what he was doing and turn around in his chair. "Come here, little one," he'd say, and I'd take my cushion and put it on the floor between his knees, and he'd take the big, flat-backed brush from his drawer and start stroking my hair with it. "What beautiful hair you have," he'd say. "Who gave you this beautiful hair?" But that was what is called a rhetorical question, which means I didn't have to answer it, and I didn't. In fact, I didn't have to say anything at all. I always waited for those times when Grandfather would brush my hair. It felt so good, so relaxing, like I was falling slowly down a long, cool tunnel.

After my illness, though, I no longer had beautiful hair. None of us who survived it do. It was because of the drugs we had to take:

First all our hair fell out, and when it grew back, it was wispy and thin and dust-colored, and you couldn't grow it past your chin or it would break off. Most people cut it very short, so that it just covered the scalp. The same thing had happened to many of the survivors of the sicknesses of '50 and '56, but it was more severe for us survivors of '70. For a while, that was how you could tell who had survived the illness, but then a variation of the same drug was prescribed for the illness of '72, and then it got harder to tell, and having short hair was just more practical: It was less hot, and it took less water and soap to clean. So now lots of people have short hair—you need money if you want to keep it long. That's one way you can tell who lives in Zone Fourteen; all of them have long hair, because everyone knows that Zone Fourteen gets three times as much water as the second-highest water allotment zone, which is our zone, Zone Eight.

The reason I started thinking about this is because last week I was waiting for the shuttle, and a man I had never seen before joined the queue. I was near the end of the queue, and so I was able to get a good look at him. He was dressed in a gray jumpsuit of the kind my husband wore, which meant he was some sort of service technician at the Farm, maybe even at the Pond, and over his jumpsuit he was wearing a lightweight nylon jacket, also gray, and a cap with a wide brim.

I had been feeling strange for the past few weeks. On the one hand, I was happy, because it would soon be December, and December was the best time of year: The weather sometimes grew cool enough for us to even wear an anorak at night, and although there were no rains, the smog that hung over the city lifted, and the store began stocking produce that only grew in the cold season, like apples and pears. In January, the storms would come, and then in February, it would be the Lunar New Year, and everyone who worked on a state site or for a state institution would get four extra grain coupons and either two extra dairy coupons or two extra produce coupons for the month, whichever you wanted. My husband and I would usually split our extra coupons, so between us, we would have eight extra grain coupons and two extra dairy coupons and two extra produce coupons. The year after we got married, which was also the first year my husband worked on the Farm, we had bought a wedge of hard cheese with our surplus coupons: He had wrapped it in paper and put it in the far back corner of our hallway closet, which he said was the coolest place in the apartment, and it had kept for a long time. This year, there was a rumor that we might get an extra day that week for bathing and laundry, which we had gotten two years ago, but not last year, because there had been a drought.

But on the other hand, despite everything I had to look forward to, I also found myself thinking about the notes. Every week on my husband's free night, I emptied out the box again to check if they were still there, which they always were. I would read all of them again, turning the scraps of paper in my hand and holding them up to the lamplight, and then I would replace them all in the envelope and put the box back in the closet.

I was puzzling over the notes the morning I saw the man in the gray jumpsuit join the queue. His presence meant that someone in the zone must have died or been taken, because the only way to get a housing assignment in Zone Eight was to wait for someone to leave it, and no one left Zone Eight willingly. And then something strange happened: The man adjusted his hat, and as he did, a long piece of hair fell loose, brushing against his cheek. He swiftly pushed it back under his hat, and looked around, quickly, to make sure no one had seen, but everyone was staring straight ahead, as was considered polite. Only I had seen him, because I had turned around, though he hadn't seen me looking at him. I had never seen a man with long hair before. The thing that interested me most, however, was how much the man resembled my husband—they had the same color skin, the same color eyes, the same color hair, although my husband's hair is short, like mine.

I have never liked it when new things happened, not even when I was a child, and I have never liked it when things aren't as they're supposed to be. When I was young, Grandfather would read mysteries to me, but they always made me anxious—I liked to know what was happening; I liked things to be the same. I didn't tell Grandfather this, however, because it was clear that *he* liked them, and I wanted to try to enjoy something he enjoyed. But then we weren't allowed to read mysteries anymore, and so I was able to stop pretending.

Now, though, I had two mysteries of my own: The notes were the first. And this man, with his long hair, living in Zone Eight, was the second. It made me feel like something had happened and no one had told me, and that there was a secret that everyone knew but that I couldn't figure out on my own. This happened at work every day, but that was fine, because I wasn't a scientist, and it wasn't my right to know what was happening—I wasn't educated enough, and I wouldn't have understood anyway. But I had always thought that I understood where I lived, and now I was beginning to worry I was wrong about that after all.

———

It was Grandfather who explained free nights to me.

When he told me I was going to be married, I was excited but also scared, and I started walking around in circles, which is something I do only when I'm very happy or very nervous. Other people get uncomfortable when I do this, but all Grandfather said was "I know how you feel, little cat."

Later, he came to tuck me into bed, and to give me the photograph of my husband to keep, which I hadn't thought to ask for earlier. I looked and looked at that picture, touching it as if I could actually feel his face. When I tried to return it to Grandfather, he shook his head. "It's yours," he said.

"When is it going to happen?" I asked him.

"In a year," he said. "So, for the next year, I'll tell you everything you need to know about being married."

This made me feel a lot calmer—Grandfather always knew what to say, even when I didn't know it myself. "We'll start tomorrow," he promised me, and then he kissed me on the forehead before turning off the light and going to the main room, where he slept.

The next day, Grandfather began his lessons. He had a piece of paper on which he had written a long list, and every month, he would pick three topics for us to discuss. We practiced conversation, and being helpful, and he taught me different circumstances in which I might have to ask for help, and how I should phrase it, and what I should do in the case of an emergency. We also discussed how I might come to trust my husband, and what I could do to be a good spouse to him, and what it was like to live with another person, and what I should do if my husband ever did anything that made me feel frightened.

I know it seems strange, but after my initial anxiety, I was less nervous about getting married than I think Grandfather thought I might be. After all, aside from Grandfather, I had never lived with anybody else. Well, that isn't completely true—I had lived with my other grandfather and my father, once, but only when I was a baby; I couldn't even really remember what they looked like. I suppose I assumed that living with my husband would be like living with Grandfather.

It was toward the end of the sixth month of my training that Grandfather told me about free nights: Every week, my husband would leave the apartment and I would have a night all to myself. And then, another night, I could leave the apartment and be by myself, and do whatever I wanted. He watched me closely as he told me this, and then waited as I thought.

"What night of the week will it be?" I asked him.

"Whichever you and your husband decide," he said.

I thought some more. "What am I supposed to do on my night?" I asked him.

"Whatever you want," Grandfather said. "Maybe you'll want to take a walk, for example, or maybe you'll want to go to the Square. Or maybe you'll want to go to the Recreation Center and play a game of ping-pong with someone."

"Maybe I can come visit you," I said. The one thing I had learned that had surprised me the most was that Grandfather wouldn't be living with us; once I was married, I would remain with my husband in our apartment, and Grandfather would move someplace else.

"I always love spending time with you, little cat," said Grandfather, slowly. "But you need to get used to being with your husband; you shouldn't begin your new life thinking about how often you're going to see me." I was quiet then, because I felt that Grandfather was trying to say something else to me without quite saying it, and I didn't know what it was, but knew that it was something I didn't want to hear. "Come on, little cat," said Grandfather at last, and he smiled and patted my hand. "Don't be upset. This is an exciting time—you're getting married, and I'm so proud of you. My little cat, all grown up and about to start a household of her own."

In the years since my husband and I were married, I have had to make use of very few of Grandfather's lessons. I have never had to go to the police because my husband hit me, for example, and I have never had to ask my husband for help with the chores, and I have never had to worry about him withholding his food coupons from me, and I have never had to pound on a neighbor's door because my husband was yelling at me. But I wish I had known that I should have asked Grandfather more questions about free nights, and how they would make me feel.

Shortly after we were married, my husband and I decided that Thursday would be his free night, and Tuesday would be mine. Or, rather, my husband had decided, and I had agreed. "Are you sure you don't mind Tuesday?" he had asked me, and he sounded concerned, as if I could say, "No, I'd rather have Thursday after all," and he would switch with me. But it was fine with me, because it didn't matter which night I had.

At first, I tried to spend my free night elsewhere. Unlike my husband, I would come home from work and have dinner with him first, and then I would change into my casual clothes and leave. It was strange being outside the apartment at night after all those years of Grandfather's reminding me that I was never to leave the house by myself, and absolutely never when it was dark. But that was when things were bad, and it was dangerous, before the second uprising.

For those first few months, I did what Grandfather had suggested and went to the Recreation Center. The center was on Fourteenth Street, just west of Sixth Avenue, and because it was already June, I had to wear my cooling suit so I wouldn't overheat. Up Fifth Avenue I walked, and then west on Twelfth Street, because I liked the old buildings on that block, which looked like versions of the building my husband and I lived in. Some of buildings' windows were lit up, but most of them were dark, and there were only a few other people in the street, also walking toward the center.

The center was open between 06:00 and 22:00, and only to residents of Zone Eight. Everyone was allowed twenty hours of time at the center per month for free, and you had to thumbprint in and then thumbprint out when you left. You could take a class in cooking at the center, or sewing, or tai chi or yoga, or you could join one of the clubs: There were clubs for people who liked to play chess, or badminton, or ping-pong, or checkers. Or you could do volunteer work, making bundles of sanitary supplies for people in the relocation centers. One of the best things about the center was that it was always cool, because it had a big generator, and during the temperate months, people would stay home and conserve their hours so they could spend more of the long summer days in the air-conditioning, rather than in their apartments. You could take an air shower here as well, and sometimes, when I was desperate to be clean and it wasn't yet a water day, I would use some of my time at the center for an air shower. You also came to the center for your annual vaccinations, and your biweekly blood work and mucus smears, and to claim your monthly food coupons and allowances, and, from May through September, the three kilos of ice per month that every resident was entitled to buy at a subsidized rate.

But until my first free nights, I had never been to the center for recreation, even though that was one of the things the center was for. Grandfather had brought me once, after the center had opened, and we had stood and watched a game of ping-pong. The center had two tables, and while people played, other people sat in chairs around the perimeter of the room and watched them, and clapped when someone scored a point. I remember thinking that it looked like fun, and it sounded like fun, too, the bright, sharp tap that the ball made as it struck the table, and I stood there for a long time.

"Do you want to play?" Grandfather whispered to me.

"Oh, no," I said. "I don't know how."

"You can learn," Grandfather said. But I knew I couldn't.

As we left the building that afternoon, Grandfather said, "You can come back, little cat. All you do is sign up for the team, and ask someone to play with you." I was quiet then, because sometimes Grandfather said these things as if they were easy for me to do, and I became frustrated because he didn't understand, he didn't understand that I couldn't do the things he thought I could, and I felt myself growing itchy and angry. But then he noticed, and he stopped walking and turned to me and put his hands on my shoulders. "You *know* how to do this, little cat," he said, quietly. "You remember how we practiced talking to other people? You remember how we practiced having a conversation?"

"Yes," I said.

"I know it's not easy for you," said Grandfather. "I know it's not. But I wouldn't be encouraging you to do this if I didn't believe, with everything I am, that you were capable of it."

And so up I went to the Recreation Center, if only because I wanted to be able to tell Grandfather—who was still alive then—that I had. But once I was there, I wasn't even able to make myself walk inside. Instead, I sat on a ledge outside the building and watched other people walk in, in twos or alone. Then I noticed that there was a window on the other side of the front door, and that if I stood at the correct angle, I could watch the people inside playing ping-pong, and it was nice, because it was almost like I was one of them, but I didn't have to actually speak to anyone.

That was how I spent my first month or so of free nights—standing outside the center and watching ping-pong through the window. Sometimes the matches were particularly exciting, and I would walk home quickly, thinking that I might tell my husband about one game or another I'd seen, even though he never asked what I did on my free nights, and never told me what he did on his free nights, either. Sometimes I imagined that I had made a new friend: the woman with the short curly hair and dimples who slammed the ball across the table, lunging back on her left heel as she did; the man who wore a red tracksuit printed with white clouds. Sometimes I imagined that I joined them at the hydration bar afterward, and I thought about what it would be like to tell my husband that I wanted to use one of the bonus liquid coupons so I could have a drink with my friends, and how he would say that of course I could, and maybe he would come and watch me play a game someday.

But after a few months of this, I stopped going to the center. For one thing, Grandfather was dead, and I didn't feel like trying any longer. For another, it was getting hotter, and I was feeling bad. And so, the next Tuesday, my next free night, I told my husband that I was tired, that I was going to stay indoors instead.

"Are you ill?" he asked me. He was washing the dinner dishes.

"No," I said. "I just don't feel like going out."

"Do you want to go out on Wednesday instead?" he asked.

"No," I said. "This will be my free night. I just won't go out."

"Oh," he said. He placed the last plate on the drying rack. Then he asked, "Which would you like, the main room or the bedroom?"

"I don't understand," I said.

"Well," he said, "I want to give you your privacy. So which would you rather have, the main room or the bedroom?"

"Oh," I said. "The bedroom, I guess." I thought about this. Was this the right answer? "Is that all right?"

"Of course," he said. "It's your night."

And so I went to the bedroom, where I changed into my night-clothes and then lay down on the bed. After a few minutes, there was a soft knock on the door, and when my husband entered, he was carrying the radio. "I thought you might want to listen to some music," he said, and plugged it in and turned it on and left, closing the door behind him.

I lay there listening to the radio for a long while. Finally, I went to use the toilet and brush my teeth and clean my face and body with hygiene wipes, and as I did, I looked into the main room, where my husband was sitting on the sofa, reading. He has a higher clearance than I do and so is allowed to read certain books, those that relate to his field, which he borrows from work and then returns. This one was a book about the care and cultivation of tropical water-grown edible plants, and even though I am not interested in tropical water-grown edible plants, I was suddenly jealous of him. My husband could sit and read for hours, and I looked at him and wished for Grandfather, who would know just what to say to make me feel better. But instead, I got ready for bed and returned to our room, and finally, after what felt like many hours, I heard my husband sigh and turn off the light in the main room, and go to the bathroom himself, and then, finally, come quietly into our room, where he changed clothes as well and got into his bed.

Ever since then, I have spent my free nights indoors. Every once in a while, if I'm feeling very restless, I'll take a walk: maybe around the Square, maybe up to the center. But usually, I go to our bedroom, where my husband has always set up the radio. I change, I turn off the lights, I get into bed, and I wait: for the sound of him sitting down on the sofa, for the sound of him cracking his knuckles as he reads, and, at last, for the sound of him shutting the book and switching off the lamp. Every Thursday for the past six and a half years, I have waited for my husband to come home from his free night, which he begins directly after work. Every Tuesday, I lie in my bed in our bedroom, waiting for my free night to be over, waiting for my husband to come back to me, even if he doesn't say a word.

———

I had gotten the idea about following my husband on his free night from the lab. This happened on a Friday. It was January 1, 2094, and Dr. Wesley, who was interested in Western history and only celebrated the new year according to the traditional calendar, assembled everyone who worked in the lab for a glass of grape juice. Everyone got some, even me. "Six more years until the twenty-second century!" he announced, and we all clapped. The juice was a dark, cloudy purple, and so sweet that it made my throat hurt. But it had been a long time since I had had juice, and I wondered if this was something that was interesting enough to tell my husband, because it was at least different from what usually happened at work, yet also not classified material.

On my way back to my part of the lab, I took a break and went to the bathroom, and as I sat there on the toilet, I heard two people come in and begin washing their hands. They were women, neither of whose voices I recognized, and they were both Ph.D.s, I think, because they sounded young and they were talking about an article in a journal they had both read.

They discussed the article—which was about some kind of new antiviral that was being engineered out of a real virus whose genetics had somehow been altered—and then one of them said, very fast, "So, I thought Percy was cheating on me."

"Really?" asked the other. "Why?"

"Well," said the first, "he'd been acting really strange, you know? Late coming home from work, and *really* forgetful—he even forgot to meet me for my six-month checkup. And he started leaving the house really early in the morning, saying he had a lot of work and had to get it done, and then he started acting strangely around my father when we went over to my parents' for Saturday lunch, kind of avoiding his gaze. So one day, after he left for work, I waited a few minutes, and then I followed him."

"Belle! You didn't!"

"I did! I was rehearsing what I was going to say to him, and what I'd say to my parents, and what I was going to do, when I realized that he was going into the Housing Development Unit. And I called out his name, and he was really surprised. But then he told me that he was trying to get us a better unit in a better part of the zone for when the baby comes, and that he and my father had been working on it together as a surprise."

"Oh, Belle—that's amazing!"

"I know. I felt so guilty for hating him, even if it was just a few weeks."

She laughed, and so did her friend. "Well, Percy can take a little hatred if it's from you," said the second woman.

"Yes," the first woman said, and laughed again. "He knows who's in charge."

They left the bathroom, and then I flushed and washed my hands and left too, and as I did, I passed the two women, still talking, but now in the hallway. They were both very pretty, and they both had shiny dark hair that they wore in neat buns at the base of their skulls, and little gold earrings shaped like planets. They were both wearing lab coats, of course, but beneath their hems I could see they were wearing colorful silk skirts and leather shoes with low heels. One of them, the prettier one, was pregnant; as she spoke to her friend, she rubbed her stomach in a slow circular movement.

I went back to my area, where I had a new batch of pinkies to move into individual petri dishes, which I had to fill with saline. As I worked, I thought of those notes my husband had kept. And then I thought of the woman in the bathroom, who had thought her husband might be seeing someone else, someone who wasn't her. But her husband hadn't been doing anything wrong after all: He had only been trying to find her a bigger unit to live in, because she was pretty and educated and pregnant, and there would be no reason to find someone else, someone better, because there wouldn't be someone better. I could tell by her hair that she must live in Zone Fourteen, and if she was a Ph.D., it meant that her parents probably lived in Zone Fourteen too, and had paid for her to go to school, and then paid more for her to live nearby. I found myself thinking of what they all ate for Saturday lunch—I had once heard that in Zone Fourteen there were stores where you could buy any kind of meat that you wanted, and as much as you wanted. You could have ice cream every day there, or chocolate or juice or even wine. You could buy candy or fruit or milk. You could go home and take a shower every day. I was thinking about this, and growing more and more agitated, when I dropped one of the pinkies. It was so tender that it turned into a smear of jelly upon impact, and I let out a cry: I was so careful. I never dropped pinkies. But now I had.

I thought about this woman who lived in Zone Fourteen throughout the weekend and Monday, and by the time it was Tuesday, and therefore my free night, I was thinking about her still. After dinner, I went straight to the bedroom instead of helping my husband with the dishes as I normally did just to use up some time. There I lay on the bed and rocked myself back and forth and talked to Grandfather, asking him what I should do. I imagined him saying, "It's okay, little cat," and "I love you, little cat," but I couldn't think of what else he might say. If Grandfather had been alive, he would have helped me figure out what I was upset about, and how to fix it. But Grandfather was not alive, and so I had to figure it out on my own.

Then I remembered what the woman in the bathroom had said, that she had followed her husband. Unlike her husband, my husband didn't leave especially early in the morning. He didn't come home late at night. I always knew where he was—except for Thursdays.

And that was when I decided that, on my husband's next free night, I was going to follow him, too.

————

The next day, I realized that my plan had a flaw: My husband never came home from work on his free nights, so either I would have to find a way to follow him from the Farm or I would have to find a way to make him come home first. I decided the second option was more feasible. I thought and thought about what I was going to do, and then I came up with a solution.

That night, at dinner, I said, "I think there's a leak in the showerhead."

He didn't look up from his plate. "I haven't heard anything," he said.

"But there's some water pooled in the bottom of the tub," I said.

He looked up then and pushed his chair back and went to the bathroom, where I had emptied half a cup of water into the tub; there would be just enough left to appear as if the spout had developed a leak. I heard him open the curtain and then turn the taps on and off, quickly.

As he did this, I remained in my seat, sitting straight, as Grandfather had taught me, waiting for him to return. When he did, he was frowning. "When did you notice this?" he asked me.

"Tonight, when I came home," I said. He sighed. "I asked the zone super to tell someone from building management to come inspect it," I said, and he looked at me. "But they can't come until tomorrow at 19:00," I continued, and he looked at the wall and sighed again, a big sigh, one that made his shoulders rise and fall. "I know it's your free night," I said, and I must have sounded scared, because my husband looked at me and gave me a small smile.

"Don't worry," he said. "I'll come home first, to be with you, and I'll go to my free night after."

"Okay," I said. "Thank you." Later, I would realize that he could have just said that he would take his free night on Friday instead. And then, later still, I would realize that the fact that he wanted to take his free night as usual meant that someone—the someone who'd sent those notes—was probably waiting for him on Thursdays, and that now he would have to find a way to tell this person that he would be late. But I knew that he would wait until the inspector came—our water consumption was monitored every month, and if you went over your allotment, you had to pay a penalty and it would be noted on your civilian records.

That Thursday, I told Dr. Morgan that I had a leak in my shower and I needed permission to go home early, which was granted. Then I took the 17:00 shuttle home, so by the time my husband got home—at 18:57, as he always does—I was making dinner. "Am I too late?" he asked.

"No," I said, "he hasn't come."

I had made an extra nutria patty, just in case, and extra yams and spinach as well, but when I asked my husband if he wanted to eat something as we waited, he shook his head. "But you should eat it now, while it's hot," he said. Nutria meat congealed unless you ate it right off the stove.

So I did, sitting down at the table and moving the pieces around with my fork. My husband sat at the table, too, and opened his book. "Are you sure you're not hungry?" I asked, but he shook his head again. "No, thank you," he said.

We sat in silence for a while. He shifted in his seat. We never talked much over dinner, but at least we were doing an activity together when we sat down to eat. But now it was like we were in two glass boxes that had been placed next to each other, and although other people could see us, we couldn't see or hear anything outside our own boxes, and had no idea of how close we were to each other.

He shifted in his seat again. He turned the page and then turned it back, rereading what he'd already looked at. He looked up at the clock, and so did I. It was 19:14. "Damnit," he said. "I wonder where he is?" He looked at me. "There hadn't been a note, had there?"

"No," I said, and he shook his head and looked down at his book again.

Five minutes later, he looked up. "What time was he supposed to be here?" he asked.

"Nineteen hundred," I said, and he shook his head once more.

A few minutes later, he closed his book entirely, and we both sat there, staring at the clock, its blank, round face.

Suddenly my husband stood. "I have to go," he said, "I have to leave." It was 19:33. "I—I have to be somewhere. I'm already late." He looked at me. "Cobra—if he comes, can you handle this on your own?"

I knew that he wanted me to be able to handle things on my own, and all at once I felt scared, as if I really were facing the prospect of talking to the building manager by myself, without my husband here; it was almost like I had forgotten that the manager wasn't coming at all, that this entire incident was something I'd invented in order to do something that should have been much scarier: following my husband on his free night.

"Yes," I said. "I can handle it."

He smiled then, one of his rare smiles. "You're going to be fine," he said. "You've met the manager before; he's a nice man. And I'll come home early tonight, while you're still awake, all right?"

"All right," I agreed.

"Don't be nervous," he said. "You know how to do this." This was something that Grandfather used to say to me as well: *You know how to do this, little cat. There's nothing to be afraid of.* And then he took his anorak from the hook. "Good night," he said, as the door closed.

"Good night," I said to the closed door.

I waited just twenty seconds after my husband closed the door before I too left the apartment. I had already packed a bag with some things

I thought I might need, including one of the small flashlights, and a notebook and pencil, and a thermos of water in case I got thirsty, and my anorak in case I got cold, though that was unlikely.

Outside, it was dark and warm, but not hot, and there were more people than usual, walking around the Square, walking home from the store. I spotted my husband immediately: He was heading briskly north on Fifth Avenue, and I followed him as he turned west on Ninth Street. It was the same route we both took every morning, at separate times, to the shuttle stop, and for a second, I wondered whether he was going to wait for the shuttle again and go back up to work. But he kept walking, crossing Sixth Avenue and through the area we called Little Eight, for its complex of high-rise apartment towers that made it feel like its own zone within Zone Eight, and then across Seventh Avenue as well, and still he kept going.

This was much farther west than I typically had reason to go. Zone Eight extended from New First Street at its southernmost point to Twenty-third Street in its north, and from Broadway on its east over to Eighth Avenue, and the river, on its west. Technically, the zone had extended farther still, but ten years ago, most of the territory beyond Eighth Avenue had been flooded during the last great storm, which meant that the people who had chosen to remain in river flats were residents of Zone Eight as well. But with every year, more and more of them were relocated, because strange things were being discovered in the river, and it was unclear how safe it was to live there.

Zone Eight was Zone Eight, and there was meant to be no hierarchy within it, no area that was considered better than any other. That was what the state told us. But if you *lived* in Zone Eight, you knew that there were in fact places—like where my husband and I lived—that were more desirable than others. There were no grocery stores west of Sixth Avenue, for example, or washing or hygiene centers except for the one that was only accessible to people who lived in Little Eight, which also maintained something called a Pantry, where you could buy nonperishable items, like grains and powdered food, but nothing that would spoil.

As I have said, Zone Eight was one of the safest districts on the island, if not in the entire municipality. Still, there were rumors about what happened near the river, just as there were rumors about what happened in Zone Seventeen, which ran along Zone Eight's north and south axes but then extended all the way to the riverbanks on First Avenue, on the eastern shore. One rumor is that the far western part of Zone Eight was haunted. I had asked Grandfather about that once, and he had taken me over to Eighth Avenue to show me that there were no ghosts there. He said that story had begun before I was born, when there had been a series of underground tunnels that ran beneath the streets, and had extended all the way to the relocation centers, although back then they weren't centers, they were districts, like Zone Eight, where people lived and worked. Then, after the pandemic of '70, they were closed, and people began telling stories that the state had used these tunnels as isolation centers for the affected, who by that point numbered in the hundreds of thousands, and then had sealed them up with cement, and everyone in them had died.

"Is that true?" I asked Grandfather. We were standing near the river by then, and speaking very softly, for it was treasonous to even discuss this. I always felt scared when Grandfather and I talked about illegal topics, but also good, because I knew that he knew that I could keep secrets, and that I would never betray him.

"No," Grandfather said. "Those stories are apocryphal."

"What does that mean?" I asked him.

"It means untrue," he said.

I thought about this. "If it's not true, why do people tell them?" I asked him, and he looked away, into the distance, to the factories on the other side of the river.

"Sometimes, when people tell stories like that, what they're really trying to express is their fear, or their anger. The state did a lot of horrible things back then," he said, slowly, and I felt that same thrill, hearing someone talking about the state that way, and that that someone was my grandfather. "Many horrible things," he repeated, after a pause. "But that was not one of them." He looked at me. "Do you believe me?"

"Yes," I said. "I believe everything you say, Grandfather."

He looked away from me again, and I worried I had said something wrong, but he only put his palm on the back of my head, and said nothing.

What remained true is that the tunnels had been sealed up long ago, and it was said that if you went close to the river late at night, you would hear the sobs and moans of the people who had been left to die within them.

The other thing that people said about the far western edge of Zone Eight is that there were buildings there that *looked* like buildings, but in which nobody lived. It took me a few years of eavesdropping on the Ph.D.s to understand what they meant by that.

Much of Zone Eight had been built centuries ago, in the eighteen hundreds and early nineteen hundreds, but a good deal of it had been demolished shortly before I was born and replaced with towers, which had doubled as clinics. Before then, the population had been very high, and people came to the municipality from all over the world. But then the illness of '50 had stopped almost all immigration, and then the illnesses of '56 and '70 had solved the problem of overcrowding, which meant that, while Zone Eight was still a high-density district, no one lived here illegally now. However, some of the zone's original buildings had been spared, especially those close to Fifth Avenue and the Square, and those close to Eighth Avenue. Here, the buildings resembled the one my husband and I lived in; they were made from red brick and were rarely more than four stories high. Some of them were even smaller, and held only four units.

According to the Ph.D.s whose conversations I listened to, there were a few of these buildings close to the river that had once been divided into apartments, the same as our building, but had over the years become places where nobody lived. Instead, you went to these buildings to—well, I did not know what you went to the buildings to do, only that it was illegal, and that when the Ph.D.s talked about them, they laughed and said things like "You'd know all about that, wouldn't you, Foxley?" This is how I surmised that these were dangerous but also exciting places that the Ph.D.s pretended they knew about but would never actually be bold enough to visit.

By this time, I was very near the river, on a street called Bethune. When I was a child, the state had tried to relabel all the named streets with numbers instead, which mostly affected Zones Seven, Eight, Seventeen, Eighteen, and Twenty-one. But it hadn't worked, and people continued to call them by their twentieth-century names. All this time, my husband hadn't looked behind him once. It had grown very dark, and I was lucky he was wearing a light-gray anorak, one I could easily follow. He had clearly walked this route many times before—at one point, he abruptly stepped down from the sidewalk to the street, and when I looked at the sidewalk, I saw there was an enormous gouge in it, and he had known to avoid it.

Bethune was one of the streets people thought was haunted, even though it wasn't near one of the former entrances to the underground tunnels. But it still had all its trees, even though they were mostly bare, and I suppose that was what made it look so old-fashioned and gloomy. It was also one of the streets that hadn't been flooded, and therefore extended all the way west to Washington Street. Here, my husband walked to the middle of the block and then he stopped, and looked about him.

There was no one on the street but me, and I quickly moved behind one of the trees. I wasn't concerned about him seeing me: I was wearing black clothes and black shoes, and my skin is fairly dark—I knew I wouldn't be visible. In fact, my husband's coloring is similar to mine, and it was by that point so dark that, had I not known to look for his anorak, I might not have seen him myself.

"Hello?" my husband called. "Is anyone there?"

I know this will sound foolish, but in that moment, I wanted to respond. "I'm here," I would have said, and stepped onto the sidewalk. "I just want to know where you go," I would have said. "I want to be with you." But I couldn't think of what he would say in response.

So I said nothing, just hid behind the tree. But I did think of how calm my husband sounded, how calm and how determined.

Then he was moving again, and I came out from behind the tree and followed him, this time with a little more distance between us.

Finally, he reached number 27, one of the final houses on the block, an old-fashioned building somewhat like the one we lived in, and he looked around again before climbing the stone steps and rapping a complicated knock on the door: *tap-ta-taptap-tap-tap-tap-ta-tap-taptap*. Then a little window slid open in the door, and my husband's face was illuminated by a rectangle of light. Someone must have asked him something, because he said something back, something I couldn't hear, and then the window shut and the door opened just wide enough for my husband to slip inside. "You're late tonight," I heard someone, a man, say before the door closed once more.

And then he was gone. I stood outside the building, staring up at it. From the street, it looked unoccupied. There was no light, there was no sound. After I had waited five minutes, I climbed the steps myself and pressed my ear against the door, which was covered in peeling black paint. I listened and listened. But there was nothing. It was as if my husband had disappeared—not into a house but into another world altogether.

––––––

It wasn't until the next day, when I was back in the safety of my room at the lab, that I comprehended fully the riskiness of the previous night's activities. What if my husband had seen me? What if someone had seen me following him and had suspected me of illegal activities?

But then I had to remind myself that my husband had not seen me. No one had seen me. And if by chance I had been recorded by some stray Fly that was patrolling the area, I would simply tell the police that my husband had forgotten his glasses when he went on his nightly walk, and that I was taking them to him.

After I returned to the apartment, I had gone to bed early, so that when my husband came home I was already pretending to be asleep. I had left him a note in the bathroom saying that the leak had been fixed, and I heard him push back the curtain to examine the showerhead. I couldn't tell if he had in fact returned earlier than he normally did, as there was no clock in the bedroom. I *could* tell he thought I was asleep, because he was very quiet, undressing and dressing in the dark.

I had been so distracted that day that it took me some time to realize that there was something amiss in the lab, and it was only when I brought over a fresh batch of pinkies to the Ph.D. cluster that I noticed that the reason they were so quiet was that they all had their headsets on and were all listening to the radio.

There were two radios in the lab. One was a normal radio, of the sort everyone had. The second was a radio that only broadcast to sanctioned research facilities around the world, so that different scientists could announce any pertinent findings and give lectures or updates. Typically, of course, such research would be shared in papers that could only be accessed by accredited scientists on highly secure computers. But when there was something urgent, it would be shared on this special radio, which broadcast a soundscreen of noise atop the person speaking; this meant that, unless you had the proper headphones to cancel the soundscreen, you would hear only a randomized, meaningless sound, like crickets chirping or a fire burning. Each person who was authorized to listen to this radio had a sequence of numbers that they had to enter first, and each sequence was registered to a different user, so the state could monitor who was listening at any time. The headphones, too, were only activated once you entered your code, and before leaving the lab for the night, the scientists locked their sets in a safe that was arranged as a series of small boxes; they each had to enter another code for their box door to open.

Now everyone was silent, frowning and listening to the radio. I placed the tray of petri dishes with the new pinkies on the side of the counter, and one of the Ph.D.s flapped his hand at me, impatiently, signaling me to go away; the rest didn't even look up from their notepads, where they were scribbling words, stopping and pausing to listen, and then writing more.

I went back to the room with my mice and watched the scientists through the window. The entire lab had gone still. Even Dr. Wesley, shut in his office, was listening, frowning at his computer.

After twenty or so minutes, the broadcast must have ended, because everyone yanked off their headsets and then hurried into Dr. Wesley's office—even the Ph.D. students, who were normally excluded from such meetings. As I saw them turn off the radio, I went over to the Ph.D.s' area and began stacking empty petri dishes on a tray, which wasn't my job. But as I did, I heard one of them say to another, "Do you think it's true?" and the other reply, "Fuck, I hope not."

Then they were in the office, and I couldn't hear anything more. But I could see Dr. Wesley speaking, and the rest of them nodding, and everyone looking very grave. I was scared then, because normally when something bad happened—when, say, a new virus got discovered—the scientists weren't scared but excited.

But now they were frightened, and serious, and when I went to the bathroom on my break, I passed the other labs on the floor, and in those, too, the only people I saw were the techs and support staff moving around, cleaning and organizing like we always did, because the scientists were all gathered in their respective principal investigators' offices, talking among themselves with the doors closed.

I waited and waited, but everyone remained in Dr. Wesley's office, talking. The glass was soundproof, so I couldn't hear. Finally, I was going to miss my shuttle and so I had to leave, though I wrote a note to Dr. Morgan explaining that I'd gone, and placed it on his desk, just in case he was looking for me.

———

It took me another week to discover some of what the scientists had overheard on the radio, and the intervening days were very strange ones. Normally, I'm able to find out information fairly quickly. The scientists are discouraged from gossiping and speculating out loud, but they all do so anyway, albeit in whispers. Besides their lack of discretion, however, the other thing that benefits me is that they rarely seem to notice when I'm around. Sometimes, that bothers me. But most of the time, I can use it to my advantage.

I have learned many things simply by listening. I learned, for instance, that Roosevelt Island, in the East River, was one of the city's first relocation centers, during the '50 pandemic, and later a prison camp, and finally, after it had become overrun with rodents carrying an infection, the state had moved the camp to Governor's Island, in the south, which had previously been a refugee camp, and had scattered thousands of poisoned food pellets that killed all the rodents, and no one had been to Roosevelt Island since except the crematorium workers. I learned that Dr. Wesley regularly traveled to the Western Colonies, where the state had built a large research facility where they kept an underground vault storing a sample of every known microbe in the world. I learned that the state was predicting a severe drought in the next five years, and that there was a team of scientists elsewhere in the country who were trying to figure out how to generate rain on a mass scale.

Aside from all of that information, I learned other things from eavesdropping on the Ph.D.s as well. Most of them were married, and sometimes they discussed romance, things that had happened with their husbands or wives. But here, they often spoke in silences, not details. They said things like "You know what happened next," and the other person would say, "I do," and I sometimes felt like saying, "What happened next? What are you talking about?" Because I didn't know, and I wanted to know. Though of course I knew not to ask.

But in the week after the radio conference, they were all unusually quiet, quiet and serious, and everyone was working much harder, though what they were working on exactly I couldn't say, and I wouldn't have understood besides. I just knew that there was something different about their behavior, and that something in the lab had changed.

Before I was to discover what that was, however, I followed my husband again. I don't know why. I suppose I wanted to know if that was what he did every Thursday, because then it would at least be something else I knew about him.

This time, I went directly from the shuttle stop to the far west end of Bethune Street, and waited. There was a house right across from the one my husband had entered, and, like all the houses that had been built back then, it had a main entrance, which was up a flight of stairs, and a second entrance that was hidden beneath the stairs. Grandfather had told me that in the old days, this door would have been protected by an iron gate, but the gate had been removed long ago to be smelted for military use, which meant I was able to stand just beneath the stairway and have a good view of the opposite side of the street.

There hadn't been much traffic that day, so I was in my hiding place by 18:42. I looked at the house, which was as abandoned-looking as it had been the previous Thursday. It was already dark, it being January, but not as dark as it had been the previous week, and I could see that the windows had been covered with black paper or black paint, something that obscured views both in and out. I could also see that, although the building was shabby, it was in decent structural repair: the staircase was old, but except for a missing piece of stone in the second step, the rest of it was solid. The compost compactor was neat and clean, and there were no gnats buzzing overhead.

Three minutes or so later, I saw someone coming west down the street, and I withdrew beneath the staircase, thinking it was my husband. But it wasn't. It was a man around my husband's and my age, but white, and wearing a button-down shirt and a pair of lightweight pants. He was walking briskly, as my husband had, and when he reached the house opposite me, he climbed the steps without checking the number first, and tapped the same rhythmic knock that my husband had the previous week. Then the same thing happened: the window sliding open, the rectangle of light, the question and answer, the door opening just enough to let the man inside.

For a while, I couldn't believe I'd actually seen this all happen. It was as if I'd willed it into existence. I had been so busy watching the event of the man's arrival that I hadn't even registered any useful details about him. "With every person you see, you should try to notice five things," Grandfather would say when I was struggling to describe someone. "What race are they? Are they tall or short?

Are they fat or thin? Do they move quickly or slowly? Do they look down or straight ahead? These will tell you a lot of what you need to know about them."

"How?" I had asked. I hadn't understood.

"Well, for example, let's say they're hurrying down the street or through the halls," Grandfather said. "Are they looking behind them? Maybe they're running from something, or someone. So that would tell you that they're frightened, maybe. Or maybe they're muttering to themselves, and checking their watch, which would let you know that they're late to something. Or let's say they're walking slowly, and looking down at the ground as they do. That might tell you that they're deep in thought, or that they're just daydreaming. But in either case, you'll know that their attention is elsewhere, and that they should—depending on the context—perhaps not be bothered. Or maybe that they *need* to be bothered, that you need to alert them to something that's about to happen."

Recalling this, I tried to describe the man to myself. He was white, as I have said, and he had been moving quickly, but not looking behind him. He had walked like the postdocs walked through the halls of the lab: looking neither left nor right, and never behind themselves. Other than that, the man was difficult to analyze. He was neither fat nor thin, young nor old, tall nor short. He was just a man on Bethune Street who had entered the house my husband had entered last week.

As I was thinking this, I heard another set of footsteps, and when I looked up, I saw that it was my husband. Once again, it was as if I had dreamed him into being, as if he wasn't quite real. He was carrying his nylon bag and was wearing his street clothes, which meant he would have changed out of his jumpsuit at the Farm. This time, he didn't look around him, didn't suspect he was being watched; he climbed the stairs and knocked on the door and was admitted.

And then everything was quiet. I waited for another twenty minutes to see if someone else might come, but no one else did, and finally, I turned and walked home. On the way, I passed a few other people—a woman, walking by herself; two men, who were discussing electrical repairs they'd made in one of the schools; a single man with bristly dark eyebrows—and with each of them, I wondered: Were they too going to the house on Bethune Street? Would they be climbing those stairs, knocking on that door, saying some secret code, and being allowed inside? And once inside, what would they do? What did they talk about? Did they know my husband? Was one of them the person who had been sending him those notes?

How long had he been going there?

Once I was back in our apartment, I opened the box in the closet again and looked at the notes. I thought there might be a new one, but there wasn't. As I was rereading them, I realized they didn't say anything that interesting—they were just everyday words. And yet I somehow knew that they were never the sort of notes that my husband would write me or that I would write him. I knew this, but I couldn't explain how they were different. I looked at them again, and then I put them all away and lay down on my bed. I realized that I wished I had never followed my husband, because what I had learned hadn't helped me at all. In fact, all I had learned was that my husband was probably going to the same place on every one of his free nights, although this was just a theory, and I couldn't prove it unless I followed him every free night from now on. But the detail that had upset me most was how, after my husband had answered the person on the other side of the door, he had laughed. I couldn't remember the last time I had heard my husband laugh, or indeed, if I ever had—he had a nice laugh. He was in another house, laughing, and I was at home, waiting for him to return.

The next day, I went to RU, as always, where the mood in the lab was still strange, the postdocs still quiet and busy, the Ph.D.s still anxious and excited. I moved among them, distributing the new pinkies, removing the old ones, lingering near the Ph.D.s I knew were naturally talkative, the ones who liked to gossip. This time, however, there was only silence.

But I was patient, which Grandfather always said was an underrated virtue, and I knew that the Ph.D.s tended to relax around 15:00 through 15:30, when most of them took a break to drink tea. They weren't supposed to drink tea around their work spaces, of course, but most of them did, especially as the postdocs were in another room then, having their daily meeting. And so I waited until a few minutes past 15:00 before I went to pick up the old embryos from the Ph.D.s' area.

For a few moments, there was just the sipping of tea, which wasn't actually tea but a nutrient-rich powder that was supposed to taste like tea and had been developed at the Farm. It always made me think of Grandfather. I was ten when tea was declared a restricted asset, but Grandfather had a small supply of smoked black tea that he had saved, and for a year, we drank that. He would measure it so carefully—just a few shreds of it per pot—but the leaves were so powerful that that was all you needed. After we finally ran out, he got the powder, but he never drank it himself.

Then, though, one of the Ph.D.s said, "Do you think it's true?"

"They're acting like it," said another.

"Yeah, but how do we know this isn't just another false positive?" asked a third.

"The genomic sequencing is different here," said a fourth, and then the conversation became too technical for me to follow, though I stayed and listened anyway. I couldn't comprehend much, but what I did understand was that there had been another new disease diagnosed, and that it was very bad, potentially disastrous.

New diseases were often being discovered at RU, and not just at RU but in other laboratories around the world as well. Every Monday, Beijing would send the principal investigators at every accredited research organization a status report listing the previous week's tally of fatalities and new diagnoses of the three to five most severe ongoing pandemics, as well as new developments they were tracking. The tallies were broken down by continent, and then by country, and then, if need be, by prefecture and municipality. Then, every Friday, Beijing would compile and send out the latest research findings—whether clinical or epidemiological—reported by the member nations. The goal, Dr. Wesley once said, was not to eradicate the diseases, because that would be impossible—it was to contain them, preferably within the regions where they were discovered. "Epidemics, not pandemics," Dr. Wesley said. "Our goal is to discover them before they disseminate."

I have worked at RU, and in Dr. Wesley's lab, for seven years, and at least once a year there was at least one scare, when there was an emergency radio announcement, as there had been the week before, and everyone in the institute grew frightened and excited, because it seemed that we were at risk of experiencing the next great pandemic, one as bad as the illnesses of '56 and '70, both of which Dr. Wesley said had "remapped the world." But in the end, every one of those threats had been contained. In fact, none of them had even affected the island; there had been no quarantine or isolation mobilization, no special bulletins, no coordination with the National Pharmacology Unit. Still, the pattern was to remain alert in the first thirty days after the discovery of a new disease, because that was the typical incubation period of most of these illnesses—even though, as everyone would admit in private, just because that had *been* the pattern of these diseases, it didn't mean that the successive diseases would behave the same way. That was why what the scientists in our lab did was so important—they tried to predict the next mutation, the next illness that would endanger us all.

I know this will be a surprising thing to hear, but many scientists can be very superstitious. I say this because, over the last few years, the alarm about these reports has grown; I think everyone believes that the upcoming plague—whatever it will be—is overdue. There had been fourteen years between the illness of '56 and the illness of '70; now it was '94, and nothing catastrophic had happened. Of course, as Dr. Morgan likes to say, we are in a much better position now than they were in '70, and this is true. Our labs are more sophisticated; there's more scientific cooperation. It's much more difficult to spread misinformation and therefore breed panic; you can't just get on a plane and unknowingly infect people in other countries; you can't just share your theories of whatever's happening on the internet with whomever you want, whenever you want; there are systems in place to segregate and humanely treat the affected. So things are better.

I was not superstitious. I may not have been a scientist, but I knew that things don't happen according to patterns, even if it may look like it. This is why I was confident that this was just another minor incident, just as the others had been, one that would excite for a few weeks longer and then vanish, another disease not even worthy of a name.

———

Every Lunar New Year, there was a limited amount of pig meat available at the grocery. Typically, the National Nutritional Unit would know by December how much pig they would be able to make available for chosen zones, and by the end of the month, a sign would go up in the grocery telling you how many half-kilo portions would be available, and how many extra protein coupons you would need to spend to purchase them. Then you had to sign up for the lottery, which was drawn on the last Sunday of January, unless the New Year came early, in which case the lottery was drawn ten days before the holiday, so you would have plenty of time to rearrange your plans if you didn't win.

I had only won the pig lottery once, the second year my husband and I were married. After that, there had been bad weather in the prefectures and colonies where the pigs were grown, and there had been very little meat. But 2093 had been a good year, with no significant climatic events, and well-controlled outbreaks, and I was hopeful that this time, we would have pig for the holiday.

I was very excited when my number was among the chosen. It had been a long time since I had had pig, and I loved the taste of it—my husband liked it, too. I had been worried that the New Year celebration would fall on a Thursday, as it had two years ago, and I would be alone, but instead it was on a Monday, and my husband and I spent the day cooking. This is something that—two years ago aside—we had done every lunar holiday since we got married, and because of that, it was the day I looked forward to most.

I had been very smart about saving our coupons for the past four months so we could have a real feast, and along with the pig, I had also accumulated enough coupons so we could make dough: Half of the dough would be set aside for dumplings, and the other for an orange-flavored loaf. But mostly, I was excited about the pig. Every year or so, the state tried to introduce a new substitute for pig and other kinds of animal meat, and while some were very successful, the pig- and cow-protein replacements never were. There was something wrong with the flavor, no matter how hard they tried. Eventually, though, they would stop trying, because those of us who still remembered what cow and pig tasted like would forget, and at some point, there would be children born who would never know in the first place.

We spent the morning cooking, and then ate an early dinner at 16:00. There was enough food so that we were each able to have eight dumplings, as well as rice and mustard greens my husband had stewed in some sesame oil that we had saved up to buy, and we each had a slice of cake. This was the one day every year when conversation with my husband was easy, because we were able to talk about the food. Sometimes, we even talked about food we had eaten when we were young, between the periods of severe rationing, but that was always dangerous, because it made you start thinking about a lot of other things from when you were young.

Now my husband said, "My father used to make the best shredded pig." It didn't seem like I needed to reply, because it was a statement, not a question, and, indeed, he continued speaking. "We had it at least twice a year, even after the rationing, and he would slow-cook it for hours, and you only needed to touch it with your fork and it would fall apart on the plate. We'd have it with runner beans and macaroni, and if there were leftovers, my mother would make it into sandwiches. My sister and I used to—" And then he stopped talking abruptly, and put down his chopsticks, and looked at the wall for a moment before picking them up again. "Anyway," he said, "I'm glad we were able to have this tonight."

"As am I," I said.

That night, as we lay in our beds, I wondered what my husband had been like before we met. I thought about this more the longer we were married, especially as I didn't know that much about him. I knew that he was from Prefecture One, and that both of his parents had been professors at a big university, and that at some point both of them had been arrested and taken to rehabilitative camps, and that he had an older sister, who had also been removed to the camps, and that because his immediate family members had been declared enemies of the state, he had been expelled from the university where he had been a graduate student. We both had been officially forgiven under the 2087 Forgiveness Act and given good jobs, but we would never be allowed to reenroll in a university. Unlike my husband, I had no desire to return—I was satisfied being a lab tech. But my husband had wanted to be a scientist, and yet he never would. Grandfather had told me this. "I can only do so much, little cat," he had said, but he never explained what he meant by that.

After Lunar New Year came Honor Day, which was always on a Friday. The state had instituted it in '71. All businesses and institutes were closed on that day, and you were supposed to spend it quietly, thinking of people who had died, not just in '70 but from any of the illnesses. The motto for Honor Day was "Not all who died were innocent, but all who died are forgiven."

Couples usually spent Honor Day together, but my husband and I did not. He went to the center, where the state sponsored a concert of orchestral music, and lectures about grieving, and I took a walk around the Square. But now I wondered if he had in fact gone to Bethune Street.

Mostly, though, I thought of Grandfather, who had not died of an illness but was dead nonetheless. We had spent every Honor Day together, and Grandfather would show me pictures of my father, who had died in '66, when I was two. He hadn't died of disease, either, but it wasn't until later that I learned that. That was also when my other grandfather had died—they had died at the same time, in the same place. It was this other grandfather to whom I was genetically related, although I can't say I missed him, because I didn't remember him at all. But Grandfather always said that he had loved me very much, and I liked hearing that, even though I didn't remember him.

I can remember almost nothing of my father as well, because I have only a few memories of my life before the illness. Sometimes I had the sense that I had been a different person altogether, someone who didn't have such a difficult time understanding other people and what they were really trying to say beneath the thing they were actually saying. One time, I asked Grandfather if he had liked me more before I got sick, and he turned his head away for a moment and then grabbed me and held me to him, even though he knew I didn't like that. "No," Grandfather said, in a funny, smothered voice, "I have always loved you just the same since the day you were born. I wouldn't want my little cat any other way," which was nice to hear and made me feel good, like I did when it was cool enough outside to wear long sleeves and I could walk and walk and never get overheated.

But one of the reasons I suspected that I might have been different was because, in the most vivid memory I have of my father, he is laughing and twirling a little girl around by her hands, spinning her so fast that she is soaring, her feet sweeping through the air. The little girl is wearing a pale-pink dress and has a black ponytail that sails behind her, and she is laughing, too. One of the only things I remember about being sick is this image, and after I got better, I had asked Grandfather who that little girl was, and he got a strange expression on his face. "That was you, little cat," he said. "You and your father. He would spin you around like that until you both got dizzy." At the time, I had thought this was impossible, because I was bald and couldn't imagine having so much hair. But then, as I got older, I thought: Suppose that *was* me, with all that hair? What else had I had that I couldn't remember? I thought of the little girl laughing, her mouth wide open, her father laughing with her. I could never make anyone laugh, not even Grandfather, and no one could make me laugh. But once I had. It was like being told I had once known how to fly.

Grandfather had always said that Honor Day was to honor me, because I had lived. "You have two birthdays in one year, little cat," he said. "The day you were born, and the day you came back to me." This is why I always thought of Honor Day as my day, though I would never say that aloud, because I knew it was selfish and, moreover, was impolite, because it disregarded all those who had died. The other thing I would never say aloud was that I had liked to hear Grandfather tell me about when I was sick; how I had lain in a hospital bed for months, and for weeks my fever had been so high that I couldn't even talk; how almost all of my fellow patients on the ward had died; how I had one day opened my eyes and asked for Grandfather. I felt cozy hearing those stories, hearing Grandfather say how worried he had been, how he had sat by my bed every night, how he had read to me every day, how he had described to me the kinds of cakes he would get for me if I got better, cakes made with real strawberries swirled into the batter, or topped with sheets of chocolate that had been stamped to look like tree bark, or sprinkled with toasted sesame seeds. Grandfather said I had loved all sweets, especially cake, when I was a little girl, but after the illness, I had lost most of my taste for them, which was just as well, since by that point sugar had also been declared a restricted asset.

Since Grandfather had died, however, no one remembered that I had once been sick, or that someone had wanted me to get better so badly that he had come to visit me every night.

That year, Honor Day was particularly lonely. The building was silent. The day after the lunar holiday, our next-door neighbors had been taken in a raid, and although they had never been loud, it turned out that they had made more noise than I had thought, because our apartment was deeply quiet without them next to us. The day before, I had checked the envelope that contained my husband's notes, and had found a new one, written in the same hand, on another scrap of paper. "I'll wait for you," it said, and that was it.

I wished, as I often did, that Grandfather were alive, or that I at least had a recent picture of him, something I could look at and talk to. But I didn't, and I never would, and thinking about that made me so upset that I got up and began pacing, and suddenly the apartment seemed so small that I was unable to breathe, and I took my keys and ran downstairs and out onto the street.

Outside, the Square was as busy as always, as if it wasn't actually Honor Day, and I joined the group of people who walked around and around it, feeling myself becoming calmer as I did. I felt less alone being with them, even though the reason we were all together was because we were all alone.

I used to come to the Square with Grandfather when he was alive.

Back then, there had been a cluster of storytellers who would congregate in the northeastern corner of the Square, which had been Grandfather's favorite place to come read outdoors when he had been younger. He once told me a story about how he had been sitting on one of the wooden benches that had then snaked all along the Square, and had been eating a pig-and-egg sandwich when a squirrel leapt on his shoulder and grabbed the sandwich out of his hands and ran away with it.

I had been able to tell from Grandfather's expression that this was a funny story, and yet I hadn't found it funny. He had looked at me and had added, quickly, "This was before," meaning before the epidemic of '52, which had originated in squirrels before being transferred to humans, and had resulted in the eradication of all North American squirrels.

Anyway, when Grandfather and I had gone to the Square, it mostly had been to listen to the storytellers. They usually assembled on weekends and on occasional weekday evenings, so people could come hear them after work, and they worked in what Grandfather called a guild, meaning that they split their earnings among themselves, and arranged their own schedules so that there would never be more than three there at the same time. You came at a certain hour—say, 19:00 on the weekdays and 16:00 on the weekends—and paid either in chits or in coins. You paid in half-hour increments, so every thirty minutes, one of the storytellers' helpers went around the audience with a bucket, and if you wanted to stay for longer, you gave him more payment, and if you wanted to leave, you left.

Different storytellers told different kinds of stories. You went to one person if you liked romances, and another if you liked fables, and another if you liked stories about animals, and another if you liked history. The storytellers were considered gray vendors. This meant that they were licensed by the state, same as the carpenters and plastic makers, but they were also much more heavily monitored. All of their stories had to be submitted to the Information Unit for approval, but there were always Flies at their sessions, and certain storytellers were known to be more dangerous than others. I remember once going to a session with Grandfather, and when he saw who the storyteller was, he had gasped. "What is it?" I had asked. "The storyteller," he whispered in my ear. "When I was young, he was a very famous writer. I can't believe he's still alive." He had looked up at the man, who was old and had a limp and was settling onto his stool; we took our places on the ground around him, sitting on pieces of cloth or plastic bags we had brought from home. "I barely recognize him," Grandfather murmured, and, indeed, there was something wrong with the storyteller's face, as if the entire left-hand side of his jaw had been removed; every few sentences, he brought a handkerchief to his mouth and blotted at the saliva that was dribbling down his chin. But once I got used to his speech, the story he told—about a man who had lived here, on this very island, on this very Square, two hundred years ago, and who had forsaken great riches from his family to follow the person he loved all the way to California, a person who his family was certain would betray him—was so absorbing that I even stopped hearing the drone of the Flies that hovered above us, so absorbing that even the money collectors forgot to circulate, and it wasn't until an entire hour had passed that the storyteller had sat back and said, "And next week, I'll tell you what happened to the man," and everyone, even Grandfather, had groaned with disappointment.

The next week, a large group of us were waiting for the storyteller to reappear, and we waited and waited, until, finally, another of the storytellers came over and said that she was very sorry to report that her colleague was suffering from a terrible migraine, and that he wouldn't be coming to the Square today.

"Will he be back next week?" someone called out.

"I don't know," the woman admitted, and even I could tell she was scared, and worried. "But we have three other excellent storytellers here with us today, and you're all welcome to come listen to them."

About half the crowd did join the circles of those other storytellers, but the rest of us, including Grandfather and I, did not. Instead, we walked away, Grandfather looking at the ground, and when we reached our home, he went into the bedroom and lay down facing the wall, which he did when he wanted privacy, and I stayed in the other room and listened to the radio.

For the next few weeks, Grandfather and I went back again and again to the Square, but the storyteller, the one who had been a famous writer, never appeared again. The strange thing was how upset Grandfather had been; after every trip to the Square, he would walk more slowly than usual back home.

Finally, after about a month of looking and waiting for the story-teller, I asked Grandfather what he thought had happened to him. He looked at me for a long time before he answered. "He was reha-bilitated," he said, at last. "But sometimes rehabilitations are tem-porary."

I didn't really understand what he was saying, but I somehow knew not to ask more questions. Shortly after that, the storytell-ers disappeared entirely, and when they finally reappeared, about eight years ago, Grandfather hadn't wanted to go any longer, and I hadn't wanted to go without Grandfather. But then Grandfather died, and I made myself start going, just a few times a year or so. But even all these years later, I still found myself wondering what had happened to the man who was going to California: Had he done so after all? Had his beloved been waiting for him? Was he in fact betrayed? Or had we all been wrong: Had they been reunited and become happy? Maybe they were in California together and happy still. I knew it was foolish, because they weren't even real people, but I thought about them often. I wanted to know what had become of them.

None of the storytellers I had seen in the years since that time with Grandfather were as good as the old man had been, but most of them were fine. And most of the stories were much happier. There was one storyteller in particular who told stories about animals who did silly things and played pranks and got into mischief, but in the end, they always apologized and everything worked out fine.

This storyteller wasn't here today, but I recognized another I liked, who told funny stories about a married couple who were always getting into mishaps: There was one in which the husband couldn't remember if it was his turn or his wife's turn to do the gro-cery shopping, and as it was their anniversary, he didn't want to ask her, because he didn't want her to be disappointed, and so he went to the store and bought the tofu himself. Meanwhile, the wife also couldn't remember if it was her turn or her husband's to go to the store, and because it was their anniversary, *she* didn't want to ask *him*, and so she also went to the grocery and bought some tofu. The story ended up with them both laughing over how much tofu they had bought, and making it into all kinds of delicious stews, which they ate together. Of course, this story was unrealistic: From where were they getting all these protein coupons? Wouldn't they have fought after realizing they'd wasted so many of them? Who forgot whose turn it was to go to the store? And yet that wasn't part of the story. The teller mimicked their voices—the man's high and worrying, the woman's low and dithering—and the audience laughed, not because it was true but because it was a problem that wasn't actually a problem yet was being treated like it was.

As I crouched in the back row, I felt someone sit next to me. Not too close, but close enough so that I could feel their presence. But I didn't look up, and they didn't look over. This story was about the same married couple, both of whom thought they had misplaced a dairy coupon. It wasn't as good as the tofu story, but it was good enough, and when the collectors came around, I put a coupon into the bucket so I could stay for the next half hour.

The storyteller announced there would be a short intermission, and some people brought out little tins of snacks and began to eat. I wished I had thought to bring a snack as well, but I hadn't. But as I was thinking that, the person next to me spoke.

"Do you want one?" he asked.

I turned and saw that he was holding out a small paper bag of precracked walnuts, and I shook my head: It was unwise to take food from strangers—no one had enough food to just offer it to someone they didn't know, and so if they did, it generally meant that something was potentially suspicious. "Thank you, though," I said, and as I did, I looked at him and realized it was the man I had seen at the shuttle stop, the one with the long curls. I was so surprised that I just stared at him, but he didn't seem offended, and even smiled. "I've seen you before," he said, and when I still didn't say anything, he tilted his head to one side, still smiling. "In the mornings," he said, "at the shuttle stop."

"Oh," I said, as if I hadn't recognized him immediately. "Oh, yes. Right."

He bent over another walnut, splitting it in half with his thumb and breaking off the remaining bits of its shell in neat shards. As he did, I was able to study him; he was wearing a cap again, but I couldn't see any hair under it, and beneath it he wore a gray nylon shirt and gray pants, of the sort my husband also wore. "Do you come to hear this storyteller often?" he asked.

It took a moment for me to realize he was talking to me, and when I did, I didn't know what to say. No one talked to me unless they had to: the grocer, asking me if I wanted nutria or dog or tempeh; the Ph.D.s, telling me they needed more pinkies; the dispenser at the center, holding out her machine and asking for my fingerprint to confirm I'd received the correct number of coupons for the month. And yet here was this person, a stranger, asking me a question, and not only asking me but smiling, smiling like he really wanted to know the answer. The last person who had smiled at me and asked me questions was, of course, Grandfather, and, remembering that, I became very upset, and started to rock in place, just a little, but when I caught myself and looked up again, he was still looking at me, still smiling, as if I were just another person.

"Yes," I said, but that wasn't really true. "No," I corrected myself. "I mean, sometimes. Sometimes I do."

"Me too," he replied, in that same voice, as if I were no different from anyone else, as if I were the kind of person who had conversations all the time.

Then it was my turn to say something, but I couldn't think of anything, and once again, the man saved me. "Have you lived in Zone Eight for long?" he asked.

This should have been an easy question, but I hesitated. In truth, I had lived in Zone Eight for my entire life. When I was born, however, there were no zones; this was simply an area, and you could move all around the island as you wanted, and you could live in whatever district you preferred, assuming you had enough money to afford it. Then, when I was seven, the zones were established, but as Grandfather and I already lived in what was now called Zone Eight, it wasn't as if we had to move, or be reassigned.

But all that seemed like too much to say, so I just said I had.

"I just moved here," said the man, after I had forgotten to ask him if he had lived in the zone for very long. ("A good thing to remember in a conversation is reciprocity," Grandfather had said. "That means that you should ask the person what they just asked you. So, if they say to you, 'How are you?,' then you should reply and then ask, 'And how are you?' ") "I used to live in Zone Seventeen, but this is much nicer." He smiled again. "I live in Little Eight," he added.

"Oh," I said. "Little Eight's nice," I said.

"It is," he said. "I live in Building Six."

"Oh," I said again. Building Six was the biggest building in Little Eight, and you could only live there if you were unmarried, had worked for at least three years for one of the state projects, and were under the age of thirty-five. You had to enter a special lottery to live in Building Six, and no one lived there for longer than two years at most, because one of the benefits of living there was that the state helped arrange your marriage. This was the kind of task that had once fallen to your parents, but fewer adults had parents these days. People called it "Building Sex."

It was unusual but not unheard-of to be transferred from Zone Seventeen into Zone Eight, and specifically into Building Six. It was more common if you were a scientist or a statistician or an engineer, someone learned, but I already knew from the jumpsuit he had been wearing at the shuttle stop that this man was a tech, maybe a higher-grade tech than I was, but still not someone with top clearance. Still, perhaps he had performed some exceptional service: For example, there were sometimes reports of how a botany tech at the Farm had quickly moved all the seedlings in his care to another laboratory when his own lab's generator failed; or, in a more extreme case, how an animal tech had thrown himself in front of his fetus jars to save them from gunfire when his convoy was set upon by insurgents.

(That person had died, but was given a posthumous promotion and commendation.)

I was wondering what the man had done to merit his move when the storyteller returned and started talking again. The new story was about the man and woman planning an anniversary present for each other. The man asked his supervisor for time off and entered the lottery for orchestra tickets. Meanwhile, the woman had also asked her supervisor for time off and had also entered a lottery, for a concert of folk music. But in their attempts to keep their plans a surprise, they had forgotten to coordinate their dates, and had gotten the tickets for the same night. In the end, though, it had all worked out, because the man's colleague had offered to trade his own orchestra tickets for a later date, so the man and the woman got to have two celebrations, and both were pleased that their spouse had been so thoughtful.

Everyone clapped and began gathering their things, but I remained seated. I was wondering what the man in the story did on his free nights, and what the woman did on hers.

Then I heard someone speak to me. "Hey," the person said, and I looked up, and the man with the long hair was standing next to me, holding out his hand. For a moment I was confused, and then I realized he was offering me help to stand, though I got up on my own, dusting off my pants as I did.

I was worried I had been rude to reject him, but when I looked at him again, he was still smiling. "That was nice," he said.

"Yes," I said.

"Are you going to come next week?" he asked.

"I don't know," I said.

"Well," he said, shifting his bag on his shoulder, "I am." He paused. "Maybe I'll see you again."

"All right," I said.

He smiled again and turned to leave. But after he had walked a few steps, he stopped and turned back around. "I never asked you your name," he said.

He made it sound as if this were unusual, as if everyone I met or worked with knew my name, as if it were rude or extraordinary to not know. I cannot say that other people were not asked for their names; I cannot say that it was unsafe to tell someone your name. I thought of the two young women scientists at work, and how people must ask their names all the time. I thought of my husband in the house on Bethune Street, the familiar way that the man at the door had said, "You're late tonight," and how, in that house, everyone would know his name. I thought of the person sending him notes, and how that person too would know his name. I thought of the postdocs and scientists and Ph.D.s at work, all of whose names I knew—they knew my name, too, though not because it was mine; they knew it because they knew what it represented, they knew that my name explained why I was there at all.

But when was the last time someone had asked me my name simply because they wanted to know? Not because they needed it for a form or for a sample or to check my records—but because they wanted something to call me, because they were curious, because someone had thought to give it to me and they wanted to know what it was.

It had been years; it had been since I met my husband seven years ago in that marriage broker's office in Zone Nine. I had told him my name, and he had told me his, and then we had talked. One year later, we were married. Three months after that, Grandfather was dead. It felt like no one had asked me since then.

So I turned to the man in gray, who was still standing there, waiting for me to answer.

"Charlie," I told him. "My name is Charlie."

"I'm pleased to meet you, Charlie," he said.

PART IV

Winter, forty years earlier

Dearest P,   February 3, 2054

Something strange happened to me today.

It was about two p.m., and I was about to catch the eastbound crosstown bus on 96th Street when, at the last minute, I decided to walk home instead. It's been raining for weeks, so much that the East River flooded again, and they had to sandbag the entire eastern part of campus, and this was the first clear day. Not sunny, but not rainy, and warm, almost hot.

It had been a long time since I had walked through the Park, and after a few minutes, I found myself wandering north. It occurred to me as I did that I hadn't been to this part of the Park—the Ravine, as it's called, which is the wildest part, a large patch of simulated nature—since I was visiting New York as a university student, and how exotic it had seemed to me back then, exotic and beautiful. It had been December, when December was still cold, and although I had seen enough of East Coast and New England foliage by then, I had still been mesmerized by how brown it had been, brown and black and chill, dazzling in its starkness. I remember I had been impressed by how noisy winter was. The fallen leaves, the fallen twigs, the thin layer of ice that had accumulated on the paths: You stepped on them and they crunched and cracked beneath you, and above you the branches rustled in the wind, and around you there was the sound of melting ice dripping onto stone. I was used to being in jungles, where the plants are silent because they never lose their moisture. Instead of shriveling, they sag, and when they fall to the ground, they become not husks but paste. A jungle is silent.

Now, of course, the Ravine looks very different. It sounds different, too. Those trees—elms, poplars, maples—are long gone, withered to death by the heat, and replaced with trees and ferns that I remember from growing up, things that still look out of place here. But they've done well in New York—arguably, better than I have. Around 98th Street, I walked through a large copse of green bamboo, one that stretched north for at least five blocks. It created a tunnel of cool, green-scented air, something enchanted and lovely, and for a while I stood in it, inhaling, before finally exiting around 102nd Street, near the Loch, which is a man-made river that runs from 106th to 102nd Street. That picture I sent you, years ago, of David and Nathaniel wearing those scarves you gave to us? That was taken here, on one of his school field trips. I hadn't been there.

Anyway, it was as I was leaving the bamboo tunnel, distracted, oxygen-dizzy, that I heard a sound, a splashing, coming from the Loch to my right. I turned, expecting to see a bird, perhaps, one of the flock of flamingos that flew north last year and then never left, when I saw it: a bear. A black bear, an adult by the looks of it. He was sitting, almost humanlike, on one of the large flat rocks on the riverbed, and leaning forward, resting his weight on his left paw as, with his right, he scooped the water, letting it run through his claws. As he did, he made a low sound, a growling. He wasn't angry, I felt, but frantic—there was something intense and focused about his searching; he looked almost like a prospector from an old Western movie panning for gold.

I stood there, unable to move, trying to remember what you were supposed to do when you encountered a bear (Make yourself big? Or make yourself small? Make noise? Or run?), but he didn't even turn toward me. But then the wind must have changed, and he must have smelled me, for he suddenly looked up, and as I took a first, tentative step away from him, he drew himself up on his hind legs and roared.

He was going to run at me. I knew it before I knew it, and I opened my mouth too, to scream, but before I could, there was a swift popping noise and the bear tumbled backward, all seven feet of him falling into the stream with a loud splash, and I saw the water staining itself red.

Then a man was by my side, another jogging toward the bear. "That was close," said the man nearest me. "Sir? You okay? Sir?"

He was a ranger, but I wasn't able to speak, and he unzipped a pocket on his vest, handed me a plastic sleeve of liquid. "You're in shock," he said. "Drink it—there's sugar in it." But my fingers wouldn't work, and he had to open it for me, and help me detach my mask so I could drink. Next to me, I heard a second gunshot, and flinched. The man spoke into his radio: "We got him, sir. Yeah. The Loch. No—one passerby. No apparent fatalities."

Finally, I was able to speak. "That was a bear," I said, stupidly.

"Yes, sir," said the ranger, patiently (I saw then that he was very young). "We've been hunting this one for a while."

"*This* one?" I asked. "So there've been others?"

"Six over the past twelve months or so," he said, and then, seeing my face, "We've kept it quiet. No fatalities, no attacks. This was the last of a clan we've been tracking. He's the alpha."

They had to take me back through the bamboo forest to their wagon to interrogate me about my encounter, and then they let me go. "Probably best not to be in this area of the Park anymore," said the senior ranger. "Word is, the city's going to shut it down in a couple of months anyway. The state's commandeered it, going to use it as some facility."

"The whole Park?" I asked.

"Not yet," he said, "but likely north of Ninety-sixth Street. You take care, now."

They drove away, and I stood there on the path for a few minutes. Next to me was a bench, and I stripped off my gloves and unbuckled my mask and sat there inhaling and exhaling, smelling the air, and running my hands over the wood, which was worn smooth and glossy from years of people sitting on it and touching it. It registered that I was lucky; to be saved, of course, and that my saviors were city rangers and not soldiers, who would surely have removed me to an interrogation center for questioning, because questioning is what soldiers do. Then I got up and walked quickly toward Fifth Avenue, and from there I caught a bus the rest of the way east.

No one was in the apartment when I got home. It was only about half past three by then, but I was too jumpy to return to the lab. I texted Nathaniel and David, put my mask and gloves in the sanitizer, washed my hands and face, took a pill so I could relax, and lay down in bed. I thought of the bear, the last of his clan, about how, when he stood, I could see that, despite his size, he was skinny, gaunt even, and that his fur had fallen out in patches. It was only now, now that I was away from him, that I could understand that what had terrified me most about him was not how large he was, or the bear-ness of him, but how I had intuited his panic, the kind of panic that resulted only from extreme hunger, the kind of hunger that drove you crazy, that drove you south, along highways and through streets, into a place you knew instinctively never to go, where you would be surrounded by creatures who only meant you harm, where you would be going toward your own inevitable death. You knew that, and yet you went anyway, because hunger, stopping that hunger, is more important than self-protection; it is more important than life. I saw, again and again, his huge red mouth opened wide, his front incisor rotted away, his black eyes bright with terror.

I slept. When I woke, it was dark—I was still alone. The baby was seeing his therapist; Nathaniel would be working late. I knew I should do something useful, get up and make dinner, go down to the lobby and ask the super if he needed help changing the filter on the decontamination pod. But I didn't. I just lay there in the dark, looking at the sky and watching night approach.

Now comes the part I've been avoiding.

I suppose, if you've read this far, you're wondering why I was walking across the Park in the first place. And you've probably guessed that it relates to the baby, because everything I have done wrong seems to relate to him in some way.

As you know, this is the baby's third school in three years, and it's been made clear to me by the principal that this is his last chance. How can it be his last chance when he's not even fifteen? I'd asked, and the principal, a sour little man, frowned at me. "I mean you're out of good options," he said, and although I wanted to punch him, I didn't, in part because I knew he was right: This is David's last chance. He has to make this one work.

The school is across the Park, on 94th just west of Columbus, in what was once a grand apartment building and had been purchased by the school's founder back in the '20s, at the height of the charter-school craze. Then it got converted into a private school for boys with "behavioral difficulties." They have small classes, and every student gets after-school therapy if he or his parents request it. It was emphasized to me and Nathaniel many times that David was very, *very* lucky to be admitted, as they have many, *many* more applicants than the school can accommodate, more than in the school's history in fact, and it was only because of our *special connections*—the RU president knows one of the trustees and wrote a letter, in part I think out of guilt that David had been expelled from the RU school, thus leading to this three-year-long shuffle— that he was there at all. (Later, I thought about the improbability of this statement: Statistically, the number of boys under the age of eighteen had decreased significantly in the last four years. So how was it that admissions had become more difficult than ever? Had they adjusted the size of the student body accordingly? That night, I asked Nathaniel what he thought about this, and he only groaned and said he was just grateful that I had known not to ask the principal that.)

Since the school year began in October—as I told you earlier, they moved it back a month after what turned out to be a localized flare-up of the virus in late August, source still unknown—the baby has been in trouble twice. The first time was for talking back to his math teacher. The second time was for skipping two of his behavioral-therapy sessions (unlike the after-school sessions, which are one-on-one and voluntary, these are conducted in small groups and are mandatory). And then, yesterday, we were called again, about a paper David had written for his English class.

"You're going to have to go," Nathaniel said last night, tiredly, as we read the email from the principal. He didn't need to say it—I had had to go to the last two conferences myself as well. Another detail I didn't mention is that the school is fiendishly expensive; after his school shut down last year, Nathaniel was finally able to find a job tutoring a set of six-year-old twins in Cobble Hill. Their parents haven't let them out of the house since '50, and Nathaniel and another tutor spend all day with them—it's impossible for him to come back to the city before evening.

Upon arriving at the school, I was led to the principal's office, where a young woman, the English teacher, was waiting as well. She was nervous, fluttery, and when I looked at her, she turned away, her hand flitting about her cheek. Later, I saw that she had tried to hide the pockmarks on her jawline with makeup, and that her wig was cheap and probably itchy, and I felt a tenderness for her, despite the fact that she had reported my son: She was a survivor.

"Dr. Griffith," said the principal. "Thank you for coming in. We wanted to talk to you about David's paper for English class. Do you know about this paper?"

"Yes," I said. It had been his assignment last week: *Write about a significant anniversary in your life. It can be about the first time you went somewhere or experienced something or met someone now important to you. Be creative! Just don't write about your birthday, because that's too easy. Five hundred words. Make sure to give your paper a title! Due next Monday.*

"Did you read what he wrote?"

"Yes?" I said. But I hadn't. I had asked David if he needed help, and he had said no, and then I had forgotten to ask what he ended up writing.

The principal looked at me. "No," I admitted. "I know I should have, I've just been so busy, and my husband has a new job, and—"

He raised his hand. "I have the paper here," he said, and handed me his screen. "Why don't you read it now." It wasn't a request. (I have cleaned up the misspellings and grammatical errors within.)

"FOUR YEARS." AN ANNIVERSARY.

BY DAVID BINGHAM-GRIFFITH

This year is the fourth anniversary of the discovery of NiVid-50, more commonly known as Lombok syndrome, and the most serious pandemic in history since AIDS in the last century. It has killed 88,895 people in New York City alone. It is also the fourth anniversary of the death of civil rights and the beginning of a fascist state spreading misinformation to people who want to believe anything they're told by the government.

Take, for example, the common name of the disease, which supposedly originated in Lombok, an island in Indonesia. The disease is a zoonosis, which means it is a disease that began in an animal and then got transferred into the human population. Zoonoses have been increasing in incidence every year for the past eighty years, and the reason is because more and more wild land has been developed, and animals have lost their habitats and have been forced to come into closer contact with humans than they were ever meant to. In this case, the disease was in bats, which were later eaten by civet cats, and then those civet cats infected the livestock, which infected humans. The problem is that Lombok doesn't have the land to sustain cattle, and as Muslims, they don't eat pork. So how can the illness really have originated there? Isn't this another case of blaming Asian countries for global diseases? We did it in '30, and in '35, and in '47, and now we are doing it again.

Various governments worked quickly to try to contain the virus, while also blaming Indonesia for being dishonest, but the American government is hardly honest itself. Everyone thought this was all good, but then all immigration to America ceased, and families were torn apart, and thousands of people either drowned at sea or were turned away to die on boats. My homeland, the Kingdom of Hawai'i, completely isolated themselves, but it didn't make a difference, and now I can never return to the place where I was born. Here in America, martial law was declared, and large camps for sick people and desperate refugees were opened on Roosevelt and Governor's Islands in New York, and in many other places, too. The American government needs to be overthrown.

My father is the scientist who did early work on the disease. He didn't discover it, someone else did that, but he was the one who found out it was a mutation of an earlier diagnosed disease called a Nipah virus. My father works for Rockefeller University and is very important. He supports the quarantines, as well as the camps. He says that sometimes you just have to hold your nose and do these things. He says that a disease has no better friend than a democracy. My other father says that he

And then it ended, just there on "says that he." I tried flicking past the screen, to see if there might be a second page, but there wasn't. When I looked up at the principal and the teacher, they were both studying me with serious expressions.

"Well," said the principal. "You can see the issue here. Or, rather, issues."

But I couldn't. "Like what?" I asked.

They both sat straighter in their chairs. "Well, for one, he had help writing this," said the principal.

"That's not a crime," I said. "Anyway, how do you know? It's not even that sophisticated."

"No," he admitted, "but, given David's difficulty with writing, it's clear he had a *lot* of help, help that goes beyond just proofreading or editing." A pause, and then, with some triumph: "He already confessed, Dr. Griffith. He's been paying a college student he met online to write his papers."

"Then he's been wasting his money," I said, but neither of them answered. "It's not even complete."

"Dr. Griffith," said the English teacher, in a surprisingly soft and melodic voice, "we take cheating very seriously here. But we both know that the bigger problem is that it's not—it's not safe for David to be writing such things."

"Maybe not, if he were a government functionary," I said. "But he's not. He's a fourteen-year-old boy whose entire extended family died before he even got to say goodbye to them, and he's a student in a private school to which my husband and I pay a great deal of money to protect and instruct him."

They sat up again. "I resent the implication that we'd ever—" the principal began, but the teacher stopped him, laying a hand on his arm. "Dr. Griffith, we would never turn David in," she said, "but he needs to be careful. Do you monitor who his friends are, who he's talking to, what he's saying at home, what he's doing online?"

"Of course," I said, because I did, but as I spoke, I felt myself flushing, as if they knew that I knew that I hadn't been watching him closely enough, and also that they knew why—I didn't want to discover that David was drifting further from us; I didn't want to have to face the fact of more misbehavior; I didn't want more evidence that I didn't understand my own son, that for years he had been becoming increasingly unknowable to me, that for years I had felt it was my fault.

I got out of there soon after with a promise to talk to David about being careful with what he said and wrote about the government, and to remind him about the anti-state language statutes that had been implemented shortly after the riots, and that we were still living under martial law.

But I didn't talk to him. I walked through the Park, I saw the bear, I came home, I took a nap. And then, before Nathaniel or David came home, I hurriedly left for the lab, where I'm sitting at midnight and writing you this letter.

I never thought we would have lived here for almost eleven years, Peter. I never meant for David to have to spend his childhood in this city, in this country. "When we're back home," we always said to him, until we didn't. And now there is no home to return to; *this* is home, except it has never felt like it, and still doesn't. From my office window, I have a direct view of the crematorium they built on Roosevelt Island. The president of RU vigorously protested it—the ash clouds would, he said, drift westward toward the university—but the city built it anyway, with the argument that if everything went as planned, the crematorium would only be used for a few years. Which has turned out to be true: Three times a day for three years, we would watch black smoke trail from its chimneys, vanishing into the sky. But now the burnings have been reduced to once a month, and the skies are clear again.

Nathaniel is texting me. I'm not answering.

But the thing I keep thinking about is the final lines of David's essay. He had written them himself—I could tell. I could see his face as he typed them out, that look of bafflement and disdain I sometimes catch him giving me. He doesn't understand why I've made the decisions I've had to make, but he doesn't have to—he's a child. So why do I feel this overwhelming guilt, this sense of apology, when all I've done is what needed to be done in order to stop the spread of illness? "My other father says": What? What is Nathaniel saying about me? We fought, terribly, loudly, the day I told him I had decided to work with the government on the containment measures. The baby hadn't been there—he had been downtown, with Aubrey and Norris—but I wonder if Nathaniel said something to him; I wonder what they talked about while I was away. How was that final sentence going to end? "My other father says that my father is trying to do what's right in order to protect us"? "My other father says that my father is doing the best that he can"?

Or was it, as I fear, something else entirely? "My other father says that my father has become someone we can't respect"? "My other father says that my father is a bad person"? "My other father says that it's my father's fault we're here, alone, with no one to save us"?

Which one, Peter? How was it going to end?

Charles

Dearest Peter,   October 22, 2054

I have to start by thanking you for talking to me about David last week—you made me feel a little better. There's more to say, but I'll say it in another email. And we can also discuss Olivier—I have some thoughts.

I'm afraid that I don't know any more about the reports coming out of Argentina than you do, only that they look potentially troubling. I talked to a friend at NIAID, who said that the next three weeks will be critical; if it hasn't spread by then, we should be fine. The Argentine government, as I understand it, is being surprisingly cooperative—meek, even. They suspended all access in and out of Bariloche, but I suspect you already know this. You're going to have to give me an update—I know a little about the epidemiological aspect of it, but my understanding is mainly limited to virology, and I doubt would be very illuminating considering what you already know.

Now some updates of my own. As I mentioned, our request for a car was finally approved, and on Sunday, one was delivered. It's a standard-issue government model, navy-blue, very basic. But with the subway system still so hampered, it made sense—it takes Nathaniel almost two hours to get to Cobble Hill in the mornings. *And* I was able to make a persuasive case that I needed to make regular trips to Governor's Island and Bethesda, and that getting a car would ultimately be cheaper than biweekly plane or train tickets.

The plan was that the car would be mostly Nathaniel's to use, but as it happened, I was called down to NIAID on Monday (a bureaucratic check-in as part of this new cross-institutional effort, unrelated to Bariloche), so I took the car and spent the night there and drove up from Maryland on Tuesday. As I was crossing the bridge, though, I got a text from the Holsons, the family whose sons Nathaniel tutors: Nathaniel had fainted. I tried calling them, but as usual these days, there was no reception, and so I turned and sped into Brooklyn.

Nathaniel has worked for this family for more than a year, but we speak about them very little. Mr. Holson, who brokers corporate mergers, spends most of his time in the Gulf. Mrs. Holson was a corporate lawyer but quit to stay home with her sons when they were diagnosed.

The Holsons live in a beautiful brownstone, two hundred years or more old, renovated with money and taste; the steps leading to the front door had been rebuilt so that the landing could be extended and the decontamination pod could be sealed within a small stone chamber of its own, as if it had always been there—once it hissed open, so too did the front door, which was painted a glossy black. Inside, the house was dim, the blinds were all drawn, and the floors were painted the same shiny dark as the door. A woman—white, small, black-haired—approached me. She took my mask and handed it to a maid, and we bowed; she gave me a pair of latex gloves to wear. "Dr. Griffith," she said, "I'm Frances Holson. He's come around, but I thought I should call you anyway, have you take him home."

"Thank you," I said, and I followed her up the staircase, where she led me to what was clearly a spare bedroom, where Nathaniel was lying on the bed. He smiled when he saw me.

"Don't sit up," I said, but he already was. "What happened, Natey?"

He said he'd just had a head rush, maybe because he hadn't eaten today, but I knew it was because he was exhausted, though I made a show of putting my hand on his forehead, feeling for fever, and then looking into his mouth and eyes for spots.

"Let's go home," I told him. "I have the car."

I expected him to argue, but he didn't. "All right," he said. "I just want to say goodbye to the boys first."

We walked across the landing and toward a room at the end of the hall. The door was ajar, but he tapped on it, lightly, before we entered.

Inside, two boys were sitting at a child-size table, assembling a puzzle. I knew they were seven, but they looked four. I had read the research about juvenile survivors, and these children were in some ways instantly recognizable to me: They both wore tinted glasses, even in this low light, to protect their eyes, and they were both very pale, their limbs soft and thin, their rib cages blocky and wide, their cheeks and hands pitted with scars. They had both regrown their hair, but it was thin and fine, like an infant's, and the drugs that helped generate hair growth were also responsible for the fuzz of fur that grew across their chins and foreheads, and along the sides and backs of their necks. Each of them had a slim tracheal tube that attached to a small ventilator pack that clipped to his waistband.

Nathaniel introduced them as Ezra and Hiram, and they waved

at me with their small, limp, salamander-like hands. "I'll be back tomorrow," he told them, and although I knew it already, I could tell from his tone that he liked these boys, that he cared about them.

"What's wrong, Nathaniel?" asked one of them, Ezra or Hiram, in a tiny, breathy voice, and Nathaniel stroked the boy's head, his hair lifting and floating from the static caused by Nathaniel's gloves. "I'm just feeling a little tired," he said.

"Do you have the sickness?" the other one asked, and Nathaniel winced, just a bit, before smiling at him. "No," he said. "Nothing like that. I'll be back tomorrow. I promise."

Downstairs, Frances was waiting, and she handed us our masks, made me promise to take care of Nathaniel. "I will," I said, and she nodded. She was pretty, but between her eyes there were two deep grooves; I wondered if she had always had them, or if she had acquired them over the past four years.

Back at our apartment, I put Nathaniel to bed and texted David to warn him to be quiet and let his father sleep, and then I went to the lab. On my way there, I thought about David, about how lucky we were that he was safe, safe and healthy. *Protect him*, I would say to myself, unclear whom I was addressing, as I walked to work, or washed the dishes, or showered. *Protect him, protect him. Protect my son.* It was irrational. But it had worked so far.

Later, while I was eating dinner at my desk, I thought about the two boys, Ezra and Hiram. It was like something out of a fairy tale: the quiet house with its gentle light, Frances Holson and Nathaniel the parents, me the skulking guest, and those elfin creatures—half human and half pharmaceuticals—whose realm it was. One of the reasons I never became a clinician is because I was never convinced that life—its saving, its extension, its return—was definitively the best outcome. In order to be a good doctor, you *have* to think that, you have to fundamentally believe that living is superior to dying, you have to believe that the point of life is more life. I didn't administer therapies to those infected by NiVid-50; I didn't have a role in developing the drugs. I didn't think about what the survivors' lives might be like—that wasn't my job. But in the past few years, now that the disease has been contained, I find myself confronted with the facts of their lives almost daily. Some, like the teacher at David's school, who was already an adult, and probably healthy, when she contracted the illness, have been able to return to a version of their lives before.

But those boys will never have a normal life. They will never be able to go outside; they will never be able to be touched by the bare hands of anyone but their mother. It's a life; it's their life. They're too young to remember anything else. Though maybe the people I was pitying wasn't them but their parents—their worried mother, their absent father. What must it have been like, to watch your children come so close to death and then, in saving them, realize that you've transported them to a place that *you* can leave but they never can? Not death, not life, but existence, their entire world in one house, your hopes of everything they'd be and see and experience buried in the backyard, never to be unearthed. How could you encourage them to dream of anything else? How could you live with the sorrow and guilt that you had condemned them to a life stripped of all that's pleasurable: movement; touch; the sun on your face? How could you live at all?

With love, Charles

August 7, 2055

Dear P, please forgive this very rushed response, but I'm racing here (for obvious reasons). All I can say is that it certainly seems to be the case. I read the same report you did, but I also got another, this one from a colleague, and I can't interpret the findings any other way. There's a multi-institute team that leaves for Manila, and from there to Boracay, tomorrow. I was asked if I could go, because this new one looks very similar to the '50 strain. But I can't—things are so bad with David now that I just can't do it. Not going feels like a dereliction of duty, but leaving would as well.

The only question now is what, if anything, can be done in terms of containment. I fear it's not going to be much. I'll keep you posted on whatever I hear, and consider this information—such as it is—not for attribution.

Love, C.

Hi dear P,   October 11, 2055

This morning I had my first MuFIDRT meeting. What does MuFIDRT stand for? I'm so glad you asked. It means: Multi-Field Infectious Disease Response Team. MuFIDRT. Written out, it looks like it might be either a Victorian-era simulacrum of a woman's genitals or a science-fiction villain's lair. It's pronounced Moofid-RT, if that helps, and it was apparently the best acronym a group of civil servants could come up with. (No offense.)

The goal is to try to formulate (well, reformulate) a global, cross-disciplinary response to what's coming by assembling a group of epidemiologists, infectious disease specialists, economists, assorted civil servants from the Federal Reserve, as well as the Transportation, Education, Justice, Public Health and Human Safety, Information, Security, and Immigration Ministries, representatives from all the major pharma companies, and two psychologists, both specializing in depression and suicidal ideations: one among children, one among adults.

I'm assuming you're at least sitting in on your equivalent group's meetings. I also assume that your meetings are more organized, calmer, thoughtful, and less contentious than ours was. By the end of ours, we had a list of things we agreed we *weren't* going to do (most of which would be illegal under the current version of the Constitution anyway), as well as a list of things whose consequences we were going to ponder based on our respective areas of expertise. The plan is for each of the member countries to try to come up with a uniform agreement.

Again, I don't know about your group, but the biggest argument in ours concerned the isolation camps, which we've all tacitly agreed to call quarantine camps instead, even though it's a deliberate misnomer. I had assumed that the split would be ideological, but to my surprise, it wasn't; indeed, anyone who had any kind of scientific background recommended them—even the psychologists, reluctantly—and anyone who didn't opposed them. But unlike in '50, I don't see how we can avoid it this time. If the predictive modeling is correct, this disease will be far more pathogenic and contagious, swifter-moving, and deadlier than its predecessor; our only hope is mass evacuation. One of the epidemiologists even suggested the preemptive removal of at-risk groups, but everyone else agreed that would cause too much of an uproar. "We can't make this political," said one of the suits from Justice, which was such an asinine comment—both stupidly obvious and impossible to address—that everyone just ignored him.

The meeting ended with a discussion of when to close the borders. Too early, and you panic everyone. Too late, and the measure becomes pointless. My guess is that they'll announce by end of November at the very latest.

Speaking of which: Given what we both know, I don't think it's responsible of us to come visit you and Olivier. I say this with sorrow and regret. David was looking forward to it. Nathaniel was looking forward to it. And I was looking forward to it most of all. It's been so long since we've seen each other, and I miss you. I know I can say this perhaps only to you, but I'm not ready to go through another pandemic. There's no choice, obviously. One of the epidemiologists said today, "This is our chance to get it right." He meant that we could do better than we did in '50: We're better prepared, more communicative, more realistic, less frightened. But we're also wearier. The problem with doing something the second time is that, while you know what you can correct, you also know what's beyond the scope of your powers—and I have never wished more for ignorance than I do now.

I hope you're doing okay over there. I worry about you. Has Olivier given you any sense of when he might come back?

Love you. Me

Dearest Peter,   July 13, 2056

It's very late here, almost three in the morning, and I'm in my office at the lab.

Tonight we went to Aubrey and Norris's. I hadn't wanted to go. I was tired, we all were, and I hadn't wanted to put on a full decontamination suit just to go to their house. But Nathaniel insisted: He hadn't seen them in months, and he was worried about them. You know, Aubrey turns seventy-six next month; Norris will be seventy-two. They haven't left their house since the first case was diagnosed in New York State, and because there are so few people who have full protective suits, they're pretty isolated. Aside from checking in on them, there was another matter on the agenda too, which involved David. So down we went.

After we parked, David slouching out of the car ahead of us, I stopped and looked at their house. I had the clear memory of my first visit, standing on the sidewalk and staring up at the windows, all golden with light. Even from the street, their wealth was unmistakable, the sort of wealth that had always been its own kind of protection—no one would think of breaking in to a house like this, even though at night, you could see all its art and goods laid out, ready to be taken, ready to be yours.

Now, though, the parlor-floor windows had been completely bricked up, which a lot of people did after the first sieges. There had been stories, enough of which had been true—people waking to find strangers in their house or apartment, not to steal but to beg for help: for food, for medicine, for shelter—that most people who lived beneath the fourth floor decided to seal themselves in. The upper windows had all been covered with iron cages, and I knew without looking that the windows themselves had been soldered shut.

There were other changes, too. Inside, the house was frayed in a way that I had never remembered it being; I knew from Nathaniel that both of their longtime maids had been among the first wave of deaths, in January; Adams had died in '50, and had been replaced with a sallow guy named Edmund, who always looked like he was recovering from a cold. He had taken over most of the housekeep-

ing duties, but not very convincingly; the inside of the decontam
chamber needed scrubbing, for example, and when we stepped into
the foyer, the force of the suction made little clouds of dust skit-
ter across the floor. The Hawaiian quilt hanging on the foyer wall
was gray along its seams; the carpet, which Adams had been vigilant
about rotating every six months, was shiny along one edge, worn by
footsteps. Everything smelled a little musty, like a sweater taken out
of a drawer after a long period of storage.

But the other change was Aubrey and Norris themselves, now
approaching us with smiles, their arms outstretched; because the
three of us were wearing suits, we could hug them, and as I did,
I could feel they'd lost weight, could feel they'd grown feeble.
Nathaniel noticed it, too—when Aubrey and Norris turned, he
looked at me, worried.

Dinner was simple: a white-bean soup with cabbage and pancetta,
good bread. Soup is the most difficult thing to eat with these new
masks, but none of us, not even David, mentioned it, and Aubrey
and Norris seemed not to notice us struggling. Meals here were
typically served by candlelight, but this time a large globe hung suspended over the table, emitting a faint buzzing sound and a bright
white light: one of those new sunlamps, meant to give the home-
bound their vitamin D. I'd seen them before, of course, but never
one this big. The effect wasn't unpleasant, but it did illuminate more
evidence of the room's faint but unignorable decay, the *grottiness*
that inevitably accumulates when a space is continuously occupied.
Back in '50, when we were self-isolating, I often thought that the
apartment wasn't really equipped for our being there all day, every
day—it needed breaks from our habitation, the windows flung open
to the air, relief from our dander and skin cells. Around us, the air-
conditioning—that, at least, was as powerful as I'd remembered it—
made deep sighs as it cycled through its settings; the dehumidifier
rumbled in the background.

I hadn't seen Aubrey and Norris in person in months. Three years
ago, Nathaniel and I had had a massive fight about them, one of our
biggest. This was about eleven months after it became evident that
Hawai'i was unrecoverable, when the first classified reports about

the looters began surfacing. Incidents like these were happening in other decimated places as well, throughout the South Pacific; marauders were finding their way there by private boats and landing at the ports. Teams of them would disembark—in full protective gear—and make their way around the island, stripping every museum and house bare of its artifacts. It was being funded by a group of billionaires who called themselves the Alexandria Project, whose aim was "to preserve and protect the greatest artistic accomplishments of our civilization," by "rescuing" them from places "that had regrettably lost the stewards responsible for their protection." The members said that they were building a museum (location unspecified) with a digital archive to protect these works. But what was actually happening was that they were keeping everything for themselves, stored in giant warehouses where it would never be seen again.

Anyway, I had become convinced that Aubrey and Norris, if not among the project's members, had at least bought some of the stolen items. I had a waking dream of Aubrey shaking out my grandmother's quilt, the one that had been meant for me and which, like every other soft good my grandparents had owned, was burned in a fire after they died. (No, I hadn't liked my grandparents, nor they me; no, that was not the point.) I had a vision of Norris wearing an 18th-century feather cape of the sort my grandfather had had to sell to a collector decades ago in order to pay for my schooling.

I didn't have any actual proof of this, mind you: I just threw out the accusation one night, and suddenly I had unleashed years of resentments, which we batted between us. How I had never really trusted Aubrey and Norris, even after they had given Nathaniel purpose and intellectual stimulation when he'd been left stranded in New York because of my job; how Nathaniel was too trusting and naïve, and had made allowances for Aubrey and Norris that I had never understood; how I hated them just because they were rich, and how my resentment of wealth was childish and silly; how Nathaniel secretly wanted to be rich, and I was sorry that I had been such a disappointment to him; how he had never begrudged me anything I wanted to do professionally, even if it meant sacrificing his own career and his own interests, and how he was grateful for Norris and Aubrey because they took an interest in his life, and what's more, David's life as well, especially when for months, for years, I hadn't been there for our son, our son who was now being expelled for "extreme insubordination" from one of the last schools in Manhattan that would have him.

We were hissing at each other, standing on opposite sides of the bedroom, the baby asleep in his own room next door. But as serious as the fight was, as real as our anger was, there ran beneath our conversation another, truer set of resentments and accusations, things that if we ever dared say them to each other would end our life together forever. How I had ruined their lives. How David's disciplinary problems, his unhappiness, his rebellion, his lack of friends, were my fault. How he and David and Norris and Aubrey had made their own family and had excluded me. How he had sold his homeland, our homeland, to them. How I had taken us away from that homeland forever. How he had turned David against me.

My other father says.

Neither of us said any of these things aloud, but we didn't need to. I kept waiting—I know he did, too—for one of us to say something unspeakable, something that would make us both tumble down and down, crashing through the floors of our shitty apartment building until we reached the pavement.

But neither of us did. The fight ended, somehow, as these fights always do, and for a week or so after, we were careful and polite with each other. It was almost as if the ghost of what we could have said had forced its way between us, and we were afraid of antagonizing it, lest it become a demon. In the following months, I almost wished we *had* said some of what we both wanted to, because then at least we would have *said* it, instead of just constantly thinking about it. But if we had—I had to keep reminding myself—then the only thing to do afterward would have been to break up.

It seemed both inevitable and right that the result of this blowup was that Nathaniel and David began spending more time at Aubrey and Norris's. At first Nathaniel claimed it was just because I was working so late, and then he said it was because Aubrey was a good influence on David (which he was; he soothed him somehow, which I never understood—even as David became more and more of a Marxist, he continued to consider Aubrey and Norris exceptions), and then he said it was because Aubrey and Norris (Aubrey, especially) had become increasingly housebound, frightened that if they left their home they'd catch the illness, and that so many of Aubrey and Norris's friends their age had died that Nathaniel felt responsible for their well-being, especially after they'd been so generous to us. Finally, I was made to go down there myself, and we had an unmemorable evening, the baby even consenting to a game of chess with Aubrey after dinner, as I tried not to look for evidence of recent acquisitions, while finding them anyway: Had that kapa weaving always been there, framed and hung over the stairway? Was that lathe-turned wooden bowl a new purchase, or had it just been in storage? Had Aubrey and Nathaniel exchanged the briefest of glances when they saw me noticing the framed shark-tooth ornament, or had I been imagining it? The entire night I had felt like I was an intruder in someone else's play, and after that, I had stayed away.

One of the reasons we had gone tonight was because Nathaniel and I had agreed that we needed Aubrey's help with David. He still had two more years of high school and nowhere to complete them, and Aubrey was friendly with the founder of a new for-profit school that was opening in the West Village. The three of us—Nathaniel, David, and I, that is—had had a shouting match in which David made it clear that he didn't intend to return to school at all, and Nathaniel and I (united again, in a way we hadn't been for what felt like years) told him that he had to. In a previous age, we would have told him he had to get out if he wouldn't go to school, but we were afraid he'd take us up on it, and then our nights would be spent not going to meetings with his principal but searching the streets for him.

And so, after we ate, Norris and Nathaniel and I went to the parlor, and Aubrey and David remained in the dining room for a game of chess. After thirty minutes or so, they rejoined us, and I could tell that Aubrey had somehow convinced David to go to the school, and that David had confided in him, and despite my envy of their rapport, I was relieved, and heartbroken, too—that some-one had reached my son; that that someone wasn't me. He seemed easier, David, lighter, and I wondered again what it was that he saw in Aubrey. How was Aubrey able to comfort him in a way I wasn't? Was it just because he wasn't his parent? But, then, I couldn't think that way, because doing so would remind me that it wasn't his *parents* David hated—it was just one parent. It was me.

Aubrey sat down on the sofa next to me, and as he poured him-self some tea, I noticed that his hand was trembling, just a bit, and that his fingernails had grown slightly too long. I thought of Adams, and how he would never have allowed his employer to pour his own tea, or to come down to dinner with guests, even us, in such a state. It occurred to me that, as much as I might have felt trapped in this house, Aubrey and Norris actually *were* trapped. Aubrey was richer than anyone else I knew, and yet here he was, just a few years from eighty, stuck in a house he could never leave. He had made a series of miscalculations: Three hours north, the Newport prop-erty sat unoccupied, now surely run over by squatters; out east, in Water Mill, Frog's Pond Way had been declared a health hazard and razed. Four years ago, he had had an opportunity—I knew from Nathaniel—to flee to a house he had in Tuscany, but he hadn't, and now Tuscany was no longer inhabitable, anyway. And it increasingly seems that, eventually, none of us will be allowed to travel anywhere. All his money, and nowhere to go.

As we drank our tea, the talk turned, as it always does, to the quarantine camps, in particular the events of last weekend. I had never considered Aubrey or Norris particularly interested in the plight of the common man, but it seemed they were part of a group that was arguing for the camps' shutdown. Needless to say, so were Nathaniel and David. On and on they went, comparing outrages and quoting statistics (some true, some not) about all the things that went on in them. Of course, none of them had ever actually *seen* the inside of one of these camps. No one has.

"And did you see that story today?" asked the baby, more ani-mated than I'd witnessed him in a while. "About that woman and her child?"

"No, what happened?"

"This woman from Queens has a baby, and the baby tests positive. She knows the hospital authorities are gonna send her to a camp, so she says she has to go to the bathroom, and then she flees back to her apartment. She's there for two days, and then there's a banging on her door, and the soldiers burst in. She's screaming and the baby's screaming, and they say she can either let them take the baby, or she can come with her. So she decides to go with her.

"They load her onto a truck with a lot of other sick people. Everyone's jammed in. Everyone's coughing and crying. The kids are peeing. The truck drives and drives, and then they stop at one of the camps in Arkansas, and they're all herded out. They sort them into groups: people who're at the beginning, middle, or end stage of the illness. The woman's baby is diagnosed to be at the middle stage. So they're taken to this big building and given a single cot that they have to share. They don't give medicine to people in the middle stage, just those in the first stage. They wait two days to see if you get sicker, and everyone does, because they don't have any medication. And once you get sicker, they move you to the end-stage building. So the woman, who's now sick herself, moves with her baby, and they both get sicker, because there's no medicine, there's no food, there's no water. And forty-eight hours later, they're dead, and someone comes through every night and moves all the dead bodies outside and burns them."

He was becoming excited telling this story, and I looked at my son and thought how beautiful he was, how beautiful and how credulous, and I was scared for him. His passion, his anger, his need for something I couldn't identify and couldn't give him; the fights he had with other students at his school, with teachers, the rage he carried everywhere: If we had stayed in Hawai'i, would he be like this? Had I made him what he was?

And yet—even as I was thinking this, I could feel myself opening my mouth, could feel the words floating from me as if I had no control over them, could feel myself raising my voice above their exclamations of horror and righteousness, their declaring to themselves what monsters the state had become, how the woman's civil liberties had been violated, how there was a price to be paid for the control of these illnesses, but it couldn't be the price of our collective humanity. Soon they would be trading the same stories that were always traded by people like this in conversations like these: The fact that different races were sent to different camps, with Blacks going to one camp and whites to another, and the rest of us, presumably, to a third. The fact that women were being offered up to five million dollars to donate their healthy babies to be experimented on. The fact that the government was *giving* people the sickness (through the plumbing, through baby formula, through aspirin) in order to eliminate them later. The fact that the disease wasn't an accident at all but something engineered in a lab.

"That story isn't true," I said.

They went quiet, immediately. "Charles," Nathaniel began, warningly, but David sat up, instantly ready to fight. "What do you mean?" he asked.

"It's not true," I said. "That's not what's happening at those camps."

"How do you know?"

"Because. Even if the government were capable of that, they wouldn't be able to keep things like that hidden from the public for long."

"You're so fucking naïve!"

"*David!*" This was Nathaniel. "Don't talk to your father like that!"

For the briefest of moments, I was happy: How long had it been since Nathaniel had defended me so unthinkingly, so passionately? It felt like a declaration of love. But, no, I barreled on. "Think about it, David," I said, hating myself even as I did. "Why would we *stop* giving people medicine? This isn't like how it was six years ago— there's plenty of medicine available. And why even have the stopgap of—what did you call it, a 'middle-stage' building? Why not just send everyone straight to the end-stage building?"

"But—"

"What you're describing is a death camp, and we don't have death camps here."

"Your faith in this country is touching," said Aubrey, quietly, and for a moment, I was almost dizzy with rage. *He* was patronizing *me*, someone whose house was stuffed full of stolen goods from my country? "Charles," said Nathaniel, standing abruptly, "we should go," at the same time that Norris put his hand on Aubrey's. "Aubrey," he said, "that's not fair."

But I didn't turn on Aubrey. I didn't. I instead spoke only to David. "And, David, if that story *were* true, then you'd have identified the wrong villain. The enemy here isn't the administration, or the army, or the Health Ministry—it's the woman herself. Yes: a woman who *knew* her baby was sick, who bothers to take her into the hospital, and then, instead of letting her get treated, steals her away. And she goes where? Back on the subway or the bus; back to her apartment building. How many streets does she walk down along the way? How many people does she jostle past? How many people does her baby breathe on, how many spores does she spread? How many units are in her building? How many people live there? How many of those people have comorbidities? How many are children, or sick, or disabled?

"How many of them does she tell: 'My baby's sick; I think she has the infection; you should keep away'? Does she call the health department, report that there's an illness in the household? Does she think of anyone else? Or does she think only of herself, only of her own family? Of course, you could say that that's what a parent does. But it's because of that, *because* of that understandable selfishness, that the government *has* to involve itself, don't you see? It's to keep all the people around her safe, all the people she herself didn't give a damn about, all the people who'll lose their children because of her, that they've *had* to intervene."

The baby had been very still and silent throughout my speech, but now he shrank, as if I'd smacked him. "You said 'we,'" he said, and something, some quality in the room, shifted.

"What?" I asked.

"You said 'that *we've* had to intervene.'"

"No, I didn't. I said 'that *they've* had to intervene.'"

"No. You said 'we.' Holy shit. Holy *shit*. You're in on this, aren't you? Holy shit. You helped plan these camps, didn't you?" And then, to Nathaniel, "Dad. *Dad.* Do you hear this? Do you hear this? He's involved! He's behind this!"

We both looked at Nathaniel, who was sitting there, slightly openmouthed, looking back and forth between us. He blinked. "David," he began.

But now David was standing, as tall and skinny as Nathaniel is, pointing at me. "You're one of them," he said, his voice high and excited. "I *know* you are. I always knew you were a collaborator. I always knew you were behind these camps. I *knew* it."

"David!" Nathaniel called out, anguished.

"Fuck you," said the baby, clearly, looking at me, vibrating with passion. "Fuck you." He wheeled, then, on Nathaniel. "And fuck you, too," he said. "You know I'm right. We've talked about this, how he's working for the state. And now you won't even back me up." And before any of us could do anything, he was running to the door, opening it; the decontamination chamber made a loud sucking noise as he left.

"David!" Nathaniel yelled, and was running to the door himself when Aubrey—who had been sitting with Norris on the sofa watching us, their eyes flicking between us, gripping each other's hands as if they were at the theater and we were actors in some particularly charged play—stood. "Nathaniel," he said. "Don't worry. He won't go far. Our security guys will watch him." (This is another phenomenon here: people hiring security guards, in full protective gear, to patrol their property all night and all day.)

"I don't know if he brought his papers," Nathaniel continued, distressed—we had reminded David again and again and again that he had to have his identity card and health certificate on him whenever he left the apartment, but he kept forgetting.

"It's okay," Aubrey said. "I promise you. He won't get far, and the team will watch him. I'll go call them now," and he left for his study.

And then there were only the three of us. "We should go," I said. "Let's get David, and we'll go," but Norris put his hand on my arm. "I wouldn't wait for him," he said, gently. "Let him stay here tonight, Charles. Security will bring him in and we'll take care of him. We'll have one of them take him home tomorrow." I looked at Nathaniel, who gave me a small nod, and so I nodded, too.

Aubrey returned, and there were apologies and thanks, but only in a muted sort of way. As we walked out, I turned and saw Norris, who looked back at me with an expression I couldn't understand. Then the door closed and we were out in the night, the air hot and humid and still. We switched on our masks' dehumidifiers.

"David!" we called. "David!"

But no one answered.

"Do we leave?" I asked Nathaniel, even after Aubrey called to tell us that David was in the security team's little stone hut that they'd appended to the back of their house, safe with one of the guards.

He sighed and shrugged. "I suppose," he said, tiredly. "He won't come home with us, anyway. Not tonight."

We both looked south, toward the Square. For a while, neither of us spoke. There was a bulldozer, the operator's way lit by a single bright light, pushing the remains of the latest shantytown into a hill of plastic and plywood. "Do you remember the first time we came to New York?" I asked him. "We were staying in that shitty hotel up near Lincoln Center, and we walked all the way down to TriBeCa. We stopped in this park and had ice cream. There was that piano that someone had set up under the arch, and you sat down and played—"

"Charles," Nathaniel said, in that same gentle voice. "I don't really want to talk now. I just want to go home."

For some reason, this was the most upsetting thing I'd experienced all night. Not Aubrey and Norris's diminished state; not how clear it was that David hated me. It would have been better if Nathaniel had been mad at me, had blamed me, had confronted me. Then I could fight back. We had always fought well. But this resignation, this tiredness—I didn't know what to do with it.

We'd parked on University, and now we began to walk. There was no one in the streets, of course. I remembered a night about, oh, ten years ago, when I was still accepting that Aubrey and Norris were going to be part of our lives, because they were a part of

Nathaniel's. They had had a dinner party, and we had left David—only seven, really just a baby—with a sitter and had taken the subway south. The party was all Aubrey and Norris's rich friends, but a couple of them had boyfriends or husbands around our age, and even I had had a good time, and after we left, we had decided that we would walk home. It had been a long walk, but it had been March, and so it had been perfect weather, not too hot, and we had both been a little drunk, and at 23rd Street, we had stopped at Madison Park and made out on a bench, among other people also making out on other benches. Nathaniel had been happy that night because he thought we'd made a bunch of new friends. This was when we were both still pretending that we'd only be in New York for a few years.

Now we walked in silence, and as I was unlocking the car, Nathaniel stopped me, turning me toward him. This evening was the first time in months that he had touched me so much, so deliberately. "Charles," he said, "were you?"

"Was I what?" I asked him.

He took a breath. His helmet's dehumidifier filter needed cleaning, and as he breathed, his face disappeared and appeared as the screen fogged over and then cleared itself. "Were you involved in setting up those camps?" he asked. He looked away, looked back at me. "Are you still involved with them?"

I didn't know what to say. I had seen the reports myself, of course—the ones published in the paper and shown on television, as well as the other reports, the ones you've seen, too. I had been in a Committee meeting the day they screened the footage that had come out of Rohwer, and someone in the room, one of the lawyers from Justice, had gasped when she saw what had happened in the babies' quarters, and shortly after had left the room. I hadn't been able to sleep that night, either. Of course I wished that we hadn't had a need for the camps at all. But we did, and I couldn't change that. All I could do was try to protect us. I couldn't apologize for that; I couldn't explain it. I had volunteered for this job. I couldn't now disavow it because things were happening that I wish hadn't.

But how to explain any of this to Nathaniel? He wouldn't understand; he would never understand. And so I just stood there, my mouth open, suspended between speech and silence, between apologizing and lying.

"I think you should stay at the lab tonight," he said at last, still in that same soft voice.

"Oh," I said, "all right," and as I did, he took a step backward, as if I had slugged him in the chest. I don't know: Maybe he had expected me to fight with him, to plead with him, to deny everything, to lie to him. But it was as if, by acquiescing, I was also confirming everything he hadn't wanted to believe. He looked at me again, but his face screen was getting foggier and foggier, and finally, he got in the car and drove north.

I walked. At 14th Street, I stopped to let a tank pass me, and then a brigade of foot soldiers, all in protective gear, the new military-issue uniforms in which the face screen is a one-way mirror, so that when you talk to anyone wearing one, all you see is yourself staring back. On and on I walked, past the barricade at 23rd Street, where a soldier directed me east to avoid Madison Park, which had been contained beneath an air-conditioned geodesic dome, and where the corpses were stored until they could be taken by one of the crematoriums. Above each corner of the park, a drone camera twirled, its strobes briefly illuminating outlines of the cardboard coffins, stacked four high in precise rows. As I crossed Park Avenue, I approached a man crossing from the other side; as he neared me, he lowered his eyes. Have you encountered this too, this general unwillingness to make eye contact, as if the illness is spread not by breath but by looking each other in the face?

Finally, I was back at Rockefeller, and I took a shower and made a bed for myself on my sofa. But I couldn't sleep, and after a couple of hours, I got up and raised the blackout shades and watched the morgue helicopters make their deliveries to Roosevelt Island, their blades flashing as the klieg lights swooped over them. Here, the crematoriums never stop, but they've suspended barge transport because of the waterway closures—the hope is that they'll deter those rafts of climate refugees, who were being dropped off late at night at the mouth of the Hudson or the East River and made to swim for shore.

And now I am very tired, tireder than I think I've ever been. Tonight, all of us are sleeping in separate places. You, in London. Olivier, in Marseilles. My husband, four blocks north. My son, three miles south. Me, here in my lab. How I wish I were with one of you, any of you. I have kept one shade open, so on the wall opposite, a square of light flickers and vanishes, flickers and vanishes, flickers and vanishes, like a code meant only for me.

Love, Me

Dear Peter,   September 20, 2058

Today was Norris's funeral. I met Nathaniel and David at the Friends meeting house on Rutherford Place. It had been three months since I had seen David, a week since I had seen Nathaniel, and out of respect for Norris, we were all excruciatingly polite with one another. Nathaniel had called me beforehand asking me not to try to hug David hello, and I didn't, but he surprised us both by patting me on the back a little and grunting a bit.

During the service, which was small and modest, I stared at David's face. He was sitting in the row in front of me, one seat to the left, and I was able to study his profile, his long bony nose, the new way he was wearing his hair, which made his head look like it was bristling with thorns. He had begun his new school, the one Aubrey had convinced him to attend after he dropped out of the other school Aubrey had convinced him to attend two years ago, and as far as I knew, there were no complaints, from them or from him. Granted, the school year was only three weeks old.

I didn't know most of the people at the service—there were some I recognized by sight, from years-ago dinners and parties—but the feeling was of emptiness: They had lost more friends than I had realized in '56, and although the room was half filled, there was also the persistent and troubling sensation that something, someone, was missing.

After, Nathaniel and the baby and I went back to Aubrey's house, where a few other people had gathered as well; Aubrey wore his decontamination suit so his guests could remove theirs. Over the past year or so, as Norris slowly died, they had begun keeping the house dim, lighting the rooms with candles. It helped, somewhat— both Aubrey and the house looked less careworn in that gloom— but also made stepping into that space feel like entering some other era, one before electricity was invented. Or maybe it was that the house now felt less occupied by humans than by some other kind of animal: moles, perhaps, creatures with small, poor, beady eyes that couldn't bear the full reality of sunlight. I thought of Nathaniel's students, Hiram and Ezra, now eleven years old, still living in their shadowed world.

Eventually, only the four of us remained. Nathaniel and David had offered to spend the night in the house, and Aubrey had accepted. I'd take advantage of their absence at the apartment to pick up a few things and take them back to the RU dormitory, where I'm still living.

For a while, we were all silent. Aubrey had leaned his head against the back of the sofa and eventually closed his eyes. "David," Nathaniel whispered, signaling to him that he should help rotate Aubrey on the sofa so he could lie flat, and the baby was standing to help him when Aubrey began to speak.

"Do you remember that conversation we had shortly after the first person in New York was reported diagnosed in '50?" he asked, his eyes still closed. None of us answered. "You, Charles—I remember asking you if this was the one we'd been waiting for, the sickness that would eliminate us all, and you said, 'No, but it'll be a good one.' Do you remember that?"

His voice was gentle, but I cringed anyway. "Yes," I said, "I do." I heard Nathaniel sigh, a soft, sad sound.

"Mmm," he said. There was another pause. "You were right, as it turns out. Because then '56 came.

"I never told you this," he said, "but in November of '50, an old friend of ours contacted us. Well, he was more Norris's friend than mine, someone he'd known since college, when they had dated for a brief period. His name was Wolf.

"By this point, we'd been living out at Frog's Pond Way for about three months. We thought, as did many people—even your lot, Charles—that we'd be somehow safer out there, that it was better to be away from the city, with all its crowds and filth. This was after the lootings had begun; everyone was scared to leave their houses. It wasn't as bad as '56—you didn't have people lunging at you in the street, trying to cough at you and infect you because they wanted you to get sick as well. But it was bad. You remember.

"Anyway, one night, Norris told me that Wolf had gotten in touch with him; he was in the area and wanted to know if he could come see us. Well. We were taking all the recommendations seriously. Norris had asthma, and the reason we'd gone out to Long Island to begin with was to avoid running into other people. So we decided that we'd tell Wolf that we'd love to see him, but for his sake as well as ours, we didn't think it was safe, though once things calmed down we'd love to get together.

"So Norris sends him that message, but Wolf writes back immediately: He doesn't *want* to come see us; he *needs* to come see us. He needs our help. Norris asks if we can video-chat, but he insists: He needs to see us.

"What could we do? The next day, we get a text at noon: 'I'm outside.' We go outside. For a while, we don't see anything. Then we hear Wolf call Norris's name, and we walk down the path, but we still don't see anything. Then we hear Wolf again, and we proceed a little farther down the path. This happens a few more times, and then we hear Wolf say 'Stop.'

"We do. Nothing happens. And then we hear some twigs being crunched behind that big poplar near the guardhouse, and Wolf steps out into the open.

"It's immediately clear that he's very sick. His face is covered with sores; he's skeletal. He's using a magnolia branch as a cane, but he doesn't quite have the strength to lift it, so it kind of drags behind him like a broom. He's carrying a small knapsack. He's holding up his pants with one hand: He's wearing a belt, but it doesn't help.

"Norris and I immediately step backward. It's obvious Wolf's nearing the end stage of the disease and is therefore highly contagious.

"He says, 'I wouldn't come here if I had somewhere else to go. You know I wouldn't. But I need help. I'm not going to live much longer. I know what an imposition this is. But I'm hoping—I'm hoping you'll let me die here.'

"He had escaped from one of the centers. Later, we'd learn that he'd approached a few other people, and all of them had sent him away. He said, 'I won't ask to come inside. But I thought—I thought maybe I could stay in the pool cottage? I won't ask you for anything else. But I want to die indoors, in a house.'

"I didn't know what to say. I could feel Norris just behind me, gripping my arm. Finally, I said, 'I need to talk to Norris,' and Wolf nodded and retreated behind the poplar again, as if to give us privacy, and Norris and I walked back up the path. He looked at me, and I looked at him, and neither of us said anything. We didn't need to—we knew what we would do. I had my wallet with me, and I took out everything I had—a little more than five hundred dollars. And then we walked again toward the tree, and Wolf reappeared.

" 'Wolf,' I said, 'I'm sorry. I'm so sorry. But we can't. Norris is vulnerable, you know that. We can't, we just can't. I'm so sorry.' I invoked you, Charles. I said, 'A friend of ours has connections in the administration; he can get you help, he can get you into a better center.' I wasn't sure if there *was* such a thing, even, as a 'better center,' but I promised it. Then I put the money down, about a foot away from us. 'I can get you more, if you need it,' I said.

"He didn't say anything. He just stood there, panting, looking down at the money, swaying slightly on his feet. And then I grabbed Norris's hand, and we hurried back to the house—by the last hundred feet, we were running, running as if Wolf had the strength to pursue us, as if he'd suddenly soar into the air like a witch and block the doorway. Once inside, we bolted the door and then went about the house checking every window and every lock, as if Wolf would suddenly charge through one of them and fill the house with his disease.

"But do you know what the worst part was? How *angry* Norris and I were. We were angry that Wolf had gotten sick, that he had come to us, that he had asked for our help, that he had put us in such a position. That was what we said to ourselves that night as we gorged ourselves, all the window shades drawn, all the security systems armed, the pool house—as if he might even now go there—padlocked shut: How *dare* he. How *dare* he make us feel that way, how *dare* he make us say no to him. That was what we thought. A friend was helpless and afraid, and that was how we reacted.

"Things were never quite the same between us after that. Oh, I know everything always looked fine. But something changed. It was as if our connection was no longer founded in love but in shame, in this terrible secret we had, in this terrible, inhumane thing we had done together. And I blame Wolf for that as well. Every day, we stayed indoors, scanning the property with binoculars. We offered the security team double pay to come back, but they said no, and so we prepared ourselves for a siege, a one-man siege. We kept all the shades drawn, the shutters closed. We lived as if we were in a horror film, like at any moment we might hear a thump against one of the windows and draw the shade to find Wolf plastered against it. We *were* able to convince the local police to monitor the death tolls for the area, but when the word came two weeks later that Wolf had been found alongside the highway, dead for apparently several days, we still weren't able to give up our watch: We stopped answering our phones, we stopped checking our messages, we stopped making ourselves available to anyone, because if we weren't in contact with the outside world, then nothing would be asked of us, and we would be safe.

"After we were given the all-clear, we returned to Washington Square. But we never went back to Water Mill. Nathaniel, you asked once why we never went out to Frog's Pond Way. This is why. We also never spoke of Wolf again. It wasn't something we had to agree on; we just both knew not to. Over the years, we tried to make reparations for our guilt. We gave to charities that helped the sick; we gave to hospitals; we gave to activist groups fighting against the camps. But when Norris was diagnosed with leukemia, the first thing he said after the doctor had left the room was 'It's punishment for Wolf.' I know he believed it. In his final days, when he was delirious from the drugs, it wasn't my name he repeated, but Wolf's. And even though I'm telling you this story like I don't, I believe it, too. That one day—one day, Wolf will come for me, too."

We were all quiet. Even the baby, who was consistent in his moral absolutism, was somber and silent. Nathaniel sighed. "Aubrey," he began, but Aubrey interrupted him.

"I had to confess to someone," he said, "which is part of why I'm telling you. But the other reason I'm telling you is because— David, I know you have a lot of resentment toward your father, and I understand it. But fear makes many of us do things that we regret, things we never thought we were capable of doing. You're so young; you've spent almost your entire life living alongside death and the possibility of death—you've become inured to it, which is heart-breaking. So you won't quite understand what I mean.

"But when you're older, you do anything you can to try to stay alive. Sometimes you're not even aware you're doing it. Something, some instinct, some worse self, takes over—you lose who you are. Not everyone does. But many of us do.

"I suppose what I'm trying to say is—you should forgive your father." He looked at me. "*I* forgive you, Charles. For—for what-ever it is you've done with—with the camps. I wanted to tell you that. Norris never blamed you like I did, so he had nothing to for-give, and no forgiveness to ask. But I do."

I realized I was supposed to say something. "Thank you, Aubrey," I said, to a man who had hung the most valuable and sacred objects from my country on his walls like they were posters in a college dorm room and just two years earlier accused me of being a stooge of the American government. "I appreciate that."

He sighed, and so did Nathaniel, as if I had somehow failed to play my part. Across the room, David sat with his face turned from us, so that I couldn't see his expression. He loved Aubrey. He respected him. I could imagine what he was thinking, and I felt for him.

I wasn't so selfish that I intended to actually ask him for his forgiveness right then. But even before I could stop myself, I was dreaming of our reunion: I'd move back in, and Nathaniel would love me again, and the baby would stop being so angry with me, and we would be a family once more.

I didn't say anything, however. I just got up and said goodbye to everyone and went to our apartment as I'd planned, and then back to the dormitory.

I have heard—we both have heard—many terrible stories about what humans did to other humans over the past two years. Aubrey's was not the worst, not even close to the worst. Over those months, there were reports of parents abandoning their children on subways, of a man who shot his parents in the back of their heads as they sat in their yard, of a woman who wheeled her dying husband of forty years to the scrapyard near the Lincoln Tunnel and left him there. But I guess what struck me the most about Aubrey's story wasn't even the story itself but, rather, how small his and Norris's life had become. I saw them clearly: The two of them in that house I used to so resent and envy, every shutter closed to blot out the light, huddling in a corner together to make themselves small, hoping that, if they did, then the great eye of illness would fail to see them, would leave them be, as if they could elude capture altogether.

Love, C.

Dear Peter,   October 30, 2059

Thank you for the belated birthday message; I'd completely forgotten. Fifty-five. Separated. Hated by my own son and much of the rest of the Western world (what I do, if not me precisely). Somehow fully transitioned from once-promising scientist into shadowy government operative. What else is there to say? Not much, I guess.

There was a rather wan celebration at Aubrey's house, where Nathaniel and the baby are now living full-time. I know I haven't mentioned this, and I suppose it's because it just happened, without either Nate or me really being aware of it. First he and David began spending more time downtown to keep Aubrey company in the weeks following Norris's death. He'd text me when this was happening, so I'd know I could go back to our apartment and stay there

for a night. I'd wander the rooms, opening the baby's desk drawers and rooting around; looking through Nathaniel's sock drawer. I
wasn't searching for anything in particular—I knew that Nathaniel
had no secrets, and that David would have taken his with him. I was
just looking. I refolded some of David's shirts; I stood over Nathaniel's underwear, inhaling their scent.

Eventually, I began noticing that things were disappearing—
David's sneakers, the books on Nathaniel's bedside table. One night,
I arrived home and the ficus tree was gone. It was almost like something in a cartoon; I left during the day and all these objects scurried
out while I wasn't looking. But, of course, they were being moved
down to Washington Square. After about five months of this slow-
drip departure, Nathaniel texted me that I could move back in, into
our home, if I wanted, and although I had been planning to refuse
him on principle—every few weeks, we briefly discussed the possibility of him buying me out of the apartment so I could find my
own, while being fully aware that he had no money to do so and neither did I—I was too weary by then, and so back in I moved. They
didn't take everything down to Aubrey's, though, and in my more
self-pitying moments, I am able to see the symbolism in this. The
baby's old picture books, a few jackets of Nathaniel's it's now far too
hot to wear, a pot permanently singed by years of burned meals—
and me: all the detritus of Nathaniel's and David's lives; all the stuff
they didn't want.

Nathaniel and I have been making an effort to speak once a week.
Sometimes these interactions go well. Other times, not. We don't
fight, exactly, but every conversation, no matter how pleasant, is a
brittle sheet of ice, and just beneath is a dark, freezing pool of water:
decades of resentment, of blame. Much of that blame involves David,
but so does much of our affinity. We both worry about him, though
Nathaniel is more sympathetic to him than I am. He'll be twenty
next month, and we don't know what to do with or for him—he has
no high-school degree, no intention of attending college, no intention of getting a job. Every day, Nathaniel tells me, he disappears
for hours, and only returns for dinner and a game of chess with
Aubrey before disappearing again. At least, Nathaniel says, he's still

tender with Aubrey; with us, he rolls his eyes and snorts when we ask him about finding a job, about finishing his degree, but he listens patiently to Aubrey's occasional mild lectures; before he leaves at night, he helps Aubrey climb the stairs to his bedroom.

Tonight, we were having cake when the decontam chamber slapped close, and David appeared. I never know what kind of mood the baby will be in when he sees me: Will he be scornful, rolling his eyes at whatever I say? Will he be sarcastic, asking me how many people I've been responsible for killing this week? Will he be, unexpectedly, shy, almost puppyish, bashfully shrugging when I give him a compliment, when I tell him how much I miss him? Every time, I tell him I miss him; every time, I tell him I love him. But I don't ask for his forgiveness, which I know he wants, because there is nothing for him to forgive.

"Hello, David," I said to him, and watched an uncertain expression cross his face: It occurred to me that he could as little predict his reaction to seeing me as I could.

He settled on sarcasm. "I didn't know we were having international war criminals over for dinner tonight," he said.

"David," said Nathaniel, wearily. "Stop. I told you—it's your father's birthday today."

Then, before he could say anything more, Aubrey added, gently, "Come sit, David, come spend some time with us." And then, when David still hesitated, "There's lots of extra food."

He sat, and Edmund brought him a plate, and the three of us watched for a while as he swiftly demolished it, leaned back, and belched.

"*David*," Nathaniel and I said as one, and the baby suddenly grinned, looking at us in turn, which made Nathaniel and me look at each other as well, and for a moment, all of us were smiling together.

"Can't help yourselves, can you?" asked David, almost fondly, addressing Nathaniel and me as a unit, and we smiled again: at him, at each other. Across from us, the baby forked into his carrot cake. "How old are you, Pops?" he asked.

"Fifty-five," I said, ignoring the "Pops" provocation, which I hated, and which he knew I hated. But it had been years since he had called me "Papa," and then another period of years in which he had called me nothing at all.

"Jesus," said the baby, but with genuine excitement. "Fifty-five! That's so old!"

"Ancient," I agreed, smiling, and next to David, Aubrey laughed. "An infant," he corrected. "A baby."

This would have been the perfect time for David to begin one of his rants—about the average age of the children removed to the camps, about the death rate among nonwhite children, about how the government was using this illness as an opportunity to kill off Black and Native American people, which was why all the recent diseases had been allowed to spread unchecked in the first place—but he didn't, just rolled his eyes, but good-naturedly, and cut himself another slice of cake. Before he began eating it, though, he untied the bandanna around his neck, and as he did, I saw that the entire right side of his neck was covered by an enormous tattoo.

"Jesus!" I said, and Nathaniel, understanding what I'd seen, spoke my name, warningly. I had already been given a list of the many topics I wasn't allowed to mention to David or inquire about, among them his degree, his plans, his future, how he spent his day, his politics, his ambitions, and his friends. But he hadn't mentioned huge disfiguring tattoos, and I rushed to the other side of the table, as if it might disappear if I didn't examine it in the next five seconds. I pulled down the neck of David's T-shirt and looked at it: It was an eye, about six inches wide, large and menacing, and radiating from it were rays of light; written in Gothic script beneath it were the words "Ex Obscuris Lux."

I let go of his shirt and stepped back. David was smirking. "Did you join the American Academy of Ophthalmology?" I asked him.

He stopped smiling and looked confused. "Huh?" he asked.

"'Ex obscuris lux,'" I said. "'From darkness, light.' That's their motto."

For a moment, he looked confused again. Then he recovered himself. "No," he said, tersely, and I could tell he was embarrassed, and then angry because he was embarrassed.

"Well, what's that for, then?" I asked.

"Charles," Nathaniel said, sighing, "not now."

"What do you mean, 'not now'? I can't even ask my son why he got an enormous"—I nearly said "hideous"—"tattoo on his neck?"

"It's because I'm a member of the light," David said, proudly, and when I didn't answer, he rolled his eyes again. "Jesus, Pops," he said, "*The Light*. It's a group."

"What kind of group?" I asked.

"Charles," Nathaniel said.

"Oh, Nate, stop with the *Charles, Charles*—he's my son, too. I can ask him what I want." I looked back at David. "What kind of group?"

He was smirking again, and I wanted to slap him. "A political group," he said.

"What kind of political group?" I asked.

"A group that tries to undo the work you've been doing," he said.

At this point, Peter, you would have been proud of me. I had one of those rare moments in which I foresaw, perfectly and vividly, where this conversation would lead. The baby would try to provoke me. I would be provoked. I would say something rash. He would respond in kind. Nathaniel would stand on the sidelines, wringing his hands. Aubrey would remain slumped in his seat, watching us with sorrow and pity and a bit of revulsion—that he should have us in his life, and that the three of us should have come to such an unhappy end.

But I did none of those things. Instead—in a display of composure not even I thought myself capable of—I simply said I was happy he'd found his mission in life, and that I wished him and his comrades all the best in their struggle. And then I thanked Aubrey and Nathaniel for dinner, and I walked out. "Oh, Charles," Nathaniel said, following me to the door. "Charles, don't leave."

I pulled him into the parlor. "Nathaniel," I said, "does he hate me?"

"Who?" he asked, though he knew perfectly well who I meant. Then he sighed. "No, of course not, Charles," he said. "He's going through a phase. And—and he's passionate about his beliefs. You know this. He doesn't hate you."

"But *you* hate me," I said.

"No, I don't," he said. "I hate what you did, Charles. I don't hate *you*."

"I did what needed to be done, Natey," I said.

"Charles," said Nathaniel, "I'm not going to discuss this with you right now. The point is, you're his father. You always will be."

Somehow, this wasn't very comforting, and after I left (I had hoped Nathaniel would try harder to make me stay, but he hadn't), I stood at the north entrance of Washington Square and watched the most recent generation of shantytown dwellers move about. A few were bathing in the fountain, and there was a family—two parents and a little girl—who had built a small fire next to the arch, where they were roasting an unidentified animal over the flames. "Is it done yet?" the little girl kept asking, excitedly. "Is it done, Daddy? Is it done yet?" "Almost, sweetheart," the father said. "Almost, almost." He pinched the tail off the creature and handed it to the girl, who squealed with joy and immediately began gnawing at it, and I turned away. There were about two hundred people living in the Square, and although they knew that one night their homes would be bull-dozed away, they kept coming: It was safer to be here than beneath a bridge or in a tunnel. Still, I didn't know how they slept, with those floodlights beating down on them, but I suppose people get used to anything. Many of the dwellers wear sunglasses even at night, or a piece of black gauze tied around their eyes. The majority of them don't have protective helmets, so from afar, they look like an army of ghosts, their entire faces wrapped in cotton.

Back in the apartment, I looked up The Light, which was much as I suspected: an anti-government, anti-science group dedicated to "revealing the truth of state manipulation and ending the age of plagues." It appears to be small, even by these groups' standards; no major attacks to their name and no major claimed incidents. But I sent an email to my contact in Washington anyway, asking them to send me their full dossier—I didn't say why I was asking.

Peter, I never ask you for these favors. But will you find out what you can, whatever you can? I'm sorry to ask. I really am. I wouldn't unless I had to.

I know I can't stop him. But maybe I can help him. I have to try. Don't I?

All my love. Charles

Dear Peter,   July 7, 2062

This is going to be a brief one, because I have to be down in Washington in six hours. But I wanted to write while I had a few minutes.

It's unbearably hot here.

The new state will be announced today at four p.m. eastern time. The original plan was to announce on July 3, but everyone agreed that people should be allowed to celebrate a final Independence Day. The thinking was that if we announced now, at the end of the day, it would be easier to lock down certain parts of the country before the weekend begins, and then give everyone a couple of days for the shock to wear off before the markets reopen on Monday. By the time you read this, it'll already have happened.

Thank you for your counsel over these past months, dear Peter. In the end, I took your advice and turned down a ministry position: I'll remain behind the scenes after all, and what I give up in influence I gain in safety. Anyway, I have enough influence regardless—I've asked Intelligence to put a tracker on David now that The Light has become so problematic, and there are plainclothes guards stationed outside Aubrey's house to protect him and Nathaniel just in case the rioting gets as bad as they fear. Aubrey isn't doing well at all—the cancer's metastasized to his liver, and Nathaniel says Aubrey's doctor thinks he only has another six to nine months.

I'll call you on your secure line tonight my time, early tomorrow yours. Wish me luck. Love to you and Olivier—

Charles

PART V

Spring 2094

In the weeks following our initial meeting, we met more and more. At first it was just a coincidence: The Sunday after we met at the storyteller's session, I was walking around the Square when I became aware of someone behind me. Of course, there were many people behind me, and ahead of me, too—I was walking in the center of the group—but this presence felt different, and when I turned, there he was again, smiling at me.

"Hello, Charlie," he said, smiling.

The smiling made me nervous. Back when Grandfather was my age, everyone smiled all the time. Grandfather said that was something Americans were known for: smiling. He wasn't an American himself, although he became one. But I didn't smile very often, and neither did anyone I know.

"Hello," I said.

He joined me, and we walked together. I had been worried he would try to have a conversation, but he didn't, and we made three laps around the Square. Then he said it had been nice to see me, and maybe he'd see me at the next story session, and then he smiled again and walked west before I even had a chance to figure out what to say in response.

The following Saturday, I returned to the storyteller. I hadn't thought I was hoping to see him, but when I did, sitting in the same spot in the back row where we'd sat on the day we met, a funny feeling came over me, and I hurried the last few feet, in case someone should take my place. Then I stopped. What if he didn't want to see me? But then he turned and saw me and smiled and waved me over, patting the ground next to him with his hand. "Hello, Charlie," he said, as I approached him.

"Hello," I said.

His name was David. He had told me that the first time we met. "Oh," I had said, "my father's name was David."

"Oh, really?" he had asked. "So was mine."

"Oh," I'd said. It seemed like there was something else I should say, and finally I said, "That's a lot of Davids," and then he smiled, very wide, and even laughed a little. "That's true," he said, "that *is* a lot of Davids. You're funny, aren't you, Charlie?"—which was one of those questions I knew wasn't really a question, and besides, wasn't even true. No one had ever told me I was funny before.

This time, I had brought some tofu skin that I had skimmed and dried myself and cut into triangles, and a container of nutritional yeast to dip them into. As the storyteller was settling into his folding chair, I held out the bag to David. "You can have some," I said, and then I was worried I sounded too gruff, too unfriendly, when really I was just nervous. "If you want," I added.

He looked into the bag, and I was afraid he'd laugh at me and my snack. But he just took out a chip, and dipped it into the yeast, and crunched it. "Thanks," he whispered, as the storyteller began, "these are good."

In that day's story, the husband and wife and their two children wake one morning to discover a bird in their apartment. This wasn't very realistic either, as birds were rare, but the storyteller did a good job of describing how the bird kept frustrating their attempts to catch it, and how father and son and mother and daughter kept crashing into one another as they ran about the house with a pillow-case. Finally, the bird is caught, and the son suggests they eat it, but the daughter knows better, and the whole family takes the bird to the local animal center, just as they're supposed to, and later they're rewarded with three extra protein coupons, which the mother uses to buy some protein patties.

After the story was over, we walked to the northern end of the Square. "What did you think?" David asked, and I didn't say anything, because I was embarrassed to admit that I had felt betrayed by the story. I had thought that the husband and wife were just husband and wife, like my husband and me, and yet suddenly they had two children, a boy and a girl, which meant they weren't like my husband and me after all. They weren't just a man and a woman: They were a father and a mother.

But it was silly to say any of this, so instead I said, "It was okay."

"I thought it was dumb," David said, and I looked up at him. "Whose apartment is that big that they can run around in it? Who's such a goody-goody that they'd actually take the bird into the center?"

This was thrilling to hear, but also alarming. I looked down at my shoes. "But it's the law."

"Of course it's the law, but he's a storyteller," David said. "Does he really expect us to believe that, if a big, plump, juicy pigeon flew into any of our windows, we wouldn't just kill it, pluck it, and put it straight into the oven?" I looked up then, and saw that he was looking back at me with a crooked little smile.

I didn't know what to say. "Well, it's just a story," I said.

"That's exactly my point," he said, like I had agreed with him, and then he gave me a little salute. "Bye, Charlie. Thanks for the snack and company." And then he left, walking westward, back to Little Eight.

He hadn't said he would see me next week, but when I returned the following Saturday, there he was again, standing outside the storyteller's tent, and again, I got that same strange feeling in my stomach.

"I thought we'd take a walk instead, if that's okay," he said, even though it was very hot, so hot I'd had to wear my cooling suit. He, however, was in his same gray shirt and pants, his same gray cap, and didn't look hot at all. He spoke as if we had made plans to meet here, as if we had an arrangement that he was now changing.

As we walked, I remembered to ask him the question I'd been wondering about all week. "I don't see you at the shuttle stop anymore," I said.

"That's true," he said. "My shift changed. I catch the 07:30 now."

"Oh," I said. Then I said, "My husband catches the 07:30, too."

"Really," David said. "Where does he work?"

"The Pond," I said.

"Ah," said David. "I work at the Farm."

It wasn't worth asking if they knew each other, because the Farm was the biggest state project in the prefecture, with dozens of scientists and hundreds of techs, and what's more, Pond employees stayed isolated in the Pond, and rarely had any reason to encounter anyone who worked in the larger enterprise.

"I'm a bromeliad specialist," said David, although I hadn't asked, because asking someone what they did wasn't done. "That's what it's called, but really, I'm just a gardener." This was unusual, too: both to describe your work but also to make it sound less important than it was. "I help crossbreed the specimens we have, but mostly, I'm just there to take care of the plants." His voice was cheerful as he said this, matter-of-fact, but I suddenly felt the need to defend his own job to him.

"That's important work," I said. "We need all the research from the Farm we can get."

"I suppose," he said. "Not that I'm doing any of the actual research myself. But I do love the plants, as silly as that sounds."

"I love the pinkies, too," I said, and as I did, I realized that it was true. I *did* love the pinkies. They were so fragile and their lives had been so short; they were poor, unformed things, and had been created only to die and be pulled apart and examined, and then they were incinerated and forgotten.

"The pinkies?" he asked. "What are those?"

So I explained a little about what I did, and how I prepared them, and how the scientists got impatient when I didn't deliver them on time, which made him laugh, and his laughter made me flustered, because I didn't want him to think I was complaining about the scientists, or making fun of them, because they did essential work, and I said so. "No, I don't think that you're disparaging them," he said. "It's just—they're such important people, but really, they're people, you know? They get impatient and in bad moods, just like the rest of us." I had never thought about the scientists like that before, as people, and so I didn't say anything.

"How long have you been married?" David asked.

This was a very forward question, and for a moment, I didn't know what to say. "Maybe I shouldn't have asked," he said, looking at me. "You have to forgive me. Where I come from, people talk much more openly."

"Oh," I said. "Where are you from?"

He was from Prefecture Five, one of the southern prefectures, but he didn't have an accent. Sometimes people transferred prefectures, but they usually did so only when they had unusual or in-demand skills. This made me wonder whether David was actually more important than he was saying; it would explain why he was here, not only in Prefecture Two but in Zone Eight.

"I've been married almost six years," I said, and then, because I knew what he was going to ask next, I added, "We're sterile."

"I'm sorry, Charlie," he said. His voice was gentle, but it wasn't pitying, and, unlike some people, he didn't turn away from me, as if my sterility were something contagious. "Was it an illness?" he asked.

This too was very forward, but I was getting used to him, and I wasn't as shocked as I would have been had someone else asked me. "Yes, of '70," I said.

"And your husband—the same reason?"

"Yes," I said, though that wasn't true. And then I was truly done with the topic, which was really not something to be discussed with strangers, or casual acquaintances, or with anyone, really. The state had worked hard to decrease the stigmatization of sterility. It was now illegal to refuse to rent to a sterile couple, but most of us clustered together anyway, because it was just easier that way: No one looked at you oddly, and moreover, you didn't have to be confronted by other people's babies and children, daily reminders of your own inadequacy. Our building, for example, was almost wholly occupied by sterile couples. The previous year, the state made it legal for a sterile person of either sex to marry a fertile person, but as far as I knew, no one actually had, because if you were fertile there was no point in ruining your life like that.

I must have looked strange then, because David touched my

shoulder, and I flinched and moved away, but he didn't seem of-fended. "I've upset you, Charlie," he said. "I'm sorry. I didn't mean to pry." He sighed. "It doesn't mean you're a bad person, though."

And then, before I could think of how to respond, he turned and left, giving me another of his salutes. "I'll see you next week," he said.

"Okay," I said, and I stood and watched him walk west until he had disappeared from sight completely.

———

I saw David every Saturday after that, and soon it was April and becoming even warmer, so warm that we'd no longer be able to take our walks, and I was trying not to think about what would happen then.

One evening, about a month after I started meeting with David, my husband looked at me at dinner and said, "You seem different."

"Do I?" I asked. Earlier, David had been telling me stories about growing up in Prefecture Five, and how he and his friends used to climb pecan trees and eat so many nuts they'd get sick. I asked him if he wasn't scared to pick the nuts, because, legally, all fruiting trees belonged to the state, but he said the state was more relaxed in Pre-fecture Five. "They really only care about Prefecture Two, because that's where all the money and power is," he said. He announced these things comfortably, for anyone to hear, but when I asked him to lower his voice, he looked confused. "Why?" he asked. "I'm not saying anything treasonous," and I had had to think about it. He wasn't, it was true, but something about the way he said it made me feel like he was. "I'm sorry," I said.

"No," my husband said. "It's nothing to apologize for. You just look"—and here he studied me, closely, looking at me for much lon-ger than he maybe ever had, so long that I began to feel anxious—"healthy. Content. I'm glad to see it."

"Thank you," I finally said, and my husband, whose head was once again bent over his tofu patty, nodded.

That night, as I lay in bed, I realized that it had been weeks now since I had wondered how my husband was spending his free nights. I hadn't even thought to look in the box for more notes. As I was thinking this, I suddenly saw the house on Bethune Street, and my husband slipping past the half-open door, the man's voice saying, "You're late tonight," as he did, and to distract myself, I thought instead about David, how he had smiled and said I was funny.

Later that night, I woke from a dream. I rarely dreamed, but this one had been so vivid that I was momentarily disoriented when I opened my eyes. I had been walking through the Square with David, and we were standing at the northern entrance, where the Square met Fifth Avenue, when he had put his hands on my shoulders and kissed me. Frustratingly, I couldn't remember the actual sensation of it, but I knew it had felt good, and that I had enjoyed it. Then I had woken up.

Over the next nights, I dreamed of David kissing me again and again. I felt different things in the dreams: I was scared, but mostly I was excited, and I was also relieved—I had never been kissed before, and I had learned to accept that I never would be. But now here I was, being kissed after all.

Two Saturdays after the kissing dream began, I was once again in the Square with David. It was now the third week of April and therefore unbearably hot, and even David had begun wearing his cooling suit. Cooling suits were effective, but because they were so puffy, they made you walk strangely, and we had to move slowly, both because the suits were bulky and because you didn't want to overexert yourself.

We were making our second lap around the Square, David telling me more stories about growing up in Prefecture Five, when, all of a sudden, I saw my husband moving in our direction.

I stopped walking. "Charlie?" asked David, looking at me. But I didn't answer.

By that point, my husband had seen me, and he came toward us. He was alone, and also wearing his cooling suit, and he raised his hand in greeting as he approached us.

"Hello," he said, as he drew near.

"Hello," David said.

I introduced them to each other, and they both bowed. They exchanged a few sentences about the weather—effortlessly, as so many people seemed to be able to do. And then my husband continued on his way, heading north, and David and I, west.

"Your husband seems nice," said David, finally, because I wasn't saying anything.

"Yes," I said. "He is nice."

"Was it an arranged marriage?"

"Yes; my grandfather arranged it," I said.

I remembered when Grandfather first spoke to me about marriage. I was twenty-one; the previous year, I had been asked to leave my college because my father had been declared an enemy of the state, even though he was long dead. It was a strange period: Depending on the week, there were rumors that the insurgents were gaining ground, followed by reports that the state had beaten them back. The official news promised that the state would prevail, and Grandfather had assured me that that would be true. But he had also said that he wanted to make sure I was safe, that I would have someone to take care of me. "But I have you," I had said, and he had smiled. "Yes," he said, "you have my whole heart, little cat. But I won't live forever, and I want to make sure that you'll always have someone to protect you, even long after I'm gone."

I hadn't said anything to that, because I didn't like it when Grandfather spoke of dying, but the next week, Grandfather and I had gone to a marriage broker. This was when Grandfather still had a little bit of influence, and the marriage broker he had chosen was one of the most elite in the prefecture; he usually only arranged marriages for residents of Zone Fourteen, but he had agreed to see Grandfather as a favor.

At the marriage broker's office, Grandfather and I sat in a waiting room, and then another door opened and a tall, thin, pale-faced man came in. "Doctor?" he asked Grandfather.

"Yes," Grandfather said, standing. "Thank you for seeing us."

"Of course," said the man, who had been staring at me since he entered. "And this is your granddaughter?"

"Yes," said Grandfather, proudly, and he drew me to his side. "This is Charlie."

"I see," said the man. "Hello, Charlie."

"Hello," I whispered.

There had been a silence. "She's a little shy," said Grandfather, and he stroked my hair.

"I see," said the man, again. Then he spoke to Grandfather. "Would you come in alone, Doctor, so we can speak?" He looked at me. "You can wait here, young lady."

I sat there for about fifteen minutes, knocking my heels against the chair legs, which was a bad habit I had. There was nothing in the room to look at, nothing to see: just four plain chairs and a piece of plain gray carpet. But then I heard raised voices from behind the other door, the sound of arguing, and I went over and pressed my ear against the wood.

The first voice I heard was the man's. "With respect, Doctor— with *respect*—I think you have to be realistic," he was saying.

"What's that supposed to mean?" asked Grandfather, and I was surprised to hear that he sounded angry.

There had been a silence, and when the man spoke again, he was quieter, and I had to concentrate hard to hear him again.

"Doctor, forgive me," the man was saying, "but your grand-daughter is—"

"My granddaughter is what?" Grandfather snapped, and there was another silence.

"Special," the man said.

"That's right," Grandfather said. "She *is* special, she is very special, and she will need a husband who understands how special she is."

I had had enough then, and I had sat down again, and a few min-utes later, Grandfather had walked briskly out and opened the office door for me and we had left. On the street, neither of us spoke. Finally, I asked, "Did you find someone for me?"

Grandfather had snorted. "That man's an idiot," he said. "No clue what he's doing. We're going to go to someone else, someone different. I'm sorry I wasted our time, little cat."

After that, we had gone to two more brokers, and both times, Grandfather had swept from the room, ushered me out, and, once we were in the street, announced that the broker was a moron or a fool. Then he said I didn't have to come with him on the appointments, as he wasn't going to waste both of our time. Finally, he found a broker he liked, one who specialized in matching sterile people, and one day, he told me he had found someone for me to marry, someone who would always take care of me.

He had shown me a picture of the man who was to become my husband. On the back of the picture was his name, birth date, height, weight, racial makeup, and occupation. The card had been debossed with the special stamp that everyone who was sterile had applied to their papers, as well as a stamp denoting that at least one of his immediate family members was an enemy of the state. Usually, cards like this listed the applicant's parents' names and occupations, but here that information had been left blank. Yet, even though my husband's parents had been declared enemies, he must have known someone or been related to someone with some influence or power, because, like me, he was not in a labor camp, or jail, or detention, but free.

I turned the picture card back around and looked at the man. He had a handsome, serious face, and his hair was cut close, neat and clean. His chin was slightly raised, which made him look bold. Often people who were sterile or related to traitors looked down, like they were ashamed, or apologetic, but he did not.

"What do you think?" Grandfather asked me.

"All right," I answered, and Grandfather said he would arrange for me to meet him.

After our meeting, our marriage date was set for one year later. As I have mentioned, my husband had been in graduate school when he was blacklisted, but he was trying to appeal his case, which was another indication that someone was helping him, and he had asked to delay the marriage until after his trial, which Grandfather had agreed to.

One day, a few months after we had both signed our promissory contracts, Grandfather and I were walking down Fifth Avenue when

Grandfather said, "There are many different kinds of marriages, little cat."

I waited for him to say more, and when he finally did, he spoke much more slowly than he usually did, pausing after every few words.

"Some couples," he began, "are very attracted to each other. They have a—a—physical chemistry, a hunger for each other. Do you know what I mean by that?"

"Sex," I said. Grandfather himself had explained sex to me, years ago.

"That's right," he said. "Sex. But some couples don't have that attraction. The man you are going to marry, little cat, is not interested in . . . with . . . Well. Let's just say that he isn't interested.

"But that doesn't make your marriage any less valid. And that doesn't mean your husband isn't a good person, or that you aren't. I want you to know, little cat, that sex is a part of a marriage, but only sometimes. And it's not all that makes a marriage, not at all. Your husband will always treat you well, I promise you that. Do you understand what I'm trying to say?"

I thought maybe I did, but then I also thought that what I thought Grandfather was saying might not be what he meant after all.

"I think so," I said, and he looked at me and then nodded.

Later, when he was kissing me good night, Grandfather said, "Your husband will always be kind to you, little cat. I have no fears," and I had nodded, though I suppose Grandfather actually *did* have fears, because he eventually told me what to do if my husband ever treated me unkindly—though, as I have already said, he never has.

I was thinking of all this when I finally returned to our apartment after saying goodbye to David in the Square. My husband came home just as I was finishing cooking our dinner, and changed out of his cooling suit before setting the table and pouring us both some water.

I had been nervous to see my husband after our encounter, but it seemed it would be a meal like any other. I didn't know where my husband went on Saturdays, except he usually wasn't gone all day. He did the grocery shopping in the mornings, and on Sundays, we did our chores together: laundry, if it was our turn, and cleaning, and then we both went to the community garden to work our shifts, though not at the same time.

Dinner that night was leftover tofu, which I had made into a cold stew, and as we were eating, my husband said, not lifting his head, "I was glad to meet David today."

"Oh," I said. "Yes, it was nice."

"How did you meet him?"

"At one of the storyteller sessions. He sat next to me."

"When?"

"About seven weeks ago."

He nodded. "Where does he work?"

"The Farm," I said. "He's a plant tech."

He looked at me. "Where's he from?" he asked.

"Little Eight," I said. "But before that, Prefecture Five."

My husband pressed his napkin to his mouth and then leaned back in his chair, looking up at the ceiling. He seemed to be struggling to speak. Then he said, "What do you do together?"

I shrugged. "We go to the storyteller's," I began, though we had not been to the storyteller in at least a month. "We walk around the Square. He tells me about growing up in Prefecture Five."

"And what do you tell him?"

"Nothing," I said, and as I said it, I realized it was true. I had nothing to tell—not to David, not to my husband.

My husband sighed, and passed his hand before his eyes, as he did when he was tired. "Cobra," he said, "I want you to be careful. I'm glad you have a friend, I am. But you—you barely know this person. I just want you to be vigilant." His voice was gentle, the same as it always was, but he was looking directly at me, and finally I looked away. "Have you considered that he might be from the state?"

I didn't say anything. Something was building inside of me. "Cobra?" my husband asked, gently.

"Because no one would want to be my friend, is that what you mean?" I asked. I had never raised my voice to my husband, had never been angry with him, and now he looked surprised, and his mouth opened a bit.

"No," he said. "That's not what I mean. I just," he started. Then he began again. "I promised your grandfather I'd always take care of you," he said.

For a moment, I sat there. Then I got up and left the table and went to our room and closed the door and lay down on my bed. There was a silence, and I heard my husband's chair scrape back, and the sounds of him washing the dishes, and the sound of the radio, and then him coming into our room, where I was pretending to be asleep. I heard him sit on his bed; I thought he might speak to me. But he didn't, and soon I could hear from his breathing that he was asleep.

Naturally, it had in fact occurred to me that David might be an informant for the state. But if he was, he was a very poor one, as informants were quiet and invisible, and he was neither quiet nor invisible. Though I had also wondered whether that too was intentional: that his unsuitability as an informant increased the likelihood that he was one. The curious thing about the informants was that they were *so* quiet and invisible that you were usually able to tell who they were. Not immediately, perhaps, but eventually; there was a quality about them, what Grandfather had called a bloodlessness, that distinguished them. In the end, though, what convinced me that David was not an informant was me. Who would be interested in me? What secrets did I have? Everyone knew who Grandfather and my father had been; everyone knew how they had died; everyone knew what they had been convicted of and, in Grandfather's case, how that conviction had been overturned, albeit too late. The only thing I had done wrong was those nights I had followed my husband, but that was hardly an offense for which one was assigned an informant.

But if it was impossible that David was an informant, then why *was* he spending time with me? I had never been someone people wanted to be around. After I had recovered from the sickness, Grandfather had taken me to activities, classes with children my own age. The parents sat in chairs arranged around the room, and the children played. But after a few sessions, we stopped going. It was all right, though, because I always had Grandfather to play with and talk to and spend time with—until the day I didn't.

As I lay there that night, listening to my husband's breathing and thinking about what he had said, I wondered if it was possible that I was actually not who I thought I was. I knew I was dull, and unexciting, and that I often didn't understand people. But maybe I had changed, somehow, without even knowing it. Maybe I wasn't who I knew I was.

I got up and went to the bathroom. There was a small mirror above the sink, which you could angle so you could see your entire body. I took off my clothes and looked at myself, and as I did, I realized I had not changed after all. I was still the same person, with the same thick legs and thin hair and small eyes. Nothing was any different; I was as I already knew myself to be.

I got dressed and turned off the light and returned to our bedroom. Then I felt very bad, because my husband was right—there was something strange about David talking to me. I was nobody, and he was not.

You're not nobody, little cat, Grandfather would have said. *You're mine.*

But this is the stranger thing: I didn't care why David wanted to be friends with me. I just wanted him to *keep* being friends with me. And I decided that, whatever his reason was, it wouldn't make a difference. I also realized that the sooner I went to sleep, the sooner it would be Sunday, and then Monday, and Tuesday, and with each day that passed, I would be that much closer to seeing him once more. And it was this understanding that made me close my eyes and, finally, fall asleep.

———

I haven't spoken for some time about what was happening at the lab.

The truth is that my friendship with David had so preoccupied me that I had less time and inclination to eavesdrop on the Ph.D.s. On the other hand, there was also less of a need for stealth, because something was clearly happening, and the scientists had begun to discuss it openly, even though they weren't supposed to. Of course, it was difficult for me to learn the details—and I wouldn't have been able to understand them even if I had—but it seemed likely that there was another disease, and that it was projected to be highly deadly. But this was all I knew. I knew it had been discovered somewhere in South America, and I knew that most of the scientists suspected it was an airborne virus, and that it was probably hemorrhagic in nature, and spread by fluids as well, which was the worst kind of illness of all, and one we were less equipped to combat because so much research and money and prevention had gone toward respiratory illnesses. But I didn't know anything else, because I don't think the scientists knew anything else: They didn't know how infectious it was, or how long its incubation was, or what the death rate was. I don't even think they knew how many people had died from it, not yet. The fact that it had begun in South America was unfortunate, because South America was historically the least forthcoming about their research and infections, and in the last flare-up, Beijing had had to threaten them with severe sanctions to make them cooperate.

It may sound surprising to hear that despite this the mood at the laboratory was pleasant. The scientists liked having something to focus on, and the initial worry had changed to excitement. This would be most of the young scientists' first major illness; many of the Ph.D.s were around my age, and like me, they would have barely remembered the events of '70, and since the travel prohibition, there were fewer illnesses in general. Outwardly, everyone said they hoped that it was just an isolated incident, and that it could quickly be localized, but later, I would hear them whispering, and sometimes I would see them smiling, just a bit, and I knew it was because they were always being told by the older scientists that they were spoiled because they hadn't actually experienced a pandemic from a professional perspective, and now they might.

I wasn't scared, either; my daily life remained just as it had been. The lab would always need the pinkies, whether the illness turned out to be something big or not.

But the other reason I was so calm was because I had a friend. About a decade ago, the state had instituted a law that ordered people to register their friends' names at their local center, but it had been quickly repealed. Even Grandfather had said it was a ridiculous notion. "I understand what they're trying to do," he had said, "but people are less idle, and therefore less troublesome, when they're allowed to have friends." Now even I had come to realize that this was true. I found myself gathering observations, things to tell David. I would never tell him what was happening at the lab, of course, but I sometimes tried to imagine the kinds of conversations we'd have if I did. At first this was difficult, because I couldn't understand how he thought. Then I realized that he would usually say the opposite of what a typical person would say. So, if I were to say, "They're worried about some new disease at the lab," then a regular person would say, "Is it very bad?" But David would say something different, maybe something very different, such as "How do you know they're worried?," and then I would really have to think about the answer: How *did* I know they were worried? In this way, it was like talking to him on days I didn't see him.

Some observations, though, I could tell him, and I did. Riding home on the shuttle, for example, I saw one of the police dogs, which were normally silent and disciplined, jump and bark and wag its tail as a butterfly flew in front of it. Or when Belle, the Ph.D., gave birth to her daughter, she sent dozens of boxes of cookies made with real lemons and real sugar to all the labs on our floor, and everyone got one, even me. Or when I discovered the pinky with two heads and six legs. Before, I would have saved these items to tell my husband over dinner. But now I thought only of what David would say, so that, even as I was observing something, part of me was thinking of the future and what his face would look like as he listened to me.

The next Saturday we met it was almost too hot to walk, even with our cooling suits. "You know what we should do?" asked David, as we moved slowly west. "We should meet instead at the center—we could listen to a concert."

I thought about this. "But then we won't be able to talk," I said.

"Well, that's true," he said. "Not during the concert. But we could talk afterward, on the track." There was an indoor track at the center, where you could walk in a loop in the air-conditioning.

I didn't say anything to this, and he looked at me. "Do you go to the center often?"

"Yes," I said, although that was a lie. But I didn't want to say the truth—that I had been too scared to go inside. "My grandfather always said I should go more often," I said, "that I might enjoy it."

"You've mentioned your grandfather before," David said. "What was he like?"

"He was nice," I said, after a silence, although this hardly seemed like an adequate way to describe Grandfather. "He loved me," I said, finally. "He took care of me. We used to play games together."

"Like what?"

I was about to answer when it occurred to me that the games Grandfather and I played—like the one in which we pretended to have a conversation, or in which I gave him observations of someone we had passed on the street—wouldn't seem much like a game to anyone but ourselves, and that calling them games would make me seem odd: odd because I would think they were games, and odd because I would need to play them. So instead I said, "Ball, and cards, things like that," because I knew those were regular games, and I felt pleased with myself for thinking of the answer.

"That sounds nice," said David, and we walked a little more. "Was your grandfather a lab tech, like you?" he asked.

This wasn't as strange a question as it sounds. If I had had a child, he would probably become a lab tech as well, or have an equivalent rank, unless he was exceptionally bright and therefore tracked at an early age to become, say, a scientist. But back in Grandfather's day, you could choose to become whatever you wanted, and then you went and did it.

It was also then that I realized that David didn't know who Grandfather was. There was a time in which everyone had known who he was, but now, I suppose, only people in the government and in science knew his name. But I hadn't told David my last name. To him, my grandfather was only my grandfather, and nothing else.

"Yes," I said. "He was a lab tech, too."

"Did he work at Rockefeller as well?"

"Yes," I said, because that was true.

"What did he look like?" he asked.

It sounds strange to say, but although I spent a great deal of time thinking about Grandfather, I could remember less and less what he looked like. What I remembered more was the sound of his voice, the way he smelled, the way he made me feel when he put his arm around me. The way I saw him most frequently in my mind was the day he was being marched to the platform, when he was looking for me in the crowd, his eyes moving across the hundreds of people who had gathered to watch and yell at him, calling my name before the executioner lowered the black hood over his head.

But of course I couldn't say that. "He was tall," I began. "And skinny. His skin was darker than mine. He had gray hair, short, and—" And here I faltered, because I really didn't know what else I could say.

"Did he wear fancy clothes?" David asked. "My maternal grandfather liked to wear fancy clothes."

"No," I said, though as I did, I remembered a ring that Grandfather had worn when I was little. It was very old, and gold, and on one side it had a pearl, and if you pressed the little latches on the sides of the setting, the pearl hinged open and there was a tiny compartment. Grandfather had worn it on his left pinkie, and had always turned the pearl inward, toward his palm. Then, one day, he had stopped wearing it, and when I had asked him why, he had praised me for being so observant. "But where is it?" I had demanded, and he had smiled. "I had to give it to the fairy as payment," he said. "What fairy?" I had asked. "Why, the fairy who looked over you while you were sick," he said. "I told her I would give her anything she wanted if she took care of you, and she said she would, but I needed to give her my ring in exchange." By this point, I had been well for several years, and I also knew that fairies didn't exist, but whenever I asked Grandfather about it, he had only smiled and repeated the same story, and eventually, I stopped asking.

But, again, this wasn't the kind of story I could tell David, and anyway, he had begun talking about his other grandfather, who had been a farmer in Prefecture Five before it was called Prefecture Five. He had raised pigs and cows and goats, and had had a hundred peach trees, and David told me about being young and visiting his grandfather and eating as many peaches as he wanted. "I'm ashamed to admit this, but I hated peaches when I was a kid," he said. "There were just so many of them: My grandmother baked them into pies, and cakes, and bread, and she made them into jam, and leather—oh, that's when you dry slices of them in the sun until they become tough, like jerky—and ice cream. And this is after she'd canned as many as we and our neighbors needed to get us through the rest of the year." But then the farm had become state property, and his grandfather had gone from owning it to working on it, and the peach trees were cut down to make room for soybean fields, which were more nutritious than peaches and therefore a more efficient crop. It was unwise to talk as freely about the past as David did, much less about governmental claims, but he did so in the same light, easy, matter-of-fact tone that he had used to discuss the peaches. Grandfather had once told me that discussing the past was discouraged because it made many people angry or sad, but David sounded neither angry nor sad. It was as if what he was describing had happened not to him but to someone else, someone he barely knew.

"Now, of course, I'd kill for a peach," he said, cheerily, as we neared the north of the Square, where we met and parted every Saturday. "I'll see you next week, Charlie," he said as he left. "Think about what you might like to do at the center."

Once I was back at home, I took out the box in the closet and looked at the pictures I had of Grandfather. The first one was taken when he was in medical school. He was laughing, and his hair was long and curly and black. In the second, he was standing with my father, who was a toddler, and my other grandfather, the one to whom I'm genetically related. In my mind, my father resembles Grandfather, but in this picture, you can see that he actually looked like my other grandfather: They were both lighter skinned than Grandfather, with straight dark hair, like I used to have. In the third picture, my favorite, Grandfather looks as I remember him. He's smiling, a big smile, and in his arms he is holding a small, thin baby, and that baby is me. "Charles and Charlie," someone wrote on the back of this photo, "September 12, 2064."

I found myself thinking about Grandfather both more and less since I had met David. I didn't need to talk to him in my head as much as I used to, but I also wanted to talk to him more, mostly about David, and about what it was like to have a friend. I wondered what he would have thought of him. I wondered whether he would have agreed with my husband.

I wondered as well what David would have thought of Grandfather. It was strange to think that he didn't know who Grandfather was, that to him, he was simply a relative of mine, whom I had loved and who had died. As I have said, everyone I worked with knew who Grandfather was. There was a greenhouse on top of a building at RU that was named for him, and there was even a law named for him, the Griffith Act, which established the legality of the relocation centers, which had once been called quarantine camps.

But it was not so long ago that many people hated Grandfather. I suppose there are people who still hate him, but you never hear about those people anymore. I first became aware of this hatred when I was eleven, in civics class. We were learning about how, in the aftermath of the illness of '50, a new government began to take form, so by the time the illness of '56 arose, they were more properly prepared, and by '62, the new state had been established. One of the inventions that had helped contain the illness of '70—which, as bad as it was, could have been much worse—was the relocation centers, which were originally located only in the west and midwest but by '69 were in every municipality. "These camps became very important to our scientists and doctors," my teacher had said. "Does anyone know the names of the early, original camps?"

People started shouting out answers: Heart Mountain. Rohwer. Minidoka. Jerome. Poston. Gila River.

"Yes, yes," my teacher said after each name. "Yes, that's right. And does anyone know who founded those camps?"

No one knew. And then Miss Bethesda looked at me. "It was Charlie's grandfather," she said. "Dr. Charles Griffith. He was one of the architects of the camps."

Everyone turned to look at me, and I felt myself grow hot with embarrassment. I liked my teacher—she had always been kind to me. When the other children ran away from me on the playground, laughing as they did, she would always come over and ask if I might like to come back into the classroom and help her distribute the art supplies for the afternoon lesson. Now I looked up, and my teacher was looking back at me, the same as always, and yet something was wrong. I felt as if she were angry with me, but I hadn't known why.

That night, at dinner, I asked Grandfather if he was the person who had invented the centers. He had looked at me then, and had waved his hand, and the servant who was pouring my milk had set down the pitcher and left the room. "Why do you ask that, little cat?" he asked, after the man shut the door behind him.

"We learned about it in civics class," I said. "My teacher said you were one of the people who invented them."

"Did she," Grandfather said, and although his voice sounded the same as it always did, I could see that he was holding his left hand in a fist, so tightly that it trembled. Then he noticed me looking, and he opened his hand and laid his palm flat on the table. "What else did she say?"

I explained to Grandfather how Miss Bethesda had said that the centers had prevented more deaths, and he nodded, slowly. For a while he was silent, and I listened to the ticking of the clock, which sat on the mantel above the fireplace.

Finally, Grandfather spoke. "Years ago," he said, "there were people who opposed the camps, who didn't want them built, who thought I was a bad person because I supported them." I must have looked surprised, because he nodded. "Yes," he said. "They didn't understand that the camps were created to keep us—all of us—healthy and safe. Eventually, people came to see that they were necessary, and that we had to build them. Do you understand why?"

"Yes," I said. I had learned this in civics class as well. "Because it meant that the sick people were in one place, so people who were healthy wouldn't get sick, too."

"That's right," Grandfather said.

"Then why didn't people like them?" I asked.

He looked up at the ceiling, which was something he did when he was thinking of how to answer me. "It's difficult to explain," he said, slowly, "but one of the reasons is that, back in those days, you would remove just the infected person, not their whole family, and some people thought it was cruel to separate people from their families."

"Oh," I said. I thought about this. "I wouldn't want to be separated from you, Grandfather," I said, and he smiled.

"And I would never be separated from you, little cat," he said. "This is why the policy changed, and now the entire family goes to the center together."

I didn't need to ask what happened at the centers, because I already knew: You died. But at least you died somewhere clean, and safe, and well-equipped—there were schools for the children to go to, and sports for the adults to play, and when you got very sick, you were taken to the center hospital, which was gleaming and white, and where doctors and nurses took care of you until you died. I had seen pictures of the centers on television, and there were pictures of them in our textbook as well. There was one, taken at Heart Mountain, of a laughing young woman holding a little girl, who was also laughing; in the background, you could see their cabin, which had an apple tree planted in front of it. Standing next to the woman and little girl was a doctor, and even though she was wearing her full protective suit, you could tell she was laughing as well, and she had her hand on the woman's shoulder. You couldn't go visit people at the centers, for your own protection, but the sick person could bring whomever he or she wanted, and sometimes whole extended families would go in a group: mothers and fathers and children and grandparents and aunts and uncles and cousins. At first, going to the centers was voluntary. Then it became required, which was controversial, because Grandfather said that people didn't like being told what to do, even if it was for the good of their fellow citizens.

Of course, by that point—this was in 2075—there were fewer people in the centers, because the pandemic had been almost contained by then. Sometimes I looked at that picture in my textbook and wished I lived in one of the centers myself. Not because I wanted to be sick, or wanted Grandfather to be sick, but because it looked so nice there, with the apple trees and wide green fields. But we would never go, not only because we weren't allowed but because Grandfather was needed here. That was why we hadn't gone to a center when I had been sick—because Grandfather needed to be near his lab, and the nearest center was on Davids Island, many miles north of Manhattan, which would have been too inconvenient.

"Do you have any more questions?" Grandfather had asked, smiling at me.

"No," I said.

That had been a Friday. The following Monday, I had gone to school, and instead of my teacher standing at the front of the room, there had been someone else, a short, dark man with a mustache. "Where's Miss Bethesda?" someone had asked.

"Miss Bethesda is no longer at this school," said the man. "I am your new teacher."

"Is she sick?" someone else asked.

"No," said the new teacher. "But she is no longer at this school."

I don't know why, but I didn't tell Grandfather that Miss Bethesda was gone. I never told him, even though I never saw Miss Bethesda again. Later, I learned that the centers may not have resembled the pictures in my textbook after all. This was in 2088, at the beginning of the second uprising. The following year, the insurgents were defeated for good, and Grandfather's name was cleared and his status was restored. But by that point, it was too late. Grandfather was dead, and I was left alone with my husband.

Over the years, I have occasionally wondered about the relocation centers: Which version of them was the correct one? In the months before Grandfather was killed, protestors marched outside our home carrying blown-up photographs they said were taken at the centers. "Don't look," Grandfather would tell me, on the rare occasions we left the house. "Look away, little cat." But sometimes I did look, and the people in the photographs were so deformed that they didn't even look like humans any longer.

But I never thought Grandfather was bad. He had done what had needed to be done. And he had taken care of me for my entire life. There was no one who was kinder to me, no one who loved me more. My father, I knew, had disagreed with Grandfather; I don't remember how I had come to know this, but I did. He had wanted

Grandfather to be punished. It was an odd thing, knowing that your own father had wanted his father to be imprisoned. But it didn't change my feelings. My father had left me when I was young—Grandfather never had. I didn't see how someone who abandoned his child could be any better than someone who had only tried to save as many people as he could, even if he had made mistakes while doing so.

———

The following Saturday, I met David in the Square as always, and he once again suggested we go to the center, and this time, I agreed, as it was by now very hot. We walked the eight and a half blocks north slowly, so as not to overtax our cooling suits.

David had said that we were going to listen to a concert, but when we paid for our tickets, there was only a lone musician at the front of the room, a young, dark-skinned man with a cello. Once we had all sat down, he bowed to us, and then he began to play.

I had never thought I cared for cello music very much, but when the concert was over, I wished I hadn't agreed to walk on the indoor track afterward and could instead go home. Something about the music made me think of the music Grandfather had played on the radio in his study when I was small, and I missed him so badly that it was difficult to swallow.

"Charlie?" asked David, looking worried. "Are you okay?"

"Yes," I said, and I made myself stand up and walk out of the room, which everyone else, even the cellist, had already left.

At the edge of the indoor track there was a man selling iced fruit drinks. We both looked at the man and then at each other, because neither of us knew whether the other could afford to buy one.

"It's okay," I said at last, "I can."

He smiled. "I can, too," he said.

We bought the drinks and sipped them as we walked around the track. There were only about a dozen other people there. We were still wearing our cooling suits—once you were in them, it was easier to just keep them on—but had deflated them, and it felt good to move as we usually did.

For a while, we walked in silence. Then David said, "Do you ever wish you could visit another country?"

"It's not allowed," I said.

"I know it's not allowed," he said. "But do you ever wish you could?"

Suddenly I was tired of David's strange questions, his tendency to always ask things that were, if not illegal, then at least impolite, subjects that you didn't think about, much less discuss. And what was the point of wishing for anything that wasn't allowed? Wishing for things would change nothing. For months, I had wished every day that Grandfather would come back—if I am to be honest, I wished for it still. But he never would. It was better not to want at all: Wanting just made you unhappy, and I was not unhappy.

I remember once, when I had been in college, one of the girls in my class had figured out a way to access the internet. This was very hard to do, but she had been very smart, and though a few of the other girls had wanted to see what it was like as well, I had not. I knew what the internet was, of course, though I was too young to remember it: I was only three when it became illegal. I wasn't sure I even understood, exactly, what it did. Once, when I was a teenager, I had asked Grandfather to explain it to me, and he had been quiet a long time, and then he finally said it was a way for people to communicate with one another across vast distances. "The problem with it," he said, "was that it often allowed people to exchange bad information—untrue things, dangerous things. And when that happened, there were serious consequences." After it was forbidden, he said, things became safer, because everyone was receiving the same information at the same time, which meant there was less chance for confusion. This seemed like a good reason to me. Later, when the four girls who had looked at the internet disappeared, most people thought they'd been taken by the state. But I remembered what Grandfather had said, and wondered if they had been contacted by people on the internet with dangerous information and something bad had happened to them. The point is that there was little purpose in wondering what it would be like to do things or go places that I would never be able to. I did not think about trying to find the internet, and I did not think of going to another country. Some people did, but I did not.

"Not really," I said.

"But don't you want to see what another country is like?" David asked, and now even he lowered his voice. "Maybe things are better someplace else."

"Better how?" I asked, despite myself.

"Well, better in lots of ways," he said. "Maybe in another place we would have different jobs, for example."

"I like my job," I said.

"I know," he said. "I like my job, too. I'm just thinking out loud."

But I didn't see how things would be any different in another country. Every place had been ravaged by the illnesses. Every place was the same.

When he was my age, however, Grandfather had traveled to many different countries. Back in those days, you could go anywhere you wanted, as long as you had the money. So, after he finished college, he got on an aeroplane and landed in Japan. From Japan, he traveled west, through Korea, across the People's Republic of China, down through India, and over to Turkey, Greece, Italy, Germany, the Low Countries. For a few months he remained in Britain, staying with friends of a friend from college, and then he began moving again: Down one coast of Africa and back up the other; down one coast of South America and back up the other. He went to Australia and New Zealand; he went to Canada and Russia. In India he rode a camel across a desert; in Japan he hiked to the top of a mountain; in Greece he swam in water he said had been bluer than the sky. I had asked him why he didn't just stay home, and he said that home was too small—he wanted to see how other people lived, what they ate, what they wore, what they wanted to do with their lives.

"I was from a very tiny island," he said. "I knew that all around me were other kinds of people, doing things I would never be able to see if I just stayed. So I had to leave."

"Was what they were doing better?" I asked.

"Not better," he said. "But different. The more I saw, the less I felt I could ever go back to where I was from." We spoke in whispers, even though Grandfather had turned on the radio so the music would obscure our conversation from the listening devices that were wired throughout the house.

But the rest of the world must have been better after all, because in Australia, Grandfather met another person from Hawai'i, and they fell in love, and went back to Hawai'i, where they had a son, my father. And then they moved to America and never returned to live at home again, not even before the illness of '50. And then it was too late, because everyone in Hawai'i had died, and by this point, all three of them were American citizens. And then, after the laws of '67, no one was allowed to leave the country anyway. The only people who remembered other places were older, and they didn't talk about those years.

After circling the track ten times, we decided to leave. But as we were walking outside, we heard the sounds of a dull thumping, and soon a flatbed truck pulled slowly into sight. In the back knelt three people. You couldn't tell if they were men or women, because they wore those long white gowns and black hoods that covered their entire heads and which must have been very hot. Their hands were bound in front of them, and two guards stood behind them, wearing cooling suits with reflective helmets. Over the drumbeat, a voice was repeating over the speaker, "Thursday at 18:00. Thursday at 18:00." They only announced Ceremonies like this when the convicted had been found guilty of treason, and usually only when they were of high rank, perhaps even state employees. Usually, state employees were punished this way if they had been caught trying to leave the country, which was illegal, or if they were trying to smuggle someone *into* the country, which was both unsafe and illegal, because it meant you could introduce a foreign microbe, or because they were trying to disseminate unauthorized information, usually via technology they weren't allowed to use or possess. They were put on a truck and driven through all of the zones, so you could look at them and heckle them if you wanted. But I never did, and neither did David, though we both stood and watched as the vehicle drove past us, and then turned south on Seventh Avenue.

After the truck had disappeared, though, something strange happened: I looked over at David, and saw that he was staring after it, his mouth slightly open; and that he had tears in his eyes.

This was astonishing and also deeply dangerous—showing even the smallest sympathy for the accused could get you noticed by a Fly, which had been programmed to interpret human expressions. I quickly whispered his name, and he blinked, and turned to me. I looked around; I didn't think anyone had seen us. But just in case, it was best to keep moving, to seem normal, and so I began walking east, back to Sixth Avenue, and after a moment, he followed me. I wanted to say something to David, but I didn't know what. I was frightened, but I didn't know why, and angry as well, at him for reacting in such a strange way.

As we were crossing Thirteenth Street, he said to me, in a low voice, "That was terrible."

He was right—it *was* terrible—but it happened all the time. I didn't like seeing the trucks go by, either; I didn't like watching the Ceremonies, or listening to them on the radio. But it was the way things worked—you did something wrong and were punished, and there was no way to change any of it: not the wrongdoing, and not the punishment.

Yet David was acting as if he'd never seen one of the trucks before. He stared straight ahead, but he was silent, chewing on his lip. We usually didn't wear our helmets on our walks together, but now he took his from his bag and put it on, and I was glad, because it wasn't typical to show emotion in public, and doing so could draw attention to you.

At the northern edge of the Square, we stopped. It was the customary place we said goodbye, where he turned left to go to Little Eight, and I turned right to go home. For a while, we stood there in silence. Our departures were never awkward, because David always had something to say, and then he would wave goodbye and leave.

But now he wasn't saying anything, and through his helmet's screen, I could see he was still upset.

I felt bad then for being so impatient with him, even if he was behaving recklessly. He was my friend, and friends were understanding of each other, even if it was confusing. I had not been understanding with David, and it was because of my guilt about this that I did something strange: I reached out my arms and put them around him.

It wasn't easy to do, because both of our cooling suits were inflated to maximum capacity, and so I couldn't so much embrace him as pet at his back. As I did so, I found myself pretending something odd: that we were married, and that he was my husband. It wasn't typical to show someone, even your spouse, affection in public, but it wasn't frowned upon, either; it was simply uncommon. Once, however, I had seen a couple kiss goodbye; the woman was standing in the doorway of their building, and the man, a tech, was leaving for the day. She was pregnant, and after they kissed, he pressed his palm to her stomach and they looked at each other and smiled. I had been on the shuttle, and I had turned in my seat to watch them, the man putting his hat on and walking away, the smile still on his face. I found myself imagining that David was my husband, and that we were a couple like that one, the kind that would embrace in public because we couldn't stop ourselves from doing so; the kind with so much extra affection that it had to be expressed in gestures because we had run out of words.

I was thinking this when I realized that David wasn't returning my gesture, that, beneath my arms, he was stiff and still, and I abruptly withdrew, stepping backward as I did.

Now I was very embarrassed. I could feel my face getting hot, and I quickly jammed my helmet on. I had done something very foolish. I had made a fool of myself. I needed to get away.

"Goodbye," I said, and began walking.

"Wait," he said, after a moment. "Wait, Charlie. Wait."

But I pretended I couldn't hear him and kept moving. I didn't look behind me. I ventured into the Square and stood in the herbalists' section and waited until I was certain he had left. Then I turned and walked home. Once I was inside the safety of our apartment again, I took off my helmet and suit. My husband was out somewhere; I was alone.

All of a sudden, I felt very angry. I am not an angry person—even when I was little, I never threw tantrums, I never screamed, I never demanded anything. I tried to be as good as I knew how for Grandfather. But now I wanted to hit something, to hurt something, to break something. But there was nothing and no one in the house to hit or hurt or break: The plates were made of plastic; the mixing bowls were made of silicone; the pots were made of metal. Then I remembered how, even though I had not been angry as a child, I had often been frustrated, and I would moan and buck and claw at myself as Grandfather tried to hold me still. So now I went to my bed and practiced the method he'd taught me when everything seemed overwhelming, which was to lie on my stomach and press my face into the pillow and inhale until I felt dizzy.

After this, I got up again. I couldn't stay in the apartment—I couldn't bear it. And so I rezipped myself into my cooling suit and went back outside.

It was now late afternoon, and the day was becoming slightly less hot. I began walking around the Square. It felt queer to be walking alone after so many weeks of doing so with David, and it was perhaps because of that that, instead of just walking around the Square, I entered it on the western side. There was nothing I needed or wanted in the Square, but despite my aimlessness, I found myself moving toward the southeastern section.

I'm not sure why, but this quadrant of the Square had a reputation for being unseemly. How this had happened was something of a mystery; as I have said, the southeastern part was mostly occupied by carpenters, and if you weren't too bothered by the sound of buzz saws and hammers, it was actually a nice place to be—the wood smelled clean and sharp, and you could stand and watch the woodworkers make or repair chairs or tables or buckets, and they wouldn't shoo you away like some of the other vendors would. And yet, for some reason, this was where you came if you wanted to find one of the people I have mentioned earlier, the people who weren't licensed and who didn't have a stall and yet who also occupied the Square, the people who could solve problems you didn't know how to ask about.

One theory I'd heard about how this had happened didn't make any sense. The southeastern part of the Square was closest to a tall brick building that had once been the library of a university that had been located nearby. After the university was closed, the building served for a period as a prison. Now it was the archive office for four of the island's southern zones, including Zone Eight. This was where the state kept its birth and death records for everyone who lived in these areas, as well as any files or notes on those residents. The front of the building was all glass, so you could look in and see the tiers of cases filled with files; in the lobby, on the street level, there was a windowless black cube, about ten feet on all sides, and inside that black cube sat the archivist, who could find any file you needed. Of course, the archive hall was only accessible to state officials, and only those officials with the highest clearance. There was always someone in the black cube, and it was one of the few buildings that were always lit, even during the hours it was illegal to turn on the lights because it was a waste of electricity. I never understood what the southeastern corner's proximity to the archive hall had to do with its illicit activity, but that was what everyone said: that it was easier to do dangerous things closer to a state building, because the state would never consider that anyone would do anything illegal so nearby. That was what everyone said, anyway.

As I have said, these people I have mentioned had no permanent station or stall, and so it wasn't as if you could just go to one area or another and expect to find them—they had to find you, instead. What you did was wander slowly among the vendors. You didn't look up; you didn't look around. You just walked, looking down at the curls of wood that covered the ground, and eventually, someone would come up to you and ask you a question. The question was usually only two or three words, and if it wasn't the right question, you just kept walking. If it was the right question, you looked up. I had never done this myself, but I had once stood near one of the woodworkers and watched it happen. There had been a young woman, pretty and fair, and she had been walking very slowly, with her hands behind her back. She had worn a green scarf on her head, and I could see some of her hair, which was thick and red and chin-length, peeking out beneath. I had watched her pace in a loop for about three minutes before the first person, a short, thin, middle-aged man, approached her and said something I couldn't hear. But she kept walking, almost like she hadn't heard him, and he moved away. A minute later, another person approached her, and still she kept walking. The fifth time, a woman walked up to her, and this time, the young woman raised her head and followed the woman, who led her to a small tent made from a tarp on the very eastern edge of the Square, then lifted one side of it and looked around her for Flies before ushering the young woman in and slipping inside herself.

I don't know what made me start walking about the southeastern quadrant myself that day. I concentrated on my feet moving through the sawdust. Sure enough, after a few moments, I felt someone following me. And then I heard a man's voice say, very low, "Looking for someone?" But I kept walking, and soon the man walked away as well.

Shortly after, I saw another man's feet approach me. "Sickness?" he asked. "Medicine?" But I kept walking.

For a while, nothing happened. I walked more slowly. And then I saw a woman's feet coming my way; I could tell the feet belonged to a woman because they were small. They drew very near me, and then I heard a voice whisper, "Love?"

I looked up and realized it was the same woman I'd seen earlier, with a tent on the eastern edge. "Come with me," she said, and I followed her to her area. I wasn't thinking about what I was doing; I wasn't thinking at all. It was as if what was happening was something I was watching, not something I was doing. At the tent, I saw her scan the sky for Flies—the same as she'd done for the young woman—and then beckon me inside.

Inside, the tent was stiflingly hot. There was a rough wooden box that had been secured with a padlock, and two dirty cotton cushions, one of which she sat on and one of which I sat on.

"Take off your helmet," she said, and I did. She wasn't wearing a helmet, but she had a scarf wrapped around her mouth and nose, and now she unwound it, and I saw that the bottom left part of her cheek had been eaten away by disease, and that she was younger than I had thought.

"I've seen you before," she said, and I stared at her. "Yes," she said, "walking around the Square with your husband. A nice-looking man. But he doesn't love you?"

"No," I said, after I had recovered myself. "He isn't my husband. He's my—he's my friend."

"Ah," she said, and her face relaxed. "I understand. And you want him to fall in love with you."

For a moment, I was unable to speak. Was that what I wanted? Was that why I had come here? But that would be impossible—I knew I would never be loved, not in the way people talked about love. I knew I would never love, either. It was not for me. It was so difficult for me to know what I felt. Other people were able to say, "I am happy," or "I am sad," or "I miss you," or "I love you," but I never knew how. "I love you, little cat," Grandfather would say, but I could only rarely say it back to him, because I didn't know what it meant. The feelings I had—what words did I have for them? The feeling I had reading the notes written to my husband; the feeling I had watching him enter the house on Bethune Street; the feeling I had listening to him return late on a Thursday night; the feeling I had lying in bed, wondering if he might someday touch me, or kiss me, and knowing he never would—what were those feelings? What were they called? And with David: The feeling I had when I stood at the north of the Square, watching him wave as he came toward me; the feeling I had when I watched him walk away from me at the end of one of our days together; the feeling I got on Friday night, knowing that I would see him the next day; the feeling I had when I had tried to embrace him, and the feeling I had when I had seen his face, the confusion on it, the way he had pulled away from me—what were those feelings? Were they all the same? Were they all love? Was I able to feel it after all? Was what I had always assumed was impossible for me something I had known all along?

Suddenly I was frightened. I had behaved rashly, dangerously, by coming here. I had lost my common sense. "I have to go," I said, standing. "I'm sorry. Goodbye."

"Wait," the woman called out to me. "There's something I can give you: a powder. You slip it into a drink, and in five days—"

But I was already leaving, I was walking out of the tarp, quickly, so that I wouldn't be able to hear what else she said, so I wouldn't be tempted to return, but not so quickly that I would attract the attention of a Fly.

I exited the Square at the eastern entrance. I had only a few hundred yards to go and then I would be back in my apartment, safe, and once I was there, I could pretend all of this had never happened; I could pretend I had never met David. I would be once again who I was, a married woman, a lab tech, a person who accepted the way the world was, who understood that to wish for anything else was useless, because there was nothing I could do, and so it was best not even to try.

PART VI

Spring, thirty years earlier

Dearest Peter,   March 2, 2064

Before I launch right in: Congratulations. A very well-deserved promotion, though I suppose it's telling that the higher you go, the less
grand and more opaque the title gets. And the less you get publicly
acknowledged. Not that that matters. I know we've spoken about this
before, but do you feel as much of a phantom as I do these days? Able
to pass through doors (if not walls) that are closed to most, but never
seen: An object of horror and fright, rarely encountered but known to
exist. An abstraction rather than an actual human being. I know some
people relish this kind of spectral existence. I did too, once.

Anyway. Yes, thank you for asking, today was indeed the final signing of the paperwork, after which Aubrey's house became, officially,
Nathaniel's house. Nathaniel will at some point pass the house on to
David, and David eventually will pass the house on to someone else,
which I'll tell you about in a bit.

Although Nathaniel had been living there for a few years now,
he had never referred to it, never thought of it, as his. It was always
"Aubrey and Norris's," and then it was "Aubrey's." Even at Aubrey's
funeral, he was telling people to "come back to Aubrey's for a reception," until I finally reminded him it wasn't Aubrey's house but his.
He had given me one of his looks, but later I heard him refer to it
as "the house." Not Aubrey's, not his, not anyone's, just a house that
had agreed to accommodate us.

I had been spending much more time at the house (see? I do
it too) this past year or so. First, there was Aubrey's death. There

was a stateliness to his dying, I always thought: He looked fairly
well, by which I mean that although he was wasted, he had been
spared so many indignities we'd both seen afflict the dying in the
past decade—no weeping sores, no pus, no drooling, no blood.
Then there was his funeral, and the sorting through of his papers,
and then of course I had to go away on business for a while, and
by the time I'd returned, the staff had been dismissed (each with
a severance specified in Aubrey's will) and Nathaniel was trying to
conceive of himself as the owner of an enormous home on Washington Square.

I was surprised, stepping into the place today, by how changed
it was. There was nothing Nathaniel could do about the bricked-
up parlor-floor windows or the bars on the windows of the upper
floors, but the overall effect was airier, brighter. The walls were
still hung with a few key pieces of Hawaiian art—the rest had gone
to the Metropolitan, which now also sheltered most of the important works once owned by the royal family, things they had meant
to keep safe and someday return, but which are now permanently
theirs—but he had changed the lighting and painted the walls a deep
gray, which made the space feel perversely sunnier. It was still full of
Aubrey and Norris, and yet their presence had been vanished.

We walked around and looked at the works. Now that Nathaniel
was their owner—a Hawaiian man with Hawaiian objects—I was
able to appreciate them more; it was less as if they were being displayed and more as if they were being shown off, if that makes sense.
Nathaniel talked about each textile, each bowl, each necklace: where
it had come from, how it had been made. As he did, I studied him.
For so long, he had wanted a beautiful house, with beautiful things,
and now he had them. Even though Aubrey's estate was much smaller
than either of us had imagined—the money having been squandered
on security services and junk-science disease preventatives and, yes,
given away in large quantities to charities—there was enough left
so that Nathaniel could, finally, feel secure. Around New Year's, the
baby, in one of his more hateful moods, had told me that Nathaniel
was seeing someone, some lawyer in the Justice Ministry—"Yeah,

he's a pretty cool guy": I didn't say that if he worked in Justice, he was by definition complicit in maintaining the quarantine camps—but Nathaniel didn't mention it, and I of course didn't ask.

After the tour, we returned to the parlor, and Nathaniel said he had something for me, something from Aubrey. One of my final visits to Aubrey had coincided with one of his more lucid moments, and during it, he asked if I wanted anything from his collection. But I had said no. I had grown to accept Aubrey, even to like him, but beneath that acceptance and affection was a knot of resentment: not, in the end, for the objects he'd collected and for the fact that he possessed more of Hawai'i than I do, but for the fact that he and my husband and child had become a family, and I had been cast out. Nathaniel had met Aubrey and Norris, and everything had started ending, so slowly that I at first couldn't tell it was even happening, and then so thoroughly that I couldn't have hoped to stop it.

I sat on one of the sofas, and Nathaniel took something out of one of the side-table drawers: a little black velvet box, about the size of a golf ball.

"What is it?" I asked him, in the idiotic way people do when they're given a gift, and he smiled. "Open it and see," he said, so I did.

Inside was Aubrey's ring. I removed it, feeling its weight in my hand, how warm the gold was. I opened the pearl lid, but there was nothing inside.

"Well?" asked Nathaniel, but lightly. He sat down next to me.

"Well," I said.

"He said he thought you hated him for this ring most of all," Nathaniel said, but serenely, and I looked up at him, surprised. "Oh, yes," he said. "He knew you hated him."

"I didn't hate him," I said, feebly.

"Yes, you did," Nathaniel said. "You just wouldn't admit it to yourself."

"Yet another thing Aubrey knew that I didn't," I said, trying and failing to not sound sarcastic, but Nathaniel only shrugged.

"Anyway," he said. "It's yours now."

I put it on my left pinkie and held up my hand for him to look at. I still wore my wedding ring, and he touched it, gently. He had stopped wearing his years ago.

At that moment, I sensed that I could have leaned over and kissed him, and that he would have let me. But I didn't, and he, as if sensing the same possibility, abruptly stood.

"Now," he said, businesslike, "when David arrives, I want you to be not just civil but encouraging, all right?"

"I'm always encouraging," I said.

"Charles, I mean it," he said. "He's going to be introducing you to—to a friend of his, who's very important to him. And he has some . . . some news."

"Is he going back to school?" I asked, just to be a brat. Even I knew the answer to that. David was never going back to school.

He ignored the provocation. "Just promise me," he said. Then, in another abrupt change of mood, he sat back down next to me. "I hate that it's like this between you two," he said. I said nothing. "Everything else aside, you're still his father," he said.

"You tell him that."

"I have. But The Light matters to him."

"Oh god," I said. I had been hoping we could get through the conversation without either one of us mentioning The Light.

At that moment, the decontamination chamber hissed, and David appeared, followed by a woman. I stood, and we nodded at each other. "Look, David," I said, and showed him the ring, and he grunted and smiled simultaneously. "Nice, Pops," he said. "You finally got it after all." I was stung but didn't say anything. And anyway, he was right: I had.

Things had been stable between us, which is to say we had, without explicitly agreeing to it, reached a détente. I wouldn't needle him about The Light, and he wouldn't bait me about my work. But this agreement could only last for around fifteen minutes, and only if we had something else to discuss: I don't mean to sound callous, but Aubrey's death had been very helpful in that regard. There were always details of his chemo to review, and his mood and water intake to monitor, and his pain management to detail. And I had been moved—moved, and, if I have to admit it, a little jealous—when I saw how carefully, how gently, the baby had cared for Aubrey in his final months: how he patted his head with a cold cloth, how he held his hand, how he talked to him in a way that many people can't to the dying, an effortless, unpatronizing patter that somehow seemed to acknowledge Aubrey even as it made clear he didn't expect a reply. He had a gift for helping the dying, a rare and valuable gift, one that could have been put to good use in any number of ways.

For a moment, we all stood there, and then Nathaniel, always having to play the negotiator, the mediator, said, "Oh! And, Charles—this is Eden, David's good friend."

She was older, in her mid-thirties, at least a decade older than the baby, a pale-skinned Korean, with the same ridiculous hairstyle as David. Tattoos crept from her sleeves and up her throat; the backs of her hands were stippled with a series of tiny stars that I would later learn formed constellations—the left hand was decorated with the spring constellations of the northern hemisphere; the right with the spring constellations of the south. She wasn't attractive, exactly—the haircut and tattoos and overdone eyebrows, the ink so thick it looked like impasto, had ensured that—but she did have a coiled quality, something lean and feral and sensual.

We bowed to each other. "Nice to meet you, Eden," I said.

I couldn't tell if she was smirking, or if that was what her smile looked like. "You too, Charles," she said. "David's told me a lot about you." This was said meaningfully, though I did not engage.

"I'm glad to hear it," I replied. "Oh, and call me Charles."

"Charles," Nathaniel hissed, but David and Eden only looked at each other and smiled, the same smirking smiles. "Told you," David told her.

Nathaniel had ordered in—flatbreads and mezze—and we went to the table. I had brought a bottle of wine, and David and Nathaniel and I all had some; Eden said she'd just drink water.

The conversation began. All of us, I could feel, were being very careful, which made for a very dull conversation. It wasn't so bad that we were left to speak of the weather, but it wasn't much better. The list of topics I was forbidden from mentioning to David was by now prohibitively lengthy, and so it was easiest to remember instead the ones on which I could engage him without taking us into perilous territory: organic farming, films, robotics, yeast-free baking. I found myself missing Aubrey, who knew exactly how to conduct us, and how to redirect anyone who strayed onto dangerous grounds.

David, I reflected, as I often did during these conversations, was still a child, and it was this—his enthusiasm for the subjects he was passionate about, the way his speech would accelerate and his voice would pitch upward—that made me wish that he had gone to college. He would have found his tribe there; he would have felt less alone. He might even have become less strange, or at the very least found people around whom he didn't seem strange at all. I could see him in a room full of young people, all of them giddy in their excitements—I could see him feeling that he finally belonged somewhere. And yet the place he had chosen instead was The Light, which, thanks to you, I can now monitor as obsessively as I want, but which I rarely have the desire to do. Once, I wanted to know everything about what David was doing and thinking—now I just want to not know, to pretend my son's life, the things that give him joy, don't exist.

But the person whom I was really watching was Eden. She was at the foot of the table, David on her left, and she stared at him with a kind of indulgent fondness, as a mother would at her unruly but gifted child. David did not include her in his monologue, but from time to time, he would glance at her, and she would nod, briefly, almost as if he were reciting lines and she was affirming that he'd gotten them correct. I noticed that she'd eaten very little—her flatbread lay untouched; there was a small dent in the scoop of hummus she'd taken, but everything else remained intact, congealing on her plate. Even her glass of water remained untasted, the round of lemon drifting toward the bottom.

Finally, when the baby had paused for a moment, Nathaniel interjected. "Before I get dessert," he said, "David, maybe you want to tell your father your news?"

The baby looked so uncomfortable that I knew that, whatever

this news was, I didn't want to hear it. So, before he could say anything, I turned to Eden. "How did you two meet?" I asked.

"At a meeting," she said. She had a slow, almost languorous way of speaking, nearly a drawl.

"A meeting?"

She looked at me disdainfully. "The Light," she said.

"Ah," I said, not looking at Nathaniel. "The Light. And what is it that you do?"

"I'm an artist," she said.

"Eden's an amazing artist," David said, eagerly. "She designs all our websites, all our advertisements—everything. She's really talented."

"I'm sure," I said, and although I had been careful not to sound sarcastic, she smirked anyway, as if I had and yet I, not she, was the butt of my own sarcasm. "How long have you been seeing each other?"

She shrugged, just a slight hunch of her left shoulder. "About nine months." She directed one of her half smiles at the baby. "I saw him and just had to have him." The baby reddened at this, embarrassed and flattered, and her smile grew a little wider as she watched him.

Now Nathaniel interrupted again. "Which brings us to David's news," he said. "David?"

"Excuse me," I said, and quickly got up, ignoring Nathaniel's glare, and hurried to the little powder room tucked beneath the stairs. Aubrey had always claimed that this was the site of many after-dinner-party blow jobs between guests when he was younger, but it had long ago been covered in a fussy black-rose-patterned wallpaper that always made me think of a Victorian-era brothel. Here, I washed my hands and inhaled and exhaled. The baby was going to tell me he was marrying this odd, weirdly seductive, much-too-old-for-him woman, and it was my duty to stay calm. No, he wasn't ready to be married. No, he didn't have a job. No, he hadn't moved out of his parent's house. No, he wasn't educated. But it was not my place to say anything; indeed, what I thought was not only not relevant, it wasn't even wanted.

Resolution made, I returned to my place at the table. "Sorry," I said to all of them. And then, to David, "Tell me your news, David."

"Well," said David, and he looked a little bashful. But then he blurted, "Eden's pregnant."

"*What?*" I asked.

"Fourteen weeks," Eden said, and leaned back, and that strange half smile moved across her face. "I'm due September fourth."

"She wasn't sure she wanted it," the baby continued, excited now, when Eden interrupted him.

"But then I thought"—she shrugged—"I might as well. I'm thirty-eight; I don't have forever."

Oh, Peter, you can just imagine what I could have said, maybe even what I should have said. But instead, with such effort I began to sweat, I just sat on my hands and closed my eyes and leaned my head back and said nothing. When I opened them—who knows how much later: it could have been an hour—I found all of them staring at me, not mockingly but curiously, maybe even a little fearfully, as if they were worried that I might actually explode.

"I see," I said, as evenly as I could. (Also: thirty-eight?! David's only twenty-four, and a very young twenty-four at that.) "And so you three will live here, with Dad?"

"Three?" asked David, and then his face cleared. "Oh. Right. The baby." He raised his chin a little, unsure if the question was a challenge or just a question. "Yeah, I guess. I mean, there's plenty of room."

But here Eden made a sound like a grunt, and we all looked at her. "*I'm* not living here," she said.

"Oh," said the baby, crestfallen.

"No offense," she said, maybe to David, maybe to Nathaniel, maybe even to me. "I just need my space."

There was silence. "Well," I said, "it sounds like you both have a lot to work out," and David shot me a hate-filled look, both because I was right and because I had seen him humiliated.

After this, there didn't seem anywhere I could go, conversationally, without starting some sort of conflagration, so I announced I had to leave, and no one stopped me. I did bring myself to hug

David, although both of us were so awkward that it was really more of a bumble, and then I attempted to hug Eden as well, her skinny, boyish body rigid in my arms.

Nathaniel followed me out. Once we were on the stoop, he said, "Before you say anything, Charles, I want you to know that I agree."

"Nate, this is crazy," I told him. "He barely knows her! She's practically forty! Do we know anything about this woman?"

He sighed. "I asked a—a friend of mine, and he said—"

"The friend in Justice?"

He sighed again, and looked upward. (He rarely looks me in the eyes these days.) "Yes, the friend in Justice. He looked into her and said there's nothing to be concerned about—just a mid-level member, a lieutenant in the organization, comes from a middle-class family in Baltimore, went to art school, no major criminal record."

"She sounds amazing," I said, but he didn't answer. "Nate," I said, "you know you're going to be taking care of this baby, don't you? You know David can't do it alone."

"Well, he'll have Eden, and—"

"I wouldn't count on her, either."

He sighed, again. "Well, it may come to that," he admitted.

I wondered, as I often did, when Nathaniel had become so passive. Or maybe not passive—there's nothing passive about raising a baby—but resigned. Was it when I moved them here? Was it when the baby began misbehaving? Was it when he lost his job? Was it Norris's death, or Aubrey's? Was it when our son joined an unsuccessful and marginal insurgency cell? Or was it years of living with me? I wanted to say, "Well, you did a great job raising a kid the first time," before I realized that the only person implicated in that statement was me.

So I said nothing. Instead, we watched the Square. The bulldozers had returned, and the most recent iteration of shantytowns had been cleared away—a soldier stood guard at each entrance, making sure no one tried to come in to reestablish it. Above us, the sky was white with floodlights.

"I don't know how you sleep, with all this light," I said, and he shrugged, resigned again.

"All the windows facing the Square are boarded up anyway," he said. He turned to me. "I heard they're shutting down the refugee camps."

Now it was my turn to shrug. "But what'll happen to all those people?" he asked. "Where will they go?"

"Why don't you ask your friend at Justice?" I asked, childishly.

He sighed. "Charles," he said, wearily, "I'm just trying to make conversation."

But I didn't know where the refugees would go. There was such movement of people—to hospitals and from hospitals; to quarantine camps and to crematoriums and to graves and to prisons—that I could no longer keep track of where any one group was at any one time.

Mostly, though, I thought about how the worst part of David's bringing a baby into this world was not his own inadequacies as a potential parent. It was the very fact of producing a new life. People do it all the time, of course—we depend on them to. But why would you do it as a lark? His life is spent trying to destroy what this country is. So why would he want to bring a baby into it? Who would want a child to grow up in this time, in this place? It takes a special kind of cruelty to make a baby now, knowing that the world it'll inhabit and inherit will be dirty and diseased and unjust and difficult. So why would you? What kind of respect for life is that?

Love, Charles

Dearest Peter,   September 5, 2064

Not words I thought I'd be writing at this age, but—I'm a grandfather. Charlie Keonaonamaile Bingham-Griffith, born September 3, 2064, 5:58 a.m., seven pounds, thirteen ounces.

Lest I start getting flattered, it was quickly clarified that the baby is named not after me but, rather, Eden's mother (deceased), who went by Charlie. A pretty girl's name, and yet she isn't a pretty girl.

Her chin is weak and her nose is blobby and her eyes are small and slitty.

Yet I adore her. I was reluctantly allowed into the mother's room that morning, and the baby was reluctantly turned over to me. Above me, David hovered, saying things like "Support the head, Pops. You've got to support the head!" as if I had not ever before held a baby, beginning with him. But I didn't mind his hectoring—it was moving, in fact, to hear him so anxious on another person's behalf, to see him so vulnerable, to watch how tenderly he held his daughter.

Now that the baby is here, many questions remain, including whether Eden will finally move in to the Washington Square house instead of continuing on in her place in Brooklyn. Also, who's going to raise Charlie, as Eden has already claimed she won't give up her "work" with The Light, and David, conventional as only young people are, feels they need to get married and cohabitate.

But for now, it was time for the four of us to be together. (Along with Eden, of course.) She's easily the best thing David has done, but before you interpret that as backhanded, I should also say that she's the best thing he could ever do. My little Charlie.

Anyway, that's it. I'm cautiously happy to hear Olivier's back in the picture. And speaking of pictures, I've of course attached about a hundred here.

Love you, C.

My dear Peter,   February 21, 2065

One of Nathaniel's qualities I've come to appreciate is his sense of responsibility to those he feels are less capable. In earlier years, this bothered me. I, for example, having been deemed capable, was considered not in need of help or attention or time. But his children, and then, after he left the school, Norris and Aubrey and David, had been classified as vulnerable, and therefore deserving of his care.

Even after Nathaniel inherited his share of Aubrey's estate, he continued to see his two former students, Hiram and Ezra, those boys I once told you about who had survived the '50 illness and then had never been allowed out of the house again. After they turned twelve, their mother hired a new set of tutors, ones that could teach them algebra and physics, but Nathaniel continued to make almost weekly trips over the bridge to visit them. Then, once Charlie arrived, he began having regular video meetings with them instead, because he's been too busy taking care of her.

As I predicted, most of Charlie's care has fallen to Nathaniel. There's a nanny, but really, it's him: David's hours are unreliable, and Eden's less so. I suppose I should add here (as Nathaniel always does) that when David *is* available, he's very sweet with the baby. But really, isn't the point as much to simply *be there*, to be consistent? I'm not sure if good behavior is as much a virtue as constancy. As for Eden: Well, I have nothing to say. I don't even know if she and David are still together, though I know David's still in love with her. But she seems to have remarkably little interest in her own daughter. She'd once told me she wanted the "experience" of pregnancy, but it doesn't seem she wanted or even considered the attendant experience of parenting. This month, for example, she's only come over twice, and never when David's around. Nathaniel always offers to bring the baby to her, but she always demurs: She's too busy, or her place is too unsafe, or she's coming down with a cold. Then Nathaniel re-offers a floor in the house, or at least money to fix up her apartment, both of which he can tell unsettle her, and neither of which she accepts.

Last week, Nathaniel asked me if I'd go out to the Holsons' and visit the boys—they'd missed their last two video appointments, and weren't returning any of his calls or messages. "Are you kidding?" I asked him. "Why don't *you* go visit them?"

"I can't," he said. "Charlie has a cough, and I should be here with her."

"Well, why don't I stay with Charlie, and you can go?" I asked him. I am always greedy for the baby: Every free night I have, I go downtown to spend with her.

"Charles," he said, hoisting the baby from one shoulder to the other, "just do this for me, all right? Besides, if something's wrong, maybe you can help them."

"I'm not a clinician," I reminded him, but there was really no point in arguing. I had to go. Somehow, Nathaniel and I have settled into a relationship that's more married than when we were actually married. Much of this is because of the baby—it feels like we're reliving our early lives together, except now both of us know exactly how disappointed we are in the other and aren't waiting to find out.

So, after my final meeting on Monday, I drove to Cobble Hill. I had last seen the boys five years ago, when their parents (well, their mother; the absent Mr. Holson was absent as usual) threw Nathaniel a belated farewell party—a farewell from Hiram and Ezra's lives as their teacher, that is. The twins were thirteen then, and looked nine or ten. They were well-mannered, handing around pieces of cake to me and Nathaniel and their housekeeper and their mother—all of us in full protective gear because the boys found it difficult to breathe in theirs—before finally taking a slice apiece for themselves. The boys weren't allowed sugar, which Nathaniel said Mrs. Holson was worried would lead to internal inflammation (whatever that means), but the cake, which was only faintly sweet, from pureed apples that had been whisked into the batter, was clearly a special treat for them. They answered my questions in their high, nasal voices, and when Mrs. Holson told them to get the card they'd made for Nathaniel, they ran off together with the same stiff-legged gait, their oxygen packs bouncing against their lower backs.

When Nathaniel had told me of Mrs. Holson's educational plans for her boys, I had thought them peculiar, even cruel. Yes, the boys might one day virtually attend college and earn a degree. They might even get jobs, working side by side as engineers or programmers, sitting behind twinned screens. But the question of what their lives would be—in their house forever, with only each other and their mother for company—had always troubled me.

I can't say that seeing them persuaded me otherwise. But I did understand that while their mother had prepared them for a world they would never inhabit—evidenced by their careful manners, their ability to look you in the eye, their conversational skills: all things, I recognized, that we had never been able to properly teach David—she had also taught them to accept the boundaries and limitations of their lives. When one of them, Hiram or Ezra (I still couldn't tell them apart), said to me, "Nathaniel said you were just in India," I had to stop myself from reflexively saying, "Oh, yes, have you been?" Instead I said that I had indeed just been there, and the other twin sighed and said, "Oh, how marvelous it must have been." It was the right answer, the polite answer (if a little old-fashioned), but there was no yearning in it, no jealousy. Further conversation revealed they knew a good deal about the country's history and current political and epidemiological disasters, even as they seemed to imply that they understood that those were not things they would ever witness for themselves; they had managed to know the world while also accepting that they would never be a part of it. However, many of us are this way: We know of India but will never be a part of it. What was stirring and disturbing about these boys was that, to them, *Brooklyn* was India. Cobble Hill was India. The back garden, which they could see from their playroom, now converted to a schoolroom, was India—places they would learn about but would never visit.

And yet, as well-behaved as they were, as smart as they were, I pitied them. I thought of David at fifteen, getting kicked out of one school after the next, the beautiful lines his body made when he tried to do a jump on his skateboard, the way he practically sprung back up after tumbling to the ground, the way he did a one-hand cartwheel in the grass at Washington Square, the way his skin seemed to glint in the sun.

The boys would be almost eighteen now, and as I knocked on their door, I thought, as I often did, of my Charlie. *Let them be safe,* I thought, *because if they're safe, my Charlie will be safe as well.* But I also thought: *If something happened to them, then nothing will happen to her.* None of it made sense, of course.

When no one answered, I entered the code Nathaniel had given me into the keypad, and then I walked inside. I could tell from the moment the decontamination chamber opened that something had died. These new helmets enhance every scent, and I tore mine off and tugged my sweater up to cover my nose and mouth. The house was as dim as ever. There was no sound, no movement: only that stench.

"Frances!" I called. "Ezra! Hiram! It's Charles Griffith—Nathaniel sent me. Hello?"

But no one answered. There was a door separating the foyer from the rest of the parlor floor, and I pushed it open and nearly gagged. I stepped into the living room. For a while, I saw nothing, and then I heard a faint sound, a buzzing, and I saw that there was a small, dense cloud hovering over the sofa. When I stepped closer, the cloud revealed itself as a swarm of black flies, whirring and humming in a tornado-like pattern. What they were circling was the form of a woman, Frances Holson, tucked up into herself, dead for at least two weeks, maybe more.

I moved away, my heart pounding. "Boys!" I shouted. "Hiram! Ezra!" But again, there was silence.

I continued moving through the living room. Then I heard something else, a faint crinkling. At the end of the space, I saw something moving, and when I got closer, I saw that it was a sheet of clear plastic, one that filled the entire doorframe that separated the living room from the kitchen, and that sealed the kitchen off from the rest of the house. There were two windows cut near the bottom right corner of the sheet: One had two plastic sleeves drooping through it, into the living area, and the other was just a plain rectangle. It was this window that had come loose, and was moving in the breeze from some unseen source.

I looked through the plastic into the kitchen. The first thing I thought was that it resembled some kind of animal's burrow: a gopher's, for example; a prairie dog's. The window shades were drawn, and every surface was covered. I unzipped the plastic wall and walked inside, and here, too, there was a stench of decay, though here the scent was not animal but vegetal. The counters were covered with dishes and pots and pans, and stacks of textbooks. In the sink, there were more pots and pans submerged in an oily scum, like someone had tried to clean them and had given up midway through.

Next to the sink sat two soup bowls, two spoons, and two mugs, all wiped clean. Pushed into every corner were bulging black garbage bags, and when I made myself untie one, I saw they were filled not with chopped-up human remains but with scraps of carrot and crumbs of bread so rotten they had gone slimy, tea bags that looked like they'd been sucked dry. The recycling bin was spilling over, a parodic cornucopia. I picked up a tin of garbanzo beans, and saw that inside, it was not just empty but meticulously empty, so clean it gleamed. The next tin, the same thing, and the next as well.

In the center of the floor, about a foot apart, divided by another stack of books, atop of which sat two laptops, were two sleeping bags, each with a pillow, and—a detail that upset me—each with a stuffed bear tucked beneath the top layer of the bag, their heads resting on the pillows, their black eyes staring at the ceiling. Around this sleeping area was a clear path, leading to a bathroom, where two oxygen packs were plugged into the wall; there were two glasses on the edge of the sink, and two toothbrushes, and a tube of toothpaste, still mostly full. The bathroom led to a laundry room, and here too nothing seemed amiss: The cupboards were stocked with towels and extra toilet paper and flashlights and batteries and laundry detergent; a set of pillowcases and two pairs of child-size jeans still lay in the dryer.

I returned to the kitchen and picked my way back through the detritus to the center of the room, where I looked around, considering what I should do next. I called Nathaniel, but he didn't answer.

And then I went to the refrigerator to get something to drink, and inside was—nothing. Not a bottle of juice, not a jug of mustard, not a stray lettuce leaf withering in the back of a drawer. The freezer, too: nothing. And then a dread moved over me, and I began opening all of the cupboards, all of the drawers—nothing, nothing, nothing. There wasn't a single edible thing in that kitchen, not even anything—flour, baking soda, yeast—that could be used to make something edible. That was why the cans were so clean: They had licked out every bit of food they could. It was why the kitchen was so messy: They had searched everywhere for something to eat.

I didn't know why they had sealed themselves—or, more likely, why their mother had sealed them—in the kitchen, except that it would have been for their safety. But once they had run out of food, I understood that they would have explored the entire house, looking for it.

I ran out of the kitchen and up the stairs. "Ezra!" I shouted. "Hiram!" Their parents' bedroom was on the second floor, and it had been overturned as well: Underwear and socks and men's undershirts vomited from the drawers; shoes were scattered outside the closet.

On the third floor, the same pattern: drawers emptied, closets in disarray. Only their own study was as tidy as I remembered it—they would have known it intimately; they wouldn't have needed to search for what they knew wasn't there.

Here, I stopped, trying to calm down. I called and texted Nathaniel again. And it was as I was waiting for him to answer that I looked through the window and saw, far below me, two forms lying facedown in the back garden.

It was the boys, of course. They were wearing wool coats, even though it was far too warm for wool. They were very thin. One of them, Hiram or Ezra, had angled his head to face his brother, whose own face was pressed into the flagstones. Their oxygen packs were still attached to their pants, the chambers long depleted. And although it was warm, the stones were cool, and this had helped preserve their bodies to some degree.

I stayed until the forensic team came, told them what I knew, and then went to the house to tell Nathaniel, who did not take the news well. "Why didn't I go over there sooner?" he cried. "I knew something was wrong, I *knew* it. Where was their housekeeper? Where was their *fucking* father?"

I made some inquiries; I argued that this could be a public-health matter, and asked that a full investigation be conducted, as swiftly as possible. Today I got the report of what happened, or at least what is thought to have happened: The theory is that, about five weeks ago, Frances Holson became sick with "an illness of unknown pathology." She, realizing it was contagious, sealed the boys into the kitchen, and asked their housekeeper to come by regularly with

food. For the first week, at least, she did. But as Frances deteriorated, the housekeeper was too frightened to return. It's thought
that Frances moved herself downstairs to be closer to her boys, and
gave them the rest of the food she'd set aside for herself, handing it
to them with sterile gloves through one of the windows cut into the
sheet. The boys would have watched her die, and then lived with the
sight of her dead body for at least another two weeks. It was thought
they ventured out to hunt for food about five days before I found
them, exiting through the door in the kitchen and climbing down
the metal stairs to the garden. Hiram—the one lying facedown—
had died first; it was thought that Ezra, who had turned his head to
face him, had died a day later.

But then there were all the things we don't know, and may never
know: Why didn't they—Frances, Hiram, Ezra—call anyone? Why
hadn't their teachers seen the disarray in the kitchen on their video
lessons and asked if they needed help? Did they not have family they
could call? Did they not have friends? How could the housekeeper
just leave such vulnerable people there alone? Why had Frances not
ordered more food? Why hadn't the boys? Had they been infected
by Frances's unknown virus? They wouldn't have starved to death in
a week, or even two. Was it the shock of being outdoors? Was it the
fragility of their immune systems? Or was it something for which
there is no clinical name: Was it despair? Was it hopelessness? Was
it fear? Or was it a kind of surrender, a giving up of life—for surely
they could have found help, couldn't they? They had a way to communicate with the outside world: Why had they not tried harder to
do so, unless, perhaps, they had had enough of life itself, of being
alive?

And most of all: Where *was* their fucking father? The Health
Ministry team tracked him down, just a mile or so away, in Brooklyn Heights, where apparently he had been living for the past five
years with his new family—his new wife, with whom he had begun
an affair seven years ago, and his two new children, five and six,
both healthy. He told the investigators that he had always made sure
Hiram and Ezra were taken care of, that he sent Frances money
monthly. But when they asked which funeral home he wanted his

sons sent to after the autopsy, he shook his head. "The city crematorium is fine," he said. "They died a long time ago." And then he shut the door.

I didn't tell Nathaniel any of this. It would have upset him too much. It upset me. How could someone disavow their children so completely, so neatly, as if they had never existed at all? How could any parent be so dispassionate?

Last night, I lay awake thinking of the Holsons. As bad as I felt for the boys, I felt worse for Frances: to have raised them, and protected them so carefully, so vigilantly, only to have them die from desperation. And as I was about to fall asleep, I wondered if the boys hadn't called anyone for help for one simple reason—because they wanted to see the world. I imagined them joining hands and walking out the door, down the steps, and into their backyard. There they'd stand, holding each other's hands, smelling the air, and looking up at the treetops all around them, their mouths opening in wonder, their lives becoming glorious—for once—even as they ended.

Love—Me

My dear Peter, April 19, 2065

Sorry for the lack of communication. I know it's been weeks. But I think you'll understand when I tell you what happened.

Eden left. And by "left," I don't mean that she vanished one night, leaving only a note behind. We know exactly where she is—in her apartment in Windsor Terrace, presumably packing her things. By "left," I mean she just doesn't want to be a parent anymore. That was how she phrased it, in fact: "I just don't think I have it in me to be a parent."

There's really not a lot else to say, and really not much reason to be surprised. Since Charlie was born, I've seen Eden maybe six times. Now, granted, I don't live in the house, so it's possible that she was coming more frequently than just Thanksgiving and Christmas and New Year's, and so on, but given how careful and anxious Nathaniel always seemed around her, I somehow doubt it. He would never speak badly about her to me—not, I think, because he thought well of her but more because he felt that if he said aloud, "Eden is a bad mother," then she really *would* be a bad mother. Though she already *was* a bad mother. I know it doesn't make sense, but this is how Nathaniel thinks. You and I know what bad mothers are like, but Nathaniel doesn't—he always loved his mother, and still finds it difficult to comprehend that not all mothers will remain mothers out of a sake of duty, much less affection.

I wasn't present for the conversation she had with Nathaniel. Neither was David, whose own whereabouts are less and less known to either of us. But she apparently texted him one day, and said that she needed to talk, and that she would meet him in the park. "I'll bring Charlie," Nathaniel said, and Eden quickly said he shouldn't, because she had a flu "or something" and didn't want to pass it on. (What did she think, that she would say she wasn't interested in Charlie anymore, and Nathaniel would shove her into her arms and run away?) So they met in the park. Nathaniel said that Eden was thirty minutes late (she blamed the fact that the subways were closed, although the subways have been closed for six months now), and that she came with some guy, who waited for her on a different bench a few yards away while she told Nathaniel she was moving out of the country.

"To where?" asked Nathaniel, after he overcame his initial shock.

"Washington," she said. "My family used to vacation on Orcas Island back when I was a kid, and I always wanted to try living out there."

"But what about Charlie?" he asked.

And here, he said, something—guilt, maybe; shame, I hope—flashed across her face. "I just think she's better here with you," she said, and then, when Nathaniel didn't say anything, "You're good at this, man. I just don't think I have it in me to be a parent."

In my new efforts at brevity, I'm going to spare you all the back and forth, the pleading, the many attempts to get David involved, the attempts at negotiation, and just say that Eden is no longer a part of Charlie's life. She signed papers terminating her rights, which leaves David as Charlie's sole parent. But as I've said, David is rarely around, which means that in fact, if not in law, Nathaniel is now her sole parent.

"I don't know what I'm going to do," Nathaniel said. This was last night, after dinner. We were sitting on the sofa in the parlor. Charlie was asleep in his arms. "I'm going to put her to bed."

"No," I said, "let me hold her," and he looked at me, that particular Nathaniel look—half annoyance, half fondness—before transferring her to my arms.

For a while, we sat there, me looking down at Charlie, Nathaniel stroking her head. I had the funny sensation that time had fallen away beneath us, and that we had been given another chance—as parents, as a couple. We were both younger and older than we were right now, and we knew everything that we might do wrong and yet nothing about what might happen, and this was our baby, and nothing in the past two decades that had occurred—my job, the pandemics, the camps, our divorce—had actually transpired. But then I realized that, by erasing all that, I was also erasing David and, therefore, Charlie.

I reached over and began stroking Nathaniel's hair, and he raised his eyebrow at me, but then he leaned his head back, and for a while, we remained there, me stroking his hair, he stroking Charlie's.

"I think maybe I should move in," I said, and he looked at me, and raised his other eyebrow.

"Do you?" he asked.

"Yes," I said. "I could help you, and spend more time with Charlie." I hadn't been planning on making this offer, but now that I had, it seemed right. My apartment—formerly our apartment—had become less a place to live and more a repository for inanimate objects. I slept at the lab. I ate at Nathaniel's. And then I went back to the apartment to change. It didn't really make sense.

"Well," he said, and he shifted a bit, "I wouldn't be opposed to that." He paused. "We're not getting back together, you know."

"I know," I said. I wasn't even offended.

"We're not having sex, either."

"We'll see," I said.

He rolled his eyes. "We're really not, Charles."

"Okay," I said. "Maybe we will, maybe we won't." But I was just teasing him. I wasn't interested in having sex with him, either.

Anyway, just an update. I'm sure you'll have questions, and please ask away. I'll see you in a few days, anyway. Maybe you can help me move? (A joke.)

Love, Charles

Dear Peter,   September 3, 2065

Thanks so much to you and Olivier for the toys: They came right on time, and Charlie loves them, by which I mean she immediately stuffed the cat into her mouth and started chomping away, which I think is a pretty inarguable indication of affection.

I don't have a lot of experience with first-birthday parties, but this one was small: Just me and Nathaniel and even David. And Charlie, of course. You may have heard the latest conspiracy theory, which is that the government invented last month's illness (to do what and to what ends are never discussed, as logic does tend to get in the way of these theories), but David seems to have bought it and tried to talk to me as little as possible over the course of the afternoon.

I was holding Charlie when he came in, looking bedraggled and unshaven, but no more so than usual, and after taking off his suit and cleaning his hands, he walked over and simply lifted her from my lap, like I was a receptacle, nothing more, and lay down with her on the carpet.

You remember David as a baby—he was so skinny and silent, and when he wasn't silent, he was crying. When I was eight, my mother, shortly before she left, told me that a parent decides what she thinks about her child in the first six weeks (or was it months?) of its life, and although I tried hard not to remember those words, they came to me, unbidden, at unwelcome moments during David's infancy.

Even now, I wonder if, somewhere deep inside me, I had never liked him, and if, somewhere deep inside him, he knows that.

That memory is partly why Charlie is such a joy—and not just a joy but a relief. She's so easy to love, to cuddle, to hold. David used to arch and buck out of my arms (and Nathaniel's too, to be fair) when I tried to hug him, but Charlie presses into you, and when you—I—smile at her, she smiles back. Around her, we're all softer, kinder, as if we've mutually agreed to hide from her the truth of who we are, as if she'd disapprove if she knew, as if she'd get up and walk out the door and leave us forever. Her pet names all involve meat. "Pork loin," we call her; "lamb chop"; "short rib"—all things that we haven't eaten in months now, ever since the rationing began. Sometimes we pretend to gnaw on her leg, making growling doglike sounds as we do. "I'm gonna eat you up," Nathaniel says, gumming her thigh as she giggles and gasps. "I'm gonna eat you right up!" (Yes, I know this is all a little disturbing if you think about it too hard.)

Nathaniel had splurged and baked a lemon cake, which all of us ate except for Charlie, because Nathaniel doesn't let her eat sugar yet, and it's probably for the best, as who knows how much sugar will be left when she's our age. "C'mon, Dad, just a bit," David said, holding a crumb out to her, like she was a dog, but Nathaniel shook his head. "Absolutely not," he said, and David smiled and sighed, almost proudly, as if he were the grandparent and was tutting over his son's unreasonably strict ways. "What can I say, Charlie?" he asked his daughter. "I tried." And then the inevitable moment came in which Charlie had to be put to bed, after which David rejoined us in the parlor and launched into one of his canned rants about the government, the refugee camps (which he's convinced are still operating), the relocation centers (which he insists on calling "internment camps"), the ineffectiveness of the decontamination chambers and helmets (with which I secretly agree), the effectiveness of herbal medications (with which I do not), and various conspiracies about how the CDC, as well as "other state-funded research institutes" (i.e., Rockefeller), are spending their time trying not to cure diseases but to manufacture them. He thinks that the state is run by a vast conspiracy, dozens of somber, gray-haired white men in military uniforms sitting in padded-wall bunkers with holograms and listening devices—the truth would be crushing in its banality.

It was the same speech, with a few variations, that I'd been listening to for the past six years. And yet it no longer upset me—or at least, it no longer upset me for the same reasons. This time, as I had the time before, I looked over at my son, still so passionate, speaking so quickly and so loudly that he had to keep wiping saliva away from his mouth, leaning toward Nathaniel, who was nodding at him tiredly, and felt a perverse sorrow. I knew he believed in what The Light represented, but I also knew that he had in part joined it to try to find a place where he belonged, a place where he might at last feel he had found his own.

And yet, for all his devotion to The Light, it did not seem devoted to him. As you know, The Light has a quasi-military power structure, with members adding tattoos of stars to the insides of their right arms as they're promoted by committee through its ranks. Eden had had three when we met her; she had added a fourth when Nathaniel had last seen her. But David's wrist was decorated with a single lonely star. He was an eternal foot soldier, relegated to (I know from your reports) scut work: procuring the bits and pieces of material that the engineers would wire into bombs, never thanked by name in the fulsome speeches from headquarters that followed each successful attack. He was a nobody, an unnamed, a forgotten. Of course, I was glad for this, for his irrelevance, for his being overlooked—it kept him safe, it kept him uninvolved. But I also realized that I had come to loathe The Light not just for what it propagated but for how it refused to recognize my son's efforts. He had joined it looking for home, and it had ended up treating him the same as everyone else had. As I say, I know this is perverse—would I have been happier if his arm had been aswim with blue stars? No, of course not. But it would be a different kind of unhappiness, an unhappiness mingled with, perhaps, a distorted pride, a relief that if Nathaniel and I were not his family, he had found one after all, no matter how dangerous or wrong. Aside from Eden, he had never brought anyone home to meet us, he spoke of no friends, he never grabbed his phone in the middle of our dinners because he was getting so many messages that he had to answer them, grinning at the screen as he tapped out a reply. Although I had never seen him in action, as it were, I had a persistent image of him on the edges of groups, of listening to conversations but never being asked to join one. I cannot prove this, naturally, but I think this friendlessness was in part what kept him from spending more time with his daughter—it was as if he feared he might infect her with his loneliness, as if she too might come to see him as someone of little consequence.

It made me ache for him. I thought again, as I often did—far too often, given that he is now twenty-five, a grown man, a father, even—of him as a small boy on the playground in Hawai'i, how the other children had run from him, how he had known even then that there was something not right about him, something that repelled people, something that would set him apart and aside for the rest of his life.

All I can do now is continue to hope for him, and to do better with and for his child. I can't say that I can use her to make up for how I failed with him, but I *do* know that it's my responsibility to try. So much has changed since David was a baby; so much has been lost. Our home, our family, our hopes. But children need adults. That much hasn't changed. And so I can try again. I not only can: I have to.

Love, Charles

My dear Peter,   January 7, 2067

It's the end of a very long day, at the end of a very long week. I returned late from the Committee—the nanny had already put Charlie to bed, hours ago; the cook had left a bowl of rice and tofu and pickled cucumbers. Next to the bowl was a sheet of paper with a thick green line of crayon forking across the page. "From Charlie, for her Papa," the nanny had written in the bottom right corner. I put it in my briefcase so I could take it to the lab on Monday.

The Committee had discussed what was happening in the U.K.—sorry, New Britain—since the election. You'll be happy to hear that everyone thought that the transition seemed much more harmonious than you do. And you'll be not at all surprised to hear that everyone thinks that, despite everything, you've made the wrong decision, and that you've been far too lenient with the population, and that you've conceded to the protestors. Everyone also agreed it was crazy that you were reopening the Underground. You know I don't entirely disagree.

After I ate, I wandered the house. This is something I've begun doing at the end of each week. It began that first Saturday after the event, when I had woken from a dream. In it, Nathaniel and I were back in Hawai'i, in the house we once lived in, but at the age we are now. I don't know if David existed in this dream—if he was in his own house, or living with us but out running an errand, or if he had never been born at all. Nathaniel had been looking for a photo, one from shortly after we'd met. "I noticed something funny in it," he said. "I have to show you. I just can't remember where I put it."

That was when I had woken up. I knew I had been dreaming, and yet something compelled me to get up and start looking as well. For the next hour, I walked from floor to floor—this is before the nanny and the cook moved onto the fourth floor—opening random drawers and taking random books from shelves and flipping through their pages. I sifted through the bowl of junk on the kitchen counter—twist ties and rubber bands and paper clips and safety pins: all the small, poor, necessary items that I remembered from my childhood, all the stuff that had remained even when so much else had changed. I looked through Nathaniel's closet, his shirts that still smelled of him, and his bathroom cabinet, the vitamins he took, even long after they had been proven ineffective.

In those first weeks, I had neither the right nor the inclination to enter David's room, but even after the investigation had finished, I kept the door shut, moving downstairs to what had been Nathaniel's room so that there was no need to ever visit the third floor. It wasn't until two months later that I was finally able to do so. The bureau had left the room very tidy. Part of this was simply a matter of reduced volume: Gone were David's computers and phones, the papers and books that had covered the floor in heaps, the rolling plastic cupboard containing dozens of tiny drawers, each filled with items, nails and tacks and bits of wire, meant for things I couldn't contemplate too hard, for if I had, I would have had to report him to the bureau myself long ago. It was as if they had erased the past decade altogether, so that what remained—his bed, some clothes, some monster figurines he had made when he was a teenager, the Hawaiian flag that had hung in whatever room he occupied from the time he was a baby—was his teenage self, just before he had joined The Light, before he and Nathaniel and I had broken from one another, before the experiment of our family had failed. The only indication that time had indeed passed after all were two framed pictures of Charlie atop the table near his bed: The first, which Nathaniel had given him, was of her on her first birthday, grinning hugely, with mashed peaches smeared over her face. The second is a short video Nathaniel took a few months later, of David holding her by her arms and spinning her around. The camera moves first to his face, and then to hers, and you can see they're both shouting with laughter, their mouths wide with happiness.

Now, nearly four months after that day, I find that hours can pass in which I think of neither of them, in which the flashes of delusion—wondering, in the middle of a dull meeting, what Nathaniel would be making for dinner, for example, or whether David would stop by this weekend to see Charlie—no longer flatten me. What I cannot stop doing is thinking of the moment itself, even though I didn't witness it, even though, when I was offered the chance to review the classified images, I declined: the explosion, the people nearest to the device bursting into bits, the jars around them shattering. I know I've told you before that the one image I did look at, before I closed the file for good, was taken that night. It was of the ground, close to where the device had gone off, in the sauces-and-soups aisle. The floor was covered with a gluey red substance, though it wasn't blood but tomato paste, and scattered through it were hundreds of nails, burned black and twisted by the heat of the explosive. On the right-hand side of the image was a man's disembodied hand and part of an arm, a watch still strapped to the wrist.

The other image I saw was the video clip documenting the moment David rushes into the store. There's no sound on the video, but you can tell by how he swivels his head that he's frantic. Then he opens his mouth, and you can see him shout something, a single syllable: *Dad! Dad! Dad!* And then he runs deeper into the store, and then there's nothing, and then the image of the door, now shut, wobbles and goes white.

It's this video clip that I've been showing investigators and ministers for months, ever since I got it, trying to prove to them that David couldn't have been responsible for the explosive, that he had loved Nathaniel, that he would never have wanted to kill him. He knew Nathaniel did his grocery shopping there; when he had realized what The Light had planned, and when Nathaniel had sent him a message saying he was going to the store, had he not run inside to find him, to save him? I could not definitively say he wouldn't have wanted to kill anyone else—though I said so anyway—but I knew he wouldn't have wanted to kill Nathaniel.

But the state does not agree with me. On Tuesday, the interior minister himself came to see me, and explained that, as David was a "prominent and known" member of an insurgent organization responsible for the deaths of seventy-two people, they would have to issue him a postmortem censure for treason. This meant that he could not be buried or interred at a cemetery, and that his descendants would be prohibited from inheriting any of his assets, which would be seized by the state.

Then a strange look came over his face, and he said, "So it's fortunate—if I may use that word in this horrible situation—that your ex-husband had specified in his will that his house and all his property would bypass your son and go directly to your grand-daughter."

I was so dazed by what he had just said about David's censure that

I couldn't understand what he was trying to communicate to me. "No," I said, "no, that's not true. It was all to go to David."

"No," said the minister, and he drew something from the pocket of his uniform, which he handed me. "I believe you're mistaken, Dr. Griffith. It reads quite clearly in his will that his entire estate is to be left to your granddaughter, with you as its executor."

I unfolded the sheaf of papers, and there it was, as if I had not been witness to the creation and signing of this will just a year ago: There was to be a trust established for Charlie, but David would inherit the house, with the provision that he must leave it to Charlie upon his death. But now here was a document, signed by Nathaniel and by me, watermarked and stamped with all three of our name seals—the lawyer's, Nathaniel's, and mine—attesting to what the minister had said. And something else: Charlie's official name on the document was listed not as "Charlie Bingham-Griffith," but as simply "Charlie Griffith"—her father's name, Nathaniel's name, edited out of existence. I looked up, and the minister looked back at me, a long, unreadable stare, before standing. "I'll leave you that copy for your records, Dr. Griffith," he said, and then he left. It wasn't until I got home that night that I held it to the light, looking at how perfect the signatures were, at how exact the seals were. And then I was suddenly frightened, and convinced the paper itself was somehow bugged, although that technology is a decade off, at least.

Since then, I have tried to find the original will, even though doing so would be both pointless and, even, perilous. I've removed all the documents Nathaniel kept from the safe, and every night I go through a few of them, watching life present itself in reverse: papers assigning Nathaniel formal, legal guardianship of Charlie, signed three weeks before the attack; papers signed by Eden forfeiting any legal claims to her daughter; Charlie's birth certificate; the deed to the house; Aubrey's will; our divorce papers.

And then I begin to wander. I tell myself I'm looking for the will, but I don't suppose I really am, because the places I look are nowhere Nathaniel would have put it in the first place, and if he *had* kept a copy in the house, it had been removed long ago, without us noticing. There was no point in looking, just as there had been no point in calling our lawyer and listening to him claim that, no, I had been mistaken, that the will as I described it had never existed. "You're under a lot of strain, Charles," he said. "Grief can make people"—he paused—"misremember." Then I became scared again, and told him I was certain he was correct, and hung up.

I am lucky, I know. Much worse has happened to relatives of insurgents, to people associated with far less deadly attacks than David has been. I am still too useful to the state. You don't need to worry about me, Peter. Not yet. I'm in no immediate danger.

But sometimes I wonder if what I'm really searching for is not the will but evidence of the person I was before this all began. How far would I have to go back? Before the state was established? Before I answered that first call from the ministry, asking if I wanted to be an "architect of the solution"? Before the illness of '56? Before the one of '50? Earlier? Before I joined Rockefeller?

How far back do I have to go? How many decisions must I regret? Sometimes I think that somewhere in this house is hidden a piece of paper with the answers, and that if I hope hard enough, I'll wake up in the month or year when I first began to go astray, only this time, I'll do the opposite of what I did. Even if it hurts. Even if it feels wrong.

Love, Charles

Dear Peter,   August 21, 2067

Hello from the lab on a Sunday afternoon. I'm just here catching up on some things and reading some of the reports from Beijing—what did you make of Friday's? We haven't discussed it, but I doubt you're surprised, either. Christ: to learn, definitively, that not only those stupid decontam chambers but also the helmets are completely use-less is going to spark riots. People went bankrupt installing them, maintaining them, replacing them for fifteen years, and now we're telling everyone that, oops, it was a mistake, get rid of them? That announcement is scheduled for a week from Monday, and it's going to be bad.

But the next five days will be the hardest. On Tuesday they'll announce that the internet will be "suspended" for an indefinite period of time. On Thursday they'll announce that all international travel, to and from other countries, including Canada, Mexico, the Western Federation, and Texas, will also be suspended.

I've been very anxious, and Charlie can sense it. She crawls into my lap and pats my face. "Are you sad?" she asks me, and I tell her I am. "Why?" she asks, and I tell her it's because people in this country are fighting, and we have to try to make them stop fighting. "Oh," she says. "Don't be sad, Papa," she says. "I'm never sad with you," I tell her, although I am—sad that this is the world she lives in. But maybe I should tell her the truth after all: that I *am* sad, all the time, and that it's all right to be sad. But she's such a happy baby, and it seems immoral to do so.

The Justice Ministry and the Interior Ministry seem certain they can quash the protests in three months. The military is ready to deploy, but as I know you saw in the last report, the number of infiltrators in the ranks has become alarming. The army says they need time to "test the loyalties" of its members (god knows what that means); Justice and Interior say that they can't spare any time. The most recent report claims that large numbers of "historically disadvantaged groups of citizens" are helping the insurgency efforts, but there's been no talk of special punishment, and thank goodness—I know I'm protected, I know I'm an exception, yet it makes me nervous all the same.

Don't worry about me, Peter. I know you do, but try not to. They can't get rid of me yet. *My* digital access isn't being curtailed, of course—for one, I need it to communicate with Beijing—and although all our communication is encrypted, I may start sending you letters through our mutual friend just as a precaution. This means they'll likely be less frequent (lucky you) but also lengthier (unlucky you). Let's see how it goes. Though you know how to reach me in an emergency.

Love to you and Olivier, C.

My dear Peter,   September 6, 2070

It's very early in the morning, and I'm writing you from the lab. Thank you and Olivier for the books and presents, by the way— I meant to write you last week, when they arrived, but I forgot. I'd hoped Charlie would be discharged in time to spend her birthday at home, but she had another grand mal seizure on Tuesday, and so they decided to keep her for a few more days; if she remains stable over the weekend, they'll let her leave on Monday.

I've obviously been spending every day with her, and most of the nights. The Committee's been almost too humane about it. It's as if they knew that one of us would have a child or grandchild who'd get infected—the odds were too great for that not to be the case—and they're relieved that it was my grandchild, not theirs. Their relief makes them guilty, and their guilt makes them generous: Charlie's hospital room is filled with more toys than she'll ever play with, as if the toys were a kind of sacrifice, and she a minor god, and by appeasing her, they'll protect their own.

We've been here at Frear for two months now. Nine weeks, actually, come tomorrow. Many years ago, when Nathaniel and I first moved to the city, this had been a ward for adult cancer patients. Then, in '56, they converted it to an infectious-disease wing, and then last winter, to a pediatric infectious-disease wing. The rest of the patients are in what used to be the burn unit, and the burn patients have been dispatched to other hospitals. In the early days of the infection, before it was announced to the public, I would hurry past this hospital, never looking up at its bulk, because I knew that this was the place best-equipped to care for the children who would get sick, and because I felt that if I never looked at the outside of it, I would never see the inside of it.

The ward is on the tenth floor and faces east to the river, and therefore to the crematoriums, whose fires have burned without pause since March. In the early days, when I was visiting as an observer, not as a guest—or a "loved one," as the hospital calls us—you could look outside and see the vans full of corpses being unloaded onto the boats. The bodies were so small that they could stack them four or five to a stretcher. After the first six weeks, the state had a fence built on the eastern edge of the river, because parents were jumping into the water as the boats pulled away, screaming for their children, trying to paddle toward the other shore. The fence prevented that, but it didn't prevent the people on the tenth floor (the parents, largely, as most of the children were insensate) from looking outside for distraction and instead encountering, in the cruelest of ironies, the place where most of their children would go next, as if Frear were simply a layover before their final destination. So then the hospital covered up all the eastern-facing windows, on this floor and all the others, and hired art students to paint on them. But as the months dragged by, the scenes the students had drawn—of Fifth Avenue, lined with palm trees and happy children walking down the sidewalk; of the Central Park peacocks being fed bread by happy children—also began to seem cruel, and eventually they were covered with white paint.

The ward is meant to accommodate a hundred and twenty patients but now holds around two hundred. Charlie is its longest-term resident. Over the past nine weeks, various other children have come and gone. Most remain for just ninety-six hours, though there was a little boy who was probably a year older than Charlie—he looked seven, maybe eight—who had been admitted three days before she was and who died last week. He was the second-longest-term resident. Everyone here is related to someone who works for the state, or related to someone to whom the state owes a favor, a favor big enough to keep them out of a relocation center. For the first seven weeks, we had a private room, and although I had been assured we would always have it, for as long as we needed, there came a point where I could no longer morally justify it to myself. So now Charlie has two roommates, in a space that could sleep three more. The other parents and I nod at one another—everyone is wearing so much protective clothing that we can only see one another's eyes—but otherwise we all pretend that the others don't exist. Only our children exist.

I've seen what you're doing over there, but here, each child's bed is surrounded by walls of transparent plastic sheeting, like the one Ezra and Hiram had lived behind; the parents sit outside and stick their hands through the gloves built into one of the walls so we can at least offer some semblance of touch. The few parents who for whatever reason had never been exposed to the earlier virus, the one that's cross-reactive to the current one, aren't allowed to enter Frear at all—they're just as vulnerable as the children, and should really be in isolation themselves. But they're not, of course. Instead, they stand outside the hospital, even in the heat, which has been almost unbearable these past few months, and look up at its windows. Years ago, when I was a child, I saw an old video of a crowd of people waiting beneath a Paris hotel for a pop singer to emerge from his room onto his balcony. The crowd here is as big, but whereas that other gathering had been restive, on the verge of hysteria, this one is quiet, eerily so, as if making any noise might upset their chances of getting inside to see their children. Though they have no hope at all of doing so, not while they're still contagious or capable of spreading contagion. The lucky ones can at least watch a livestream of their children lying, unresponsive, in bed; the unlucky ones, not even that.

The children enter Frear as distinct people, but within two weeks of being treated with Xychor, they look more alike than different. You know what it looks like, too: the shrunken faces, the softened teeth, the hair loss, the boil-covered extremities. I read the report from Beijing, but here, the fatality rate is highest among those ten and younger; adolescents are much more likely to survive, though even those rates of survival—depending on whose reports you're seeing—are grim.

What we don't know yet, and won't know for another decade or so at least, is Xychor's long-term consequences. It wasn't made for children, and it certainly shouldn't be administered to them in the doses it is. One thing we *do* know, as of last week, is that its toxicity alters—we don't know how—pubertal development, which means there's a strong possibility that Charlie will be sterile. After I heard this in one of the Committee meetings I managed to attend, I barely made it to the bathroom before I started crying. I had kept her safe for so many months. If I had been able to keep her safe for just nine more, we'd have a vaccine. But I couldn't.

I knew from reports that she would be changed, and she is, though among the many things I don't yet know is how much. "There will be damage," I read in the latest report, which then outlined, in vague terms, what that damage might be: Cognitive differences. Slowed physical reflexes. Stunted growth. Sterility. Scarring. The first is the most terrifying, because "cognitive differences" is so meaningless a phrase. Her new quiet, where she'd once chattered away—is that a cognitive difference? Her sudden affectlessness—is that a cognitive difference? Her new formality—"Who am I, Charlie?" I asked her, the first day she regained consciousness. "Do you know me?" "Yes," she said, after studying me, "you're my grandfather." "Yes," I said, and I was beaming, smiling so hard my cheeks hurt, but she was only staring at me, silent and inexpressive. "It's me. Your Papa, who loves you." "Grandfather," she repeated, but that was all, and then she closed her eyes again—is *that* a cognitive difference? Her halting conversation, her new humorlessness, the way she studies my face, her expression composed but slightly puzzled, as if I were another species and she were trying to interpret me—is that a cognitive difference? Last night I read her a story she had loved, about a pair of talking rabbits, and when I was finished, where she would have normally chimed "Again!," she instead looked at me, her eyes blank. "Rabbits can't speak," she said, finally. "That's true, sweetheart," I said, "but it's a story." And then, when she said nothing in response, only continued to stare at me, her face unreadable, I added, "It's make-believe."

Read it again, Papa! Do the voices better this time!

"Oh," she said at last.

Is *that* a cognitive difference?

Or is her new seriousness—her use of "Grandfather" makes her sound slightly disapproving, like she's aware that the title is grander than I deserve—an inevitable result of all the death she's seen? Even though I've been careful not to discuss it with her, the severity of her illness, the now hundreds of thousands of children who have died, she must have intuited it anyway, mustn't she? Already her roommates have been replaced seven times in two weeks, the children turned in a single exhalation to corpses and hurried out of the room beneath a tent of muslin so Charlie, asleep anyway, wouldn't witness their departure—there have been some of these kindnesses, even now.

I stroked her scalp, which is stubbly with scabs and the first fine bristles of new hair. I thought again of the sentence from the report that I now repeat to myself multiple times a day: *These findings remain speculative until we have a larger sample set of survivors to study, as does the duration of these effects.* "Go to sleep, little Charlie," I told her, and whereas, before, she would whine a bit, plead for another story, she instead closed her eyes immediately, an act of submission that made me shiver.

Last Friday, I watched her sleep until about eleven p.m. (or 23:00, as the state would now have it), until I finally made myself leave. Outside, the streets were empty. For the first month, they made a curfew exception for the parents who wait on the street, and who would sleep on the pavement on blankets they brought from home; typically, the other parent, if there was one, would relieve the sleeper at dawn, bringing them food and taking their place on the sidewalk. But then the state became afraid of riots and banned overnight gatherings, even though the only thing those people wanted was what was inside the hospital. Naturally, I was in favor of this dispersal, if only from an epidemiological perspective, but what I hadn't realized until everyone left is that the small, human sounds of this gathering, the sighs and snores and murmurs, the sharp flick of someone flipping the page of a book, the glug of water being swigged from a bottle, somehow balanced the other noise: the refrigerated trucks idling at the docks, the cottony thud of sheet-wrapped bodies being stacked atop one another, the boats chugging to and fro. Everyone who worked on the island had been trained to do so in silence, out of respect, but sometimes you heard one of them exclaim, or swear, or occasionally cry out, and you couldn't know whether it was because they had dropped a body, or because a shroud had come loose, revealing a face, or because they were simply overwhelmed by the work of burning so many bodies, bodies of children.

The driver knew where I was going that night, and I was able to lean my head against the window and sleep for half an hour before I heard him announce our arrival at the center.

The center is on an island that, half a century ago, was a nature preserve for endangered birds: terns, loons, ospreys. By '55, the terns were extinct, and the next year, another crematorium had been erected on the southern shore. But then the island flooded in the storm, and sat abandoned until '68, when the state started quietly rebuilding it, constructing artificial sand beds and concrete barrier walls.

The walls are meant to protect the island from future floods, but they're also a necessary obfuscation. It was never the intention, but this center has ended up serving mostly children. There was a debate over whether we should allow parents in or not. I argued that we should—the majority of them were immune. But the psychologists on the Committee argued we shouldn't—the problem was, they said, that they would never recover from what they saw there, and this trauma, on such a mass scale, could lead to social instability. Finally, a dormitory was built for the parents on the north side of the island, but then there was that incident in March, and now no parents at all are allowed. So instead, the parents have built a shantytown— the richer people have actually erected tiny houses from brick, the poorer from cardboard—on the coast in New Rochelle, though all they can see from there is the wall that surrounds the island, and the helicopters lowering themselves from the sky.

There had been, as you recall, a good deal of debate about where we should locate this center. Most of the Committee had argued for one of the former refugee camps: Fire Island, Block Island, Shelter Island. But I had fought for this island: far enough north from Manhattan so there'd be few unexpected visitors; not too far for the helicopters and boats, which could easily float downriver to the crematorium now that the waterways have been reopened.

But though I never said so, the reason I really chose this place was because of its name: Davids Island. Not singular—David's—but many, as if this land were inhabited not by an ever-changing population of (mostly) children, but by Davids. My son, in duplicate, at all different ages, doing all the things my son had liked to do at various points in his life. Building bombs, yes. But also reading, and playing basketball, and running about like a crazed puppy to make me and Nathaniel laugh, and spinning his daughter around, and climbing into bed next to me when it was thundering and he was frightened. The older Davids would be parents to the younger Davids, and when one finally died—though that wouldn't be for a very long time, as the oldest inhabitants were still only thirty, the age my David would have been, had he lived—he would be replaced by another, so that the population of Davids always would remain the same: never increasing, never diminishing. There would be no misunderstandings, no concerns that the younger Davids might be somehow different, somehow strange, because the older Davids would understand them. There would be no loneliness, because these Davids would not have ever known parents, or classmates, or strangers, or people who wouldn't play with them: They would only know one another, which is to say themselves, and their happiness would be complete, because they would never know the agony of wanting to be someone else, for there was no one else to admire, no one else to envy.

I come here sometimes, late, when even the residents of the shantytown have gone to sleep, and sit at the edge of the blackish, brackish water and look out onto the island, which is always lit, and think about what my Davids might be doing now: Maybe the older ones are having a beer. Maybe some of the teenagers are playing volleyball under those bright white lights, the ones that never switch off and transform the water around the island into a shimmer of oil. Maybe the younger ones are reading comic books under their covers with a flashlight—or whatever it is kids do these days when they're goofing off. (*Do* they still goof off? They must, mustn't they?) Maybe they're cleaning up after dinner, because the young Davids have been taught to be helpful, they have been taught to be good people, to be kind to one another; maybe there's a pile of them flopped on a bed many yards wide, in which they all sleep in a jumble, one's breath hot against the back of another's head, one's hand stretching out to scratch his thigh and scratching his neighbor's instead. But it won't matter: They'll both feel it anyway.

"David," I say to the water, quietly, so as not to wake the parents who sleep behind me. "Can you hear me?" And then I listen.

But no one ever answers.

Love—Charles

My dear Peter,   September 5, 2071

Today was Charlie's seventh birthday party, which we weren't able to have on Thursday, as we'd planned, because she wasn't feeling well. I didn't get to mention it when we talked, but for the past month she's been having petit mal seizures: They only last eight to eleven seconds, but she's been experiencing them more frequently than I had realized. She had one at the neurologist's office, in fact, but I hadn't noticed it until the doctor pointed it out to me—a long, silent stare, her mouth slightly open. "That's what you have to look for," her doctor said, but I was too ashamed to admit that she often looked like that, that I had seen her wear that expression before and had thought it simply part of who she now was, not a sign of any neurological condition. An aftereffect of Xychor, again, especially for children who were given the drug before puberty. The doctor thought she'd grow out of them without medication—I couldn't bear to put her on another, especially one that might further deaden her—but isn't certain "what the developmental damages will be."

After these seizures, she's limp, acquiescent. Since coming home, she's been so wooden; when I reach out a hand to her, she teeters backward with a kind of stiff-limbed rigidity that would be comical if it weren't so dismaying. Now I know just to pick her up and hold her next to me, and when she begins to squirm—she no longer likes being held—I know she's recovered.

I try to make things as easy for her as I can. The Rockefeller Child and Family Center has closed for lack of students, and so I enrolled her in a small, expensive primary school near Union Square, where each student has her own teacher, and where they agreed she could begin in late September, once she gains a little more weight and grows a little more hair. I, of course, don't care whether she has hair or not, but it's the one aspect of her appearance that seems to make her self-conscious. Anyway, I was happy to keep her at home with me for a while longer. The school's dean suggested I get her an animal, to give her something to interact with, and so on Monday I got her a cat, a small gray thing, and presented her with it when she woke up. She didn't exactly smile—she rarely smiles these days—but she did immediately express an interest in it, taking it in her arms and looking into its face.

"What's his name, Charlie?" I asked her. Before the sickness, she had named everything: people she saw on the street, the plants in their pots, the dolls on her bed, the two sofas downstairs that she claimed resembled hippos. Now she looked up at me with her newly disquieting gaze, in which you can see either profundity or nothingness.

"Cat," she said, finally.

"How about something more—descriptive?" I asked her. ("Make her describe things to you," her psychologist said. "Make her keep talking. You won't necessarily be able to reawaken her imagination, but you can remind her that it's there for her to use.")

She was quiet for so long, staring at the kitten and stroking its fur, that I thought she'd had another seizure. Then she spoke again. "Little Cat," she said.

"Yes," I said, and my eyes grew hot. I felt, as I often do when watching her, a deep ache, one that radiates from my heart to every part of my body. "He *is* little, isn't he?"

"Yes," she agreed.

She's so different now. Before the illness, I would watch her from the doorway of her bedroom, unwilling to interrupt her play by speaking, listening to her talk to her stuffed animals, using one pitch of voice to command them and another to inhabit each one, and feel something inside me swell. When I was in med school, I remember a woman, the mother of a child with Down syndrome, had come to talk to us about the manner in which the doctors and geneticists had discussed her daughter's postnatal diagnosis with her, which ranged from heartless to clueless. But then, she said, on the day she and her baby were being discharged, the attending resident had come to say goodbye to them. "Enjoy her," he had said to this woman. *Enjoy her*: No one had ever told her that she might delight in her baby, that her baby might be a source not of troubles but of pleasure.

And in the same way, I had always enjoyed Charlie. I always knew I did—that enjoyment, that pleasure I took in the fact of her, was inextricable from my love for her. Now, though, that enjoyment is gone, replaced by some other sensation, one deeper and more painful. It's as if I cannot see her without experiencing her in triplicate: the shadow of who she once was, the reality of who she is, the projection of who she might become. I mourn one, am bewildered by the next, and fear for the third. I had never realized just how much I had assumed about her future until she emerged from her coma so changed. I knew I wouldn't be able to predict what New York, this country, the world might look like then—but I always knew that she'd be able to meet her future bravely and forthrightly, that she had the self-possession and charm and intuition to survive.

But now I fear for her constantly. How will she live in this world? Who will she be? That image I hadn't even realized I had, of her banging into the house, a teenager, after visiting a friend, me lecturing her for being late—will that still happen? Will she be able to walk through the Village—sorry, Zone Eight—alone? Will she have friends? What will become of her? My love for her at times feels terrible, huge, dark: a wave so towering and silent that there is no fighting, no hope against it—you can only stand and wait for it to smother you.

I understand that this dreadful love is being compounded by a growing awareness of how the world that we live in—a world that, yes, I helped create—is not one that will be tolerant of people who are fragile or different or damaged. I have always wondered how people knew it was time to leave a place, whether that place was Phnom Penh or Saigon or Vienna. What had to happen for you to abandon everything, for you to lose hope that things would ever improve, for you to run toward a life you couldn't begin to imagine? I had always imagined that that awareness happened slowly, slowly but steadily, so the changes, though each terrifying on its own, became inoculated by their frequency, as if the warnings were normalized by how many there were.

And then, suddenly, it's too late. All the while, as you were sleeping, as you were working, as you were eating dinner or reading to your children or talking with your friends, the gates were being locked, the roads were being barricaded, the train tracks were being dismantled, the ships were being moored, the planes were being rerouted. One day, something happens, maybe something minor, even, like chocolate disappears from the stores, or you realize there are no more toy shops in the entire city, or you watch the playground across the street from you be destroyed, the metal jungle gym disassembled and loaded into a truck, and you understand, suddenly, that you're in danger: That TV is never returning. That the internet is never returning. That, even though the worst of the pandemic is over, the camps are still being built. That when someone said, in the last Committee meeting, that "certain people's chronic procreation was welcome for once in history," and no one reacted, not even you, that everything you had suspected about this country—that America was not for everyone; that it was not for people like me, or people like you; that America is a country with sin at its heart—was true. That when the Cessation and Prevention of Terrorism Act was passed, allowing convicted domestic insurgents the choice between internment and sterilization, it was inevitable that Justice would eventually find a way to extend that punishment to first the children and then the siblings of those convicted insurgents.

And then you realize: I can't stay here. I can't raise my grand-daughter here. So you reach out to some contacts. You make some discreet inquiries. You reach out to your best, your oldest friend, your former lover, and you ask him to help get you out. But he can't. No one can. You are told by your government that your presence is essential. You are told that you'd be allowed to travel on a limited-term passport, but that a passport cannot be issued for your grand-daughter. You know that they know that you would never leave without her—you know that she is the reason you have to leave; you know she is how they will ensure that you never will.

You lie awake at night; you think of your dead husband, your dead son, the bill being proposed that would make a family like the one you once had illegal. You think of how proud you once were: how you once bragged about being a young lab chief; how you volun-teered to help build the systems you now want to escape. You think of how your safety is guaranteed only by your ongoing participation. You want nothing more than to scroll back through time. It is your dearest dream and wish.

But you can't. You can only try to keep your granddaughter safe. You are not a brave man—you know that. But, as much of a cow-ard as you are, you will never abandon her, even as she has become someone you can't access and don't understand.

You ask every night for forgiveness.

You know you'll never receive it.

Love, Charles

I was nervous on the day I met my husband for the first time. This was in the spring of 2087; I was twenty-two. The morning I was to meet him, I woke earlier than usual and put on the dress that Grandfather had gotten for me somewhere—it was green, like bamboo. There was a sash around the middle that I tied in a bow, and long sleeves, which hid the scars I had from the sickness.

At the marriage broker's office, which was in Zone Nine, I was taken to a plain white room. I had asked Grandfather if he would be there for the meeting with me, but he had said that I should meet with the candidate alone, and he would be right outside, in the waiting room.

After a few minutes, the candidate entered. He was nice-looking, as nice-looking as he was in his picture, and I felt unhappy, because I knew I wasn't nice-looking myself, and his attractiveness would make me less so. I thought he might laugh at me, or look away from me, or turn around and leave.

But he did none of those things. He bowed to me, deeply, and I bowed back, and we introduced ourselves. Then he sat, and I sat, too. There was a pot of powdered tea and two cups, and a little dish with four cookies. He asked if I wanted some tea, and I said I did, and he poured me some.

I was anxious, but he tried to make the conversation easy. We already knew all the important things about each other: I knew that his parents and sister had been declared guilty of treason and had been sent to labor camps, and had later been executed. I knew that he had been a graduate student in biology, and that he had been studying for his doctorate before he was expelled for having traitorous relatives. He knew who Grandfather was, and who my father was. He knew the disease had left me sterile; I knew that he had chosen to be sterilized rather than be sent to the rehabilitation camps. I knew he had been a promising student. I knew he was very smart.

He asked me what I liked to eat, what kind of music I liked, if I was enjoying my job at Rockefeller, if I had any hobbies. Meetings between relatives of state traitors were usually recorded, even meetings such as these, so we were both careful. I liked that he was careful, and that he hadn't asked me any questions that I wouldn't be able to answer; I liked his voice, which was soft and gentle.

But I still hadn't known if I wanted to marry him. I knew I had to be married someday. But getting married would mean it would no longer be just me and Grandfather, and I wanted to delay that for as long as I could.

Finally, though, I decided I would. The next day, Grandfather visited the broker to finalize the arrangements, and soon, a year had passed, and it was the night before my marriage ceremony. We had a celebratory dinner, for which Grandfather had found apple juice, which we drank from our favorite teacups, and oranges, which were dry and sour but which we dipped in artificial honey for sweetness. The next day I would again see the man who would be my husband; he had failed in his attempt to appeal his expulsion, but Grandfather had found him a job at the Pond, which he would begin the following week.

As we were finishing our meal, Grandfather said, "Little cat, I want to tell you something about your future husband."

He had been serious, and quiet, all through dinner, but when I asked him if he was angry at me, he had only smiled and shaken his head. "No, not angry," he said. "But this is a bittersweet moment. My little cat, all grown up and getting married." Now he continued: "I have debated whether to tell you this or not. But I think—I think I must, for reasons I will explain."

He got up to turn on the radio, and then he sat down again. For a long time, he was silent. Then he said, "Little cat, your future husband is like I am. Do you understand what I mean by this?"

"He's a scientist," I said, though I already knew that. Or he was an aspiring scientist, at least. That was a good thing.

"No," Grandfather said. "Well, yes. But that's not what I'm trying to say. I'm trying to say that he is like—he is like me, but also like your other grandfather is. Was." He was quiet, then, until he saw I understood what he was trying to say.

"He's a homosexual," I said.

"Yes," Grandfather said.

I knew a little about homosexuality. I knew what it was; I knew Grandfather was one, and I knew it had once been legal. Now it was neither legal nor illegal. You could be a homosexual. You could have homosexual intercourse, even though it was discouraged. But you could never get married to someone of your same sex. Technically, all adults could reside with another person to whom they weren't related, which meant you could be two men or two women and live together, but very few people chose to do that—if you were two people living together and weren't married, you would receive food coupons and water and electricity tokens for only one person. There were only three kinds of dwellings: dwellings for single people, dwellings for married couples (no children), and dwellings for families (one for families with one child; one for families with two or more children). Until you were thirty-five, you could live in a single-person residence. But then, according to the 2078 Marriage Act, you had to get married. If you were married and got divorced or were widowed, you had four years to get remarried and were eligible for a state-sponsored re-partnering within two years. There were a few exceptions made, of course, for people like Grandfather. The state also honored all preexisting legal homosexual unions, but only for twenty years after the law's passage. The point is that it was illogical to choose to live with someone to whom you weren't married; it was almost impossible for two people to survive on a single person's benefits. A society was more stable and healthier when its citizens were married, which was why the state tried to dissuade people from alternative arrangements.

Other countries had banned homosexuality for religious reasons, but that was not the case here. Here, it had been discouraged because it was the duty of adults to produce children, as the country's birth rate had fallen to catastrophic levels, and because so many children had died in the illnesses of '70 and '76, and so many of the survivors had been left sterile. Moreover, the way the children had died had been so horrific that many parents and former parents had been reluctant to have more children, because they were certain that those, too, would die in an equally horrific manner. But the other reason homosexuals had been targeted was because so many of them had joined the '67 rebellion; they had sided with the insurgents, and the state had had to punish them and, moreover, keep them under control. Grandfather had once told me that many members of racial minority groups had also joined the rebellion, but punishing them in the same way was counterproductive, as the state needed everyone they could to replenish the population.

But even though homosexuality was not illegal, it was also not something people discussed. Aside from Grandfather, I knew no other homosexuals. I thought of them neither one way nor another. They were simply not people who affected my life in any significant way.

"Oh," I said to Grandfather now.

"Little cat," Grandfather began, and then stopped. Then he started again. "I hope someday you'll understand why I decided this match was the best one for you. I wanted to find you a husband who I knew would always look after you, who would always take care of you, who would never raise a hand to you, who would never shout at or diminish you. I am confident this young man is that person.

"I could have not told you. But I *want* to tell you, because I don't want you to think it's your fault that you and your husband don't have sexual relations. I don't want you to think it's your fault if he doesn't love you in some ways. He will love you in other ways, or at least show love for you in other ways, and those are the ways that matter."

I thought about this. Neither of us said anything for a long time. Then I said, "Maybe he will change his mind."

Grandfather looked at me, and then he looked down. There was another silence. "No," he said, very softly. "He will not, little cat. This is not something that he can change."

I know this will sound very foolish, because Grandfather was so smart, and as I have said, I believed everything he said. But even though he had told me otherwise, I have always hoped that he might have been wrong about my husband, that one day, my husband might grow to be physically attracted to me. I wasn't sure how, exactly, this would happen. I know I am not attractive. I also knew that even if I *was* attractive, it wouldn't have mattered to my husband.

Yet for the first two or so years of our marriage, I had a dream of how he might fall in love with me. It wasn't a typical dream but, rather, a waking one, as I never had it while I slept, though I always wished I would. In it, I was lying in my bed, and suddenly I felt my husband get into bed next to me. He held me, and then we kissed. That was the end of that dream, but sometimes I had other dreams, in which my husband kissed me while we were standing, or that we went to the center and listened to some music and held hands.

I understood that Grandfather had told me the truth about my husband before I was married so I wouldn't think it was my fault that my husband wasn't attracted to me. But knowing the truth didn't make it easier; it didn't make me stop wishing that maybe my husband was an exception, that maybe our life would end up being different than Grandfather had told me it would. And even though it hadn't, it was difficult to stop hoping. I had always been good at accepting things as they were, but it was harder for me than I had expected to accept this. Every day I tried; every day I failed. There were some days, some weeks, even, when I didn't hope that maybe, maybe Grandfather had been wrong about my husband— that maybe someday he would love me back. I knew it was more realistic and ultimately less distressing to spend my time working on accepting, rather than hoping. But hoping, though it made me feel worse, also made me feel better.

I knew that whoever was writing my husband those notes was a man—I could tell from the handwriting. Knowing this made me feel bad, but not as bad as it would have if the notes had been written by a woman: It meant that Grandfather had been right; that my husband was as he had said. But it still made me unhappy. It still made me feel that I had failed, even though Grandfather had said that I wasn't to think like that. In a way, I didn't need to know who the person was, just as I didn't need to know what happened in the house on Bethune Street—whatever more I learned would be useless, just extra details. I would be unable to change them; I would be unable to correct them. Yet I still wanted to know—it was as if knowing was better than not knowing, as difficult as knowing would be. It was for this same reason, I suppose, that Grandfather had told me about my husband.

As unhappy as my husband's inability to love me made me, however, David's inability was worse. It was worse because I hadn't truly comprehended how I had felt about him; it was worse because I knew that at some point, I had begun thinking that he might like me as well, that he might like me in a way my husband couldn't. And it was worst of all because I had been wrong—he hadn't felt for me what I felt for him.

The following Saturday at 16:00, I stayed indoors. My husband was taking a nap in our bedroom; he had been tired lately, he said, and needed to lie down. But after ten minutes, I went downstairs and opened the door to our building. It was a bright, hot day, and the Square was very busy. There was a crowd of people waiting in front of the metal merchant whose stall was closest to the northern edge. But then some of them moved aside, and I suddenly saw David. Although it was hot, the air quality was good, and he was holding his helmet in one hand. With his other hand, he was shielding his eyes, and he was turning his head back and forth, slowly, looking for something or someone.

I realized then he was looking for me, and I shrank against the door before remembering that I had never told David where I lived—all he knew was that I lived in Zone Eight, just like him. I was thinking this when he seemed to look directly at me, and I held my breath, as if it would make me invisible, but then he turned his head in the opposite direction.

Finally, after another two minutes or so, he left, looking back over his shoulder one last time as he moved west.

The next Saturday, the same thing happened. This time I was waiting at the door exactly at 15:55, so I could watch him approach, stand at the center of the north edge of the Square, and, for the next eleven minutes, look for me before finally leaving. The next Saturday, the same thing; and again the next.

It made me feel good that he still wanted to see me, even after I had embarrassed myself. But it made me sad as well, because I knew I could no longer see him. I know this sounds silly, or even childish, because even though David didn't feel for me as I did him, he still wanted to be my friend, and hadn't I been saying all along that I wanted a friend?

But I just couldn't see him again. I know that sounds illogical. But it took so much energy and discipline for me to remind myself to not hope for my husband's love that I didn't think I had enough strength to remind myself not to hope for David's love, either. It was too difficult for me. I would have to learn to forget or ignore my feelings for David, and I wasn't going to be able to do that if I kept seeing him. It was better to pretend I had never met him at all.

―――――

At the top of the building where I worked, there was a greenhouse. This was not the greenhouse that had been named for Grandfather— that was atop a different building.

The greenhouse at Larsson Center was not a working greenhouse but, rather, a museum. Here the university maintained a specimen of each of the plants that had been engineered at RU for use in anti-viral medications, dating all the way back to 2037. The plants were grown in individual clay pots and arranged in rows, and although they didn't look all that remarkable, they each had a label beneath them listing their Latin name, and the name of the lab that had developed them, and the drug they had contributed to. The bulk of botanical research had been long ago transferred to the Farm, but there were still a few RU scientists who collaborated in the development program.

Anyone could come visit this greenhouse, though few people ever did. In fact, few people ever came up to the roof at all, which was mysterious to me, as it was very pleasant. As I mentioned earlier, the entire campus is under a biodome, which means it's always climate-controlled, and near the greenhouse there were a few tables and benches so you could sit and look over the East River, or at the rooftops of the other buildings, some of which are dedicated to growing vegetables and fruits and herbs that the cafeteria uses to make food for the employees of the university. Anyone who worked at Rockefeller could buy lunch at the cafeteria at a subsidized rate, and I often brought my lunch up to the roof, where I could eat alone but not feel self-conscious about it.

It was especially nice to sit on the roof in the summer. You almost felt like you were outside, except better, because unlike actually being outside, you didn't have to wear your cooling suit. You could just sit there in your jumpsuit and eat your sandwich and look at the brown water beneath.

As I ate, I thought, as I often did, about David. It had been almost a month since I had seen him last, and although I was trying my best to forget him, I still saw things every day that I thought he might be interested in hearing about, and it took a great effort to remind myself that I wasn't going to see him again, and that I should stop making observations and storing them to share with him. Though then I remembered that Grandfather had said that you don't have to make observations only so you can tell someone else; that making them just for the sake of making them was a good thing. "Why?" I had asked him, and he had thought about it for a moment. "Because we can," he had said, finally. "Because it's what humans do." Sometimes I worried that my lack of interest in making observations meant I wasn't human, though I know that wasn't what Grandfather had intended.

I was thinking about this when the elevator doors opened and three people, a woman and two men, stepped off. I knew instantly from how they were dressed that they were state employees, and I could tell that they were in the middle of an argument, as one of the men was leaning toward the other, and they were all whispering. Then the woman looked over and saw me and said, "Oh, Christ—people, let's try someplace else," and before I could offer to go away, they got back in the elevator and left.

Grandfather had always said that the people who worked for the state and the people who didn't were united in their desire to never encounter one another: The state didn't want to see us, and we didn't want to see them. And for the most part, it didn't happen. The ministries were all in one zone, and the state workers had their own shuttles and grocery stores and clusters of apartment buildings. They didn't live in just one zone, though many of the senior members lived in Zone Fourteen, the same as many of the senior scientists at RU and senior engineers and researchers at the Farm and the Pond.

It was well-known that there was an office of state employees at every biological research institution in the country. It was necessary, so they could watch over us. But although we all knew there was an office at RU, no one knew where it was or how many people worked there. Some people said it was fewer than ten people. But others said it was more, many more, maybe as many as a hundred, two for almost every principal investigator here. There were rumors that their office was many layers underground, even beneath the supposed additional labs with the supposed additional mice, and the supposed operating rooms, and that these underground offices connected to special tunnels, where there were special trains that could take them back to their ministries, or even all the way down to Municipality One.

But other people said that they were just in a small set of rooms in one of the lesser-used buildings, which was probably the truth, though RU wasn't so large a campus that you didn't cross everyone at some point or another, and yet I had never seen these state employees, though I had recognized them the moment I did.

Their presence here was actually a relatively recent development. When Grandfather had begun working at Rockefeller, for example, it was just a research facility. The labs received funding from the state, and they sometimes worked with various ministries, especially the Health and Interior Ministries, but the state had no jurisdiction over any of their work. After '56, though, that changed, and in '62, when the state was established, it was given oversight of all the country's research facilities. The following year, the forty-five states were divided into eleven prefectures, and in '72, the year after the zones were established, the state was one of ninety-two countries that signed a treaty with Beijing, allowing them full access to all scientific institutions in return for funding and other resources, including food and water and medicines and other humanitarian supplies. This meant that, while every federal project was monitored by the state, only the state employees who oversaw institutions such as RU ultimately reported back to Beijing—Beijing didn't care about other domestic enterprises, only the ones that worked with illnesses and illness prevention, as we did.

Along with the people who were visibly members of the state, you also had to assume that there were a number of scientists and other researchers who worked for both the institute and the state. This didn't mean they were informants—the institute would be informed of their dual responsibilities. Grandfather had been one of those people: He had begun as a scientist, but eventually he had also worked with the state. When I was born, he had been very powerful. But then his power had diminished, and when the insurgents briefly took control of the country the second time, he had been killed for his association with the state, and for what he had done to try to stop the spread of disease.

The point is that it was strange to see these state officers moving about the campus so openly and behaving so strangely. So I suppose it wasn't that surprising that, about a week or so later, I returned from eating my lunch on the roof to find five of the Ph.D.s excitedly whispering in one corner of the break room about an announcement that had just come down from the Health Ministry that all the containment centers in our prefecture were to be closed, effective immediately.

"What do you think it means?" asked one of the Ph.D.s, who

always began these conversations with the same question, and whom I would sometimes later hear repeating the answers he'd heard to other people.

"It's obvious," said another, who was large and tall, and whose uncle was rumored to be one of the interior minister's deputies, "it means this new thing is not only real but projected to be highly deadly, and easy to spread."

"Why do you say that?"

"Because. If it were easy to treat, or to contain, then the old system would still be fine: Someone gets sick, you hold them for a week or two and see if they get better, and then, if they don't, they get transferred to a relocation center. It's worked perfectly fine for the past, what, twenty-five years, right?"

"Actually," said another of the Ph.D.s, who rolled his eyes when the interior minister's deputy's nephew said anything, "I've never thought the system that effective. Too much of a margin for error."

"Yes, the system has its flaws," said the interior minister's deputy's nephew, irritated at being contradicted. "But let's not forget what the containment centers accomplished." I had heard the interior minister's deputy's nephew defend the containment centers before; he would always remind people that the centers gave scientists the opportunity to conduct real-time human research, and to identify subjects among their residents for drug trials. "Now they're guessing that, whatever this is, they either won't have time for the stopgap of the containment center, or there'll be no point because the morbidity rate will be so high, and so fast, that it's best and most efficient to just send all cases straight to the relocation centers and to get them off the island as soon as possible."

He sounded very excited about this. They all did. A big new disease was definitely coming, and now it was their time to witness it, to try to solve it. None of them seemed scared; none of them seemed worried that they might get sick themselves. Maybe they were right not to be scared. Maybe this disease wouldn't affect them—they knew more about it than I did, so I couldn't say that they were wrong.

On the shuttle ride home, I thought of the man I had seen two years ago, the one who had tried to escape the containment center and had been stopped by the guards. Ever since, I had looked out the window whenever we passed the center. I don't know why I did—the center no longer existed, and anyway the facade was completely mirrored, so you couldn't see inside at all. But I still continued to look, as if, one day, the same man might appear again, this time walking out of the center in his regular clothes because he had been cured, and he was going home to wherever he had lived before he had gotten sick.

———

The next few weeks at the lab were extremely busy for everyone, including me. This made it more difficult to eavesdrop, because there were far more meetings among the scientists, many of them led by Dr. Wesley, and therefore far less time for the Ph.D.s to gather and discuss what had happened in those meetings, and less time for me to try to listen to them.

It took me several days to understand that even the older scientists were taken aback by what was happening. Many of them had been Ph.D.s or postdocs themselves during the '70 illness, but the state was much stronger now than it had been then, and they were made confused and even anxious by the constant and multiplying presence of state employees: the three people I'd seen on the roof, but dozens of others as well, from many different ministries. They would be organizing the response to the illness, and they would be taking over not only our lab but all of RU's labs.

The new disease was not yet named, but all of us were under strict orders to discuss it with no one. If we did, we could be charged with treason. For the first time, I was happy that David and I were no longer speaking, as I had never had to keep a secret from a friend and so was unsure how good I'd be at it. But now that was no longer a problem.

Since I had stopped seeing David, I had renewed my Thursday-night monitoring of my husband. There was no more to see than there had been—just him approaching the door of the house on Bethune Street, knocking his special knock, saying something I couldn't hear into the opening, and then disappearing inside—and yet I continued to watch him, standing beneath the stairwell of the house across the street. Once, the door opened slightly wider than usual, and I saw the person inside, a white man about my husband's age with light-brown hair, poke his head out and quickly look left and right before pulling the door shut again. After the door closed, I would stand there for a few minutes longer, waiting to see if anything more happened, but it never did. Then I would go home.

Everything, in fact, had returned to how it had been before I had met David, and yet things were also different, because I had felt like somebody else when I had had David as a friend, and now that I no longer did, it was difficult to remember who I actually was.

One night, about six weeks after I had last met up with David, my husband and I were eating dinner when he said, "Cobra, are you all right?"

"Yes," I said. "Thank you," I remembered to say.

"How is David?" he asked, after a silence, and I looked up.

"Why are you asking?" I said.

He lifted one shoulder and let it fall. "I just thought I would," he said. "It's so hot now—are you two still walking, or are you spending more time at the center?"

"We aren't friends anymore," I said, and across from me, my husband was silent.

"I'm sorry, Cobra," he said, and now I shrugged. Suddenly I was mad: I was mad that my husband wasn't jealous of David or of my friendship with him; I was mad that he wasn't relieved that David and I were no longer friends; I was mad that he was so unsurprised.

"Where do you go on your free nights?" I asked him, and I was pleased to see him look startled, and lean back in his seat.

"I go to see friends," he said, after a silence.

"What do you do with them?" I asked, and he was silent again.

"We talk," he said, at last. "We play chess."

Then we were both silent. I was still angry; I still wanted to ask him questions. But I had so many that I didn't know where to begin, and besides, I was scared: What if he told me something I didn't want to hear? What if he got angry at me and shouted? What if he ran out of the apartment? Then I'd be alone, and I wouldn't know what to do.

Finally, he stood and began gathering the dishes. We had had horse that night, but neither of us had finished our servings; I knew my husband would wrap the leftovers in paper so we could use the bones to flavor our porridge.

It was Tuesday, and my free night, but as I began walking toward our bedroom and my husband set down the dishes to bring me the radio, I stopped him. "I don't want to listen to the radio," I said. "I want to go to sleep."

"Cobra," my husband said, stepping close to me, "are you sure you're all right?"

"Yes," I said.

"But you're crying," my husband said, even though I didn't think I was. "Did—did David hurt you in some way, Cobra?"

"No," I said. "No, he didn't hurt me. I'm just very tired and would like to be left alone, please."

He moved away from me, and I went to the bathroom and then to my bed. A few hours later, my husband came in. It was unusual for him to go to bed this early, but we had both been working long hours, and he was very tired, as was I. Yesterday there had been an early-morning raid that had woken us both. But although we were both tired, only he fell asleep quickly, while I stayed awake, watching the searchlight move across the ceiling. I imagined my husband at Bethune Street playing chess with somebody else, but as hard as I tried, I could only envision the inside of the house looking like our own apartment, and the only other person I could see playing with my husband was not the man who had opened the door for him, but David.

———

By mid-July, I felt like I was living in two worlds. The lab had been transformed: The rooftop of Larsson had been made into an office for a team of epidemiologists from the Health Ministry, and a section of the largest of the basement passageways was converted into an office for some employees of the Interior Ministry. The scientists hurried about looking worried, and even the Ph.D.s were silent. All I knew was that whatever had been found was very dangerous, so dangerous that it had overshadowed even the excitement surrounding its discovery.

But outside of RU, everything continued as it always did. The shuttle picked me up; the shuttle dropped me off. There were groceries at the store, and there was one week when horse was even discounted, as it occasionally was when there was a surplus of meat from the factories out west. The radio played music when it was supposed to and bulletins when it was supposed to. You saw nothing of the preparations that I knew from school had happened in advance of the '70 illness: There was no increase in military personnel, no requisitioning of buildings, no reinstatement of the curfew. On the weekends, the Square filled with people, as usual, and although David had stopped waiting for me, I still stood at the front door and looked out its window every Saturday at the same time we had once met, looking for him as he had looked for me. But I never saw him. A few times, I wondered if I should have bought the powder from the vendor and slipped it into David's drink, as she had said, before remembering that it hadn't been David who had chosen to stop seeing me—I had been the one who had chosen to stop seeing him. I would wonder then whether I should go to the Square and let that woman find me again—not for the powder that would make David fall in love with me but for a different powder, a powder that would make me believe that someone could love me at all.

The one thing that was different outside of work, I suppose, was that my husband was home more than usual, often sleeping in his bed or napping on the sofa. He even came home earlier on his free nights, and when he did, I could hear that he moved slowly, even heavily. Normally, he walked lightly, but now his walk was different, and when he climbed into bed, he groaned, quietly, as if he were in pain, and his face often looked puffy. He had been working extra hours at the Pond, just as I had been working extra hours at the lab, but I didn't know if he knew what I knew, which wasn't very much, anyway. People who worked at the Pond and the Farm did vital jobs, but just as I didn't know what they were actually doing in those jobs, they often didn't, either. It could be that he was staying late, for example, because a lab—maybe even a lab at RU—had urgently requested a certain kind of material from a certain kind of plant, but just as I didn't know why I was preparing the mice, he wouldn't know why he was preparing a sample. He would just be told to do it, and he would. The difference was that I wasn't curious about why I was told to do anything; it was enough for me to know that my work was necessary, that it was useful, and that it had to be done. But my husband had been two years away from completing his doctorate when he was declared an enemy of the state and expelled from his university—he would want to know why he was asked to do things. He would even, perhaps, want to contribute an opinion. And yet he never would.

I remember that, once, I had been very upset after one of my lessons with Grandfather about the sort of questions I should ask people. I was often frustrated after our sessions, because I was reminded of how difficult it was for me to do and say and think things that seemed to be so easy for other people. "I don't know how to ask the right questions," I said to Grandfather, even though that wasn't exactly what I wanted to say, even though I didn't know how to say what I really wanted to say.

Grandfather had been quiet for a moment. "Sometimes not asking questions is a good thing, little cat," he said. "Not asking questions can keep you safe." Then he looked at me, really looked at me, as if he were memorizing my face and might never see it again. "But sometimes you need to ask, even if it's dangerous." He stopped again. "Will you remember that, little cat?"

"Yes," I said.

The next day at work, I went to see Dr. Morgan. Dr. Morgan was the most senior postdoc at the lab, and he oversaw all the techs. But even though he was the most senior, the Ph.D.s didn't want to be like him. "God help me if I turn out like Morgan," I sometimes heard one of them say to the others. This was because Dr. Morgan didn't have a lab of his own and was still working for Dr. Wesley, seven years after he'd begun. In fact, Dr. Morgan and I had joined

Dr. Wesley's lab in the same year. Grandfather had told me that every lab would have at least one postdoc who never left, who stayed on and on, but I should never mention that fact to them, or remind them of how long they'd been there, or ask them why they hadn't gone somewhere else.

So I never had. But Dr. Morgan had always been nice to me, and, unlike many of the other scientists in the lab, he always said hello to me if he saw me in the hallway. Still, I rarely sought him out except to ask for permission to leave early or come in late, and as I didn't know the best way to approach him, I spent about five minutes waiting near his station while most of the lab was away eating lunch, not knowing what to do and hoping he would eventually look up from his work.

Finally, he did. "Someone's watching me," he announced, and turned around. "Charlie," he said. "What are you doing, just standing there?"

"I'm sorry, Dr. Morgan," I said.

"Is something wrong?" he asked.

"No," I said. Then I couldn't think of what else to say. "Dr. Morgan," I said, quickly, before I lost my nerve, "will you tell me what's happening?"

Dr. Morgan looked at me, and I looked back at him. There had always been something about Dr. Morgan that reminded me of Grandfather, though for a while, I couldn't figure out why: He was much younger than Grandfather, just a few years older than I am. He was a different race. And, unlike Grandfather, he wasn't acclaimed or influential. But then I realized it was because he always answered me when I asked a question—other people in the lab, even if I asked them, would tell me I wouldn't understand, but Dr. Morgan never said that.

"It's a zoonosis, and definitively a hemorrhagic fever," he finally said. "And it's spread by both respiratory aerosols and droplets as well as by bodily fluids, which makes it profoundly contagious. We don't yet have a clear sense of its incubation period, or of how long the period is between diagnosis and death. It was identified in Brazil. The first case in this country was found about a month ago, in Prefecture Six." He didn't need to say that this was a lucky thing, as Prefecture Six was the most sparsely populated of the prefectures. "But since then, we know it's been spreading—we don't yet know how fast. And that's all I can say."

I didn't ask whether that was because Dr. Morgan didn't know more or because he couldn't tell me more. I just thanked him and returned to my area, so I could think about what he had told me.

I know that the first thing someone might wonder is how this disease got here in the first place. One of the reasons there hadn't been a pandemic in almost twenty-four years is because, as I've said, the state closed down all the borders, as well as banned all international travel. Many countries did the same. In fact, there were only seventeen countries in total—New Britain, a cluster in Old Europe, and a second cluster in Southeast Asia—with reciprocal movement rights for their citizens.

But although no one was allowed to come in and no one was allowed to go out, it didn't *actually* mean that no one came in and no one went out. Four years ago, for example, there was a rumor that a stowaway from India had been found in a shipping container at one of the ports in Prefecture Three. And as Grandfather always said, a microbe can travel in anyone's throat: a person's, of course, but also a bat's or a snake's or a flea's. (This is a figure of speech, as snakes and fleas don't have throats.) As Dr. Wesley always said, all it took was one.

Then there was another theory, one I would never repeat—though other people did—that the state invented the diseases themselves, that half of every research institute, even RU, was dedicated to making new illnesses, and the other half was dedicated to figuring out how to destroy them, and that whenever the state thought it needed to, it deployed one of the new diseases. Don't ask me how I know that people thought this way, because I couldn't say—I just do. I *can* say that my father thought this way, and it was one of the reasons he was declared an enemy of the state.

But though I had heard these theories before, I didn't believe them myself. If that had been true, then why wouldn't the state have deployed an illness in '83 or '88, during the uprisings? Then Grandfather would still be alive, and I would still have him to talk to.

I would also never say this, but sometimes I wished there *would* be another disease from far away. Not because I wanted people to die but because it would be proof. I wanted to know for certain that there were other places, and other countries, with people living in them and riding their own shuttles and working in their own labs and making their own nutria patties for dinner. I knew I would never be able to visit these places—I didn't even *want* to be able to visit them.

But sometimes I wanted to know that they existed, that all those countries that Grandfather had been to, all those streets he had walked on, were still there. Sometimes I even wanted to pretend that he wasn't dead at all, that I hadn't seen him be killed with my own eyes, but that, when he dropped through the platform hole, he had instead landed in one of the cities he had traveled to when he was young: Sydney or Copenhagen or Shanghai or Lagos. Maybe he was there, and thinking of me, and although I would miss him just as much, it would be enough for me to know he was still alive, remembering me as he sat in a place I couldn't even begin to know how to imagine.

———

Over the next weeks, things began to change. Not in any immediately obvious way—it wasn't as if you saw lines of transport trucks or military mobilizations—and yet it was becoming clear that something was happening.

They did most of the work at night, so it was when I was on the shuttle, heading north to RU, that I began noticing the differences. One morning, for example, we lingered longer at the checkpoint than usual; another, there was a soldier who scanned our foreheads before we boarded with a new kind of temperature wand I'd never seen. "Move it along," said the soldier, but not meanly, and then, though none of us had asked, "Just some new equipment the state is testing." The next day, he was gone, but in his place was a different soldier, standing and watching us, one hand on his weapon, as we boarded the shuttle. He said nothing, and did nothing, but his eyes moved back and forth across us, and when the man in front of me was stepping up, the soldier held out his hand. "Halt," he said. "What's that?" and pointed to a splotch the color of smashed grapes on the man's face. "Birthmark," said the man, who didn't sound scared at all, and the soldier took a device out of his pocket and beamed a light at the man's cheek, and then read what the device said and nodded, waving the man onto the shuttle with the tip of his weapon.

I cannot say what other people on my shuttle route did or didn't notice. On the one hand, so little changed in Zone Eight that it was impossible not to recognize things that had. On the other hand, most people weren't looking for changes. But I have to assume that most of us knew, or suspected, what was happening: Every one of us worked for state-run research institutions, after all; those of us who worked for places that studied biological sciences perhaps knew more than those who worked at the Pond or the Farm. Still, none of us said anything. It was easy to believe nothing was happening if you tried.

One day, I was in my usual seat on the shuttle, looking out the window, when I suddenly saw David. He was in his gray jumpsuit and he was walking down Sixth Avenue. This was just before we had to stop for the Fourteenth Street checkpoint, and as we waited our turn in the queue, I saw him turn right on Twelfth Street, heading west and disappearing from sight.

The shuttle inched forward, and I turned back around in my seat. I realized that it couldn't have been David after all; it was an hour past his usual shuttle time—he would already have been at work at the Farm.

And yet I had been so sure I had seen him, even though it was impossible. For the first time, I felt a kind of fear about everything that was happening—the illness, how little I knew, what was going to happen next. I was not afraid of getting sick myself; I wasn't sure why. But that day on the shuttle, I had the strange sensation that the world was truly being split, and that in one world, I was riding the shuttle to my job taking care of the pinkies, while in another, David was going somewhere completely different, somewhere I had never seen or heard of, as if Zone Eight were actually much bigger than I knew it to be, and within it were places that everyone else knew about, but that I somehow did not.

————

I was always thinking of Grandfather, and yet there were two days on which I thought about him especially hard. The first was September 20, the day he was killed. The second was August 14, the day he was taken from me, the last day I ever spent with him, and though I know this will sound strange, this date was even more difficult for me than the actual day of his death.

I had been with him that afternoon. It was a Saturday, and he had come to meet me at what had been our apartment but was now my husband's and my apartment. My husband and I had only been married since June 4, and of all the things that were strange and difficult for me about being married, the strangest and most difficult was not seeing Grandfather every day. He had been resettled into a very tiny flat near the eastern edge of the zone, and for the first two weeks of my marriage, I had gone over to his building every day after work and waited in the street, sometimes for several hours, until he came home. Each day, he would smile but also shake his head. "Little cat," he would say, patting my hair, "it'll never get easier if you keep coming over here every night. Besides, your husband will worry."

"No, he won't," I would say. "I told him I was coming to see you."

Then Grandfather would sigh. "Come up," he would say, and I would go upstairs with him and he would put down his briefcase and give me a glass of water, and then he would walk me home. On the way, he would ask me questions about how work was, and how my husband was, and whether we were comfortable in our apartment.

"I still don't understand why you had to leave," I would say.

"I told you already, little cat," Grandfather would say, but gently. "Because it's your apartment. And because you're married now— you don't want to hang around your old grandfather forever."

At least Grandfather and I still spent every weekend together. Every Friday, my husband and I invited him over for dinner, and he and my husband would talk about complicated scientific matters I couldn't understand past the first ten minutes of conversation. Then, on Saturday and Sunday, it would be just the two of us. Things were very hard for Grandfather at work then—the capital had fallen to the insurgents six weeks earlier, and the insurgents had held enormous rallies, promising to reinstate technology to all citizens and to punish the leading members of the regime. I was worried, hearing that, because Grandfather was part of the regime. I didn't know if he was a leading member, but I knew he was important. But so far, nothing had happened, except that the new government had instituted a 23:00 curfew. Everything else, though, seemed exactly the same as it had been. I was beginning to think that nothing would change in the end, because in reality, nothing had. It didn't matter to me who was in charge of the state: I was just a citizen, and would be either way, and it wasn't my place to worry about such things.

That Saturday, August 14, was a typical day. It was very hot, and so Grandfather and I met at 14:00 at the center and listened to a string quartet. Then he bought us some iced milk, and we sat at one of the tables, eating the milk with little spoons. He asked how work was, and if I liked Dr. Wesley, who had once worked for Grandfather, many years ago. I said I liked work, and that Dr. Wesley was fine, both of which were true, and he nodded. "Good, little cat," he said. "I'm glad to hear it."

For a while, we lingered in the air-conditioning, and then Grandfather said that the worst of the heat would have broken, and we could go look at the vendors' offerings in the Square, which we sometimes did, before I went home.

We were only three blocks from the northern entrance when the van pulled alongside us, and three men in black got out. "Dr. Griffith," one of them said to Grandfather, and Grandfather, who had stopped to watch as the van approached, standing next to me with his hand on my shoulder, now took my hand and squeezed it, and turned me to face him.

"I have to go with these men, little cat," he said, calmly.

I didn't understand. I felt like I was going to collapse. "No," I said. "No, Grandfather."

He patted my hand. "Don't worry, little cat," he said. "I'm going to be fine. I promise you."

"Get in," said another of the men, but Grandfather ignored him. "Go home," he whispered to me. "You're only three blocks away. Go home, and tell your husband I was taken, and don't worry, all right? I'll be back with you soon."

"No," I said, and Grandfather winked at me and climbed into the back of the van. "No, Grandfather," I said. "No, no."

Grandfather looked out at me and smiled and began to say something, but then the man who had told him to get in slammed the doors shut, and then all three men got into the front seat and the van drove away.

By this point, I was shouting, and although some people stopped to look at me, most did not. Too late, I began to run after the van, which was driving south, but then it turned west, and it was so hot, and I was so slow, that I tripped and fell, and for a while I remained on the sidewalk, rocking myself.

Finally, I stood. I walked into our building and up to our apartment. My husband was there, and when he saw me, he opened his mouth, but before he could speak, I told him what had happened, and he went immediately to the closet and took out the box with our papers, and removed some. Then he went to the drawer beneath my bed and took out some of our gold coins. He put them all in a bag, and then he scooped some water into a mug for me. "I have to go see if I can help your grandfather," he said. "I'll be back as soon as I can, all right?" I nodded.

I waited all night for my husband to return, sitting on the couch in my cooling suit, the blood from the scrapes on my forehead drying in place and making my skin itch. Finally, very late, just before the curfew began, he returned, and when I asked, "Where is Grandfather?," he looked down.

"I'm sorry, Cobra," he said. "They wouldn't let him out. I'm going to keep trying."

I began moaning then, moaning and rocking, and my husband

finally got my pillow from my bed so I could moan into it, and sat on the floor by my side. "I'm going to keep trying, Cobra," he repeated. "I'm going to keep trying." Which he did, but then, on September 15, I was notified that Grandfather had lost his trial and was to be executed, and five days later, he was killed.

Today was the six-year anniversary of the day Grandfather was taken, which my husband and I always commemorated with a bottle of grape-flavored juice we bought at the store. My husband would pour us each a glass, and we would both say Grandfather's name aloud, and then we would drink.

I always spent the day alone. Every August 13 for the past five years, my husband would ask, "Do you want to be alone tomorrow?" and I would say "Yes," though in the last year or so, I began to wonder whether that was actually true, or whether I was saying yes only because it was easier for us both. If my husband instead had asked, "Do you want company tomorrow?," would I not also have said "Yes"? But there was no way I would ever know this for sure, because last night, he had asked as usual if I wanted to be alone, and as usual, I said I did.

I always slept as late as I could on that day, because that meant there was less of it to use up. When I finally rose, around 11:00, my husband was gone, his bed as neatly made as ever, a bowl of porridge left for me in the oven, a second bowl inverted over it so the surface wouldn't dry out. Everything was the same.

As I was walking toward our bathroom after I had washed out my bowl, however, I noticed there was a piece of paper on the ground near our front door. For a few moments I stared at it, because I was for some reason afraid to pick it up. I wished my husband were here to help me. Then I realized that perhaps it was a note to my husband from the person he loved, and this made me even more afraid—it was as if, by touching it, I would be proving that this other person existed, that he had somehow gotten into our building, and climbed the stairs, and left a note. And then I was angry, because although I knew my husband didn't love me, how could he care for me so little that he wouldn't tell this person that this was the worst day of my life, that every year on this date all I thought about was what I had once had, and how it had been taken from me? It was that anger, finally, that made me stoop and snatch the note from the ground.

But then my anger disappeared, because the note wasn't for my husband. It was for me.

Charlie—meet me at our usual storyteller today.

It wasn't signed, but it could only be from David. Now I was confused, and I began to walk in a circle, deliberating aloud about what I should do next. I was too embarrassed to see him: I had misinterpreted his feelings for me, and I had behaved stupidly. When I thought of him, I remembered the look on his face before I had pulled away from him, and how it had been not mean, but worse—it had been kind, even sad, and that was more shameful than if he had pushed at me, or made fun of me, or laughed at me.

But I also missed him. I wanted to see him. I wanted to feel as I had when I was with him, the way only Grandfather had ever made me feel, as if I were special, as if I were a person of interest.

I paced for a long time. Once again, I wished there were something to clean in the apartment, something to organize, something to do. But there wasn't. The hours passed slowly, so slowly that I almost went to the center for a distraction, but I didn't want to put on my cooling suit, and I didn't want to leave the apartment, either—I don't know why.

Finally, it was 15:30, and although it would take me just five minutes, less, to reach the storyteller's tarp, I left anyway. It was only on the walk over that it occurred to me to wonder how David had known where I lived, and how he had gotten into our building, which you needed two keys to access, as well as a fingerprint scan, and suddenly I stopped, and almost turned around—what if my husband was right, and David *was* an informant? But then I reminded myself, again, that I knew nothing, and was nobody, and I had nothing to hide and nothing to say, and anyway, there were other explanations: He could have seen me go home one day. He could have handed the note to one of the neighbors who was entering the building, and asked them to slide it beneath my door. It would have been unusual to do so, but David was unusual. Yet this reasoning led to another unpleasant thought: Why did he want to see me after all this time? And if he *did* know where I lived, why had he not tried to communicate with me earlier?

I was so consumed by my thoughts that it wasn't until I became aware of someone speaking to me that I realized I had been standing at the edge of the storyteller's tarp, not moving. "Are you coming in, miss?" asked the storyteller's assistant, and I nodded, and spread my piece of cloth on the ground, near the back.

I was arranging my bag at my side when I felt someone standing near me, and when I looked up, it was David.

"Hello, Charlie," he said, and sat down next to me.

My heart was beating very fast. "Hello," I said.

But then neither of us could say anything more, because the storyteller had begun to speak.

I cannot say what the story was that day, because I was unable to concentrate—all I could do was think about my questions and my doubts—and so it was with surprise that I heard the audience applaud, and then David say to me, "Let's go to the benches."

The benches were not really benches, but a line of cement blockades that had been used years ago for crowd control. After the insurgents were defeated, the state had left a row of them in front of a building on the east side of the Square, and sometimes people, especially old people, sat there and watched as the pack that circumnavigated the Square walked past. The benefit of the benches was that they were private, even though they were in the open, and you could stop there and rest. The drawback was that they were very hot, and in the summertime, you could feel the heat rising from the stone even through your cooling suit.

David picked one of the benches at the southern end, and for a few moments, neither of us spoke. We both had our helmets on, but when I reached up to unstrap mine, he stopped me. "No," he said. "Leave it on. Leave it on and look straight ahead, and don't react to what I'm going to say." And so I did.

"Charlie," he said, and then he stopped. "Charlie, I'm going to tell you something," he said.

His voice sounded different, more serious, and once again, I was scared. "Are you mad at me?" I asked him.

"No," he said. "No, not at all. I just need you to listen, all right?" And he turned his head toward me, just slightly, and I nodded, just slightly as well, to show I understood.

"Charlie, I'm not from here," he said.

"I know that," I said. "You're from Prefecture Five."

"No," he said. "I'm not. I'm from—I'm from New Britain." He looked at me again, quickly, but I kept my face blank, and he continued, "I know this is going to sound . . . strange," he said. "But I was sent here, by my employer."

"Why?" I whispered.

Now he did look at me. "For you," he said. "To find you. And to watch over you, until it was safe." And then, when I didn't speak, he continued, "You know that there's a new illness coming."

For a moment, I was so shocked that I couldn't speak. How did David know about the illness? "It's real?" I said.

"Yes," he said. "It's real, and it will be very, very bad. As bad as '70—worse. But that's not why we need to leave immediately, though it certainly complicates matters."

"What?" I asked. "Leave?"

"Charlie, eyes front," he whispered, quickly, and I repositioned myself. It was unwise to display anger or alarm. "No bad emotions," he reminded me, and I nodded, and we were silent once again.

"I work for a man who was great friends with your grandfather," he said. "His dearest friend. Before your grandfather died, he asked my employer to help get you out of this country, and for six years, we've been trying to do that. Earlier this year, it finally looked like it might be possible, like we might have found a solution. And now we have. Now we can get you out of here, and take you somewhere safe."

"But I'm safe here," I said, when I could speak, and once again, I felt his head move, just a bit, in my direction.

"No, Charlie," he said. "You're not safe. You will never be safe here. And besides," and here he shifted on the block, "don't you want another kind of life for yourself, Charlie? Someplace where you can be free?"

"I'm free here," I said, but he kept talking.

"Somewhere you can—I don't know, read books or travel or go where you want? Somewhere you can—you can make friends?"

I couldn't speak. "I have friends here," I said, and when he didn't answer, I added, "Every country is the same."

And now he did turn to me, and through the tint of his face screen, I could see his eyes, which were big and dark, like my husband's, and were looking straight at me. "No, Charlie," he said, gently, "they're not."

I got up then. I was feeling strange—things were happening too fast, and I didn't like it. "I have to go," I said. "I don't know why you're telling me these things, David. I don't know why, but what you're saying is treason. Making up stories like this is treasonous." I could feel my eyes turn hot, my nose begin to drip. "I don't know why you're doing this," I said, and I could hear my voice becoming louder and panicky. "I don't know why, I don't know why," and David swiftly stood and did something extraordinary: He pulled me to him and held me and said nothing, and after a while, I held him back, and although at first I was self-conscious, imagining that people must be looking at us, after some more time I didn't think about them at all.

"Charlie," said David, somewhere above my head, "I know this is a great shock for you. I know you don't believe me. I know all this. And I'm sorry. I wish I could have made it easier for you." And then I felt him slip something into my cooling suit's pocket, something small and hard. "I want you to open this only when you're back at home, and alone," he said. "Do you understand me? Only when you're absolutely certain you're not being watched—not even by your husband." I nodded against his chest. "Okay," he said. "Now we're going to separate, and I'm going to walk west, and you're going to walk north and go up to your apartment, and then I'm going to send you a message about where our next meeting will be, all right?"

"How?" I asked.

"Don't worry about that," he said. "Just know I will. And if what's in your pocket now doesn't convince you, then you just won't show up. Though, Charlie"—and here he inhaled; I could feel his stomach retracting—"I hope you do. I've promised my employer I won't return to New Britain without you."

And then he abruptly dropped his arms and left, walking west: not too fast, not too slow, as if he were just another shopper in the Square.

I remained standing there for a few seconds. I had the odd sensation that what had happened had been a dream, and that I was dreaming still. But I wasn't. Above me, the sun was hot and white, and I could feel sweat trickling down my side.

I turned the cooling suit up to its maximum level and did as David had told me. Once I was in my apartment, though, with the front door safely locked behind me and my helmet removed, I felt like I was going to faint, and I sat down, right on the floor, resting my back against the door and inhaling big gulps of air until I felt better.

Finally, I stood. I checked the locks on the door again, and then I called my husband's name, even though it was clear he wasn't at home. Yet I still checked every room: the kitchen, the main room, our bedroom, the bathroom. I even checked the closets. After that, I returned to the main room. I drew the blinds on the windows, one of which looked onto the back of another building, the other of which looked into an air shaft. And only then did I sit on the sofa and reach into my pocket.

It was a package about the size of a walnut shell, of brown paper wrapped around something hard. The paper had been secured with tape, and after peeling it off, I found that beneath the first layer of paper was a second, and then a layer of thin white tissue, which I also tore away. And then I was left with a small black pouch made of a soft, dense fabric and pulled tight with a drawstring. I loosened the drawstring and held out my palm and shook the bag, and into my hand fell Grandfather's ring.

I hadn't known what to expect, and only afterward did I realize that I should have been scared, that I could have been carrying any-thing: an explosive, a vial of viruses, a Fly.

But in certain ways, the ring was worse. I cannot quite say why, but I'll try. It was as if I was learning that something I had known to be one way was actually another. Of course, that had already hap-pened: David had told me he was not who he said he was. But I had been able to disbelieve him until I saw the ring. I had had what Grandfather had once called "plausible deniability," which means you can pretend to not know something while knowing it as well. And so, if David was telling me the truth about himself, then were the other things he said also true? How did he know about the dis-ease? Had he really been sent to find me?

Were other countries not like this one after all?

Who *was* David?

I looked at the ring, which was as heavy as I remembered, its pearl lid still smooth and shiny. "It's called nacre," Grandfather had explained. "It's a kind of calcium carbonate that a mollusk produces, building layers and layers of it around an irritant—like a speck of sand—in its mantle. You can see it's very strong."

"Can humans make nacre?" I had asked, and Grandfather had smiled.

"No," he said. "Humans have to protect themselves in other ways."

It had been almost twenty years since I had seen the ring, and now I clenched it in my fist: It was warm and solid. *I had to give it to the fairy,* Grandfather had said. *The fairy who looked over you while you were sick.* And although I had always known he was teasing, and although I knew there were no such thing as fairies, I think this is what made me saddest of all: That Grandfather hadn't had to pay a price for me returning to him after all. That I had just come back to him anyway, and that, one day, he had sent the ring someplace else, to someone else, and now that it had been returned to me, I no longer knew what it meant, or where it had been, or what it had once stood for.

————

We met again the following Thursday. That morning at work, I had gone to the bathroom, and when I returned to my desk, there was a small folded piece of paper tucked beneath one of the boxes of saline, and I grabbed at it, looking around to see if anyone was watching me, although of course no one was: It was only me and the pinkies.

When I reached the center at 19:00, he was already there, standing outside, and held up his hand to me. "I thought we'd walk around the track," he said, and I nodded. Inside, he bought us both fruit juices, and then we began to walk, slowly but not too slowly, at our regular pace. "Keep your helmet on," he'd said, and so I did, opening the little slot around the mouth when I wanted to take a sip. It was cool inside the center, but some people kept their helmets on anyway, just out of laziness, and so this raised no suspicions. "I'm glad to see you," David said, in a low voice. "Your husband's on his free night," he added, and it was not a question but a statement, and as I turned toward him, he shook his head, just slightly. "No amazement, no anger, no alarm," he reminded me, and I redirected my gaze.

"How do you know about our free nights?" I asked, trying to stay calm.

"Your grandfather told my employer," he said.

It may seem odd that David had not asked to meet in my apartment, or in his. But aside from the fact that I would not want him in my apartment, and would not be willing to go to his, the reason is that it was simply safer to meet in public. In the year of the uprisings, before the state's return to power, it was widely assumed that most private spaces were being monitored, and even now, you had to deeply trust someone before visiting his or her apartment.

For a while, neither of us said anything. "Do you have any questions for me?" he asked, in that same quiet voice, which sounded so unlike the David I knew. But, then again, I had to remind myself, the David I knew did not exist. Or maybe he did, but he was not who I was talking to now.

I had many questions, of course, so many that it was impossible to know where to begin: What to say, what to ask.

"Don't people in New Britain sound different?" I asked.

"Yes," he said. "We do."

"But you sound like you're from here," I said.

"I'm pretending," he said. "If we were somewhere safe, I would use my regular voice, and I would sound different to you."

"Oh," I said. For a while we were silent. Then I asked him something I'd been wondering for a long time. "Your hair," I said, "it's long." He looked at me, surprised, and I was proud of myself for having surprised him. "Some of it fell out of your cap that first day I saw you in the shuttle queue," I said, and he nodded.

"It's true, I had long hair," he said. "But I cut it, months ago."

"To fit in?" I asked him, and he nodded again.

"Yes," he said, "to fit in. You're very observant, Charlie," and I smiled, just a bit, pleased that David thought I was observant, and pleased because I knew Grandfather would be proud of me for noticing something that perhaps some other people would not have.

"Do people in New Britain have long hair?" I asked.

"Some do," he said. "Some don't. People wear their hair how they like."

"Even men?" I asked.

"Yes," he said, "even men."

I thought about this, a place where you could wear your hair long if you wanted—if you were able to grow it long, that is. Then I asked, "Did you ever meet my grandfather?"

"No," he said. "I was never so lucky."

"I miss him," I said.

"I know, Charlie," he said. "I know you do."

"Were you really sent here to get me?" I asked.

"Yes," he said. "It's the only reason I'm here."

Then I didn't know what to say again. I know this will sound vain, and I am not a vain person, but hearing that David had come just for me, just to find me, made me feel light inside. I wished I could hear it again and again; I wished I could tell everyone. Someone had come here to find me: I was his only reason. No one would believe it—I didn't believe it myself.

"I don't know what else to ask," I finally said, and once again, I could feel him looking at me, just a bit.

"Well," he said, "why don't I begin by telling you the plan," and he looked at me again, and I nodded, and he began to talk. Around and around the track we went, sometimes passing other walkers, sometimes being passed by them. We were neither the fastest nor the slowest there, neither the youngest nor the oldest—and if you were watching us all from above, you wouldn't have been able to tell who was talking about something safe, and who was, at that moment, discussing something so dangerous, so impossible, that you wouldn't have thought they could still be alive at all.

PART VIII

Summer, twenty years earlier

Dearest Peter,   June 17, 2074

Thank you for your lovely, kind note, and apologies for this late reply. I wanted to write earlier, because I knew you'd be anxious, but I hadn't found a new courier I can trust completely until now.

Of course I'm not angry with you. Of course not. You did everything you could. It was my fault—I should have let you get me out when I (and you) had the chance. Again and again, I think: If I had asked you just five years ago, we would be in New Britain now. It wouldn't have been easy, but it at least would've been possible. Then, invariably, my thoughts grow more dangerous and more despairing: If we had left, would Charlie still have gotten sick? If she hadn't gotten sick, would she be happier now? Would I?

Then I think that maybe this, her no-longer-new way of thinking, of being, has perhaps better equipped her for the realities of this country after all. Maybe her affectlessness is a kind of stolidity, one that will see her through whatever this world becomes. Maybe the qualities whose loss I mourned on her behalf—an emotional complexity, a demonstrativeness, even a rebelliousness—are actually ones about whose disappearance I should feel relief. In more hopeful moments, I can almost imagine that she's somehow evolved and become the sort of person who's better-suited for our time and our place. *She* isn't sad about who she is.

But then the old cycle replays itself: If she hadn't gotten sick. If she hadn't taken Xychor. If she had grown up in a country where tenderness, vulnerability, romance were still, if not encouraged, then at least tolerated. Who would she be? Who would I be, without this guilt, this sorrow, and the sorrow about the guilt?

Don't worry about us. Or, rather, *do* worry, but not any more than you would. They don't know I tried to escape. And as I know I keep reminding the both of us, they still need me. As long as there's disease, there'll be me.

With thanks and love. (As always.) Charles

Dear Peter,   July 21, 2075

I'm writing this to you in haste, because I want to make sure I catch the courier before he leaves. I nearly called you today and might still, even though it's been harder and harder to get a secure line. But if I figure out a way in the next few days, I will.

I think I mentioned that at the start of the summer, I began letting Charlie go out on brief walks by herself. And when I say brief, I mean brief: She can walk one block north to the Mews, and then east to University, and then south to Washington Square North, and then west to home. I had been reluctant, but one of her tutors encouraged it—she'll be eleven in September, she reminded me; I had to let her out in the world, just a little.

So I did. For the first three weeks, I had security follow her, just to make sure. But she did exactly as I'd told her, and I watched from the second-floor window as she climbed the stairs to the house.

I hadn't wanted her to know how nervous I had been, and so I waited until dinner to talk to her about it. "How was your walk, little cat?" I asked.

She looked up at me. "Good," she said.

"What did you see?" I asked.

She thought. "Trees," she said.

"That's nice," I said. "What else?"

Another silence. "Buildings," she said.

"Tell me about the buildings," I said. "Did you see anyone in any of the windows? What color were the buildings? Did any of them have flower boxes outside? What color were their doors?" It helps her, these exercises, but they also make me feel like I'm coaching a spy: Did you see anyone suspicious? What were they doing? What were they wearing? Can you identify them from these pictures I'm showing you?

She tries so hard to give me what she thinks I want. But all I want is for her to one day come home and tell me that she saw something funny or beautiful or exciting or scary—all I want for her is the ability to tell herself a story. She looks at me occasionally as she talks, and I nod or smile to show her I approve, and whenever I do, there's that awful squeezing in my chest, that sensation only she is capable of causing.

In late June, I began letting her go alone. When I'm not home, her nanny is to wait for her arrival; it only takes her seven minutes to make the loop, and that's allowing her plenty of time to stop and look at things as she goes. She's never been curious to go any farther, and it's too hot, besides. But then, at the beginning of the month, she asked if she could walk into the Square.

Part of me thrilled to this: My little Charlie, who never asks for anything or to go anywhere, who seems at times devoid of appetites and desires and preferences at all. Though that isn't true—she knows the difference between sweet and salty, for example, and she prefers the salty. She knows the difference between a pretty shirt and an ugly one, and she prefers the pretty. She knows when someone's laughter is mean and when it's joyful. She can't articulate why, but she knows. I remind her constantly: It's fine to ask for what she wants; it's fine to like someone, or something, or someplace, more than another. It's fine to dislike, too. "All you have to do is say," I tell her, "all you have to do is ask. Do you understand me, little cat?"

She looks at me, and I can't tell what she's thinking. "Yes," she says. But I don't know if she does.

I wouldn't have allowed her into the Square at all six months ago. But now that the state has taken over, you can only enter it if you're a resident of Zone Eight—there are guards posted at each of the entrances to check people's papers. I had been worried, after last year's conversion of the rest of Central Park, that they were going to repurpose all the parks as research facilities, even though that hadn't been the original plan. But in a rare alliance, the health and justice ministers partnered to persuade the rest of the Committee that a lack of public gathering spaces would *increase* treasonous activity, and force potential insurgent groups underground, where we'd be less able to monitor them. So we won this round, but barely, though it now seems that Union Square will eventually go the way of Madison Square and become, if not a research facility, then an all-purpose, state-run staging site: one month a makeshift morgue, the next a makeshift prison.

Washington Square, however, is a different matter. It's a small park, in a residential zone, and therefore has been of no great concern to the state. Over the years, the shantytowns were built, and then destroyed, and then rebuilt, and then re-destroyed: Even from my vantage at the upstairs window, I could sense something rote about their destruction, a halfheartedness in the way the young soldier by the northern gate twirled his baton by its loop, the way the bulldozer operator leaned back her head and yawned, one hand on the controls, the other dangling out the window.

Four months ago, though, I woke to the sound of something large falling with a dull crash, and looked outside to see that the bulldozer had returned, but this time to unearth the trees on the western side of the Square. Two bulldozers worked for two days, and when they were finished, the transplant team arrived and bound up the fallen trees' roots in great tangles of burlap and clods of soil, and then they too disappeared, presumably to Zone Fourteen, where they're relocating many of the mature trees.

Now the Square sits empty, denuded of trees except for a strip that extends from the northeast corner to the southeast corner. Here, there are still benches, still paths, still a few remnants of the playground. But this, I have to imagine, is temporary; in the rest of the park, workers spend the day pouring cement across areas that had once been covered with grass. One of my colleagues in the Home Ministry said the space will be converted into some kind of outdoor bazaar, with vendors who will compensate for the loss of stores.

So it was here, to this final remaining section of green, that I let Charlie venture. She was to confine herself only to this area, and she was to talk to no one, and if anyone approached her, she was to go straight home. For the first two weeks, I watched her—I had set up a camera in one of the upstairs windows, and as I sat in the lab, I could see her on the screen, walking briskly to the southern end of the park, never stopping to look around her, and then resting for a few seconds before marching back. Soon she was home again, and the second camera showed her walking inside, locking the front door behind her, and going to the kitchen for a glass of water.

She usually walks late in the afternoon, when the sun's lower in the sky, and as I talk or write, I can still see her movements, a stripe on the screen moving farther away from the camera and then closer, her round little body and round little face receding from view and then returning.

Then came this past Thursday. I was on a Committee call. The topic was the cooling suit, which will likely be introduced next year, and differs from your version because ours comes with a full hard-shell helmet with a pollutant-filtering shield. Have you tried one yet? You don't walk so much as waddle, and the helmet is so heavy that the manufacturer is incorporating a neck brace into the design. But they're truly effective. A group of us tested them out one evening, and for the first time in years, I didn't reenter the lab and immediately begin coughing and wheezing and sweating. They're going to be expensive, though, and the state is investigating whether we can reduce the price from astronomical to extraordinary.

Anyway, I was half listening to the call, half watching Charlie begin her walk through the park. I went to the bathroom, got some tea, returned to my desk. One of the interior ministers' was droning on, still in the midst of his presentation about the difficulties of producing the suits on a mass scale, and so I looked back at my screen—only to see that Charlie was missing.

I stood, as if that would help matters. After reaching the southern end of the park, she usually sits on one of the benches. If she has a snack with her, she eats her snack. And then she stands and begins moving north. But now there was nothing: just a state employee sweeping the sidewalk, and, in the background, a soldier, facing south.

I accessed the camera and swiveled it to the right, but there were only the soldiers in their navy-blue uniforms, an engineer corps, it seemed, taking measurements of the Square. Then I swiveled the camera to the left, as far as I could.

For a while, there was nothing. Just the sweeper and the soldier and, on the northeast corner, another soldier, rocking back and forth on the balls of his feet: one of those casual, carefree gestures that startle me more than anything else—that, even with everything that's changed, people still rock on their feet, they still pick their noses, they still scratch their behinds and belch.

But then, at the very edge of the southeast corner, I saw something, a movement. I magnified the image as much as I could. There were two boys—young teenagers, I thought—both standing with their backs to the camera, talking to someone else who was facing the camera. I could only see this person's feet, their white sneakers.

Oh, I thought. *Oh, please.*

And then the boys moved, and I saw that the third person was Charlie, in her white sneakers and red T-shirt dress, and she was following those boys, who didn't even look around them, as they began walking east on Washington Square South.

"Officer!" I shouted at the screen, uselessly. "Charlie!"

But of course no one stopped, and I sat and watched as all three of them vanished from sight, strolling offscreen. One of the boys had his arm draped loosely around her neck; she was so short that the top of her head fit just beneath his armpit.

I told my secretary to have a security unit deployed, and then I ran downstairs to my car, calling and re-calling the nanny as we drove south. When she finally picked up, I yelled at her. "But, Dr. Griffith," she said, quaveringly, "Charlie's right here. She just got home from her walk."

"Give her to me," I snapped, and when Charlie's face appeared on the screen, her expression the same as always, I nearly sobbed. "Charlie," I said to her. "Little cat. Are you all right?"

"Yes, Grandfather," she said.

"Don't leave," I told her. "Stay right there. I'm coming home."

"All right," she said.

At home, I dismissed the nanny (leaving it intentionally unclear whether that dismissal was for the day or forever) and went upstairs to Charlie's room, where she was sitting on her bed, holding the cat. I had been fearing torn clothes, bruises, tears, but she looked the same as she always did—a little flushed, maybe, but that could have been the heat.

I sat down next to her, trying to calm myself. "Little cat," I said, "I saw you in the Square today." She didn't turn from me. "On the camera," I told her, but she remained silent. "Who were those boys?" I asked, and, when she still didn't speak, "I'm not angry, Charlie. I just want to know who they are."

She was silent. After four years, I've grown used to her silences. She isn't being insubordinate or stubborn—she's just trying to think of how to answer, and it takes time. Finally, she said, "I met them."

"All right," I said. "When did you meet them? And where?"

She frowned, concentrating. "A week ago," she said. "On University Place."

"Near the Mews?" I asked, and she nodded. "What are their names?" I asked, but she shook her head, and I knew she was getting upset—that she didn't know, or didn't remember. It was one of the things I was always reminding her: *Ask people's names. And if you forget, ask them again. You can always ask—you have every right.* "It's okay," I told her. "Have you seen them every day since you met them?" Again, a shake of her head.

Finally, she said, in a small voice, "They told me to meet them in the park today."

"And what did you do?" I asked.

"They said we should go on a walk," she said. "But then—" And here she stopped, and pressed her face into Little Cat's back. She began to rock herself, which she does when she's upset, and I rubbed her back as she did. "They said they were my friends," she said, at last, and she hugged the cat so tightly that he yelped. "They said they wanted to be friends," she repeated, almost in a moan, and I pulled her close to me, and she didn't resist.

The doctor has said there won't be any permanent damage: minor tearing, minor abrasions, some bleeding. She suggested a psychologist, and I agreed, not telling her that Charlie already sees one, along with an occupational therapist and a behavioral therapist. Then I turned the video over to Interior and ordered a full search—they found the boys, fourteen-year-olds, both residents of Zone Eight, sons of research fellows at Memorial, one white, the other Asian, within three hours. One of their parents is a friend of a friend of Wesley's, and he sent a note asking for mercy for his son, which Wesley hand-delivered to the house yesterday, his face expressionless. "It doesn't matter to me, Charles," he said, and when I crumpled the note and handed it back to him, he just nodded, and wished me good night, and left.

Tonight, as I have for the past three nights, I'll sit near Charlie's bed. On Thursday, about thirty minutes after she had fallen asleep, she began to make a low growling noise deep in her throat, twitching her shoulders and head. But then she stopped, and after watching her for another hour or so, I finally went to bed myself. I wished, as I often did, for Nathaniel. I also wished, as I rarely did, for Eden. I suppose, though, that what I was really wishing was for someone to be responsible for Charlie alongside me.

I can't say that what happened was my greatest fear for her—my greatest fear is that she'll die—but it was close. I had tried to talk to her about her body, about how it was hers only, about how she didn't have to do anything she didn't want to. No, that's not accurate. I hadn't *tried*—I *had*. I knew she was vulnerable; I knew something like this could happen. Not even that—I knew it *would* happen. And I knew we were lucky—that, as bad as it was, it could have been worse.

When I was an undergraduate, a professor of mine had said there were two types of people: those who wept for the world, and those who wept for themselves. Weeping for your family, he said, was a form of weeping for yourself. "Those who congratulate themselves on their sacrifices for their families aren't actually sacrificing at all," he said, "because their family is an extension of their selves, and therefore a manifestation of the ego." True selflessness, he said, meant giving of yourself to a stranger, someone whose life would never be entangled with your own.

But hadn't I tried to do that? I *had* tried to make things better for people I didn't know, and it had cost me my family, and therefore my self. And yet the improvements I had attempted are now in dispute. I cannot do anything else to help the world—I can only try to help Charlie.

Now I am very tired. I'm crying, of course, I suppose selfishly. I don't know, though, of anyone who doesn't cry for themselves these days—sickness makes the self indivisible from strangers, and so, even if you're thinking of them, those millions of people with whom you navigate the city, you are by definition wondering when their lives might brush against yours, each encounter an infection, each touch a potential death. It's selfishness, but there seems to be no other way—not now.

My love to you and Olivier—Charles

My dear Peter,   December 3, 2076

Years ago, when I was traveling through Ashgabat, I met a man in a café. This was in the '20s, when the Turkmen Republic was still known as Turkmenistan, and still under authoritarian rule.

I had been in university then, and this man had engaged me in conversation: What brought me to Ashgabat, and what did I think of it? Now I realize he was likely a spy of one sort or another, but then, being callow and stupid, as well as lonely, I was eager to share my thoughts about the inhumanity of an autocratic state, and how, although I wasn't arguing for democracy, there was a difference between a constitutional monarchy of the sort I lived in and the dystopia he lived in.

He listened patiently as I bloviated, and then, when I was finished, said, "Come with me." We walked to one of the open windows. The café was on the second floor of a building on a narrow tributary, a shortcut to the Russian Market, one of the last streets in the city not to be razed and rebuilt in glass and steel. "Look outside," the man said. "Does this look like a dystopia to you?"

I looked. One of the great dissonances of Ashgabat was watching people who were dressed for the 19th century navigate a city that had been built for the 22nd. Below me, I saw women in bright-patterned head scarves and dresses hefting bulging plastic bags, and men zipping by on motorized handcarts, and schoolchildren shouting to one another. It was a sunny, crisp day, and even now, even as it's no longer possible to remember the feeling of winter, I can still recall cold by visualizing the scenery of it: a gaggle of teenage girls' cheeks stippled with scarlet; an elderly man tossing a just-roasted potato from hand to hand, the steam shimmering before his face; a woman's wool scarf fluttering around her forehead.

It had not been the cold that the man had wanted me to see, though, but the life being lived in it. The middle-aged women, bags stuffed with groceries, gossiping in front of a blue-painted doorway, the group of boys playing soccer, the two girls walking down the street eating meat buns, their arms linked—as they passed beneath us, one of them said something to the other and they both began giggling, covering their mouths with their hands. There was a soldier, but he was leaning against the side of a building, his head resting against the brick, his eyes closed, a cigarette balanced on his lower lip, relaxing in the pale sun.

"So you see," my companion said.

I think about that exchange often these days, as well as its underlying question: *Does this place* look *dystopic?* I ask it often about this city, where, in the absence of shops, there is still commerce, conducted now in the Square, but still populated by the same kinds of people—strolling couples, children wailing because they've been denied a treat, a strident woman haggling with a truculent vendor over the price of a copper pan—as before. In the absence of theaters, there are still people gathering for concerts at the community centers they're establishing in every zone. In the absence of the number of children and young people that there should be, there is more care, more love, lavished on the ones who remain, although I know firsthand that that care can resemble something more dictatorial than loving. The answer, implicit in the man's question, was that a dystopia doesn't *look like* anything; indeed, that it can look like anywhere else.

And yet it also *does* look like something. The things I have described are elements of the sanctioned life, the life that can be lived aboveground. But out of the corner of our eyes, there is another life, one we see in glimpses, in movements. There is no television, for example, there is no internet, and yet messages are still relayed, and the dissidents are still able to telegraph their reports. I sometimes read of them in our daily briefings, and while it typically takes only a week or so to discover them—a surprising, or perhaps unsurprising, number of them are related to state employees—there are always those who elude us. There is no foreign travel, and yet every month there are reports of attempted defections, of dinghies capsizing off the coast of Maine or South Carolina or Massachusetts or Florida. There are no more refugee camps, and yet there are still reports— fewer, admittedly—of escapees from even worse countries than this, found and packed into a poorly made boat and sent back out to sea under armed guard. To live in a place like this means to be aware that that little movement, that twitching, that faint, mosquito-like buzzing, is not your imagination but proof of another existence, the country you once knew and you know must still exist, beating onward just beyond the range of your senses.

Data, investigation, analysis, news, rumor: A dystopia flattens those terms into one. There is what the state says, and then there is everything else, and that everything else falls into one category: information. People in a young dystopia crave information—they are starved for it, they will kill for it. But over time, that craving diminishes, and within a few years, you forget what it tasted like, you forget the thrill of knowing something first, of sharing it with others, of getting to keep secrets and asking others to do the same. You become freed of the burden of knowledge; you learn, if not to trust the state, then to surrender to it.

And we try to make the process of forgetting, of unlearning, as easy as we can. It is why all dystopias seem so generic in their systems and appearance; there is the removal of the vehicles of information (the press, the television, the internet, books—even though I think we should have kept television, which can easily be made useful), and an emphasis instead on the elemental—the things gathered or made by hand. Eventually, the two worlds, the primitive and the technological, are united in endeavors such as the Farm, which looks like an agrarian project but will be powered by the most sophisticated irrigation and climatic systems the state can afford. Eventually, you hope, the people working there will forget how that technology was once applied, and what it was once capable of doing, and how many ways we once depended on it, and what information it could provide.

I look at you, and what you're doing over there, Peter, and I know we're doomed. Of course I do. But what can I do now? Where can I go? Last week they changed my profession on all my state papers from "scientist" to "senior administrator." "A promotion," said the interior minister, "congratulations." And while it is, it also isn't. If I were still classified as a scientist, I'd in theory be able to attend foreign symposiums and conferences, not that the invitations have exactly been flooding in. But as a state administrator, there is no reason, no need, for me to ever leave here. I am a powerful man in a country I cannot leave, which by definition makes me a prisoner.

Which is why I'm sending you this. I don't think I'll ever be stripped of my possessions. But it's valuable, and I suppose I think that if the day comes when Charlie and I *are* able to leave, we won't be able to take our money or our things. We might not be able to take anything at all. So I'm asking you to keep this safe for us. Maybe someday I'll be able to reclaim it from you, or have you sell it so we can use the money to settle elsewhere. I understand how naïve this all sounds. But I also know that you, being kind, aren't laughing at me. I know you're worried for me. I wish I could tell you not to be. For now, I know you'll protect this for me.

Love, Charles

My dear Peter,   October 29, 2077

Sorry I've been so quiet, and, yes, I will send you regular updates, if only to say, "I'm here and alive." You're kind to want to hear them. And thank you for the new courier—much safer, I think, to have the person be from your side rather than ours, especially now.

Everyone is still astonished that you're ceasing relations with us. I'm not saying this in an accusatory way, not that it would make a difference—but it just seemed like one of those threats that would never be realized. The bigger fear is not so much *your* lack of recognition, however, but that you might inspire other places to do the same.

Yet we also understand perfectly why it's happened. When the Marriage Act was first discussed, six years ago, it had seemed not just impossible but silly. There had been that study from the University of Kandahar about how rising rates of unrest in three different countries were linked to the percentage of unmarried men over the age of twenty-five. The study failed to take into account other socially destabilizing effects, such as poverty, illiteracy, illness, and climatic disaster, and was eventually discredited.

But I guess it had had more of an effect on certain members of the Committee than I (and perhaps they) had realized, though when the proposal was revived and re-presented this past summer, it was framed differently: Marriage would be a way to encourage repopulation, and to do so within a state-supported institution. The proposal was coauthored by a deputy minister from Interior and another from Health, and was thorough and almost troublingly rational, as if the entire point of marriage was not an expression of devotion but an acquiescence to the needs of the society. Which it perhaps is. The deputy ministers explained the system of rewards and incentives for marriage, which could be used, they argued, as a way to ease the population into the concept of a comprehensive welfare state. There would be housing allowances, and what they're calling "procreation incentives," which essentially means that people would be rewarded, in either benefits or cash, for having children.

"I never thought I'd see the day when free Black people would be celebrated for making more free Black people," said one of the justice ministers, dryly, and everyone stiffened.

"The society needs all people, of all kinds, to contribute to its rebuilding," said the deputy interior minister.

"I guess desperate times call for desperate measures," the justice minister responded, quietly, and there was a strained silence.

"Well, then," said the deputy interior minister, finally, in a conclusive way.

There was another silence, this one unhappy as well, but also anticipatory, as if we were all actors in a play and at a particularly charged moment, one of us had forgotten his lines.

Finally, someone spoke. "Ah, what is the definition of marriage here?" he asked.

Everyone in the room either looked down at the table or up at the ceiling. The man who had asked the question was a deputy in the Pharmacology Ministry, newly arrived from the private sector. I knew little else about him except that he was white, and probably in his early fifties, and that both of his children and his husband had died in '70.

"Well," said the deputy interior minister, at last, and then she too fell silent, looking around the room almost beseechingly, as if someone might answer for her. But no one did. "We will of course honor all preexisting marital contracts," she said, after a pause.

"But," she continued, "the Marriage Act is meant to encourage procreation, and therefore"—again, a cast about the room for help; again, no takers—"the benefits will be given only to unions between biological males and biological females. This is not to say," she added, quickly, before the pharmacology minister could speak, "that we are proposing any moral . . . penalty upon those who do not fit this definition, only that such couples will not be eligible for state incentives."

People began shouting questions at once. Of the thirty-two people in that room, at least nine of us—including, I was fairly certain, one of the authors of the proposal, a rabbity little woman—would not be eligible for state benefits if this act passes. If there had been only two or three of us, I would be more worried—in such situations, people tend to vote against their own interests because they think it offers them greater personal protection. But in this case, there are too many of us for such a proposal to be realized, not to mention the fact that there are too many unanswerables: Would this mean that barren couples' marriages would become ineligible for state benefits? What about same-sex parents who had biological children, or have means to have more? What would happen to widows and widowers, of whom there were now historic numbers? Were we actually, *really* talking about paying citizens for having children? What if they had children and the children died—would they keep their benefits? Was this effectively eliminating a fertile person's right to choose to have children or not? What if the fertile person was physically or mentally unfit—would we still be encouraging them to have children? What about divorce? Wouldn't this be encouraging women to stay in abusive marriages? Would a sterile person be allowed to marry a fertile person? What if a person had transitioned to another gender—would this legislation not leave them in an irresolvable legal gray area? From where was the money coming to support this plan, especially as two of our primary trading partners were expected to cease relations with us? If procreation is so essential to the country's survival, would it not make more sense to pardon state traitors and encourage them to have children, even in a controlled environment? Why wouldn't we just adopt some of the refugees' children, now orphans, or import children from climatically ravaged countries, and thus divorce the idea of parenthood from biology? Were the authors really suggesting that we exploit a national and existential trauma, the disappearance of a generation of children, to advance a moralistic agenda? By the end of the session, both of the proposal's authors seemed about to cry, and the meeting disbanded with everyone in a foul temper.

I was walking to my car when I heard someone call my name, and turned and saw it was the pharmacology minister. "It's not going to happen," he said, so firmly that I almost smiled: He was so young, and so certain. Then I remembered that he had lost his entire family, and that he deserved my respect for that alone.

"I hope you're right," I said, and he nodded. "I have no doubt," he said, and then bowed and walked off toward his car.

We shall see. Over the years, I've been astonished at and dismayed by and fearful of how acquiescent the public has proven to be: Fear of disease, the human instinct to stay healthy, has eclipsed almost every other desire and value they once treasured, as well as many of the freedoms they had thought inalienable. That fear was yeast to the state, and now the state generates its own fear when they feel the population's is flagging. Monday begins the third consecutive week of debates about the Marriage Act, and it looks like we may be able to stop this after all—your condemnation helped, certainly. I don't see how this proceeds without alienating us completely from Old Europe, but of course I've been wrong before.

Keep your fingers crossed for all of us. I'll write more next week. Send my love to Olivier. And save some for yourself.

Charles

February 3, 2078

Dear Peter—the act passed. It'll be announced tomorrow. I don't know what else to say. More soon. Charles

Dear Peter,   April 15, 2079

It's very early, just dawn, and I can't sleep. I haven't been sleeping at all, it seems, these past few months. I've been trying to go to bed earlier, closer to eleven instead of past midnight, and then I lie there. Sometimes I don't so much fall as slip into a liminal state between wakefulness and slumber, one in which I'm acutely aware of both the mattress beneath me and the sound of the fan wicking away above me. In these hours, I relive the events of the day, yet in this replay, I'm sometimes participant and sometimes witness, and I never know at which moment the camera might swing on its dolly and my perspective will shift.

Last night I saw C. again. He's not exactly my type, and I can't imagine I'm his. But we both have the same security clearance and rank, which means that he can come to my house or I can go to his and we can have our respective cars wait outside to drive us home afterward without any questions or difficulties.

You forget, sometimes, how much you need to be touched. It's not food or water or light or heat—you can go for years without it. The body doesn't remember the sensation; it does you the kindness of allowing you to forget. The first two times, we had sex quickly, almost brutally, as if we might never have the opportunity again, but the past three instances have been more leisurely. He lives in a state-appointed townhouse in Zone Fourteen, bare of anything but the essentials, one mostly empty room opening into another.

Afterward, we pretend the listening devices don't exist—we have that privilege, too—and talk. He's fifty-two, twenty-three years younger than I am, only twelve years older than David would have been. He speaks, sometimes, about his sons, the younger of whom would have been sixteen this year, just a year older than Charlie will be this September, and his husband, who had been in the marketing department of the pharmaceutical company where he'd once worked. C. had considered killing himself after they had died, all within six months, but in the end, he hadn't, and now, he said, he couldn't remember why.

"I can't remember why I didn't, either," I said, though as soon as I spoke, I realized that was a lie.

"Your granddaughter," he said, and I nodded.

"You're lucky," he said.

You'll recall it had been C. who'd been so certain that the Marriage Act would fail. Even now, even as we were meeting in semi-secret, he continued to argue that it'd be overturned imminently. "What's the point of having marriage for people who aren't going to have children?" he asked. "If the point is to raise more children in general, why not use some of us as child-carers, or assign us other supportive roles? Isn't the whole point to try to get maximum advantage out of all our citizens?" When I once suggested the inevitable conclusion—that, despite the Committee's promises, the Marriage Act will only lead to the eventual criminalization of gayness on moral grounds—he contradicted me with such fury that I had no choice but to gather my things and leave. "What's the point of that?" he asked me, again and again, and when I said that the point was the same wherever and whenever homosexuality was criminalized—to create a useful scapegoat on whom the fortunes of a faltering state could be blamed—he accused me of being bitter and cynical. "I believe in this state," he said, and when I said I had, once, too, he had told me to get out, that we were too distant from each other philosophically. For weeks, there was silence. But then need drew us back together, the source of our reunion the same thing we could no longer discuss.

Afterward, he walks me to the door; we embrace, rather than kiss, confirm our next encounter. At Committee meetings, we're cordial. Not too distant, not too friendly. I imagine no one can tell anything different. At our last encounter, he told me that safe houses have started cropping up, mostly at the far western edges of Zone Eight, for people who can't meet as we do in a private house. "They're not brothels," he clarified. "They're more like gathering places."

"What do people do there?" I asked.

"The same things we do here," he said. "But not just sex."

"No?" I asked.

"No," he said. "They also talk. They go there and talk."

"About what?" I asked.

He shrugged. "The things people talk about," he said, and as he did, I realized: I no longer knew what people talk about. If you were to listen to us on the Committee, you would think that all people talk about is how to overthrow the state, how to escape the country, how to cause mayhem. And yet what else is there to discuss? There are no movies, no television, no internet. You can't, as we once had, spend an evening debating an article or a novel or bragging about a vacation to someplace far away. You can't discuss the person you've just had sex with, or how you were interviewing for a new job, or how much you wanted to buy a new car or apartment or pair of sunglasses. You can't do these things because none of those things are possible any longer, at least not openly, and with their elimination has also disappeared hours', days' worth of conversations. The world we live in now is about survival, and survival is always present tense. The past is no longer relevant; the future has failed to materialize. Survival allows for hope—it is, indeed, predicated on hope—but it does not allow for pleasure, and as a topic, it is dull. Talk, touch: the things C. and I kept reuniting to find—somewhere downtown, in a house by the river, there were other people like us, talking to each other just to hear the sound of someone responding to them, proof that the self they remembered still existed after all.

Later, I went home. I had a female guard from Security sit downstairs on the nights I knew I'd be out, and after I had dismissed her, I climbed up to Charlie's room and sat on the edge of her bed, staring at her. She's one of those children who look like neither their mother nor their father. Her nose resembles Eden's perhaps, and I suppose she has David's long, thin mouth, but somehow nothing in her face reminds me of either of them, and I am grateful for that. She is her own creature, one unfreighted by history. She was wearing a pair of short-sleeved pajamas, and I ran my fingers over her arms, which are pocked by little craters left behind by the scars. Next to her wheezed Little Cat, a sore on his right foreleg oozing pus, and I knew that I would soon have to take him to the clinic, have him injected with poison, come up with a lie to tell Charlie.

In bed, I thought about Nathaniel. If I'm lucky, I can conjure him as a source not of shame or self-flagellation but of neutrality. When I'm with C., I can sometimes close my eyes and pretend he's Nathaniel at fifty-two. C. looks and smells and sounds and tastes entirely different than Nathaniel did, but skin is skin. I dare not admit this to anyone but you (not that there's anyone else left to tell), but increasingly I have these dreams in which I revisit scenes and moments from my life with Nathaniel but in which David—and later, Eden, and later still, even Charlie—are missing, as if they never existed. These dreams are often banal: Nathaniel and I, getting older and older, arguing about whether we should plant sunflowers or not, or, once, trying to chase a raccoon out of our attic. We seem to live in a cottage by the sea in Massachusetts, and although I never see the outside of the structure, I have a sense of what it looks like anyway.

In the daytime, I sometimes speak aloud to Nathaniel. Out of respect, I rarely discuss work, for that would upset him too much. Instead, I ask him about Charlie. After that first incident with those boys, I had told her about sex, and sexual threats, in a much more complete way than I had told her before. "Do you have any questions?" I had asked her, and after a silence, she had shaken her head. "No," she'd said. She still doesn't like to be touched by anyone, and while I sometimes mourn for her, I envy her, too: To live a life without desire (not to mention imagination) would once have been something to pity, but now it might ensure her survival—or at least increase her chances. Yet her distaste has not stopped her from wandering off again, and after the second incident, I sat down with her again. "Little cat," I began, and then I didn't know what else to say. How could I tell her that those boys weren't attracted to her, that they saw her only as something to use and toss aside? I couldn't, I couldn't—I felt traitorous even thinking the words. In those moments, I wished that someone felt lust for her, that even if that lust was muddied with cruelty, it would at least be passion, or a form of it—it would mean that someone saw her as lovely and special and desirable; it would mean that someone might one day love her as deeply as I do, but differently, too.

More and more frequently these days, I think about how, of all the horrors the illnesses wreaked, one of the least-discussed is the brisk brutality with which it sorted us into categories. The first, most obvious one was the living and the dead. Then there was the sick and the well, the bereaved and the relieved, the cured and the incurable, the insured and the uninsured. We kept track of these statistics; we wrote them all down. But then there were the other divisions, the kind that didn't appear to warrant recording: The people who lived with other people, and the people who lived alone. The people who had money, and the people who didn't. The people who had connections, and the people who didn't. The people who had somewhere else to go, and the people who didn't.

In the end, it hadn't made as much of a difference as we thought it would. The rich died anyway, maybe more slowly than they should have; some of the poor survived. After the first round of the virus had whipped through the city, scooping up all the easiest prey—the indigent and the infirm and the young—it had returned for seconds, and thirds, and fourths, until it was only the luckiest who remained. And yet no one was truly lucky: Is Charlie's life lucky? Perhaps it is—she is here, after all, she can talk and walk and learn, she is able-bodied and lucid, she is loved and, I know, capable of loving. But she is not who she might have been, because none of us are—the illness took something from all of us, and so our definition of luck is a matter of relativity, as luck always is, its parameters designated by others. The disease clarified everything about who we are; it revealed the fictions we'd all constructed about our lives. It revealed that progress, that tolerance, does not necessarily beget more progress or tolerance. It revealed that kindness does not beget more kindness. It revealed how brittle the poetry of our lives truly is—it exposed friendship as something flimsy and conditional; partnership as contextual and circumstantial. No law, no arrangement, no amount of love was stronger than our own need to survive, or, for the more generous among us, our need for our people, whoever they were, to survive. I sometimes sense a faint mutual embarrassment among those of us who lived—who had sought to deprive someone else, maybe even someone else we knew, or a relative of someone we knew, of medication or hospitalization or food if it meant we could save ourselves? Who had reported someone they knew, perhaps even liked—a neighbor, an acquaintance, a colleague—to the Health Ministry, and who had turned up the volume on their headphones to muffle the sounds of them begging for help as they were led away to the waiting van, shouting all the while that someone had been misinformed, that the rash that had spread across their daughter's arm was only eczema, that the sore on their son's forehead was only a pimple?

And now the illness is under control, and we are back to considering the incidentals of life once more: whether we might be able to find chicken rather than tofu at the grocery; or whether our children might be admitted into this college versus that one; or whether we might be lucky in this year's housing lottery, and move from Zone Seventeen to Zone Eight, or Zone Eight to Zone Fourteen.

But behind all these concerns and minor anxieties is something deeper: the truth of who we are, our essential selves, the thing that emerges when everything else has been burned away. We have learned to accommodate that person as much as we can, to ignore who we know ourselves to be. Most of the time, we're successful. We must be: Pretending is the cost of sanity. But we all know who we really are. If we have lived, it is because we are *worse* than we ever believed ourselves to be, not better. Indeed, it feels at times as if all who remain are those who were wily or tenacious or scheming enough to survive. I know that this belief is its own kind of romance, but in my more fanciful moments, it makes perfect sense—we are the left-behind, the dregs, the rats fighting for bits of rotten food, the people who chose to stay on earth, while those better and smarter than we are have left for some other realm we can only dream of, the door to which we're too frightened to open, even to peek inside.

Charles

Dear Peter,   September 15, 2081

Thank you, as always, for Charlie's birthday gifts, which are especially welcome this year. The rationing has been so severe that it's been fourteen months since she's had any new clothes, much less a dress. Thank you too for letting me take credit for them with her. I wished, as I often do, that I could tell her about you, that I could tell her that somebody else, somebody far away, cares about her as well. But I know it's not safe to do so.

Today I went in to speak with the dean at her school. Last year, when she was in eleventh grade, I started getting suspicious that the school would discourage her from attending university, despite the fact that all her teachers have been supportive, and even if they hadn't, Charlie's math and physics scores would guarantee her acceptance to a technical college at the very least.

I've been trying for years to articulate to myself the scope of Charlie's deficiencies. As you know, there still remains so little research on the long-term effects of Xychor on those children who received the drug in '70, in part because, obviously, there are relatively few survivors, and in part because the guardians and parents of those who *have* survived have been reluctant to subject their children to further research and testing. (I myself am one of those selfish people who are inhibiting greater scientific understanding by withholding permission for my child to be studied.) But the papers that have been published, from here and various institutes in Old Europe, which are better funded, have been unhelpful, and I've yet to see my Charlie reflected in any of the descriptions I've read. I want to clarify, though, that I haven't sought an explanation because I feel I need to understand her any better than I do in order to love her more. But some part of me is always hoping that, if there are others like her, then she will someday see someone she recognizes, someone who feels like home. She has never had a friend. I don't know how deeply she feels loneliness, or even if—unlike her poor father—she has the capacity to recognize it. But my dearest wish is that someone will someday take that loneliness from her, preferably before she's able to identify the sensation for what it is.

So far, though, there's been no one. I still can't tell how much she comprehends about what she doesn't comprehend, if you know what I mean. Sometimes I fear that I've been fooling myself, that I'm searching for a humanity within her that's been wiped out entirely. Then she'll say something astonishingly perceptive, so insightful that I become horrified that she might have sensed I ever doubted her humanness. Once, she asked me if I had liked her better before she got sick, and I felt as if someone had socked me in my solar plexus, and had to grab her and hold her to me so she couldn't see my expression. "No," I told her. "I have always loved you just the same since the day you were born. I wouldn't want my little cat any other way." What I couldn't say, because it would confuse her, or sound too much like an insult, is that I loved her now *more* than

I had; that my love for her was terrible because it was more ferocious, that it was something dark and seething, a misshapen mass of energy.

At the school, the dean reviewed with me a list of three math-and-sciences colleges she thought might be appropriate for Charlie: all within two hours of the city, all small and well-defended. All three guaranteed their graduates employment in a Grade Three or higher facility. The most expensive of these colleges was for females only, and this was the one I chose for Charlie.

The dean made a note. Then she paused. "Most Grade One state employees opt for twenty-four-hour security for their children," she said. "Would you like to use the college's service, or continue your own?"

"I'll continue with my own," I said. The state, at least, would pay for that.

We discussed a few more details, and then the dean stood. "Charlie will be finished with her last class," she said. "Shall I get her and you two can go home together?" I told her I'd like that, and she left her office to tell her assistant.

As she did, I stood and looked at the photographs of her students which hung on her wall. There are four all-girl private schools left in the city; this one is the smallest, and attracts what the school calls "studious" girls, though the word is a euphemism, as not all of them are especially academically gifted. Rather, the word is meant to convey their charges' fundamental shyness, their "delayed sociability," as the school calls it.

The dean returned with Charlie, and we said goodbye and walked out. "Home?" I asked, once we were in the car, "Or a treat?"

She thought. "Home," she said. On Mondays, Wednesdays, and Fridays, she has an additional life-skills tutorial class, where she works with a psychologist on verbal and nonverbal communication. This always leaves her tired, and she leaned her head against the seat and closed her eyes, both because she was genuinely depleted and, I think, because she wanted to avoid the questions she knew I'd ask and which she would struggle to answer: What happened in school today? How was music class? What did you listen to? How did the music make you feel? What do you think the musician was trying to say? What was your favorite part of the composition, and why?

"Grandfather," she'd say, frustrated, "I don't know how to answer you."

"You *do* know, little cat," I'd say. "And you're doing so well."

More and more, I wonder what her adulthood will be like. For the first three years after she recovered from the illness, my only concern was keeping her alive: I monitored how much she ate, how much she slept, the whites of her eyes, the pink of her tongue. Then, after the first incident with the boys, I thought mostly of protecting her, though that surveillance was more complicated, since it relied as much on my oversight as it did on hoping she understood whom she could trust, and whom she couldn't. Obedience would ensure her survival, but had I trained her to be *too* obedient?

Then, after the second incident, I began to think about how she would continue through her life—how I could defend her from people who tried to take advantage of her; how she might live after I die. I had always assumed that she would be with me for her entire life, even as I always knew as well that it wouldn't be the entirety of *her* life that she would be with me but the entirety of mine. Now I am nearly seventy-seven, and she is seventeen, and even if I live another ten years—if I don't die myself, or if I'm not disappeared, like C.— I'll still leave her with decades of her own to contend with.

But on the one hand, maybe the society that is coming will be easier for her in certain aspects. There are marriage brokers (all state-licensed) opening up offices, promising they can find a spouse for anyone. Wesley will guarantee her a job, and the points system will guarantee that she will always have food, always have shelter. I would prefer to stay alive to watch over her as she enters middle age, but I only *need* to stay alive to make sure I can settle her with someone who will take care of her, that I can secure her a position someplace where I know she'll be well-treated. This knowledge makes doing the work I do easier. I had long ago stopped believing I was doing anything to help science, or humanity, or this country or city, but knowing that I'm doing it to help her, to safeguard her, makes life bearable.

Or at least that's what I'm able to believe—some days more than others.

Love to you and Olivier. Charles

My dear Peter,   December 1, 2083

Happy birthday! Seventy-five. Practically a baby, still. I wish I had something to send you, but instead, you're the one sending me presents, if a picture of you and Olivier on vacation can really be considered a present. And thank you for the beautiful shawl, which I'm going to give Charlie when she comes home for the holidays in two weeks. The new courier's working out wonderfully, by the way—even more discreet than the last one, and a lot faster, too.

The house is almost fully converted. Although there have now been two speeches in Committee meetings about my generosity, it wasn't as if I really had a choice—when the military asks to commission a private house, they're not asking: They're ordering. Anyway, I was lucky to hold on to it as long as I did, especially in wartime. I *did* ask for the unit of my choice, which they granted: They've carved out eight apartments, and ours is on the third floor, facing north, consisting of what used to be Charlie's bedroom and playroom, which is now the living room. I'm sleeping in the bedroom until she gets home, after which I'll move to the living room. As the house was in her name to begin with, she'll keep the apartment once she marries, and I'll be relocated to another flat in the zone, which was also part of the compromise.

Despite the fact that I'm now living in what is, technically, military barracks, there are no attractive soldiers strutting about. The other apartments have instead been given to various operations technicians, beetley men who look away when I pass them on the staircase, and from whose apartments I sometimes hear the shrill of distorted radio-wave messages.

You mentioned in your last letter that I sounded sanguine about the whole situation. I think the better word is probably "resigned": The proud part of me was appeased by the fact that I was among the last three people on the Committee to have his house commissioned, and the practical part knew that, with Charlie off in college, I didn't need this large a residence anyway. Also, the house was never truly mine: It was Aubrey and Norris's, and then it was Nathaniel's. But I—like Aubrey's collection, the final pieces of which I donated one by one to the Metropolitan and then, when the museum was closed down, to various private organizations—could only be said to have occupied the place, never to have possessed it. Over the years, this house, which had once been so symbolic to me—a repository of my resentments; a projection of my fears—had become, finally, just a house: a shelter, not a metaphor.

I *am* concerned about how Charlie will react. She knows it happened; I went up to visit her at school a few weeks ago, and when I asked if she had any questions, she shook her head. I'm trying to make it easy for her, as easy as I can. For example, there aren't a huge number of paint colors to choose from these days, but I told her she could pick whichever she liked, and perhaps we could even draw a pattern on the bedroom wall, even though neither of us is very good at drawing. "Whatever you want," I tell her. "This is your apartment." Sometimes she nods and says, "I know," but other times, she shakes her head. "It's not mine," she says, "it's ours. Yours and mine, Grandfather," and then I know that, despite her best efforts, she's been thinking of her future, and that it scares her. I change the subject then, and we speak of something else.

C. had always been convinced that there were more of us working at high levels in the state than we even knew, which he said made things more dangerous for us, not less, as those people would seek to make examples out of anyone who flagrantly disobeyed the laws in order to protect themselves, as happens in the irrational logic of the vulnerable. He had argued that the Marriage Act could never have passed without a plurality of us on the Committee and beyond, and that our internalized shame and guilt at being unable to reproduce had led to a dangerous kind of compensatory patriotism, the kind that drove us to create laws that ultimately endangered us. "But," he had said, "no matter how bad it gets, there will always be loopholes for us, as long as we follow the rules in public." This was shortly before he was disappeared. A year later, as you know, I began going to one of the safe houses he'd told me about, and which still endure, intact, while so many other things have been destroyed or co-opted or reinvented. With Charlie away at college, I go more and more frequently, and now that the house has been converted, I suspect I'll go still more.

The changes have also made me think about Aubrey and Norris. It's been years since I've thought of them, but recently, I've found myself talking aloud to Aubrey in particular. This house still feels like his, even for as long as I've lived in it—now almost as long as Aubrey himself. In my conversations with him, he's angry, angry but trying to conceal it. But eventually, he no longer can. "What have you fucking done, Charles?" he asks me, in a way he never would have in life. "What have you done to my house?" And although I tell myself I've never cared about Aubrey's opinion, I never have anything to say in response.

"What have you done, Charles?" he keeps asking, again and again. "What have you done?" But every time I open my mouth to answer, nothing comes out.

Love to you and O.—Charles

Dear Peter,   July 12, 2084

Last night I dreamed of Hawai'i. The night before, I had been in my favored house of ill repute, sleeping alongside A., when the sirens began to wail.

"Jesus, Jesus," said A., scrabbling for his clothes, his shoes. "It's a raid."

Men began crowding in doorways, buttoning their shirts and buckling their belts as they did, their faces blank or terrified. It was safer to be silent in these raids, and yet someone—a young man who does something in Justice—kept repeating, "What we're doing isn't illegal; what we're doing isn't illegal," until someone else hissed at him to shut up, that we already knew that.

We stood there, waiting, about thirty of us across four floors. Whoever they were trying to find wasn't guilty of homosexuality—the person might be under suspicion for smuggling, or forgery, or theft—and although they couldn't charge us for who we are, they *could* humiliate us for it. Why else, then, would they arrest this person when they knew he was here, instead of quietly, at his residence? It was for the spectacle of leading us, single file, out of the house, our hands raised above our heads like criminals, for the mortifying pleasure of tying our hands and having us kneel on the curb, for the sadism of asking us to repeat our names—*Louder, please, I didn't hear you*—and shouting it to their colleague to run through the database: *Charles Griffith. Thirteen Washington Square North. Says he's a scientist at RU. Age: Eighty in October.* (And then a smirk: *Eighty? You're still doing this at* eighty? As if it were absurd, obscene, that someone so old should still want to be touched, when really, it is the sensation you come to crave the most.) And then there was the discomfort of the hours spent in a crouch in the street, your head bent as if in shame, the suspect long since removed, waiting for the theater to end, for one of them to get bored and release us, the sound of his fellow soldiers' laughter as they climbed back into their cars. They were never physically abusive with us, they never called us names—they couldn't; too many of us had too much power—but it was clear they disdained us, and when we finally stood and turned for the house, you could see the street darkening again, the neighbors who had watched us through their windows, never saying a word, returning to bed now that the show had concluded. "I wish they'd just make us illegal," someone, a young man, had grumbled after the last raid, and a number of people had begun shouting at him, asking him how he could be so ignorant and stupid, but I understood what he was trying to express: If we were illegal, we would know our position. As it was, we were nothing—we were known but not named, tolerated but not recognized. We lived in a constant state of uncertainty, waiting for the day we would be declared enemies, waiting for the night when what we did would, in the space of an hour, a single signed document, be transformed from regrettable to criminal. The very word for what we were had somehow, at some point, disappeared from the vernacular—to us, we were only "people like us": "Do you know Charles? He's one of us." Even we had become euphemistic, unable to say what we are.

They almost never raided the inside—as I said, too many of us had too much power, and it was like they knew that the amount of contraband they'd find inside would entail so much processing that they'd be able to do little else for the following week—but there were chutes in each room that you could toss your possessions down, and the first place we went after going back indoors was the safe box in the basement, where we'd retrieve our books and wallets and devices and whatever else we had dropped, and then we would leave, probably without even saying goodbye to the person we'd been with, and the next time we came, neither of us would mention it, we would pretend it had never happened.

Two nights ago, we had been waiting three minutes for the bang on the door, for the loudspeaker announcing one of our names, when we realized that the sirens weren't for us after all. Again, there was a soundless exchange of glances—the people on the first and second floors looking up to us on the third and fourth, all of us wondering—when, finally, a young man on the first floor cautiously unlocked the door and then, after a pause, dramatically flung it open, standing in the center of the frame.

He shouted, and we came rushing downstairs to see that Bank Street had become a river, the water racing east. "The Hudson River's flooded," I heard someone say, in a quiet, awestruck voice, and then, right after, someone else said, "The safe box!" and there was a hustle down to the basement, which was already filling with water. A chain was formed to move the books and equipment we'd stored there to the attic, and after, we stood at the first-floor windows, watching the water rise. A. had a communication device, a kind I had never seen before, one different from my own—I never asked what he did, and he never told me—and he spoke into it, a few terse words, and ten minutes later, a flotilla of plastic dinghies appeared.

"Get out," said A., whom I had known only to be passive and somewhat whiny, but who had suddenly transformed into someone declarative and stern: his work persona, I assumed. "Everyone, queue up for the boats." The water was now lapping up the front steps.

"What about the house?" someone asked, and we all knew he was asking about the books in the attic.

"I'll handle them," said a youngish man, whom I had never met, but who I knew to be the house's owner, or manager, or keeper—it was never clear which, but I knew he was responsible. "Go."

So we did. This time, whether because of who A. was, or because of the equalizing nature of the crisis, there were no jokes from the soldiers, no sneers: They held out their hands, and we grabbed them and were lowered into the rafts, and the whole exchange was so matter-of-fact, so collegial—we needed saving, and they were here to save us—that you could almost believe that their disgust for us was an act, that they respected us as much as they did anyone. Behind us, another fleet of boats was arriving, and now there was a loudspeaker announcement: "Residents of Zone Eight! Evacuate your units! Descend to your front doors and wait for help!"

By now the water was rising so rapidly that the boat was actually bobbing on the water, as if atop a wave, and the puny motor was becoming choked with leaves and twigs. A block east, on Greenwich Street, we were joined by other motorized rafts moving east, from Jane and West 12th Streets, all of us making our slow way to Hudson Street, where corps of soldiers were stacking sandbags, trying to hold the river back.

Here there were emergency vehicles, and ambulances, but I climbed out of the raft and left, walking east, never looking behind me: It was best not to get involved where you didn't need to; there was no honor, no use in it. I hadn't gotten too wet, but my socks squished as I walked, and I was glad I hadn't worn my cooling suit, despite the heat. At West 10th and Sixth Avenue, a platoon of soldiers jogged by me, groups of four each holding aloft a plastic raft. They looked weary, I thought, and why wouldn't they be? Two months ago, the fires; last month, the rains; this month, the floods.

When I finally got home, everything was quiet, though whether that was because of the hour or because some of the inhabitants had been conscripted to help with the efforts, I didn't know.

The next day—Tuesday: yesterday—I went to work and did little but listen to radio reports of the flood, which had consumed a significant part of Zone Eight and all of Zones Seven and Twenty-one, from what had been the highway all the way east to, in some instances, Hudson Street. The Bank Street house had, presumably, been ruined; someone will let me know for sure one way or another. Two people had died: An elderly lady had fallen down the stairs of her house on West 11th Street trying to reach the boat and had broken her neck; a man on Perry Street had refused to vacate his basement apartment and had drowned. Two streets had been somewhat spared, purely from happenstance: The army had felled three massive, diseased trees on Bethune and Washington early Monday morning, which had mitigated the flooding there. And on Gansevoort, the army had been digging a trench on Greenwich to reroute a deteriorating sanitation pipe, and this too had minimized the damage. Whereas, a few years ago, I would have been outraged by the flood—its inevitability the result of years of governmental inaction and arrogance—I found that this time I could summon little of anything. Indeed, I felt nothing but a kind of weariness, and even that I experienced not as a sensation but as an absence of one. I listened to the radio and yawned and yawned, staring out my office window at the East River, which David had always said looked like chocolate milk, watching a small vessel inch its way north: maybe to Davids Island, maybe not.

But if I could not find it in myself to feel anything about the flood, there would be others who would: the protestors who gathered each day in the Square and were removed each night. I had expected a surfeit of them when I returned home—they had long ago discovered who among us were on the Committee, and they had an unerring sense of when we'd arrive home each night. It didn't matter how often we changed drivers, or how much we tried to upend our schedules—the car would approach home, and there they'd be, with their signs and slogans. They're allowed to do this;

they cannot congregate outside state buildings, but they can outside of ours, which I suppose is more apt—it's the architects they hate even more than what we've built.

Last evening, though, there was no one, just the Square with its vendors and people shopping its stalls. This meant that the floods had given the state a reason to conduct a roundup of the protestors, and for a moment, I dawdled in the street despite the heat, watching regular people doing regular things, before going into the house and up to the apartment.

That night, I dreamed of when I was a teenager at my grandparents' farm in Lā'ie. It was the year of the first tsunami, and although we had been (just) far enough inland to not be directly hit, they had always said that they wish we had been, for then we could have collected the insurance money and begun anew, or not at all. As it was, the farm was too intact to be forsaken, but also too damaged ever to be productive again. The hill that had provided shade for my grandmother's herb garden had been destroyed, and the irrigation channels were filled with seawater—you would pump it away and then it would return, for months. Salt had affixed itself to every surface: The trees, the animals, the vegetables, the sides of the house were all streaky with white. The salt made the air sticky, and when the trees fruited that spring, the mangoes, the lychees, the papayas all tasted of salt.

They had never been happy people, my grandparents: They had bought the farm in a rare romantic moment, but romance is ephemeral. Yet they kept working at it long past the point when it ceased to be enjoyable, partly because they were too proud to admit they'd failed, and partly because they had limited imaginations, and couldn't think of what else they might want to do. They had wanted to live as their own grandparents had dreamed of living, before Restoration, and yet doing anything because your ancestors wanted to do it—fulfilling someone else's ambition—is a poor motivation. They had berated my mother for not being Hawaiian enough, and then she left, and they had had to raise me. They had berated me for not being Hawaiian enough, too, while at the same time assuring me I never would be, and yet when I left as well—for why would I stay someplace I had been told I would never belong?—they resented that just as much.

But the dream was not so much about them as it was a story my grandmother had told me when I was a child, about a hungry lizard. All day, the lizard would stalk across the land, grazing. He ate fruit and grass, insects and fish. When the moon rose, the lizard would go to sleep and dream of eating. Then the moon would set and the lizard would wake and begin eating again. The lizard's curse was that he would never be full, although the lizard didn't know this was a curse: He wasn't that intelligent.

One day, after many thousands of years had passed, the lizard woke, as usual, and began looking for food, as usual. But something was wrong. Then the lizard realized: There was nothing left for him to eat. There were no more plants, no more birds, no more grasses or flowers or flies. He had eaten everything; he had eaten the stones, the mountains, the sand, and the soil. (Here my grandmother would sing a lyric from an old Hawaiian protest song: *Ua lawa mākou i ka pōhaku / I ka 'ai kamaha'o o ka 'āina.*) All that was left was a thin layer of ash, and beneath that ash—the lizard knew—was the core of the earth, which was fire, and although the lizard could eat many things, he could not eat that.

So the lizard did the only thing he could. He lay in the sun and waited, dozing and saving his strength. And that night, as the moon was rising, he drew himself up on his tail and swallowed the moon.

For a moment, he felt wonderful. He'd had no water all day, and the moon was so cool and smooth in his stomach, as if he'd swallowed an enormous egg. But as he was relishing the feeling, something changed: The moon was rising still, trying to escape him so it could continue its path in the sky.

This must not happen, the lizard thought, and he quickly dug a hole, narrow but deep, or as deep as he could before he reached the fire at the earth's center, and stuck his entire snout inside of it. This will keep the moon from going anywhere, he thought.

But he was wrong. For just as it was the lizard's nature to eat, it was the moon's nature to rise, and no matter how tightly the lizard clamped its mouth, the moon rose still. But so tight was the hole in the earth where the lizard had stuck its snout that the moon was unable to exit his mouth.

And so the lizard exploded, and the moon burst forth from the earth and continued its path.

For many thousands of years after that, nothing happened. Well, I say nothing happened, but in those years, everything that the lizard had eaten returned. Back came the stones and the soil. Back came the grasses and the flowers and the plants and the trees; back came the birds and the insects and the fish and the lakes. Overseeing it all was the moon, which rose and sank each night.

That was the end of the story. I had always assumed it was a Hawaiian folktale, but it wasn't, and when I asked her who had told her that fable, she would say, "My grandmother." When I was in college, and taking an ethnography class, I asked her to write it down for me. She scoffed. "Why?" she asked. "You already know it." Yes, I told her, but it was important for me to hear it as she would tell it, not as I remembered it. But she never did, and I was too proud to ask her again, and then the class ended.

Then, several years later—we were barely communicating by then, pulled apart by mutual lack of interest and disappointment—she sent me an email, and in the email was the story. This was during my Wanderjahr, and I remember getting it while I was at a café in Kamakura with friends, although it wasn't until the next week, when I was on Jeju, that I read it. There it was, the familiar old inexplicable story, just as I'd remembered it. The lizard died, as he always did; the earth restored itself, as it always did; the moon glowed in the sky, as it always would. But this time, there was a difference: After everything had grown back, my grandmother wrote, the lizard returned, although this time he was not a lizard, but *he mea helekū*—a thing that goes upright. And this creature behaved in exactly the same way as his long-deceased ancestor had: He ate and ate and ate, until one day he looked about him and realized there was nothing left, and he too was forced to swallow the moon.

You know of course what I'm thinking. For a long time, I

assumed that it would be a virus that would destroy us all in the end, that humans would be felled by something both greater and much smaller than ourselves. Now I realize that that is not the case. We are the lizard, but we are also the moon. Some of us will die, but others of us will keep doing what we always have, continuing on our own oblivious way, doing what our nature compels us to, silent and unknowable and unstoppable in our rhythms.

Love, Charles

Dear P,   April 2, 2085

Thanks for your note, and for the information. Let's hope it's true. I have everything ready just in case. Thinking about it makes me squirrelly, and so I won't discuss it here. I know you said not to say thank you, but I'm saying it just the same. But I really do need it to happen, more than before, which I'll explain.

Charlie's been fine, or at least as fine as can be expected. I explained the Enemies Act to her, and while I know she understands it, I don't know that she fully comprehends the effect it will have on her life. She just knows that it's the reason she's been expelled from college, three months before she was to have graduated, and why we had to visit the zone registrar to have her identity document stamped. But she doesn't seem particularly troubled or shaken or depressed, for which I'm relieved. "I'm sorry, little cat, I'm sorry," I kept telling her, and she shook her head. "It isn't your fault, Grandfather," she said, and I wanted to cry. She's being punished for parents she never knew—isn't that punishment enough? How much more must she endure? It's also ludicrous—this act won't stop the insurgents. Nothing will. In the meantime, there are Charlie and her new tribe of the extralegal: the children and brothers and sisters of enemies of the state, most of them long since dead or disappeared. In the last Committee meeting, we were told that if the insurgents can't be quelled, or at least controlled, then "more severe restrictions" will have to be implemented. No one clarified what that meant.

As you can probably see, I've been in a far worse state than she has. I keep turning her future, which has at times—as I don't need to tell you—filled me with dread, over and over in my head. She had been doing well at school—she had even enjoyed it. I had dreamed of her earning her master's, maybe even her doctorate, of her finding a position in a small lab somewhere: nowhere fancy, nowhere flashy, nowhere prestigious. She could go to a research facility in a smaller municipality, have a good, quiet life.

But now she is prohibited from ever earning her degree. I had immediately gone to my acquaintance at Interior, whom I begged for an exception. "Come on, Mark," I told him. He had met Charlie once, years ago; after she'd come home from the hospital, he had brought her a stuffed rabbit. His own son had died. "Enough of this. Let her have another chance."

He had sighed. "If the mood were different, I would, Charles, I promise you," he said. "But my hands are tied—even for you." Then he said that Charlie was "one of the lucky ones," that he'd already "pulled some strings" for her. What that means, I don't know, and I suddenly didn't want to know. But what *is* clear is that I'm being pushed aside. I've known it for a while, but this was proof. It won't happen immediately, but it will happen. I've seen it before. You don't lose your influence at once—you lose it by degrees, over months and years. If you're lucky, you just become insignificant, assigned a meaningless job where you can do no harm. If you're unlucky, you become a scapegoat, and although it sounds like a perverse sort of bragging, I know that, given what I've implemented, what I've planned, what I've overseen, I am a candidate for some kind of public disavowal.

So I have to act quickly, just in case. The first thing is that I have to find her a job at a state institution. It'll be difficult to do, but she would be safe, and she would have it for life. I'll go to Wesley, who won't dare say no to me, even now. And then, as absurd as it sounds, I have to find her a husband. I don't know how long I have—I want to make sure I've placed her in a good situation, and if it's not, I want to be able to fix it for her. That at least I can do.

I'll wait to hear from you.

Love to you and Olivier, C.

My dear Peter,   January 15, 2086

Yesterday we had a bit of relief from the heat wave, which is expected to move north tomorrow. The past few days have been agony: more deaths, and then I had to use some of my coupons to replace the air conditioner. I'd been saving them to buy Charlie something nice, something to wear for our appointments. You know I don't like asking you for these things, but would you mind sending me something for her? A dress, or a blouse and a skirt? The drought means there's very little fabric coming into the city, and when it does, it's prohibitive. I'm attaching a picture of her here, and her sizes. Normally, of course, I'd have the money, but I'm trying to save as much as I can to give to her when she gets married, especially as I'm still getting paid in gold.

Certain expenses, however, can't be avoided. It was A. who introduced me to this new marriage broker, the same person he used to arrange his own marriage, to a widowed lesbian. If I needed proof of how diminished my reputation is, it's that I couldn't immediately get an appointment with this broker, although he's known to help anyone who's affiliated with a state ministry at a senior level. Yet it took A., whom I rarely see anymore, to secure a meeting with him.

I hadn't liked him from the start. He was tall and bony and unable to make eye contact, and he made it clear in every way he could that he was seeing me as a favor.

"Where do you live?" he asked, although I knew he already knew the basic information of my life.

"Zone Eight," I said, playing along.

"I usually only see applicants from Zone Fourteen," he said, which I also already knew, for he had told me this by letter before we even met.

"Yes, and I'm very grateful," I said, as blandly as I could. For a moment, there was silence. I said nothing. He said nothing. But finally, he sighed—what more could he do, really?—and took out his pad of paper to begin our interview. It was stiflingly hot in his office, even with the air-conditioning. I asked for a glass of water, and he looked affronted, as if I'd asked for something impossible, like brandy or scotch, and then called for his secretary to fetch me some.

And then the real humiliation began. Age? Occupation? What rank? Where exactly did I live in Zone Eight? Assets? Ethnicity? Where had I been born? When had I been naturalized? How long had I been at RU? Was I married? Had I ever been married? To whom? When did he die? How? How many children had we had? Was he my biological child? What had been his father's ethnicity? His mother's? Was my son living? When did he die? How? I was here on behalf of my granddaughter, was that correct? Who was her mother? Why, where was she? Was she living? Was my granddaughter my son's biological child? Had she or my son had any health problems or conditions? With each answer, I could feel the air around me change and change and change, getting dimmer and dimmer and dimmer, the years crashing and colliding into one another.

Then came the questions about Charlie, although he had already seen her papers, the scarlet "Enemy Relation" stamp x-ed across her face: How old was she? How much education had she had? What was her height and weight? What were her interests? When had she become sterile, and how? For how long had she taken Xychor? And, finally, what was she like?

It had been a long time since I had had to describe so precisely what Charlie was and wasn't, what she could and couldn't do, what she excelled at and what she struggled with: I think I last had to do this when I was trying to secure her a place at her high school. But after I told him the fundamentals, as best I could, I found myself still talking—about how attentive she had been to Little Cat, how, when he was dying, she would follow him from room to room until she had understood that he didn't want to be followed, that he wanted to be alone; about how, when she slept, her forehead furrowed in a way that made her look not angry but inquisitive and thoughtful; about how, although she could not give me a hug or kiss, she knew, always, when I was sad or worried, and would bring me a cup of water or, when we'd had it, a cup of tea; about how, as a child, just home from the hospital, she would sometimes slump against me after her seizures and let me stroke her head, her hair light and thin and as soft as down; about how the one thing that remained from her pre-sickness life was her scent, something warm and animal, like hot, clean fur after it's been in the sun; about how she could be resourceful in ways you wouldn't expect—she was rarely defeated, she would always try. After a while, some part of me realized that the broker had stopped taking notes, that the room was quiet except for my voice, and yet still I talked, even though it felt with every sentence like I was ripping my heart from my chest and then replacing it, again and again—that terrible, awful pain, that overwhelming joy and sorrow I felt whenever I spoke about Charlie.

Finally, I stopped, and into the silence, which was now so complete it vibrated, he said, "And what does she want in a husband?" And here again, I felt that anguish, because the very fact that it was I having this appointment, I and not her, was really all the broker needed to know: Everything else I said about Charlie, everything else she was, would be eclipsed by this fact.

But I told him. Someone kind, I said. Someone protective, someone decent, someone patient. Someone wise. He didn't have to be rich, or educated, or clever, or good-looking. He just had to promise me that he would protect her forever.

"What do you have to offer him in return?" the broker asked. A dowry, he meant. I had been told that, given Charlie's "condition," I would likely have to offer a dowry.

I told him my offer with as much confidence as I could, and his pen paused over the paper, and then he wrote it down.

"I'll need to meet her," he said, at last, "and then I'll know how to direct my search."

And so, yesterday, we went back. I had debated about whether I should try to coach Charlie, and then had decided not to, because it would be both pointless and anxious-making for her. Consequently, I was much more nervous than she was.

She did well, as well as she could. I have lived with her, and loved her, for so long that it sometimes takes me aback when I watch other people meeting her, when I understand anew that they don't see her as I do. I know this, of course, but I allow myself the luxury of incomprehension. And then I look at their faces, and there it is again: my heart being ripped from its veins and arteries; my heart being replaced, sucking back into my chest.

The broker told her that he and I were going to talk and that she could wait in the reception area, and I had smiled and nodded at her before following him inside, almost shuffling, as if I were back in school again and had been summoned by the headmaster for causing trouble. I had wished I might faint, or tumble to the floor, something to upset the moment, to garner some sympathy, some sign of humanity. But my body, as always, performed as it ought to, and I sat and stared at this man who could secure my child's safety.

For a moment, there was silence, each of us staring at the other, before I broke it: I was tired of this theatricality, of how this man understood our vulnerability and how he seemed to enjoy it. I didn't want to hear him say what I knew he would, but I also wanted him to say it, because then this moment would be over, would be becoming the past. "Do you have anyone in mind?" I asked him.

Another silence. "Dr. Griffith," he said, "I'm sorry, but I don't think I'm the broker for you."

Another heart rip. "Why not?" I asked, even as I didn't want to ask, because I didn't want to hear the answer. *Say it*, I thought. *I dare you to say it.*

"With respect, Doctor," he said, next, though there was no respect in his voice, "with *respect*—I think you have to be realistic."

"What's that supposed to mean?" I asked.

"Doctor, forgive me," he said, "but your granddaughter is—"

"My granddaughter is what?" I snapped, and there was another silence.

He paused. I could see him recognizing how angry I was; I could see him realizing I wanted to have a reason to fight with him; I could see him preparing to be careful.

"Special," he said.

"That's right," I said. "She *is* special, she is very special, and she will need a husband who understands how special she is."

I must have sounded as livid as I was, because his voice, until then devoid of compassion, changed somewhat. "I want to show you something," he said, and tugged a thin envelope from the bottom of a stack on his desk. "Here are the matches I found for your grand-daughter," he said.

I opened it. Inside were three cards, of the sort that you have to give to a broker. Stiff pieces of paper, about seven inches square, with the applicant's photo on one side and their data on the other.

I looked at them. All of them were sterile, of course, the red "S" debossed across their foreheads. The first man was in his fif-ties, thrice widowed, and the old illogical part of me—the part that remembered those Gothic television shows about men murder-ing their wives, disposing of their bodies, and eluding the law for decades—recoiled, and I turned his card facedown, rejecting him before I could read the rest of his data, which probably revealed that his wives had all died of the illness, not by his hand (and yet what kind of bad luck was that, to have three wives die, but a bad luck that bordered on criminality?). The second was a man in, I guessed, his late twenties, but with an expression so furious—his mouth a mean seam, his eyes astonished and bulging—that I had a vision, again from those old television shows I still sometimes watch late at night in the office, of him hitting Charlie, of him hurting her, as if I could read his potential for violence in his face. The third was a man in his early thirties, with a plain, placid face, but when I studied his information, I saw that he had been listed as "MI": mentally incom-petent. This is a broad designation, one that comprises all kinds of deficiencies of the sort that had once been known as mental disease, but also mental disability. Charlie does not have this designation. I had been willing to ask you to send money to bribe anyone I had to in order to prevent this, but I hadn't needed to in the end—she had passed their tests; she had saved herself.

"What are these?" I asked, my voice shrill in the quiet.

"These are the three applicants I could find who would consider your granddaughter," he said.

"Why were you looking for applicants before you even met her?" I asked, and as I did, I realized that he had determined who Charlie was from her files well before he had met her, probably well before he had even met me. Meeting her hadn't changed his mind—it had confirmed the idea of her he'd already had.

"I think you should try someone else," he repeated, and handed me another piece of paper, on which was typed three other brokers' names, and I understood that he had known from even before this meeting that he wasn't going to help me. "These people will have candidates that are more . . . in keeping with your needs."

Thank god he didn't smile, or I'd've done something stupid and male and animal: swung at him, spit at him, swept everything off his desk—the kind of things someone on one of those old television shows would have done. But now there was no one to perform for, no camera but the tiny blinking one I knew was secreted in the ceiling panels somewhere, dispassionately recording the scene below: two men, one elderly, one middle-aged, handing pieces of paper to each other.

I recomposed my face and left with Charlie. I held her as close to me as she'd allow. I told her I'd find someone for her, although something inside me was crumbling: What if no one wanted my little cat? Surely *someone* would see how dear she is, how much she's loved, how brave she is? She survived, and yet she is being punished for surviving. She wasn't like those applicants—leftovers, dregs, the unwanted. I thought this even as I also understood that to someone, they too weren't leftovers or unwanted, even—the heart ripping out again—that their someones might be looking at Charlie's card and thinking, "*This* is what they expect him to settle for? Surely there's someone better. Surely there's someone more."

What world is this? What world has she lived for? Tell me it'll be okay, Peter. Tell me and I'll believe you, this one last time.

Love, Charles

Oh, dear Peter,   March 21, 2087

How I wish we could speak on the phone. I wish that often, but I wish it desperately tonight, so much so that before I sat down to write you, I spent the past half hour talking aloud to you, whispering under my breath so I wouldn't wake Charlie, asleep in the other room.

I haven't written about Charlie's marriage prospects as much as I might have because I wanted to wait until I had something happier to say. But about a month ago, I found a new broker, Timothy, who was known to specialize in what a colleague of mine called "unusual cases." He had used Timothy to find someone for his son after his son was declared MI. It had taken almost four years, but Timothy had found him a match.

With each broker I'd met, I had tried to act more confident than I'd felt. I'd admit I'd seen a few of their colleagues, but never specified just how many. Depending on the person, I would try to make Charlie sound choosy, mysterious, brilliant, aloof. But every relationship would end the same way, sometimes even before I had a chance to bring Charlie in to meet them; the same kinds of candidates would be presented to me, sometimes candidates I'd seen before. That pale and placid young man marked MI had been shown to me three times since I first was given his card, and each time I saw his face, I felt a mix of sorrow and relief: sorrow that he too was still unmatched; relief that it wasn't just Charlie. I thought of her card, now foxed on the edges, being shown and reshown, of clients or their parents flicking it to the side. "Not her," I imagined them saying, "we've seen her before." And then, at night, to one another, "That poor girl, still on the market. At least our son isn't that desperate."

But this time, I was honest. I detailed exactly which brokers I'd seen. I told him about all the candidates I'd been presented or met with, on whom I'd taken notes. I was as honest as I could bear to be without crying or being disloyal to Charlie. And when Timothy said, "But beauty isn't everything. Is she charming?" I waited until I was sure I could control my voice before I said she wasn't.

At our second meeting, I was given five cards, none of which I'd seen before. Something unsettled me about each of the first four. But then there was the final card. He was a young man, only two years older than Charlie, with large dark eyes and a strong nose, looking straight into the camera. There was something inarguable about him—his handsomeness, for one, but also his steadiness, as if someone had tried to convince him to be ashamed of himself and he had chosen not to be. Over his picture were two stamps: one that declared him sterile, the other that declared him an enemy relation.

I looked up at Timothy, who was looking back at me. "What's wrong with him?" I asked.

He shrugged. "Nothing," he said. He paused. "He chose sterilization," he added, and I shuddered a bit, as I always did when I learned that about someone: It meant that fertility hadn't been taken from him by disease or medicine; it meant that he had chosen to be sterilized in order to keep from being sent to a reeducation center. You chose your body or your mind, and he had chosen his mind.

"Well, I'd like to arrange a meeting," I said, and Timothy nodded, though as I was leaving he called me back.

"He's a fine person," he said, a strange turn of phrase these days. I had investigated Timothy before I made my first appointment—in his previous life, he had been a social worker. "Just have an open mind, all right?" I didn't know what this meant, but I agreed, though having an open mind was also an anachronism, another concept of long ago.

The day of our meeting arrived and I was nervous again, uncommonly so. I had come to sense that, although Charlie was still young, she was nearing the end of her options. After this, I would have to expand my search beyond this municipality, beyond this prefecture. I would have to hope Wesley would grant me one more favor, after the previous favor he'd granted me, in which he'd given Charlie a job, a job she liked. I would have to wrest her from that job, and I would have to resettle her elsewhere, and then I would have to find a way to follow, and I would need Wesley's help. I would do it, naturally, but it would be difficult.

The candidate was already there when I arrived, sitting in the small, unadorned room that all brokers' offices maintained for such meetings, and as I entered, he stood and we bowed. I looked at him as he settled back into his chair, and I into mine. I had assumed that Timothy's entreaty meant that he would look significantly different, worse, than his photo, but this was not the case: He looked like his image, a trim, attractive young man, the same vivid dark eyes, the same unfrightened gaze. His father had been West African and Southern European; his mother had been South and East Asian—he resembled my son, just a bit, and I had to look away.

I knew the facts of him from his card, and yet I asked the same questions anyway: where he had grown up, what he had studied, what he did now. I knew his parents and sister had been declared enemies; I knew it had cost him the final years of his doctoral studies; I knew he was appealing the decision now that the Forgiveness Act had passed; I knew he had had a professor, a well-known microbiologist, who was helping support his case; I knew that if he agreed to the match, he wanted to delay the marriage by up to two years so he could try to finish his degree. He confirmed all this information; his account did not differ from what I knew.

I asked about his parents. He had no immediate living family. Most relatives of state enemies, when asked about their relations, became either angry or ashamed; you could see them swallowing something back, some surplus of feeling, you could see them practicing what they'd learned about keeping their emotions small.

But he was neither angry nor ashamed. "My father was a physicist; my mother was a political scientist," he said. He named the university where they had taught, a once-prestigious place before it had been subsumed by the state. His sister had been an English-literature professor. They had all joined the insurgents, but he had not. I asked him why, and for the first time, he looked troubled, though I couldn't tell whether it was because he was thinking about the camera hidden in the ceiling or about his family. "I said it was because I wanted to be a scientist," he said, after a pause, "because I thought—I thought that I could do more by becoming a scientist, by trying to help that way. But in the end—" And here he stopped again, and this time, I knew it was because of the camera and recorder.

"But in the end, you were wrong," I finished for him, and he looked at me and then to the door, quickly, like it was about to be broken down by a squad of officers, ready to drag us off to a Ceremony. "It's all right," I said, "I'm old enough to say what I want," even though I knew that wasn't true. He knew, too, but he didn't correct me.

We kept talking, now about his aborted dissertation, about the job he hoped to secure at the Pond as he appealed his case. We talked about Charlie, about who she was, about what she needed. I was—I didn't know why, at the time—honest with him, more honest even than I'd been with Timothy. But nothing seemed to surprise him; it was as if he had already met her; it was as if he already knew her. "You must always take care of her," I heard myself saying, again and again, and he nodded back to me, and as he did, I understood that he was agreeing to the marriage, that I had found someone for her after all. And at some point, somehow, I had another realization. I realized what it was that Timothy had tried to communicate to me about him; I realized what it was I recognized in him—I realized why he would be willing to marry Charlie. It was obvious, once I knew—I had known it since before I met him.

I interrupted him as he was mid-sentence. "I know who you are," I said, and when he didn't react, I said, "I know what you are," and then his mouth opened, just slightly, and there was a silence.

"Is it obvious?" he asked, quietly.

"No," I said. "I only know because I'm one, too," and now he sat back in his seat, and I could see something in his gaze change, could see him look at me again, differently.

"Can I ask you to stop?" I asked, and he looked at me, that determined, defiant, brave, foolish boy. "No," he said, softly. "I promise you I'll always take care of her. But I cannot stop." There was a silence.

"Promise me you'll never do anything that will get her in trouble," I said, and he nodded. "I won't," he said. "I know how to be discreet." *Discreet*—what a depressing word to hear used by someone so young. It was a word from before my grandfather's time, not a word that should have had to make a reappearance in our lexicon.

My disgust must have shown on my face, for his own became worried. "Sir?" he asked.

"Nothing," I said. Then I asked, "Where do you go?"

He was quiet. "Go?" he echoed.

"Yes," I said, and I'm afraid I sounded impatient. "Where do you go?"

"I don't understand," he said.

"Yes, you do," I said. "Jane Street? Horatio? Perry? Bethune? Barrow? Gansevoort? Which one?" He swallowed. "I'm going to find out anyway," I reminded him.

"Bethune," he said.

"Ah," I said. That made sense. Bethune attracted a more bookish sort. The man who ran it, Harry, a fussy queen who was very high up in Health, had dedicated two of the floors to libraries that looked like they were from an old-fashioned drawing-room comedy; the bedrooms were above. There were also rumors of a dungeon, but frankly, I think those were begun by Harry himself, to make the whole operation sound more exciting than it was. I had begun frequenting Jane Street, which was much more businesslike: You came in, you had your fun, you left. Anyway, it was a relief—I did not relish the thought of looking up only to see my granddaughter's husband peering down at me.

"Do you have someone?" I asked.

Another swallow. "Yes," he said, quietly.

"Do you love him?"

This time, there was no hesitation. He looked directly at me. "Yes," he said, and his voice was steady.

Suddenly I was very sad. My poor granddaughter, whom I was marrying to a man who would protect her but would never love her, at least not in the way we all need to be loved; this poor boy, who would never be able to have the life he should. He was only twenty-four, and when you're twenty-four, your body is for pleasure and you're constantly in love. I saw, suddenly, Nathaniel's face when I had first met him, his rich dark skin, his open mouth, and I turned away, because I feared I might cry.

"Sir?" I heard him ask, his voice soft. "Dr. Griffith?" This was the voice he would use to speak to Charlie, I thought, and I made myself smile and turned back to him.

We came to terms that afternoon. He didn't seem to care much about the dowry, and after we'd signed the papers of intention, we walked downstairs together, his marriage card in my briefcase.

On the sidewalk, we bowed again. "I'm looking forward to meeting Charlie," he said, and I said I was sure Charlie would be excited to meet him, too.

He was leaving when I called out his name, and he turned and walked back to me. For a while, I didn't know how to begin. "Tell me," I began, and then I paused. Then I knew what I wanted to say. "You're a young man," I said. "You're handsome. You're bright." I lowered my voice. "You're in love. Why are you doing this now, so young? Don't mistake me—I'm glad you are," I added, quickly, although his face hadn't changed. "For Charlie's sake. But why?"

He stepped closer to me. He was tall, but I was taller still, and for a second, I thought, ridiculously, that he might kiss me, that I would feel the brush of his lips against mine, and I closed my eyes, just for a moment, as if doing so would make it happen. "I want to be safe, too, Dr. Griffith," he said, just louder than a whisper. He stepped back then. "I have to keep myself safe," he said. "I don't know what I'll do otherwise."

It wasn't until I got home that I cried. Charlie was still at work, thank goodness, and so I was alone. I cried for Charlie, for how much I loved her, and for how I hoped she would know that I did what I thought best for her, how I had chosen her safety over her fulfillment. I cried for her perhaps-husband, for his need to protect himself, for how limited this country had made his life. I cried for the man he loved, who would never be able to make a life with him. I cried for the men in the cards I'd seen and rejected on Charlie's behalf. I cried for Nathaniel, and David, and even Eden, all of them long disappeared, none of whom Charlie remembered. I cried for my grandparents and for Aubrey and Norris and for Hawai'i. But mostly, I cried for myself, for my loneliness, and for this world I'd helped make, and for all these years: all the dead, all the lost, all the vanished.

I don't often cry, and I had forgotten how, beneath the physical discomfort, there was something exhilarating about it as well, every part of the body participating, the machinery of its various systems lurching into movement, plumping the ducts with liquids, pumping the lungs with air, the eyes growing shiny, the skin thickening with blood. I found myself thinking that this was the end of my life, that if Charlie accepted this boy, I would have discharged my final duty—I had protected her from harm, I had seen her to adulthood, I had found her a job and a companion. There was nothing else I could do, nothing else I could hope to do. Any life I had beyond this point would be welcome, but unnecessary.

Not too many years ago, Peter, I thought for certain that I'd be able to see you again. We'd have lunch together, you and me and Charlie and Olivier, and then maybe the two of them would go somewhere, to a museum or a play (we'd be in London, of course, not here), and then you and I would spend the afternoon together, doing something you did every day but which had become exotic to me—a trip to a bookstore, for example, or a café, or a boutique, where I'd buy something frivolous for Charlie: a necklace, maybe, or a pair of sandals. As the afternoon grew long, we'd go back to your house, the one I will never see with my own eyes, where Olivier and Charlie would be making dinner, and where I'd have to explain some of the ingredients to her: *This is shrimp; this is sea urchin; these are figs.* For dessert, there'd be chocolate cake, and the three of us would watch her eat it for the first time, watch as an expression I hadn't seen since before she got sick bloomed across her face as we laughed and applauded, as if she'd done something marvelous. We'd have our own rooms, but she'd come into mine because she would be unable to sleep that night, so overwhelmed would she be by all she'd seen and heard and smelled and tasted, and I'd hold her as I had when she was a little girl, feel her body twitch with electricity. And the next day we'd get up and do it again, and then the next, and the next, and although much of her new life would eventually become familiar to her—I falling back into it within days, the old memories reasserting themselves—she would never lose her new expression of awe, she would look about her with her mouth always slightly open, her face pitched to the sky. We would smile to see it; anyone would. "Charlie!" we'd call, when she got into one of her trances, to wake her up, to remind her of where and who she was. "Charlie! All of this is yours."

Love, C.

My dearest Peter,   June 5, 2088

Well, it's official. My little cat is married. It was, as you can imagine, an emotionally complicated day: As I stood and watched the two of them, I experienced an unusually vivid bout of one of those time jumps I've been having more and more frequently—I was back in Hawai'i, I was holding hands with Nathaniel, we were looking toward the sea, in front of which Matthew and John had positioned that bamboo chuppah. I must have looked strange, because at some point my now grandson-in-law glanced over at me and asked if anything was wrong. "Just old age," I said, which he accepted; to the young, anything unpleasant can be blamed on or attributed to old age. Outside, we heard troops marching by, the shouts of the insurgents in the distance. After they had signed their papers, we returned together to what is now their home and had some cake made with real honey that I had bought them as a special treat. None of us had had cake in months, and although I had feared conversation might be stilted, I needn't have worried, because all of us were so focused on eating that there was little need to speak at all.

The insurgents have now taken the Square, and although the apartment faces north, we could still hear them chanting, and then the loudspeakers blaring above them, reminding everyone of the 23:00 curfew, warning that anyone who failed to obey the order would be arrested immediately. That was my cue to go home to my new apartment, a single room in an old building on 10th and University, just four blocks from Charlie: I moved in last week. She had wanted me to stay with them, just for another week, but I had reminded her that she's an adult now, a married adult, and that I would come see her and her husband for dinner the next day, as we'd agreed. "Oh," she had said, and for a moment, I thought she might cry, my brave Charlie who never cries, and I had almost changed my mind.

It's been many years since I've slept in a place alone. As I lay there, I thought of Charlie, her first night as a spouse. For now, there's only a single, narrow bed, the one Charlie slept on, and the sofa in the living room. I don't know what they'll do, if they'll get a double bed, or if he'll want to simply sleep apart—I couldn't bring myself to ask. I instead tried to concentrate on the image of the two of them standing at the open door of their apartment, waving at me as I walked down the stairs. I had at one point looked up and had seen him put his hand on Charlie's shoulder, just lightly, so lightly that she might not even have felt it. I had talked to her beforehand; I had told her what to expect—or, rather, what not to expect. But would this be enough of an explanation for her? Would she still hope her husband might come to love her in a different way? Would she hope to be touched? Would she blame herself when she was not? Had I made the wrong decision for her? I had spared her pain, but had I also denied her ecstasy?

But—I have to remind myself—at least she will have someone. I don't only mean someone to look after her, to stand in front of her against the world, to explain things that to her are indecipherable. I mean that she is now part of a unit, the way she and I were once a unit, the way that Nathaniel and David and I were. This is not a society made for the single and unattached—not that the old society was, either, as much as we all pretended otherwise.

When I was Charlie's age, I scoffed at marriage, thinking it an oppressive construction; I didn't believe in a relationship legislated by the state. I had always thought that I didn't view an unpaired life as a lesser one.

And then, one day, I realized that it was. This was during the third quarantine of '50, and in retrospect, I can see that that was one of the happiest times of my life. Yes, it was anxious, and dangerous, and, yes, everyone was frightened. But it was the last time we were all together, as a family. Outside was the virus, and the containment centers, and people dying; inside was Nathaniel and David and I. For forty days, and then eighty days, and then a hundred and twenty days, we never left the apartment. In those months, David became softer, and we were able to become close again. He was eleven, and I can look back now and understand that he was trying to make a choice about the person he would become: Would he choose to be someone who once more tried to have the kind of life his parents led, the kind of life we expected he would lead? Or would he choose to become someone else, finding another template for who and how he could be? Who would he be? The boy of the year before, the one who threatened his classmates with a syringe—or a boy who might one day use a syringe in a different way, in the way a syringe is meant to be used, in a laboratory or hospital? In later years, I would think: If only we had had a few more weeks with him close to our side, away from the world; if only we could have convinced him that safety was valuable, and that we could be the ones to provide it to him. But we hadn't had a few more weeks, and we hadn't been able to convince him.

It was in the middle of the second forty days that I got an email from a long-ago friend from medical school, a woman named Rosemary who had moved to California for her postdoc when I had returned to Hawai'i. Rosemary was brilliant and funny and had been single for as long as I had known her. We began a correspondence, our messages part workaday matters and part sweeping updates from the past twenty years. Two members of her staff had gotten sick, she wrote; her parents and closest friend had died. I told her about my life, about Nathaniel and David, about how we were together in our small apartment. I realized, I wrote her, that it had been almost eighty days since I had seen another person, and although that realization had been astonishing, what had been more so is that I had yearned for no one. David and Nathaniel were the only people I wanted to see.

She responded the next day. Wasn't there anyone I really missed, she asked; wasn't there anyone I couldn't wait to see when the strictures had been lifted? No, I wrote back, there wasn't. I meant it.

She never wrote again. Two years later, I heard from a mutual acquaintance that she'd died the year before, during one of the illness's rebounds.

I have thought about her often since then. I came to understand that she was lonely. And although I cannot have been the only person she attempted to find who was as lonely as she was—we had spoken so infrequently that she must have tried a dozen others before she reached out to me—I wished that I had lied to her: I wished I had told her that I *did* miss my friends, that my family *wasn't* enough. I wished I had thought to find her before she was driven to find me. I wished I hadn't, subsequent to her death, been so grateful that I hadn't had to live her life, that I had my husband and my son, that I would never be that alone. Thank goodness, I had thought, thank goodness that isn't me. That pretty fiction we told ourselves when we were younger, that our friends were our family, as good as our spouses and children, was revealed in that first pandemic to be a lie: The people you loved the most were in fact the people you had chosen to live with—friends were an indulgence, a luxury, and if discarding them meant you might better protect your family, then you discarded them quickly. In the end, you chose, and you never chose your friends, not if you had a partner or a child. You moved on, and you forgot them, and your life was no poorer for it. As Charlie got older, I'm ashamed to say I thought of Rosemary more still. I would spare her that fate, I told myself—I would make sure she wasn't pitied as I had come to pity Rosemary.

And now I have. I know that loneliness cannot be fully eradicated by the presence of another; but I also know that a companion is a shield, and without another person, loneliness steals in, a phantom seeping through the windows and down your throat, filling you with a sorrow nothing can answer. I cannot promise that my granddaughter won't be lonely, but I have prevented her from being alone. I have made certain her life will have a witness.

Before we left for the courthouse yesterday, I had looked at her birth certificate, which we had to bring as proof of her identity. This was the new birth certificate, the one issued to me by the interior minister in '66, the one that disavowed her father—it had protected her for a while, and then no longer.

When Charlie's parentage had been erased, so too had her name: Charlie Keonaonamaile Bingham-Griffith, a beautiful name, bestowed with love and diminished by the state to Charlie Griffith. It was a reduction of who she was, because in this world, the world I had helped make, there was no intentional excess of beauty. The beauty that remained was incidental, accidental, the things that nothing could vanquish: the color of the sky before it rained, the first green leaves on the acacia tree on Fifth Avenue before they were picked.

It had been Nathaniel's mother's name: Keonaonamaile, the fragrant maile. I gave some to you once—a vine whose leaves smelled of pepper and lemons. We wore leis of them for our wedding—the day before, we had hiked into the mountains, David between us, the air around us wet, and had cut a rope of it that was growing between two koa trees. It was a lei you wore for weddings, but also for graduations and anniversaries: a special-occasion plant, back when there were so many plants that some were considered special and some were not, and you could just take them from the tree, and then the next day you would throw them away.

That day, we walked back downhill, our shoes squelching in the mud, David between us holding on to one of each of our hands. Nathaniel had cut enough maile so that we could each wear a length of it around our necks, but David had wanted to wear his wound around his head like a crown. Nathaniel helped him, tying the vine around itself and settling it on his forehead.

"I'm a king!" David had said, and we had laughed back at him. "Yes, David," we'd said, "you're a king—King David."

"King David," he said. "That's my name now." And then he turned serious. "Don't forget," he said. "You have to call me that, okay? Do you promise?"

"Okay," we said. "We won't forget. We will." It was a promise.

But we never did.

Charles

PART IX

Autumn 2094

O ver the following weeks, David and I discussed our plan. Or, rather, it was his plan, and it was being shared with me. On October 12, I would leave Zone Eight. He wouldn't tell me how, exactly, until just before. Until then, I was to do nothing out of the ordinary. I was to maintain all my daily rhythms: I was to go to work, I was to go to the grocery, I was to take the occasional walk. We would continue to meet every Saturday at the storyteller's, and if David needed to communicate with me between those meetings, he would find a way to send me word. But if I didn't hear from him, I wasn't to worry. I was to prepare nothing, and pack nothing beyond what I could carry in my tote bag. I would not need to bring clothes, or food, or even my papers: New ones would be issued to me once I was in New Britain.

"I have a lot of extra chits I've saved up over the years," I told David. "I could exchange them for coupons for extra water or even sugar—I could bring those."

"You won't need those, Charlie," David said. "Bring only things that mean something to you."

At the end of our first meeting after our talk on the benches, when I had begun to believe him, I had asked David what would happen to my husband. "Of course your husband can come," he said. "We've prepared for him as well. But, Charlie—he may not want to."

"Why not?" I had asked, but David hadn't answered. "He loves to read," I said. On that walk on the track, I had asked David lots of questions about New Britain, but he had said that he would tell me more about it on our travels—that it was too dangerous to share too much now. But one thing he *had* said was that in New Britain you could read whatever you wanted, as much as you wanted. I thought of my husband, how he made himself read slowly, because you could only borrow one book every two weeks, and he had to make each one last. I thought of him sitting at our table, resting his right cheek in his right hand, completely still, a small smile on his face, even when the book was about the care and feeding of tropical water-grown edible plants.

"Yes," David said, slowly, "but, Charlie—are you sure he'd want to leave?"

"Yes," I said, although I wasn't sure at all. "He could read any book he wanted, over there. Even the illegal ones."

"That's true," said David. "But there might be other reasons he'd want to stay here, in the end."

I considered this, but I couldn't think of any. My husband had no family here except for me. There would be no other reason for him to stay. And yet, like David, I also somehow wasn't confident that he would want to leave. "What do you mean?" I asked, but David didn't answer.

At our next meeting, before the storyteller began, David asked me if I'd like his help in talking to my husband. "No," I said. "I can do it myself."

"Your husband knows how to be discreet," David said, and I didn't ask how he knew this. "So I know he'd be smart about this." There seemed to be something else that he wanted to say, but he didn't.

After the storyteller's session, we walked. I had assumed our meetings would be complicated, full of information for me to memorize, but they were not. Mostly, they seemed to be opportunities for David to make sure I was remaining calm, that I was doing nothing, that I trusted him, although he never asked if I did.

"You know, Charlie," he said, suddenly, "homosexuality is completely legal in New Britain."

"Oh," I said. I didn't know what else I could say.

"Yes," he said. Once again, he seemed to want to say something else, but once again, he didn't.

That night, I thought about how much David already knew about me. In some ways, it was disturbing, even frightening. But it was also relaxing, even comforting. He knew me the way Grandfather knew me, and that knowledge had of course come from Grandfather himself. David had not met Grandfather, but his employer had, and so in a small way it felt as if Grandfather were actually alive and with me still.

Yet there were certain things I did not want David to know. I had come to realize that he understood that my husband did not love me, and would never love me, not the way a husband is supposed to love his wife, and not the way that I had hoped I would be loved. It made me ashamed, because while loving someone is not shameful, it *is* shameful not to be loved at all.

I knew I would need to ask my husband if he wanted to come with me. But the days passed and I did not. "Did you ask him?" David asked at our next meeting, and I shook my head. "Charlie," he said, not meanly but not gently, either, "I need to know if he's going to come. It affects things. Do you want me to help you?"

"No, thank you," I said. My husband may not have loved me, but he was still my husband, and it was my responsibility to talk to him.

"Then do you promise you'll ask him tonight? We only have four weeks left."

"Yes," I said. "I know."

But I didn't ask him. That night, as I lay in bed, I clenched Grandfather's ring, which I kept under my pillow, where I knew it'd be safe. In the other bed, my husband slept. He had been tired again, tired and breathless, and on his way to the kitchen with our dishes, he had stumbled, although he caught himself on the table before he dropped anything. "It's nothing," he'd said to me. "Just a long day." I had told him to go to bed, that I would do the dishes, and he had argued with me a little, but then had left.

All I had to do was say his name, and he would wake, and I would ask him. But what if I asked him, and his answer was no? What if he said he wanted to stay here instead? "He will always take care of you," Grandfather had said. But if I left, it would be the end of always, and then I would be alone, all alone, with no one but David to protect me, and no one who remembered me, and who I was, and where I had once lived, and who I had been. It was safer not to ask at all—if I didn't ask, I was both here, in Zone Eight, and also not, and as October 12 drew closer and closer, that seemed like the best place to be. It was like being a child, when all I had to do was follow directions, and I never had to think about what might happen next, because I knew that Grandfather had already thought of everything for me.

———

For many weeks, I had been keeping two things secret: The first was knowledge of the new illness. The second was knowledge of my departure. But while only one other person knew the second thing, many people—all of the people in my lab; many of the people at RU; various employees of the state; generals and colonels; unseen people in Beijing and Municipality One whose faces I couldn't even imagine—knew the first.

And now more people were learning of it as well. There had been no official announcement in the various zones' newsletters, no radio bulletin, yet everyone knew that something was happening. One day at the end of September, I walked outside to discover that the Square was completely empty. Gone were the vendors, their tents, even the fire that constantly burned. And it was not just empty but clean: There were no wood shavings on the ground, no bits of metal, no snippets of thread blowing through the air. It had all vanished, and yet I had heard nothing during the night, no sound of bulldozers, no industrial scrubbers or sweepers. The cooling stations were gone as well, and the gates to each of the four entrances, which had been removed long ago, had been replaced, and locked.

The mood on the shuttle that morning was very tense, less of a silence than a complete absence of sound. There was no recognizable protocol for disease preparedness, because the state had changed so much since '70, but it was as if everyone already knew what was happening, and no one wanted to hear their suspicions confirmed.

At work, there was a note waiting for me beneath one of the

mouse cages, the first since David and I had begun meeting at the storyteller's. "Rooftop greenhouse, 13:00," it said, and at 13:00, I went to the roof. There was no one there but a gardener in his green cotton suit, watering the specimens, and before I could wonder how I was going to search for David's next note in the greenhouse if the gardener wouldn't leave, he turned and I saw it was David.

He quickly raised his finger to his mouth, gesturing me to be silent, but I was already weeping. "Who are you?" I asked. "Who are you?"

"Charlie, quiet," he said, and came over and sat down next to where I had fallen to the ground, and put his arm around my shoulder. "It's all right, Charlie," he said. "It's all right." He held me and rocked me, and eventually I was quiet. "I disabled the cameras and microphones, and we have until 13:30 before the Flies return," he said. "You saw what happened today," he continued, and I nodded. "The illness is all over Prefecture Four now, and it'll be here soon as well. The worse it gets, the harder it's going to be for us to leave," he said. "So the date's been moved up: October 2. The state will make an official announcement the next day; testing and evacuations to the relocation centers will begin that evening. They'll instate a curfew the following day. It's cutting it too close for my taste, but there was so much rearranging that this was the best I could do. Do you understand me, Charlie? You have to be ready to leave on October 2."

"But that's this Saturday!" I said.

"Yes, and I apologize," he said. "I miscalculated—I was told the state wouldn't announce until October 20 at the earliest. But I was wrong." He took a breath. "Charlie," he said, "have you talked to your husband?" And, when I didn't say anything, he turned me by my shoulders to look at him. "Listen to me, Charlie," he said, his voice stern. "You *must* tell him. Tonight. If you don't, I'll assume you're going to leave without him."

"I can't leave without him," I said, and I began crying again. "I won't."

"Then you must tell him," said David. Then he looked at his watch. "We have to leave," he said. "You go first."

"What about you?" I asked.

"Don't worry about me," he said.

"How did you get in here?" I asked.

"Charlie," he said, impatiently, "I'll tell you later. Now go. And talk to your husband. Promise me."

"I promise," I said.

But I didn't. The next day, there was another note waiting for me: *Did you?* But I crushed it into a ball and burned it in a Bunsen burner.

That was Tuesday. On Wednesday, the same thing happened. Then it was Thursday, three days before we were to leave, my husband's free night.

And that night, my husband didn't come home.

———

Now, if I was asked, I could not say why I decided to trust David. The truth was that I did not in fact trust him, or at least not completely. This David was different from the David I had known: He was more serious, less surprising, scarier. Yet the other David had been scary, too; he had been so reckless, so unusual. In some ways, this David was easier for me to accept, even as I felt that with each day I knew him less. Sometimes I would hold Grandfather's ring and think of all David knew about me, and tell myself that David was someone I could believe in, that he was someone who would protect me, that he had been sent by someone Grandfather had trusted. Other times, I examined the ring, holding the flashlight beneath the covers as my husband slept, wondering if it was Grandfather's after all. Hadn't his been bigger? Had the gold been dented on the right side? Was it real, or a copy? And what if he hadn't sent it to this friend after all? What if it had been stolen from him? Then I would think: It wasn't worth his lying—I wasn't worth kidnapping. No ransom would be paid for me; no one would miss me. There was no reason for David to want to take me.

And yet there was no reason for him to want to save me, either. If I was not worth taking, I was also not worth saving.

And so I cannot say why I decided to go, or even that I had really decided. It seemed too far off, so unlikely, like a make-believe story. All I knew was that I was going somewhere better, somewhere Grandfather wanted me to go. But I knew nothing about New Britain, other than it was a country, and it had once had a queen, and then a king, and that they spoke English there, too, and that the state had ceased relations with them back in the late '70s. I suppose it seemed a bit like a game, like the kind I had played with Grandfather in which we pretended to have conversations—this was a pretend conversation, too, and my leaving would be pretend as well. At our last meeting, I had argued with David again about leaving the extra chits behind, for what if I needed them later, when I returned, when David interrupted me. "Charlie, you're never coming back," he said. "Once you leave this place, you will never return. Do you understand me?"

"What if I want to?" I said.

"I don't think you will," he said, slowly. "But at any rate, you can't. You would be captured and killed in a Ceremony if you tried, Charlie."

I said I understood, and I thought I did, but maybe I didn't. One Saturday, I had asked David what would happen to the pinkies, and he had said I couldn't think about the pinkies, and that they would be fine: Another tech would take care of them. And then I got upset, because although I knew I wasn't the only one who could handle the pinkies, I sometimes liked to pretend I was. I liked to pretend that I was the best at preparing them, the most careful, the most thorough, that no one else could be as good as I was. "You're right, Charlie, you're right," he'd said, and after a while, I calmed down.

That Thursday, as I waited for my husband, I thought about the pinkies. They were such an important part of my life here, and I decided that when I went in to work tomorrow, on what David had reminded me would be my last day at Rockefeller University, ever, I should steal a petri dish of them. Just one dish, with just a few pinkies in just a little saline. David had said I should bring only what was personally meaningful to me, and the pinkies were meaningful.

I had lots of room in my bag. The only things I had packed

were half of the gold coins we kept under my bed, and four pairs of underwear, and Grandfather's ring, as well as the three photographs of him. David had said not to bring clothes, or food, or even water— all those would be provided to me. As I was packing, I had suddenly thought I might pack the notes my husband had kept, but then I had changed my mind, just as I had changed my mind about taking all of the gold coins. I told myself that, when my husband decided to come with me, he would carry the other half. Once packed, the bag was still so small and light that I could roll it into a tube and stuff it into the pocket of my cooling suit, which was now hanging in the closet.

I knew that I would need to talk to my husband tonight, and so, rather than changing into my sleep clothes, I lay down on my bed fully dressed, thinking that if I was less comfortable I'd not fall asleep. But I fell asleep anyway, and when I woke, I could tell that it was very late, and when I checked the clock, it was 23:20.

Immediately, I was frightened. Where was he? He had never stayed out so late, not ever.

I didn't know what to do. I paced the main room, clapping my hands together and asking myself aloud where he was again and again. Then I realized that I knew where he was: He was at the house on Bethune Street.

Before I could get scared again, I put my papers in my pocket, in case I was stopped. I got the flashlight from under my pillow. I put on my shoes. And then I left the apartment and walked downstairs.

Outside, everything was very quiet and, without the light from the fire in the Square, very dark. There was only the occasional spotlight, swooping in slow circles, illuminating the side of a building, a tree, a parked wagon, for a moment, before they were again left in darkness.

I had never been out so late before, and although it wasn't illegal to be out at this hour, it also wasn't typical. You just had to look like you knew where you were going, and I did know where I was going. I walked west, through Little Eight, looking up at the apartments and wondering which one was David's, and then crossed Seventh Avenue, and then Hudson. As I was crossing Hudson, a troop of soldiers walked by, and turned to look at me, but when they saw who I was, just a short, plain, dark-skinned Asian woman, they continued on without even stopping me. On Greenwich Street, I turned right and began walking north, and soon I was turning left on Bethune and walking to number 27.

As I was about to climb the stairs, I stopped, overtaken by fear, and for a while I rocked myself, and I could hear myself whimpering. But then I walked up, stumbling on the missing stone in the second step, and knocked out the rhythm I had memorized from months ago: *tap-ta-taptap-tap-tap-tap-ta-tap-taptap.*

At first, there was silence. And then I heard someone coming down a flight of stairs, and the little window slid open, and a sliver of a man's face, a reddish face with blue eyes, was looking out at me. He looked at me, and I at him. There was a brief silence. Then he said, "There was never any more inception than there is now; nor any more youth or age than there is now," and, when I didn't answer him, he repeated it.

"I don't know what to say in response," I said, and before he could slide the window shut, I added, "Wait—wait. My name is Charlie Griffith. My husband hasn't come home, and I believe he's in your house. His name's Edward Bishop."

At this, the man's eyes widened. "You're Edward's wife?" he asked. "What did you say your name was, again?"

"Charlie," I said. "Charlie Griffith."

The little window slammed closed then, and the door opened, just a few inches, and the man on the other side, a tall, white, middle-aged man with thin, pale-blond hair, beckoned me inside and locked the door behind us. "Upstairs," he said, and as I followed him, I looked to my left and saw a door that was ajar a few inches, through which I could see the glow of a lamp.

The staircase had been laid with a carpet in a dark red-and-blue pattern of swirling shapes and lines, and creaked as we moved up it. On the second landing, there was another door, and I realized that the house had been converted into a series of apartments, one per floor, and yet it was still being used as a single house, the way it had originally been built: The staircase wall had been painted with roses, and the painting extended past the second story, all the way up. Drying laundry—socks and shirts and men's underwear—had been draped over the banister.

The man knocked on the door and turned its handle at the same time, and I followed him inside.

The first thing I thought was that I had somehow returned to Grandfather's study, or at least the version of it I could remember from just before I got sick. Every wall was covered with bookcases, and in them were what looked like thousands of books. There was a rug on the floor, a bigger, more intricately patterned version of the one that covered the staircase, and there were soft chairs and an easel in one corner with a half-completed painting of a man's face. The large windows were hidden with dark-gray curtains, and there was a low table on which were stacked more books, as well as a radio and a chessboard. And, in the far corner, opposite the easel, was a television, which I hadn't seen since I was a child.

Just in front of me was a sofa, not the kind we had at home but something deep and comfortable-looking, and on that sofa was a man, and that man was my husband.

I ran over to him and knelt by his head. His eyes were shut, and he was sweating, and his mouth was partly open because he was gasping for breath. "Mongoose," I whispered to him, and I took one of his hands, which were crossed over his chest, and which was sticky and cold. "It's me," I said. "Cobra." He made a faint moaning noise, but nothing else.

Then I heard someone say my name, and I looked up. It was a man I'd not noticed before, with dark-blond hair and green eyes, about my age, who was also kneeling by my husband, and who I then saw was cupping my husband's head in one hand and stroking his hair with the other. "Charlie," the man repeated, and I was surprised to see that there were tears in his eyes. "Charlie, it's good to finally meet you."

"You have to get him out of here," someone else said, and I turned and saw it was the man who had let me in.

"Jesus, Harry," said another voice, and I looked up and saw that there were three other men in the room, all of whom were standing a few feet away from the sofa and looking at my husband. "Don't be so heartless."

"Don't you lecture me," said the man from the door. "This is *my* house. He's putting us all at risk by being here. He has to get out."

Another of the men started to protest, but the man who had been stroking my husband's hair stopped them. "It's okay," he said. "Harry's right; it's too risky."

"But where will you go?" asked one of the men, and the blond man looked back at me.

"Home," he said. "Charlie, will you help me?" and I nodded that I would.

Harry left the room, and two of the other men helped the blond man stand my husband up, even though he groaned as he did. "It's all right, Edward," said the blond man, who had his arm around my husband's waist. "It's all right, sweetheart. It's going to be okay." Together, they began to move him slowly down the stairs, my husband groaning and panting with each step, the blond man soothing him and stroking his face. At the base of the staircase, the door to the ground-floor apartment was now fully ajar, and the blond man said he had to get his and my husband's bags, and entered.

I followed him, though I wasn't aware that I had until I found myself in the room, and all of the men within it staring at me. There were six, though I was unable to register any of their faces, only the room itself, which was decorated like the room upstairs but grander, the furnishings fancier, the fabrics richer. Then I noticed that everything was frayed: the edge of the carpet, the seams on the sofa, the spines of the books. Here, too, there was a television, though it was also silent, just a black screen. Here, too, the walls had been removed, transforming what could have been a one-bedroom apartment into a single large space.

Then the men were gathering near the doorway, and one of them was holding the blond man against him. "Fritz, I know someone who can help," he was saying, "let me tell him," but the blond man shook his head. "I can't do that to you," he said. "You'll be hanged or stoned for sure, and so will your friend," and the other man, as if admitting he was correct, nodded and stepped away from him.

I was looking at them when I felt someone watching me, and I turned to the left and saw one of the Ph.D.s, the one who always rolled his eyes at the interior minister's deputy's nephew.

He stepped closer to me. "Charlie, right?" he asked, quietly, and I nodded. He looked toward the foyer, where the two men were still holding my husband upright, surrounded by other men. "Edward's your husband?" he asked.

I nodded. I could not speak, could barely even nod, could barely even breathe. "What's wrong with him?" I asked.

He shook his head. "I don't know," he said, and he looked worried. "I don't know. It seems like heart failure to me. But I know it's not—it's not the illness."

"How do you know?" I asked.

"We've seen some of the affected," he said. "And it's not that—I know it. He'd be oozing blood from his nose and mouth if it were. But, Charlie: Don't take him to the hospital, whatever you do."

"Why not?" I asked.

"Because. They'll assume it's the illness—they don't know as much as we do—and he'll be sent straight to one of the containment centers."

"There are no more containment centers," I reminded him.

But he shook his head again. "There are," he said. "They just don't call them that anymore. But it's where they're taking early cases, to—to study them." He looked back at my husband, and then at me once more. "Take him home," he said. "Let him die at home."

"Die?" I asked. "He's going to die?"

But then the blond man was approaching me again, this time with both his and my husband's bags slung over his shoulder. "Charlie, we have to go," he said, and I followed him, again without my knowing it.

Some of the men kissed the blond man on the cheek; others kissed my husband. "Goodbye, Edward," one said, and then they all said it: "Goodbye, Edward—goodbye." "We love you, Edward."

"Goodbye, Edward." And then the door opened, and the three of us stepped into the night.

———

We walked east. The blond man was on my husband's right, I on his left. My husband's arms were looped around our necks, and we each had an arm around his waist. He could barely walk, and his feet dragged behind him much of the time. He wasn't heavy, but because the blond man and I were both shorter than he was, he was difficult to guide.

At Hudson Street, the blond man looked around us. "We'll cut across Christopher, and then go past Little Eight and east on Ninth Street before turning south on Fifth," he said. "If we're stopped, we'll say he's your husband and I'm his friend and he—he got drunk, all right?" It was illegal to be publicly drunk, but I knew that, in this circumstance, it was better to say my husband was drunk than sick.

"All right," I said.

We were silent as we walked east on Christopher Street. The streets were so empty and dark that I could barely see where we were going, but the blond man moved quickly and surely, and I tried to keep up. Eventually, we reached Waverly Place, which formed the westernmost border of Little Eight, which was well-lit with spotlights, and we flattened ourselves against a nearby building to avoid being seen.

The blond man looked at me. "Just a little longer," he said to me, and then again, softly, to my husband, who coughed and groaned. "I know, Edward," he said to my husband. "Almost there, I promise— we're almost there."

We moved as quickly as we could. To my left, I could see the towers of Little Eight, their windows now mostly black. I wondered what time it was. Ahead of us, I could see the large building that had been built several centuries ago as a prison. Then it became a library. Then it became a prison again. Now it was an apartment building. Behind it was a cement playground, but it was usually too hot for the children to use.

It was just as we were approaching this building that we were stopped. "Halt," we heard, and we did, abruptly, almost dropping my husband. A guard, dressed all in black, which meant he was a municipal officer, not a soldier, had stepped in front of us, holding his weapon at our faces. "Where are you going at this time of night?"

"Officer, I have my papers," the blond man began, reaching for his bag, and the guard snapped, "I didn't ask for your papers. I asked where you were going."

"Back to her apartment," said the blond man. I could tell he was afraid but trying not to be. "Her husband—her husband had a little too much to drink, and—"

"Where?" asked the officer, and I thought he sounded eager. Officers got extra points for arresting people for quality-of-life crimes.

But before we could answer, we heard another voice, one saying, "*There* you are!" as if he were greeting someone, a friend who was late to meet him for a concert or a walk, and the blond man and the officer and I turned and saw David. He was approaching us from the west, not in his gray jumpsuit but in a blue cotton shirt and pants, similar to what the blond man was wearing, and although he was moving quickly, he also wasn't hurrying, and he was smiling and shaking his head. In one hand he carried a thermos, in the other, a small leather case. "I *told* you to stay put—I've been looking all over the complex for you," he said, still smiling, to the blond man, who had opened his mouth in surprise but now shut it and nodded.

"I'm sorry, officer," David said to the man in black. "This is my foolish big brother, and his wife, and our friend"—he nodded at the blond man—"and I'm afraid my brother had a little too much fun tonight. I went to get him some water from our flat, and when I came back, these three"—he smiled at us, fondly—"decided to take off without me." And here he smiled at the officer, and shook his head a little, and rolled his eyes upward. "Here, I have all three of our papers," he said, and handed the case to the officer, who had still not lowered his weapon, and who had been looking at each of us in turn as David spoke, but who accepted the case and unzipped it. As the officer pulled out the cards, I saw a flash of silver.

The officer read the papers, and as he read the final one, he suddenly straightened, and saluted. "Apologies," he said to David. "I didn't know, sir."

"No apologies necessary, officer," David said. "You're doing exactly what you're supposed to."

"Thank you, sir," said the officer. "Do you need help getting him back home?"

"That's very generous of you, officer, but no," David said. "You're doing a fine job here."

The officer saluted again, and David saluted back. Then he took my place at my husband's left side. "Oh, you silly man," he said to my husband. "Let's get you home."

None of us spoke until we had crossed Sixth Avenue. "Who are—" the blond man began, and then, "Thank you," and David, no longer smiling, shook his head. "If we pass another officer, let me handle it," he said, quietly. "If we're stopped, no one should look worried. You have to seem—exasperated, all right? But not scared. Charlie, do you understand?" I nodded. "I'm Charlie's friend," he said to the blond man. "David."

The blond man nodded. "I'm Fritz," he said. "I'm—" But he couldn't continue.

"I know who you are," David said.

The blond man looked at me. "Fritz," he said, and I gave him a nod to show I understood.

We reached home without being stopped again, and once he had closed the front door behind us, David handed me the thermos and then picked my husband up in his arms and carried him up the flights of stairs. I didn't understand how he did this, as they were about the same size, but he did.

Inside, he took my husband to our bedroom, and even through everything that was happening, I felt a burn of embarrassment, that both David and Fritz should be seeing how we slept, not touching, in separate beds. Then I remembered that they already knew, and felt even more embarrassed.

But neither of them seemed to notice. Fritz had sat next to my husband on his bed and was stroking his head again. David was holding my husband's wrist and looking at his watch. After a few moments, he gently laid my husband's arm down by his side, as if he was returning it to him. "Charlie, will you get me some water?" he asked, and I did.

When I returned, David was kneeling by the bed as well, and he took the water I gave him and held it to my husband's lips. "Edward, can you swallow any? Good; good. A little more. Good." He set the mug on the floor next to him.

"You know this is the end," he said, though it was unclear to whom he was speaking: me or Fritz.

It was Fritz who answered. "I know," he said, quietly. "He was diagnosed a year ago. I just thought he'd have a little more time."

"With what?" I heard myself ask. "Diagnosed with what?"

They both looked at me. "Congestive heart failure," Fritz said.

"But that's treatable," I said. "That can be fixed."

But Fritz shook his head. "No," he said. "Not for him. Not for relatives of state traitors," and as he said this, he began to cry.

"He didn't tell me," I said, when I could speak again. "He didn't tell me." And I began to pace, to flap my hands, to repeat myself— "He didn't tell me, he didn't tell me"—until Fritz left my husband's side, and grabbed my hands in his own.

"He was trying to find the right time to tell you, Charlie," he said. "But he didn't want to worry you. He didn't want you to be upset."

"But I *am* upset," I said, and this time it was David who had to take me and sit with me on my bed, and rock me back and forth, just the way Grandfather used to.

"Charlie, Charlie, you've been so brave," he said, while rocking me. "It's almost over, Charlie, it's almost over." And I cried and cried, even though I was ashamed to be crying, and ashamed to be crying for myself as much as for my husband: I was crying because I knew so little, and because I understood so little, and because, although my husband had not loved me, I had loved him, and I think he had known that. I was crying because he *did* love someone, this someone who knew all about me and about whom I knew nothing, and I was crying because this someone was now losing him as well. I was crying because he had been sick and he hadn't thought to tell me or been able to tell me—I didn't know which, but it didn't make a difference: I hadn't known.

But I was also crying because I knew that my husband was the only reason I would have stayed in Zone Eight, and now my husband was dying, and I would not stay either. I was crying because we were both leaving, to different places, and we would be doing so separately, and neither of us would ever return, back to this apartment in this zone in this municipality in this prefecture, ever again.

———

We waited the rest of the night and all day Friday for my husband to die. In the early morning, David had left to register all three of our absences from work at the center. Fritz, who was unmarried, also lived in Building Six, just as David had said he himself did, and so we didn't need to worry about his spouse missing him, as he had none.

When David returned, he gave my husband a little more of the liquid in his thermos, which made my husband's face relax and made his breaths deeper and longer. "We can give him more if he really begins suffering," he said, but neither Fritz nor I said anything in response.

At noon, I made some lunch, but no one ate it. At 19:00, David reheated the lunch in the oven, and this time, all three of us ate, sitting on the floor in my husband's and my bedroom, watching him sleep.

None of us said anything, or not much. At one point, Fritz asked David, "Are you from the Interior?" and David smiled, a bit, and said, "Something like that," which made Fritz stop asking questions. "I'm in the Finance Ministry," he said, and David nodded. "I guess you knew that already," Fritz said, and David nodded again.

I suppose it would be natural to wonder if I asked Fritz about how and when he and my husband had met, and how long they had known each other, and if he was the person who had sent my husband those notes. But I did not. I thought about it, of course, over many hours, but in the end, I didn't. I didn't need to know.

I slept in my bed that night. David slept on the sofa in the main room. Fritz slept next to my husband in his bed, holding him even though my husband couldn't hold him back. When I heard someone saying my name, I opened my eyes to see David standing over me. "It's time, Charlie," he said.

I looked over to where my husband was lying, very still. He was breathing, but barely. I went and sat on the floor next to his head. His lips were a faint purplish blue, a strange color I had never seen on a human. I held his hand, which was still warm, but then I realized that it was warm only because Fritz had been holding it.

We sat there for a very long time. As the sun began to rise, my husband's breathing became harsh, and Fritz looked over at David, who was sitting on my bed and said, "Now, please, David," and then looked over at me, because I was his wife, and I nodded, too.

David opened my husband's mouth. Then he took a piece of cloth from his pocket and dipped it into the thermos, and then wrung the cloth into my husband's mouth before wiping it around his gums, the inside of his cheeks, and his tongue. And then we all listened as my husband's breathing became slower, and deeper, and less frequent, and then finally stopped altogether.

Fritz was the first to speak, but it was not to us, but to my husband. "I love you," he said. "My Edward." I realized then that he had been the last person to speak to my husband, because when I had finally seen him, on Thursday night, he was no longer responsive. He bent to kiss my husband on his lips, and although David looked away, I did not: I had never seen someone kiss my husband, and I never would again.

Then he stood. "What do we do?" he asked David, and David said, "I'll take care of him." Fritz nodded. "Thank you," he said, "thank you so much, David. Thank you," and I thought he was going to cry again, but he didn't. "Well," he said. He looked at me, next. "Goodbye, Charlie," he said. "Thank you for—for being so kind to me. And to him."

"I didn't do anything," I said, but he shook his head.

"Yes, you did," he said. "He cared about you." He sighed, a long, shaky sigh, and picked up his bag. "I wish I had something of his," he said, "something to remember him by."

"You can have his bag," I said. Earlier, we'd looked through his bag, as if it might contain a cure, or another heart, but there had only been his work uniform, and his papers, and a small twist of paper holding a few cashews, and his watch.

"Are you sure?" Fritz asked, and I said I was. "Thank you," he said, and carefully placed my husband's bag in his own.

David and I walked Fritz to the door. "Well," he said again, and then he did begin to cry. He bowed to David, and then to me, and we bowed back to him. "I'm sorry," he said, because he was crying. "I'm sorry, I'm sorry. I loved him so much."

"We understand," David said. "You don't need to apologize."

And then I remembered the notes. "Wait," I told Fritz, and I went to the closet and took out the box and opened the envelope, and removed the notes. "These are yours," I said, as I gave them to Fritz, and he looked at them and began crying again.

"Thank you," he told me, "thank you." For a moment, I thought he would touch me, but he didn't, because it wasn't done.

And then he opened the door and slipped out. We listened to him walk down the stairs, and down the hallway, and then there was the sound of him opening the front door, and letting it fall shut behind him, and then he was gone, and everything was silent once more.

Then the only thing to do was wait. At 23:00 precisely, I was to be waiting at the banks of Charles and Hudson Streets, where a boat would meet me. This boat would take me to another boat, a much bigger boat, and that boat would take me to a country I'd never heard of, called Iceland. In Iceland, I would be placed in isolation for three weeks, to make certain I wasn't carrying the new illness, and then I would board a third boat, and that boat would take me to New Britain.

But David would not be meeting me at the shore. I would have to do it myself. He had some things to finish here, and so I wouldn't see him again until I landed in Iceland. Hearing this, I began to cry once more. "You can do it, Charlie," he said. "I know you can.

You've been so brave. You *are* brave." And finally, I wiped my eyes and nodded.

In the meantime, David said, I should stay inside and try to sleep, though I must be careful to leave with enough time. He would make sure my husband's body was picked up and cremated, although not until after I had left. We were lucky the weather was cooperating, he said, but he still fit my husband into his cooling suit and turned it on, though he left his helmet off.

"It's time for me to go," he said. We stood at the door. "Do you remember the plan?" he asked. I nodded. "Do you have any questions?" he asked. I shook my head. Then he put his hands on my shoulders, and I flinched, but he held on. "Your grandfather would be proud of you, Charlie," he said. "I am, too." He released me. "I'll see you in Iceland," he said. "You'll be a free woman."

I didn't know what that meant, but "I'll see you," I said in return, and he saluted me, as he had saluted the officer on Thursday night, and then he left.

I went back to my husband's and my room, which was now my room, and which tomorrow would be somebody else's room. I took three of the remaining coins from the drawer beneath my bed. I remember Grandfather telling me that certain cultures put gold coins over the eyes of their deceased, and some put coins under the dead person's tongue. I can't remember why they did this. But I did the same: One coin over each eye, one beneath his tongue. The rest of the coins I put in my bag. I wished I had remembered to give the extra chits we had to Fritz, but I had forgotten.

And then I lay down next to my husband. I put my arms around him. It was a little difficult because of the cooling suit, but I was still able to do it. It was the first time I had been so close to him, the first time I had touched him. I kissed his cheek, which was cold and smooth, like stone. I kissed his lips. I kissed his forehead. I touched his hair, his eyelids, his eyebrows, his nose. I kissed and touched him for a long time. I talked to him. I told him I was sorry. I told him I was going to New Britain. I told him that I would miss him, that I would never forget him. I told him I loved him. I thought of Fritz saying that my husband had cared about me. I had never imagined that I would actually meet the person who had written my husband those notes, but now I had.

When I woke, it was dark, and I was anxious because I had forgotten to set my alarm. But it was only just after 21:00. I took a shower, even though it was not a water day. I brushed my teeth, and put my toothbrush in my bag. I was afraid if I lay back down I would fall asleep again, so I instead sat on my own bed and stared at my husband. After a few minutes, I put his cooling helmet on, so his face and head wouldn't begin to rot before he could be cremated. I knew it didn't make a difference to him, or to anyone, really, but I didn't want to think of his face turning black and soft. I had never spent so much time around a dead person, not even Grandfather—it was my husband who had overseen his cremation, not me, because I had been too upset.

At 22:20 I stood. I was wearing a plain black shirt and pants, as David had instructed. I put my bag over my shoulder. At the last minute, I added my papers, which David had said I wouldn't need, but which I thought I might if I were stopped on the way over to the western banks. Then I took them out again, and put them under my pillow. I thought of the petri dish of pinkies I would now never be able to retrieve. "Goodbye, pinkies," I said aloud. "Goodbye." My heart was beating so fast that I was having trouble breathing.

I locked my apartment for the final time. I slid the keys beneath the door.

And then I was outside and I was walking west, almost like the walk I had taken just two nights ago. Above me, the moon was so bright that, even when the spotlights had arced away, I could still see where I was going. David had told me that after 21:00 the majority of the Flies would be diverted in order to form clusters around the hospitals and monitor high-density zones, in anticipation of tomorrow's announcement, and, indeed, I saw only one or two, and instead of their normal drone, there was only silence.

I reached the banks by 22:45. I sat on a dry patch of land to keep myself from pacing. Here there was absolutely no light. Even the factories across the river were dark. The only sound was of the water slapping against the cement barriers.

Then, very faintly, I heard something. It sounded like a whisper, or like wind. And then I saw something: a faint blob of yellowish light that seemed to float over the river like a bird. Soon it grew bigger, and more distinct, and I saw that it was a small wooden boat, the kind I knew from pictures that people used to row across the Pond back when it had been an actual pond.

I stood, and the boat drew to the shore. There were two people inside it, both dressed completely in black, one of them holding a lantern, which he lowered as they approached land. Even their eyes were covered in thin pieces of black gauze, and I struggled to see them in the poor light.

"Cobra?" one of them asked.

"Mongoose," I replied, and the man who had spoken reached out his hand and helped me into the boat, which rocked beneath me, and I thought I might fall over.

"You'll stay down here," he said, and helped me crouch into the space between him and the other oarsman, and once I had made myself as small as possible, they covered me with a tarp. "Don't make a sound," he said, and I nodded, even though he wouldn't have been able to see me do so. And then the boat began to move, and the only noise was the sound of the oars slicing through the water, and the men's breathing, in and out.

After David had told me he wouldn't be meeting me at the banks, I had asked him how I would know that the people coming to get me were the right people. "You'll know," he'd said. "There's no one else at the banks at that time. Or ever, really." But I had said I needed to know for certain.

Two weeks after my husband and I were married, there had been a raid in our building. It was the first raid I had experienced without Grandfather, and I was so terrified that I hadn't been able to stop moaning, moaning and batting at the air and rocking. My husband hadn't known what to do, and when he tried to reach for my hands, I slapped him away.

That night, I had a dream that I was at home after work, making dinner, and heard the sound of keys turning in the lock. But when the door opened, it was not my husband but a group of policemen, shouting and ordering me to get on the floor, their dogs lunging at me and barking. I woke up, calling for Grandfather, and my husband had gotten me a glass of water and then had sat next to me until I had fallen asleep again.

The next evening, I was making dinner when I heard the noise of keys in the locks, and although of course it was only my husband, in the moment I was so frightened that I dropped the entire pan of potatoes on the floor. After he had helped me clean them up, and as we were eating dinner, my husband said, "I have an idea. Why don't we have a pair of code words, something we can say when we're entering the apartment, so we'll each know it's the other? I'll say my word, and you'll say yours, and then we'll both know that we are who we say we are?"

I thought about it. "What words will we use?" I asked.

"Well," my husband said, after thinking. "Why don't you be—let's see—a cobra?" I must have looked surprised, or offended, because he smiled at me. "Cobras are very fierce," he said. "Small, but quick, and deadly if they catch you."

"And what will you be?" I asked.

"Let's see," he said, and I watched him think. My husband liked zoology, he liked animals. The day we met, there had been a report on the radio that Magellanic penguins had been declared officially extinct, and my husband had expressed sorrow over that, had said that they were resilient animals, more resilient than people thought, and more human than people knew as well. When they were sick, he said, they toddled away from their flock so they could die alone, with none of their kin to watch them.

"I'll be a mongoose," he said at last. "A mongoose can actually kill a cobra, if it wants to—but they very rarely do." He smiled again. "It's too much work. So they just respect each other. But we'll be a cobra and a mongoose that do more than just respect each other: We'll be a cobra and a mongoose that unite to keep each other safe from all the other animals in the jungle."

"Cobra and Mongoose," I repeated, after a pause, and he nodded.

"A little more dangerous than Charlie and Edward," he said, and smiled again, and I saw that he was teasing, but teasing in a nice way.

"Yes," I said.

I had told David that story on one of our earliest walks, back when he was still a tech at the Farm, and my husband was still alive. And so, as we stood at my door before he left, he said, "What about using code words—like Cobra and Mongoose? That's how you'll know the people coming to meet you are who they should be."

"Yes," I agreed. It was a good idea.

Now I stayed crouched in position beneath the middle plank seat. The boat bobbed and rocked, and yet it kept moving, the sounds of the oars stroking through the water steady and swift. Then, rumbling through the bottom of the boat, I heard the sound of a motor, and as I listened, it grew louder and louder.

"Oh shit," I heard one of the men curse.

"Is that one of ours?" the other asked.

"Too far to tell," said the first, and swore again.

"What the fuck is that craft doing out here?"

"Fuck if I know," said the first man. He swore once more. "Well, there's no way out. We just have to take our chances, and hope it's one of ours." He nudged me with his foot, not hard. "Miss: Be very quiet and keep very still. If it's not one of our people—"

But then I could no longer hear him, because the sound of the motor was now too loud. I realized that I had never asked David what I should do if I was caught, and that he had never told me. Was he so certain everything would unfold as he had described? Or was this in fact the plan, and was I being delivered to people who would hurt me, who would take me somewhere and do things to me? Surely David, who knew so much and had foreseen so much, would have told me what I was to do if something went wrong? Surely I wasn't so helpless that I wouldn't have thought to ask him? I began to cry, quietly, folding a piece of the tarp into my mouth. Had I been wrong to trust David? Or had I been right, and had something happened to him? Had he been arrested, or shot, or disappeared? What would I do if I was caught? Officially, I was nobody: I didn't even have my papers with me. Of course, they could do whatever they wanted to me even if I had my papers, but without them, it would be that much easier. I wished I had Grandfather's ring in my hand, so I could squeeze it and pretend I was safe. I wished I was at home, and my husband was alive, and I hadn't seen or experienced any of the things I had in the past three days. I wished I had never met David; I wished he were with me now.

But then I realized: No matter what happened, this was the end of my life. Perhaps it was the actual end. Perhaps it was just the end of the one I had known. But either way, my life mattered less to me, because the person to whom it had mattered most was gone.

"You," I heard someone say, but over the motor, I couldn't tell if it was one of the people in the boat with me, or in the other boat, which I could feel was pulling alongside us, or to whom they were speaking. And then the tarp was being pulled away from me, and I could feel the breeze on my face, and I lifted my head so I could see who was speaking to me, and where I was going next.

PART X

September 16, 2088

Dearest Peter,

I'm writing fast, because this is the last chance I'll have—the person who's going to find a way to get this to you is standing just outside my cell but has to leave in ten minutes.

You know that I'm going to be executed in four days. The insurgency needs a face, and the state needs a sacrificial lamb, and I was the compromise. I managed to get some concessions from both of them in return for being publicly hanged in front of a braying crowd, however: that they would leave Charlie and her husband alone, that she would never be punished for me; that Wesley will always treat her decently. No matter which side triumphs, she'll be protected—or at least not harassed.

Do I trust them? No. But I also have to. I don't care about dying, but I can't bear to leave her here, in this place, alone. Of course, she won't be alone. But he can't stay here, either.

Peter, I love you. You know I do, and I always have. I know you love me, too. Please take care of her, my Charlie, my granddaughter. Please find a way to get her out of this country. Please give her the life that she should have had, if I had gotten out of here earlier, if I had been able to save her. You know she needs help. Please, Peter. Do everything you can. Save my little cat.

Who would have thought that New Britain, of all places, would one day be heaven, and this place so spectacularly rotten? Well, you did, I know. And so did I. I'm sorry for it. I'm sorry for it all. I made the wrong decisions, and then I made more and more of them.

My only other request—not to you, but to someone or something—is this: Let me come back to earth someday as a vulture, a harpy, a giant microbe-stuffed bat, some kind of shrieking beast with rubbery wings who flies over scorched lands, looking for carrion. Wherever I wake, I'll fly here first, whatever they're calling it then: New York, New New York, Prefecture Two, Municipality Three, whatever. I'll pass by my old house on Washington Square and look for her, and if I don't find her, I'll fly north to Rockefeller and look for her there.

And if she's not there, either, I'll assume the best. Not that she's been disappeared, or died, or interned somewhere, but that you have her, that you managed to save her in the end. I won't even circle above Davids Island, or the crematoriums, or the landfills or prisons or reeducation or containment centers, trying and failing to detect her scent, cawing her name as I do. Instead, I'll rejoice. I'll kill a rat, a cat, whatever I can find, eat it for strength, and stretch my ribbed wings wide and let out a squawk, a sound of hope and anticipation. And then I'll turn east and begin my long flight across the sea, flapping my way toward you, and her, and maybe even her husband, all the way to London, to my loves, to freedom, to safety, to dignity—to paradise.

ACKNOWLEDGMENTS

I am most grateful to Dr. Jonathan Epstein of the EcoHealth Alliance, and to the scientists at Rockefeller University who gave me valuable insights and access in early stages of my research: Drs. Jean-Laurent Casanova, Stephanie Ellis, Irina Matos, and Aaron Mertz. Profound thanks go to Dr. David Morens of the National Institutes of Health and the National Institute of Allergy and Infectious Diseases, who not only brokered these introductions, but also good-naturedly gave of his time during a real-world pandemic to read about an imaginary one.

My deep gratitude to Dean Baquet, Michael "Bitter" Dykes, Jeffrey Fraenkel, Mihoko Iida, Patrick Li, Mike Lombardo, Ted Malawer, Joe Mantello, Kate Maxwell, Yossi Milo, Minju Pak, Adam Rapp, Whitney Robinson, Daniel Schreiber, Will Schwalbe, Adam Selman, Ivo van Hove, Sharr White, Ronald Yanagihara, and Susan Yanagihara, as well as Troy Chatterton, Miriam Chotiner-Gardiner, Toby Cox, Yuko Uchikawa, and everyone at Three Lives Books in New York for the extraordinary support, faith, and generosity they've extended to me in realms professional and personal. Thank you too to Tom Yanagihara and Haʻalilio Solomon for their assistance with ʻŌlelo Hawaiʻi. Any remaining mistakes—not to mention the decision to remap Oʻahu's topography to suit the narrative—are mine.

I am extraordinarily lucky to have two agents, Anna Stein and Jill Gillett, who have not only never asked me to compromise, but whose patience and dedication have never dimmed. I am also extremely grateful to Sophie Baker and Karolina Sutton, who protected and fought for this book with zeal, and all my editors, publishers, and translators abroad, especially Cathrine Bakke Bolin, Alexandra Bori-senko, Varya Gornostaeva, Kate Green, Stephan Kleiner, Päivi Kovisto-Alanko, Line Miller, Joanna Maciuk, Charlotte Ree, Daniel Sandström, Victor Sonkine, Susanne van Leeuwen, Maria Xilouri, Anastasia Zavozova, and the staff of Picador UK.

Gerry Howard and Ravi Mirchandani took a chance on me when no one else would; I will always be grateful to them for their advo-cacy, passion, and belief. I am so grateful to have Bill Thomas on my side, and for his steadfastness and calm; thank you, Bill, and every-one at Doubleday and Anchor, in particular, Lexy Bloom, Khari Dawkins, Todd Doughty, John Fontana, Andy Hughes, Zachary Lutz, Nicole Pedersen, Vimi Santokhi, and Angie Venezia, as well as Na Kim, Terry Zaroff-Evans, and, always, Leonor Mamanna.

I would not have conceived of this book, much less written it, were it not for a series of perspective-altering conversations and exchanges with Karsten Kredel, who I am privileged to count as both trusted editor and beloved friend. One of the greatest gifts of the past five years has been my friendship with Mike Meagher and Daniel Romualdez, whose hospitality, advice, and generosity have brought me immeasurable comfort and pleasure. Kerry Lauer-man has been a source of humor and good counsel for more than a decade.

Finally: I am blessed to have met Daniel Roseberry, whose wis-dom, empathy, wit, imagination, humility, and constancy make my life richer and more wondrous; I could not have endured the past two years without him. And nothing of who I am—as an editor, a writer, and a friend—would be possible without my first and favorite reader, Jared Hohlt, whose love and compassion have sustained me more times and in more ways than I can count. My devotion, not to mention this book, are for them.